The Matriarch
Tale of the Degeli Witches

A novel by James W. Dereniak

Copyright © 2013 by James W. Dereniak

http://thedegeliwitches.com

ISBN: 978-0-692-23710-6

Second Edition

Cover design by my good friend,

Jason Bergsieker

Type set in Adobe Caslon Pro

Cover font: CuttyFruty.com

Jessica Lapointe

Dedicated to Friendship, Love, & Understanding

To my long time friend, Janice Vandenheuval, who read and re-read my novel with delicate, constructive criticism. To a fellow author, Eric Foulkrod, whose criticism almost brought me to tears. However, it was well deserved and needed. I also give thanks to Jason Bergsieker for the design of my cover and for being an eye-opening friend. To Karen Lamb (Daffy), I give thanks for her years of friendship and partnership.

Kim Settimo has many thanks for her time and effort in teaching me much about grammar. I still have a ways to go; however, like so many things...it will come together. And when I get the money, I'll hire someone!

Thanks to Regina Pelinski for her polish translation. Special thanks to Rocco LaTorre for he was kind enough to meet a stranger at the mall and help translate the spells to Italian. To Giuseppe Ciccone, for his Italian translations and Jessey Sterling for the French translations, I thank you.

I would also like to say thanks to Matt Twomey for his assistance with the hydraulics for the cellar and his friendship and Karen Twomey for her constant love, support and answering bizarre questions.

To a wonderful author of the *Grimoire Chronicles* and a long time friend, Sally Dubats, I thank you.

Last, but certainly not least, I would like to thank my Mom, Anna Mae Dereniak, for her honesty & love, and for listening me read the same chapter twenty thousand times.

With fond memories and dedication to those who are no longer with us: My great aunt, Elizabeth Settimo, grandmother, Katie, grandfather, Jimmy, cousin Betty Settimo, cousin Bob Formento, great uncle, Sam Settimo, Vicki Eaton(A dear friend), Cousin Robert Miller, Mary Urbisci (My neighbor when I was a kid), Loretta B Olkowski (grandma in-law), Larry Lamb, (Daffy's husband), Carol & Bud Coy, (Coy's parents), Gracie Shultz, (God mother), Al Person, (Burlie's father) Andy Boscagila, (A moose's companion), & Tom & Gloria Emery (My second parents)

Meet the Degeli Family on Page 505

(I've slowly introduced each character and gave reminders of who they are throughout. However, I've included a family tree for interest.)

The Matriarch
Tale of the Degeli Witches

Morning Coffee

When Azzurra found her voice, she spoke with a tone that was unlike her own. "Marta, are you saying you spoke with your Aunt Tessa?"

Memories of over forty years ago played in Azzurra's head like a movie... the phone calls, the flashes of light. Her heart quickened, muscles tensed and temper boiled.

Marta dipped biscotti in a cup of coffee and took a bite. She loved Sunday mornings with her mother. To start the day with fresh brewed coffee, cookies and biscotti, and if she was really lucky, cannoli — a rich custard-filled shell baked with chocolate chips throughout.

Marta took another sip of coffee and decided on more sugar, then responded. "Yeah, Ma, I told you, I bumped into her yesterday. You OK?"

Azzurra gave no sign that she heard her daughter...the movie was still playing in her head.

Marta reveled in the flavor of the biscotti and continued. "Well anyway, she looks terrible, didn't keep herself up very well — look who's talking — I'm terrible, and what a thing to say." She swallowed and her raspy voice filled the air once more. "Like I'm some hot tamale." She laughed, dipped the biscotti into the coffee and took another bite.

She continued describing the meeting with her Aunt Tessa — her mother's sister, who they hadn't seen for almost forty-one years. "There was just something about her that made me think how awful she looked — I mean it's been years since I've seen her. I was just a little girl." She swallowed the remains of her biscotti. "I'm not even sure if the word *awful* is the right word, more like horrid, something horrid about the way that woman looked. I felt it in my bones…not necessarily how she actually looked…I mean…I don't know. It's just weird — the feeling I got." Marta took a bite of biscotti. "Where did you get these or did you bake them? They're really good."

Marta finally looked across the table and noticed her mother's stone face. She dabbed her mouth with a napkin and placed it gently on the table next to the cup and saucer filled with her mother's hazel nut coffee. It was her Aunt Katie's set of antique cups and saucers they drank from that Sunday morning.

"Ma…what's the matter?"

Azzurra stood and walked to the kitchen sink. She looked immaculate as always, and for her age of 71, she was simply a beautiful woman. Age had done its fair share, for her skin had not the same luster, her eyes had not the same sparkle and her lips had become a bit thinned, but overall, Azzurra had aged as gracefully as she could have hoped.

Azzurra placed her hands on the ledge of the kitchen sink — she felt dizzy…sick to her stomach. She looked out the window at the neighbor's large apple tree. The family movie continued playing in her head…so real… so recent, yet another lifetime ago — someone else's life.

Marta noticed her mother wore the outfit her father had bought her a few years back. She wore black pin-striped slacks with a maroon silk blouse from *Spiegel's*. One accessory you could always count on Azzurra wearing was a white apron. She also wore the purple ballerina slippers that he had bought her on his last Christmas. She thought to herself, *"Maybe she's just missing Dad…it's only been three months."*

Azzurra looked at the pewter cat that sat on the kitchen sink's ledge. Black onyx eyes stared up to her. Attached to the cat was a small pewter basin that was used to hold a scouring pad for the pots and pans she cleaned on a daily basis.

She brushed a hand through her gray hair, closed her hazel eyes and took in a slight breath. When she opened them, she caught her reflection within the ovens' door. A face with smooth olive skin and the look of dread, stood before her.

The trickling of water that came from the Blessed Mary etched at her nerves. She felt the cool September breeze through the opened window. Azzurra's mind raced. By speaking to Tessa, Marta could have very well opened doors, that even Tessa herself, thought were closed. She felt a rush of panic course through her and faced her daughter, placing a hand on her head as though feigning a headache. Azzurra's temper rose fiercely as her insides roared with the anger of years past. "Stupid!" Azzurra yelled. She pointed at her daughter and walked closer. "Stupid! I told you never to speak to that woman...yet you spoke to her! If I had a pan I'd hit you over the head with it!"

Marta's face became blank as her mouth slid open. She knew full well that the physical threats upon her or her brother and sister were empty — having heard them a dozen times. It was more of an Italian custom to threaten one with physical harm. At least that's the story — which come to think of it, had been decades since she heard that phrase — *if I had a pan*.

Azzurra began to pace the kitchen.

She was closest to Marta out of the three children and now the angriest she'd ever been with one of them. She tried to convince herself to calm down, that it was not Marta's fault. Azzurra gathered her strength, looked up to the ceiling, said a quick prayer, and took her seat at the table.

Marta spoke. "Ma, I can't believe you called me stupid. What the hell's the matter with you?" The color drained from her face. It was worse than she thought, something was horribly wrong, and it had nothing to do with her father.

Azzurra took in a deep breath. "I'm going to tell you something Marta — you may think that I'm old and have my funny ways, and that the things I say are silly and superstitious; that I have not a clue as to what's going on in this world. That all the old stories of our family, they were tales that were meant for Halloween...but I'm going to tell you something Marta..."

Azzurra stood and brushed her hands across the apron and walked away from her daughter. She thought of how life could change in a matter of minutes. The film in her head plagued her once more and she felt her blood pressure rise. She walked up to the table and pointed a finger at her daughter. Fear harpooned into her gut.

"...you're the one that doesn't have a clue! You're the one that is a silly woman who won't listen to her mother who damn well knows what she is talking about!" She raised her voice and slammed a hand on the table. "Now what have I told you about speaking with Aunt Tessa?" She had a glare that could have thrown Marta right off her chair.

Marta responded. "Ma, for the love of God…I bumped into her at the fruit market yesterday…we spoke for a little bit. I was polite, kept it short, and that was it! What the hell is the matter with you?" She tugged at her collar. "I'm gonna need to see my therapist again and start taking pills if you don't tell me what's gotten into you." Her leg bounced up and down rapidly.

The ranch home absorbed the soft sounds of the birds' morning song as Azzurra and Marta waited…Azzurra for the strength she needed and Marta, for an answer.

Marta was a little lady, just like her mother, reaching a height of five foot one. At 46, she was the fun aunt, the cool cousin and the crazy second cousin. Her black hair, streaked with gray, was combed away from her face, reaching just below chin level. She pulled at the collar of her sweat shirt once again.

Outside — blue skies erupted with swirls of black and gray. There was a slight rumble of thunder and the temperature dropped several degrees.

A storm was brewing — a storm that had nothing to do with Mother Nature.

Azzurra and Marta's attention was thrown to the sliding glass door. A gust of wind blew the blinds as it swooped through the screen. Chimes blasted the air.

Azzurra stood, braced a hand on her lower back, then hurried through the living room to the sliding glass door, and slid it closed. A shiver edged up her spine. She looked to the fountain of the Blessed Mary — the trickle of water had stopped. Her heart raced as she looked outside and then back to the fountain.

Azzurra continued to stare at the fountain — heart racing. She thought to herself that she was too old for this. She looked at her daughter, then to the storm and then back to the fountain. Something was approaching.

Marta looked through the sliding glass door to the storm. Lightning flashed as the winds whipped the trees. They looked at each other in silence. Marta felt horribly uncomfortable and did what she always did when feeling that way — she removed herself from the situation. With a sudden rise to her feet, she headed to the front door.

"Ma, I love you…but call me when you've calmed down." She could not remember the last time she was so annoyed with her mother and at the same time…scared. Halfway down the hall, she realized she forgot her purse. She turned around, walked back to the table and took what she had forgotten.

Azzurra gathered all the strength she could muster, and with a force she hadn't used in her voice for nearly forty-one years she commanded. "Marta! Sit!" She pointed to Marta's chair.

With no hesitation, Marta sat.

Azzurra slowly walked over to her chair, sat down, inhaled a large breath and smoothed her apron. She took a sip of coffee from the delicate saucer her sister Katie bequeathed her. She dabbed the sides of her mouth with a napkin, took an Italian cookie from the tray and spoke softly. "Tell me what my sister said. Do not leave a thing out Marta. I want you to describe what she looked like: what she wore, the tone of her voice, the manner in which she stood and everything you said as well."

* * * *

Aunt Tessa

The wind whipped the apple tree into a mangled monstrosity of limbs. Rain pelted the ground, spattered the windows and rushed down the gutters. A low deep rumble purred in the distance; it grew into a loud boom and rattled the windows. Azzurra stood and returned to the kitchen window. She slid it closed and looked across the yard once again.

She watched as the apple tree's branches fought against the wind. Her eyes focused on the whirls of black clouds that were moving fast through the shield of rain. Lightning flashed before them. She gave a slight jump and heard a loud snap. Azzurra looked to the apple tree. A large branch was lying on the ground.

Azzurra shook her head slightly. The weather was so nice and peaceful. What a difference a few minutes can make. The tree would never be the same.

She returned to her seat and looked to her daughter.

"What was that?" Marta asked.

"Mary's apple tree lost a big branch." She paused. "I loved that tree. It was so beautiful and the apples were delicious." She looked back to the kitchen window. "I hope it doesn't die."

Marta took a sip of coffee. "I swear Michigan's weather is getting more and more un-predictable. They said it was supposed to be a beautiful day today. Where? It's like a hurricane out there." She looked through the glass sliding door to the storm.

A moment later she heard her mother clear her throat. Azzurra was staring at her, waiting for what she had asked — details of the conversation with her aunt. Marta closed her eyes and tried to recall every bit of yesterday's conversation.

She opened her eyes. "OK Ma, here's what happened. I was looking at the Greek pastries; the ones shaped liked triangles, when I heard a voice from behind me. *"Marta...Marta Stephani...is that you?"*

Marta began to bounce her leg once more. "I looked up and that's when I saw them. I forgot to tell you her daughter, Celia, was there too. I would have never recognized her. I mean, we were kids the last time we met, but Aunt Tessa, I sort of remembered. She must have recognized me from photos from Uncle Augusto or Aunt Gabriella. Anyway, it was funny after all these years shopping there and I've never bumped into them before."

She looked up and to the right, trying to recall the meeting. "Anyway, what Aunt Tessa looked like...now let me remember. She had black hair. I mean, that black-blue hair and it was a horrible dye job if you ask me. I mean come on...jet black hair...for the love of God Ma, she's older than you. She had the same hair style I remembered from the photos, you know, with it swooped back, away from her face and teased on top."

Marta raised a hand to the right side of her head. "She had one silver streak on the right side of her head just above the temple stretching back an inch or two above her ear. It was odd."

Marta heard her boss' voice in her head...*Details...it's all about the details.* "She wore this weird purple lipstick or maybe it was more of a deep plum, anyway it looked horrid with her skin tone. She wore thick eyeliner to accent her swollen eyes." Marta opened her eyes. "Reminded me of Alice Cooper or you know that Goth look that's going on. Anyway, she didn't age all that horribly, I mean, if she just got some sleep and had a makeover she'd be a pretty woman. Like I said before...it was the feeling I got that made her look horrid."

Marta tried to smile at her mother. "Ummm, she had deep lines on her forehead, some deep crow's feet and pursed, tight lips. She was thin, I mean really thin and had long nails. She wore a black dress with a deep orange

7

— no, it was more like a rust colored scarf that was tied around her neck and draped across the front of her dress. She wore black high-heels that were at least three inches but they were dull black with matching nylons."

Both ladies jumped as the thunder struck. The wind howled outside. Azzurra and Marta glanced to the rain spattered sliding glass door. Marta continued.

"That scared the hell out of me! Now let's see…Celia, what did she look like…OK…Celia aged worse than I — like I have room to talk. Lord knows I haven't aged all that well and I certainly don't have the men knocking on my door. Anyway, she had more gray in her hair than me and it was shoulder length, brushed back, with a swoop to the front, on the left side — weird style."

She took some biscotti and placed it on a napkin. "She had deep lines on her chin, crow's feet and sallow cheeks — very hardened. I think her mother actually had less wrinkles. She had a medium build and was very curvy. Wish I had more of her figure, but hell, what are you gonna do? She wore a navy dress, kind of plain and ugly, but I did notice she had brown…*brown* flats on — for the love of God, Ma, brown flats with a navy dress? I've never liked brown and blue…but that's just me?"

Marta took a sip of her cooling coffee.

"They waited for me to answer. I said *"Aunt Tessa?"* She said *"Yes dear, it is your long lost Aunt Tessa and I'm sure you remember your cousin, Celia."* She was kind of weird, Celia. She did like this bow-thing to me and then smiled and said *"Greetings"*. I almost busted out laughing. I mean what the hell kind of *hello* is that! *Greetings!* She was out there, Ma. Well, anyway, that's all I said to Celia with the exception of bye at the end. Oh, wait. I did say nice to see you again. I wanted to be polite."

"So I walked over, I mean, it was ten feet away and I felt stupid talking across the blueberry pies and people would stare. So you know, I went over and said, *"Yea well, you're not lost. You're right here!"* I felt weird Ma. I knew there was a falling-out and didn't know what to say, so I laughed, she laughed and then she said. *"Oh yes, I'm here all right. How's your mother? How is she getting on without your wonderful father beside her?"*

Marta took another sip of coffee and bounced her leg faster.

"I couldn't believe she mentioned Dad. I guess it's polite. Anyway, there was just something sinister about mentioning Dad. Maybe it's just me." She swished a hand at her mother and continued.

"Anyway, her voice was light and friendly, you know that fake politeness. She stood very straight and dignified. I told her, *"Ma is Ma. She misses my Dad but she's doing just fine, and she is as healthy as ever."And* then she said *"Oh, I'm so pleased to hear that. Do tell my long lost sister, I said hello, won't you, and give her my best. Will you dear.*" I told her that I would and said she should try some of the blueberries — they were delicious. It was strange the way she referred to you as *long lost* after she said that about herself. Anyway, I smiled to Celia and said bye to them both…as I turned, Aunt Tessa cleared her throat."

Another bolt of thunder shook the house. The lamp flickered; the room was lit by a quick flash of lightning and then sank into darkness. Azzurra stood and turned on the kitchen light. She had a feeling about who was causing the storm and if it was him, she was going to give him an ear-full when she saw him.

Azzurra sat down and waited for Marta to continue.

Marta imitated her Aunts voice. *"Marta dear, how is your cousin Olivia doing? Is she well, the poor thing?* I said that I thought so, that it had been a while since I saw her. It was weird — almost sent chills up my spine. I mean to ask about Aunt Katie's daughter after the huge fight between them? Well, Aunt Tessa gave another fake smile and said to Celia, *"I told you she'd be fine."* She then turned to me. *"Well, do take care, Marta."* She nodded again and they walked away."

Marta leaned back in her chair. "That was it. I swear on Dad's grave. Oh, I bought a dozen of the Greek pastries…never mind. I guess that wasn't important." She took a breath. "So, now can you tell me what the hell is going on?"

Azzurra took a sip of coffee and dabbed her mouth with a napkin. She leaned forward, placed her forearms on the table and said, "I'm still angry that you spoke with them Marta…but at least now…I know there's trouble."

* * * *

The Cellar

Azzurra stood and began to gather the plates, biscotti and cookies. "It will all make sense, once I've explained everything." She walked toward the kitchen sink. "In time, I will tell you everything. Unfortunately, now is not that time. You'll just have to be patient and trust me." She threw the napkins in the trash and moved the biscotti and cookies to the other side of the counter.

"I've changed my mind — I'm no longer angry with you. As a matter of fact, I'm glad you spoke to them. There have been things throughout the years that have always bothered me and now, I have an answer."

The trees, deforming into the wind's minions, shown for a brief moment as the dark skies lit up the yard and then sank back into darkness.

Azzurra placed the biscotti and the cookies on a crystal platter — lining them in a circular pattern. She was calm for some reason, confident, secure.

She placed the last bit of biscotti in the center of the platter. "And let me tell you something Marta, as far as the men coming knocking on your door, you're right, they will not come knocking on your door. That's why you need to get out there and join the rest of the world. There is not a thing wrong with the way you have aged. You're my daughter and I would tell you."

"Now, let me tell you something else." She leaned down to her daughter and took her cheeks in the palms of her hands. "You are a beautiful woman. If you take some time with your hair and use some makeup...although you don't need too much sweetheart, just a pinch for color. Spend a bit more time in picking clothes that would compliment your figure and show a lot more confidence, you will be surprised at what comes your way."

She winked at Marta and slapped her cheeks. "Now here's what I want you to do, you need to call your brother and sister sometime today and invite them over for pasta supper on Wednesday." She began to remove her apron. "Do not take no for an answer." She waved a finger at Marta. "That should give me some time to get...well to prepare myself for how I'm going to explain everything to the three of you."

She opened the pantry door and hung her apron. "Now, another thing, you are to say nothing to anyone and do not call Olivia. I will call my niece when the time is right. You can tell your brother and sister everything, but do not call anyone else. You will just have to be patient."

Azzurra placed the crystal lid on the cake platter, now lined with Italian cookies and biscotti — home baked by Azzurra herself. She pointed a finger at her daughter. "I think I'll make some brownies a bit later." She walked past Marta and into the back bedroom. A moment later she returned with her purse and a sweater. "You and I have to go someplace. I'll need you all day tomorrow too, so you'll have to find a way out of work."

Marta's mouth dropped open. "Out of work...I haven't called in sick for over twenty years!"

Azzurra set her purse on the table and laid the black sweater over the chairs' edge. "Well it's about time you did." She then placed her palms on Marta's cheeks once again. "Now, you and I have always had a special con-nection — my daughter, my friend. Not that I don't love Marie and Nicco, but it's always been you and me sweetheart." She squeezed her daughter's cheeks together. "Tell Nicco or Marie and I'll deny it!"

Azzurra stood. "I have to go to the cellar...I'll be right back." When she reached the basement door, she turned to her daughter. "Could you shut off the coffee pot sweetheart, you can leave your Aunt Katie's cups and saucers; I'll do them a bit later, they'll be fine." She opened the door, walked down a step, turned, winked at Marta, and closed the door.

Her eyes took their time adjusting to the light as she looked around the cellar.

Bottles of pickled cucumbers sat on their shelves. There was a bag of potatoes that would be mashed, baked or fried. Canned tomato paste sat next to cans of black olives, flour, sugar and dozens of spices. Azzurra stood in the center of the cellar trying to remember how to open the panel.

Now let me see, which one are you? She said to herself. Her eyes moved to a bottle of wine that read, *Castello Banfi Brunello di Montalcino.* She picked up a nearby footstool and placed it under the shelf. Azzurra reached for the bottle and twisted it to right, and then the left. She smiled to herself. She then pulled the bottle of wine toward her and carefully stepped down.

There was a click of a hydraulic system releasing pressure. A four by three foot section of the panel dropped below floor level on a roller track. It slid back and to the right and down the wall. She flicked a switch that revealed a circular stairway that led down twelve feet into the earth. Some of the stones were chipped and cobwebs were strewn throughout.

She had a flashback of the kids asking about the light switch by the pantry shelves that never seemed to do anything. She or Franco would say it was there before they moved in and they had no idea.

Azzurra stepped down the dimly lit stairs, brushing the cobwebs away. She heard another thunder strike from above and could still hear the rain pelting the house.

Within minutes she found the items she was looking for, placed them in a purple velvet bag and headed back up the stone steps. She flicked the switch down and watched the panel close. She opened the basement door and heard the tail end of her daughter's conversation.

"...I've never seen her like this. She wants you here Wednesday night for supper..."

"...Nicco, she won't take no for an answer."

"...I don't know; tell Tracy there's a family emergency or something."

"...OK, good. Oh, can you call Marie and tell her the same thing?"

The thunder struck again. Marta jumped and inhaled a quick breath. "Yea, it's that damn storm."

"...well it's storming something terrible here: lightning, rain, winds, the whole bit. Anyway listen, Ma said I have to go with her someplace, don't ask I have no idea."

"...all right, I'll see you Wednesday. Don't forget to call Marie."

"…all right, Bye." She hung up. "Ma, where did you go?"

Azzurra stood near the kitchen sink, trying to brush some of the dust from the velvet bag. "I'll tell you soon enough, Marta." She turned to her daughter. "And thank you for calling Nicco and not saying that I was crazy… although I didn't hear the whole conversation. Now, Marta we are off to our first destination." She smiled and winked.

"OK Ma, I'm going along with this, but it had better all make sense in the end or I'm taking pills!" She grabbed her purse from the table and took a sip of the now cold coffee. "What about the storm?"

Azzurra exchanged her slippers for a pair of black pumps and then grabbed her purse and sweater. She clutched the velvet bag close to her body and walked briskly past her daughter. "Enough with the pills Marta… you shouldn't joke about such a thing." She waved a finger at her daughter. "Don't worry about the storm" She looked up to the ceiling "I just had my hair done, so it better be over soon!"

Marta narrowed her eyes and glanced up to the ceiling and then back to her mother. "It was my problem…You OK there Ma?"

"I'm fine, now let's go." Azzurra headed for the front door.

"Where are we going?" Marta asked.

Azzurra turned. "We are going to the cemetery."

* * * *

The Cemetery

The entrance of the Detroit cemetery was the same as Azzurra had remembered, beautiful and horrid at the same time. She drove the car through the old wrought iron gates that she hated so much. Sunlight streamed through the trees.

Memories bubbled like a kettle ready to release steam, brought back to life by simply entering a familiar place. She and Franco drove past the same rustic, black gates so many years ago. Katie was in front of them — in the hearse.

The landscaping was beautiful and calm. Large oaks, maples, weeping willows and pines towered above the ground.

Azzurra's heart sank; it never seemed to get easy to visit this place. Through the windshield, she saw a flock of ducks flying toward the chapel and mausoleums located at the end of the narrow road.

The gravel beneath the wheels crunched as Azzurra pulled the Lincoln to the side of the road, stopping in front of the mausoleums.

"Ma, I can't believe this cemetery is still so beautiful." Marta opened the car door and stepped onto the grass.

"Well, just because it's old, doesn't mean it's not needed. People are still getting buried here, you know." She turned and looked across the landscape at a man setting up chairs in front of an open grave.

Marta squinted in the sunshine and blocked the light with her hand. Her eyes followed her mother's. "Ma, is it safe here?" When her mother didn't answer, she turned — Azzurra was gone.

"Ma, wait up!" Marta called.

Stone steps led to a plateau that was flanked by mausoleums. Her mother stood near a beautiful birch tree.

Marta was out of breath when she reached the top of the plateau. A sign read, "No Artificial Flowers, They Will Be Removed".

Marta fanned herself with a collapsed, foot-long umbrella. "You know Ma, I can't believe how the storm cleared the moment we stepped out of the house." She looked to the sky. "Although, it looks like another storm is brewing."

"There better not be another storm, if he knows what's good for him." Azzurra began to walk toward the halls of the dead.

Marta rolled her eyes. "Who are you talking about, Ma?"

"Not now, Marta." She turned and walked in the direction of her sister's resting place.

Narrow paths lead through the gardens which were flanked by 12 halls of mausoleums. The mausoleums were open, which meant that visitors could enter through either side. Japanese maples, weeping pines, and green leafy hostas, intertwined with ornamental bushes and shrubs. Rows of boastful boxwoods, lilac trees and bright red burning bushes, joined the landscape.

Azzurra looked up into the sky. She shielded her eyes from the sun and watched for a moment.

"Is it St. Catherine's?" Marta asked, as she read the etched name at the top of one of the halls.

"She wanted St. Catherine's that time, but there were none left. It's St. Aloysius." Azzurra approached the last hall on the right. She stopped and turned to face her daughter. "Marta, I want you to stay over there, near St. John's. I have to do this alone."

The sky above them rumbled.

Marta took a breath and sat on one of the several benches that were placed throughout the gardens. She watched as the groundskeepers set a casket lowering device in place. "All right, I'll wait here."

"Now promise me you won't come into the hall unless I call for you." Azzurra waited for an answer.

Marta adjusted herself toward her mother. "I promise Ma."

Marta watched her mother walk into the entrance of St. Aloysius and sighed. One day her mother would be in her own vault. Her heart sank. When had her mother turned 71? Where had the time gone?

St Aloysius housed nearly 240 residents. Large, stone squares were in shades of dark granite. Some of the stones were adorned with small photos of the departed. The names and dates were etched in white. Azzurra stood at the entrance of the great hall, while her sister, Katie, rested near the rear entrance.

Azzurra could see a large oak tree at the opposite end of the hall. She entered with small footsteps, taking in the names and photos as she passed. Some of the residents had not yet arrived as their dates of departing were blank.

She spoke aloud. "Now let me see, where are you?" If memory served her right, it would be the bottom row, third one from the end, on the left.

Azzurra approached the stone that listed her sister's name and her departure date. Her body felt heavy, weighed down as she read the words... Katherine E *Marinacci and Dante A Marinacci.*

"Well it's been a long time now, hasn't it?" A sharp pang stung at her heart. Several minutes passed as she stared at the names that were etched.

Azzurra shook her head to rid the memories. The breeze picked up within the tunnel of the dead. Leaves blew past her feet and it felt cold against her silk blouse as a chill rose up her spine. She placed the black sweater over her shoulders and spoke out loud. "Now let me see...oh it's been such a long time. I hope I remember how to do this."

A slow, guttural rumble of thunder began in the distance. The rumble grew louder and then cracked. She looked to the large oak tree. Its leaves and branches began to move in the increasing breeze.

She placed the velvet bag down and loosened its sash with care. Azzurra removed the items one by one and placed them gently in front of her, directly below the remains of Katie and her brother-in-law, Dante.

Her eyes focused on the stone plate above Katie and her brother-in-law. A photo of a cute Italian couple stared back at her. They had not been there at her last visit. They were James Colyica 1905–1977 and Catherine Colyica 1911–1970. "Hello. My name is Azzurra. I'm here to see my sister."

The temperature dropped several degrees as the skies darkened and the winds grew in strength.

Azzurra knelt down on the velvet bag, picked up the chalk and began to draw on the pavement. Several minutes later she sat back and admired her work. There was a star at the top of the circle and an eye at the bottom. Two arrows were drawn on either side of the circle, pointing to its center and her sister's full name was written in the middle.

She placed the oil burner on her sister's name, removed a cork from a bottle and poured river water into the basin of the oil burner. With a large wooden match, she lit a candle and placed it under the basin. Azzurra contemplated for a moment or two before taking the sage. Holding the sage over the candle, it caught fire and began to produce a plume of smoke, which was thicker than she anticipated. She got to her feet and made large sweeping motions with her arm, smudging the area, ridding the hall of negative energy. Her words echoed as she spoke her sister's full name.

Katherine Elizabeth Degeli Marinacci

***

Marta pulled her hair away from her eyes as she looked up into the sky. Swirls of black clouds were forming as drizzles of rain fell onto her face. She deflated with a sigh and looked back toward St. Aloysius. *"I should have had a shot of Baileys in my coffee this morning.*

Marta fumbled in her purse for a cigarette, placed it between her lips and lit the end. She took a deep drag and then gave a frightful scream. A reddish brown blob of something caught her peripheral vision. Her head spun around as she brought the umbrella high above her head, ready for the attack. It was a squirrel. He darted up a nearby weeping willow.

Her mother's voice came from inside the hall, "Marta calm down. It's just a squirrel."

Marta reached in her purse, pulled out her cell phone and flipped it open. This strange event was not going to be experienced alone. She was calling her sister, Marie.

***

After a few minutes of smudging, Azzurra placed the sage in a small bowl and let the smoke swirl in the air. She removed a small lock of Katie's hair from a plastic bag and placed it into the water. Azzurra spoke the incantation.

17

"Beyond the grave I speak to thee
Hear my words and come to me
Bring me the soul that use to be
Here on Earth and walked with me
Katherine Elizabeth Degeli Marinacci"

Lightning flashed across the sky, lighting up St. Aloysius. The sound of rain entered the mausoleum as did the rustle of the trees that fought against the wind.

Azzurra carefully removed her necklace that Katie had given her for her sixteenth birthday and placed it into the small basin of water. She waited patiently as the smoke from the sage spiraled in the air.

Water began to swirl in the basin. It churned and bubbled. With each bubble the water rose from the basin. After several minutes, it molded itself into a Merlin Falcon that flapped its wings. Water spattered to the ground which immediately retracted and re-joined the bird. It hovered over the basin, looking at Azzurra, waiting for instructions.

The Merlin Falcon was about 10 inches in height with a 27 inch wing span. Azzurra spoke to her favorite messenger. "Oh hello…I need you to find Katherine Elizabeth Degeli Marinacci." She then spoke into the bird as if recording her voice. "Katie, this is Azzurra, please come now. I need you." She nodded and told the bird "Thank you."

Azzurra made a wish that Katie would still be within the Earth's realm. Her eyes followed the bird as he flew past her and out the entrance toward the large oak tree.

***

Marta's eyes widened as she saw smoke coming from the opposite entrance of St. Aloysius. *What the hell is she doing?*

She took a long drag from her cigarette. "Marie…Marie…there's smoke coming out of the entrance. I'm a wreck. I'm so glad that I haven't quit smoking, although a drink about now would come in handy too."

Her scream echoed the great halls. It was the same squirrel.

The skies erupted with rain. Marta opened the umbrella. It exploded outward into a large black canopy. A gust of wind caught the umbrella; it tugged out of her hands and flew into the air, and over the roof of a mausoleum. Marta screamed as the sudden jerk pulled her forward, toppling her over the bench into the begonias. Rain drenched her in moments. She frantically looked for her phone; it was in a hostas plant. Lightning flashed across the gardens, thunder cracked and the wind struck her. Marta screamed again and reached for the phone, stood and bolted into St. Johns.

18

The winds howled through the tunnel. Marta's eyes darted in every direction; her heart thudded, pulse raced and her palms began to sweat. She placed the muddy phone to her soaked head. Marta's voice dropped as she panted into the phone. "I'm all right. Just a squirrel and I lost my umbrella."

***

Azzurra sat patiently waiting and laughing to herself. *She's afraid of her own shadow that girl. God only knows how she'll defend herself.*

Within a few minutes, the Merlin Falcon soared through the entrance. She waited —forgetting how the rest was supposed to work. Was she to ask the bird something or would Katie just come?

Thunder echoed through the hall and lightning flashed once again.

"Basil, if you don't stop this storm, I'm going to be mad! Now I will call for you when I'm ready. I don't want to get you into trouble. Now that's enough!" Azzurra placed hands upon her hips as the falcon hovered near her shoulder.

Thunder cracked once more, then the rain faded into drizzles and the sun peaked out from behind the clouds.

"Thank you Basil!" She looked at the Merlin Falcon. "Is she on her way?"

The Merlin looked out the entrance toward the large oak tree. Sun was shining behind its large branches that gently blew in the breeze. A rainbow appeared far in the distance. Azzurra stared out at the large oak. A mist was forming just in front of the tree. A halo of lights fell from the sky as the tree branches glistened in its bath.

It was a kaleidoscope that appeared before her. Beautiful reds, purples, oranges and greens melded with the landscape. A fluffy reddish brown squirrel appeared at the entrance. He watched as the mist spread.

A silky white shape formed in front of the tree, floating several feet in the air. The shape hovered for several moments within the beams of light then shifted into a shape of a young woman. She glided over the wet blades of grass.

The woman was showered in a rainbow of color. Oak branches waved gently through her thin existence. She wore a medium blue dress and satin slippers. Dark hair fell in waves to her shoulders. Katie slowly walked into the entrance of the open garden mausoleum — into her resting place.

Azzurra was frozen with joy, with fear and with sorrow. She smiled at her sister. "Katie, I can't believe it's you."

* * * *

Katie

Katie's eyes narrowed and her jaw tightened as she stood in silence. She turned toward the oak tree — something else was on its way. Oranges, greens and purples filled the entrance of the Great Hall once again. A small shape of watery white exposed itself, wriggling its four legs as it hovered in the air. A little black and white dog appeared, just as thin and transparent as the Spirit before. When his legs reached the grass, they took him toward his mother, best friend and companion. A tiny bark came from him as he made a breezy entrance into St. Aloysius.

Azzurra placed hands to her mouth and cried out. "Oh my word, It's Blackie!"

Katie looked down at her long time friend as he wagged his tail at Azzurra. She then looked at her sister, crossed her arms and spoke. "You used Magick."

Azzurra's heart raced, eyes avoiding her sister. She was surprised to hear Blackie's growl. "Blackie, you leave that squirrel alone." Katie spoke firmly. The fluffy squirrel sat on his hind legs watching the reunion. He wrinkled his nose and stared at Blackie.

Azzurra watched the squirrel, thankful for the few extra seconds he gave. After exhaling a breath, she focused on her sister. "Katie, please don't be mad. When you hear what I have to tell you, you will understand why I used Magick."

Azzurra's heartbeat slowed and she placed her hands upon her hips. Her voice strengthened with confidence. She felt calm and somehow new exactly what to say. "Now, I'm not going to pretend it's not good to see you and if you want to stay mad, well, then too bad, but let me tell you something Katie. That Vow Dad made us take, that you made me swear I'd uphold on your death bed...well, it was for nothing, because our sister, Tessa, has never stopped using Magick!"

Katie's mouth opened as Azzurra continued. "That's right Katie. I believe she's been using Spirits to attack your daughter, Olivia." Azzurra nodded curtly.

Katie sighed, placed a hand on her chest and said nothing. The soft breeze that rustled the trees was the only sound the Great Hall possessed. Her voice was defeated when she finally spoke. "Azzurra, I can't believe it — she's using Magick, after all the things that have happened. Doesn't she see what using Magick has done to our family? The Evil it brought into our lives?" Katie placed a hand to her forehead and began to pace. "I must have been a damn fool to have made you take that stupid Vow, knowing full well what Tessa was like." Her arm fell to her side with a purposeful slap. "With the family not using Magick, you were all sitting ducks. Dad would have understood if we didn't take the Vow. Besides, it's the people who are evil, not the Magick."

Katie turned to face the entrance of St. Aloysius. Memories of Azzurra and her other sister, Arianna, came to focus. They were beside her as she lay in the bed, hooked up to an IV, a heart monitor and a dozen tubes, begging them to take the Vow. "I was upset; I was on my death bed." She shrugged and turned to face her sister. "I'm not mad at you Azzurra. I'm disappointed that the Vow that Dad wanted us to take, the Vow that we should have honored him by — was for nothing." Katie closed her eyes, sighed once more and then opened them. "I knew something had happened the moment I saw Merlin and heard your voice. I knew you wouldn't have broken the Vow unless something awful had happened."

Thin wisps of white silky clouds moved gently above them. "I really thought everything would have ended. Well, at least the use of those damn Spirits." Katie said.

"Oh, Katie, I think it's the same as it was when you were alive, but it's been so subtle that you couldn't tell whether it was life taking its toll, or the work of the dead." Azzurra bent down and called Blackie away from the squirrel. He was lying on his back grunting at his new friend. "Has Blackie been with you the whole time?"

Katie nodded. "He hasn't left my side since the day I died, except once."

Katie stood in front of her sister. After all these years, she was once again mulling over life's problems with her best friend. A smile broke across Katie's face; her eyes widened and filled with tears. Azzurra looked beautiful — forty years older but her sister was still beautiful. She felt her cheeks flush and that tingling feeling around her nose that she hadn't felt in decades. "Oh Azzurra, it's so good to see you!"

Azzurra burst into tears. She opened her arms and ran to her sister. To her horror, she went right through her and stumbled out the end of the Great Hall. A light scream escaped as Blackie barked and the squirrel darted away.

"Azzurra, are you all right?" Katie called after her. "What the hell were you thinking? I haven't become solid yet. You can't do that." With those words, Katie became solid and began to laugh. "I was a little slow. I'm sorry."

Azzurra turned to face her sister, flushed red, as she placed her hands over her face and began to laugh. Through the muffle of her hands, she spoke. "Oh Katie...I'm so stupid. I should have waited. You were still a ghost. I went right through you." She wrapped her arms around herself and shivered. "Oh, that was so cold." She laughed harder.

Blackie became solid as well and ran in circles in front of Azzurra. He'd stop, look at her, then bark and do circles again.

The two sisters embraced with laughter and tears of happiness. It had been a long time since the two of them had a laugh together.

As little girls, they would gather around the kitchen table for dinner with the rest of the family. Their mother would warn them that their father was in a bad mood, so there was to be no silliness at the table.

Their father, Pasquale, owned a barber shop off Kelly road in Detroit. It was the one place where he got along with everyone. He chatted with his customers about everything under the sun...even sports. However, the stress of competitive barber shop franchises, which charged half the price, fueled his bad temper.

When he was in a bad mood, Pasquale would enter the dining room with a ridiculous, over exaggerating "bad mood" attitude. He'd then make an announcement that he didn't want any talking that night and no goofing at the table.

Azzurra and Katie would start to laugh, knowing full well how it would end. They tried to pretend that they had sneezed or choked or coughed, while their mother and sister, Arianna, made noises to try and cover up their smuggled laughter. Gabriella, their other sister, would pretend nothing was wrong, Tessa would get angry, while their brother, Augusto, would roll his eyes. Everything they did to cover up the laughter, was unsuccessful, for in a few moments their father would slam a hand down on the table. "I said no goofing!" Well, now it was to the extreme, from laughter to tears as they cried eating their dinners — two sisters — two peas in a pod.

Azzurra hugged her sides as Katie covered her face in laughter. All those years later and they're still laughing. This time it was at Katie's resting place, in the Great Hall of St. Aloysius.

**

Marta crouched down near the entrance of St. Johns, peering in the direction of the mausoleum where her aunt was laid to rest. Her voice was quick, sharp and raised an octave as she spoke into her cell phone. "Marie there is barking and she's laughing...no, I don't think she's barking. There's an odd glow coming from the entrance. Maybe it's just the reflection of the sun." She looked around, trying to ascertain if she was correct. "Oh my God what do I do? Thank God I didn't quit." Her eyes grew wide as she inhaled deeply from her cigarette; with her hand trembling, she looked wildly at the entrance of the Great Hall wondering what in the hell her mother was doing.

* * * *

The Vow

$\mathcal{R}$ainwater dripped from the large oak's branches, flowed in tiny rivers through the hostas and begonias, and trickled off the rooftop of the mausoleums. Light sprinkles from the clearing skies were all that remained of Basil's storm. A fluffy reddish brown squirrel was joined by a sleek black squirrel; they peeked around the corner, tiny eyes watching the two women as they calmed their laughter and sunk into conversation. The women reminisced about old times and what the after-life was like; did Katie find Blackie or did Blackie find her? They spoke of their parents and how they had left the Earth's realm. Azzurra asked about Dante, Katie's husband.

Katie placed hands upon her hips and answered her sister. "Well, you know what that husband of mine did? God love him Azzurra, but sometimes I could still take a pan and hit him over the head with it. He's off with your husband...that's right, my husband Dante and your husband, Franco, gallivanting God only knows where — in a crisis no less."

With a wave of her arm, Katie conjured a chair and sat. "When that husband of yours died a few months back, the two of them went off to explore the other planets and such. What nonsense, and I might as well just come out and say it — it's bullshit!" Katie reached down and picked up Blackie and scratched the little Terrier behind his ears. His eyes filled with joy and closed half way.

Azzurra's eyes widened. "You mean to tell me, that Franco, my husband, the man I devoted my life to, the man I loved and have known since I was a teen — didn't attend his own funeral! He didn't even see if he could try to comfort me — after all those years." Her hands flew to her hips.

"Azzurra, I hate to tell you this…the boys were off within a few minutes of Franco's death. They were laughing and reminiscing, then Dante mentioned to go to the planets and they left. I should have conjured a pan and hit them both over their heads."

Katie continued and waved a finger at Azzurra. "I told them I had a feeling something was wrong…you know me and my feelings, never been wrong yet. Of course that's why I've never moved on, never felt right about what happened with Olivia. She was so withdrawn and stuck in that horrible marriage. So I never left the Earth's realm in search of Ma and Dad. Of course Dante wasn't going to leave without me, so…here we are." She conjured a chair for Azzurra and gestured with a hand to be seated.

Katie continued. "Well, I asked Franco if you were all right. He said that you were fine, not to worry; that you were the tough one." She looked down at her grunting dog. "It was good to see Franco after all those years. You know, I've always liked him. Well anyway, he said it was wonderful to see me, we chatted for a bit, and they left."

Katie adjusted herself and smoothed her dress. "I know it's a shame, not even to attend your own funeral. If I wasn't sure it wouldn't make me sick to my stomach, I would have spit!" She placed a hand on her chest. "I was there though. The Higher Sprits allow us to attend the funerals of family and friends, you know. They really don't like us being around our loved ones. They say it's too much of a deterrent to move on. Anyway, his funeral was very nice, Azzurra. You did a wonderful job…just like mine. Oh and thank you for the blue dress and satin slippers, they're beautiful. You didn't have to go through the fuss though; a housecoat would have been fine."

Blackie looked up at Katie and grunted.

Azzurra seated herself on the chair, not quite sure if it would vanish or not. "He's been gone not even three months; never showed up to his own funeral…that son of a…I've been missing him something terrible and he's out having the time of his death! You wait till I get hold of him." She raised her voice and crossed her arms over her chest. "Thank you Katie; let's see how Franco's going to get out of this one." Azzurra glanced at her watch and began to tell the story of Tessa and Marta's conversation.

After listening to the details of the conversation, Katie looked to the large oak tree. She saw the squirrels looking at them. Blackie began to cry and wriggle in her arms. "First you growl at him, now he's you're new best friend? Oh look, now there are two squirrels…he's not as fluffy." She turned Blackie's head further from the squirrel's direction. "So what do you think it means?"

"Well Katie, the way I figure it, there's trouble. When she said 'lost' she was referring to the fact that she's been removed from this side of the family and is quite bitter. When she said that I was lost, well she was right, I had no clue that she was still fussing with her Magick."

Katie shook her head. "Oh, she is definitely up to something Azzurra. How could you've kept such a stupid Vow?"

Azzurra slapped a hand on her lap. "You were on your death bed! What was I supposed to do, deny your dying wish?" She swished a hand at her sister and continued. "Beee." Which was a word the older generation used to mean; *for the love of God, or what a mess or I can't believe that.*

Blackie jumped off Katie's lap and headed over to the water bird that hovered near Azzurra. The bird squawked and fluttered his wings.

Azzurra continued. "Marta said Tessa stood straight and dignified. Her tone was polite and fake. She always puts on that pretense in front of her enemies and Spirits she doesn't trust."

"Was she all in black with a splash of rust? Did she wear dull black shoes?" Katie asked.

"Yes, she did. That's how I knew she was still practicing — her and her stupid clothing rituals." Azzurra rolled her eyes.

Katie responded. "Blackie, leave that bird alone! You know, she never forgave me for that argument. I simply didn't want the family to use Spirits anymore. So, I asked Dad to put a ban on them and have everyone take the Vow. You would have though I asked her to cut off her right arm. I just thought that beckoning Spirits to do your bidding was too dangerous. There's plenty of other Magick that is safe to do." Katie swished a hand in the air. "So she got mad and has been attacking Olivia to get back at me for asking her to give up the power of Spirits."

"Well, I think there's a lot more to the story, Katie." Azzurra shifted uncomfortably. She didn't meet Katie's eyes and her heart rate leapt. "I was so stupid; I should have known something was wrong with Olivia."

Katie called Blackie to her. "You would have never realized that it was the influence of Spirits or those dam Culls."

Azzurra wrinkled her face and contorted her mouth when Katie spoke of Culls. It had been years since she heard that horrible word. They stalk you randomly or are sent by someone. They cling to your body and whisper terrible things in your ears, feasting on your thoughts. Culls twist your deepest fears, doubts and weaknesses against you by plaguing your dreams and whispering to you morning, noon, and night. They were nasty, ugly little demons.

Katie looked down and adjusted the hem of her dress and scolded Blackie as he approached her with his ears flat to his head. "I told you to stay away from that bird, now you scared him back into his bottle." She looked up to her sister. "You know, after I died, I had a bad feeling about making you stick to that Vow, but what are you gonna do…I was dead."

"Well Katie, when you asked me to keep the Vow, you thought the war was over. How were you to know?" Azzurra said. "Has everyone else moved on? Have you seen Aunt Francine or Gilbert…any news of Anna?"

"They all moved on. As for Anna, neither I nor anyone else has seen her, and she did not cross over — the Higher Spirits told me that much." She shook her head. "Basil of course never moved on— he and I talk all the time."

"I worry why Basil never moved on." Azzurra glanced up. "Poor Anna never knew what happened to her. You were right Katie; we should have given up that part of Magick when we were teens." Azzurra stood.

Katie looked up and spoke softly. "I've always said it; you may as well sit down with the Devil himself! Beee…No wonder I'm not resting in peace. Who could rest with all this mess?" She turned and looked out at the large oak tree.

Katie wrapped her arms around her shoulders and shivered. She stood silent for a moment and then she spoke. Her voice was low. "Have you seen her lately? Have you seen my Olivia?"

Azzurra replied. "I saw her a week after Franco passed. I stopped by her house. Olivia and I could always talk about things and Walter doesn't bother me. He's always liked me for some reason. Carlotta won't stop by, she's afraid she'll cause trouble for Olivia, so she says she doesn't see her sister too much." She took a few steps toward Katie.

Azzurra watched Katie closely and treaded with care. Her voice was soft and soothing. "Well, I won't lie — she's stressed — tired eyes, didn't look well. She's having a lot of issues with Walter. He's always accusing her of something, saying awful things to her and he's fighting with the kids something terrible. David moved out — couldn't take it anymore. They got into a big fight about parking his car in the driveway. Michael and Rose are still home. She's afraid they'll leave her and she'll be alone with him." Azzurra approached her sister's side. Katie was still staring out to the oak tree, her eyes filled with tears.

"Katie, I've always known Walter was a hard man, so I thought nothing of it. As for the kids — well, they grew up with him, so they're bound to have issues. Besides all kids go through things, mine did." She paused a moment. "Don't worry Katie, we'll help her. It may not be Culls; maybe it's only Spirits that are manipulating her thoughts." Azzurra took her sister's hand. A tear fell from Katie's eye.

"Azzurra, we have to ask the Higher Spirits to break the Vow." Katie's voice cracked.

Azzurra replied. "We will Katie. We'll have to ask them to let you into her house, so you can talk with her, explain the situation?"

Katie looked down. "My poor Olivia." She turned to her sister and sighed. She nodded once and cleared her mind, feeling a sudden strength. Her voice was even when she spoke. For some reason she felt protected. "You will also need to contact Basil and recruit more Spirits. I hate to say it, but you have to fight Spirits with Spirits. I will check for any activity around Olivia's house. See if someone can tell me if anything strange has happened or if they saw any Spirits going in and out."

Azzurra added. "I've all ready opened the secret room. I'll need to get things in order down there. We'll need to also ask the Higher Spirits if they will grant us Guardians for Olivia and the rest of the family — explain to them that nobody knows Magick. The Guardians will remove the demons and protect her and the others — while us, the older generation, well…we'll have to fight."

Katie squinted. "You said Celia was there, right?"

'Yes, Tessa's daughter was there. Marta said she was really out there too."

"That means Celia knows Magick." Katie nodded.

"You're right. I bet you the other side of the family taught them everything." She looked down at Blackie then up to her sister. "Katie, our kids are in so much danger."

Katie began to pace back and forth. Blackie followed her. "Don't panic Azzurra. We have to think about this. We'll have to be careful about what family we call, they could be in cahoots with Tessa. You'll have to call for Basil as soon as they let you."

Azzurra stood. "You're right; I shall call upon my Basil. I'm sure his powers have grown and he would have learned new things too. And when you do see him, tell him that he had better stop with the storms — the Higher Spirits don't like us messing with the weather. It could cause havoc all across the east coast and Canada." She placed her hands on her hips. "He'll just have to be patient."

Katie paused and placed a hand upon her forehead and nodded. "Oh Azzurra, how in the hell are you going to tell the kids they're Witches?"

***

Marta stood staring at the burial. The last bit of dirt was being placed on the grave; the chairs were being stacked as the last two mourners walked arm and arm away from the grave site. She balanced the muddy cell phone on her shoulder as she spoke with her sister.

"...and lead us not into temptation, but deliver us from evil. Amen"

Marta turned to look at the entrance of St. Aloysius. "For the love of God Marie, it's been over two hours. My phones about dead and not a single damn bird has been around...not even that horrifying little squirrel. Marie, I'm gonna take pills! I swear...pills!"

***

"Katie, everything will be fine." Azzurra started to pace with her sister as she spoke. "We shall call upon the family. All of those that are willing to help, that is. We'll speak with Olivia and Carlotta. We'll call Arianna and Mateo, Augusto, Bernardo, and of course Bella, from New York — they'll be on our side. Then there's Thom from San Francisco, good old Thom. He'll be there for us. I'm sure we can count on Drago and Kimberly; they've always been there in times of crisis. Oh that Kimberly is going to be so mad."

"What about Gabriella and Nicolai?" Katie asked.

"Well, now Katie, you know I love our sister, but I'm not sure about her. Remember the last time? Nicolai keeps his mouth shut, but Gabriella has a big mouth and never listens to anyone."

Katie stopped pacing and looked at her sister. "That's ridiculous, Gabriella is fine. We'll just have to tell her to keep her mouth shut this time. You know her, never liked anyone fighting...always wanted to forgive. She'd always say *we all make mistakes...none of us are perfect*. I guess that's why she still speaks with Contessa. Gabby just has a soft heart, no reason to not include her." Katie paused and then continued. "Now, we have to strengthen the Witches of our families. Dear God, you're all in your seventies and eighties." She shook her head. "Beee, what a damn mess were in."

Azzurra narrowed her eyes and stood straight; she winced a bit and held her back. "I'm not dead yet. I just have to see the chiropractor more often and

I'll be fine. I'm as tough as I was back then, you know. I'm not afraid of those Spirits or Tessa." She balled a tiny fist and shook it in the air.

Katie laughed. "Look at you, Miss Toughie over there." Her eyes narrowed. "But you're right. You're one of the most powerful Witches alive, Azzurra. You have the inheritance of the Degeli bloodline and every Witch that was in our family. The lineage is handed to you — no one else. We don't even know how powerful you'll be."

Azzurra took in a deep breath. "Oh Katie, I forgot I had the lineage." She clasped hands over her mouth.

Katie rolled her eyes and swished a hand at her sister. "Beee, you forgot you inherited the lineage, and you say not to worry." She noticed the reddish brown squirrel peeking around the corner of the mausoleum. "He's an odd squirrel. Blackie come here and leave him alone."

"He's a brave little squirrel, isn't he? I wonder where the black one went." Azzurra nodded. "This one's cute though…fluffy."

Katie continued. "Listen, I'll go to the Higher Spirits right now and ask them to break the Vow. I'll ask them to let you call for Basil too. I'll try to convince them to keep things quiet and explain to them what's happening. I'll ask them about assigning Guardians for the family as well." She shook her head. "Doesn't Tessa know what the Higher Spirits will do to her when her time comes? What a stupid girl!"

Azzurra shook her head in agreement. "We have a lot of work to do Katie."

"Well, we're going to pull out all of our old books, Enchantments, Spirits, and Wands — because that dirty little bitch isn't going to get away with this. We will call the whole family back…for an all-out, old-fashioned, Witches War!" Katie placed hands upon her hips and nodded once in agreement with herself.

Azzurra smiled. "Oh, it's good to have you back Katie. It's good to have you back."

* * * *

All in Good Time

Azzurra held the velvet bag close to her chest as she exited St. Aloysius. Her footsteps slowed as she approached what looked like her daughter. Marta stood at the entrance of St. John...hair flat, eyes narrowed and jaw clenched. Her grey, muddy sweatshirt was stretched below the calves.

"Marta! What happened to you?" Azzurra asked.

Marta's heart began to race. "First of all, I have spent my normally calm and relaxing Sunday morning in a cemetery! Then, there is a freak storm that seems to follow us, a horrifying squirrel that attacks people and I thought I heard you laughing with someone. I also could have sworn I heard a dog barking, not to mention the smoke, bright lights and I lost my umbrella!" She violently heaved her purse over her shoulder. "I've been on the phone with Marie. She missed church because I threatened to take pills if she hung up and now, thanks to me, she's a wreck."

"I'm sorry, but it couldn't be helped." Azzurra said. "Thank you for being patient and waiting for your mother." Azzurra waved a finger at Marta.

"Although, I have to say, you're afraid of your own shadow Marta. That squirrel, did not attack you."

Marta took a breath, looked up into the sky, screamed and followed her mother to the car.

Azzurra opened the passenger side door and turned to face her daughter. "All I said was that the squirrel didn't attack you. Now can you please stop with the screaming?"

Marta snatched the keys from her mother's outstretched hand and walked to the driver's side of the Lincoln. "He could have been rabid and terrifying."

"You're right sweetheart; maybe that cute fluffy red squirrel was terrifying."

A strange guttural sound came from Marta as she slammed the car door shut.

Azzurra's mind raced. For forty years there had been silence. For forty years their Magick had remained dormant. Their lives were at peace. Now, in the cooling September breeze, another Witches War was brewing — A war between families. What they had thought was peace, a truce made all those years ago, had been veiled by evil just below the surface...scratching and tearing at Olivia's soul. Katie needed to convince the Higher Spirits to assist them, to free her daughter from the torture inflicted by an old family feud. Nicco, Marie and Marta needed to know the truth of what happened almost four decades ago — the family secret needed to be told.

Azzurra sat in the passenger seat clutching the velvet bag. Her eyes were focused straight ahead. "Marta, I'm sorry if you're upset. All I can tell you... is that I'll explain everything at Wednesday's supper. I'll tell the three of you then — the Lord knows I don't want to have to say it more than once."

Marta took a deep breath. "Ma, I'm sorry. I didn't mean to snatch the keys from you like that. I didn't' sleep well, I'm getting a headache and today was just weird."

Azzurra faced her daughter. "I know sweetheart. Just try to be patient with your mother...it's not easy for me either." She sighed. "Now, I want you to come over between 9:30 and 10:00 tomorrow morning. I'll make some pastries and maybe eggs in a raft."

Marta smiled. "With raspberry filling?"

"OK, sweetheart...raspberry filling." Azzurra placed a hand to her mouth. "Oh, we missed Church again...well, maybe next week."

"Who's going to hear Father Bernardo?" Marta rolled her eyes. "You'll just have to explain that a family emergency came up."

"Oh I'll be telling him what's going on all right, and he won't like it one bit." Her mind raced to Katie. "Wait till Katie see's I still use her cups!"

Marta cocked her head to one side. "Ma...she's gonna *see* you use her cups? What...from the grave?"

Azzurra waved a finger toward her daughter. "All in good time Marta, all in good time."

* * * *

A Damsel in Distress!

Roberta's voice welcomed everyone to a cool September, Monday morning on *WWJ* radio. Marta reached lazily to her alarm, fumbled for the large button and pushed.

It raised its head, yawned, and focused on the sleepy woman.

The waft of fresh coffee gently stroked Marta's nostrils as she headed for the shower. The events from yesterday still fresh in her mind. What had her little Italian mother been keeping from her all these years?

After a quick shower, Marta sat on a tiny stool in the bathroom and reached for the moisturizer. The idea of taking time while applying makeup seemed a nice thought. Her mother's words came to mind. *There is not a thing wrong with how you have aged, I'm your mother and I would tell you.*

Marta reached for her deep red lipstick and froze. She had been applying lipstick in last night's dream, sitting on this very same stool. The vision of herself fixated in the mirror with tears streaming down her cheeks — startled her. Sadness filled her as she saw herself throw the lipstick at the mirror. Marta shook her head — the flash of last night's dream faded.

Marta checked herself in the mirror. Black slacks, which she hadn't seen since her early thirties, fit her well and displayed a nice pair of legs. A royal-blue silk buttoned-down blouse made her blue eyes sparkle. Slipping on a black blazer that Marie gave her years ago, she grabbed a pair of shoes from a box in the back of her closet. She adjusted the strap of the black opened-toed heels, looked down and thought *when did I buy these?*

For jewelry, she chose a mother of pearl heart pendent necklace that Olivia had bought her and a pair of silver half-moon earrings. The half moon's dangled inside a beveled hoop with a diamond baguette which sat in the arch of the moon...a Christmas present from her mother.

Marta made a final check in the mirror before heading to work. She pulled a couple of wisps of hair over her forehead and double checked the back of her head for an even fluff. She unbuttoned the second button of her blouse feeling a bit daring and sassy and headed out the door.

It went with her, eyes sleepily closing and opening.

Marta sped out of the driveway at 7:15am; the ETA to the office would be 8:50, by 9:15 she would leave for her mother's. She made a right turn on the main road and headed for downtown Detroit, via I-75.

The 17th floor elevator doors opened and Marta entered the law firm of Buchman, Hyatt and Findlay off Jefferson Avenue. Her mind raced for an idea of how to go home sick. In the twenty five years at the firm, never once had she missed a day of work — until her father's death. She was the most dependable paralegal they had ever known. The partners treated her wonderfully, due to the influence of Mr. Buchman, the senior partner. Marta received top salary, benefits, vacation, an awesome 401k and on her 25th anniversary — a two year lease on a red Miata convertible.

Mr. Buchman had harbored feelings for his paralegal for twenty-five years. Marta was the talk of the firm and his partners resented his preferential treatment. No matter how many times he asked her to dinner, movies or the theatre, his affections were never returned. She was friendly and polite and their friendship blossomed, but friendship wasn't on his mind. It wasn't that Marta didn't have feelings for him; it just never occurred to her that *he* had feeling for her.

Friends and co-workers would try and tell her differently but she insisted that Mr. Buchman was far too handsome and wealthy to be interested in her. *He likes me because I make him laugh...we're pals, besides he's my boss, things could get messy.*

After a while, Tom Buchman assumed that Marta wasn't interested and settled for friendship. He did all but hold up a sign that read, I Want to Date You!

Marta set her purse in the bottom filing cabinet drawer and went over the day's schedule. Berry Findlay was on his way to court. Edward Hyatt would be in Hawaii and Tom Buchman would be in bright and early, as his trial wasn't until 2:00.

Thoughts twirled in her brain, flipping from one idea to the next, trying to decide the best way out of work. She came to the conclusion that she would tell a limited version of the truth.

Marta strummed her fingers across the desk, waiting for Mr. Buchman to arrive. A note on his desk seemed the easy way out, but it would be rude, after all those years. He deserved a face to face. Good mornings were exchanged with JoAnn and Barbara and Tony — a long time friend, computer wizard, and make us laugh guy.

Marta winked at Tony. His rough handsome face broke into a dazzling white smile. A puppy brown eye winked back at her as his muscles flexed to move the copier machine he was repairing. Jeans stretched across tight, thick thighs and a cute butt. JoAnn, Barbra and Marta all watched him work. Tony had it all, looks, personality and brains.

"Hey Tony, how the hell are you today?" Marta asked.

"I'm doing just dandy, you?" A smirk spread across his face. "Wow, lookie at you, Miss Hot and Sassy today. Two buttons undone, a necklace, fancy earrings, a silk blouse...I knew you'd clean up well. Who's the man?" Tony laughed.

Marta blushed. "Oh Tony, there's no man. I just felt kind of perky today that's all. But this old broad will take a compliment when I can....thanks honey." She reached in the air and grabbed the compliment. "Clean up well...I'll give you clean up well." She shook a fist at him.

Tony shook his head and began to work on the copier. "If you only knew how to play your cards Marta..."

"...JoAnn?" Marta called over to her co-worker and friend.

"Yea, Marta." JoAnn was placing her purse in the bottom drawer of her desk. She was in her thirties, attractive and brunette.

"Where's Mr. Buchman?" Marta asked.

JoAnn grinned and raised an eyebrow. "He should be in any minute — had to do an errand this morning."

Marta swished a hand at her friend as Barbra entered from the kitchen that was around the corner. She stirred her coffee as she spoke. "Did I hear you asking about Tom?" Her blonde hair was in an up-doo. Barbra was full figured, pretty and Marta's age…46.

Marta rolled her eyes. "If you two ladies don't be quiet…pow, right in the kissers!"

Marta approached the fish tank, located several feet behind her desk. It sat upon an ornate oak cabinet. The tank held 1500 gallons of water and housed beautiful salt-water fish. Marta picked up a container of food, opened the tanks lid and sprinkled a few flakes into the water. A large yellow Tang swam to the top. A Clownfish made his way to the side of the tank greeting Marta's wriggling fingers.

Marta went to her desk. She contemplated booting up the computer to check email but decided against the fuss. She checked her reflection in the monitor and pulled a few wisp of hair in place.

"You're looking very nice today…and asking about Mr. Buchman…what in the world could this mean?" Barbra smiled and looked to JoAnn.

Tony faked a cough and muffled words. "She finely got a clue!"

Marta decided to try and explain to Barbra, Tony and JoAnn, why she needed to leave. She picked up a stone paper-weight from Mackinaw Island and began tossing it back and forth in her hands. "Listen I have a family…" Marta screamed, stumbled backward and fell into the chair. The rock flew out of her hands and over her head. There was an unmistakable sound; a loud sharp tink against glass. Tony and JoAnn asked if she was alright. Barbra rushed over.

Marta got up from the chair and whirled around to look at the tank. A group of white and orange Butterfly fish were darting frantically through the water. A yellow and blue Damsel was in distress, while a large black and orange trimmed Pinnatus Bat swam in crazy circles, annoying a yellow Sea Horse. "No!" Marta screamed and leapt back from the tank. Short breaths came and went. She twisted on her heel and fell to the carpet, hitting her head on the desk.

Tony rushed to his friend's side and helped her to her feet. The crackle of glass filled the room. Marta's eyes grew twice their size as she saw the tank's glass grow a spidery web of tentacles. They inched in quick darting splays of white and reached out to the sides of the tank. The fish looked at Marta.

"Marta, are you alright?" Barbra asked.

"What have I done?" Marta made her way around the desk and grabbed onto a ficus tree. She peered through its branches as Tony called out that the tank was going to break. Barbra and JoAnn ran. A horrible crunching sound pierced the room followed by a loud gush. The 1500 gallon tank released its water and terrified residents.

The water hit Marta's desk, knocking her backward. She tried to stabilize herself with the ficus tree. The branches tangled within Marta's arms as she rolled over with the tree and did a somersault, and slammed against the carpet.

"The fish...save the fish!" Marta moaned. She placed a hand on her lower back and rolled over trying to get up. Tony helped her to her feet.

Mr. Buchman pushed open the glass doors "What the hell happened?" He looked up to see JoAnn appearing from behind her desk and Barbara standing against the wall.

Barbra and JoAnn screamed *the fish!* Mr. Buchman yelled over the commotion as his other two paralegals ran toward the kitchen looking for containers to house the fish. "Marta, forget the fish! Your head! That's a huge bump...should I call an ambulance?"

"No! I hate those things...I'm fine! I really am...ow, my back!" She clung onto Tony.

Marta's eyes took in the disaster that was the office. "Oh! Look what I've done!" Her eyes widened as she noticed Mr. Buchman pushing buttons on his phone. "No! Really I'm fine!" She grabbed his phone and pushed *end*. "I'll just see my chiropractor today, that's all. The fish! Save the fish!"

"I've got a large salad bowl, put them in here!" JoAnn screamed. A moment later, Barbara appeared with a large ceramic bowl, water spilling out the sides. JoAnn swore and headed back to the kitchen to fill her bowl with water.

Mr. Buchman insisted that she take the rest of the day off work and that Tony would drive her to her mother's. She shouldn't be alone. He'd have her car dropped off at her mother's later.

Tony grabbed Marta's purse from the filing cabinet, found her keys and gave them to Mr. Buchman. He then guided Marta out the glass doors of Buchman, Hyatt and Findlay. "Marta, what the hell happened?"

Marta answered. "I'm not sure Tony. I thought I saw....in the monitor... Oh Tony, I'm not crazy, I swear...I'm not."

"Maybe it's the stress of loosing Mr. F?" Tony guided her to the elevator doors. "You should have taken more time off."

Marta looked through the glass doors at Mr. Buchman...Tom. He was pale and breathed heavy as he watched her being escorted by Tony. The look on his face told her what he had been trying to tell her for twenty five years. Her heart raced as she watched him gently glide a dazed clownfish into JoAnn's bowl.

* * * *

A Train Wreck!

*A*zzurra heard the front door open and dusted her hands off on her apron. She took the coffee pot from the warmer, walked to the table and filled their cups. Homemade Danish with raspberry filling and a dozen Italian cookies and cannoli sat on the table.

"Hi Sweetheart, come on in." Azzurra called out to her daughter.

Azzurra heard a man's voice. She returned the coffee pot to its warmer, stood still and listened. *Was that Tony?*

Her daughter entered the kitchen. A black blazer hung stretched, wrinkled and disheveled over a pair of slouched shoulders; dark hair was matted and flat — framing a smudged makeup face. The blue silk blouse was torn at the collar. Marta limped, carrying the heel of a shoe. A large bruise shined on her forehead.

"MARTA!" Azzurra ran to her daughter. "Marta what happened to you!?"

Marta looked at her mother and shook her head as tears welled. "Don't ask. I'm a murderer. I've killed them all!"

Tony began to explain to Azzurra. "Mrs. A, Marta freaked out at work. Completely lost it! Maybe she should have taken more time off...dunno, but I think she's a train wreck. Lost it like there was no tomorrow, wigged out over something she thinks she saw in the monitor, which was off by the way. You should have seen her, she screamed so loud, scared the hell out of JoAnn & Barbra, and then she threw a rock at the fish tank...well not on purpose, she fell backward onto her chair and the rock just followed the law of gravity. The whole tank's gone...all the fish to their deaths. They knew it was her too. It was like they stared at her with contempt, the poor little things. JoAnn, Barbra and Tom are trying to save them." He hugged Azzurra. "I think she needs a drink Mrs. A." He started to laugh.

"What the hell was that Tony?" Marta punched his arm. "That was supposed to make Ma and me feel better? I feel awful! Those poor fish, it's all my fault. Maybe I am a train wreck...oh Ma it was awful!"

"Sorry, I can't help it. You looked hysterical!" Tony laughed again and mimicked her screaming.

"Tony, you're not going to get any Danish if you're not nice." Azzurra slapped his chest and waved a finger at him.

"I'm trying to lighten things up. I'm joking. But seriously, I think she needs a drink." Tony headed for the cabinet that held the liquor.

Azzurra looked into her daughter's face. "What do you mean you saw something?"

"Ma, I can't — Tony's right. I need a drink." Marta walked over to Tony who was pouring a Southern Comfort on the rocks.

Azzurra followed in pursuit. "Marta, I'm serious. I want to know what you saw."

"Ma, for the love of God, I don't know! I glanced in the monitor and saw it in the reflection...it was there!" She covered her mouth. Tony put his arm around her and handed her the drink.

"What did you see?" Azzurra demanded.

Marta opened her eyes and lifted her head that was resting on Tony's chest. She took a sip of SoCo and breathed deeply. Her eyes met Tony's... then her mother's. "I don't know Ma. I can't remember. I just know the feeling. I know it's weird, but I know something was there —something awful but I don't know."

Tony looked at Azzurra then spoke. "Marta, take a good gulp and then lay down for a while." A smile broke across his lips, then a grin. "Mr. Tom Buchman was very upset...very upset indeed and Marta got all dressed up today, asking about him." He mouthed a loud whisper to Azzurra. "He gave her the look...and she noticed."

Marta hit his strong chest. "Tony! I'm gonna get mad!"

"All right, all right...I'm sorry." He held her tight then mouthed to Azzurra. "I'll tell you later."

Azzurra nodded and mouthed "We'll have some Danish and cookies."

Azzurra guided Marta to the sofa, let her finish her SoCo and laid her down. Tony helped himself to some Bailey's in his coffee and sat at the table.

"She may have a concussion, but her pupils are fine and she's holding a conversation. I wouldn't let her sleep for more than an hour and we'll need to ask her who she is when she wakes, check her pupils again and any check for signs of confusion." He grabbed a raspberry Danish and several cookies.

Azzurra joined Tony. "You think she's all right, Tony?"

"Yea, seriously though, I think she needs to take some time off work, Mrs. A." He took a bite of the Danish. "These are awesome!"

"Tony, did you get my card thanking you for coming for Franco?" Azzurra smiled at him.

"Sure did and there is nothing I wouldn't do for this family." Tony took a bite of a cookie. "I'll have to hit the gym hard today."

"Now Tony, your birthday is coming up next week, I have some things going on, so your birthday dinner will have to be a bit later."

"Thank Mrs. A. You just let me know. Can't believe I' m gonna be forty five. Where the hell did the time go?"

"Well, we're all aging honey, what are going to do?" She reached for his hand. Her tone changed. "Tony, what do you think it was? What did she see?" Azzurra leaned in close to him, peeked over to Marta on the sofa and then back to Tony.

Tony shook his head. "Not sure, post traumatic stress I guess. Honestly Mrs. A, one minute we were joking about Tom and she started to tell us something about a family something or other, then she wigged out."

Azzurra gave a deep sigh and narrowed her eyes.

"Mrs. A...she did tell me in the car about some weird dream last night. Something about a mirror and lipstick — anyway, she kept checking to see if both earrings were there and kept grabbing her necklace. The poor thing kept saying strange things like, I can't lose them and I'm so stupid and she hates me. Don't have a clue as to who *she* was. Then it got really weird. She began to wipe off her lipstick and makeup, but it was rough and panicked. I think she's tired and freaked out about Mr. F."

Azzurra looked over to Marta who was sound asleep on the couch. "Oh Tony, maybe you're right. She hasn't said much about her father's death. She's always asking how I'm doing and I never even thought to ask her how she's doing." Both hands flew to her mouth as she looked at Tony. "I'm a horrible mother!"

"That is nonsense! You've been through thick and thin with your kids and with me too. You, Mrs. A, are the best Ma in the world. I mean, come on...he was your husband and you've known him forever. So you forgot, bid deal. Besides, when I asked Marta about her dad, she shrugs her shoulders and says that she's fine. He was suffering and she's glad he's resting in peace. She does the same thing to JoAnn and Barbra too."

Azzurra reached for Tony's hand once again. "Thank you sweetheart — have another Danish."

Tony's cell rang. It was Mr. Buchman. Azzurra could hear his deep voice from Tony's cell. After several minutes, Tony asked Azzurra if it would be all right if JoAnn brought Marta's car to the house. Tony would drive Joann back to the office. Azzurra nodded.

The moment Tony hung up Azzurra spoke. "Tell me about Tom? What happened? What do you mean the look?"

Tony spent the next half hour talking about Marta and Mr. Buchman. JoAnn arrived and sat for a cup of coffee and some cookies. When Tony asked about the fish, she grimly replied. "There are casualties and thousands of dollars of damage and the suite on the 16th floor is damaged too." The three grimaced and then discussed Marta for the next fifteen minutes.

Azzurra thanked JoAnn for attending Franco's funeral and for the beautiful card and flowers. She thanked Tony once again for driving Marta home. Tony and JoAnn left with a bag of cannoli, cookies and Danish— assuring Azzurra that they would say hello to Barbra and Mr. Buchman for her.

Fifteen minutes and I'll wake her. Azzurra thought to herself. *I'll need to check for a concussion and ask her if she is confused, pupils and who she is.*

Azzurra put the remainder of the sweets away. Katie's cups were placed in the sink along with Tony and JoAnn's mugs and Marta's glass. She put the lid on the cake platter, turned around and gave a frightful, short scream.

"Katie! Oh my word, you scared the day lights out of me! I have to get used to you popping in like that." She placed her hands over her chest. "Katie, what's wrong?" She glanced over to Marta who was still sleeping.

Katie stood in front of the stove in her blue dress and slippers. Blackie spotted Marta and ran toward the couch — both remained semi transparent.

"Blackie, come back here." Katie said. "Why is Marta home?"

Azzurra began to explain the morning's events. "I don't know Katie. Maybe it is about Franco. You don't think something's going on, do you?"

Katie shook her head. "No, I don't. You know, Marta has always been afraid of her own shadow and somewhat of a klutz. The stress of being in the cemetery yesterday probably gave her nightmares. She'll be fine and you're a wonderful mother." Katie called for Blackie once more and scolded him. "If she wakes up and see's you, she'll have a heart attack." He crept toward her, ears flat to his head.

Marta began to stir. "Quick, you better get out of here, come by tonight." Azzurra nodded to Katie. "You'll have to tell me what the Higher Spirits had to say. Is everything all right? You seemed upset when you first arrived."

Katie nodded. "Everything's all right. Well, kind of. I spoke with the Higher Spirits and well, they haven't given their final decision. What they said makes sense but...I'll stop by this evening and tell you everything." She looked to Marta. "You should keep an eye on her, just in case."

Azzurra nodded.

Katie picked up Blackie. She glanced in the kitchen sink. "Azzurra, you use my cups." She smiled at her sister.

"I always have Katie, and I always will." Azzurra replied.

Katie took Blackie's paw and waved as she and he, faded out of sight.

* * * *

Marta

"What's your name?" Azzurra looked deep into her daughter's eyes.

"Ma, I'm fine." Marta sat up on the couch, rubbed her head and then stood.

"Humor your mother...does your head hurt? Are you confused? Who are you?" Azzurra reached for Marta's arm and gently guided her.

"I am Marta Stephani. My head hurts just a bit and the only thing I'm confused about...is you." Marta paused and went into her own thoughts. She envisioned Mr. Buchman just before the elevator door opened. He was a devilishly handsome man in his early fifties, confident cocoa eyes, distinguished salt and pepper hair and a grin that made you melt. She shook her head. "Ma...I think everyone has been right all these years. Mr. Buch...I mean Tom, has a thing for me." Her eyes widened and her stomach lurched.

"Well it's about time. Any longer and he may have met someone else. He's been divorced for 15 years and he may not stay single forever." Azzurra felt Marta's forehead. "Now, don't get nervous. It's Mr. Buchman...Tom, the man you've known for twenty some years."

"You're right. You're absolutely right." Marta winced and placed a hand on her lower back.

"You should see the chiropractor today." Azzurra walked to the phone that was on the kitchen wall. "I'll call him. JoAnn brought your car here while you were asleep. You can get adjusted and then you'll have to do some errands for me." Azzurra pushed 11 buttons and waited for the phone to answer. A moment later the receiver was placed back in its cradle.

"I told them you'd be there in five minutes." Azzurra walked over to her daughter and gently touched the bump on her forehead.

"Does it look bad, Ma?" Marta asked.

"No, not really." Azzurra lied. "I'm going to keep an eye on you though. Now, you better get going. You can go home after the adjustment, change your clothes and come back here. You should wear comfortable shoes. Oh and tell Dr. Kaiser and the ladies I said hello."

"Ma, what do you mean *you*? Aren't you coming with me today? I thought we were running around together?" Marta raised an eyebrow.

Azzurra replied "These are simple things you can get on your own, you won't need me. I'll get the important items from the Vendor."

Marta thought to herself that her mother couldn't possibly be using the internet for the shopping. Her mother never touched a computer. She decided not to ask about the Vendor...all in good time.

Marta gave her mother a quick hug. Azzurra stood back abruptly. Her eyes widened with shock. "Marta!"

"What's the matter now, Ma?" Marta said as she walked to the door.

"Marta, stop walking away from me!" She hurried over to Marta and turned her daughter around by the shoulders and looked into her eyes. It was gone. The look of loathing, anger and disgust was gone. "Are you angry with me Marta?"

"I'm just worried about you Ma. With Dad gone, the cemetery fiasco and those poor fish...I named the clown fish Oopsy, you know, after Oopsy the Clown. I guess I'm just freaked out. Don't worry Ma, I'm fine"

Azzurra spoke out loud. "I hope so, Marta...I hope so."

Her hand cupped her mouth as she made her way to the kitchen window, deep in thought. Her neighbor stood near the large branch that lay on the ground next to the apple tree, shaking her head. Flashes of the day's events appeared before Azzurra's eyes. Her daughter had seen something in that monitor, something that frightened her. Tony said that she had been acting fine up until today.

Azzurra shook her head to rid the thoughts, at the same time she heard a voice. Mary, her neighbor, had walked over to the fence and was calling her name. Azzurra opened the window all the way and called out to her friend. "I'm sorry Mary. I guess I was lost in my own thoughts. I feel awful about your tree. I hope it survives."

"Oh, me too Azzurra." Mary turned to look at the broken tree. "It will never be the same."

"I know Mary. That's what I'm afraid of." Azzurra's eyes filled with dread.

Mary narrowed her eyes. "Are you OK Azzurra?"

"I will be Mary...I will be. I'm a tough old lady."

"Well, I'm just a few years younger than you and sometimes I wonder if I'm going to make it through the day. Oh, by the way, Eleanor and Carol would love to get together and play some Pinochle. They said it would do us all good."

"That sounds wonderful, but it's going to have a wait a bit. I have some things going on with the family that I need to sort out first." Azzurra saw the look of understanding slide across her friend's face.

"That's all right. I'll tell Eleanor & Carol that you'll call when you're ready. Let me know if you need anything Azzurra." Mary smiled, waved and walked back to her broken apple tree.

Well, if things were going to get done, she needed to get the day moving. Azzurra took off her apron and hung it in the pantry. She went to the hallway and sat down at the writing desk, looking over the note that she wrote the night before.

Dear Marta

> *You will need to purchase three sets of the following...for Nicco, Marie and yourself.*

> *Eye droppers*

> *Large pots (black cast iron)*
> *Bunsen burners*
> *Lighters (the long kind)*
> *Stone mortars and pestles*

Incense holders and/or bowls
Incense stick: Lavender and Sandalwood will do
Boxes of long wooden matches
Sage (bundle for smudging)
Azzurra added to the note.

Three dozen tapered candles (any scent is fine)
At least six dozen votive candles
One white Silk Scarf
One Cactus Plant
One Ivy Plant
One Feather(any color)
I will get the rest of the supplies from the vendor. Thanks for
doing this sweetheart.

Love Ma xxoo

Azzurra lowered her pen and examined the list. She went to her purse and pulled out her wallet. The *MasterCard* would have to do for Marta.

Azzurra wondered to herself if the vendor took credit cards and decided that she would go to the bank and withdraw some cash after Marta got back.

It was nearly forty-five minutes later when Marta walked into the kitchen dressed in a pair of jeans, tennis shoes and a navy blue sweater.

"You look very nice sweetheart. I like that sweater on you — it brings out your eyes." Azzurra stood and walked to the refrigerator and pulled out a gallon of milk. She retrieved a glass from the cupboard and poured Marta a full glass and set it on the table next to the note. "How about a sandwich with your milk, this way you're not running around on an empty stomach?"

"Ma, we just had all those cookies and Danish...OK, sounds good." Marta sat at the kitchen table. "Thanks, I like this sweater too. I found it in the back of the closet, haven't worn it in years." She picked up the note. "I feel so much better. Dr. Kaiser says Hi, by the way." She stretched her back and took a sip of milk.

As Azzurra made Marta's sandwich she explained the note on the table. "Those are the things I want you to pick up today. Make sure you ask if you don't know where to get them. This will save me a lot of time; I don't want to have to buy things from the vendor that I don't have to. They can be expensive." She kissed Marta on the top of her head. "Thank you for taking the day off work to help your mother."

Azzurra handed Marta the credit card and informed her that there was no need to pay her back.

They sat and chatted about the items on the list as Marta ate her lunch.

"The mortar and pestle are the small bowls that you see at the pharmacist. They have the little grinders that look like mini baseball bats. You know what I mean, don't you?" Azzurra asked.

"Oh yea, Witches use them to make their potions." She nodded in agreement with herself.

Azzurra spit out her coffee and dabbed her mouth with a napkin. "Yes, sweetheart, those are the ones."

Marta shook her head and twisted her neck. "My neck is feeling stiff again." She swore and closed her eyes. A few seconds later she opened them. Her leg bounced up and down. She took the last bite of her sandwich and drank the rest of her milk.

"You OK, honey? Azzurra asked.

"Yea, my neck feels so heavy, my head still hurts too. I took two *Tylenol* when I was home. Don't tell Dr. Kaiser." She stood and gave her mother a hug and left to do the errands, without saying another word.

Azzurra grabbed her purse with her mind still on her daughter. She recalled her jumpiness at the cemetery, screaming about the squirrel, the disaster at the office and now her neck being heavy after an adjustment from the Chiropractor. "I am keeping an eye on you, Marta." She said aloud.

* * * *

A Witches Vendor

Azzurra drove to the bank and withdrew a thousand dollars. She made it back to the house near 1:00. The day's schedule was busy. Katie would be there that evening with information from the Higher Spirits and she would call for Basil as well, if the Higher Spirits allowed.

The first order of the afternoon was to call upon the Witches Vendor. Then the secret room needed to be cleaned and organized as well. She gathered the supplies for the vendor spell and looked up the incantation. Now it was time to make room for him to arrive.

The tiny pads under the feet of the coffee table made it slide across the wooden floor. She slid a light-green upholstered classic armchair to the side. Moved two classic American floor lamps, a magazine rack and slid another pastel purple armchair out of the way. Azzurra sat on the traditional, beige and forest green sofa and thought to herself that perhaps a visit to the chiropractor a week early would be a good idea. Her lower back felt horrible. After her visit with the vendor, it would be time for another *Advil*.

A note of supplies for the vendor sat upon the sofa. It contained everything from crystals, books and herbs to various kinds of enchanted objects. Sachets, vials and potion bottles were for Marie, as she was sure that Sachets and Elixirs were her calling. Marta would need a wand, for if her gut was right, Wands was going to be Marta's calling, just like her mother. Perhaps she would give Marta her mother's wand.

Azzurra thought about the Witches Vendor, which she hadn't seen in over forty years. It was the old fashioned way that a Witch was to buy supplies. She remembered her mother telling her to use the vendor for items that you can't get at mortal stores.

Merek Kroll, the family vendor, would be the person to call upon. God only knows if he's still in business after all these years. Perhaps he moved on and is no longer in the earth's realm. The thought of using anyone else made Azzurra uncomfortable.

Merek Kroll was an older Polish gentleman. Azzurra traded her Italian recipes of soups, entrees and desserts for recipes of pirogues and guampkies. He had been dead when she was a little girl.

Next to the note of supplies sat a crystal platter with the ingredients that she needed to cast the spell.

To Summon a Witches Vendor
Comfrey
Soloman's Seal
Wormwood
Horehound
Three Citrines
Irish Moss

She knelt down in front of the sofa and looked around at the large living space. The thought of him arriving with a horse and carriage did not make her happy, she'd just vacuumed. If Merek Kroll was still in the earth's realm, there would be a large old-fashioned vendor's trolley.

Azzurra removed items from the crystal platter and placed several vials of herbs and stones on the floor. Three citrine stones were to be placed in a triangle on the platter. One by one, she placed the stones that would promote success in the transaction. The brass incense burner was placed in the center. She ground the herbs into their own stone mortars and opened the lid of the incense burner. After placing the charcoal disk at the bottom of the burner, she lit it with wooden match. Facing south, she added a sprinkle of the Soloman's seal for wisdom, upon the charcoal, thanking it for its contributions and properties. The wormwood was added for repelling negativity and spell-binding. The smell of the wormwood almost made her gag, but what are you going to do? Pinching her nose slightly she repeated the beneficial properties of the wormwood and asked it to blend in harmony with the Soloman's seal. Horehound was sprinkled next, for a sharp wit. Once again, she spoke the ritual and then added Irish moss, thanking it for its help with money transactions. A pinch of lady's mantle was added as the last ingredient. It was used to heal and promote love in a relationship — never a bad idea to add lady's mantle to any spell, was Azzurra's motto. She thanked the properties of the lady's mantle.

Azzurra closed her eyes and visualized what she had wanted to have happen. Opening her eyes, she spoke the incantation.

> *Now let it be known for what I seek*
> *The Witches Vendor in which I beseech*
> *From cauldrons, to sachets, to Witches' hats*
> *To wands and cloaks and wings of bats*
> *Here my call across the skies*
> *Bring to me my desired supplies.*
> *Merek Kroll*

Azzurra stood from where she knelt and sat on the sofa. If he was busy, he may not arrive till late that evening. She recalled her mother's words. "Azzurra, he may not be here for hours so you girls will just have to be patient."

Poof!

"Azzurra Stephani, I can't believe it! I can't believe my eyes! It's you! What have you been up to all these years?" He spoke with a thick Polish accent. Azzurra stood up rather quickly and greeted a long-time family friend.

"I've kept myself busy, very busy raising the kids. Of course, they're all grown now, but I've just been staying out of sight is all. You know of the feud between me and my sister, Tessa." She opened her arms and waited for him to give her a hug.

Merek Kroll turned solid and walked down from his trolley. His arms wrapped around Azzurra. Her legs left the ground as he spun her in a circle. Azzurra let out a scream. Maybe she put too much lady's mantle in the spell, she thought.

"Never could stand that bitch sister of yours! She was nothing but a useless, good-for-nothing woman. I really should be nice...but she gets under my skin. And if I remember, she couldn't' cook to save her life! What a waste of God's good air. If she wasn't so nasty...who cares about the cooking... look at your sister Arianna, now she is good woman. Who cares that she can't boil water? It matters only if you're a good person. But Tessa is a royal bitch, I say." He paused, straightened his wool black cap and took a good look at Azzurra, debating whether he should continue and decided he may as well. "When I heard what happened, I stopped doing business with her whole family and anyone who I knew that liked her! Never could stand her or that damn cousin of yours, Debra. And as for that daughter of hers, Celia, what an evil thing she turned out to be. I really shouldn't be mean. They say we should have patients for everyone…but what a bitch. I've heard some things, you know. How they are related to the Degelis, I'll never know. I shouldn't have said that. Maybe deep down, they are nice…just misguided." He stood tall and smiled wide at Azzurra.

Merek wore grey striped trousers with a black frock coat, vest and a white dress shirt. He must have been in his sixties when he died, which was sometime in the early 1900's. She remembered seeing him for the first time at the age of seven.

Azzurra chatted with Merek for a while. She avoided talking about the current situation. Merek asked about why she broke her father's Vow never to use Magick. However, when he noticed the look on Azzurra's face, he apologized, saying that it was none of his business and there was no need to explain.

Azzurra trusted Merek; however, she didn't want to get him involved. He would know soon enough. She informed him of Franco's passing and a conversation ensued for several minutes. Merek said how sorry he was for her loss and they hugged again. He adjusted his black bow tie and winked, held out his arm and escorted her to the trolley.

Measuring 12 feet wide by 8 feet in depth and 10 feet in height, the vendor trolley took up most of the remaining space in living room. "Now, if there is anything you need that I don't have on my trolley, I'll be sure to find it for you, my dear. However, I'm sure your desires were met." Merek stepped onto the trolley and looked down at Azzurra.

The top part of the trolley had a red and white stripped awning that stuck out three feet. Rich looking cloaks in reds, blacks and charcoals were hanging on the far left. Rugs of all sizes floated near the cloaks. Wands of different textures, lengths and colors were displayed behind Merek, stacked in tiny slits that resembled a bee hive. Books of every size, shape and style lined the lower part of the trolley in an ornate, redwood bookshelf. Spinning vials, decanters that changed colors and mason jars of eel eyes, spider legs and various other animal parts sat on top of the red-wood shelves. Elixirs were labeled on ornate tables of pine and cedar. Cabinets that housed herbs and square patches of cloth were in large dressers, some draped over the opened drawers. Clocks, pens, feather quills, rings, necklaces, hats and athames were displayed amongst the shelving that wrapped the length of the trolley near the top.

Azzurra knew this could take some time. It had been nearly forty years since she used Magick and she needed advice on how to fight a Witches War for the new millennium.

Azzurra looked up to Merek and asked him for the first item on her list. "Merek dear, I would like to purchase a book for the modern day uses of a wand."

* * * *

Apothecaries & Hutches

Streaks of rain were frozen in time, along with the wind and the lightning — forever engraved on the back of an antique pocket watch. The storm brewed over the Degeli estate that once bustled with life. A pallid yellow haze from the gas lantern, bathed the narrow stone steps that led to the front door. Weeping willows, pines and oaks stood strong against the wind and rain — displayed through the soft light of the lantern and feeble attempts by the moon. The scene would be a reminder of one of the most deadly spells the Degeli family had ever known.

Franco had been given the watch by Pasquale Degeli, Azzurra's father. He explained the spell and how it worked, that it was passed down from generation to generation. He trusted Franco, who came from a powerful family of Witches himself. Franco had the power to recast the spell, when the time was right — when Pasquale had passed away. Augusto, Azzurra's brother, did not want the family watch and since his only son refused the heritage, Pasquale thought it fitting to release its power to Franco. After all, he was the husband of the most powerful Witch of all time.

Custom made, the Degeli pocket watch had an original black background, until it became enchanted; now displaying the Degeli manor during a summer storm. Tiny crystal hands marched around the storm, pointing to white roman numerals. The outside was made of gold with painted enamel. It displayed faint clouds and the soft beams of the full moon. Several shooting stars surrounded the scroll of the letter D.

Azzurra stared at the Degeli pocket watch with its long gold chain. Her own mind painted with memories of the past. This would be the first time the enchantment would be cast by a woman.

Her eyes moved over the secret room, taking in the memories of the past 49 years. Merek Kroll had brought the purchased items to the secret room and they spent the last few hours cleaning and organizing. It was wonderful to catch up with an old friend. By six in the evening they were finished. Before he left, Merek promised he would stop by the house Wednesday to deliver the remainder of the supplies. The secret room hadn't looked so wonderful and full of life in years.

Elixirs were organized alphabetically upon an antique mahogany apothecary. It stood eight feet tall by six feet wide by two feet in depth. It had three rows of drawers at the bottom, each containing five squares. The faces of the drawers were painted a hunter green with gold etching of its contents. The shelves were trimmed in the same green. On the left side of the apothecary were several different sized cubbies that housed various antique bottles filled and labeled neatly with their purpose. The bottom shelves had glass doors that protected their elixirs while the top shelves were left open. The right side of the apothecary had tiny pigeon holes that were of different sizes that housed potion bottles, herbs and incense. Sitting on top of the apothecary, were several measuring instruments, a Bunsen burner, and a cast iron cauldron.

To the left of the apothecary was a hutch filled with spell books, manuals and papers. On one of the shelves sat an antique gilded Alabastrite clock with two, rather thin cherubs. The hutch was made of pine with a distressed appearance of chipped maroon paint.

Another hutch, made of maple, was opposite the apothecary. There was an aged box with its lid opened. It reminded her of a wooden egg carton with velvet lining, except it didn't have eggs. It housed several spheres that were creamy white and swirling before her eyes. Azzurra had no idea what they were, but she dusted them off and set them gently in their place. Merek Kroll seemed very interested in these spheres and mentioned that he thought he remembered when Franco purchased them.

The hutch also held a pair of glasses, Azzurra's wand, several quills, a large oval shaped mirror, knives and one large crystal ball — all displayed on the hutches' shelves. There was a mannequin hand holding several large ornate rings and bracelets and an antique jewelry box. A mannequin head wore several types of gold and silver gemstones necklaces, and an angel pendent dating back to the 1700's.

To the right of the maple hutch was a pristine armoire made of solid oak and finished with cherry. Doors were open and revealed several garments, including two cloaks: one deep red and the other, a plum. There was an assortment of shirts and dresses, a tuxedo and a black velvet gown. Several hats were on the bottom shelf, from top-hats to old tabbies. Two drawers were at the bottom with large ornate handles.

A large round oak table sat in the middle of the cellar. It was used to cast their spells. The rim was four inches thick and deeply etched with stars and moons. The legs were large and shaped like bird claws.

On the far wall sat an elegant Wooton desk dating back to the 1870's. It was made of walnut and consisted of three sections: the main desk, two doors, which contained letterboxes, pigeon holes, shelving, drawers, and hidden compartments. The third section was a folding desk platform. The desk was extremely unique, beautiful in character and in history. The legs were short and thick. The top face had large brass trophies on either side with two large brass horses facing each other, matching the brass ornate hinges. The Wooton housed written potions, letters, manuals and the history of the entire Degeli family, old ink-well pens, ink bottles, pencils and vials of hair from every family member, labeled neatly with the person's name. It may have not been that functional for the everyday person with its tiny compartments and pigeon holes, but for the Degelis, it was perfect.

Azzurra closed the pocket watch and traced a shooting star with her finger. It would be Nicco's watch soon. He, of course, will become the master of Enchanted Objects.

The vision of the Degeli's watch floated across her memory. Azzurra was sitting with Franco under the enchanted gazebo, when he cast the spell on the pocket watch, which captured the storm that night. Marta's voice startled her back to reality. She placed the watch on the Wooton desk and headed up the stone steps.

"How are you feeling sweetheart?" Azzurra entered the kitchen.

"I was wondering where you were. I put everything in the front room." Marta stood with her purse and car keys in hand.

"I can make you something for dinner?" Azzurra approached the front room and noticed the bags on the floor by a designer chair by *Bokja*.

"No thanks, I got everything on the list Ma and I'm exhausted. Besides I promised Marie I'd call her. She's still a wreck from yesterday, said she's been eating all day." Marta rolled her eyes and then shook her head to wake herself.

"Well OK. Thank you, honey. How's your head?"

"It's fine." Marta hugged her mother goodbye and just before she reached the front door she turned and spoke. "Oh, Mr. Buchman called four times today to check on me."

Azzurra smiled at her daughter. "Well, that's wonderful. I knew he would. He'd be worried about you."

"Yea." Marta turned, twisted her neck, and walked out the door.

Azzurra shook her head and narrowed her eyes, still focusing on the closed front door.

Azzurra's mind wondered where about Katie. She should be there soon with news from the Higher Spirits. To keep herself busy, she began an Italian recipe called Bousaloon. A sirloin steak rolled with egg, salami, cheese, garlic and bay leaves. After hearing the grandfather clock strike nine times, she removed the Bousaloon from the oven and let it cool on the counter. Pondering where her sister could be, she began to pace the kitchen. *Well she can't be tired, she'd dead. She probably needed to get her sense of time back after all these years.*

At eleven chimes of the clock, Azzurra sat at the writing desk in the front hall, wondering if she should call her sister, Arianna. She should have called her earlier but there was little time...and now it seemed too late.

At midnight, Azzurra's mind was racing with worry. Basil could not be called unless permission came from the Higher Spirits. Waking Arianna now, would do nothing except worry them both.

The clock chimed two times. Tired and unable to keep her eyes open a moment longer, Azzurra went to bed. When she woke at six chimes and Katie still hadn't shown, the awful reality sank in — something was wrong. Something had happened to Katie.

* * * *

The Nightmares of Hags & Culls

Crisp, clean and fresh — Azzurra saw the trickle of sunlight that came through the window. It shown across the room and onto her dresser, revealing the little dust particles that could be seen whirling and whizzing through the light. The morning breeze felt cool as it seeped through the cracked window. It was the dawning of yet another morning. With age, came the heightened sense of noticing Mother Earth; her smells, sounds and beauty that bloomed to view, that would have gone un-noticed in youth. You witness the sun first peeking up from its night slumber, the crickets that have gone quiet and the birds that begin their busy day. Azzurra was aware of these simple but beautiful moments. Mornings were nothing to be taken for granted and now, at her age of 71, it was a beautiful thing that was given by Mother Nature — even though she was a nervous wreck.

It was now six am, Tuesday morning — exhausted and unable to sleep another wink, Azzurra decided to make coffee. Several scenarios played in her mind as she prepared the coffee. Perhaps Katie spent the night trying to convince the Higher Spirits to assign Guardians to protect the kids? Maybe they gave Katie permission to speak with Olivia and that's where she spent the night? Her thoughts turned dark...maybe Tessa's Spirits were stronger than Katie and they had banished her?

Powerful Witches and Spirits had the ability to banish mortals and other Spirits. The Degeli family had the ability to accomplish such a spell. Tessa, unfortunately, was part of that lineage.

If the spell was weak or performed on a very powerful Witch, the Spirit could find its way back within hours. The Higher Spirits punished those severely who cast such a spell. If the spell was successful, the Spirit would be thrown into a different dimension. It could take them years or even centuries to return to their own time. They would be isolated and alone in a vast expanse of blackness.

Azzurra kept telling herself that Katie was not banished, so there was no sense in worrying. She poured coffee into an old mug scrawled with the word "Mom", added plenty of sugar and cream, and headed for the secret room. A thought entered her mind...birds...have to feed the birds. After a quick trip to the back yard and a hello to her neighbor Mary, she retrieved her mug of coffee, warmed it up and once again headed for the basement.

Sitting at the Wooton desk, she set the mug of coffee on a napkin and donned her reading glasses. A book lay open on the ornate desk, *Protection Spells for Today's Witch*. A couple of strong Defense spells and some Enchanted Objects would suffice for the time being.

Flashes of one of her most favorite enchantments came to mind. The spell had been cast after her honeymoon with Franco. It still worked and sat upon the kitchen sink. With a few words, the cat would come to life and clean the dishes, while the soap dispenser applied the soap as needed. The only mistake made when casting the spell was to envision them getting along with each other. The cat would attack the dispenser if it splattered him with soap.

The enchantments today, however, would be for protection. Her mind thought about the objects to enchant. The Degeli pocket watch came to mind. Would Nicco be ready to receive such a spell? Much too powerful... she'd ask for Katie's opinion. Her mind leapt easily to another question — where in the world was Katie?

Azzurra shook her head to clear her mind. Enchanted jewelry for the girls, grandchildren, nieces and nephews needed to be cast.

Her fingers tapped across the antique Wooton desk. Marie had the power of Sachets & Elixirs; Marta would take up Wands, while Nicco had the most difficult of the powers...Enchanted Objects. All of their supplies were neatly organized in boxes waiting to be given to them at Wednesday's supper.

A deep sigh of frustration heaved from her chest. The Apothecary was full of potions that she had no idea what they did. Hutches were lined with books about demons whose names had no meaning. Then, there were the milky, swirling spheres in what looked like an egg carton on the cherry wood hutch. She had absolutely no clue as to their purpose.

"Katie?" Azzurra spoke out loud...nothing. After forty years of not casting a single spell, her nerves were rattled at the thought of not being up to the task. She thought of the messenger bird she cast to call forth Katie. He was big, had a personality and performed well — maybe she's just being silly.

The warmth of the mug of coffee felt good against her palms. Azzurra had never been ready for the Witches War nearly forty one years ago. For this Witches War, time and the element of surprise were on her side...or so she hoped.

Azzurra stood and felt a wince of pain in her lower back. After doing some stretches that the chiropractor had demonstrated...her back released. Getting old was not glamorous.

Her eyes scanned several books that Merek Kroll had placed in the pine hutch. They were bound in beautiful leather and had a rustic appeal. The titles were foreign and somewhat gruesome: *Ghouls of the 21st Century*, *Devilish Ferries and their Hags, Gossamer...Modern Uses, Shadow People & The Emergence of Jumbies, Dover Demons & Their Cousins, Gaki, Nephilims & Shapeshifters*, and finally *Vetala & Zombies, What You Don't Want to Know, But Should*. Azzurra's eyes glazed over. Out of the corner of her eye she spied a purple dyed leather bound book, *The Nightmares of Hags & Culls*. Pulling it from the shelf, she sat at the Wooton desk and began to read.

Fifty five minutes later, Azzurra closed the book. A chill ran up her spine. Goosebumps sprouted everywhere and her mouth became dry at the thought of Olivia being attacked by either Hags or Culls. Focusing back on *Protection Spells for Today's Witch*, she thumbed through the pages and came across a familiar protection spell...*Protezione.*

Protezione worked against Spirits, Lower Level Demons, Ghouls, Poltergeists, Mortals, and powerful Witches or Wizards. A disclaimer informed the reader that the spell had little effect upon Upper Level Demons, such as the Dover Demon. Further down on the page, there was another spell to enchant an object. *Oggetto di Protezione.* Next to that was the translation from Italian to English: *Object of Protection.* It was always best to use your native tongue on defense or attack spells...to increase the intensity.

An old memory came to mind. Whenever they had visited her Cousin Debra's parents...Stella and Sabino Degeli, her mother would make sure they all wore their horn necklaces, cast with the spell of *Oggetto di Protezione*.

Azzurra looked over the ingredients.

Rose Quartz Crystals
Tiger Eye
Dragon's Blood Resin
Black Salt
Burdock
Ginger
White Sage
River Water

Ginger? Azzurra would have never thought to add ginger. *See you can always learn something new,* she thought to herself.

Under the preparation there was a tip about spell binding:

The most important aspects of any good spell caster will be the act of Visualization. The caster must concentrate on the person to protect and should visualize how the object will behave during and after the enchantment.

Azzurra stood and walked to the maple hutch and opened an antique jewelry box. Franco's bracelets and rings, cuff-links and necklaces lay neatly organized. Nicco didn't care much for necklaces and cuff-links were too dressy. The enchantment should be something he could wear every day. A bracelet or ring would have to do. Once she spoke with Katie, she'd make a decision as to whether or not the pocket watch should be enchanted.

Azzurra brought the sterling silver antique dragon's bracelet to the round, bird-footed table in the middle of the secret room and laid it down. She placed four votive candles at North, South, East and West, surrounding the bracelet. Azzurra closed her eyes for several minutes and visualized how the enchantment should behave.

She leaned on the table and began to read the spell from the book. Another sting of back pain struck — forcing her to shift her position. When her eyes focused on the book once more; she inadvertently skipped a line that gave instructions to face South...she was facing North. The spell would not solidify correctly and could backfire or simply do nothing.

Several moments later the spell was ready for the incantation. Black salt surrounded the bracelet which helped in the binding of the spell. Four pink rose quartz crystals were placed next to each votive, providing a calm mind, even in dangerous situations. The smell of white sage lingered in the air that was used for smudging the bracelet clean of negativity.

Tiny whispers were spoken. Azzurra continued to repeat the effects of the spell over and over, giving the precise details of how the enchantment should work.

She submerged the bracelet into river water and then blotted it dry with a blue towel. This was to ensure the cleansing of spells Franco may have placed. A deep red tiger's eye was placed above the bracelet for acute awareness and attention. She held the bracelet over the burning coal of burdock, letting the swirls of incense seep across every inch. This would give protection. The dragon's blood resin produced a thick smoke and the scent was powerful. She placed the smoldering dragon's blood resin next to the bracelet and then lifted the bracelet with the blue towel, holding it above the smoke. Whirls of smoke engulfed the bracelet providing protection and the banishment of negativity.

Azzurra continued to visualize the effect and set the bracelet down. Incense of ginger was added to boost the power and solidify the spell. It was time for the final step...the incantation.

"Protezione
Protezione
Chiamare per protezione
In times of trouble
In times of doubt
The power created, I bring about
Dwell within this object I see
Let it come to rescue thee
Nicholas Franco Stephani
Protezione
Protezione
Chiamare per protezione
So Mote it be"

She raised the bracelet into the air. *Nothing will be able to get to Nicco with this enchantment*...or so she thought. Azzurra spent most of the afternoon enchanting objects. There was a ring for Marta that was purchased from Merek Kroll. It had the enchantment built in, but she needed to finalize the spell and bind it to Marta. The ring would change colors depending on the type of danger it sensed and react accordingly with an incantation. Marie had a green thumb, so the cactus and ivy were enchanted to attack and protect. A silk scarf would also alert Marie if anything dangerous was near and protect. There was also a necklace for Marie's daughter, Katherine and a 18th century silver necklace for Tracy, who was Nicco's girlfriend of ten years. A pre-enchanted necklace for Olivia, three rings for Olivia's kids and a ring for her husband, Walter, were also enchanted. Earrings for Olivia's sister, Carlotta, and rings for her two kids, Dino and Elizabeth, completed the enchantments. Once she notified the rest of the family, every niece and nephew would be protected. Nicco's dragon bracelet remained the only enchanted object with a dangerous flaw.

Near 4:00pm she headed up the stone steps to have dinner and do some nervous cooking or baking. Azzurra debated on calling Arianna but decided that with Katie missing, it would only cause worry. If she didn't hear from Katie by Wednesday morning, she'd make the phone call to her youngest sister.

The clocked chimed 10 times and the kitchen emanated with the smells of cannelloni. Azzurra yawned — sleep was calling. Upon climbing into bed, her stomach lurched...Wednesday's supper was tomorrow and not one thought was given as to how to explain the family secret to her children.

Azzurra's eyes popped open near 2:00am. Flashes of funerals, Katie, Tessa and the anticipated dinner with the kids forbade her from sleeping another minute. Azzurra slipped on her robe and ballerina slippers and headed for the kitchen to make a pot of decaf coffee. While the coffee brewed, she entered the large bathroom, which was straight down the hallway and began to brush her hair in the mirror. The soft glow from the bedroom and kitchen light bathed the hall between them in dim light.

The reflection of the mirror showed eyes with large, dark circles. Azzurra sighed in frustration and continued to brush her hair. The feeling came over her so fast that she gave a slight gasp —someone was there. Frozen in fear, her heart leapt. Of all the protection enchantments cast that afternoon, the only person without one...stood in the mirror. Senses tingled to life. Ears heightened their perception, smells became acute and the sixth sense roared with warning. Azzurra's eyes slid from the mirror toward the premonition. Something stood at the end of the hall with its eyes upon her. Terror raged from her gut and catapulted into her heart. A man stood at the end of the hall, radiating a white light. It was Spirit, a tall man dressed in white. The man tilted his head up and to the left and then fixated on his target once more. Before she could scream, before she could react, he glided down the hall and stood beside her. The brush clunked into the sink, as she opened her mouth to scream. Terror swallowed the sound. Azzurra was alone and not at all prepared for battle.

* * * *

The Vicar

"*I* mean you no harm. I am a Vicar sent by the Higher Spirits. I need a word with you." The man's voice was deep and determined.

Azzurra's heart slowed after a plummet of relief. The body's defenses were retreating and a sense of complete calm took over. "A Vicar, thank the Lord. You gave me quite a scare young man." Her face flushed red with embarrassment of being caught off guard.

The Vicar continued. "As I've stated, I was sent by the Higher Spirits, your sister, Katherine Degeli Marinacci, petitioned the Higher Spirits for their assistance on Sunday evening."

He stood at attention, the highest ranking official to the Higher Spirits. The Higher Spirits were the members who remained within the earth's realm. They oversaw the dead and their interaction with the living. They are the most powerful beings on this side of the earth's realm.

Azzurra could tell his mind wandered in places other than the present. Vicars could glimpse the future and see the past. They held the power, authority and wisdom that could destroy anything on this planet, bound by their oath to the Higher Spirits.

"Your sister requested that the Higher Spirits assign a Guardian to her daughter, Olivia Jasienski and other members of the family. I was sent to investigate whether or not we should grant the request." His deep brown eyes saw into her.

Azzurra spoke carefully. "I've been waiting for Katie, she never showed last night and I'm very worried."

The Vicar turned solid and continued. "It was near zero five hundred hours when the Higher Spirits agreed to hear her case." The Vicar looked away from her as though speaking to someone next to him. He then returned his attention. "Your sister left at near zero eight hundred hours. I've sent an inquiry to locate her. There was a report of an Energy Disbursement Spell in the area, however, it failed." He tilted his head slightly to the left as if listening to a voice.

Azzurra had no idea what an Energy Disbursement spell could be, but nodded. "Thank you young man...I will try not to worry. It's in my nature to worry. I'm a mother." Azzurra smiled at him. She wanted to give him a little pat on the chest but thought it best not to touch him.

He angled his body to the left as if looking at someone then returned his focus. "Your sister has quite the tongue on her." He arched his brow. "She even spoke her Lord's name in vain."

Azzurra almost vomited. She clenched her chest and put a small hand over her mouth, then released it and spoke with a gulp. "I...I...I...oh that Katie and her mouth. You must forgive her young man. She means nothing by it, but I will definitely have a word with her. I've told her before she curses a bit too much. She's always sworn like a sailor. But I don't, I never swear that much. I guess sometimes I do, when I'm really mad, but it takes a lot to get me mad..." Her face was beet red.

The Vicar continued, interrupting her. "...I have positioned myself here as a courtesy to you. I have completed my investigation upon the family members under attack and will submit a report within the hour to the council of Higher Spirits."

Her embarrassment left her. There was something about him, the way he made you feel. The feeling she possessed at that moment was as if nothing in the world could harm her, at least not while he was around. It was as if any pain, anger or frustration from God's world of people, plagued by their own demons....all disappeared. To have this feeling, to let the earth's troubles slip away from you as if you were a little child still wrapped in your dad's arms — those strong arms that protected you, loved you and made you feel that he was the strongest, wisest man in the world and no one could ever love you more.

Azzurra continued to daydream, his patience allowing the time. A moment later her mind shifted to Katie. "Now let me see…am I right to say that she had the meeting with the Higher Spirits near 5am and left near 8am on Monday morning?"

"Yes, Ma'am. Since that time, I have investigated all family members that were attacked by Spirits or other entities. As of this time, I have not been told to investigate who may have orchestrated the attacks upon your family. I realize that you and Katie both feel that your sister, Contessa, is responsible. I will need to prove that she is involved. Sometimes we conclude what the painting depicts before the painter is finished, influenced by sour memories." He took a few steps, turned as if to speak to someone and then turned back to Azzurra. "The council will then investigate if the Spirits are acting of their own accord or have been sent by a Witch."

"Does that mean that there is proof of someone attacking my family?" Azzurra raised a hand to her chest.

He nodded once very quickly and spoke clear and deliberate. "Your sister had asked for protection for the following members of your family; Olivia, Walter, Rose, David, and Michael Jasienski; Carlotta, Elizabeth and Dino O'Reilly; Marie, Steven and Katherine Giordano; and Nicco and Marta Stephani and Tracy Deluca. I would think that a Guardian would be placed for Olivia and Walter with not much hesitation, but I am unable to say for certain about the rest of the family."

"Walter? I would have never thought to ask to protect him. I'm glad my sister was thinking. Tracy too…she lives with Nicco and could be in danger." She thought to herself, *why would Tessa attack Olivia's husband?* "May I ask why only Olivia and Walter?" Azzurra looked into his deep brown eyes for an answer.

"The others are not in immediate danger. I am sure you are aware that interfering with the behavior of Spirits whom choose to stay within the Earth's realm is something the Higher Spirits would rather not be involved with…unless it means grave danger for a mass of people. Walter and Olivia are the only members who have been attacked by Spirits for several years if not decades. They are weak, distressed and almost at a loss to function in normal society."

Azzurra's heart sank. The feeling subsided almost immediately.

He continued. "If your sister, Contessa, is responsible, she has made a grave mistake by the attack upon Walter, as he is a mortal man with no powers to defend himself and is not blood related. Olivia has no knowledge of her powers, which is another issue. There are other matters that I am not privy to disclose at this time. Furthermore, Contessa had taken the Vow never to use Magick along with the rest of the family. That Vow was broken and is punishable by the Higher Spirits. I might add that you, as well, have broken the Vow when you summoned your sister from the dead and cast the spells of protection this afternoon." He gave a slight tilt of the head.

Azzurra's face became pallor with dread. She would be punished along with Tessa. "There was nothing else I could have done. It was either the safety of my family or breaking the Vow. If you want to punish me, well then do so, but I would not change what I've done and I would do it again."

The Vicar looked straight into Azzurra's eyes. "I would not be concerned with your breaking the Vow at this time. However, I do stress the importance of not breaking it again. Until I meet with the council, you are forbidden to cast another spell." He then turned and walked down the hall. He stopped halfway and faced Azzurra.

Azzurra took notice of his appearance for the first time. The light that exuded from his being was strong, yet very soft and gentle. His suit was immaculate and tailored to his body. It exemplified the presence of strength and power. Crisp, clean and classic, came to mind when viewing this spectacular man. He stood at attention, resembling the discipline of the US Armed Forces. The suit's white slacks hugged his strong legs then flared, giving a slight break against white patent leather shoes. The white silk shirt, fastened with flat mother of pearl buttons, gleaned against a strong torso. A thin pattern of white, slightly raised stripes ran vertically down the shirt. French cuffs, held in place by large round diamond cuff-links, added a touch of class and elegance. The white Regency Brocade tailcoat fastened with large opal buttons. Azzurra had never seen a tie such as the one he wore. It was made of gemstones that hung neatly in place over his solid chest. Five strands of gemstones contrasted against the pure white that he wore; the center strand sparkled with diamonds while the others were mixtures of blue sapphires, crimson rubies, holly blue-violet agates, light purple amethysts, sea green peridots and blood red garnets. His jet black hair, strong jaw and deep brown eyes made him one of the most attractive men Azzurra had ever seen.

"Are you willing to reinstate Basil as your Wand Spirit?" The Vicar was alert and concentrated on the outer walls of Azzurra's home.

"Yes." Azzurra's voice was soft. "I wish to reinstate him, although I have not spoken to him to abide by the laws of the Vow our family has taken."

"He is outside the house, anxious and annoyed. The Higher Spirits will also determine if your family can break the Vow and call forth your old Spirits and use Magick once more, to its full extent. I would see no reason for refusal. I shall speak with Basil and let him know that you are not to call for him until you are granted permission. He may choose to guard you on his own accord. However, he is not to communicate with you. There is to be no contact with other Spirits with the exception of your sister, Katie."

"Thank you for speaking with him. He is a very good man and I love him with all my heart. I promise not to call forth any other Spirits as well." She took a few steps toward the Vicar.

"Is there anything else before I take my leave?" The Vicar stood at attention with his hands clasped behind his back.

Azzurra nodded and smiled. "Why yes, there is my friend, there certainly is. I would like to know your name." Azzurra squinted at him.

The Vicar once again looked into her eyes. A slight smirk slid across his face. "I am a Vicar to the Higher Spirits. My name is Aiden Sinclair and you may address me as Vicar Sinclair." He nodded and gave a slight bow.

"Well, Vicar Sinclair, it's very nice to meet you. I can't tell you how much I appreciate your assistance. You'll let me know the moment you hear something, either about the protection for my family or my sister's whereabouts?"

"I will Ma'am." The man in white turned to leave, halted, returned his attention and spoke sternly. "I may take better caution Ma'am. You stated that you felt your family was in danger, yet you were unprepared to protect yourself. I could have killed you in an instant if I had wanted. I suggest you go to your secret room and gather some protection for yourself."

Azzurra narrowed her eyes.

The Vicar spoke. "I have forbidden you from using Magick until the Higher Spirits grant permission. However, if you do break my request you will explain the reason for doing so. The Higher Spirits will forgive you if they see fit, which I can tell you, they will." He tilted his head toward Azzurra with a slight nod. His eyes met hers.

Azzurra couldn't help but to feel that he was a man you wouldn't want to anger. Her face turned red as she replied. "I will do what I must and explain later. Thank you Vicar Sinclair. It's been forty years. I thought of my family before myself."

"You are the most powerful Witch this family has ever known. Without you, they will not prevail." He bowed slightly, looked up into the ceiling and then vanished.

A chill ran up Azzurra's back. She took in a large breath and decided to head for the secret room and cast a protective enchantment for herself. Upon entering the kitchen she released a frightful gasp. By the stove, Katie had just appeared.

* * * *

Energy Discombobulating Spell?

The monotonous ticking of the grandfather clock penetrated her ears. Soft, continuous and accurate...it was the only sound that permeated the kitchen. Azzurra stood with tiny hands clasped to her face, eyes wide open and heart racing for the second time that morning. Katie stood near the stove: weak, disoriented and distressed. Her hair was matted with dirt, the medium blue dress was frayed, torn and her blue satin ballerina slippers were spotted with sand.

"If I were alive, I'd be exhausted!" Flickering in and out of being solid, Katie collapsed to her knees.

"Oh my Lord, Katie! Are you all right? Where the hell have you been?" Azzurra hurried forward.

It sounded as though Katie was trying to catch her breath. Deep heaves rose from her chest as her energy tried to stabilize. "I will be fine...don't panic. I'll start to regenerate shortly." Katie brushed her hair away from her face. "I was attacked."

"Katie! What can I do? Are you hurt? Should I touch you?" Azzurra's back gave a sharp twist of pain as she adjusted her position beside her sister.

Katie's eyes were half closed as she nodded to Azzurra. "It will help to regenerate."

Azzurra took a moment, then raised a hand and laid it upon her flickering sister. A sharp intake of breath and a tingling sensation of warmth rushed through her body.

Katie smiled then closed her eyes and leaned against the dishwasher. Her hair adjusted itself and returned to the beautiful dark waves. Her dress mended. The dirt and sand floated from the dress, hair and skin and then evaporated. A moment later, her dress sparked with satin hems and a beautiful sheen. The slippers shined. Katie's eyes opened and took notice of her sister who was fading fast; Azzurra had fallen against the cabinet, eyes closed. Katie turned solid and rested her hand upon her sister's head. A flash of bright blue light surrounded the tiny figure that was drained of energy. A moment later, Azzurra opened her eyes, feeling refreshed and energized.

"Azzurra, how do you feel?" Katie began to help her sister to her feet.

"Oh Katie, I'm fine. You're OK?" Azzurra's back felt light and painless.

"Yes, I'm fine, thanks to you." Katie guided Azzurra to the kitchen table and sat her down in Franco's chair. Katie took the chair to its left.

"Are you sure you're fine?" Katie asked.

"Yes, I feel better than when I woke. Thank you Katie." Azzurra stood and walked to the counter. She took one of Katie's old cups and saucers from the cabinet and fixed herself some coffee. When she returned to her seat, she took a tiny sip, rested her forearms on the table and spoke. "Where have you been? I've been worried sick, pacing around the house, baking and cooking incessantly and I almost got myself killed!"

Katie answered. "I was outside of Olivia's home, chatting with a neighbor's dead mother. She's a very nice lady by the way. Her name is Sarah, beautiful silver hair with bright green eyes. Anyway, I began to ask her if she saw anything strange coming from Olivia's house, when Blackie began to bark. He was growling and his fur was on end. It was something in Olivia's yard that got him riled." Her voice began to rise. "I should have done something right then, but I stood there like a dumb bitch." She slammed a hand on the table. "I looked over and saw two young men...both had long hair, one blonde, the other brunette. They were watching Sarah and me. Well, I didn't think fast enough and before I knew it those dirty little bastards, sons of bitches, no-good, rotten little freaks — banished my ass!"

Azzurra gasped. "Banished?"

"Blackie snarled and yelped and the next thing I knew I was surrounded by darkness. Oh Azzurra, it was terrible. The wind tore at me from every direction. I couldn't get my bearings. I felt sick and knew my energy was being sucked from me." She raised a hand to her left shoulder and rubbed gently. "I felt this prickling sensation and expanding, like I was blowing up from the inside. Oh, Azzurra it was awful." Katie covered her face for a moment, then looked up and continued. "Then something struck my arm. I felt as though I was going to explode. I was so damn mad! I concentrated on every last drop of energy that I had and cast a protective shield around myself. Bright lights flashed, like strobe lights...it was sickening. I willed myself someplace else. Don't ask me why sand came to mind. I'm so stupid sometimes. Anyway, I saw clouds and the sky and began falling. I had not one ounce of energy left. I landed in a mountain of sand, I think somewhere in Egypt. I remember seeing a pyramid. I was so weak I couldn't' do anything but lay there. I kept flickering in and out of being solid." Her eyes widened at the memory. "I barely had enough strength to will myself here. What day is this? How long have I been gone?"

"It's early Wednesday morning. I think it's near three or four." Azzurra examined her sister. "Oh Katie, that's awful! Are you sure you're OK?" Azzurra looked at Katie's arm and gently lifted her hand away. "That was not an ordinary Banishing spell."

"What do you mean?" Katie looked down at her arm.

"Katie, you're hurt. I think it's a hole. Pieces of your arm...they're missing." Azzurra examine the hole on Katie's left upper arm. It was the size of a silver dollar.

Katie gasped. "Those dirty little bastards! Look at my arm!" She placed a finger into the hole and twisted her arm around; a finger was wiggling out the other side. "I'm sure I'll regenerate. At least I hope so. I don't feel pain — just a strange sensation."

"What kind of a spell makes part of you missing?" Azzurra put her hands to her face. "You know Katie, Vicar Sinclair mentioned something about an Energy Discombobulating Spell or Dislodgement Spell that someone had cast, but it didn't work. I wonder if that was the spell they cast on you?

Katie rubbed her arm. "I've never heard of an Energy Dislodgement Spell. You've met the Vicar?"

"He's a Vicar to the Higher Spirits. I guess you know him already. Well, he's been assigned to the family. He's investigated which family members were being attacked by Spirits. So far he thinks that Walter and Olivia will be the only ones granted a Guardian, although I'm hoping the kids will too." Azzurra glanced down at Katie's arm.

"The Vicar is a very nice man. I'm sure he'll do everything he can. Now, what the hell do you mean you almost got yourself killed? How did you meet the Vicar?"

Azzurra explained the entire embarrassing episode of when she met Vicar Sinclair. How a dozen enchanted objects had been made and not one was produced for her own use. Her face reddened as she explained how he appeared while she was brushing her hair and was taken off guard. How she was scolded for not thinking of protecting herself.

"Well, he has a point now, hasn't he? Without you we're all sitting ducks. It makes sense about Walter too. I always thought that Walter was a bit too mean and too hot tempered. If Spirits were interfering, Olivia will have a new husband when all this is said and done. I'm glad I asked them to look into him as well." Katie continued to rub her arm.

"I bet you're right Katie. She'll see a different man in Walter...and she'll be a new person herself." Azzurra took a sip of coffee.

"Isn't the Vicar handsome?" Katie's glanced down.

Azzurra smiled at the thought of the Vicar. "One of the most handsome men I've ever seen." They laughed. A moment later, Azzurra's eyes widened with panic. "Katie! Where's Blackie?"

Katie clutched her heart. "Oh my Lord, Blackie! I completely forgot about my little Blackie. Oh, I'm a terrible mother!" She rose from her seat and began to pace. "Azzurra I have no idea. It happened so fast. I have to go and look for him. If anything happened to my little Blackie, I'll never forgive myself!" She placed a hand to her chest. "I hope nothing has happened to Sarah either. She was such a nice lady."

"I'm sure he's fine. He probably ran off someplace and why would they attack Sarah?" Azzurra rose. "Will it be safe to go back there?"

"Don't worry about a thing! I'm prepared this time and there is no way those little bastards will get me a second time. I have to find him. What will I do without Blackie?" Katie hugged Azzurra. "I'll be fine. Now, you need to get some rest, it's early yet. I'll stop by later this morning."

Azzurra watched her sister fade from sight. Katie would be just fine. She's way too mad and determined to be in danger. She placed her cup and saucer in the sink and headed for the cellar. Within the next couple of hours, she and her house would be protected for the largest Witches War the Degeli family had ever seen.

* * * *

Achar

For several minutes the scream of the tea kettle went unnoticed. Thinking she should check on the water, the woman entered the room, hurried to the stove and turned the gas burner off. The sound of the tea kettles whistle subsided. Filled with a bit of disgust, she shook her head — to not hear the whistle of the tea kettle until she entered the room irritated her. She placed the metal infuser, filled with Chamomile tea, into a cup and added the steaming water. Setting the timer on the stove for three minutes, she waited. The woman caught her reflection in the oven's door and adjusted the silver streak in her hair. The timer moved on. Icy blue eyes fell upon the cup, taking in the colors, pattern and the memories. For over forty years the cup sat, unnoticed, untouched and unwanted in her china cabinet. Today, something was happening, something was different. Her tiny hand reached for the cup and an aged finger traced the rim. The delicate handle was trimmed with gold as were the three tiny feet that held the cup upon a matching saucer. Roses intertwined with green vines that crept up the sides of the porcelain antique cup. The tiny finger continued to trace the rim, the handle and the edge of the saucer as the timer moved on. Her mind flooded with the memories of the cup, the cup her sister gave her months before she died. It was beautiful, but had she taken it from the cabinet any time before this Wednesday morning, she would have smashed it against the wall.

The memories continued to change with the timer. Images of being with her sisters, laughing, crying, and then screaming and speaking such horrid things. The cup came to her months before it happened, before the start of the deadliest Witches War Michigan had ever seen. The tiny finger traced the rim, remembering her sister and for the first time not feeling angry, but a sense of solace.

The memories faded at the harsh sound of the timer. Tessa pushed the button to silence it, removed the infuser to the sink and carried the cup and saucer to her favorite reading chair. Still feeling comforted by something so old, she set the antique cup and saucer on the table and donned her reading glasses. She turned on the Capodimonte porcelain lamp and reached for the thick book. Removing the bookmark and setting it upon the table, she began to read a page from *The Castor, the Scepter & Time*.

After several moments, her eyes darted up from the page. Something was there. Her eyes searched the room, senses tingling. She set the book on the end-table and reached into the pocket of her royal blue housecoat to clench a wand. "Who's there?"

The room remained silent. Contessa's blue eyes scanned the pristine room adorned with antique furniture. After 73 years of being a Witch, she didn't have to hear in order to tell when something entered the room. Nathan, her husband, would still be hunting and her daughter, Celia, always rang the bell, opened the door and shouted loudly before entering. Fingers tightly gripped the wand within the housecoat. Her heart quickened as she continued to scan the room, eyes moving to the adjacent kitchen, resting near the refrigerator. Deveroy, her Wand Spirit, always revealed himself. The reading glasses slipped down her nose as she spoke once more. "Who's there...Deveroy?"

A deep voice penetrated the room. She knew the voice and immediately became annoyed. "It is I, Achar." The Spirit revealed himself in front of the refrigerator. "I have brought you news...good news."

"Achar, I do not like it when you lurk around before revealing yourself. It's rude." Contessa released her wand, removed her reading glasses and placed them on the table next to her book.

She turned and faced one of her household Spirits. "You gave me a fright, Achar. I am not young anymore and do not need to be frightened first thing in the morning."

"I'm sorry. I didn't mean to frighten you." Achar grinned. "A little jumpy? Do you expect to be attacked?"

77

"Of course not, but I have opened myself up to the Spirit world, have I not? Lord only knows what may show up." Contessa's heart slowed. She squinted at Achar.

"Having trouble with your eyes Tessa?" He turned solid and leaned against the refrigerator.

"Things seem a bit blurry lately. Perhaps it's time for everyday glasses. But what are you going to do? I'm up in age." Contessa's voice was strong, almost monotone. She stood erect and proper. She regretted the last words spoken.

"Golden years they call them. But you're right — what are you going to do?" He slipped his hands in his jeans pocket and took a few steps forward. "Are you not pleased to see me? It's been weeks...or were you expecting Deveroy?"

Contessa's voice was flat. "Of course I'm happy to see you. It has been a while." She felt a sharp pain in her thigh but did nothing to address what she felt. She casually shifted her position. "I did expect Deveroy. He's been very scarce lately and I miss him. You know how close he and I are, with no offense to you, Achar dear."

"Oh, I do know how close you are. It amazes me at the change in your behavior when I arrive with Deveroy, then when I arrive without him." Achar jerked his head one way, then the other, attempting to crack his neck — an old habit.

"Achar, there is no need to be offended. Deveroy is like the son I never had..." Her words were cut off with lump that lodged in her throat. She continued. "You said you have news?"

"Very well, I am not offended and yes, I do bring you news." Achar angled his head down and raised his eyes to focus upon Contessa.

Contessa reached in her housecoat and clasped her wand. She enunciated each word. "Then what news do you bring?"

"You are always different around me. I've done nothing to you, yet you stay distant. You are comfortable around Deveroy, even Stephan. But with me you are cold and distant. You think I'm a fool that I shouldn't notice these things?" He bolted straight up and he once again attempted to crack his neck. "I've done everything you have ever asked of me, yet you do not like me." His jaw clenched, eyes narrowed and forehead furrowed.

"You just said you weren't offended, now you speak such silly things. Enough of this. I am sorry you feel that way but there is nothing either of us can do about that. Now tell me, what news is there?" Contessa remained focused on Achar, wand clasped.

"Why of course Tessa, enough of my silly behavior." He angled his head to the side. Jet black waves of hair fell to his shoulders. With the cocky arrogance of the 23 years he had lived, he smirked, accenting a defined jaw line. His white shirt was open three buttons, revealing darks tufts of hair. He began to roll his sleeves up to his forearm, his gaze never leaving Contessa. Silence filled the room as he finished rolling up his sleeves. Achar's jaw tightened, his full lips formed a devilish smile. He glanced down at his scuffed sneakers and then focused back to Contessa. "Deveroy...the son you never had eh? Are you thinking to replace him with your long lost Vincent? After all, Vincent is the reason why Deveroy and I haunt Olivia and her family. Revenge for what your sister did to your son...which I am more than willing to do. All I ask — is that you treat me well."

Contessa forced herself not to respond for a moment. Feeling another sharp pain in her thigh she shifted her position again. She enunciated each word with care. "Do not say his name!" Her eyes gleaned a cold, emotionless woman. "Achar, every mother has a unique relationship with her children. Each child is special in a different way. Deveroy and I are close. It does not mean that you and I are not close in a different way. You remind me more of Celia, distant, cunning and therefore, I act appropriately. Now, as you are one of my household Spirits that abide by my bidding, I bid you to drop your feelings of inadequacy and tell me the news you have come to tell."

Achar's eyes looked up to the ceiling. He crossed his arms, one hand clenched into a fist. "I have destroyed her. Is your thigh giving you troubles?" Achar stood erect and placed his hands in his jeans pockets once more.

"My thigh is fine. Destroyed? What do you mean? Who are you talking about?" Contessa placed a hand on the counter.

Achar walked into the living room and leaned against the entertainment center. He then picked up a framed photograph. "Katie...Katie has been destroyed." He strode over to Contessa, smiling, showing her the picture he held. "Why do you ask us to haunt her family and yet you keep a picture? You are no longer close with them. Augusto and Gabriella speak to you only out of pity."

Contessa's voice dropped in tone, her eyes narrowed. She pointed at Achar with her tiny, aged finger. "You put that picture back! Don't ever touch that again." Contessa calmed herself. "Katie? What do you mean destroyed? She's dead. What more can be done?"

Achar returned the picture to its place and walked over to the end-table, picking up the book Contessa had been reading. She turned to face him. He slid his black eyes to her with a sideward gaze. "Keep reading Tessa. You don't know half of what you think you know. There are spells, things you have no idea exist. An Energy Disbursement Spell, scattering her atoms into millions of tiny particles across the universe. It will take her centuries to regenerate." He turned to face her. "If she can."

"That's horr..." Contessa began.

Achar over-articulated each word. "Are you not happy?" He attempted to crack his neck once again. "For what reason did we torture Olivia and Walter?" He raised his voice. "Because of Vincent! He was two years old when Katie had him killed. Your little baby boy — so innocent...so cute, with big brown eyes..."

Contessa clenched her wand ready to attack. Her voice reached the anger she hadn't displayed in over 40 years. "...stop it! Do not speak my son's name!" She screamed. "Don't you ever say his name again or so help me I shall command Lamia to destroy you with the same spell you used to destroy Katie. Now leave me!"

Achar's eyes widened. "You command Lamia! Hah!" He glanced down at her housecoat pocket. "I am sorry. I shouldn't have said that." He stood quite for a moment. "You seemed almost sad at your sister's demise. I thought I would remind you of what she had done." He walked toward her. "Do not think of using your wand. You're not quick enough anymore...besides, I am on your side."

Contessa stood erect and spoke evenly. "I am pleased Achar. Katie deserved what she got and now we can put it all to an end. I would like to see Deveroy. Please tell him to come to me...never mind, I shall summon him myself."

Achar stepped back. "I shall tell Deveroy as well." He looked into Contessa's eyes. "Deveroy did nothing. It was I who cast the spell. Katie was snooping around. If she found out what was really going on with her daughter, she would have come after you. I did it for you...believe me or not." Achar bowed, keeping his eyes upon Contessa.

Contessa calmed herself. "Thank you Achar. You did the right thing. I'm not sure why Katie was at Olivia's. She hasn't been there in decades. I can't imagine why Azzurra would have summoned her. Maybe Katie was just missing her daughter." There was a long pause of silence. "I wonder if she's been to see Carlotta." Contessa placed a hand on her forehead as though feigning a headache. "Thank God for the Vow Father made us take." She thought back to her father's words. "Azzurra won't dare break it. At least, I don't think she would. Yes, Achar, thank you. I won't pretend that I'm please with such a gruesome spell, but it was necessary."

Achar stood, placing his hands in his pockets once more. "I'll go and find Deveroy. We'll send the Cull away and fetch a couple of other Celestials. We shall finish Olivia off this eve...Walter too, perhaps the kids."

Contessa rounded on him. "There had better not be a Cull there! I told you no Culls! Oh, how I hate those things. Leave the kids be. They have nothing to do with what Katie had done." She placed a hand on her stomach and began to pace. "When did this happen?"

"It was Monday." He answered.

Contessa took a deep breath. "And you've waited until now to tell me? What did you mean about Lamia? What do you mean not in my command?"

Achar smiled — eyes half closed. "Nothing...I was making it up." He could feel panic, and if he had been alive...his heart would be thudding. He calmed himself. "You don't look very happy about the loss of your sister." He walked toward Contessa. "After Deveroy chats with you, he and I will finish off Olivia. Maybe I'll get Walter to kill her."

"Leave them be. Leave Walter, forget Olivia. They've suffered enough. It's done. Katie paid for what she did...she's gone." Contessa walked to her reading chair and sat. She placed her hands over her mouth as she whispered to herself. "Katie's atoms scattered across the universe — for the love of God."

Achar approached her. "I shall leave them be. You are right; they have suffered enough...just like you have. Your son Vincent's death is avenged. Everything can stop now...just what you wanted."

Contessa looked up into Achar's face. She smiled weakly and nodded. "Yes, enough is enough." She stood and examined his face. "I am not too old to have sent you to the middle of the Pacific Ocean in a tomb that would hold you there for eternity. Don't ever suggest that I am too old again."

He saw it in her eyes, the look of loathing for him. Achar's black eyes turned cold. He would tell Deveroy that she commanded them to kill Olivia, Walter and the kids by any means he wished. He would block her summons to him and would tell him nothing of his visit. He once again tried to crack his neck, smirked and then vanished.

Contessa felt exhausted...mentally and physically. Tiny steps took her to the entertainment center where she picked up the photograph. It revealed herself standing between Azzurra and Katie. Arianna, Gabriella and Augusto stood to Katie's left. Her finger traced the picture, resting on Katie. A drop of salty water splattered against the glass frame. "You deserved it." Deep heaves rose from her chest. She slid to the floor and hugged the picture frame to her chest. Sobs escaped her as she continued to say one word over and over. "Katie."

* * * *

Wednesday Morning

Tiny eyes watched her as she slept, whispering to each other. They giggled and laughed as Azzurra's eyes fluttered and then began to open. A powerful enchantment brought them to life, and now, for the first time, they were going to meet their creator. The Cherubs large puppy-brown eyes widened and their faces glowed with excitement. They placed their instruments upon a plateau of the clock, one harp and one flute and took their positions, flanking the ancient time piece. One adjust his toga and giggled, the other straightened the wreath upon his head, sneezed, blushed bright red and covered his mouth.

Made of gilded Alabastrite, the clock was produced with fine details. The tower resembled a harp that was slender at the top and ballooned in the middle. The time piece displayed intricate black hands that ticked around a mother of pearl background, telling the time of 9:35am. The bottom of the tower flared into a solid base. Several large swirls of Alabastrite, molded into two dragons, formed to the sides of the clock.

The silly Cherubs chuckled as they prepared for their first performance of duty. One raised his flute to his mouth, while the other conducted. Azzurra

* * * *

82

greeted them good morning and listened to the soft sounds of *Morning Has Broken* by *Cat Steven's*. The tune grew louder the more Azzurra woke and then came to a soft conclusion. The Cherubs took a slight bow and sat in their seats on opposite sides of the tower. They giggled and blinked with excitement.

It was a tradition on her mother's side of the family to use the clock as a method for protection. She remembered her grandmother telling the story of where the Alabastrite clock came from and the powerful enchantment placed upon the majestic piece. When her grandmother had passed away, her mother re-cast the enchantment with the traditional minor adjustments. Each generation personalized the spell, making it unique and even more powerful. In the early hours of Wednesday morning, it was Azzurra's turn to cast the spell and add her own adjustments.

Through every generation, the clock would sense ill intentions of anyone within the room. Azzurra's adjustment was to widen the protection to include the house, not just the room the clock resided within. The fact that she inherited the power from every Witch in her family, gave her the confidence that the spell would be successful.

The enchantment would be able to discern between a Witch, mortal or other celestial being. A chime would begin and the cherubs would sound trumpets in alarm. The mortal or Witch with ill intentions would hear a separate high pitch tone that would render only that person unconscious.

If the enchantment sensed a Spirit or other entity, the clock would once again sound its alarms. In addition, the clock would produce a large white light that emanated from the face. The light would capture the entity and pull it into the clock, keeping it prisoner. If Azzurra was not home when the clock's enchantment triggered, the Cherubs would inform her of the particulars upon her return.

Some Spirits or other celestials would be able to escape the clock's prison if they were powerful enough. The distraction of the clock's efforts, would give Azzurra enough time to defend herself in another manner.

Along with the ancient clock, Azzurra also produced an enchanted necklace with an angel pendant. Her sister, Arianna, had given her the pendant years ago and she thought it would be perfect to provide protection no matter where she went. A beautiful silver chain let the pendant hang to the middle of her chest. The angel was carved from an oval blue agate, surrounded in silver trim. When the angel sensed danger, its mouth would open, releasing a high pitch, rendering the same effects as the enchanted clock. Her tiny hands would expel the beams of light to capture the intruder within the piece.

Azzurra looked at the pair of cherubs staring up at her...their eyes sparkled with excitement. She leaned down and tickled one of them under his chin. They giggled. "You two are so cute!"

A moment later she was on her feet and decided that she would wear Franco's last gift given to her. For some reason she thought it would give her strength. She placed purple ballerina slippers on her feet and donned the robe. Looking in the bedroom mirror, she fussed with her hair. It was a beautiful plum robe with embroidered black stars and moons throughout. The style reminded her of the old days when being a Witch was an everyday, normal thing. She left the top three buttons undone and raised her arms, letting the large bat-wings flare. After a thoughtful sigh, she headed to the kitchen.

Her mind began to churn as she prepared the coffee...things to accomplish. There was pasta sauce to make, cheesecake and perhaps some homemade bread would be nice. It had been years since the house was filled with the smell of home baked bread. The kids would be thrilled. One thing her mother had taught her was to never bring bad news to someone on an empty stomach. However, if she was going to have strength for the day, breakfast was in order.

Azzurra made one of her favorite morning dishes...Eggs in a Raft that her mother used to make. She buttered two slices of bread on both sides and then took a small juice glass and carved a hole in the center of each slice. She grilled both sides then placed one egg in the middle of each slice and began to cook; adding a sprinkle of marjoram, salt and pepper for taste. The name changed depending on where you heard it however, she always knew it as Eggs in a Raft.

After breakfast and a brief look at the morning paper, she instructed the pewter cat and soap dispenser to clean the dishes. Azzurra reminded them not to fight and watched them for a couple of moments. She scratched the cat behind his tiny ears and tapped the top of the dispenser. The cat arched his back and purred, while the dispenser expelled soft bubbles.

Azzurra took a worn out wicker basket from the bottom of a cabinet and headed for the Cellar. Ingredients for the pasta sauce, Italian cream cheese and ricotta for the cheesecake and bread were placed in the basket and then carried up to the kitchen. The cat was drying a plate, while the soap dispenser sat quietly. Azzurra thanked them and put the clean items away. A moment later she remembered that the birds needed feeding. Several minutes later and a good morning to couple of squirrels and a spunky Blue Jay she headed back into the house.

While everything simmered, rose and baked, a phone call to Arianna and the rest of her siblings was long overdue. It was now 11:45am.

Azzurra screamed. "Oh my Lord, Katie! I have got to get used to you popping in like that. You scared me again." Azzurra gave a tiny swish of a hand toward her sister.

"Beee Azzurra, it's only me. Talk about Marta being afraid of her own shadow." Katie glided over to the stove and peered in the pot. "It's funny to see you jump like that, though." Inhaling the scent of the sauce, she smiled. "Thank goodness I can still smell." Katie turned to her sister. "I wanted to make sure you had plenty of time to sleep in, didn't want to come too early and my sense of time is off you know." She turned solid and hugged Azzurra good morning.

"I was just wondering where you were and poof...you showed up. It's so good to see you Katie." Azzurra eyes widened with joy. "I slept very well and got a lot of things done this morning. And thank you for reminding me. I've been so scattered I don't know where my head is anymore...it's about Marta. For the Love of God, something is wrong with that girl!" Azzurra placed her hands upon her hips.

"What do you mean?" Katie asked.

"She's not herself, I think she..." With a terrifying thought, Azzurra paused and then spoke. "Culls!"

Katie placed a hand to her chest and began to pace. "Now don't panic. I'll have Basil check for a Cull. What makes you think it's a Cull?" She shook her head. "I can't believe Tessa would send a Cull. She hated those things?" She went to the stove and began to stir the sauce with quick, violent circles. "Why now? Why send the Cull after Marta after all these years? It doesn't make sense. It has to be something else. How bad is that girl's period?"

Azzurra took in a deep breath and swished a hand at her sister. "Oh Katie, it's not her period! I know my daughter and there is something wrong with her. I sensed anger from her. Really deep seeded, like she loathed me. Then Tony said she acted very strange in the car, smearing off her makeup in a panic and talking about bad dreams. Damn it! I'm so stupid sometimes. Katie...it's a Cull!" She placed hands upon her hips and waited for her sister's response.

"All right, if it's not her period...then why now? Why after all these years would Tessa send something that she can't stand herself?"

Azzurra took the spoon from Katie and gently stirred the sauce. She then began to clean up the spatters of sauce on the stove. "Well Katie, I don't know why she decided to do it now, but we're going to find out." She pointed a finger at Katie.

Katie replied. "I think you're crazy, Tessa would not use Culls! I know my sister."

"You don't know your sister!" Azzurra slammed a hand on the counter top. "After all the things I've seen that girl do, I would not be surprised!"

"All right, all right! Now don't get upset and start slamming counter tops. We'll figure this mess out. You said Celia was there…maybe Celia sent the Cull?" Katie placed a hand to her chin and thought. "I'll send Basil to her work; make sure she doesn't do anything stupid, like ruin her chances with Mr. Buchman. If there is a Cull around her neck, the Lord only knows what mess he can cause. If she's not sleeping…having nightmares and hearing whispers from a demon all the live long day…she's bound to do stupid things. As for the anger toward you, kids will blame us mothers for everything that is wrong in their lives. Nothing we ever did was exactly what they needed. The Cull is sure to bring that out and maybe that's why she's mad at you. I wouldn't worry about it though. You and Marta are very close. You've both have always spoken your minds. We'll just need to act fast, that's all."

"I didn't even think about Celia. I bet you're right, Katie."

Katie raised a hand and splayed her fingers. Small white streams of what looked like vapor, shot from her finger tips, swirling and moving rapidly forming a circle. Katie looked into the orb, whispering instructions. Azzurra could hear Basil's name, Marta and the office. Within a moment, it darted up and dissolved through the ceiling.

"Oh, Katie! You don't need a messenger bird? That was so nice. Was that vapor?" Azzurra looked up to the ceiling.

"I haven't had to use a bird in decades, but they are cute though. I enjoyed seeing your Merlin Falcon and no, it's not vapor. Its thoughts transcended into living matter." Katie took the spoon once more and began to stir the sauce. Noticing the look on Azzurra face, she tapped the spoon against the side of the pot and placed it on the spoon rest.

Azzurra wiped another part of the stove then rinsed the cloth in the sink. "That sounds difficult…thoughts into living matter. I'll stay with my falcon, thank you. Will Basil send word if he thinks it's a Cull?" She placed the cloth in the cat's basin and began pacing the floor.

"Don't start your pacing, you'll get me nervous. Yes, I told Basil to send word the moment he knows." Katie said.

"My poor Marta, she's walking around with a Cull around her neck, haunting her every waking and sleeping moment." Azzurra shook her head. The thought of what Olivia must be going through after years of being attacked by a Cull, terrified her. She said nothing so as to not upset Katie. "How's the sauce smell?"

"It's smells wonderful. I can smell the basil and just enough garlic. We don't know that it's a Cull yet." Damn I wish I could eat. Don't worry about Marta, she'll be fine. What else are you making — salad? If Basil tells us it's a Cull, we'll have to destroy it in front of her, so this way she knows why she's been having such terrible thoughts. She'll be terrified, but what are you gonna do?" There was a slight pause. "Bread, are you baking bread?"

"You're right Katie, she will need to see it, or she'll think she's going mad. Yes I'm baking bread. It's rising in the other room. Basil will just have to stay with her. Beee, what a damn mess. I haven't thought about salad but you're right, I should make one…maybe Greek?"

"Perfect…nothing to heavy…always feed them first then tell them the bad news. Ma always told us that. Do not worry about Marta, she'll be fine. Basil will be with her all day. Are you gonna make homemade pasta?" Katie looked at Azzurra's white apron. "You still keep them in the pantry?" She opened the pantry door and pulled out an apron.

"Oh Katie, I can't make homemade pasta. That's a lot of work and I'm not sure if I have time. I hope the bread is done in time. I'm not used to getting up so late. Then I have to call Gabriella, Arianna and Augusto. I really should call Father Bernardo, but I think I'll assign that to Augusto. Then there's Kimberly and Drago, I should call them. They've been there through thick and thin — I know they'd want me to call. Oh, I have way too much to do. I think I'll make garlic butter." She nodded knowing Katie understood every word.

"You make your calls. Have Augusto call the Father, good thinking who wants to deal with him. He's going to be so mad. Forget Kimberly and Drago until we know for sure. I hate to have them bothered, if they still take their vacations in October, I'd hate to have them miss it for nothing. We'll talk to everyone else and see what they think. Garlic butter is nice, you should do that. I'll make the pasta. You still have the pasta machine in the cellar right?" Katie tied the apron around her back.

"Oh Katie, that was so old. It's long gone. You think I should wait to call Drago and Kimberly eh? You're right. They go to Florida every September or October." She swished a hand. "Katie that's a lot of work — it's ok, I have *Delallo* pasta. That's fine."

"Nonsense! We need to make sure this dinner is wonderful, I don't even know what *Delallo* is and there is nothing like homemade pasta. Beee, they still go to Florida of all the places in the world. You wait till I talk to those two. I'll do it by hand. Blackie where are you?" Katie looked up toward the ceiling. There was a sudden bark and Blackie appeared. He turned solid and ran toward Azzurra and barked for her attention.

"You found him! I forgot about him. The poor thing! Oh Katie I'm so glad. Where was he?" Azzurra bent down to pet him and pinch his cheeks

"Blackie was with that nice lady I told you about…Sarah. She grabbed him and fled the moment of the attack. I was so glad she was OK — I would have felt awful. Blackie's been a damn mess ever since. Getting lost every five minutes and he thinks I have all the God damn day to pet him. I hope he gets over this soon, driving me crazy." Katie picked him up. "I'm right here. You're safe, my little sweetheart. No one is going to hurt you while Mommy's around." She put him down. "He's a damn wreck this dog. Nothing I say helps."

Azzurra slapped Katie's arm softly. "Poor little thing, he's scared, that's all. Be patient. He'll be fine." She placed her hands on her hips once again and narrowed her eyes at her sister.

"What? He is driving me nuts this dog. I have other things to worry about than…"

Azzurra interrupted her. "…I'm not talking about Blackie. I'm talking about your mouth. When I spoke with the Vicar Sinclair, he said your mouth was just awful up there and you even took the Lord's name in vain. In front of the Higher Spirits no less! Katie, shame on you and your tongue, I always said you swear too much. He said you need to mind yourself." She waved a finger at her sister.

Katie swished a hand back at Azzurra. "Oh damn it, I forget about that? I didn't swear that much. Was the Vicar mad? He's such a nice man. I would hate to upset him, although, I can't remember taking the Lord's name in vain."

Azzurra replied. "He wasn't mad, but you need to mind yourself. He doesn't seem the type of man you would want angry with you, nor does he seem like the type that when he suggest you to do something, that you should ignore what he says." She started to laugh.

Katie spoke through laughter. "Well damn it! I get mad Azzurra." She covered her mouth laughing and then continued. "I'll try and watch my mouth. The Higher Spirits won't send me to hell for a little swearing — at least I hope not." She looked up to the heavens.

After several minutes and promises to Azzurra to watch her language, Katie headed to the basement to begin the pasta. Just before she reached the steps, she paused and turned to face her sister. "What did you plan on telling our siblings and Father Bernardo?"

"Well, I'm going to tell them everything that has happened so far. I'll just call Arianna and Augusto. I'll have them call Gabriella and Father Bernardo. I'm not going to demand anything. If they want to help they can. If they don't, well then it's just you and me Katie."

"I think that's a good idea. Let them offer help. This way, they can't blame us for getting them into another Witches War. Wait on Drago and Kimberly and I would wait on good old Thom in San Francisco and Bella in New York, just in case it turns out not to be a Witches War." Katie nodded in confidence.

"OK Katie. I'll start making the phone calls and thanks for doing the pasta. The kids will be thrilled." Azzurra said.

"I'm glad to do it Azzurra. Come Blackie. Let's go downstairs and cook some pasta." Blackie followed her to the basement.

Azzurra poured herself some coffee, added some cream and lots of sugar. She placed a small bowl of potato chips next to the phone. It was always a good thing to have something to snack on while having a long phone conversation. Azzurra pulled a notepad from the writing desk drawer in the front hall and took a seat. She picked up the receiver, pushed the buttons and waited for her sister to answer.

* * * *

Arianna

It was the third ring when Arianna picked up the receiver. Azzurra heard the soft voice of her younger sister say hello. "Arianna, its Azzurra. I've got news for you."

"Oh, I thought something was up. I hadn't heard from you in a while." Arianna's voice cracked.

Azzurra's voice hardened "Well now Arianna, you have a phone too! I'm not going to be the one that always has to call. If you are thinking of me and want to call, well, then pick up the phone and call." Her heart thudded a bit faster.

"Well, I don't know. I always think you're busy and wait for you to call." Arianna offered in her typical gentle tone.

Azzurra tapped a hand on the desk. "I'm going to tell you something Arianna — I'm the one who just lost a husband. Do you think it would occur to you to call and see how I'm getting along after losing my Franco? No, it does not occur to you nor does it occur to Augusto or Gabriella. Do you think that my own brother and sisters would call? Father Bernardo hasn't even called me! What? Am I the one who died?"

Azzurra continued. "I'll tell you something else too...Kimberly and Drago, Bella from New York and even Thom in San Francisco called to check on me! Carlotta, Katie's daughter called just last week and even Olivia, with a Cull wrapped around her neck, called a couple of times since Franco's funeral!" Azzurra took a breath and sank into silence.

Arianna paused for several uncomfortable seconds and then responded. "Well, in all fairness, out of all the years, you have always called everyone. If we don't hear from you, we think you may be busy. It may not be right, but that's the way it is. And I do apologize. You just lost Franco and I should be the one calling to see how you are doing...and well, I didn't. I'm sorry. My mind is so scattered these days. I'm not sure if I'm coming or going. I love you Azzurra. Let's not fight. We've always been there for each other. Whatever you need, I'll be there."

Azzurra made a deep sigh in the receiver, paused a moment and then replied. "I love you too Arianna. You're right, let's not fight. But if you don't call me next, I'm gonna be mad. I'm telling you now." Azzurra waved a finger at the receiver.

"I promise I will...if I remember." She added with a smile to her voice. "I burnt my sauce again. Then I was going to take it to the sink to empty it and forgot my pot holders and touched the sides and dropped the pot. It went all over the kitchen floor...what a mess. I've been cleaning for hours. Mateo's so patient. He asked if I wanted help cleaning it up, but I told him it was my mess. Sometimes he gets annoyed with me. He says I'm gonna hurt myself one of these days. I guess he's right. I do such stupid things, Azzurra."

Azzurra's heart sank. After Katie had passed, Azzurra took over where she had left off. Katie was forever teaching Arianna how to cook, how to sew, clean and what to do with Scott when he was small. One of the last things Katie had told Azzurra on her death bed was to watch over Arianna. "That girl is a klutz. She'll kill herself one day," Katie would say. But nowhere in the family could you find a bigger heart than Arianna. She possessed a natural instinct to read people and was extremely quick witted. The kitchen was a disaster zone for her and housework was not her thing, but that never stopped her from cleaning or preparing meals every night. It may be the third dinner she made, having burned the last two, but nevertheless it was made. Salad and dessert were always served with dinner. Her only child, Scott, never complained and married a woman just like his mother.

"Well honey, you're not stupid. I think sometimes you just move too fast. When you have something on the stove, place the oven mitts right next to it, so you don't forget. I've told you before you should get the pots and pans that don't heat the handles, but then again, you touched the sides and there's not too much you can do. The sides get hot…what are you going to do? I do dumb things like that all the time. Thank God, that Mateo is a gem. I've always liked him, Arianna." Azzurra nodded into the phone then took a bite into a chip.

"Azzurra, you've never burned a dinner in your life. Neither did Katie. But I accept that I'm a bit of an awful cook, but I try. Scott actually loves my cooking and Mateo has never complained…although there have been times when I took the dishes from them, threw everything away and ordered a pizza. They would both tell me that it wasn't that bad, that it was just fine. But I knew better and in the disposal it went. I should have never put grapes in with chicken. I read it somewhere or perhaps someone gave me the recipe." Azzurra heard Arianna take a sip of something.

"Katie and I both told Mateo when he married you that if didn't have patience with you, he'd hear from the two of us. He got mad that time. He said there was no need to tell him such things." Azzurra bit into another chip.

"Well, Azzurra, sometimes I do such dumb things. I just don't pay attention and my mind is everywhere else except the present. Muma never had patience with me. She always made you and Katie help me. Gabriella was too busy all the time, Tessa would roll her eyes and Augusto made me nervous explaining things. That poor Muma would shake her head and walk away. Then I start laughing and forget it. Nothing gets done."

Azzurra laughed. "Oh, Muma didn't mind. She just didn't want to upset you."

"Oh Azzurra, the other day, I did Mateo's laundry and put some type of grease cleaner in the washer instead of soap. The bottles look alike. All of his brand new shirts looked shredded, like the material just evaporated. I think I need glasses in my old age. I just couldn't see the bottle right. That was one of the few times Mateo got mad. He now has huge labels on the bottles. I told him that it was his fault for putting that bottle on my laundry shelf. I should have looked though. That was a lot of money in shirts. Then yesterday, I was watering my plants and I was going to bring one of them to the sink to wash her leaves and give her a nice drink. You know it's good for the plants. Anyway, I tripped on the hem of my nightgown and fell foreword. Well, the poor thing right through the kitchen window. Broken glass was everywhere. Damn old windows are paper thin. I told Mateo we need new windows. He said why, so plants don't go flying through them? Well, then I started to laugh. He just shook his head and walked away. He came back in with the plant…poor thing. I think she'll make it though. He helped me clean everything and then went online to find someone to replace all the windows. They are old…better heating to replace them. So the guy comes out next week. I can't wait, Azzurra. All new windows! I should have thrown the plant through the window years ago."

Azzurra realized why her sister never called. Arianna was too busy cleaning up the messes she made all day. Azzurra started to laugh, picturing the plant flying through the window. Like Katie, she and Arianna could laugh. For the next ten minutes, they laughed and over exaggerated everything that could have happened.

"Well honey, things happen, what are you going to do?" Azzurra's face was red as she dabbed her eyes with tissue. "Were you alright when you fell? For the love of God, you're going to kill yourself, Arianna." Azzurra began laughing all over again. She covered her face with a tissue.

Through tears of laughter Arianna replied. "Oh, I'm alright. Mateo was so funny. He said I was lucky I didn't throw myself out the window." There was an eruption of laughter on both ends of the receiver. "Oh Azzurra, my sides hurt."

After a couple of minutes, their laugher died down and Azzurra made a note on the pad of paper to remind her to make a joke to Mateo about the windows.

"Let me grab some more coffee and some cookies," Arianna told her sister.

Azzurra had a flashback of Arianna's cookies and thought to herself, "*I hoped she bought them from the store.*"

She heard the rustle of Arianna getting herself comfortable, then heard a crash of something breaking and heard Arianna swear. *Thank God she only has one of Katie's old cups. She would have broken everyone of them by now.*

Arianna came back to the receiver and Azzurra asked what broke.

"It was Mateo's mug. I don't know why I grabbed his mug. Well, maybe he can glue it back together. Oh, I bought some cookies yesterday from Nino's. They're really good." Azzurra heard her take a bite. "So are you doing okay Azzurra? How are you holding up without Franco?"

The sisters sank into a half hour conversation about the loss of Franco and how things were different but she was coping well. Azzurra then changed the subject to the matter at hand.

Arianna listened intently while Azzurra filled her in on the meeting between Marta and Tessa and how she had summoned Katie from the dead. She explained that Katie was attacked at Olivia's house and the fear that Olivia has been attacked by Tessa and her Spirits for over forty years. Arianna cringed at the word Cull and gasped when she heard that Marta may have one around her throat as well.

After explaining that the kids were coming over for dinner so that she could break the news to them, Azzurra waited for a response. After a moment's pause, Arianna spoke. "You know Azzurra; I've never felt right about everything. I was more like Katie when it came to Tessa. You get mad, but after all she's your sister and you try to forgive and forget. But I tell you something Azzurra, she's sick in the head that girl. She's always messing with the dark Magick and those damn Spirits — never satisfied with her lot in life. Then she goes and marries that God-awful husband of hers, Nathan. I think he influences her. I never thought she'd stop using Magick, even though Dad made us take that Vow." Arianna took a sip of coffee and a small bite of a cookie.

"I'll tell you something else too, Azzurra." Arianna's voice began to rise. "I agree with you that she's the one doing things to Olivia. I don't hear from Olivia anymore and I've been so worried. I've been meaning to call but I keep forgetting." She could hear that Arianna was pacing in the kitchen. "I, for one, will not stand around and let our sister torture Katie's daughter." Her voice rose again. "It's just not right. I think we should ask the Higher Spirits to break that Vow and teach our older sister a lesson she won't soon forget." Arianna slammed a hand on the counter top.

Azzurra smiled to herself. "Katie and I feel the same way Arianna."

Arianna's voice became light and excited. "Oh, Azzurra, I can't wait to see Katie! It's been years!"

"Do you really think we'd be doing the right thing? Oh, I have to check the sauce. Hang on a second Arianna." Azzurra put the receiver down, went to the stove, lifted the lid, stirred the sauce a bit, then turned the burner to off and covered the sauce. A moment later, she returned to the phone. "I'm back."

Arianna replied. "I think the time has come that we gather the family together and use Magick again. Dad would agree that we need to protect the family. I always felt Tessa was behind Katie's son's death and now I think it's high time she pays. The family needs to come together and fight."

"Oh Arianna...don't say a word about Katie's Angelo. I've never spoken to her about Tessa having something to do with his death. And without proof, we can't. My God, I would be afraid to see Katie's wrath."

"You're right Katie...I mean Azzurra. We can't mention a thing. I'll talk to Mateo about everything. He's going to be beside himself. I should call the others. You have your hands full with getting dinner ready." Arianna spoke softly then bit into another cookie.

Azzurra thought for a moment. "I'm going to call Augusto." She knew Arianna got nervous talking with him. "I'll have Augusto call Father Bernardo and you can give Gabriella a call. We'll have to discuss which family members to call and decide who we can trust. Can you come over tomorrow, you and Mateo? We can discuss it then."

"Tomorrow? I'm not letting you tell the kids they are witches all by your-self. You just lost Franco. I'll be there by 6 and we can do this together"

"Oh Arianna, it would make me feel better if you were here tonight."

"I'll call Gabriella, but are you sure we should do that? I love her dearly, but remember the last Witches War?

"Well, Katie thinks Gabriella will be OK. What do you think?"

"Augusto still speaks with Tessa. He says keep your enemies close so you know what they're up too. Well, a lot of good that's done. But he says Gabriella doesn't speak to Tessa but once in a blue moon. Gabriella called me just last week to say hello. She told me Tessa was upset with her for not calling. I think Gabriella will be fine. We'll just have to remind her to keep her mouth shut this time.

"Well then, I guess if you and Katie think it's a good idea, then I say call Gabriella." Azzurra paused for a moment then raised her voice. "Augusto calls you. Gabriella calls you. You wait till I get a hold of those two. They are going to hear an earful from me. I have not heard from either of them in two weeks!"

"Now don't get upset. Listen, I'm going to run and tell Mateo and then start getting ready. Do you need me to bring anything?" Arianna asked.

"You're right, but they are going to hear it from me. I'm fine, just bring yourself and tell Mateo everything. Don't forget to call Gabriella."

Azzurra heard Arianna call for Mateo. "Azzurra, you need to make yourself a protective charm. Maybe you can pull Muma's old clock out. Give it a good enchantment, just like the old days. Beee I need to do some protec-tive charms too. I'll tell Gabriella to do the same. Tell Augusto to pull out his old wand. Oh, and tell Katie hi, and I can't wait to see her!"

"I've already enchanted the clock and a pendant for myself and several other objects for the kids. You need to tell Mateo everything the moment we hang up. You'll need protective charms for yourselves, Scott, Gracie and the kids too. Don't forget now Arianna. This is important. Promise me when you hang up, you'll go straight to Mateo." Azzurra said.

"I promise, I'll tell Mateo right now." Azzurra heard her call for Mateo once again to come to the kitchen.

"Thank you. I'll tell Katie you can't wait to see her. I'll see you at 6:00 then." Azzurra reached in the desk drawer and opened the phone book to Augusto's number.

"Thank you Azzurra. See you." She spoke away from the phone. "I'll be off in a second. I have news to tell you from Azzurra. Remind me to call Gabriella and make protective charms." She placed the receiver back to her mouth. "I'll see you tonight. Beee what a mess this is. See you soon." Arianna hung up and in the background, Azzurra heard Mateo's voice *Charms. What the hell do we need charms for?*

Azzurra stood, glanced at her watched and gasped. It was now 1:15pm. She finished the cheesecake and about an hour later she sat at the desk in the hallway once more. This time there would be no laughing. This time she'd be speaking with her brother, Augusto.

* * * *

Augusto

"*H*ello...Augusto?" A memory of her brother at his wedding appeared before Azzurra's eyes. Anna, his new wife, smiled at the video camera and waved as they sliced the first piece of cake together. "Augusto? Is that you?"

"Yea, Azzurra, who else do you think would be answering my phone." He cleared his voice while Azzurra rolled her eyes before speaking.

"Well, Augusto, I haven't heard your voice since the funeral, maybe I forgot what you sounded like." Her hand lightly slapped the small writing desk. Silence filled the air along with the memory of Augusto and Anna kissing at the head table, prompted by the clinking of utensils upon glasses.

"Well, I've been busy Azzurra — busy with the church. Father Bernardo is running me ragged. I have been thinking of you though...believe me or not. Besides, I was going to call you anyway but I just wasn't sure what it meant and I didn't want to worry you for nothing." His voice dropped and lost its tone. He cleared his throat. "I was thinking of you though." Another pause, "Believe me or not."

Azzurra furrowed an eyebrow. She looked at her notepad and read the last few notes; *remember to laugh with Mateo about the plant through the window. Arianna is ready to fight. Augusto is crabby again.*

Anna tossed the bouquet over her shoulder and laughed. The memories played in slow motion as Azzurra spoke to her widowed brother. "Well, Augusto, if things were happening that you didn't want me to worry about, you could have still called and asked how I was getting along without Franco and kept your mouth shut about what was on your mind. Now, am I right?" Azzurra slapped her palm a bit harder on the desk.

Labored breath caused Augusto to pause for another awkward moment. "Don't start with me Azzurra. I'm tired and don't feel like fighting. I'm not sleeping and I'm hearing things. Besides, you have Arianna, call her." Another cough escaped from him.

Azzurra went to open her mouth and then stopped. She scratched the note about Augusto being crabby and jotted down another. *Something is wrong with Augusto.*

Anna and Augusto waving from the back window of the limo came to mind. Azzurra shook her head and spoke. "What do you mean Augusto? Things have been happening here too. That's why I'm calling as a matter of fact. Is it a bad feeling or is there something actually happening?"

Another silence made Azzurra think he hung up the phone. When she began to speak, Augusto cut her off. "I know you were there every day when I lost my Anna. You all were…and I'm sorry, Azzurra — I'm sorry I haven't done the same for you."

Azzurra felt a deep ache somewhere low in her chest. Anna was gone…the one person on this earth that brought out a gentle, patient man. She began to respond but once again, he cut her off.

"It started right after Franco's funeral and hasn't stopped." Augusto said.

"Augusto, talk to me." Azzurra began to draw geometric shapes on the notepad.

"You're gonna think I'm crazy but I swear I'm hearing her voice. Anna's near and something's wrong — like she needs my help or guidance. I hear her at night and sometimes when I'm just sitting here reading. I hear my name and she sounds desperate, scared." His voice pitched to a higher note near the end, a second later, when he continued, his voice became deep and strong.

"Something's not right Azzurra, I feel it in my bones. Maybe I'm going crazy at my old age. Maybe I'm getting dementia. I also think something is wrong with Olivia. She doesn't return my calls. Her kids say she's been withdrawn from the family, crabby and looks God-awful." His hand hit the kitchen table. "Damn it Azzurra! Something is definitely wrong and I'm not going insane. I don't have dementia and Anna and Olivia are in trouble." He went to stand, but thought it best not to.

"Well, you're not going crazy Augusto, I'll tell you that much. Your feelings are right on. You've always had the most accurate feelings of all of us. Although, I'm not sure what's going on with Anna. I'll ask Katie if she can see her anywhere." She made another note: *Ask Katie about Anna. Augusto hearing her voice…scared, desperate…needs help. He confirms Olivia.*

"What do you mean ask Katie? What have you done Azzurra?" Augusto slowly rose to his feet and placed a hand onto the table for stability.

Azzurra replied. "Well, Augusto…I've had to summon Katie back from the grave. We are all in a mess. Olivia has been attacked by Tessa's Spirits. Marta has a Cull wrapped around her and Katie was discombobulated while outside her daughter's house. That's right, Augusto. We are about to enter another Witches War!" Azzurra nodded to herself.

Augusto sat. He took his kerchief from his pocket and dabbed his forehead. "Maybe that's why Anna's not resting. For the love of God Azzurra…I'm Eighty years old! Who the hell has the energy for a Witches War?"

Azzurra began to scribble out the shapes she drew. "Listen to me Augusto. I'm not sure why Anna's voice is plaguing you at this time. Maybe you're right. She's not resting. Katie and Basil will be able to search for her. You'll have to be patient. We'll help her Augusto. Her Spirit has been missing since the end of the first Witches War. Maybe it's time we have an answer as to what happened to her."

"Is Katie all right? You said she was discombobulated. By whom and what the hell do you mean…discombobulated?"

"She's fine Augusto. I'll fill you in later. It was a nasty spell…part of her arm is missing." Azzurra swished a hand through the air.

Augusto tried to stand, lost his balance and fell back into his seat. He swore. "Never heard of a Discombobulating Spell. And thank you Azzurra, I know you'll do all you can for Anna. Besides, you inherit the legacy. Do you remember?"

"Of course I do. Katie reminded me. Now, I want you to pull yourself together and not worry about Anna." Azzurra drew a triangle and then began a rectangle below that.

"Olivia attacked, A Cull around Marta…I can't believe Tessa would do this." He fanned himself with his kerchief.

Azzurra spent the next half an hour guiding her brother through the last three days of events.

Augusto cleared his voice and replied. "I'm glad you contacted Merek Kroll. He's a good man. I'm also glad you opened the secret room too. You made enchantments...also very good. However, I'm not pleased about the Vicar Sinclair. Father Bernardo won't be pleased either."

"What do you mean?" Azzurra stopped her drawing. "I thought he was very nice."

"I'll speak to the Father about it and if I'm right, I'll fill you in. I'm glad Katie's back. She'll be a huge asset. Have you called Arianna or Gabriella? If we tell Gabriella, she has to keep her mouth shut this time." Augusto shook his head.

"Katie feels it's safe to tell Gabriella and I can't argue the point. I've called Arianna. She's calling Gabriella and you can call Father Bernardo. Katie is here making pasta for the kids. I have to tell them everything Augusto. They'll be here at six."

"OK, I'll call Father. What about Thom in San Francisco and Bella in New York? Kimberly and Drago...should we call them?"

"Katie thinks we should wait on them." Azzurra glanced down to her watch and gave a slight gasp.

"Ok, I will." Augusto breathed into the phone. His mind leapt for a brief moment to his wedding...standing in front of the altar and tears running down Anna's cheeks as she said *I do.*

"Augusto I have to go. I need to finish the bread. Listen; be at my house with Father Bernardo tomorrow at two o clock. We'll discuss what to do and whom to call then." Azzurra placed the pencil on the notepad and stood. Her tiny hand clasped the silver chain around her neck that held the enchanted angel. Augusto told her that he'd see her the next day at 2:00 and hung up the phone.

Azzurra hung up and darted to the back room to where the bread was still rising. It was near 3:00. She carried the bread pans, one by one, to the kitchen and began the process of kneading the bread for a second time. The bread was placed in the oven by 3:30.

Katie entered the kitchen with Blackie just as Azzurra shut the oven door. "The noodles are set to be cooked by 6:15. Thank goodness for a little bit of Magick. Now, you get yourself in the shower and I'll set the table, get the vegetables started and all the sides. You have olives right?" She brushed her dress free of some debris and then waved her hand. Tiny particles of ingredients popped, sparkled and vanished. "How did it go with Augusto and Arianna?"

"Olives are in the cellar and it went very well...I think." Azzurra filled her sister in on the recent phone calls. They sat at the kitchen table.

"I'm so depressed. All this food and I can't eat a damn thing." Katie looked down to Blackie. "Neither one of us can eat...can we?" Blackie's ears went flat to his head.

Azzurra smiled at her sister. It felt just like old times...her and Katie sitting at the kitchen table. "Well, Katie honey, what are you going to do? At least you won't gain any weight. I'm fighting to keep my weight down." She stood and began to walk down the hall toward the bedroom. "Thanks for all your help Katie. I would have never made it without you."

Katie smiled as she watched her sister make her way down the hall. Her heart sank. When the Witches War was over, she'd have to once again say goodbye to her sister. She stood and walked to the dining room and spoke aloud. *Enjoy it while you can, Katie...nothing last forever.*

* * * *

Banished!

*L*ights flashed before her eyes as she spun around in the endless darkness. Floating and twirling like a feather falling through a never-ending breeze. Lights came and went from every direction, flickering faster and faster. Were they in her mind? Were they real? Or was it part of the curse? Time...space...a sense of being in space...no, not space...it's time...no, not time — somewhere in between. Nothing makes sense.

Control your thoughts...and you master the mind. Master the mind and you control all. *Think Anna, think! There must be a way out! The lights...use the lights! Light is energy! Use the lights! Bring the energy to you...but how?*

There were times the dancing of lights ceased to exist. Blackness swallowed her. Anna's body glided through the tremendous, hallow vortex.

Was this some type of limbo after her death...or was she still alive? Screams of frustration and fear raged, vibrating off the black walls. The strobe lights flickered. *Close your eyes. No, open them! I must keep them open! No, for the love of God, keep them closed!*

Time evaporated. How long had she been trapped in this ebony whirlpool? Constant spinning and flashing had been her existence in the beginning. Time moves on and with time comes change and this void was no different. As time ticked on, the void morphed into something that twirled in slow motion. The lights flashed farthing in the distance...drifting away from where she floated. Then she heard it...voices. For the first time she heard voices.

The ambiance of people began to fill the tunnel from just outside the blackness. There were voices of men and women. Things, there were sounds of things — cars, gun fire, rain, wind, walking, crowds, music, animals, sirens.

Voices teased her. She longed for the sound of thunder or a car's horn. The distance varied. Sometimes they were within reach, sometimes they were barely audible.

Banished in this wretched vortex of madness, when will it be over? Images accompanied the ambient sounds. Quick, frustrating snapshots of people she knew. It was as though she had a glimpse of the past...or the future. The blackness transformed into a large drive-in movie screen that revealed a life...her life. Images of Augusto, her mother and father taunted her. *Augusto? Mom? Dad?*

Anna tried to imagine sleeping in bed, just sleeping...dreaming. Maybe she could make the images appear...or was she already doing that. No, they were appearing of their own accord. It was part of the vortex.

Astral Projection! If she could will her Spirit into another place, she could free herself from this prison. Send her soul to someplace else, but where? The confusion always obliterates sense, replacing it with distress...anxiety...anger.

As time passed, the void looped in a recurring pattern. The images and sounds were being rewound. The same laughter...the same conversations, the same blaring car horns! Repeating over and over, sometimes fast, other times in still frames that flipped frame by frame. Astral Projecting toward the familiar voices, images or sounds, caused the vortex to slow...lights dimmed...spinning came to a floating rotation. Reaching and willing her soul toward the voices, toward the images, only exacerbated her desperation as they floated past her and faded away. The voices of friends and family...so close and yet no one knew she existed.

Time! It all had to do with time. It came and went so fast. If she could recognize the event, she would know the time period and will herself into that time. But is that what she wanted, to go back in time?

The video clips of the past played before her. Father Bernardo stood upon the altar, Augusto looking hansom in his tux. Azzurra and Katie were there...Mom and Dad...then blackness. New images, flashes of things she did not recognize began to display upon the black screen. Mt. Olivet Cemetery...is Katie dead? Who were those children?

If this was her life that she was falling through, how does she step out of the blackness and into that life? When did the loop stop...her death? Would it stop at the current date? If she could recognize the event of her death, maybe she could Astral Project herself out of the funnel and into the scene of her death. But when was her death? If the loop stopped at her death she would be in the wrong time period. How long was she dead? A day, a month or was it years?

A voice came to Anna. It was Augusto. He was calling to her. Something awful was about to happen. Augusto needed her. Her voice leapt from her throat. *Help me Augusto!*

* * * *

Ten Minutes Till Six

*A*zzurra applied the finishing touches of lipstick and checked the results in the mirror. Her mind raced with thoughts of how the pending evening would unravel. Looking up to the ceiling, Azzurra spoke a soft prayer to her mother, Luciana, asking her for strength, guidance and clarity.

After taking a deep breath, Azzurra decided to help Katie in the dining room. She was thankful that Franco converted Marie's bedroom into one of her favorite rooms. *The dining room is an intricate part of family connection —* spoken a thousand times by her mother.

The Degeli Manor, the house Azzurra grew up in, housed a large formal dining room and a smaller casual dining room. She remembered feeling awkward as a child in the formal room, afraid to touch a thing. As an adult, the feeling morphed to that of a great fondness.

Azzurra's father, Pasquale, had insisted that when he and their mother passed on, Azzurra and her family should move into the old manor. Azzurra never could. Neither could any of her siblings. So, they pay for the up-keep and renovations, but the house stood empty. The secrets of the Degeli manor lay dormant.

Azzurra's dining room could seat 6 comfortably and 10 rather uncomfortably. A cherry finished china hutch held her crystal, silver, china and flatware. The oak table, finished with black cherry, sprouted four, uniquely carved legs. The matching chairs had white pattern cloth seats and an elegant backing that complemented the table. There were six chairs — two at the ends and two flanking each side. The remaining chairs were set into pairs against the hunter green walls.

The dining room also boasted a large gargoyle & marble severing buffet and a toasted sienna chandelier. Floor plants and hanging vines and ferns mingled with landscape paintings that would give the room its final appeal.

When entering the dining room, Azzurra found Katie seated, folding a beige linen napkin.

Azzurra smiled. The room looked beautiful. *Lancaster by Spode* lay upon the table, one setting in front of each chair. *Lancaster* displayed a bold thick band of cobalt blue, trimmed by hand with raised 22 carat gold. The plates sat on a beige table cloth. *Reed and Barton, 18ᵗʰ Century* pattern flatware flanked the plates while the *Lismore Collection* stemware by *Waterford* sparkled above them.

Two, *NambÃ* crystal candle sticks adorned the center of the table with elegantly carved white tapers. Delicate crystal salt and pepper shakers, by *Waterford,* were placed at each setting for a personal touch. Azzurra also noticed two bottles of Chardonnay wrapped in cloth within wine buckets on the buffet, next to an assortment of red wines.

"Katie, you've done a beautiful job. It looks wonderful! Thank you very much. I don't know how I would have made this day without you." Azzurra spoke from the entrance. "You've set six places? There's me, Arianna and the kids. That makes five?"

Katie continued folding a napkin. "I thought I would set one for Franco. You know, out of respect." She placed the napkin gently on the table and flattened it with care. "I had so much fun. Although, I forgot if the dessert spoon goes above the dessert fork, or below — I have no idea if I got that right." She stood and began to place a napkin at each setting, fussing until it looked just right. She cleared her throat. "I'm gonna grab some flowers from the yard and put them in a nice vase as the center piece. I'll move the candlesticks just a bit." She smoothed her dress and took another deep breath, dabbing the corner of her eye with the back of her finger. "I thought the *Lancaster Blue* would be best as the *Stratford Flowers* is a bit too springy and the *Blue Italian* didn't seem right for the occasion."

"Thank you for thinking of Franco, Katie." Azzurra took a few steps forward. "Are you all right Katie? How's your arm? You seem down."

"Oh, I'm fine." Katie paused for a moment, eyes focused on her aged sister. She sighed once more. "I'll get the vase. I placed both red and white wine glasses. White is chilling; red is placed on the buffet." She took a large *Tiffany* crystal vase from the hutch and walked out of the room.

Azzurra followed. "You're right, Katie — I like the *Blue Italian,* but not for this occasion. *Lancaster* is so elegant and strong. And the Lord knows I'm going to need all the strength I can get. You sure you're OK?"

Katie swished a hand toward her sister. "I'm fine, just a little melancholy." She entered the kitchen, Azzurra behind her.

Poof! Merek Kroll popped in the living room, without his trolley cart. The ladies jumped. Katie and Azzurra rolled their eyes to each other.

"Look at us, afraid of our own shadows." Azzurra laughed and then spoke to Merek. "Merek dear, it is ten minutes till six. The kids are due any moment. So you can't be here. They'll have a heart attack before I tell them they're Witches."

Katie stood back and smiled brightly at a long time family friend.

"Is that who I think it is? Katie? Katie Marinacci! My God, it's really you! Come here and give this old man a big hug!" Merek turned solid, hurried around the coffee table and hugged Katie.

Katie blushed. Azzurra interrupted their conversation. "You two have to catch up later. Right now I need to get you out of here. After today, you can pop in anytime you wish Merek dear."

Katie told Merek she'd catch up with him later and headed out to the yard to pick some flowers. She held up a finger to her sister. "I know Azzurra, I'll be careful that the kids don't see me. I'll go to Spirit form. I hardly think they'd recognize me anyway." She slide the door closed.

"I've always liked her. A shame she passed on so young…such a terrible thing." Merek's eyes widened as he waved a hand in the air and shook his head. "I won't ask any questions. It's none of my business. I know you ladies have things to do." He then pointed at Azzurra. "I take it that royal bitch sister of yours is the reason for conjuring the dead." He raised a hand and shook his head once more. "I really shouldn't say that. It's not nice. But she is a bitch. I shouldn't have added that." He swore under his breath and spoke. "If you should need me for anything, do not hesitate for a moment, my dear." He placed his hands behind his back and stood proud.

"Thank you so much Merek. You've always been there for our family. I won't forget that."

"Don't say another word. I know I have to high-tail myself out of here. I just wanted to drop off a few things, like I promised. Can I come back tomorrow?"

"Yes. That would be wonderful. Come around 2:00. The rest of the family will be here and you can catch up with everyone then." Azzurra took a few steps toward an old friend.

"Say no more my dear lady." He raised his hand to halt her. "Say no more, and thank you. I shall take you up on your offer and say hi to the family at 2:00 tomorrow." He winked and tipped his hat, said good-day and vanished.

Azzurra hurried to the coffee pot. The pot was full of fresh brewed raspberry, chocolate coffee. The sliding door opened by itself and then closed. Katie appeared holding a bouquet of beautiful white calla Lilly's. Azzurra furrowed an eyebrow. "Katie, where did you pick those?"

Katie swished a hand toward her sister. "I turned your sunflowers into calla Lilly's. Sunflowers just would not have matched the table. Now these will be perfect." She walked to the sink and started to fill the vase with water.

"Oh my Lord, Katie, I forgot you can do Magick." Azzurra raised a hand to her chest.

Katie rolled her eyes. "Azzurra, for the love of God we're Witches. May as well start acting like one. I've been using Magick all day. You should start using Magick too. You know — practice. As soon as you get the OK from the Higher Spirits, that is." She lifted the vase from the sink and wiped the bottom dry with the kitchen towel.

"I am so stupid sometimes. I kept thinking, my Lord, Katie got everything done so fast. Pasta, salad, dressings…and the table looks so beautiful, the coffee is made. I said to myself, beee she's fast." She held a small hand over her face and began to laugh.

"And you tell me not to worry when you can't even remember you're a Witch!" Katie set the vase down on the counter.

"Well it's probably a good thing I forget. Vicar Sinclair forbad me to use Magick. But he was a bit odd. He said if I did, I would just have to explain myself." She clasped a hand over her mouth. "I called upon the cat and soap dispenser. That wasn't an emergency! Oh Katie, I'm going to be in trouble!"

"Big deal." She swished a hand. "Just tell them you were preparing for a Witches War and didn't have time to do the dishes. They'll understand." Shrugging her shoulders she continued. "I can't believe you thought I got everything done without Magick" Another swish. "Beee, you think I'm like that mouse. Oh, what's his name, Speedy Gonzales?" They laughed.

Azzurra glanced at the clock and panicked. "Oh my Lord, it's almost six!" She headed for the front door, then to the dining room and then hurried back to the kitchen.

Katie busted out laughing and sat at the kitchen table. Azzurra stopped, shook her head, sat down opposite Katie and began to laugh at herself.

The laughter was brought to an abrupt halt at the site of Vicar Sinclair.

* * * *

Free Will

When Azzurra began to speak, the Vicar raised his hand for silence. "I am aware of the dinner with your children and have made adjustments. They will be late. Your sister, Arianna, will be late of her own accord." He looked to Katie and glanced down to her arm where the silver-dollar sized hole could be seen. "I see that you have recovered from your attack with only minor damage. Might I have a closer look?"

Katie extended her arm to the Vicar. Blackie gave a short bark, spun in a circle, sat down and looked up to the Vicar. After taking a moment to examine Katie's arm, the Vicar spoke. "You were not banished. You were the victim of a Disbursement Charm. The pieces of your arm will find their way back to you sometime in the near future. It has been in your benefit that the spell was performed by a Spirit who did not possess the power needed for such a spell."

Katie began to feel the effects of the Vicar. The worries that consumed her so strongly in the dining room, lifted gently away from their intension. They morphed into a calm resolution that everything would be the way that it should.

"What in the world is a Disbursement Charm?" Azzurra questioned.

The Vicar turned his attention to her. "The Disbursement Charm is an attack spell worthy of the most powerful Magickal beings. Your sister, having been a powerful Witch and a Soul, made it difficult for the spell to be completed. If they had succeeded, her atoms would have been scattered over time and space and could have taken centuries to reform. The caster of such a spell will feel the effect of his actions upon leaving the Earth's realm." He glanced up and to the left with a swift tilt of the head. Azzurra and Katie followed his eyes to empty air.

Azzurra asked another question. "Vicar Sinclair, you said it was a Spirit, can you tell us the name?"

"Yes, he is one of Contessa's Spirits, referred to as Achar. However, I am unaware at this time whether his involvement has been the result of following a command from Contessa, influenced by someone else, or an act of his own Free Will. I will confirm."

"Achar...I'm not sure I remember him." Azzurra took a few steps closer to the kitchen table. The Vicar stood near the entrance of the hall. "Well, thank goodness you found the culprit that attacked my sister and you can now stop him from attacking anyone else."

Katie turned to the calla Lilies and began to arrange them haphazardly. She shook her head and whispered something to herself.

The Vicar spoke. "I cannot. When Achar decides to leave the Earth's realm or when the time comes in which everyone must leave, he will feel the effects of what he has done. However, until then, he, like you, has Free Will. Therefore, I cannot intervene." Blackie cocked his head, then looked to Katie and gave a soft cry. He then looked to Azzurra.

Azzurra frowned and narrowed her eyes. "Achar is same Spirit that has been attacking Olivia and Walter. Am I right?" The Vicar nodded. "Achar is the same Spirit who has most likely sent a Cull to wrap itself around my daughter's throat and torture her with horrid thoughts. Am I right?" Her tone released hostility.

Katie shook her head several times, whispering more thoughts as she continued to fuss with the flowers. Blackie lowered his ears flat to his head.

The Vicar nodded. "You are correct. There is another Spirit involved as well — a Spirit by the name of Deveroy. Celestials have also interfered with the lives of Olivia and Walter. There are other parties involved in their instruction. However, I will not reveal them." The Vicar moved slightly toward Azzurra who withdrew.

The Vicar addressed the sisters. Katie shifted her focused. "I have the results of the inquiry from the Higher Spirits. They have granted a guardian to be assigned to Olivia and Walter. They are the only family members that have been granted protection. I will be serving as their guardian, guide and healer." His eyes moved to Katie and then back to Azzurra. "They have also given Katie permission to come and go among mortals and to utilize her powers to their full extent. This is permitted as long as the threats from your sister, Contessa, or other members of your family, remain. Furthermore, you and your family may break your father's Vow, without penalty. You may begin using Magick. The Higher Spirits have also granted permission to call forth your Wand Spirit, Basil. He may enlist other Spirits to aid him in his endeavors."

Azzurra's hazel eyes fixed on the man in white, void of all emotion, except one. Her voice had the same tone that revealed itself Sunday morning — a tone unlike her own. "I'm going to tell you something, Vicar Sinclair. As a woman and a mother, I will do whatever it takes to protect my family. I will use the Magick I was born to use. I will learn new spells and incantations, because a mother's instinct is to protect her loved ones. I will pray to the Lord for guidance and protection. However, I am not stupid. A Witch or Wizard in their 70's or 80's, who have not so much as boiled water by Magick in over forty years, will not be very useful in a full-out Witches War! Am I right Vicar Sinclair?"

The Vicar nodded in agreement. Azzurra's face turned flush. "My children, nieces and nephews do not know they possess powers. They have had no involvement in Witchcraft their entire lives, and you and the Higher Spirits are aware of this. Am I right, Vicar?" The Vicar acknowledged her with another nod.

Azzurra approached the kitchen table, eyes narrowed upon the Vicar, lips tense. "Now let me tell you another thing. This Spirit, Achar, has tortured Olivia and Walter for God only knows how long. He is responsible for the attack upon Katie and most likely the same Spirit who has sent a damn Cull upon my daughter! Am I right Vicar?" She slammed her hand upon the kitchen table.

"Azzurra, calm down and watch your tone." Katie moved toward her sister. Black gave a soft whimper and crawled under the table.

The Vicar clasped his hands behind his back and gave a nod.

"I'm going to tell you another thing, Vicar. If you think that the older generation can just pick up where we left off — you're wrong! Katie's atoms were separated from her body. Arianna can't water a plant without throwing it through the damn window. Augusto is hearing his dead wife's voice and too damn crabby for a Witches War and I was taken off guard in my own home! For the love of God Vicar, she is using Spirits, demons and the Lord only knows what else! How are we to protect our loved ones? Am I to see my entire family die!?" She pointed a finger at the Vicar. "A demon has wrapped itself around my daughter's throat and you're going to stand there and tell me, that as a man representing God's kingdom…as a compassionate, high ranking official to the heavens…that my family can just f*****g protect ourselves!" Azzurra slammed a hand on the kitchen table.

"Azzurra, for the love of God apologize!" Katie covered her mouth with both hands as Blackie yelped, darted out from the table and bolted behind the sofa. "Azzurra he can't. He just can't! You don't understand." Katie turned to face the Vicar. "She didn't mean that Vicar. My sister's just upset." She placed hands on her hips and faced Azzurra. "Talk about my language! The F word Azzurra! I don't even say that word!" She took a hold of Azzurra's hands and squeezed. "Azzurra, honey, try to understand…he…can't."

"He can't, or he won't!" Azzurra flung Katie's hands away, turned and pointed at the Vicar once again. Her voice was low and threatening. "I'm going to tell you something Vicar. If something happens to my family because…"

The Vicar's voice boomed over Azzurra's, forcing silence. "…because of Free Will!" He slammed his hand on the table. Blackie yelped from behind the sofa. His voice deepened with a threat of anger. "I am forbidden to interfere with the behavior of mortals and/or Spirits that have not yet left the Earth's realm. When the Universe was created, it was created with Free Will. It means that everyone has the right to make their own decisions — what you would call, good or bad. It is the design of the Universe that every living creature has the right to Free Will. The Higher Spirits, Vicar's, Guardians and other Spiritual beings are respectful of the Universal design of Free Will. I cannot interfere with Spirits or mortals that are simply exercising their right. Katie chooses to stay within the Earth's realm. Basil is waiting on his own accord to protect his beloved Witch. They are exercising their Free Will. Your Creator, your God, your Bible, every religion that speaks of love, as end result, reveal the same philosophy. You reap what you sew. The energy that is given in this life will mimic itself in death. Achar will need to feel what it is like to act upon such disturbed energy. It is not that he should be punished; it is not for us to judge or impose punishment for his actions. He simple put forth the energy within his actions to cast such a spell and he will know the consequences. It is what you call punishment and far more complex than Karma. Contessa's day will come. Everyone's day will come and what they exude, here on Earth, will indeed, come back to them. It is unavoidable. It is not in the right of knowing all that I know, to interfere with Free Will. Does it frustrate me to have to stand by and do nothing to protect good people — people who have good hearts and souls. Yes, it does. The Degeli family has chosen to practice Magick. No one should judge you for that decision. I will not, nor will the Higher Spirits. To judge, is not in the nature of the Universe. Your family has chosen to become one of the most powerful clans of Witches this century has seen. Consequences for using certain types of Magick are the same for every creature's own decision…to steal a car, protect a loved one, break into a home, save a life, gossip and afflict cruelty to animals or other beings. These are decisions that are given to everyone under the Universal Law. But whatever energy is pushed out, you will receive, because the Universe is reacting to your commands. It is for these decisions that everyone must accept the consequences. I will assist as much as I can. But it must be limited so as to not force the Will of others. It is better that the human race be guided in their actions, learn their own skills and know their own downfall. Reap what they sew. The being you refer to as Mother Nature, is simply invoking the same energy you release. She will respond the way you have treated the Earth, each other and other beings. I am a Vicar, blessed with knowledge that only a being of my nature may understand. I ask that you have patients. I cannot and will not be able to heal Walter and Olivia completely. I will provide them with the feeling of love, protection, knowledge and understanding of their full potential. However, it will be up to them to interpret, digest, feel and change. They will need assistance and understanding from loved ones. It is with a heavy heart that neither the Higher Spirits nor I can interfere. You chose, by Free Will, to make the Vow never to use Magick again. You chose, by Free Will, not to tell your children that they are Witches and now, because you have Free Will, you shall choose how to defend your family. I shall be at your side. However, I will not take away the Free Will of mortals and or Spirits. You have opened the gates that allow celestial beings to enter your family and you must and will protect yourselves as a consequence. You must have faith. You must show love, compassion and understanding within your heart…and must never speak to me that way again."

Azzurra collapsed to the floor, placed her face into the palms of her hands and cried.

Katie knelt beside her and laid a hand upon her sister's head. Blackie peeked out from behind the sofa, looked up to the Vicar, then to his mother. He then hurried to Azzurra's side, lied down next to her and placed his head upon her thigh.

Several moments later, Katie whispered softly to her sister and helped her to her feet. Blackie sat down in front of the Vicar and looked up at him.

Azzurra raised her head and met the Vicar's eyes. "I'm sorry Vicar. I guess I'm afraid for my family. I'm up in age…and tired…and I'm foolish. Forgive me."

Katie handed her a tissue. Azzurra dabbed her swollen eyes and looked down.

The Vicar approached Azzurra, lifted her chin and looked into her eyes. "You are more powerful than you realize. You must not fail in your desires. Trust your nature." He smiled at Azzurra. His deep brown eyes swam with emotion.

Azzurra's breathe shuttered. "I'm sorry Vicar. Vicar *Sinclair*, that is. I'm sorry."

He placed strong arms around her and held tight. "You are always forgiven. It is in nature to be forgiven, as long as your heart is sincere."

Azzurra melted into a feeling of calm, happiness and love.

Katie swished an arm in the air. "Vicar…Vicar *Sinclair*…I liked referring to him as just plain old Vicar. Why did you have to be so formal? Beee this girl. Anyway, Vicar *Sinclair*, I understood everything you said. However, I do have a question about Demons. Can you, or the Higher Spirits, get involved if Demons are being used?"

The Vicar cupped his hands behind his back, glanced upward, and then faced the sisters. "You may simply call me Vicar, Katie." His mouth slid into a grin, which faded as quickly as it came. "Demons, and or other such entities, that have had no human form in their existence can be interfered with, as long as the mortal does not wish the presence of such a demon."

"Thank you, Vicar. I have a feeling our sister, Tessa, is using a lot more than your average Wand Spirit these days. Culls *are* demons and as far as we know Marta, Olivia and most likely Walter have demons wrapped around their throats. Although…it could be Celia who sent the Culls, not Contessa, we just don't know yet." Katie said.

The Vicar winked at Kate. "I have decided to remove the demons from Walter and Olivia. You, or a member of your family, will remove the Cull that has attached itself to Marta."

"With all this talk of demons, Culls and Celestial beings, who feels like dinner?" Azzurra took a deep breath and sighed.

The Vicar looked up and to the right, narrowed his eyes and then returned his focus to Azzurra. "I have just been informed that Contessa is not aware that you have summoned Katie. Achar confessed that he cast the Disbursement Charm to her. He thinks he succeeded in Katie's destruction. It is also known that the attack was not ordered by Contessa. Achar acted of his own accord or by the command of someone else, other than your sister. Your sister is disturbed at the thought of Katie's atoms spread over the universe. She thought it gruesome and wept at the thought of Katie's demise. Perhaps you have painted a picture of Contessa that is disturbed by previous encounters." He looked to the women and then continued. "The Higher Spirits are very interested in this Witches' War." His eyes moved from one sister to the other.

"I will take my leave, your guest are arriving. I will inform you of when I shall take guardianship over Walter and Olivia. I will notify you within 24 hours. There are repercussions to consider before I make such a move. Should anyone realize that a Vicar has been placed as Olivia's Guardian, should anyone realize that Katie has been summoned or Basil has be reinstated as your Wand Spirit, it may cause a reaction sooner than what you are ready to receive.

He focused on Azzurra. "Azzurra, you will need to summon your Spirit, Basil. He is beginning to annoy the Higher Spirits with his weather interruptions." He turned to Katie. "Katie, if you would, I need a word." He held out his arm.

"I will Vicar." Azzurra acknowledged.

Katie nodded and wished Azzurra luck with the kids and said that she would return as soon as possible. They embraced. Katie reached down, picked up Blackie and stood next to the Vicar. She hooked an arm through the Vicars, took Blackie's paw and waved. She, Blackie and the Vicar, vanished.

The front door opened and the voices of Marta and Marie entered the room. Wednesday's supper had arrived.

* * * *

Wednesday Supper

The Dining Room

"Canadian geese, there were dozens of geese. I couldn't get across the road. Two minutes from you and you'd think I could make it to dinner on time. People just sat and watched as all these geese waddle across the road. They were cute though. Their little butts wiggling back and forth." Marta took off her leather jacket and placed it on the *Bokja* arm chair. "Damn, I think I'm getting a headache."

"I couldn't find my keys. I swear to God I had them in my hands and was heading out the door and then I didn't have them. Took me fifteen minutes to find them and they were right there on their hook. I swear I looked there a thousand times. That is so annoying when you can't find something. Sorry Ma." Marie struggled to remove a light sweater. Her ring became caught on the sleeve. "Oh for Heaven's sakes, Marta, can you help me?"

The door opened once more and closed. Nicco squeezed past his sisters. "Car died Ma. Not even a year old and the car died right in the middle of the road. People kept beeping and swearing at me to get off the road. Like I would if I could, you know. Then, suddenly, poof the damn thing started. At least we're all late, eh." Nicco turned to Marie. "Got trouble there Marie?" He laughed and went to hug his mother. "Sorry Ma!"

"Nicco, sweetheart, things happen, what are you going to do? Not like I'm going anywhere." She pinched his cheek and gave him a hug.

"Ma...the cheeks." Nicco blushed.

"I can't help it. You still have cute cheeks and I love to pinch them." She turned and opened her arms to Marie who was finally free from her sweater.

"Damn, now there's a snag." She examined her ring that did the damage. She looked up and noticed her mother standing with her arms open. "Oh, Ma, I'm sorry." She gave her mother a quick hug and moved over so Marta could have a turn. Marie spoke again. "Ma, I'm sorry. I was paying attention to my ring and didn't even notice you standing there with your arms opened. I'm sorry Ma."

Azzurra waved a hand to her daughter and hugged Marta. "Marie, it's all right. Leave your sweater here and I'll fix it tomorrow — if you're busy and don't have time." She took in her daughter appearance. "You look so cute, Marie. I love that dress on you."

"I have time to fix it, but thank you." She glanced down to her dress. "You always say you love this dress. It's OK."

"I like the haircut Marie, very cute on you and I like that dress too." Marta commented.

"The haircut is cute, Marie. Maybe a little too short, but it's very nice." Azzurra added.

"Thanks Marta." Marie turned to her mother. "Ma, you always say it looks too short. I like it this way." She focused on her sister. "Marta, you look...let me see you." She spun her sister around. "Marta! My Lord! You took time with your hair! Is that make-up? And look at those curves you're showing off! When did you get those slacks?"

"I didn't mean anything by it Marie. Marta, you do you look very nice sweetheart. I like those slacks on you, they show your figure very nicely, and what a nice sweater. I like orange on you, very sharp." Azzurra spoke as she examined Marta closer. "How do you feel? How's your head?"

Marie gasped. "Oh, Marta, what happened? That bruise is awful." She spoke to her mother. "Oh my Lord, is this part of what happened...you've been attacked?" She placed a hand to her chest. "That's what this is all about? Marta! You've been attacked?"

"No, no…I was not attacked, for the love of God. I fell at work. I'll explain everything later." Marta swished a hand through the air. "I'm fine, Ma. I think I'm getting a headache though." She placed a hand over the bump on her head and rubbed gently.

"That looks awful, Marta. You may have a concussion." Marie leaned on her toes and tried to look over Marta's hand.

Nicco burst into the conversation. "Who cares? My God, the hair, the dress, the slacks, the makeup! Oh, that bruise looks terrible! Can we eat? I'm starving!"

The three women retorted.

"Gee thanks, Nicco. Sorry that the bruise on my head is causing you distress!"

"That bruise is awful! Nicco, you should be ashamed!"

"Nicco, I'm gonna get mad. How dare you treat your sister that way!"

"He's hungry again…always an idiot when he's hungry."

It went on for at least two minutes until Nicco interrupted them. "You're right! I'm sorry Marta about your head, it looks terrible. And I agree, that orange looks spectacular on you. Marie, I can't believe that haircut, simply stunning!" He put his fingers to his lips and gave a kiss to the air.

"Yea, but Ma thinks it's too short."

"I like the orange too. It's fun."

"I didn't mean anything by it Marie. I said it looks cute?"

"She didn't mean anything by it, Marie. She used to tell me to put a comb through my hair once in a while."

"Marta sweetheart, you got your hair cut too. It looks very nice."

"What? Not too short like mine, eh?"

"Marie would you drop it, she didn't mean anything. And I did get it cut. Thanks, Ma. I got it done Tuesday. It was getting to be a mess. Not too much off the top but just shaped up a bit."

Nicco walked over to the dining room entrance, peeked in and then turned to face his family. "The dining room looks great. Maybe we should head in."

"Thanks honey, Katie…I mean…I did it. I mean…of course I did. Who else would do it? Thanks honey." Azzurra looked to Marie.

"It's just because I'm fat. It's too short and it makes me look fat. Is that it, Ma?"

"Marie! I'm going to get mad! I didn't mean anything by it! I wish you would stop describing yourself as fat. That is an awful thing to say! Perhaps overweight or slightly plump, it sounds so much nicer."

"Ma, you shouldn't have said that!"

"I can't believe you just said that!"

"Now what? What did I say?"

"You shouldn't have said that, Ma."

"I didn't mean anything by it. I hate that word fat. I think plump is cute."

"Ma, enough with the words already!"

"I can't believe she just said it again. Just like the neighborhood kids."

"What neighborhood kids?"

"Neighborhood kids?"

"They all called me a fat cow today."

"Oh my Lord, Marie!"

"What kids?"

"Neighborhood boys. Just because I yelled at them the other day for using foul language when they were playing kickball in the street."

"That's awful."

"Oh Marie, sweetheart, don't pay attention."

"Just ignore them, Marie. Damn kids, I would have never spoken to an adult that way."

"Oh Ma, it was just awful! It brought back memories of high school."

"Oh, Marie, you look beautiful, honey. You're mother wouldn't lie to you. You're my daughter and I would tell you the truth."

121

"You do, Marie. I just love the hair and the dress and look how nice your nails are."

"You like them? It's a new color…"

"FOR THE LOVE OF GOD, CAN WE PLEASE EAT?" Nicco's screamed.

The three women stopped and stared at Nicco. "We have to wait for your Aunt Arianna. She should be here any minute…or should we be rude and start without her?" Azzurra hurried past her son.

"Ma, did you make salad? I'll put it on the table and get the dressing." Marie stormed by Nicco and hit him on the back of his head as she passed.

"Is that homemade bread I smell? Oh Ma, what a treat." Marta pushed her shoulder into Nicco as she passed. Nicco threw his arms in the air as the front door opened.

"Aunty Arianna!" He hurried forward. "Let me take that for you." Nicco took the platter covered with plastic wrap and hugged his aunt. "It's so good to see you. How's Uncle Mateo? Is he here?"

"No, no sweetheart he stayed home. I just wanted to give support to my sister. He sends his love." She pinched Nicco's cheeks.

"The cheeks Aunty A, the cheeks! What support? Something strange has been going on? Something weird happened Sunday. I guess Ma went to the cemetery. Marta said it was creepy. Do you know what's going on?" Nicco hooked his arm with hers and began to escort his aunt to the kitchen.

"Don't ask Nicco. I'm not telling. How's Tracy? Have you proposed to that poor girl yet?" Arianna looked up to her nephew.

Nicco stopped. He looked down to his favorite aunt and took in her appearance. She was aging, just like Ma. Thin brunette hair with a smattering of gray was pushed away from her face and combed to the left. "I'm not telling." Nicco pinched her nose.

The ladies turned the corner from the kitchen, chattering. Their hands full of food. "Arianna, come on in honey. Nicco, why are keeping her in the hallway?"

"Ma, I didn't keep her in…"

"…Aunty A!" Marie hurried to the dining room, placed the salad and dressings on the table and rushed out of the entrance to greet her favorite aunt. "I love the dress. I love the spattering of maroon and hunter green? You didn't' have to make anything Aunty."

122

"Just a little something sweet, that's all." Arianna reached out to hug her niece. "Thanks honey. Nice fall colors." She pinched Marie's cheek and added. "Marie, honey…you look beautiful. I love the haircut!" She placed her purse on the chair.

"Thank you Aunty A." Marie moved aside for Marta.

"Aunty A, how the hell are you?" Marta hugged her favorite aunt. "I like that dress too. When did you get it?"

"Oh, I bought it a couple of weeks ago. Thank you, sweethearts, Mateo really likes it too." Arianna complimented the orange that Marta wore.

"Can I hug my sister please?" Azzurra squeezed in between Marie and Marta and hugged her sister. "You didn't have to make anything, but thank you. And thank you for being here. It means a lot to me not to be alone."

"My pleasure, I shall always be there for my sister. I'm not sure how those turned out. I may not have baked them long enough, but we'll see." Arianna shrugged her shoulders.

"You want me to take your shawl, Aunty A?" Marta asked. "Or you think you may get chilled? Ma keeps the house cool."

Nicco stood by the dining room entrance. "Why don't we head into the dining room? We can start the salad and I'll pour the wine. Ma made home baked bread."

"Oh, I'll keep it on, thank you. I'm always chilled. You got your hair cut too. Oh, it looks so cute, Marta." Arianna touched Marta's bump lightly. "How's the bump sweetheart?"

"Yea, Marie's haircut makes her look fat!" Marta's said.

"Marta!" Marie shouted.

Arianna's eyes widened as she backed away from Marta. She gave a slight shiver. "Never mind honey. She's not herself." Arianna patted Marie's shoulder.

"Let's just head in and we can chat over salad." Nicco closed his eyes slowly and then opened them.

Marie looked toward Marta and shook her head. "Are you OK Marta? You look stressed or in pain. You mad at me?"

"I'm in pain because I have a frickin' headache Marie because of my God damn bruise that no one gives a shit about! It's always worrying about how it's going to affect Marie! Poor, Marie!" Marta placed her hands upon her hips.

Marie clutched her chest and took in a deep breath.

"Maybe we should eat. We'll all feel better." Nicco stood at the entrance, his arm stretched to the wall, bracing himself.

Azzurra turned Marta toward Nicco and ushered her through the dining room entrance. "It's all part of the evening's discussion, Marie. Don't take it seriously. She's not herself."

"A Cull is wrapped around your sister's throat, sweetheart." Arianna place an arm around Marie and guided her past Nicco, who sighed with relief. Azzurra made a slight noise and shook her head toward her sister.

"Oops, sorry." Arianna covered her mouth.

Nicco took a deep breath and walked into the dining room. He lit the candles and then began to pour wine for everyone. "I'm sorry I yelled. I haven't eaten much today and you all know how crabby I get when I haven't eaten. Marie, they are stupid kids whose opinions don't mean a damn thing to you, so why get upset? You have a wonderful husband, a beautiful daughter and you're gonna let a bunch of kids bother you. They said it because they were mad. Forget it OK. I love you and you're a beautiful woman." He kissed the top of her head.

"Thank you, Nicco. You're right. I know you are. It just hurts, that's all." Marie unfolded her napkin and placed it on her lap, glaring at Marta.

Marta grunted something under her breath.

"What's a Cull? And what do you mean Marta's not herself?" Marie asked, narrowing her eyes at her sister.

"That was a nice thing to say Nicco and he's right, Marie." Azzurra moved to the head of the table at the opposite side of the room, placing Marta to her right. "I'll let you have dessert sweetheart. That was a very sweet thing to say to your sister."

Marie smiled at her mother. "I'm sorry Ma. I know you didn't mean anything. I was so upset from those damn boys." She turned to her sister. "Marta, are you upset with me?"

"No, she's not upset." Arianna and Azzurra spoke together, both ladies swishing their hands toward her.

"Well Aunty A said there was a Cu..." Marie started.

"...Nothing! Nothing Marie, never mind. Just have some salad." Azzurra shook her head at her sister and unfolded the napkin roughly.

"Marie, I'm fine. It's been a rough couple of days. I'm sorry for snapping. I've been ripping Ma's head off too. I just don't feel myself lately." Marta said.

"It's because of the Cul..."Arianna covered her mouth and shook her head.

Azzurra cleared her throat loudly. "And we were worried about Gabriella's mouth!" She eyed her sister.

"I'll say grace, so we can eat." Nicco interrupted.

The ladies glared at him.

Arianna sat next to Marta; Nicco sat directly to Azzurra's left while Marie was seated next to Nicco, across from her aunt. They all looked to the empty seat, opposite Azzurra. "You set a place for Dad." Marie asked.

"Oh Ma." Marta replied.

"That was sweet." Arianna offered.

"Yea, yea touching. Here's grace." Nicco began but was interrupted for the next five minutes.

"Now, you may say grace." Azzurra said, slapping a hand on the table.

Nicco said grace.

"Bless us Oh Lord and these thy gifts, which we are about to receive, through thy bounty, through Christ Oh Lord. Amen."

The dinner started with a salad: fresh greens tossed in olive oil, white wine vinegar, dried oregano, a large garlic clove, garbanzo beans, a sliced red bell pepper, very thinly sliced red onions, sliced fresh fennel, goat cheese, thinly sliced prosciutto and sliced pitted black olives with a dash of salt and pepper. The fresh baked bread smelled like heaven. There was also a colorful tray of pickles, black olives, Italian olives and radishes that were displayed in a crystal relish tray.

Nicco took his portion of salad and passed it to Marie. Azzurra took the relish tray and placed some pickles and olives on her butter dish, not feeling much like eating. Marta took the bread and passed it to Azzurra who passed her the relish tray, which was passed to Arianna. It went on like this for a few minutes until everyone had what they wanted.

Outside, the wind began to gather in strength.

Marta wanted to ask her mother what she had to tell them, but didn't want to upset her, so she kept quite. Marie couldn't stop wondering why they were there — a formal dinner, on a Wednesday evening. Aunt Arianna's comment about Marta's throat gave her the willies. Nicco's blood sugar began to settle and a sense of calm engulfed him. He could have cared less about the news.

The trees began to bustle in the increasing wind.

About twenty minutes later, Marie and Marta cleared the salads plates while Azzurra went to the basement to get the pasta and Arianna removed the sauce from the stove. Nicco refilled wine glasses and pulled another loaf of bread.

Nicco placed the angel hair pasta and meatballs in a thick marinara meat sauce on the table. All of them took another slice of bread and lathered it with garlic butter. Nicco took his mother's plate and gave her some pasta, then ladled sauce on top. He did the same for Marie, Marta and his aunt, leaving himself for last. He then passed the parmesan cheese and scallions around the table which were sprinkled atop their pasta.

There was a sudden rumble of thunder. Crack! Lightning flashed across the room. The five of them jumped in their seats. The lights flickered, leaving them for a brief moment in candlelight.

"Gee, that was loud! It scared the hell out of me," Marta said as she sprinkled a large amount of parmesan cheese over her pasta.

"Everyone's windows rolled up?" Arianna asked.

"Yea."

"Yep."

"Yes."

"What's with the weather lately? We've been having such freak storms. I mean, I know this is Michigan, but gee." Marie spoke as she sprinkled scallions over her pasta.

The thunder rolled again and the rain started to come down. The wind howled and some of the tree branches near the house scraped the roof.

A chill ran up Marta's spine.

"How's the dinner, kids?" Azzurra smiled at her children.

"Good Ma."

"Delicious, Ma."

"I love it Ma."

The thunder rolled throughout the skies. The lightning streaked through the room as the lights flickered. The five of them looked up to the chandelier.

"Maybe we should check the news. There may be a tornado warning up or something." Nicco put down his fork and dabbed his mouth with his napkin. He began to rise from the table.

"Oh sit down. It's fine. It's just Basil." Azzurra swished a hand at her son. Arianna began to choke on her food

The kids stopped chewing, drinking and rising from the table.

"What?"

"Basil?"

"Who's Basil and what does he have to do with the storm?"

Arianna turned red. Azzurra flushed and fanned her face with a napkin. "Oh, I mean the basil in the sauce is wonderful. It really makes the sauce." She shoved a huge amount of pasta into her mouth. Arianna began to laugh as she tried to stop choking. Marta patted her aunt on the back.

Nicco slowly sat back down. Marta took large gulp of wine while Marie began to eat faster.

"Yea, the basil does make the sauce, Ma." Marta spoke slowly.

"I was thinking to myself how fresh basil makes the difference and meant to say don't worry, it's nothing. I just had basil on my mind, that's all." Azzurra smiled awkwardly but looked as though she had cramps.

"Your mother is just tired, kids. It's not easy being without Franco." Arianna explained.

The three chimed in, agreeing with their aunt.

"Ma, I can't believe you did all this today, all by yourself, too. I would have come over and helped." Marie dabbed her mouth with a napkin. "The table looks beautiful and these calla Lilies are stunning." Marie reached for the parmesan cheese.

"Ma, is this homemade pasta? It's really good." Nicco rolled his fork up with a bountiful amount of pasta.

"Oh it was nothing. Katie made the pasta." Azzurra replied.

Arianna spit her wine across the table.

Azzurra realized what she said and covered her mouth with a napkin. Several swearwords were muffled.

Marie choked on a meatball. Marta spit up her wine, and Nicco's water went down the wrong pipe.

Azzurra looked at her three kids shaking her head. She turned to her sister, who was laughing in a napkin. The thunder rolled again and then cracked like a whip. She looked up past the kids and noticed at the entrance of the dining room, Katie had appeared. She was laughing.

"It's not funny, Katie!" Azzurra spoke out loud. She quickly covered her mouth. This time, she pulled herself to the side of her chair and started to laugh.

"She meant to say my name! Oh Azzurra, how much wine have you had." Arianna said. She then noticed Katie, who winked at her. "Katie!"Arianna covered her mouth with a napkin. The kids turned to the entrance, but Katie had vanished. They all stared at their aunt.

Nicco was still choking on his water. Marie was patting him on his back as she tried to clear her throat from a meatball. Marta was dabbing up the wine she and her aunt had spit across the table.

"Ma, are you all right?" Marta asked. "You're creeping me out."

"Nicco, oh Nicco swallow honey. Is he all right Marie?" Azzurra asked. She glanced at the doorway. Katie reappeared, still laughing.

"Ma, I'm fine. What the hell do you mean Aunt Katie made the pasta?" Nicco held his chest and put a napkin to his mouth. Marie stopped patting him on his back. He nodded to her that he was ok. "Thanks Marie."

"Oh, it's nothing. It's just that Katie always helped me at dinner parties and I remembered how she taught me how to make homemade pasta. I've had her on my mind a lot lately. I'm fine. Eat your dinner."

"I made the pasta. She meant to say my name." Arianna announced.

Azzurra deflated. Marie scrunched her eyes and tilted her head at the pasta. Marta looked aghast and then examined her plate. Nicco rolled a large amount of spaghetti on his fork and spoke. "Who cares who made it? This is good pasta, Aunty A. Thanks." He shoved the fork into his mouth.

"Does this have something to do with what you're going to tell us tonight?" Marie asked. She turned to Nicco shaking her head.

"All in good time Marie, but since you asked, as a matter of fact it does. Eat your dinner."

Arianna leaned across the table toward Nicco. "Thank you sweetheart for believing me, but I confess, I didn't make the pasta."

"Who cares? It's good." Nicco spoke with a mouthful.

"Nicco, don't talk with your mouth full." Azzurra scolded.

The rain started to bombard the ground with sharp pellets. The wind blew violently, whipping the trees in every direction. Crack! More lightning struck. The lights flickered and silence filled the room.

Azzurra's mind raced. *Just watch your mouth and don't say another word.* She looked to Arianna, who shook her head.

Nicco was trying to convince himself his mother was not hallucinating. Marie was nervous and began eating too fast again, which made her stomach upset and Marta began to pick at her food, glancing over to her aunt.

Azzurra announced that she needed to start the coffee, and excused herself from the table.

In the kitchen, she placed both hands on the counter and took a breath. Arianna rushed beside her. "You're doing fine. Don't worry. Just take a deep breath and the right words will come to you. Where's Katie?" Katie appeared in her ghostly form in front of the kitchen sink.

Arianna screamed Katie's name. Katie turned solid and they hugged. Azzurra threw her arms in the air. Katie turned to Azzurra. "Oh Azzurra, they think you're crazy!" Katie began to laugh.

"No one believed me. I could have made the pasta. Nicco did, but then again he didn't care." Arianna swished a hand in the air.

Azzurra placed her hands upon her hips. "Katie, Arianna, I'll laugh about this later. Right now, I'm too upset. I don't know how to tell them they are

Witches. And would you please tell Basil to give me a half an hour and I'll call for him. Tell him he is to stop this storm. He's going to flood my garden and tell him he is annoying the Higher Spirits as well!"

"I'm sorry Azzurra, you're right. I wouldn't want to be in your shoes. I'll go and tell Basil to stop the storm, right now. Here, I already made the coffee, it will refill itself. Oh that smells so good. I love chocolate and raspberry!" She turned to Arianna. "Arianna, give your sister support and stop saying such nonsense like, 'I made the pasta!'" She smiled and gave both sisters a half hug and vanished.

Azzurra shook her head and looked to Arianna. "I forgot the coffee was made. She didn't mean anything by it Arianna, let it go" Azzurra grabbed the coffee pot and they headed back to the dining room.

Nicco had cleared the plates and placed them on the buffet. Marta was serving the desserts and as their mother and aunt entered the room. They all heard the sudden break in the wind and rain and looked toward the window. Marta shivered.

Marie looked up to her mother, who was pouring her coffee. "That was fast. I thought you had to brew it?"

Azzurra stopped and stared at Marie for several long uncomfortable seconds. She never answered. Marie shrank in her seat.

Azzurra poured Nicco's coffee. After Nicco, she poured her own, then Marta and Marie. After pouring Arianna coffee, she placed the coffee pot on a warmer that was on the buffet table and pressed the button to keep the coffee hot.

Azzurra took her seat at the head of the table. "Eat your desserts and then we'll talk."

The crickets began their chain of music. Water released itself from the gutters and millions of droplets plunged from the trees to the ground.

No one spoke a word. They sat quietly eating the chocolate chip stuffed cannoli. They had each taken what looked like angel wings dusted with powdered sugar that their Aunt Arianna had made, but no one attempted to eat them, not even the baker.

About ten minutes later Nicco stood and refilled everyone's coffee, he examined the full pot, shrugged his shoulder and took a seat.

They focused on their mother — and waited.

Azzurra took a deep breath and dabbed her mouth with a napkin. She placed her forearms on the table and looked past the kids. Katie stood at the entrance to the dining room, smiled and gave thumbs-up. Azzurra looked to Arianna who winked. "Kids, I have something to tell you. I only ask that you do not interrupt and let me finish. I will answer all your questions after I'm done. Do I have your word?" Her voice was soft but had the presence of control.

They all agreed.

Azzurra took another deep breath and began to speak.

* * * *

Ciro & Adalina

"My grandparents were born and raised in Livorno, in Northern Italy. Now at this time, my Grandfather, Ciro, was in the business of making shoes, which extended to a clothing line that became very successful. My Grandmother, Adalina, stayed home and raised the kids and ran the household."

"Back then, it was very common to have 12 children However, my grandmother had a hard time of it. The poor thing had several miscarriages, even lost one of her babies in the ninth month." Azzurra shook her head slightly. "God willing though, she did have four children. One of those children, of course, was my father, Pasquale. As you know, Sabino is his brother, Francine his sister and Bernadette died when she was 7." Azzurra took a sip of coffee and placed her forearms on the table.

"Ciro, my grandfather, had a very different view of how his family should live their lives. I mean it was different from other members of the family. You see, they didn't like that he made clothes and shoes; a very conventional way of making a living. You know how family can be." She almost regretted making them promise not to interrupt. Marta frowned and Nicco seemed distracted by his coffee.

132

"Let me see, maybe if I say it this way — my Grandfather Ciro refused to use the same means of earning a living as the rest of the family, so they resented him."

Marie tried to stifle a yawn. "Well, Grandfather Ciro had loved his brothers and sisters…twelve in all, but what are you going to do? If they were mad, they were mad. He had four children to think about and wanted to set an example."

"You see, he never felt right about making money the way other members of the family did. It wasn't morally right. The same argument had been made generations before. It's not to say that Grandfather Ciro never used the family gifts — I really shouldn't call them gifts as they were more of a craft that had been mastered throughout the years." Nicco looked up from his coffee.

"Now, like I said, my grandfather didn't always feel that it was wrong to use the family…let me say…practice. However, after reading old diaries of ancestors and seeing how using the practice had caused family feuds and even deaths, he decided that he no longer wanted to use the family practice. There were certain types of practices that could be used, that he felt, would harm or hurt nobody. You see, he felt that if you used the practice the way the other family members were doing, you were no better than a common thief."

Marta narrowed her eyes as Marie leaned in a bit closer.

"There was also a certain part of the practice that was far too dangerous and had no business being taught. My own father, Pasquale, didn't quite feel that way…but that's another story."

Azzurra took a sip of water and continued. "When Grandfather Ciro tried to explain why he didn't want to live his life in that manner, well, it didn't go over very well. The other family members thought he was judging himself to be better than they." She looked at Nicco and Marie then over to Marta.

"Grandfather Ciro's parents were killed early in their years, which meant that the only family he had were his brothers and sisters. His wife, Adalina's family lived in Southern Italy, so the distance kept them out of the feud. Besides, once they heard about the feud, they would side with him or against him. My grandfather had little support and after much thought, he and Grandma Adalina decided to go against the family ways of life in hopes that it wouldn't cause a family feud. Unfortunately, it did just that."

"Now, let me see. I'm not sure who it was, but one of my grandfather's brothers refused to allow him to raise his children away from the family practice and threatened to take the children away from him. Well, you can image how that went over. Grandfather Ciro was just furious and he was not a man you wanted to be around when riled, neither was Grandma Adalina."

Azzurra took a rather large gulp of wine, dabbed her mouth and continued. "Certain family members believed that the family practice was their birthright. They thought of this as a gift from God and thought that it should be utilized. How they thought that God would tell them to steal and be dishonest, I have no idea, but this is the way they thought. He and Grandma Adalina, did, however, convince two sisters and one brother to join him."

"So the three sided with my grandparents and tried to convince the rest of the family that they should live normal, conventional lives; saving the family practice for chores and recreation."

"Well, now I can't remember who got it first." She paused a moment and looked toward Katie. Katie did a quick hand movement and produced a card with the name Alessandra.

"Oh yes, that's right…Alessandra. That's it, now I remember." She smiled at Katie and gave a tiny wink. The kids looked toward the dining room entrance. Katie had vanished and then reappeared in a faint transparency as the kids turned back toward their mother.

"Well poor Alessandra. She was the first to be killed. If they would have just lived their lives and tried not to convince the others to give up the family practice, who knows? To tell you the truth, I don't think they would have allowed them to do so. After several deaths, they left Italy and moved to the Degeli manor and the war faded. The same war that was waged for generations has begun again. I told you when you were small about the feud between Tessa and your Aunt Katie. Your father and I forbad you to speak with Tessa, Sabino and Stella. Drago and Benny were our first cousins and of course Franco and I kept in touch with them behind our parents back. We knew they were good people. We were there when Drago met Kimberly and when Benny decided to become a priest."

"Anyway, this is not an ordinary family feud, because if it were, I would not bother you with such nonsense. This feud involves an attack upon my family, particularly Katie's family. You have all heard the stories of family members placing curses on one another. Jinxes and Hexes…the Evil Eye."

Nicco's eyes squinted, Marie placed a hand to her chest and Marta looked to her Aunt, narrowed her eyes and then focused back to her mother.

Azzurra paused and then continued. "I've told you stories of your Great Aunt Stella and Uncle Sabino. I've forbad you to never speak to Aunt Debra or Uncle Carlo…to avoid and run if you saw your Aunt Tessa or Uncle Nathan. Stories…so many stories of what happened at the Degeli manor were never spoken to anyone outside our family." Azzurra lowered her voice to an unexpected whisper. "I've kept things from you." Nicco, Marta, Maria and Arianna leaned toward Azzurra. "Things that I was hoping to never speak of. The Degeli manor housed such horrid, hideous memories….memories of the monstrosities that occurred within those walls caused by the family practice. Monstrosities of what happened in that house are written within the family books. Evil seeped into our lives and some of our souls. There are aspects of the practice that nobody in their right minds ought to have learned." Azzurra closed her eyes and then opened them.

"When Marta ran into your Aunt Tessa this past Saturday, I realized that the war that started over forty years ago, between Katie and Tessa, wasn't over. That it had been going on for a very long time. Olivia is being attacked and tormented by the family practice. Her soul is being drugged with evil thoughts and twisted memories that should not be remembered. Marta, you too were attacked and we need to protect ourselves." Marta's eyes widened as Nicco and Marta focused on their sister.

"They will not stop at the destruction of Olivia and her family; they will not stop at the demise of this family. Your Aunt Arianna, Uncle Mateo, Uncle Nicolai, Aunt Gabriella, Uncle Augusto and I are in grave danger." Azzurra paused, inhaled a deep breath and spoke. "Now, this is our War...a Witches War."

Arianna raised her shawl over her nose and shivered. Nicco, Marie and Marta did not speak or react.

Azzurra continued. "What I'm trying to say is that we all come from the Degeli family, and whether we like it or not, we all have inherited the same genes. You see, we practiced to be Witches. We enchant objects, control Spirits, create sachets and elixirs and use wands."

Marie looked to her Aunt and then back to her mother and whispered. "Ma, are you saying you and Aunty Arianna and the rest of the family are Witches?"

Nicco added in whisper. "Ma, just sit still." He turned to Marie and Marta. "Maybe we should call an ambulance?"

Azzurra deflated while Arianna swished a hand toward Nicco. "Nicco, your mother does not need an ambulance. Marie, put that damn bread down and listen to your mother. You're gonna be sick." She looked to Azzurra. "Go on honey."

"I thought I was prepared for this. I swear I did." Marta said. "You expect us to believe in Witches and Magick. Casting spells and using wands? Members of the mob I would have believed, but Witches? Come on Ma?"

"We are not members of the Mafia and you need to be quiet and listen!" Arianna slapped a hand on the table.

"It is not a matter of believing." Azzurra replied. "I am telling you this because we are about to have another Witches War. Your Aunt Tessa has already begun using Spirits and demons."

Nicco spoke softly. "Ma, I'm sorry…enchanted objects, haunted houses?"

Azzurra lightly slapped a hand on the dining room table. "I'm telling you the truth. You two are Witches, and you, are a Warlock."

"Ma, stop it! Oh my Lord, she's really gone! Ma, listen to me. I'm Marie and there is no such thing as Magick." She looked to Marta, shook her head and spoke. "Sachets and elixirs…Spells…maybe she read a book and thinks it's real." After turning to her Aunt, she asked. "Why are you going along with this?"

Azzurra looked to her sister Arianna who shrugged her shoulders, smirked and then nodded to the dining room entrance and winked.

Azzurra took a sip of coffee, rested her forearms on the table and spoke. "Katie, can you help explain to the kids that I'm I know the difference between a novel and reality?"

The three of them looked toward the dining room entrance and right before their eyes, their Aunt Katie appeared.

"Boo!" Katie yelled.

* * * *

Aunt Katie

Screams echoed the dining room. Marta stood so fast, her chair knocked over as she bolted behind her mother. Marie let out a scream that threatened to shatter the wine glasses as she too fled to her mother and stood behind Nicco. Their screams were silenced as Katie began to speak.

"Oh, for the love of God, will you look at these kids! All behind their mother! What Fraidy cats. I held you as babies and changed your diapers!" Katie turned solid. She glanced down to see Blackie's appearance beside her. "Now come here and give your Aunty a hug."

Screams erupted once more. Azzurra slammed a hand on the dining room table and spoke over the screams. "If you kids don't shut up I'm going to hit you all over the head with a pan! Now I'm right here. Aunty Arianna is here too! I had to use a summoning spell to raise your Aunt Katie from the grave. And look, there's Blackie. You kids remember the pictures I showed you." Azzurra called for the little terrier to come to her. Blackie barked and ran toward her. Screams erupted once more.

"Oh, I can't believe this! Do you hear me screaming? Katie, honey, don't take offense. You look beautiful!" Arianna rose and looked to her nieces and nephews. "Now, I know it's been a very long time since you've seen your aunt, you were too young to remember. But this is indeed your Aunt Katie... our sister. Now shut up and listen."

"Beee, sure they were too young. I've been gone a long time. But I will tell you kids this much, I've watched over you. That's right. Marie, you have a wonderful husband, Steven. I was at your wedding. They allow us to attend weddings you know and your daughter, Katherine, is beautiful and you've done a fine job raising her." She focused her attention on Marta. "Marta, you have grown at that job and it's not because your boss has been in love with you forever. But I tell you, if you don't wake up and smell the roses. And Nicco..." She turned to face her nephew. "...look how handsome Nicco is. Although I think Tracy is perfect for you, you should propose to that sweet girl and be happy." Katie nodded once in agreement with herself. "Now give your Aunty a hug."

The three looked toward their mother then to their Aunt Arianna. "Will you give your poor aunt a hug? I called her back from the dead so she can help us and you're all being rude. Now that is not how I raised you." Azzurra motioned for them to go to their aunt.

"Go on. Give your Aunty Katie a hug." Arianna gestured as well.

Marie spoke first in a weak feeble attempt at kindness. "Aunt Katie, is that really you?"

Nicco had become pale and didn't say a word.

Marta peeked out from behind Nicco's shoulder and gulped

"It's good to see you kids." Katie opened her arms as tears welled up.

"Aunt Katie?" They all spoke her name incredulously.

"Katie, don't be offended they'll hug you later. You three sit or so help me I will conjure a pan and you're all going to get it!" Azzurra motioned for them to be seated.

As Nicco took his seat, he looked up to his Aunt Katie and shivered. "No offense Aunty Katie...I'm a bit freaked out."

"It's OK, honey. No offense." Katie said as she seated herself in Franco's chair.

Arianna began the discussion. "We have things that must be discussed this evening and one little demon to dispel of." Arianna made a head nod toward Marta.

"Dear God! That thing that you said earlier, Aunty A...the thing wrapped around Marta's..." Marie couldn't finish and placed her hands to her mouth.

"That's right. You kids all need to see this, so that you realize what we are up against and to take this serious." Katie looked to Azzurra.

"I have not been attacked...nothing is wrong with me. So I'm a little crabby?" Marta said.

"Shush" Arianna patted her hand.

Crack! The sound of thunder made everyone jump and Blackie leapt into Katie's lap. The kids jumped at Blackie's sudden move. Blackie lowered his ears and whimpered. The wind whipped at the trees as the lightning flashed through the room.

Azzurra shook her head. "You're right Katie; the kids will need to see this." She looked up to the ceiling. "Basil. Will you stop with the storms! My poor plants are still outside!" She looked to Katie. "Does Basil know how to get rid of the Cull?"

Katie shrugged her shoulders. Arianna spoke. "If he doesn't, I do." She nodded once. "I've looked up a spell and I know how to make him reveal himself too."

"Beee, this girl can't boil water but she knows how to dispel of a demon." Katie laughed.

Arianna slapped a hand on the table. "Katie!"

Azzurra laughed. "Well, it's true honey. Don't be upset. We love you."

Nicco gulped at the sound of demons. Marie guzzled some wine and Marta just stared at her Aunt Arianna.

"I was the best at Enchanted Objects and I can use a Wand." Arianna gave a nod in agreement with herself.

"Thank goodness. I've been far too busy to think of how to get rid of it. Let me call Basil before he floods my garden." Azzurra looked once again. "Basil, would you please come down here and make yourself present?" She addressed Katie. "No wonder the Higher Spirits are getting annoyed."

"Be nice now Azzurra. He's just been waiting a very long time for you to call him back." Katie stroked Blackie's head. "And I don't want to hear any screaming from you three. Basil is your mother's Wand Spirit and he's a wonderful man."

The kids all looked to their mother for comfort. Azzurra nodded sweetly and waited for Basil's arrival.

Several moments passed when Azzurra turned to Katie and spoke. "Well, what is he waiting for? He's been driving everyone crazy with his tirades and now he's taking his time getting here?"

"You hurt his feelings. You and your mouth tonight, did she tell you she used the F word while yelling at the Vicar tonight?" She asked Arianna.

Arianna's mouth opened with shock. "The F word...in front of a Vicar... Azzurra, shame on you!"

"You know Katie — you had to say something, now didn't you." Azzurra turned to her other sister. "It wasn't anything. I was upset. I'll tell you later."

"What's a Vicar?" Marie asked. Her question was ignored.

"Now, Azzurra be nice. He only wants to see you and there you are saying he's throwing a tirade and annoying everyone. You need to apologize."

Azzurra rolled her eyes, cleared her throat and spoke with a smile in her tone. Basil...Basil honey, I'm sorry sweetheart. I didn't mean to hurt your feelings. I've missed you so very much. I've been upset, you understand. I made cannoli. They smell wonderful, and I have Bousaloon in the refrigerator, I can heat it up and you can smell." She looked to her children. "Which reminds me, you kids need to take some food home with you. I've been baking and cooking all day and I don't want good food to go to waste." She looked up to the ceiling. "Basil, come on down and say hi to the kids and Arianna."

Marta saw him first. There was a dashing young man who had appeared in the doorway of the dining room. His was looking down. The others heard Marta's gasp and looked toward the door. Nicco and Marie took in deep breaths. Basil had already turned solid. Blackie barked as the man slowly raised his head full of dark waves. His green eyes pierced the room as his mouth slid into a smile. His Irish accent broke the silence.

"I've missed you as well, Mum."

* * * *

Basil

*A*zzurra hugged her Wand Spirit and long time friend. She took a napkin and dabbed her eyes. Basil looked around the dining room table to observe familiar faces in which he hadn't spoke with in decades. Three pair of eyes stared at him in silence.

His hair tussled loosely into dark waves. A black trench coat came just below the knee, sewed with large black buttons that were etched in gold dragons. His white silk shirt was fastened with a silver clasp at the neck. Black pants, which had large pockets in various places, the right thigh, left lower thigh and right calf, hugged his strong legs. The pockets had buttons with gold dragons. Black, scuffed leather, boots came up three inches above the ankle, with large silver buckles that were loose. A black onyx ring adorned his right ring finger, while one studded diamond earring pierced his earlobe. His green eyes sparkled as he spoke.

"Everyone…I am Basil, but your Mum and the rest of the family pronounces it like the herb, which I am accustomed to."

"Isn't Basil, I mean Basil an English name?" She spoke his name properly and then switched it to the herb pronunciation. Katie shook her head at Marie. She was ignored once again.

"Miss Katie, you were very right. My feelings were hurt and that's the reason for my delay." He turned to Arianna. "Miss Arianna, what a pleasant surprise. You look beautiful." He bent down and gave her a hug and kiss.

"Thank you, sweetheart. It's good to see you too." Arianna replied.

"I didn't mean to hurt your feelings. Can you forgive an old woman for being impatient?" Azzurra asked.

"Thank you Mum, and of course I accept your apology." Basil watched his Witch make her way back to the head of the table, slower than he remembered. He felt a pang in his heart. She's getting on in age and with that comes a weakness — a weakness never before noticed.

Basil greeted Marta first with a simple nod, apologizing for the cold greeting, saying that he would explain later. He then turned to Marie. He confessed that he had been the voice of *Mousey*, a childhood friend.

"I'd take my middle and index finger and make an arch and he'd talk to you saying he was going eat your nose — because Mousey always loved noses! Kind of a silly thing I did, but you'd laugh, and you laughed hard too. It used to warm my heart to hear you laugh."

Marie placed hands to her face. "Oh my Lord, I do remember Mousey. I remember him. He sounded like *Sylvester the Cat*." Marie stood and hugged an old time playmate. Quickly back away, apologized and sat quickly. "Oh, my Lord, he's real...all of this is real."

Marta narrowed her eyes toward Marie. "Marie, you were like three years old? How the hell do you remember that?"

Azzurra looked to Basil in question.

"So I came back a few times, after I was told not to. I visited the kids. I did. Several years after we departed, I played games with them. So you see... she was probably near six or seven. I'm sorry. It was wrong of me. I used to play with Marta and Nicco too, until I was warned that it may not be in my best interest to do so. The Vicar warned me that contact with any member of the Degeli's would not bode well with the Higher Spirits. I should do as I was told. So I said my goodbyes and stopped visiting. It broke my heart." He looked toward the floor. "I'm sorry Mum."

"Don't be silly, Basil. Marie never laughed harder than when she was with you."

"Thank you, Mum. And you…must be Nicco." Basil stepped behind Marie and shook Nicco's hand.

"I think I remember you. At least I think I remember the accent." To everyone's surprise and even Nicco's, Nicco gave Basil a hug. He wasn't sure why, but he just wanted to hug this strange man. "I'm sorry." He sat down quickly, face turning beet red.

"Don't be sorry, Nicco honey." Azzurra said. "Basil would spend hours playing with the three of you…doing voices, all sorts of silly things. You kids adored him."

"Beee, Basil was a like a big kid himself when it came to the three of you," Katie added.

Nicco took a large sip of wine and then filled his glass again.

"Basil was everyone's favorite." Arianna added. "My Scott adored him too."

"Not to be rude, but we'll need to cut the greetings short. There is business to attend. Again, I'm sorry Marta. I'll explain my fear about those things later." Basil winked then turned to Azzurra. "Mum, I've been talking with the Vicar and the Higher Spirits and I know we have to prepare the kids for a Witches War. The Cull needs to be removed. But Mum, I was listening and I'm not sure if seeing the Cull would be a benefit to them all."

"But how will they know the danger if they don't see it with their own eyes?" Arianna asked.

"I agree with Arianna. They should see it so they know what they are up against." Katie added. Blackie barked.

"Basil, why do you feel they shouldn't see the Cull?" Azzurra asked.

"Well, Mum. I think it maybe too traumatic. I mean, they just met their dead Aunt Katie, not to mention myself. And you want them to see this demon. He's a wee bit horrible Mum. It may give them nightmares." Basil looked to Arianna and then to Katie.

"Oh dear Lord, they're talking about that thing around Marta's…" Marie covered her mouth.

"What thing around Marta? What the hell's a Cull? Ma, I don't want to meet it!" Nicco slurred.

Marta sat silent. Her thoughts were of a favorite Teddy bear that used to speak with an Irish accent. He would always introduce himself as Mr. Teddy Bear.

"You may have a point. I think the two of you should go with your Aunt Katie in the kitchen. No need to see the Cull. Bring out some spumoni after it's done," Arianna suggested.

Azzurra stood. "Arianna's going to take care of the Cull. It will be good practice. I've had no time."

"All right, but don't complain later when these kids don't take things seriously." Katie stood and narrowed her eyes to Basil.

"Don't be upset Miss Katie. I really believe it's going to be too traumatic." Basil turned to Arianna. "You'll be able to rid the demon from her, eh?"

"Of course honey and I think you're right. Enough of the looks, Katie, he has a point." Arianna pointed a finger at her sister.

"Basil, I want you to stay in case her spell doesn't work." Azzurra instructed.

"My spell will be just fine." Arianna turned to Marta. "I'll get that little devil off your throat."

Marie screamed while Nicco stood. "There's a devil around her throat!?"

Marta stood. "There is nothing around my throat, Nicco!" She pulled down her collar for proof.

"Nicco, there is nothing to be getting on about. We've disposed of them before. Marta will be just fine." Basil assured him. "Miss Katie, will you kindly take Nicco and Marie to the kitchen."

"All right you two...come with me." Katie began to usher Marie and Nicco threw the entrance of the dining room. As they exited, she turned to Azzurra. "She needs to see that Cull or she'll think the thoughts were her own. Very dangerous Azzurra." Katie said as she left the room.

Arianna spoke to Marta. "I don't think Marie and Nicco need to see it, but Marta honey, you do." She winked at her niece.

"Have you all gone crazy? There is nothing around my throat! So I've been crabby. We all get crabby. Look at Nicco. Does he have a thing wrapped around his throat? I'm fine." Marta looked to her Aunt Arianna. "This is ridiculous!"

"You do have something wrapped around your throat and it's the reason why you've been having all those horrible thoughts...dreams and the head-ache." Azzurra turned to Basil. "Honey, would you turn that painting into a mirror please."

"Of course Mum. I agree with Miss Katie. Although it may be traumatic for Marta, I think she'll be all right. She's tough like her Mum." Basil winked at Azzurra. With a hand gesture, the painting on the wall became a reflective surface. "How's that Mum?'

Azzurra looked into the reflection and saw Arianna and Marta seated at the table. "Perfect."

"Where are my manners? Mum, I'm so sorry…about Franco. I didn't even ask how you were getting on without him. And I'm sorry Marta… about your father." He leaned on Franco's chair.

"I'm doing just fine and thank you for asking. You're more considerate than my brother and sisters. Do you want to smell the cannoli sweetheart?"

Basil nodded and Azzurra handed him a small plate with some cannoli. "You can sit in Franco's seat. He wouldn't mind sweetheart. I know you can't eat them, but sit and smell while Arianna and I get rid of that Cull."

Basil sat down in Franco's chair, whispering to himself and then raised the plate of cannoli to his nose. He slowly let the smell sink into his senses.

"Mum, I love your cannoli. Got to be the best in the entire world, they are. I do miss eating. It has to be the one thing I miss most…well almost." His mouth slid into a grin.

Arianna interrupted. "Enough smelling! It's time to get rid of that Cull." She pulled a Wand from her purse and set it upon the table.

* * * *

The Cull

It opened its eyes, blinked and shook its head to rid the sleep. Its matted hair flopped around a bulbous shaped head. Red-veined eyes tried to focus. A clump of dark hair stuck out at an odd angle above a furrowed forehead. Wonder plagued the small mind. Had someone mentioned the word Cull? A yawn escaped from its mouth revealing three crooked fangs. Its large eyes focused on a woman sitting next its host. She was adjusting something green around her shoulders and speaking to the host's mother and a young man it had never seen before.

Its tail hung around the host's shoulder while its head rested upon the other. Another blink, another yawn, had it missed something? Did they know it was there? Fear leapt to the tiny demon's brain as it heard the word Cull again. There was no mistaking the word. They were speaking about it and it needed to flee. But she was so good, so much food. It would convince its host to leave. It had done it just a few days earlier.

Tiny whispers emanated from its mouth, setting panic into its host. *Leave! They are ganging up against you!* It searched its host's memory for the woman speaking to the mother, and the young man. Who was the young man? Images and sound erupted. It shook its head violently. Completely awake, its large ears twitched and lay flat upon the head. The woman, wrapped in green, was her Aunty Arianna. *The man, forget him, leave…leave now* the demon told itself.

There is nothing wrong with you. Nothing is around your throat. They always knew you were different. Get out! It was working. Its host had stood. She was telling her Aunt Arianna that she was leaving and that there was nothing wrong with her. The whispers kept filling its host ears. Over and over again it whispered the need to leave. The woman, her aunt, spoke again, telling its host to step in front of the mirror.

"…if you see nothing, then you may leave." The woman in a green wrap was speaking. It narrowed its eyes, trying to focus on its host. *Should I leave? Just forget her and flee? Ah, but so good…so good…you must stay!* It looked from the mother to the strange man who stood and walked to the side of its host. Her mother stood opposite its host, while the aunt stood behind, looking into the mirror. *Leave! Damn you mortal woman!*

Its host spoke. "I see only my reflection."

Good, now leave.

The aunt placed a hand through it and on its host shoulder. "I haven't said the incantation yet. Are you both ready?" The demon looked to its host's mother and to the strange man, who both nodded. *Ready? Ready for what?*

The demon lowered its head to the bosom of its host and contemplated what to do next. Its eyes focused on its host, trying to make her leave…tiny whispers.

"*Rivela ciò che non può essere visto!*"
(Reveal what cannot be seen)

It heard the words and knew what they were. It bolted its head up from its host's chest, claws clenching. The reflection had revealed a grotesque looking creature. Its jowls filled with air. Confusion stabbed at its brain. She was screaming…screaming so loud. *Stop it! Stop screaming!* It let out a scream of its own, screeching at the top of its lungs. The Cull howled in disgust at its own appearance and the threat of losing its host. *She's mine!* The aunt was holding a wand and began an incantation. *Shut her up!*

"*Distruggi un de…*

It screeched and leapt from its host to the throat of the aunt casting the spell. *You will not finish!* It reached the woman and had broken the incantation. The woman fell back. Its claws were ready to swipe at her flesh. It would fight! It was full of its host energy and would slash this meddlesome old woman! The man shouted something and it felt burning all around its sagging, leathery skin. The woman was gone. Thoughts swirled in the demons head. *Where did she go?* Confusion, pain, hitting something hard, more pain, burning! *The man, kill him!* The demon flung itself upon the throat of the man with all the speed it could muster. Strong from a good feast, it placed its rancid mouth against the man's ear and began extracting thoughts and energy. It was working! The man was full of dark little secrets. He was delicious!

A scream escaped from the man. In a quick glance, it saw its former host, huddled with her mother upon the floor. A spell of protection must have been cast. It saw a great white shield surrounding them. *Feast upon him. Oh so good…run…no he is too good. Flee. Flee now! They are too powerful for you!*

It decided to leave. One last swallow of emotion from the young man and it would flee into the floorboards and out of sight.

"Rilascio!"

The aunt's voice came from behind. The spell forced it to release its mouth from the man's ear as it screamed in pain. It felt queasy and dizzy as it struck the wall once again. *Down, down, go down into the floorboards.* It scrambled to right itself and looked up to the man. The aunt was pointing a wand and began an incantation. *Leave!* A bright blue light grew from the man's hand. A moment later it struck. It howled in pain as it felt its insides boil. Swelling, confusion, pain, regret, hunger…nothing.

* * * *

Spumoni

The sound of the clocks ticking etched at everyone's nerves. It seemed to be getting louder with every passing second. Their eyes were focused on only one thing...the woman at the head of the table. They saw grey hair, slightly mussed and aged hands covering a face. The clock kept ticking, filling the room with that soft annoyance, waiting for Azzurra to begin the conversation and tell them what they should do next.

Azzurra lowered her hands and raised her head. "I do not want any questions. I do not want any screaming. And I will not hear any arguing." Her eyes moved from Basil to Arianna. "I do not care that Basil's spell was cast before you finished your incantation. So he had been quicker than you at destroying the Cull. The Cull is gone and that's what matters." Her eyes took in Marta and then focused back to Arianna. "Will she ever come out of this catatonic state or is my daughter lost?"

"She'll be fine. I may have burned too much Calamus root during the incantation to calm her. Maybe I should have had Gabriella make the sachet, but there really wasn't time." Arianna lowered her voice. "She'll be fine...by tomorrow."

149

Azzurra stared at her sister for several uncomfortable seconds and then spoke again. "Katie, I thank you for keeping Nicco and Marie in the hall while we handled the Cull."

"You're welcome." Katie replied quickly. Blackie cried softly.

Azzurra cupped her hands together and rested them against her mouth, thought for several seconds and then spoke. "Basil, would you please remind me to put on my angel necklace and to alert the Cherubs that they should return to their duty before I go to bed."

"Yes, mum." Basil replied.

Azzurra took in a breath, paused for a moment, then continued. "Thank you Basil." She addressed her children. "I know you are all tired and would like to go home. However, that is not possible. Now, your Aunt Arianna has prepared sleeping drafts for all of you to take before bedtime, so do not worry about nightmares or a restless sleep." She addressed her sister. "You had Mateo help you with the sleeping drafts?" Arianna nodded and winked at the kids.

"Basil, I am exhausted, but I think it would be in the kids' best interest to know what the war between Katie and Tessa was about. Therefore, I would be appreciative if you would fill them in on the general story. Please do not make it long and drawn out...and save any theatrics for another time."

Basil's eyes narrowed a bit. "Yes Mum."

"Maybe you kids should have some spumoni before we begin," Katie offered.

Nicco, Marie and even Marta turned to look at their aunt. Nobody spoke as they returned their attention back to their mother.

"Well, maybe later." Katie reached down and picked up Blackie, who grunted loudly. "Go on Basil dear. Tell the story."

* * * *

The Feud

"It was forty one years ago…almost to the date. It was October, I remember because Halloween was approaching and I love that holiday so. Anyway, I remember Mum bought an enormous pumpkin to go inside the fireplace. He was so cute, big and orange with a huge silly face. Now let's see, the fall air was crisp. There was a coolness that was refreshing, you know what I mean…that briskness in the air, meant for heavy sweaters but not yet for winter coats and such."

"I remember I was playing with Angelo, Katie's little one you see. We were playing in his room. Now, Carlotta and Olivia were outside playing ball with their cousins. The cousins, which of course were you three." Basil made eye contact with Nicco, Marie and Marta and continued. "Angelo was two years old. He was a cute little tike, with chubby cheeks and large brown eyes. Big puppy eyes, they were. Now, let me see…Carlotta would have been 11 and Olivia would have been 4. My, what wee tikes they were. And you, Miss Katie, would have been 32, a year before your death age. Now Nicco would have been 7, Marta 5 and Marie would have been 2 years old, same as Angelo. I remember Angelo wanting to go outside to play with Olivia and Carlotta. Anywhere his sisters were, he wanted to be. It was brisk, like I said, so I wanted to get him into something a wee bit warmer."

"I heard the bell and then pounding on the door…the front door that is. Well, it was your Aunt Tessa. She was raging mad, that woman. You see

151

kids; don't mind me calling you that, I mean no disrespect by calling you kids. It's just gonna take me a wee bit to get used to you being adults."

The small antique clock ticked in the nearby hutch and the tiny music of crickets lent to the ambiance of the room.

"I walked into the kitchen to where the commotion was happening. I held Angelo in my arms. Contessa looked up and retorted loudly, *How dare you tell me that I shouldn't use Spirits when that thing stands there holding your baby!* I didn't like the way she spoke of me at all. You see, I was not a THING and I got angry and I told her so. Miss Katie asked me to calm down, not to take it personally and asked if I would take Angelo outside with the rest of the kids. Mum scolded Contessa for the way she spoke to me and said that I was her Wand Spirit, not Katie's."

"You see, Miss Katie didn't see any reason to have Wand Spirits or any Spirits. She thought that they could be very dangerous and with good reason. She agreed with your Great Grandfather Ciro and Grandma Adalina, that you could do plenty of Magick on your own without the use of Spirits. However, your mother felt as long as you knew your Spirit well and didn't ask for things you shouldn't, well then, there would be no harm. But your mother always stood by Miss Katie."

Katie and Azzurra eyes squinted. "And I'd still stand by you today Katie." Azzurra confirmed.

"Now Contessa knew this and it had always bothered her — the close-ness between your mother and Miss Katie that is. Was it right to defend blindly one sister and not the other…who knows?"

Katie and Azzurra looked at each other and then to Arianna, who shrugged her shoulders.

"Perhaps if Contessa had been more likeable, she would have had sisters she had always dreamed of. Of course things happen that build a foundation of hurt, mistrust and anger. You see kids, your Uncle Dante…Miss Katie's husband, had been on a date with Contessa at a wedding. He met Miss Katie and fell in love. That scar runs deep. It was not that your Aunt Katie threw herself at Dante either. Contessa would never listen to how many times Dante's calls were refused by Miss Katie. Miss Katie would have nothing to do with him. Well, Contessa and Dante had not spoken in almost a year and finally Miss Katie conceded to a date."

Katie waved a hand in the air and looked to Azzurra. "Oh that Dante was so handsome in his Navy suit with the big bell bottoms and the white hat. Oh Azzurra, remember when we meet him at the pier?"

"Sure I remember — that's the first time I saw Franco. He was so handsome too. Both men in their Navy uniforms, they were so young back then. Every woman wanted their attention. But Dante liked Katie...what are you going to do." Azzurra replied.

Basil raised an eyebrow and then continued. "Other events fueled the ill feelings between Contessa and Miss Katie. Miss Katie asked her father to ban the family from using Spirits. Now Miss Katie, of course, understood that I was her sister's Wand Spirit, and we got on very well. Her request was to rid the family of Spirits with little known background and non-trust. Your grandmother, Luciana, agreed with her daughter Katie, but didn't know how to decide which family Spirits to keep and which to send away. Her fear was that a Witches War could begin by telling Spirits they were no longer needed. Pasquale, your grandfather, told the girls it would be between them and they should decide. He would make no such family decision; that whoever wanted to use Spirits could and whoever didn't...shouldn't."

"I, of course, was a bit worried. As a family Spirit to Azzurra I didn't want to leave. It felt like home for the first time in decades. Since I wasn't crossing over anytime soon, I really didn't want to lose my second family. I will tell you something though...Miss Katie had a good point. I've seen it before and she was very right to be nervous. Several family members were getting newer Spirits and the older Spirits were deciding to move on, so it left the family with a lot of young, immature Spirits — or older Spirits, with little known background."

"You see kids, Spirits can be dangerous. They get bored and want to stir things up for a wee bit of fun. Spirits have been known to kill people just to promote some excitement in their otherwise boring existence. There is also a type of bitterness that exists in some Spirits. They detest the living because they are no longer able to participate in the pleasures of the physical world. I know of an entire generation of a family that was destroyed by the influence of bitter Spirits."

The clock ticked in the background as the spumoni melted. Marta stared at the flickering candles that sat upon the dining room table, seeming to take in Basil's words and feeling numb. Marie's face was pallid and Nicco's eyes were glassy.

"So you understand the concern about the use of Spirits. Now, where was I? That's right, Contessa, Miss Katie and Azzurra were having a go in the kitchen and Miss Katie asked me to take Angelo out of the room. Angelo began to squirm in my arms with all the yelling, you see. Just as I was about to close the door, I heard Miss Katie slam her hand on the kitchen counter and yell at Contessa. *Are you that stupid Tessa? What the hell is the matter with you? You know yourself that Spirits will trick and deceive you and will cause family fights just to keep them from getting bored off their ass.* I lingered a bit before closing the door. *You think that you know these dirty little bastards, but you know nothing about them. Where they came from? How they died? For all you know, these Spirits could be murderers afraid to cross over and accept what they have created for themselves. For the Love of God, you're inviting them into your home! For all you know you could be inviting the Devil himself into your home!* I closed the door and let Angelo play with his sisters and cousins. Katie was right and I became worried for the family.

Basil paused as the clock chimed 11 times. "Let me continue. Contessa left that day very riled. She demanded that Miss Katie stop speaking to their father about disbanding the Spirits. Your Aunt Gabriella agreed with Contessa, but would have never spoken to Miss Katie that way. Your Aunt Arianna agreed with Miss Katie and your Uncle Augusto as well. But they were not there that day and did not hear the fight. Only Mum and Miss Katie were present."

"It was a couple of days later. I was playing the game of *Sorry* with Nicco and Marta. I had Marie on my lap when I heard the phone call that started everything…that changed the family forever." He looked at Azzurra and back to Katie.

"One of the few times I've ever heard Mum scream like that." His voice dropped in volume and texture. "She kept saying *Katie…it can't be, oh my Lord, not Vincent…not Vincent!* I told the kids to stay there and placed an invisible barrier on the bedroom's entrance that would not allow them to cross over nor hear a thing. I appeared in the kitchen to where your mother stood. She had dropped the phone, tears streaming down her cheeks. I held her for a few moments as she cried in my chest that Vincent…your cousin who was 2 years old at the time…your Aunt Tessa's and Uncle Nathan's son…was found dead that morning."

* * * *

Vincent

*A*rianna reached for one of the angel wings that she had baked, took a bite and quickly rejected it into a napkin. Katie rolled her eyes and made a quick hand jester. The dessert disappeared and a powdered sugar, crispy, salt-free plate of angel wings appeared in its place. Arianna thanked her sister and helped herself to the fresh dessert.

"Sorry Basil, go on dear," Katie apologized.

"Well, like I was saying…the phone call was to announce the death of Contessa's son, Vincent. Now I won't say…"

"…who killed Vincent?" Marie asked.

Azzurra answered. "No one killed Vincent. It was unfortunate. It was simply his time to go. We have…"

Katie lightly slapped a hand on the table. "…you can't say that Azzurra! We have no idea if his death had been the result of Spirits or not." Blackie jumped to the floor and lay by Basil.

"Fine, you're right Katie. We don't know for sure what happened, but my instinct is to say that there were no Spirits involved in his death." Azzurra took a large sip of wine.

"I thought we wanted to keep this short…might I continue?" Basil's voice possessed a tinge of sarcasm.

Katie and Azzurra narrowed their eyes toward Basil while Arianna let out a soft laugh.

Basil continued. "Vincent was dead, at just two years old mind you. Miss Katie had relayed the information to your mother, who was devastated. I appeared at Franco's work and brought him straight home. I may have done it a wee bit too fast, it really upset his stomach. Other family members began their phone calls to discuss the little one's death. It was Father Bernardo who conveyed that Contessa refused an autopsy. Never did it cross her mind that there may be foul play…well, at least at first."

"Shortly thereafter, family from San Francisco, New York, New Orleans and Phoenix were talking about his death. After speaking with the cousins, rumors began that Contessa no longer believed her son's death to be that of an accident. Finger pointing began. Unfortunately, your Aunt Katie had said something that was horribly misconstrued. You see kids; your Aunt Katie believed that Spirits were indeed involved. She was overheard speaking with her siblings at the parlor. Cousins heard her say that she thought one of Contessa's Spirits killed Vincent and that she should have never kept those Spirits in service. Miss Katie had said that Contessa was foolish and now look what happened." Basil paused to take notice of Katie.

"You're right Basil, and I still think something was wrong with his death." Katie looked to Azzurra and nodded once in agreement with herself.

Azzurra looked to Arianna and rolled her eyes.

"Now Mum, Miss Katie had every reason to think that there was something unnatural with his death. I myself didn't feel as though the thought of Spirits were farfetched. However, everyone was aware of the argument between Miss Katie and Contessa and how Miss Katie felt about the use of Spirits. Miss Katie had been speaking with her siblings, Gabriella, Mum, Arianna and Augusto. They all knew what she meant by those words. However, the cousins that overheard your Aunt Katie speaking told Contessa that Katie wished her son's death. That it would be a good lesson for her to learn about the use of Spirits. That it was because of Contessa that her son was no longer among the living."

Arianna shook her head. "That was stupid. Katie would never wish such a thing."

156

"It was indeed, Miss Arianna. Miss Katie's words should have been a warning to us all that day. But certain cousins had Contessa's ear and they were less than upstanding. All of them associated with Spirits with shady backgrounds. They twisted Miss Katie's words, they did. Those cousins were responsible for the start of the first Witches War between the Degelis in Michigan."

Nicco's loud words were a bit slurred. "Who, which cousins started the war?"

"I think that's obvious, Nicco...those from New Orleans and Phoenix, Aunt Angelica and Aunt Dorthea." Marie took a sip of wine.

"You would be correct, Marie. Now, I'll save the details of the first Witches War for another time. However, you should know that Dorthea and Angelica were some of the nastiest people I had ever met. Debra and Carlo were no better. They all came from Sabino and Stella Degeli, your Grandfather Pasquale's brother."

"How Father Bernardo ever became a priest growing up in that family, God only knows." Katie swished a hand in the air. "Uncle Gino and Aunt Francine's were wonderful people. Sometimes family members just go astray."

Arianna added. "Your Great Aunt Francine was your Grandfather Pasquale's sister and she and her husband, Gino, were nothing like their other brother, Sabino and his wife, Stella. Now, Francine and Gino's kids... almost every one of them are decent."

Marta's words were monotone when she spoke. "Aunt Beatrice, from San Francisco and Aunt Bella, from New York were Aunt Francine's children. Aunt Beatrice married Uncle Thom and Aunt Bella, married Uncle Gilbert."

"See! I told you she'd come around." Arianna patted Marta on the cheek. "That's right honey. Good old Uncle Thom and Aunt Bella are still with us."

Nicco and Marie asked Marta if she was all right. Azzurra shushed them and asked for Basil to continue.

"You would be right, Marta. But to make a long story short...that was the beginning of the feud which led to the biggest Witches War the Midwest had ever known. There were about a dozen deaths in that war. It was just after the death of one of your cousins that your grandfather decided to put a ban on Spirits." Basil said.

"Oh there was a big fight...right there in the funeral home. We had to do so much Magick just to cover things up." Arianna looked to Azzurra.

Katie picked up Blackie and placed him on her lap. "Contessa also listened to the wrong people, no brains of her own — like I would wish death upon Vincent to make a point."

"But what happened? Who died?" Marie asked.

Azzurra answered. "That story will be for another time. We were lucky to survive ourselves. Poor Anna…never knew what happened to her."

"I still say she was Banished." Arianna slapped the table lightly.

"Well Arianna, you may be right. I've never seen her and the Higher Spirits told me that she never crossed over." Katie scratched behind Blackie's ears. He grunted.

"Anna was Uncle Augusto's wife?" Marie asked.

"Yes honey, we never knew what happened to your Aunt Anna. Your Uncle Augusto found her dead in their bedroom just as the Witches War was thought to be over." Arianna answered.

"Thank goodness for Kimberly and Drago that time, always there for us…good people." Katie added.

"The main point being that the war began with Vincent's death." Azzurra looked to Marta.

Basil shifted in his seat and spoke. "Vincent's funeral went on without any further outburst and so far there had been no other deaths. But it was a couple of days later that the thought of a Witches War occurred to us."

"Well, Aunt Beatrice and Uncle Thom knew something was wrong… and so did Uncle Drago and your Aunt Kimberly." Arianna added.

"The story would be told quicker without interruptions." Basil smirked.

Arianna, Azzurra and Katie all looked at Basil then to Nicco, who spoke.

"I like Uncle Tom. He's a stitch." He imitated his uncle in a loud voice. "Paaaapostrous!" He thought for a moment. "I don't remember Aunt Beatrice."

"She died years ago honey." Azzurra answered.

"Uncle Gilbert is dead too. Did he die in the war?" Marie added.

"Another time Marie…Basil honey, continue." Azzurra spoke.

"A crucifix, right through chest. Oh, whose funeral was that at — Nicholas'?" Arianna asked.

Marie placed a hand to her chest. Nicco's mouth went to open then closed, while Marta slowly looked to her Aunt Arianna.

"Another time Arianna…it's getting late." Azzurra voice began to rise.

"Blood everywhere…it was awful…poor Gilbert." Arianna patted Marta's hand.

Azzurra let a hand fall to the table.

Basil raised his voice. "After they laid little Vincent to rest, everything went downhill. Shortly after the funeral, your Aunt Katie received a phone call from your Aunt Contessa. Debra, Dorthea and Angelica were the three cousins that spoke with Contessa about what Miss Katie said. Contessa was calling Miss Katie that day to ask if what they said was true…did Katie wish for Vincent's death. Miss Katie told Aunt Tessa that she was stupid to believe the bullshit. That those three bitches could go straight to hell and she could join them if she was that stupid." Basil paused for a brief moment.

"I should have been nicer. After all, she just lost her son. If I could take that phone call back I would." Katie said.

"What do you mean Katie? It was stupid on her part. How could she think you would say something like that?" Azzurra swished a hand at her sister.

"Basil and I have spoken about this before and…being dead brings certain things to light with more understanding. Basil is very good at taking both sides fairly and this should be a lesson to us all. Had I not been so hot tempered, perhaps I would have realized that she was just hurting and confused and wanted to make sure that I was with her…that I was on her side. That I was suffering along with her. Me and my big mouth, but what are you gonna do. If I only knew then what I know now."

"Your right Katie, maybe we all could have been a bit more understanding. After all, Tessa is our sister." Arianna patted Azzurra hand.

"I have no comment." Azzurra replied.

"Mum, I love you so very much, but don't you see? Miss Katie's anger was nothing compared to the loss of Vincent…of what Contessa was feeling. Miss Katie should have been more understanding. I know you love your sister so, but you have to stop and think. If you lost one of your kids, how would you feel? Maybe you wouldn't say the most rational things either." Basil said.

Azzurra shook her head slightly. Arianna softly agreed with Basil while Blackie jumped down from Katie's lap and onto Basil's.

Katie rested her forearms on the table as she spoke. "Vincent was so cute. Oh how he would laugh with a deep voice…ha ha ha. Big eyes and chubby… reminded me of my Angelo. He always grabbed my nose…reminded me of

Basil's silly game of Mousey with Marie. Thick dark hair...all wavy, oh, he was so adorable."

Azzurra's eyes gleamed over to a cold sheen of glass. Katie looked to Azzurra and took in a breath. "Azzurra, sometimes you do irrational things when it comes to your children, as you very well know. I've not visited Olivia in over twenty years. Why...because it hurts me to see my daughter live like that. I wouldn't wish her life on my worst enemy. I've seen Carlotta and her kids, Elizabeth and Dino, but I could not bring myself to see Olivia. It hurt too much to see her like that, so I stood away. I didn't know she had a Cull wrapped around her throat. But nevertheless, I stood away. Is that right, that I should have abandoned my child? Maybe not, but I did. Was it right for Tessa to believe that I wished Vincent's death? No. But sometimes the pain and hurt a mother feels makes her do some things that she wouldn't otherwise have done. Death...Death opens your eyes. After I died I had a sense of others that I did not have when I was alive. I wish I could take that conversation back. I wish I could have been supportive to her. Maybe Gilbert and Beatrice, Aunt Francine and Anna would still be here."

"Stop it Katie. Don't do that to yourself!" Azzurra stood.

"Azzurra you have not lost a child...and I'm telling you I was wrong to speak to her that way." Katie said.

"But she should not have accused you of wanting Vincent's death! You don't do that to your sister. She's supposed to be flesh and blood!" Azzurra said.

Arianna sat up and adjusted her shawl. "You're not listening Azzurra. I know you get stubborn when it comes to this, but did you not just hear what Katie said? She is absolutely right. I wish I would have handled things differently myself."

"I am listening Arianna and do not tell me that I'm not!" Azzurra turned to face hers sister.

Arianna's lips tightened before she spoke. "Don't say you're listening when I know very well you're not! You didn't lose a child! You're not dead. So how could you say that Katie's wrong? You are blindly defending what she did. Contessa lost Vincent...something you cannot understand until it happens to you. Katie lost Angelo; I lost...Listen with an open heart will you please!"

"I think we're getting a wee bit off topic." Basil's spoke.

Katie raised a hand toward Arianna and spoke. "Azzurra, when I lost Angelo, I thought I would die. I'm simply asking you to try, for a moment, to put yourself into Tessa's shoes. I don't want us making the same mistakes in this war that we made in the last."

"Did you see Angelo…when you passed, Katie? Was he there?" Arianna asked with a sideward glance toward Azzurra.

"Mom and Dad left the Earth's realm and took him. If only I had known that he crossed over when he first died. I would have been comforted somewhat. Thoughts rattled my mind. Is he alone? Was he crying and looking for me? I heard him crying in my mind. Dante would hold me and tell me that he was with Mom and Dad — that the Higher Spirits would comfort him. Nothing he said helped. It wasn't 'til after I passed away that I thought what Tessa may have been going through. It took my own death. Don't be angry Azzurra…please." Katie's said.

Arianna reached for Azzurra's hand.

"Aunt Katie, you said that you thought Vincent's death may have been caused by a Spirit… was Angelo's?" Marie asked carefully.

Azzurra and Arianna held their breath for a brief moment. Katie answered. "No honey. He had a bad valve in his heart. It ran in the family. Besides, there was no way a Spirit could have touched him. I had him protected." Katie paused, deep in thought. "But I remember, I will always remember the night we found him. The night my Angelo died."

* * * *

Angelo

A soft, watery light showered the boy's room. Two small girls stood near his crib. The youngest whimpered next to an elder sister, who remained silent. It was two in the morning and a chill ran through the room and their bones. The wind rolled outside as a cold breeze slipped in the room through an opened window. The glow of the nightlight revealed a tiny boy in his crib. He was wearing *Scooby Doo* pajamas. He lay still with his eyes open, facing the mobile of tiny moons and stars.

The smallest of the girls began to cry louder. She looked down, placed tiny hands over her face and began to sob.

"Olivia, be quiet!" Carlotta turned her sister around by the shoulders and faced her. She knelt to her knees and once again pleaded for her silence. She lowered her Olivia's hands. "Listen to me. Be quiet and listen to me...I put..."

A women's voice interrupted the eleven years olds words. "What are you two doing in your brother's room? Carlotta, why are you telling Olivia to be quiet? Olivia come here sweetheart. What's the matter? It's late and you girls are going to wake your brother."

Olivia looked up to her mother and began to speak. Carlotta stepped in front of her sister, interrupted her words and methodically spoke to her mother. "He's dead."

Katie staggered back. Her heart did something…something she would never find the words to describe. Her mind whirled with the words her daughter just spoke. Something inside her plummeted to a place that should have not existed. Words failed. Through the force of instinct, she turned, flicked the light on and looked to the tiny boy. A scream expelled from her lungs, harsh and deep. The sound echoed around the room, the house…the sound of pain, agony and despair. The sound erupted like a howl, a creature in pain…the pain that only a parent could feel.

The girls covered their ears, their own hearts and bodies reacting to their parent. Olivia's screams were drowned by her mother's lament. Carlotta closed her eyes and held Olivia. Katie rushed to her son and picked him up. Dante rushed into the room, hurried to the side of his wife and looked to his son. The little boy's eyes perpetually stared over his mother's shoulder. He howled in anguish. Katie fell to the floor and cradled her son, rocking back and forth as Dante sobbed into his wife's hair.

***

Katie continued describing the story to all who sat at the table. She recalled sitting with Arianna on the floor of the kitchen. She explained that the police checked him for strangulation marks. There was nothing. There were no pillows or strange objects near him, nothing that would have caused him to stop breathing. He was too old for SIDS. She remembered seeing Dante still talking with the police. Carlotta was speaking to a female officer while Olivia was being questioned by yet another female officer.

Katie described how she rocked back and forth, covered in a blanket as Arianna rubbed her shoulders and kissed her head. The memory came back, so real, so intense. Her thoughts continued out loud. She recalled Azzurra's entrance. Her voice carrying through the hall, quick, labored, and defeated. She remembered Azzurra's expression as she rushed into the kitchen and by her side. It was as though Azzurra had lost her own child. They held each other and cried.

Katie kept repeating what the police had told her; that there was nothing in the room or crib. She explained how Carlotta and Olivia said he wasn't moving when they entered his room. "Is it the Spirits? Was my Angelo killed by the Spirits? The same thing happened to Vincent! We all caused this! It's our fault!"

Azzurra grabbed her sister by the shoulders and told her that it was not the Spirits. That it was not her fault. That Angelo was in his crib, safe and sound from harm. Arianna asked if he wore the Patron of Saint Anne necklace that had been given to him by his grandmother, Luciana. Katie nodded. "He was wearing the necklace when we found him."

"Then he could not have been attacked by a Spirit." Azzurra assured her.

***

Carlotta had been the one who let the police enter the home. Neighbors had called, telling the police that there were screams coming from the house. Carlotta explained to the police what had happened. She remained calm and collected.

The police report would state that the eldest daughter, Carlotta, 11, had met her younger sister, Olivia, 4, in the hallway. It had been two in the morning and they heard their younger brother, Angelo, 2, crying. They wanted to comfort him. Just before entering the room, the cries subsided. They entered the room together and tried to wake their brother. They couldn't.

The report would also read that Olivia had stated that she had entered the room without her older sister. Olivia was crying and sobbing and difficult to comprehend, repeating over and over that she had seen an Angel. Carlotta insisted that her sister was wrong and they entered the room together and that her sister always saw Angels. Both parents were reported as saying they did not hear their son crying. The father stated that it was unusual not to hear him. That he and Katie slept light and would have woken had he been crying.

***

Katie could remember sitting with Azzurra, Gabriella and Arianna at the doctor's office shortly after. Dante would not attend. Since the Patron Saint of Saint Anne had been enchanted with a powerful protection charm and it had still been around Angelo's neck the night he died, they were convinced that it was nothing supernatural and made an appointment with the doctor to discuss the possibilities. The doctor convinced them that sometimes, a child's heart may not fully develop and that it could have been a deformed valve. The Doctor assured them that, given the family history of heart disorders, it was most likely the cause of death. They opted, like Tessa, to not have an autopsy. It was just over forty years ago.

Katie's eyes came to focus. She was sitting in the dining room with her family. The memory had subsided and all eyes were upon her. She had been silent for while, lost in thoughts that had been burned in her mind. Basil sat beside her. Marie wore a look of pain. Nicco looked ill while Marta sat expressionless. Arianna and Azzurra looked to each other and then to Katie. They had heard their sister re-live the night her son died a thousand times. The details were etched in their minds and hearts; the words, the emotion, the pain. And they knew that without proof, without knowing for certain, their theory of what really happened to Angelo should be kept from Katie.

****

The End of the First Witches War?

*K*atie shook her head to rid the memories and took a deep breath. She called for Blackie, who leapt to her lap.

Marta spoke. "I'm sorry Aunty Katie. I never knew what happened to Vincent or Angelo."

"I'm fine sweetheart. Don't you worry about me, I'm tough." Katie dabbed her eyes with the back of her palm and squeezed Blackie.

Nicco and Marie extended sympathetic comments to their aunt as well, while Azzurra looked to Arianna, shaking her head ever so slightly.

Azzurra cleared her throat. "Now that you kids know some of the story, I hope you realize the urgency and importance that you do as we ask…for your own safety."

Nicco and Marie nodded. Marta grunted, shook her head and said she wanted pudding.

Nicco laughed. "She's gone again."

"Nicco, be nice. She's fine." Arianna pointed a finger at her nephew.

Azzurra looked up to the ceiling, mouthed something and continued. "I think it's important to understand that Tessa feels that her son, Vincent, was killed by a Spirit that was sent by Katie or at the very least, that Katie felt she deserved her son's death. That my father, Grandpa Pasquale, spoke to us on his death bed, just six months after Vincent's death. Arianna, Katie, Tessa, Gabriella, Augusto, Mom and I were there. He pleaded with us to take a vow, swearing never to use Magick again. That it had caused the recent deaths and that the use of Spirits should be banned as well. Now, your Grandfather Pasquale was the head of the family. What he said should have become law.

"We stood around his bed and agreed not to use Magick but we did not take the vow. You see, when you take a Witches Vow, you must abide by its rules or be severely punished upon crossing over. Tessa agreed as did each of us that day, but no vow was taken. He passed away within a few hours."

Arianna added. "Beatrice and Gilbert were killed after he passed. Something had to be done. Mom cast an extremely powerful spell that watched over the family. It would let her know if anyone used Magick or Spirits. Both sides were exhausted and lost loved ones. Debra, Dorthea and Carlo lost members of their family and of course we had losses too."

"Mom died just two weeks after Dad. The enchantment died with her." Azzurra continued. "Dorthea, Debra, Carlo, Sabina and Stella...the lot of them swore they were not responsible for her death. We all agreed on a truce. However, no one took the vow. A month later Anna died mysteriously."

Arianna shook her head. "Anna could astral project, which meant that her soul could leave her body at will — very dangerous. Her husband, your Uncle Augusto, begged her not to let her soul wander around without a body. Basil warned against it as well. But a week after Mom died, Anna came to Azzurra and me with a plan. We begged her not to go and a few hours later, Augusto found her dead. Dorthea and Debra swore they had nothing to do with Anna's death. They performed an autopsy and found nothing wrong. We concluded that her soul may have lost connection with her body, causing her death."

Basil added. "But we never saw her in the afterlife. I was able to look for her immediately after passing and never saw hide or hair. Miss Katie inquired with the Higher Spirits and they confirmed that Anna had not crossed over."

"A month later, my Angelo dies. It had been eight months since Vincent's death and eight months of a Witches War. Since Angelo wore the necklace, we didn't think his death had anything to do with the war. Tessa was supportive during his death and cried with the rest of us." Katie let Blackie to the floor in favor of Basil's lap. "I wanted everyone to take the vow...but no one would listen to me."

"Katie, we were worried we'd be sitting ducks." Arianna protested.

"Arianna's right, we would have been sitting ducks. No one wanted to take that vow, because none of us trusted the other side." Azzurra's voice lowered. "A few months after Angelo's death, Katie received the news that her heart was failing."

"It was on your Aunt Katie's death bed that we all took the vow. Tessa was there, along with me, Azzurra, Gabriella and Augusto." Arianna continued. "We all cast the enchantment that we would never break the vow, governed by the Higher Spirits. It was the end of the first Witches War. Or so we thought."

* * * *

Say Goodnight, Katie

Marie let out a slight scream, Nicco jumped while Marta stared at the man in white —the third Spirit that appeared before their eyes that evening.

Basil rose to his feet and bowed. "Vicar, I must apologize for the storms. It won't happen again, I give my word." Basil looked to Azzurra.

The Vicar responded. "It had better not. The residents of New York are not happy with you."

Basil quickly took his seat, eyes wide. He gulped and looked toward Katie. She shook her head and told him not to worry, New York had storms before.

"Katie, I hope you've been practicing the technique of transformation I showed you yesterday. Have you done what I've asked? Have you added further enchantments to the house?" The Vicar asked. "It will provide the family with a stronghold."

"I haven't had time, but I will. I promise." Katie slapped a hand on the table. "Damn it! I knew I was forgetting something."

"Nicco, Marie and Marta…I am Aidan Sinclair, a Vicar to the Higher Spirits assigned to the family." Nicco stood and reached around Marie to shake his hand. The Vicar simply bowed his head.

Arianna whispered loudly. "It's not appropriate to touch a Vicar." Nicco replied that he understood and took his seat. Marie said hello to the man in white, while Marta giggled then shook her head. Azzurra tapped her hand on the table and looked toward Arianna.

"She'll be fine. Give her some time, will you. Beee you're so uptight this evening." Arianna said.

The Vicar continued. "Basil, might I ask that you recruit some of your faithful friends. Use caution and be discrete. You are now the family Spirit. You will protect not only your Witch, but the family as well."

"I will. And yes, I shall recruit some of my most trusted allies." Basil stood.

Marie screamed. Across the table, Marta had placed a finger through the hole in Katie's arm. Marta's eyebrows furrowed as Katie shook her head. "Marta dear, will you please remove your finger from my arm?"

Arianna took Marta's hand and pulled it away. "It was a Discombobulating Spell. The pieces of her arm will come back." She looked to Azzurra and then whispered something encouraging about Marta.

The Vicar spoke with an even tone. "Disbursement Charm…the spell is called a Disbursement Charm. That brings me to another point." He turned to Azzurra. "Right now, Achar, the Spirit who cast the spell, thinks that Katie has been destroyed. He has passed the information to Tessa as you well know, but others may know of her demise. They need to continue to believe that she has been destroyed. It must look as though Katie randomly visited Olivia and happened to be at the wrong place at the wrong time."

"Yes, Vicar, Katie will stay out of sight." Azzurra answered. She shook a finger at Katie. "No more going in the backyard to pick flowers."

Katie swished a hand toward her sister. "I was corporeal."

The Vicar continued. "Since the spell was cast outside of Olivia's home, near mortals, they should have realized that a Vicar would investigate. This will explain my presence. I will pay Olivia a visit tonight under the guise of investigating the Disbursement Charm. We must keep it from being known that Azzurra was aware of the attack on Olivia all these years. Once they realize that Azzurra summoned Katie and knows about Olivia, it will only be a matter of time before another Witches War begins."

"Yes Vicar. We understand." Azzurra nodded.

"Good, I shall take my leave." He looked to Katie. "Say goodnight, Katie. You have spells to cast." He nodded to the room and vanished.

"I guess that's our cue Blackie. Come on. Let's go downstairs and get to work." Katie hugged the kids' goodnight, kissed Azzurra and Arianna and left the room with Blackie on her heels.

Azzurra stood. "Before you kids leave, I have to give you some protective enchantments and some Bousaloon." She left the room. Several moments later, she reentered with a paper grocery bag. She reached in the bag and set a scarf on the table, followed by a ring, a bracelet and a necklace.

"OK, now let me see. Marie, don't let me forget, I have two plants on the kitchen counter that I want you to take home with you tonight. They are next to the *Tupperware* of food. They are enchanted and should help protect you if something evil enters the house." She handed Marie a silk scarf. "Now, I want you wear this scarf at all times. It's also enchanted."

"Thanks Ma." She glanced at her watch. "Oh my Lord, I should have called Steve hours ago! It's already 2:30am!" She picked up the scarf. "Do I have to wear this all the time?"

"You want to be safe don't you? It's cool out so nobody will think it's strange. Be creative. I just saw a girl wear one as a belt. Maybe I should have made you jewelry. Oh well, you have a scarf." Azzurra took the ring that lay on the table.

"Marta, when you come out of your coma, I want you to wear this." The silver ring had a small purple stone in the middle.

"That's a cool stone, Ma. Neato." Marta stammered.

"I'll make sure she gets home, Mum. I'll send her car home as well." Basil grimaced toward Arianna.

"Marta…it stays purple if there is…never mind sweetheart. I've stuck a note in the book, A MODERN DAY WITCH. It will tell you how to use it. Read it tonight." Azzurra swished a hand at Marta then took the bracelet."

"She'll be fine in about a half hour. I swear." Arianna smiled.

"I'll cleanse her aura before I leave, should speed up the process a wee bit." Basil jerked his head toward Marta.

"Thank you Basil." Azzurra narrowed her eyes toward Arianna and then turned toward Nicco. "Nicco honey, wear this bracelet at all times, even in the shower. I have a necklace for Tracy." Nicco finished clasping the bracelet and took the necklace. "Thanks, Ma." He looked at the necklace and grimaced. *Tracy will never wear that.*

"Marie honey, are you sure you don't want me to fix your sweater?" Azzurra nodded.

"No Ma, I'll fix it tomorrow. Thank you."

Nicco stood. "What about Mr. Buchman? What happened? Marie told me something happened with your boss...romantic stuff."

"Do you really think now is the time Nicco?" Azzurra swished a hand at him. "She doesn't even know who she is, let alone Mr. Buchman. Tomorrow honey."

"Yea Ma, forgot." Nicco said.

Azzurra stood. "I want everyone here tomorrow evening after work. We will teach you the basics. Arianna, can you be here tomorrow?"

"Of course I will be here. We'll ask Gabriella to join us too." Arianna replied.

Marie stood as did Marta. Basil took Marta's arm and wished everyone a goodnight. "Come on now Marta, time to go home. Hang on tight and don't let go."

"Wait! I was going to give them a sleeping elixir. However, I'm thinking an enchantment may be better. Mateo was busy today...I lied. What are you gonna do?" She looked toward Azzurra and smiled weakly.

"Arianna, if all three of my kids are loopy tomorrow, I'm going be mad." Azzurra walked around the table and stood near the entrance. "Basil, would you make sure the plants, cars and food get to their houses?"

Basil nodded.

Arianna spoke. "They will be fine. This spell will give them a full night's sleep, even though it's after 2. I promise. This is better than the elixir I made. I used to cast this spell for Scott when he was little. Now, once the spell is done, everyone may leave. They'll only have a few minutes." She picked up her wand and placed Nicco, Marie and Marta next to each other and spoke the incantation.

> *"Thoughts of trouble, thoughts of strife*
> *Let the mind fill with delight*
> *Rid the nightmares and sleepy tight*
> *This wish for thee I give tonight."*

* * * *

Sleep Tight, Olivia

The reflection in the mirror revealed what could not be hidden…the reality of a broken soul. How many times had she looked into the mirror and wanted to see something else…someone else. The truth of the matter was that the reflection did belong to someone else. Someone she hardly recognized. A reflection of dark hair, sallow cheeks and sunken brown eyes belonged to a woman she no longer knew or liked.

Into the reflection her mind traveled…flashes of the changing years…flashes that ripped a bit of who she had been, year after year. Now, Olivia stood in the bathroom…tired, depressed and lifeless. Something had eaten away the spark of life.

The spark of life, her father had told her, was the ability to see within one's soul the excitement of life…adventure…curiosity. As a little girl, her father had told her that she had the spark…a twinkle in the eye…a zest for life. When did the spark die? Bit by bit, darker and darker, the spark faded. Each event triggered the slight breeze that the spark fought against. Eventually the spark went out.

How to gain the strength to keep it lit? Her sister, Carlotta, had been her strength — her force to keep the spark. It's hard to keep two sparks lit.

Her lifeless eyes saw visions of her brother, Angelo, lying in his crib, wearing Scooby Doo pajamas and those eyes…nothing; they were empty, completely void of anything living inside. That was the first of many attempts to snuff the spark. Why the memory was so vivid, she did not know. A four-year old should never have remembered such details.

The reflection sickened her. It was as though a cloud had settled above the flame, a cloud that covered the sun for so many years. Forty years and nine months marked the second biggest gust that threatened her existence. It was the death of her mother. She could see her mother as though it were yesterday, her eyes, her face. She could see her mother smile weakly and then slip into death. Empty eyes, just like Angelo…so vivid…so much detail. How was there so much detail?

Walter had been an igniter. He brought a spark that she hadn't felt in years. They had met when she was sixteen and had been married by twenty-one. Carlotta loved him, said he was the perfect man for her. Her father, Dante, liked him as well. When did it change? When did Walter change?

His change must have been the ice breaker. The one breeze that altered her life, that re-wrote who she had been and who she would become.

Olivia leaned into the mirror for signs of life. If it had not been for her children…if it had not been for a strong will, she would a blasted her brains out years ago.

David, her oldest son, had argued with Walter again that evening. The voices raged from the garage, through the house and up into her room, where sleep kept her most of the time. *Ignore them…just sleep…sleep until it goes away. There is nothing you can do.*

The front door burst open. Large, heavy footsteps make their way to the room, where he knew his wife would be. The bedroom door flies open.

"Olivia! Do you know what that dumbass son of yours did? That stupid son of a bitch changed his motorcycle's oil in my garage and didn't put so much as a towel down! Now, there is oil on my garage floor! I have a stain on my frickin' floor! I told that son of a bitch that if he ever did that again, I'd knock his head right through the garage wall. You know what he had the nerve to tell me? *Well then your garage wall will be damaged.* I should have knocked his teeth out for a smart-ass crack like that. I told him to clean that mess up and he is to no longer use my garage to change his oil or anything! He can do it at his apartment, in the frickin' street! I'll fix his ass."

A few moments later, Carlotta had called…her lifesaver. Olivia conveyed the story to the only person she confided in…her sister. Aunty Azzurra and Aunty Arianna were always there, but Carlotta was a rock…a rock that she needed.

Carlotta pleaded with Olivia to come over, sit with her for awhile and relax. She even suggested coming to Olivia. Walter didn't scare her in the slightest. Years ago Olivia would have gotten in the car and left. It was different since Carlotta's divorce. Her rock had had her own troubles, so the rock had to be pushed away.

Carlotta insisted that she was coming to the house this Saturday and taking her to lunch. "I'm not feeling well, Carlotta, I can't." Her sister's response was that she should bring a bucket and keep it next to her. They were going to lunch.

The reflection played the memories from the day's events. Mechanically, her arm opened the medicine cabinet and pulled out the toothpaste. A hand reached into the back of a ceramic hippo and pulled a purple tooth brush up to the mirror. Paste squeezed out upon the purple tooth brush. *Brush Olivia…brush back and forth.*

Rose and Michael still lived at home. *Defend them or they'll move away too.* She'd be left alone…with him. Her eyes became heavier…deeper… darker. Something inside…way deep inside, there was a voice that sounded so familiar…so strange. It spoke the words to say. "Walter, for God sake calm down. Try asking him to clean it up. If you would have taught him to put down newspaper without bitching at him in the first place, you wouldn't…" Another voice would always win.

The reflection showed the front teeth being brushed, back and forth, then in small circles.

The other voice would see the future…hear the conversations…hear Walters's response: *Why do you always stick up for those damn kids?* She would tell herself not to say a thing…it would only make it worse.

Small circles, back and forth… over and over the front teeth.

Something inside him explodes…wild, violent and angry. Walter had grown to be a raging inferno.

Her hand had stopped brushing. Time had stopped. The reflection showed an arm placed near a face, a toothbrush in a mouth but no movement. The arm came down; she spit into the sink and rinsed the brush. A hand placed it back into the hippo. The toothpaste was placed back into the cabinet. A mundane task completed.

Another task…the sheets were pulled from her side of the bed. A glance at the clock told her it was 2:17am. Don't wake him. Nighttime always seemed to dodge sleep. It had been 11:00 when she first attempted to sleep. The dreams kept her from sleeping very long. Dreams of Angelo plagued her mind, dreams of her mother and the last smile. Then there was the thing that came to visit her almost nightly.

Is Walter awake? It always comes when he is sleeping. Perhaps he's pretending to be asleep…it won't come if he is awake. The pillow felt soft upon her neck as her eyes grew heavy. *Don't come…let me sleep, let me sleep.*

Not the slightest sound came from Walter…heavy deep breaths of sleep were void, completely still. He was pretending sleep.

Mary…before sleep took over…she'd say a prayer to the Mother Mary, a prayer for guidance, a prayer for strength. The first words were spoken softly, released silently from her lips.

Her heart lurched and skipped a beat, then began to pound heavy, palms broke into a sweat. Pounding…her heart thudded against her chest. Her eyes flew open. The bed on her side slowly sank as *it* took its seat. It had come to see her again.

Without thinking, her leg moved toward the indention, knowing that there would be nothing there. There was never anything there…just the feeling of the bed sinking…the feeling as if someone sat down. A gasp escaped as her foot hit something. Something sat upon her bed!

Olivia bolted upright, heart racing, pulse thudding, mind whirling. Maybe it's Rose? Maybe Rose needs to talk and she is sitting at the end of the bed. Darkness…nothing could be seen but a shadow of a person. "Rose?" Clouds moved away and moonlight revealed the silhouette of a young man with dark long hair. He lifted his head…his eyes unnaturally white and glowing.

The man shook his head methodically.

"Walter! Walter, wake up!" Heavy breathes made it hard to speak. Her voice was being sucked into her chest.

The man spoke. "He's not waking!" In a blink, the man glided into the air and hovered within an inch of Olivia, eyes staring into hers. "You wanted him dead?" The man's arms stretched out, a glow emanated from his body, eyes bright with white light, breath foul and rank. Olivia's heart thudding, screams swallowed into the pit of her stomach. A screech erupted from the man…a screech beyond nature.

"Ma what was that?" Michael called from his room. Rose's voice cracked, asking the same question.

A voice reached out from her throat and screamed. "Get out! Run! Leave the house!" The man grabbed her face and lifted her forward. "They're not going anywhere!" The man was gone. The bedroom door flew off its hinges as it raced toward her children.

Gasping, she reached for Walter. Commotion in the hall, Rose and Michael's doors opening then slamming, screams from Rose...Michael calling for his sister.

"Walter!" From the depths so deep, she screamed his name. "Walter! Walter! Walter! Wake up!" Frantically, she reached for the bedside lamp, flicking it on just before it crashed to the floor. The brief moment of light revealed a blonde man sitting next to Walter. A beast lay upon her husband. The man watched the beast lapping at Walters's mouth with a long, black tongue. Walter's eyes were open, empty...void of life.

From a place within her soul that had long been dormant — rage appeared. The need to protect her family rushed into every ounce of her being.

"Get away from him!" Olivia screamed. Her hand flew up, fingers splayed and the release of energy expelled from her palm.

The beast flew away from Walter and smashed into the drywall. It howled in pain. The moonlight exposed the blonde man, who looked to the beast, which was rising. The man looked back to Olivia and then fled through the wall.

"Rose! Michael!" Olivia crawled over the bed toward the entrance. The moonlight revealed the room's contents once more. The beast stood over seven feet tall, covered in black fur, hunched shoulders and fangs, drool oozing out its mouth. It growled and swiped a paw across Olivia. A blast of pain shot into her shoulder, then the side of the face, back of the head and the thigh as she flew across the room, hitting the far wall. Scuffling through the broken jewelry stand and smashed lamp, she scurried to her feet, blood trickling down her head. "Rose! Michael!

Heavy breathing, tearing, growling and snorting came from Walter's side of the bed. Olivia staggered to the door, Rose's and Michael's screams, driving her forward. The room lit up once again, revealing the beast. It was in frenzy. Spatters of warmth splashed across her face. It was ripping Walter apart. The beast's tore into the sheets, the bed, into Walter's flesh. A large head peered up at Olivia, eyes glowing red. Blood and skin were hanging from its mouth. It roared and flung itself upon Olivia.

Olivia turned and raised a hand once more. A blast of white light shot from her palm, hitting the beast. It howled in pain and slammed into the wall above Walter. Rose's screams stopped. Michael shouted for his sister, then his mother. Olivia screamed that she was coming. She turned to run. Paws wrapped around her legs and pulled her down with a tremendous force. Her body was dragged across the carpet. Soft and wet, her body hit the bed. She screamed.

Olivia flipped herself over and began to crawl over the remains of her husband, tears streaming down her cheeks, heart racing and muscles tense. Her eyes caught the beast as it leapt toward her. She raised her arms for protection. The beast yelped and large swooshes of warmth crossed over her.

Silence...nothing happened.

A feeling flushed through her body...feelings that hadn't been there in years: safe, content, alive. Nothing was going to harm her. She lowered her arm, eyes searching the room. The beast was gone. A man in white stood in the entrance. His tie glowed with sparkles of gem stones — two were blinking red. The man raised a hand toward the hall and two green lights entered the tie. They blinked. His hand rose toward her. A red light released from her throat, glided toward the man and joined the other blinking gems.

Handsome and tall with dark hair, the man tilted his head up and to the right then lowered his gaze upon Olivia. A bright light filled the room. It was so powerful that her eyes went blind with white. A short snore and Walter turned in his sleep. She was in bed, covers pulled to her neck. The man stood at her bedside, his lips parted into a slight smile. Before falling into the deepest, most restful sleep she had ever had, she heard his voice. "Sleep tight, Olivia."

* * * *

A Panther, a Bubble & a Water Bird!

Azzurra made her way down the old stone steps that led to the secret room. Thoughts catapulted her memory to three years prior when she had walked down these very steps with Franco. The diagnosis of cancer prompted their decision. Together, they had placed the ingredients for the Summoning Spell in the purple velvet bag. Together, they had agreed that if the time came to break the vow, Azzurra would call for Katie.

"Good morning, Katie." Azzurra watched her sister place the cat and soap dispenser from the kitchen sink upon the round oak table.

"Good morning Azzurra. I just completed the last of the Transformation Spells that would make the house a stronghold for the family. Not that I don't trust your angel or those cute cherubs, but the Vicar thought we needed something that would be more...well...independent and transportable." Katie placed a vase of water next to the soap dispenser and cat.

Azzurra reached for the angel necklace that hung around her neck. "She's strong, Katie and goes wherever I go. She's transportable?" She walked over to the vase and looked inside. "What are the cat and soap dispenser supposed to do? Is this water? Are you going to give a demon a bath?" A slight chuckle escaped.

"Go ahead. Make fun. But wait 'til you see what I've done." She looked around the room. "You're right, the cherubs and angel are strong. However, they are stuck in the bedroom and the angel is around your neck, only protecting you. Now, these enchantments can go anywhere and will protect the entire family." Katie searched the floor. "Blackie…Blackie where are you? That dog is afraid of his own shadow. Must be hiding from the cat."

Azzurra looked around the room and a sudden image of Anna came to mind. "Katie, oh my word, I forgot to tell you. Augusto told me that he's been hearing her voice. She's been calling for him. He swears he's not hearing things and says that he feels she's in trouble and needs his help. What do you think it means Katie?"

Katie looked under the table. "It means Anna's in trouble and needs his help."

Azzurra placed hands upon her hips.

"I'm serious Azzurra. I didn't mean to be a smart ass. I've always felt that her disappearance was too strange. I think she's been banished and she's reaching the end of the banished realm and is calling out to him. I think Augusto will need to help guide her out of the darkness." Katie peeked around the pine hutch, which revealed no sign of Blackie.

"You think so, Katie? But how could she have been banished for so long? Do you think Debra or Dorthea or even Stella and Sabino are that powerful? I mean to have banished her for over forty years?" Azzurra peeked behind the apothecary.

"Maybe someone else is involved. Maybe they weren't lying. Maybe they didn't banish her. Let's talk with Augusto this afternoon. He'll be here at 2:00. Poor Anna…lost for over forty years. I can't imagine what it must be like." Katie crossed her arms. "Blackie, you come out this instant!"

A tiny bark came from the armoire. The sisters turned toward the bark. A little black and white Terrier inched his head out from under a plum velvet cloak. Katie swished a hand in the air. "Beee, I told you that the cat wasn't going to hurt you. Now come out and say good morning to Azzurra.

Blackie looked at the pewter cat and soap dispenser and ducked his head back under the cloak.

"Forget him. Listen, don't worry about Anna. This is good news. It's the first time anyone has heard from her since her disappearance. I think there was a very good reason why Anna was banished. She knew something that she shouldn't have known." Katie rubbed her hands together and walked over to the table. "Now, I need to show you something. Are you ready?" Azzurra's eyes widened, shaking her head. "Bee, there is nothing to be afraid of. Now stand back." Katie positioned a hand over the pewter cat and spoke an incantation.

"Dimostra il tuo potere!"
(Demonstrate your power!)

Before their eyes the pewter cat morphed — the skin peeled back revealing black fur. The head stretched out from a tiny body, fangs protruding from its mouth. The body oozed from its head, stretching out two giant paws, a huge chest and strong hind legs. The tail writhed out of its body as it leapt from the table and to the floor. A large roar filled the room. The panther looked toward the armoire. Blackie yelped.

Large green eyes darted across the room as its tail swished through the air. His eyes focused upon Azzurra and Katie. Azzurra's palms muffled a scream. The panther roared again and bowed toward the sisters. He moved toward Katie and nudged her hand over his head. Katie patted his large forehead between the eyes. He closed them slowly then opened them, roaring a bit softer. He slinked to Azzurra, looked up and roared again. He bowed then nudged his head against her arm. Azzurra scratched behind his ears. He roared loudly. Blackie yelped again, the cloak shaking violently.

All 155 pounds of cat rolled on the floor, resting on his back. Giant paws lay upon his chest.

"He will come to life when he senses an evil Spirit, demons or mortals that intend to harm you or a loved one. Self-healing with razor sharp claws, he can travel in the blink of an eye and depending on the circumstance — he can become solid or attack in Spirit form. His teeth can tear through anything: metal, bone and dislodge energy in a Spirit. Sammy has artificial intelligence and yes, he will still clean your dishes." Katie nodded once.

"Sammy. I like that name for him. Oh my word, he's huge!" Azzurra placed hands to her mouth once again.

"The Vicar told me everything I needed to know to create him. Isn't he cute?" Katie looked to the table at the soap dispenser next to a vase of water. "Now, let me show you the soap dispenser." Sammy roared and rolled onto his belly. Katie spoke the same incantation.

"Dimostra il tuo potere!"
(Demonstrate your power!)

The soap dispenser move slightly and gave a soft hiccup noise. A tiny bubble oozed from its tip, growing in size…growing, growing and growing. It swirled with white, bubbly film and morphed to irregular ovals and then back to circles near the size of a medicine ball. It hovered in the air. Azzurra laughed softly. "It's cute, but what does it do?" She clasped a hand to her face.

"Well, it can grow to any size that it needs. Morph into any type of container and the bubbly film will render a mortal or Witch unconscious. It will also disperse a mean energy discharge to Spirits or demons. The constant discharge will weaken the entity and hold him captive in the bubble. Not sure what kind of demons it can hold, but I'm sure it will do damage to lower-level to mid-level demons. I wouldn't hold my breath for upper-level demons. But you never know." Katie reached out and poked at the morphing bubble. The bubble glowed blue. "It will be able to sense any friend or family member and offer assistance in healing as well. The dispenser will dispense as many bubbles as needed. It can travel with you, or you can instruct any bubble to follow you or give it commands."

"Oh Katie, that's incredible!" Azzurra poked at the bubble as the panther roared at the morphing blob. The Bubble glowed purple, then sent white film up Azzurra's arm. Azzurra gasped and then sighed in relief. "Oh, Katie, my back, it just loosened right up! No more *Advil's!*"

Katie laughed and spoke to the Bubble. "Shrink down sweetheart. We need to make room for Merlin." The Bubble glowed blue and then shrunk down to a size of a softball and hovered over the panther. "Don't you swat that Bubble, you'll regret it Sammy."

The panther roared and flipped onto its back once again. Katie called to the vase of water. "Ok Merlin, come on out and say hi."

The water churned and then began to swirl in the vase. It rose up and formed a funnel. Round and round it swirled. Water began to splatter on the table, and then retracted back into the funnel. The shape contorted into that of a Merlin falcon, the same Merlin from Azzurra's summoning charm.

"Oh Katie, it's the messenger bird." Azzurra's eyes grew large as she watched the bird flap its wings, water splashing to the ground and then rising up to rejoin the bird.

"When you cast the spell for the messenger bird, you gave him personality and he came to life. Because of your powers, he didn't evaporate when the message was completed. He'll respond to any command without being summoned. It's part of the enchantment. Now, he's not just a messenger bird. Basil came up with this one. He had to leave by the way. The Vicar summoned him about something. Anyway, he can change into any shape needed to protect or attack. His size can vary from a centimeter to 60 feet tall. He can fly large distances in the blink of the eye, produce various sounds and mimicry and hold passengers. Merlin also has the ability to breathe water and produce high winds." Katie leaned into the water bird. "Change into some shapes for us sweetheart…nothing too big."

The water bird exploded outward, spraying water on Katie, Azzurra, Sammy and The Bubble. The water retracted back toward the bird in a split second, and formed into a butterfly. He exploded outward again and became a beaver, then a sword and shield — splitting itself in two. It exploded again and morphed into a large bear, then a small dragon and finally back into a Merlin falcon.

"I forgot to tell you, he can split himself in multiple parts if he feels the need." Katie reached out and patted the top of the water bird. He made a soft caw, deformed with her finger then reshaped.

Azzurra shook her head. "I can't believe all this Katie. You and Basil did a wonderful job!"

"Keep them upstairs. Nothing will enter or even come near this house! It's defiantly a stronghold. We can take them with us or send them wherever we wish. The angel stays with you, the cherubs will be in your bedroom and these three will be everywhere else!"

Azzurra's eyes widened with delight. Sammy roared, the Bubble glowed purple and the Merlin changed into a ferret. The sisters laughed.

Basil appeared and interrupted. "Mum, Miss Katie, Olivia had been attacked!"

* * * *

$\mathcal{D}$everoy

$\mathcal{T}$he sun felt hot, almost blistering as the man lay in the mound of sand. Wiping his crusted eyes with a couple of fingers, he took in the blazing sun that shown above. He tried to focus on his surroundings through the glare. Pain, he felt pain…why? How was he feeling this kind of pain? He placed his palms upon the hot sand and hoisted his body up a few inches. Solid…he was in solid form and something told him there was no sense in trying to return to Spirit.

Deveroy turned and pushed himself to his knees. He placed his hand above his eyes and searched the area. A lump of something human lay in the sand, some fifty feet away. The wind gusted. His blonde hair blew over his face, obstructing the view. The lump in the sand must be Achar!

His weak legs pulled him to his feet. Heavy and tired, the feeling became an annoyance as he pushed through the desert sand, toward his friend.

"Leave him be. Do not go to him." A thick voice came from behind. The wind picked up and blew into his face, blinding him. He shielded his eyes.

Feeling the wind subside, Deveroy opened his eyes and turned behind him and then back to Achar. The voice warned once again not to go toward his friend.

Deveroy twisted to face the voice. A man stood, dressed in a fine white suite with a gemstone tie. He shielded his eyes from the sun. His voice cracked when he spoke. "My friend and I are in trouble, I think he's hurt. Can you help me?"

"I will not help. Your friend will awaken soon. Before he awakes you will answer my questions or suffer severely." The man looked to the right and then focused back on Deveroy.

Deveroy squinted; the man came into clear view. He stood ten feet away, comfortable and calm in the middle of the desert. Deveroy wanted to cast a fireball but knew that it would be the wrong thing to do. Besides, something inside him revealed that there would be no fireball to cast. "Is he alright? Who are you? Did you bring us here?"

"I will ask the questions. What were you and Achar doing at the home of Walter and Olivia Jasienski, early this morning near 2:30? Why were you in the company of demons?"

Deveroy paused a moment then pivoted and began to trudge toward Achar.

Pain! A blast of pain hit his chest. A blue light flashed before his eyes, burning and stinging. The sight of Achar blurred. The man in white stood before him as he was spun around by an invisible force. Deveroy tried to catch his balance but fell into the sand. On all fours, he looked up to the man in white. "What do you want? Who are you?" He yelled.

"I told you, I will ask the questions." The man's voice lowered. "You have thirty seconds to answer me or you will feel pain once again."

"I don't know what you're talking about!" Deveroy stepped backward and screamed for Achar.

Pain shot through his stomach, chest and eyes. His head was throbbing in agony. His thin body was thrust once again to face the man. Pain like he had never felt, pierced his body. It felt as though his insides were being ripped apart.

Falling to the sand, Deveroy released his body. The pain subsided. He smeared his hair away from his eyes and focused on the man in white. "We were told to scare her...to haunt her...Achar and me." His eyes squinted in the sun.

"Thank you. I do not wish to harm you further." The Vicar smiled upon Deveroy. "Who told you to haunt her? Did you cast the Disbursement Charm upon a nearby Spirit?

Deveroy shook his head. The man in white raised a hand. "No! Don't, please! Tessa asked us years ago if we could seek revenge for her. A Spirit named Basil...he belonged to the family...to her sister, Azzurra. He killed Contessa's son, Vincent. Basil killed him in his sleep. The haunting started out simple...doors slamming, opening...lights flicking on and off. Then a man asked us to place the Culls and told us to work with demons. I don't know who he is...some man...long grey hair. I don't know his name, I swear. Please, I'm telling you the truth."

"I asked you another question. Did you cast the Disbursement Charm?" The man in white stepped forward.

A soothing feeling washed over Deveroy. A feeling of a cooling breeze, calm...peace...protection, swept over his body and into his brain. "What are you?" Deveroy asked.

The man in white smirked and shook his head.

"I'm sorry, please don't. I did it! I cast the spell. Let Achar go. Please." His pounding heart slowed, the wind died down and the pain subsided. The heavy feeling dissipated.

The Vicar squatted and looked into Deveroy's eyes. "You lie. I ask that you be respectful to tell the truth when I ask you a question."

"Get away from him!" A voice called from behind. Achar's hands shot out in front of him, fingers splayed. Nothing...the spell he cast did nothing.

Deveroy spiraled in the sand and faced his friend. Achar buckled in pain. He screamed and howled in agony. His body floated fifteen feet in the air and slammed to the sand with a tremendous force. He lay still.

"Achar!" Deveroy faced the man in white. "Is he all right? Please don't."

"He is not all right. Achar's soul is dark, tainted by evil. Yours however, is not. I am sorry that you are stressed, scared...I mean you no harm." The man in white looked into the pale blue eyes of Deveroy.

"Please! He's all I have. He didn't mean to hurt Katie. I know he didn't. You don't understand!"

"I do understand. I understand all things and he did mean to harm Katie. You are not alone. He is not all that you have. You have Contessa. She loves you dearly. Damiano loves you as well, so does Medeia and Dormava."

Safe...the feeling of contentment engulfed Deveroy's body.

"I am a Vicar to the Higher Spirits. My name is Aiden Sinclair. I do not intend to harm you again. I will not say the same for your friend. He is healing but feels as a mortal does. You will both return to your Spirit forms shortly."

Without thinking, without hesitation Deveroy spoke. "I'm Deveroy. I'm sorry for everything." He gulped and looked up to the man. "Why am I feeling all this, this dread...disgust...exhaustion? My life is flashing before me. The things I've done, in life and in death. Let me go back to feeling contented and loved...please."

"I will not, you must feel them. Feel what you've done and release those emotions that accompany them. So you went astray, made poor choices and now you will let them go. I will help you."

"I don't want to! You don't know what I've done...what I feel. You know nothing about me!" He yelled.

"I do. I know what you've done in the 27 years that you lived and everything you've done after your death. I know what Achar has done. And I do know how you feel. Your life was like a towel. When the towel is purchased, it is soft, white, fluffy and absorbent. Tiny pores in the towel are used to clean up spills...mistakes...trouble. The threads are finely sewn together, created to withstand, created to last a lifetime. It is the perfect towel. It is beautiful. Without the experience of life, it stays white and perfect. It does not change. Then, a spill happens. Nothing serious, but the towel has gained experience. It is cleaned and placed away to be used once again when the time is needed. Another spill, it is bigger this time, takes more scrubbing. It stains the towel. It was made to be washed. It was made to change...all things must change. It is placed back upon the shelf. Years go by and the spills vary from tiny accidents to catastrophic mistakes. It is now aging." He raised a hand to the side of Deveroy's face, gently smearing away a tear with his thumb. "One day, the towel is needed for yet another spill. Your eyes focus on the towel, and for the first time you notice the change: tiny rips, frayed edged, holes and stains that cannot be hidden. When did it change? When did your life become a filthy rag? You felt the rag was no longer absorbent, white or useful. So what did you do?" Deep brown eyes penetrated Deveroy's soul. "You threw it away." A gasp escaped Deveroy as tears rushed down his face. "The towel was made for spills. The towel was made to clean the most disgusting of life turmoil's. In your life, you made the mistake of becoming a rag. In death, you will realize that there is always new thread. There is never a time when the towel should become a useless rag." A tear rose from the Vicar's eye, swelled over his lid and streamed down his cheek. "There is always hope. There is always love...and understanding...and there is always forgiveness."

* * * *

Without a Wand

The panther bolted upright, roared toward Basil and began to pace. Katie reached for the table for balance. "Is Olivia alright? What happened?"

"I don't have much time. I need to find two more of my mates. I think they may still be in Europe, but yes, she is fine. Actually, she is more than fine." Basil looked to the Bubble. "Something's very cute about that Bubble."

Katie and Azzurra's eyes narrowed toward Basil. Blackie barked from behind the cloak. "Sorry. Miss Katie. You should be proud of your daughter. She fought to protect her family. She cast two Energy Blasts. The second was powerful, visible, and strong. Both were without her knowledge of what she was doing. Both were done…without a wand!"

Katie replied. "What do mean, Basil? A mortal Witch doesn't have the power to cast that kind of spell without the assistance of a Spirit through a wand." She looked to Azzurra who shrugged her shoulders.

"Are you sure Basil? Are you sure she cast the spell?" Azzurra took a couple of steps toward Basil. The Bubble glowed purple, floated to Azzurra and released more white film to her back. She sighed.

"Yes, Mum…well kind of. I mean, she never said the spell. It just happened. The Vicar destroyed the demon and both Culls, but he told me that Olivia had cast two powerful Energy Blasts at the demon…without the use of a wand." Basil reached out to the Bubble. It turned a crimson red and then morphed into an irregular shape.

"Without a wand…what could this mean? When I was alive I could cast minimum protective spells, expel heat and cold and levitate things, but in a battle…you need a Wand Spirit." Katie turned to Basil. "What do you think it means?"

"The Vicar was tight-lipped about the no wand thing, said that it wasn't his place." Basil looked toward the Merlin who looked up to him and blinked his eyes. "He turned out grand Miss Katie."

"Basil, focus please." Azzurra said.

"Sorry Mum. The Vicar is with Achar and Deveroy as we speak. He is setting the scene that he was investigating the Disbursement Charm. He revived Walter and Rose and repaired the house. Walter and Rose were mortally wounded, but he took care of everything, he did — brought them back from the dead. They are well rested and may not remember the event."

"You said they are fine…Rose and Walter? Is Michael alright?" Katie asked.

"As a matter of fact, the Vicar informed me that Deveroy could not get near Michael. He tried to attack him but could not. He fled to help Achar with Rose. I think Michael, as you well know, is the next generation of power, and in time will be more powerful than Mum." Basil patted Sammy on the head.

"Casting an Energy Blast without a wand? Michael? Azzurra, you know what this means?" Katie looked to her sister.

"No, Katie I don't." Azzurra replied.

"It means that we are more powerful than we ever imagined." Katie looked to Basil, who nodded. "Wait 'til the rest of the family hears this."

"We don't know for sure Miss Katie. For all we know, Olivia's Energy Blasts could be a fluke and Michael may not be the designee of the Degeli lineage. The Vicar would confirm nothing." Basil poked at the Bubble which glowed once again a crimson red.

Azzurra looked to Katie. Blackie peeked out from behind the cloak and whined, then darted back. "Katie, I hate to say it, but something is not right about that Vicar." Azzurra waved a finger toward her sister.

"The Vicar is a good man." Basil interjected, still poking at the Bubble.

Katie sighed. "Basil honey, it's not that he isn't a good man. But my sister is right. Something doesn't make sense about the Vicar."

* * * *

Nathan

Soft, gentle and powerful, the music played as the woman stood near the glass sliding door wall. She gazed out into the yard, letting the music fill her soul. *Bach's Prelude in C Major* resonated within her senses. Contessa's lips curled into a slight smile, eyes closed ever so slowly, then reopened, feeling the music penetrate as the breeze outside rustled the ash tree that she would not let die.

Her eyes focused on the tree, being thankful, once again, that she had been born a Witch. Without that power, without her caring about such a silly tree, it would have died along with the rest of the ash trees as the Emerald Ash Borer ate its way through so many states. She would not let her tree succumb to such an awful fate. As a Witch of one the most powerful families in history, no little beetle was going to kill her tree.

Contessa took a sip of tea and smiled.

"Tess? I'm home honey." Nathan entered his home, closing the door behind him. "Tess?" He shook his head and called once again over the music. He placed his suitcase to the side and removed his shoes. "Contessa?"

Contessa reached for the volume of the stereo and turned down the music. Did she hear something? "Is someone there?" She set her tea on the side table, next to her book and headed toward the front door. Nathan should be coming home today. Maybe it's him. "Nathan? Celia? Is that you?

Nathan entered the kitchen. "Tessa, would you please cast a spell to improve your hearing, I've been calling you?"

"I will not cast a spell to improve my hearing...because I don't know of one." She smiled and kissed her husband on the cheek. "Didn't catch a thing, did you? Let me make you something to eat."

"Not a damn thing. I can't even get a deer with three Witches and my son-in-law. That's it Tess, I'm not going any more. Too damn annoying! Stephan screams for the deer to run for their lives. Lamia and Marcus are off scaring other hunters and Alfonso's not very good...love him Tess, but it's not in his heart."

"Well don't say anything to Celia. She thinks you like hunting with Alfonso. Our daughter doesn't need to be thinking you're mad at her husband again. What would you like honey? How about a fried baloney sandwich, with onion and mustard? Maybe a side of chips, I just bought the Sun Chips that you like?"

"That sounds wonderful." He angled his head and listened to the music. "I like this one." He made his way over to his wife, holding his back. "How's my honey doing? Did you miss me?"

"Nathan, you're 78 years old. You have no business being out in the woods for days. I don't care that the Spirits make you comfortable and provide warmth. You're just too old...now your back hurts. I'll get some *Tylenol*." Contessa headed to the bathroom.

"I'm not too old, 78 is young yet." He brushed his hand through his thick grey hair and looked at the aged skin of his hands. Silently, he agreed with his wife. He was too old. "I left my suitcase by the front door."

"I'll get it later dear. Here take these." She handed him two *Tylenol*, then went to the cupboard, brought down a large glass, filled it with water and gave it to him. "I'll start your sandwich. Sit down honey."

Nathan sat in his chair at the kitchen table, rolled up his flannel sleeves and unbuttoned his shirt one more from the top. "Yea...I think I'm done. No more hunting." He brushed his hands over his jeans and stood, walked to the sink and began to wash.

"Did you at least have fun with Alfonso? He wasn't upset was he?" Contessa reached in the refrigerator. "Honey, did you eat enough...you look thin to me."

She pulled out the lunch meat container, stacked the bread, cheese, an onion and mustard upon the container and walked over to the counter.

"I'm fine, why do you always ask about Alfonso and me?" He took a towel and dried his hands. "Alfonso and I get along better than Celia and I; can't ask that girl anything without her ripping my head off. I don't know how Alfonso stays married to her. I will always love her…but I just don't like her." He shook his head and seated himself back at the table. "I hope Felicia and Fredrick take after their father. I want to be close to my grandchildren."

"That's an awful thing to say about your daughter. Would you please take the *Tylenol*?" Contessa hesitated, poured oil in a pan, and lit the burner. "Actually, I'm not sure how he stays married to her either." She laughed to herself. "Talk about crabby…very distant too, secretive and what a nasty streak."

"She's always been crabby and distant." Nathan rested his elbows on the table, rubbed his face with his hands and yawned. "The girls must have stayed with Celia. They never showed up."

Contessa began to slice an onion and tossed them into the sizzling pan. "Now you know very well that Dormava and Medeia don't like to hunt. Of course they would stay behind with Celia. They are her Spirits after all, and don't refer to them as girls. They don't like that. Did Damiano join you?" She began to stir the onions with a spatula.

"No, Damiano did not join us. He is another one I don't understand. He seems to like Alfonso and me but yet he won't join us at events. I don't think he likes Lamia to tell you the truth." *Bach's Mass in B Minor* began. He scrunched his nose and shook his head.

"Actually, I know for a fact that he doesn't like Lamia." Contessa reached in her housecoat and pulled out her wand. With a quick flip toward the stereo, it skipped the song and began to play *Beethoven's Moonlight Sonata*.

"Stephan was there. He made Alfonso and I laugh so hard. Lamia and Marcus have no patience with him, but he always makes a trip fun, even though he is the reason no deer came near us." Nathan chuckled.

Contessa placed two slices of baloney in the pan and began to poke at them. "Stephan tries my patience as well. Nice fellow, but he's a bit too dramatic for me." She prodded the baloney a bit harder.

Nathan turned to face his wife. "Have you seen Achar or Deveroy? They never showed up?"

Contessa rolled her eyes as she flipped the baloney over in the pan. "You know very well Deveroy does not like Lamia and despises hunting. I haven't seen him in well over a week." She noticed Nathan's look as he glanced down to her wand sticking out of her housecoat. "He is not in my wand...not sure why I used my wand to change the music...just an old habit I guess. But I have not seen him. I'm a bit worried. It's not like my Deveroy."

Nathan rolled his eyes. "I thought he said he'd be there. He's probably with Damiano."

"Achar showed up here though...that pest. He really gets on my nerves. If it wasn't for Deveroy I would dismiss him." She nudged the onions roughly away from the baloney and turned down the burner. She turned to the cupboard and pulled out a plate. "I could have taken a pan and hit him over the head with it."

"Achar, why the hell is Achar entering my home when I'm not here? I will speak with Lamia about him. What did he want?" Nathan arched his back slightly and took a sip of water.

"He was just being an ass, is all. Would you take your *Tylenol*, please? He crept around for a while before he revealed himself, gave me a fright." Contessa jumped when Nathan's fist hit the table "Now don't get upset dear. I scolded him for that. Kept talking nonsense and wouldn't give me a straight answer as to where Deveroy has been. I don't think he is with Damiano either."

She turned the burner off, swore, and then placed two slices of wheat bread in the toaster. "I forgot to toast the bread. It will be another minute."

"What the hell do you mean?" Nathan turned to face Contessa once more.

"Well I know you like it toasted and I forgot..."

"...not the damn bread...Achar. What nonsense is he talking about? Why won't he tell you where Deveroy is? He's a bad influence on Deveroy, I'll tell you that much. I'll tell you another thing. I don't want them near Olivia and Walter anymore. Enough is enough!" He rubbed his eyes with the back of his hands.

"Funny that you should say that, Achar said Katie showed up to the house." Contessa looked down to the toaster and closed her eyes.

"Katie!" Nathan rose to his feet. "What the hell do you mean Katie showed up? She hasn't been to see Olivia in over twenty years!"

"Well maybe she missed her daughter, is all." The toast popped, a deep breath expelled from her mouth. "Nathan, don't get worked up. Everything is fine."

"Don't tell me not to get worked up. What happened when Achar saw Katie?" Nathan approached his wife.

"He said he cast a Disburpalating Charm or something like that. Katie's been Disberma…."

"…Disbursement Charm? That ass can't do a Disbursement Charm! It would never stick. Don't worry about Katie. She'll be just fine." Nathan waved a hand toward his wife.

"Oh you think so!" She faced her husband. "Nathan, you really think she's alright? I couldn't sleep a wink last night, thinking that her atoms were scattered everywhere. That's an awful spell." Tears welled in her eyes. "But then I kept thinking that she deserved it. She sent Basil after our Vincent…"

Nathan raised a hand. "…stop it Tess. Please. We are not evil demons. That is a horrific spell that should never be cast. Achar's spell will have brought a Vicar to investigate the Charm. No Witch or Wizard will cast that spell and not pay the price. They will find out who cast that spell and he'll be in trouble…you mark my words."

Tessa sighed. "Oh, thank God she's OK. I hope they punish that Achar. I keep telling Deveroy to stay…"

"…I'm worried about what Katie will be thinking." Nathan placed the toast on the plate. "She goes to visit her daughter and gets attacked? She'll investigate why there were Spirits around Olivia's house." He stopped and looked into the pan of fried baloney. "If she finds out that Deveroy and Achar have been haunting Olivia's family. Katie will force them to spill their guts and tell her who sent them. That will lead straight to us." His eyes met Contessa's.

"I didn't think of that. I tried to summon Deveroy but he didn't answer. Maybe something has happened. We will just tell Deveroy and Achar to stay away. I told Achar already…enough is enough…when Katie comes back she'll find nothing there." She grabbed the spatula and moved the baloney and onions to the toast. She looked up to Nathan. "Did you place Culls at the house?"

"Culls, no I did not place Culls at the house! I hate those damn things." Nathan peeled a slice of tiger cheese from the block and placed it on the bread.

"Achar mentioned that he would send the Culls away. If Katie gets there and finds Culls she'll be livid!" Contessa leaned against the counter.

"Livid? She'll come right after us!" He paused then continued. "Tess, this is not good. You should have sent a message to me. I would have come home!" Nathan grabbed the mustard and squirted circles on the cheese.

"Don't get upset dear. Things will be alright. Let's send someone to Olivia's house to make sure there is no evidence of Culls or Demons. If Katie sees nothing, she won't know anything about Culls. We should also send Lamia after the boys and find out where they have been." Tessa grabbed a bag of Sun Chips and a small bowl.

Nathan stood still. "OK, we'll check to see if anything is strange at Olivia's. Just for safe measure. I'll send Stephan to investigate Azzurra's... make sure nothing odd is happening. If Katie thought that we were involved in attacking Olivia, she'd go straight to Azzurra."

"But what of the vow they took?"

"If Katie thinks that her family is in danger, she'll break the vow. Forget that it's punishable by the Higher Spirits. She'll see Azzurra." He looked down to his sandwich.

"Oh, Nathan there's more." Contessa's eyes began to flood. "I saw Marta."

"What!" Nathan slammed a hand down next to the sandwich.

"It was an accident. Celia was with me. She was odd...Celia. I don't know about that girl sometimes. We spoke a bit. I asked for Azzurra and about Franco." She covered her mouth. "Oh no, I shouldn't have done that."

"Contessa, what the hell were you thinking?" Nathan waited for an answer. Nothing came. "Please tell me you were not dressed in that stupid garb, ritual shit you wear, that damn scarf and shoes!"

"It's not stupid! Celia and I were shopping at the Witches Market and we stopped at Nino's on the way home. I wanted some fresh fruit. Oh Nathan, I'm so stupid! I asked about Olivia!" Tears flooded out of Contessa's eyes.

Nathan threw the sandwich to the floor. "Damn it! Azzurra will know you broke the vow, that you use Magick, that Celia knows Magick! Dear God Contessa! How could you do something so stupid?" He slammed his hand once again on the counter top.

Contessa placed her face in her hands and began to sob. Nathan reached for her and brought her close to him. "I'm sorry Tess, I shouldn't have yelled. It's all right. Nothing's wrong. Marta may not have mentioned it to Azzurra. Come here, I'm sorry for yelling. Things will be OK." He brought his wife's head to his chest.

"I'm sorry Nathan. I wasn't thinking." Tessa whispered.

Nathan pulled his wife away and looked into her eyes. "I'm just being paranoid. Things will be fine. Even if Marta mentioned something, it doesn't mean anything. Don't be upset."

Contessa placed a hand upon her husband's chest. "If Azzurra thinks that Olivia has been attacked…that her horrible marriage is due to interference of a Cull…she'll break that vow and the first spell she'll cast…is a summoning charm for Katie."

* * * *

The Master Player

There had been a time when everything seemed exciting — an adventure waiting to be explored. Life had been worth living...worth exploring. With each tick of time, there came the opportunity to meet someone new, someone that made your pulse quicken. People were like books waiting to be opened and their chapters read. That's the intriguing part of getting to know someone. Everyone has their own story.

As time ticked by, it brought change. Deveroy felt the change in his soul. He knew that something deep down desired release. The change ate at him, gnawed at his insides until the desire to meet new people simply evaporated. Their chapters were all alike...boring and selfish...cruel and disappointing.

Deveroy knew that things happen for a reason...plotted, written and controlled. Play the game right and you win. Play it wrong and you lose.

It's like kings and queens upon a chessboard. He would often explain this to Achar. We are all pieces upon a chessboard, controlled by a Master Player. Sometimes he makes you a king and sometimes the Master Player makes you a pawn. It doesn't matter. Every person becomes a piece upon a chessboard. Some are on his end of the board, some are not. Some play the game for a long time. Some are removed quickly.

Time ticks by and the pieces make their moves. Through time comes change; through change comes the disloyal souls. Allies are now foes and foes become allies. Do not trust anyone completely. Trust is a weakness that comes back to destroy you. Things change...that's life. People change from pawns to knights, from knights to kings, all in a blink of an eye.

The most important element of all, is that each piece know what they are — a bishop, a pawn or a rook. Each one knowing how they must move — who has control over whom. That's the way the pieces were designed. The decision has been made by the Master Player.

Pawns do what they are told. They will stick their necks out to see if there is danger — all for the greater good.

Deveroy knelt in the desert sand at the Vicar's feet. He had never met a Vicar before this moment. However, he knew it was the Vicar who made him feel such wonderful joy. He knew he could trust this man. He knew that everything he felt, everything he knew, was wrong.

Achar stood in the distance, watching and trying to listen to the Vicar's words.

The Vicar spoke. "I cannot keep either of you. It is not in the right of a Vicar to do so. You will both return to Spirit form soon. I will ask you both to not go near Olivia, Walter or their children again and pray for forgiveness."

He looked into Deveroy's pale blue eyes, searched his heart...his desires... his soul. "You are not a pawn upon a chessboard controlled by a Master Player. You *are* the Master Player and you may become any piece of your liking. If your heart is right, you will be forgiven for all you have done. If you should desire change...if you desire new thread...ask and I will be there."

Before he had a chance to ask, before thoughts transcended to words, Deveroy knew that he and Achar would no longer be allies.

* * * *

Stephan

Tessa placed a metal tea infuser on a napkin, looked up and stared out into the yard. The sun shined as the wind blew the crisp air. Her eyes focused on the ash tree, leaves on the cusp of gold. Thoughts slipped in and out of focus as she watched her tree blow gently in the breeze. Stephan should be here any moment. He would go to Azzurra's and make sure there were no signs of anything unusual...like a family meeting. Nathan's voice became loud and annoyed as he spoke with Celia about the whole debacle. He held the cell phone to his chest, looked up, took a breath and began speaking to his daughter once again. What happened to her peaceful afternoon?

The Rooibas tea felt smooth, warm and calming. Contessa dabbed her mouth with a napkin and replaced the tea cup back upon the saucer. It was Katie's cup she drank from.

"Dahling, I'm here! I came as soon as I received the summons. It was only after I did some shopping, took a tour of the Pyramids...again...never get tired of them, and did my hair that I rushed to be by your side in this time of need. Stephan is here!" Stephan produced a mirror and checked himself, fluffing the top of his hair. "My stars, I should have gotten a haircut before

I died. Look at this! It's a mop! I should have added highlights as well. Way too dark, it makes me look drab. I should have done a Liza and chopped all my hair off. And look at my hips. Who gains weight after death? Oh, that would be me!" Stephan adjusted the hem of his dress and took a seat opposite Contessa. "Why couldn't I have been tall, these heels are killing me. Oh, Tess this dress is hideous, isn't it?" His large gray eyes widened even more, waiting for an answer.

Contessa took another sip of tea, set the cup down and inhaled a breath. "Stephan, I told you before I don't like it when you wear dresses. I've also told you that red, is not your color. Now I summoned you over 20 minutes ago and it's rude to keep me waiting." Contessa stood. "Why on earth would you wear lace? That high collar neckline and sleeves makes you look like a potato stuffed in a lace sack!"

Stephan's lips began to quiver. Tears welled in his eyes as he pulled a red kerchief made of lace from his bra and began to sob.

"Nathan! Get off the damn phone, he's having another breakdown." Contessa placed her hand to her forehead.

"I was kidding about shopping and the Pyramids! I came here as soon as my makeup looked right. I supposed the hot red lipstick looks awful too!" Stephan dabbed at his eyes, mascara running down his cheeks and soaking into the red kerchief.

"Every time I call for you, you show up with some nonsense story and looking ridiculous! Now, the family may be in trouble. Have you seen Deveroy or Achar?" Contessa placed her hands upon her hips.

"Trouble? Oh my stars! Stephan is here to save the day!" He made a hand jester which removed his makeup. He stood and tucked the kerchief back in his bra. "I haven't seen those sweet things since I left to save the deer. Do you think they're in trouble? Oh, I would hate for anything to happen to them. They are adorable, those two!"

Nathan interrupted. "Everyone is on their way. Stephan, the family is in trouble. I need you to stop your goofing around. You know Contessa doesn't like it when you wear dresses. Now I'm gonna get mad if I have to ask again." Nathan placed the cell phone into his pocket.

Stephan saluted to Nathan and spun around *Wonder Woman* style and made a loud thunder crack. With his hands on his hips he stood proud in his new US Civil war costume. "I am at your service!" He pointed to Contessa. "She was mean to me…said I looked like a giant potato in a lace potato sack. It was very hurtful."

"Well now, a man of your size really shouldn't be wearing lace now should he?" Nathan turned to his wife. "You really should try and be nicer. Stephan has always been there for us."

Contessa shook her head and rolled her eyes. "I'm sorry Stephan. I shouldn't have been so rude. Next time, will you please come as soon as I summon you?"

"No one can do it that fast honey." Stephan rolled his eyes and straightened his uniform.

Nathan laughed. "Stephan, listen to me. Lamia will be here soon and if you don't want to see her, let me tell you what I need you to do for us." He took Contessa by the shoulder and hugged her close.

"Lamia! That Bitch! I want to a see her like I want to see someone eating monkey brains." Stephan scrunched his face and rolled out his tongue, shook his shoulders and then stood at attention.

"Good, now listen up. We need you to go to Azzurra's house. I trust you to be discreet. A Vicar may be lurking around. He'll be investigating a Disbursement Charm Achar cast upon Katie."

"Oh my Stars, a Disbursement Charm! That's awful! Cute little Achar cast such a…wait a minute. He doesn't have the power for such a spell, the poor thing, always trying to play with the grownups." He pulled out a nail file and began working on one of his thumbs. "Katie! Oh my stars. I'm going to get to see Katie! I always thought she had such beautiful hair!" Stephan placed the nail file back into the pocket of the uniform and looked up into the ceiling.

Nathan narrowed his eyes. "You are not to approach Katie if you see her. The purpose is to find out if Azzurra has had contact with Katie and if they have cast any protective enchantments around the house. We think they may have found out that we've been haunting Olivia all these years."

"Well now, that is just a mean thing to do, now isn't it? I told both of you not to haunt that poor thing. God only knows she could have had a beautiful marriage without all that interference. I still can't believe sweet Deveroy and Achar agreed to haunt them…very shameful."

"We know all that…" Nathan began.

"…what about Vincent? My Vincent…" Contessa began.

"…Oh for the love of Egypt, if I hear about Vincent one more time!" He placed a hand on his hip. "Contessa, that was over forty years ago. Poor Olivia had nothing to do with it and neither did Walter. If the two of you had any brains you would have gone after Basil. He's the one that should pay for all of this. I never met him personally, but I'm told he's very cute!"

Contessa looked to Nathan and flung her hands in the air. "Nathan?"

"Stephan, I understand what you're saying and unfortunately I think you're right. We did a lot of things wrong. We called off the haunting. Did you know anything about Culls being placed at the house?" Nathan took his wife's hand and squeezed.

"Culls!" Stephan screamed and fell to his knees! He placed his hands in his thick, wavy, dark hair and screamed again, then stood and straightened his uniform. "No. I know nothing about Culls. Ask that bitch, Lamia. She probably placed them."

"I'll check with Lamia. She'll be here any minute. Let me make this fast. You should go to the neighbor's houses first. Pretend you're just people watching and then go to Azzurra's. Keep an eye out for a Vicar. They wear all white and are very powerful beings."

"I know what a Vicar looks like. Most are extremely handsome. I don't think this outfit is right." He looked down to his US Civil War costume. "Now, there is no danger, is there? I won't have to fight anybody, will I?"

"There should be no danger. Now run along before Lamia gets here. Thank you, Stephan. Thank you for doing this." Nathan took Stephan by the shoulders and smiled. "Be safe now."

"Be safe? You just said there would be no danger! That's it! I'm wearing the wrong outfit! I need something extravagant?" Stephan smiled and made a dramatic hand jester.

The theme to *Lawrence of Arabia* filled the room. Stephan unsheathed a sword and let out a loud note of a high "C". He stood in his new outfit... an Egyptian uniform of ancient times with a beautiful embroidered purple headdress. "Now I think I need a camel. Don't worry, I'll make him smallish."

"Oh my word, a camel? I just vacuumed! Nathan, really?" Contessa walked away from them.

Nathan chuckled. "Stephan hurry, Lamia will be here any minute. Send me word the moment you know if anything has happening."

"My camel is outside. I'm sure he's offended too. Off to war...a safe war that is!" Stephan bowed and then vanished.

* * * *

Lamia

Lamia appeared, turned solid and acknowledged Nathan and Contessa. Soft locks of dark wavy hair cascaded over her shoulders. Red lips revealed a sensual, innocent and captivating smile. Her face resembled a porcelain doll, an Angel. She was 43 years of age when she took her last breath and for two hundred and forty seven years she explored the Earth and all it had to offer. It was rare for younger women to achieve the type of seductiveness she exuded, confidence...manipulation. Her skin, soft and silky, poured into one of the most beautiful dresses Contessa had ever seen. White silk and lace woven together caressed a strong, curvaceous body. Lamia stood before them, absolutely refined, classic, sexy and stunning. The only flaw that beheld this gorgeous creature was her lack of empathy or concern for any living creature, other than herself.

Lamia spoke. "Contessa...Nathan, Celia informed us of the matter at hand. She and Alfonso are on their way."

Four Spirits appeared. Two men flanked Lamia, while two women stood to the rear.

"Thank you, Lamia." Contessa nodded slightly to each of the family Spirits that appeared. "Damiano, Marcus, Medeia and Dormava...always good to see you." They all acknowledged her with a slight bow.

"How much has Celia told you?" Nathan moved forward.

"We understand that Katie has returned and there's been an attempt at a Disbursement Charm. We also understand that Azzurra may have been alerted to the interference with Olivia's life." Lamia slid a manicured red finger nail softly over the kitchen table.

Nathan spoke. "We need you to question the boys...Deveroy and Achar. They are missing and don't respond to Contessa's Summoning Charm." He turned to his wife.

"I'm worried. Deveroy has never gone a week without paying a visit." Contessa hooked arms with her husband.

Lamia brought a hand to her neck and lightly grazed her skin. A glance toward Damiano and then to Marcus prodded another smile. A sparkle twinkled in her eye. "You are attached to Deveroy by affection and esteem, are you not?"

Contessa said nothing

"Marcus, would you please bring the boys here so that I may question them." Lamia ordered.

Nathan and Contessa glanced toward each other.

Marcus crossed over to the living room. His green eyes narrowed as he pushed his fingers through his rumpled dark hair and away from his olive-skinned face. He took a deep sigh. His black T-shirt strained against a strong chest. When he spoke, it was with an Italian accent.

"I'll summon them. So as long as a powerful being is not holding them, they should appear." He rubbed his palms against his black jeans, an old habit when he was about to cast a spell that he did not want to cast.

Lamia narrowed her eyes. "Marcus, I asked you to cast the spell. Now would you please oblige me and stop rubbing your jeans. It looks foolish."

Marcus looked up to the ceiling, scratched the stubble of his square jaw line and closed his eyes. He spoke the incantation.

"Across the skies, I beckon thee
Come across, you cannot flee
I command to thee with the power that be

Achar and Deveroy appeared in front of Marcus. Achar stood while Deveroy appeared on his knees.

"Deveroy!" Contessa rushed to his side, knelt down and looked into his eyes. "Are you all right? What happened? I've been trying to summon you all day! Dear God, you look awful. Tell me what happened."

Deveroy turned solid and placed his arms around Contessa. He released her after a tight squeeze. "I'm fine." He looked to Achar, then around the room. Barely moving his lips, he spoke again. "I will tell you later." He brushed his long blonde hair away from his face, then stood and spoke to the room at large. "We are fine. We were at the pyramids…hoping to scare Stephan but we couldn't find him."

Contessa looked over to Achar. "Very well, perhaps you were simply out of range? That is rather far. Stephan did say he was at the Pyramids."

Silence filled the room for a brief moment. Lamia destroyed that silence. "Contessa, they were indeed within range. You are a powerful Witch and the summons should have reached them. They either ignored you or it was blocked." Her eyes glinted as they widened and then relaxed. "Now, Contessa dear, would you please allow me to question these handsome young men?" Lamia strode past Marcus and stood in front of Achar in Contessa's living room.

Deveroy brushed the sand from his faded blue jeans, made a hand movement and the sand evaporated. "Sorry." He spoke to Contessa. Achar turned solid and siphoned the sand from his thin body and the carpet.

"Lamia would like to ask…." Contessa began.

Lamia interrupted. "…the Disbursement Charm failed, as everyone realized it would. No offense dears." She circled the pair of them and placed a hand upon the shoulder of Achar, rubbed her thumb against the white material and looked into the young man's cold black eyes. "It was you who cast the spell, Achar." She glided a finger nail over his cheek, down his neck to a button of his shirt. Her finger pushed downward, releasing a button. She slid a hand into the tuffs of hair on his chest. She then placed a finger under his chin and angled his face upward. "You cast that spell and you failed. Did you know to whom you cast the spell upon?"

His eyes slid toward Deveroy, and then back to Lamia. "Yes I did, Katie, Olivia's mother."

"Did it occur to you that Katie will wonder why she was attacked when she attempted a visit to her daughter? A mother will investigate. I never had the instinct of motherhood myself. However, I do understand what a mother feels...what she thinks and how she reacts." She turned to face Deveroy. "Will she not wonder why she was attacked?"

Deveroy did not respond.

Damiano stepped forward and into the living room. He spoke to Achar. His tone was light and somewhat humorous. "Oh come on, the boys just thought they were doing the right thing...go light on them, will ya?"

Achar looked downward and then into Damiano eyes. "Yea, I thought I had enough power. I mean...I'm over a hundred years old." He looked over to Medeia and Dormava and smiled. "I guess not, eh."

"It's all right sweetheart. Damiano is right...no harm has been done." Media spoke.

Lamia placed several fingers into Achar's hair and stroked his long, dark mane. "You thought, because you are over a hundred years old, that you could cast a spell of that magnitude and not inform one of us before casting it? You thought nothing that the spell was cast upon the mother of a Witch we have been haunting for over three decade's?"

Achar gulped and looked toward Media and Dormava.

"Do not look to them for answers. Now, what made you attempted such a spell?" Lamia asked; her voice on the tinge of anger.

Achar crossed his arms over his chest. Lamia's fingers played with his dark locks. He stiffened. "We were interfering with Olivia and Walter, like we were told to do. I recognized her mother, Katie, speaking with another Spirit outside the neighbor's house. It was that stupid dog that saw us." His eyes narrowed and voice dropped. "I hate dogs. It barked and growled. That's when Katie looked over and saw us. I cast the Disbursement Charm to get rid of her. I read about it, it sounded like a cool spell. I didn't want her to find out that we've been haunting her daughter. It would have caused trouble." He shook his head to remove Lamia's hand. "It should have worked. I'm over a hundred years old!"

Lamia glanced to her dislodged hand and placed it back into his dark mane. Achar's lips tightened. She gently ran her fingers through his hair, down his forehead and over his nose. She rested a finger tip upon his full lips. "Shush, you are always making a fool of yourself." She traced a finger nail over his chest, around and under and then glided down his belly. "Does it hurt to think that Damiano thinks you a fool?"

"Lamia, please, let's not get..." Damiano began.

"Quiet! You and Medeia have not a clue as to what this could mean." Her eyes focused upon Achar's black eyes. "You thought that because you are over a hundred years old that you should have been able to cast such a powerful curse? You thought that you, a sniveling little boy, could possibly cast a spell of that measure?"

Damiano released a deep sigh and took a few steps forward. Contessa grabbed Nathan's arm, pulled him nearer and looked up to him. Dormava and Medeia took a few steps closer.

Nathan cleared his throat. "Let us focus at the matter at hand, Lamia."

"I am, dear Nathan, I am." She looked up to the ceiling and then traced a finger nail down Achar's arm.

Deveroy looked to Contessa, eyes pleading.

"Lamia, please be nice." Contessa said. "There is no need to be condescending and rude."

"I am being nice. I have not struck him for his stupidity, have I?" Lamia smiled. She leaned down and peered into Achar's eyes. "You are a pathetic little boy who tries to play with the adults. The question would remain; do you offer anything that anyone would be pleased by? I think not. Not even when you were alive did anyone desire you for very long. I am sure they were disappointed after getting to know you…physically or mentally. You are a handsome little toy, I must admit. However, you have nothing that would interest anyone who possesses skill or brains. You are a sniveling snot-nosed brat that lacks the power of controlling your desires, hiding your fears and asking for assistance when it is needed!" She grabbed his mane and forced him to his knees.

"Contessa, please!" Deveroy pleaded.

"Nathan?" Contessa spoke.

Nathan shook his head. Damiano stepped in front of Deveroy.

"Not one person is coming to your aid. They know you deserve this. Contessa is only upset because it distresses her beloved Deveroy. The mothering ladies are waiting cautiously in the kitchen. And Marcus, well, he is in his own world. Damiano has moved slightly closer to Deveroy, not you."

"This is making everyone uncomfortable. Please stop this Lamia. You are being mean and cruel." Contessa placed a hand upon Deveroy's shoulder.

Nathan took Tessa's arm and moved her closer to him.

"Cruel? I am not being cruel. If honesty and the truth are cruel, well then so be it. But everything I said is simply the truth." Lamia said.

She turned to face Achar. "I don't mean to be cruel sweetheart; it's just that you annoy me so incredibly, that at times I could peel off your skin and just listen to you scream, simply to clam my annoyance." She placed a hand upon his handsome cheek. "But I won't sweetheart." She gently pushed into his chest. He stumbled backward and bumped into the sofa. She took in a deep breath and placed her hands on her hips. "You may have ruined all that I have worked for! Damiano and Medeia do not understand the consequences of your idiotic actions. You cast that spell for what? To try and impress this puppy dog you found?" She flung a hand toward Deveroy. No, no, of course not...puppies are cute but not enough to impress. No, it was not to impress him." She turned to address the room. "Ah, but if it is not he you choose to impress, then who?" She slid a finger down Achar's cheek and rested it upon his lips. "Damiano, doesn't really like you and his attentions are else ware, the ladies do nothing but mother you...so it must be Marcus."

"Lamia, I will ask you for the last time to stop this torment! I will not have this in my home!" Contessa cautioned.

Medeia stepped into the living room. She flung her dark hair over a shoulder and looked to Lamia. She placed a hand upon her hip, red leather stretching across her voluptuous body. "Let's not get nasty, there is no need for such words ..." Lamia cut her off and made sweeping arm gesture. Medeia's body rose three feet and flew across the room and into the kitchen's drywall. Her body flopped to the ground and lie still.

"Stop this! Stop this immediately!" Contessa flung a hand forward and swished it in a half circle toward Lamia. Lamia raised a hand but was forced to lower it to her side. "You will not attack anyone in my home! We are all on the same side and you will not treat Medeia or any other Spirit with such contempt! Do I make myself clear?" Her fingers splayed in the direction of Lamia's face.

Nathan shook his head.

Dormava hurried to the aide of Medeia, who struggled to her feet. Damiano reached for Deveroy and pulled him away from Lamia.

Lamia narrowed her eyes. "I'm sorry, Madam. I'm not sure what came over me. You know I get a temper rather quickly." Lamia's voice became deep and monotone. She knew that Contessa had the power of Spirits...the power to control the dead. She also knew that Contessa came from one of the most power family of Witches the United States had ever seen.

Contessa spoke, an edge to her voice. "I don't need Deveroy or my wand to have you do my bidding. Apologize to Medeia."

"Tessa, don't." Nathan warned.

Lamia's eyes narrowed and she smiled with a slight curl to her red lips. "Why Contessa, when did you realize that you don't need a Spirit in your wand for such a powerful spell?" Contessa said nothing. Lamia turned to face Medeia. 'I am sorry, Medeia. Are you hurt dear?"

"How dare you do that to me?" Medeia escaped Dormava's attempt at holding her back and rushed toward Lamia. Dormava swore. Contessa's arm flung toward Medeia, making another half moon with her hand. "Do not attempt to retaliate! I will not have this in my home!" Medeia froze and calmed.

Lamia strode over to Damiano, gently touching his chest. "Release Deveroy, would you dear. I have some questions for him. I sense that he has had contact with someone, and that someone is the reason they did not respond to Contessa's summons."

Everyone looked to Deveroy.

Deveroy inched behind Damiano while Damiano squared off to block Lamia. Marcus held up a hand to Dormava and Medeia.

"Lamia, I realize that Achar may have interrupted a process, a process in which I am not sure I understand. Katie may think it is a simple random haunting. Olivia's negative energy would have been a beacon for other negative energies. So Achar's presence and he attacking Katie was simply a matter of time. The only reason why other Spirits have not closed in on her home is because we forbid it. Katie will understand this. She will know how depressed and negative Olivia is." Contessa looked to Nathan and then back to Lamia. "However, Nathan and I agreed to stop the haunting. Enough is enough. So I do not see the reason for your temper, unless I do not know everything. Now tell me, what is going on?" After a few seconds Contessa spayed her fingers and twisted her wrist. "Answer me!"

Lamia's eyes narrowed, her mouth contorted as she spoke, low and deep. "I am angry at such stupidity. It is he who will be angry — he who has the plan." She again attempted to raise a hand, but her body would not agree to her minds demands. She swore under her breath.

"Who are you talking about? Who will be angry?" Contessa's wrist flipped and she stabbed at Lamia.

Lamia closed her eyes tightly and began to speak. "The…

"…it is my fault. Please, I'm sorry. I should have never attempted such a spell. Forgive me, Lamia. I'm sorry." Achar's black eyes searched the room for support, they feel upon Deveroy.

Contessa relaxed her arm. "Of course this is your fault…and I'll tell you another thing, Achar. You are to never enter my home again without Nathan present or without Deveroy. Do I make myself clear?"

"Yes." His eyes darted quickly to Lamia.

Contessa turned and spoke to the room at large. "I may be old, but I'm a Degeli. And don't any of you forget that!"

"Madam!" Lamia's voice had become even and sweet. She glanced toward Achar, and then continued. "I have upset you and I am sorry for that. Let me take the boys elsewhere for questioning. Shall I fix your home?"

"I will fix the damage you caused. Thank you, Lamia…and thank you for that apology." Contessa gave a nod to her Spirit. "Where will you take them? You will be kind…no violence?"

"Of course I shall. Your command is my wish." She curtly gave a nod. "Marcus will see to it, that I am kind. Won't you, Marcus dear?"

"Yes." He rubbed his jeans with the palm of his hand.

"All settled then. I shall have Deveroy back to you by this evening so you two may chat — attached together by affection and esteem, how sweet." She turned and motioned for everyone to come closer. "Oh and I expect to hear the results of Stephan's inquiry with Azzurra."

Medeia and Dormava stepped into the living room. One dressed in red leather, the other in black. Achar and Deveroy looked to Damiano.

"It was nice to see you again." Damiano shrugged his shoulders.

Lamia spoke. "Very well then, everyone ready?"

"I'll see you this evening Deveroy." Contessa smiled to him and lightly touched his shoulder. He smiled back.

Lamia raised an arm high above her head. One by one, they all turned to Spirit form. "Until this evening, Contessa." She, Damiano, Marcus, Dormava, Medeia and the boys vanished.

"Contessa, you should not have treated her that way." Nathan approached his wife.

"And be belittled in my own home?" Contessa retorted. "Deveroy will tell me what's going on this evening. He whispered to me."

Nathan spoke. "Something is wrong with Lamia. I know you have fought before, but this was different. Who was she talking about? Who is going to be angry? Who did the boys speak with that blocked your summons? She's up to something and we are clueless."

Contessa's eyes darted over the room. "I don't know. That damn Achar spoke and I became distracted." She raised a hand to her lips. "You're right Nathan, something is going on."

"I think it was a mistake to have controlled her like that. She may decide to no longer be in our service." Nathan looked into his wife's face.

"Of course she is in our service. You saw her. She couldn't do a thing. She'd best remember that before she hurts Deveroy. She wouldn't dare hurt him, would she?" Contessa looked to the floor, then to her husband. "Oh Nathan, should I have let her take him? What if you're right? What if she hurts Deveroy? What if I am losing control?"

"I shouldn't have said anything. Deveroy will be fine." Nathan rubbed her shoulders.

"You're right, Nathan. I'm a Degeli. One of the most powerful Witch's the world has seen this century. I have the power of Spirits. I am the only one in my family that has that power. I am a Degeli. There is nothing Lamia or any other Spirit can do about that." Contessa rested her head into her husband chest, sighed and then whispered, "God help us if I'm wrong."

* * * *

The Degeli Family

The brisk breeze felt refreshing as the woman snipped off the dead heads of the orange mums. She noticed a silver Chevy Traverse, pull into the driveway across the street. She didn't recognize the SUV, but when the woman exited the vehicle, she knew at once who had pulled into Azzurra's driveway. Eleanor stood and called out a hello.

"Oh, hello Eleanor, how are you?" Arianna replied.

"I'm well, thank you. Just pruning my mums, how are you? How's Azzurra doing? Mary said she spoke with her the other day...I hope everything is OK." Eleanor stepped across her yard and waved hello to Mateo.

"I'm fine, thank you. Azzurra's holding up well. Just a family get-together, you know, being supportive during a rough time. She misses Franco. You remember my husband, Mateo?" Arianna motioned.

"Of course I do. Well, do tell Azzurra that the ladies are all waiting on a nice game of pinochle when she's back on her feet." She waved again as she headed back to her flower bed. "It was nice to see you Arianna...Mateo."

Arianna and Mateo replied that it was nice to see her too and headed to Azzurra's front porch. "Do you think I look too dull? Maybe I should have worn something brighter, more cheerful?"

"You look beautiful. I think the colors are fine. It's September." Mateo rang the bell.

"Mateo honey, I forgot the cookies in the car. Would you grab them for me?" Arianna adjusted the maroon shawl around her shoulders.

"I'll get them." Mateo made his way down the porch, unlocked the SUV and opened the door.

"Katie!" Arianna screamed. Mateo looked around to see that Katie had opened the door to greet her sister.

"Arianna...shush!" Mateo called out. He looked toward Eleanor who froze during a snip, mouth gaping as she looked across the street, stretching her neck. He looked back to the front porch; both Arianna and Katie had entered the home. He hurried into the house.

"Katie you should not have opened the door!" Mateo gave his sister-in -law a hug.

"I forgot I'm dead and not supposed to be seen. What are you going do?" Katie hooked Mateo's out stretched arm and escorted him into the kitchen. "You look so handsome Mateo! You've aged well, honey."

Mateo placed the cookies on the table and looked down to his sister-in-law. He may have aged well but to him he was still old. His skin had not the same strong, smooth tone as in youth. His blue eyes still sparkled, although it wasn't with the excitement of life, it was with the knowledge of life — very different. Mateo still maintained a strong, solid build. He ran four miles once a week, stretched and did yoga with Arianna. "This aging thing sucks, Katie." He ran his fingers through his thick grey hair and looked down to Katie. He smirked. "But then again, what's the alternative?" He paused and tapped Katie's nose. "You look beautiful, Katie."

"Arianna says you've been a wonderful husband, patient, kind and loving. I've seen your Scott, just as handsome as his father, and he married a beautiful wife and the children are wonderful."

"Well, Katie, I have a secret to tell you." He smiled over to Arianna who was chatting with Azzurra at the kitchen sink. Azzurra was showing her the pewter cat and a soap dispenser. Arianna stood with her hands clasped over her mouth. "We've been married for over 45 years and I'm still crazy about her and I will always feel lucky to have had her as my wife."

Katie beamed. "Oh Mateo, she feels the same." They hugged again as the front door opened.

Gabriella called out. "Azzurra, the door was opened honey, so we thought we would walk in? What's the matter with Eleanor across the street? I waved hi but she's kneeling in front of a mum with her mouth wide opened. She never said a word."

Azzurra hugged Mateo quickly as she made her way to the front door. "Nicolai honey, you don't need to take off your shoes. Its fine, come on in." Azzurra greeted her brother-in-law with a hug.

"Nicolai honey, good to see you. It's Katie's fault. She opened the door to let Arianna in and now Eleanor's in shock." Azzurra swished a hand through the air. "I told her to be careful, but does she listen?"

Gabriella placed her purse on the *Bokja* chair and turned to face her sister. "You're mad at me, aren't you?" She crossed her arms. Gabriella wore a beautiful black pant suit with a stunning blazer, diamond earrings and a garnet and silver broach. Her thin legs took a stance of defiance as she glared at her sister.

"Don't start with me Gabriella. I'm the one who lost a husband and have you bothered to call to see if I'm dead or alive? I'll tell you. No, you have not! I'm hurt that not one of my sisters will take the time out of their day to give me a call and ask how I'm getting along without Franco!" Azzurra turned and slapped Nicolai on his shoulder.

Gabriella relaxed. "Oh Azzurra, I just figured that if you wanted to talk, you would call me. You're always the one who makes the phone…"

"…I don't want to hear it! If you don't start picking up that damn phone, I'm gonna be mad!" She looked to Nicolai and slapped his arm. "If your husband died, I'd be sure to call you." Azzurra took in a breath. "Now, let's not fight. I'm not mad. Katie is dying to see you." Azzurra stood back and shook her head. "Gabriella honey, you look beautiful. How do you do it?"

"I'm sorry. I will call you, I promise." She gave her sister a hug. "Well, it's an all day job Azzurra and I'm exhausted. It cost a fortune but I'm fighting age with every cent I have!" She shook her dark hair. The short bob bounced back into place, leaving a slight curl at the ends. Gabriella laughed and leaned against Nicolai.

"I keep telling her that enough is enough. I'm afraid that one of these days she'll come home and I won't recognize her. Thank God, she still looks like a human being." Nicolai laughed.

"Where's is she? Where's Katie?" Gabriella's feet took her toward the kitchen. "Katie! Katie!

The kitchen erupted with screams.

"You had better make her call me Nicolai or you're going to hear from me." Azzurra leaned up and gave him a kiss on his cheek. "You look good sweetheart. You did something to your eyes?"

Nicolai opened his black eyes wider. "She thought I could use a little Botox. I had a little tuck under the chin too. She wants me to dye my hair, but I think grey looks good on me."

"Oh Botox…It looks so natural. No one would ever believe you're in your seventies, and Gabriella looks stunning, no one would take her for 68 either. It's expensive though, isn't it?" Azzurra looked closely at Nicolai.

"Let's just say that if I hadn't made the money over the years, we'd both look like hell." Nicolai rolled his eyes and adjusted his brown tweed jacket.

"Well, let's go say hi to Katie." Azzurra hooked his arm. "That rust color shirt with that jacket is very handsome Nicolai."

They entered the kitchen and Katie rushed to hug Nicolai. Gabriella was dabbing her eyes with a tissue and holding Arianna's hand.

"The door was open. We're coming in." A gruff voice spoke.

Azzurra rushed to the front door, telling Katie to stay in the kitchen.

"What the hell is all that screaming about?" The gruff voice came again.

"It's called a greeting Augusto. You should try it sometime." Father Bernardo spoke. His arms opened to hug Azzurra. Azzurra gave him a cold hug.

"Now don't be mad. If you came to church, I would have asked how you were getting along without Franco." Father Bernardo looked over his round glasses to Azzurra

"So I have to go to church to get a phone call from my cousin the priest! You don't have enough brains to think that maybe I wasn't up to going to church." Her hands flew to her hips.

Augusto interrupted the Father. "Oh, would you shut up about Franco. For years you've always called us. It's your own damn fault for always making the calls. You spoiled us! Now, it's going to take some time to adjust. I see you're getting along without Franco just fine. You're breathing." Augusto kissed Azzurra on the cheek and slowly made his way to the kitchen.

Azzurra flushed. "Augusto..."

Father Bernardo took her by the arm and gently guided her back. "Leave him Azzurra. He's been miserable. Can't stop with the Anna thing...day and night. He called me last night at 1:00 in the morning to tell me he is hearing her voice again. Please, be patient Azzurra."

"I'll be patient when I put a pan over his head! There is no need to be that rude." Azzurra turned and almost knocked her cousin over. "Oh Father, I'm sorry, are you all right? He's lucky Katie didn't hear him. She has no patience with him." Azzurra adjusted Father Bernardo's black cap upon his thin grey hair. "You look cute Father. Look at you? Are you shrinking?"

"Thank you Azzurra and yes, I think I am shrinking. I think I should have gone to your chiropractor like you suggested. I would have been better off. My back is giving me problems." Father Bernardo adjusted his collar to let some air into his neck. "Oh, it's warm in here." He began to remove his beige sweater that revealed his priestly attire.

"I turned the temperature up, Gabriella gets cold. I'll make you an appointment with the Chiropractor. Now Father, Gabriella and Nicolai are here. No word about face lifts or how they should just age gracefully. They are fighting age with every dime they have." Azzurra placed his sweater on the chair.

"I told them before that they need to age gracefully. Let them age the way God intended. She doesn't look like a plastic doll, does she?" Father took Azzurra's arm.

"No Father, she and Nicolai look wonderful. Now, don't say anything." Azzurra looked into his grey eyes.

"I promise not to mention a thing. Now where's Katie? I have to make sure she hasn't killed Augusto." Azzurra escorted him to the kitchen.

Gabriella stood blocking her husband from Augusto. Nicolai spoke over his wife's head. "How dare you speak to my wife like that? Just because you look like hell at your old age doesn't mean she has to. Gabriella, move! I'm gonna bash his brains in!"

"Enough!" Father Bernardo's voice, tiny but effective, interrupted. "There will be no bashing of brains! I can't leave you alone for a minute and you're rude to someone. Now sit down at the table and be quiet!" Father approached Gabriella. "You look beautiful Gabby. Just ignore him."

Katie spoke across the room. "I tell you one thing Augusto; you're a mean old bastard. I haven't seen you in forty years and that's the greeting I get?"

She glared at him. "I'll tell you another thing, you talk to Gabriella like that again and you'll regret it."

Father Bernardo defused the tension with an elaborate display of affection for Katie. Augusto grumbled something at the table. Arianna sat next to him and held his aged hand, assuring him that they are trying to figure out a spell that would bring Anna back.

Basil appeared and greeted the family. Hugs and kisses were given and more tears spilled. Augusto tried to see who had appeared but couldn't distinguish his features. He adjusted his glasses and spoke. "Who's Drasil?"

"Basil, honey, Basil is here. You remember, Azzurra's Wand Spirit." Arianna answered.

"Oh, hi Basil, how are you, my dear boy?" Augusto shouted. He tried to stand and fell back into his seat. Arianna smoothed out his navy turtleneck and told him to sit still.

"Well now, if it isn't Augusto. Still annoying the ladies, I see." Basil smiled and bent down to shake Augusto's hand. Augusto nodded and said hello.

Basil enlarged the table and added chairs, as everyone seated themselves. Azzurra took the seat at the head. "I forgot to start the coffee." She began to rise.

"Beee...this girl, you'd think she never knew Magick." Katie waved an arm and steaming cups of coffee appeared before everyone. Cream and sugar appeared with some Italian cookies, a relish tray and dip.

"Thank you Katie. I forgot." Azzurra began to fix herself some coffee.

Katie rolled her eyes. "We're all dead."

Everyone laughed. "Oh, Katie stop it, I'm fine." The next several minutes were filled with laughter and exaggeration on Azzurra forgetting something and killing them all.

"Who brought these?" Augusto pulled the cellophane off the tray of cookie. He bit into the cookie and spit it out in a napkin. "Damn it, Arianna, these must be yours! You mixed up the salt and sugar again! What the hell is the matter with you? Never learned to cook or bake!"

Mateo was on his feet. "I'm going to knock your head in that wall you old, balding bastard!" Arianna placed a hand on his arm and asked him to please sit.

"Who do you think you're insulting? That's my wife?" Mateo charged.

"Well, she's my sister and these cookies are garbage." Augusto ignored Katie and Father Bernardo. Azzurra began to curse at her brother. Nicolai and Gabriella told him that he's nothing but a mean old man. Mateo tried to get around Basil, who blocked him from getting to Augusto. Arianna stood, slammed a hand on the table and spoke to a silent room.

"Augusto is right! I should never have tried to bake cookies today. My mind was on Anna, and Katie and the Witches War. I was distracted...I'm always a bit distracted. Mateo, sit please and don't upset me. I will handle my brother. Basil, everyone...please sit." She looked down to Augusto who held his head down. "I'm going to tell you something Augusto. When I woke this morning, my heart fluttered thinking that I was going to see Katie again today. I wanted this one time to bake cookies that were good, that tasted sweet and were soft and chewy. I burned the first batch, broke the blender, broke two bowls and jammed the new blender." Her eyes began to fill with tears. "I did not! And will never! Give up the attempt to bake something nice for my family. Because it's about the love of family! It's about, that not once has my husband or my son complained about my cooking." Tears streamed down her cheeks. "I bake to express myself. I bake because I love to give to people. Do I wish I was a good baker? Sure I do. But it hurts me to be insulted by you Augusto! And I will tell you this much. You ever insult me again...I will not stop my husband from pounding your head into the $@#!ing wall!" Arianna sand into Mateo's chest and began to cry.

"Beee, everyone is saying the "F" word and they complain about my swearing." Katie swished a hand through the air.

Augusto took a gulp and looked up to the room. Every person and Spirit stared at him with contempt. Father Bernardo made the sign of the cross. Basil was the only one standing, arms folded and looking down at Augusto. He gently laid a hand upon his sister's back. "I'm sorry, Arianna. Please, don't be upset. You're right. I am an old bitter fool. Can you forgive me sweetheart?"

Arianna lifted her head from Mateo's chest, turned to her brother and hugged him.

Basil spoke to the room. "Well now, this went like every Degeli family gathering I've been to. Hysterical laughter, a bit of cursing, threats across the table and tears. Now, what do you say we discuss the real reason for the family meeting? We are in grave danger and need to discuss defending ourselves and our loved ones." He took a seat next to Mateo. Eyes focused on one person...Azzurra.

* * * *

Breaking the Vow

Azzurra began to describe the events that took place since Sunday. Marta's meeting during morning coffee, the meeting with Contessa and Celia, all the way through the attack on Katie. The family sat and listened without interruption. When she finished, Azzurra took a sip of coffee and waited for a response.

Gabriella spoke first. "I know the Spirits that attacked Katie, they are Achar and Deveroy. One has long dark hair, the other has long blonde. I saw Deveroy a few years back on a visit with Tessa. He seems like a nice boy, can't imagine him casting such a spell. Achar, however, is a nuisance, up to no good. Tessa can't stand him." Gabriella took a few carrots and placed it on a napkin.

"I think I remember him…" Father Bernardo began.

"…there she goes again! Deveroy tried to destroy Katie. A piece of her arm is missing, and you think he's a sweet boy!" Augusto turned to face his sister.

"I did not say that Augusto." Gabriella warned.

219

Nicolai, her husband, raised his voice. "Augusto, she is simply stating that Deveroy does not seem the type to cast such a spell and I agree. I've met him several times..."

Katie shook her head and interrupted. "...so are we saying that the Spirit who has haunted my family for forty-one years is a precious darling, a sweet innocent boy?"

Azzurra responded. "Of course not, Katie, now don't get upset. Let's move this along. We are all familiar with Achar and Deveroy. The thing we need to focus on is who is giving the orders or are they acting on their own accord. The Vicar spoke to the boys. He does not believe that Deveroy cast the spell and as far as they are aware, the Vicar was investigating a Discombob...oh whatever that spell's name is." Azzurra looked at Father Bernardo when he choked on his cookie.

"Vicar...that's right. That's what I wanted to say." He cleared his throat. "What is a Vicar involved in a family of Witches for?" Father Bernardo turned to Basil. "Basil, why is there a Vicar involved?"

Augusto spoke. "There should be no reason why a Vicar is involved..."

"...quiet Augusto, let Basil answer." Father Bernardo interrupted.

"Well, Mum and Miss Katie feel it's odd as well, but I see no reason why he should not be involved." Basil looked to Azzurra.

"Why not, honey?" Azzurra asked.

"Because he needs to keep balance, Miss Katie has already said how powerful she thinks the family has become. Olivia defended herself against a level two or three demon without a wand. Do I need to say more?" Basil looked to the room.

"Well, of course you need to say more, my boy. I don't understand." Augusto responded.

Father Bernardo spoke. "I was afraid of this. Basil is right. I should have seen it myself. The family must have grown in power. With that power, comes greed for more power. Something that would cause catastrophic plight to mortals must be at stake. Someone more powerful than Contessa is calling the shots."

Katie responded to Basil. "Basil, we asked you earlier if you thought anything was odd about the Vicar and you said no."

Everyone looked to Basil. "Well, Miss Katie, there is nothing odd about the Vicar. I've said nothing new, now have I?" Basil's eyes shifted down to Blackie.

"Basil, answer Katie please." Azzurra asked.

"Mum, please don't ask. I will not answer. I've given my word." Basil looked to the room. "I've taken an oath to protect the family. I've spoken to the Vicar...yes that is true...but I've sworn to him that I would not repeat what we've discussed. Why do you think I keep pressing upon you that we need to fight? We need to teach the kids Magick and everyone must prepare for the biggest Witches War this century has seen."

Father Bernardo raised his voice. "Teach the kids! You will not teach the kids Magick! We shall pray for guidance and ask God to protect us. I cannot believe that a Vicar would suggest a family of Witches to use Magick!"

Mateo spoke. "Not teach the kids! Are you out of your mind, Father?" Arianna placed a hand on her husband's.

"We'd all be killed." Nicolai added.

"I agree. It's odd that a Vicar would suggest using Magick." Augusto said.

Katie shook her head. "We have to teach the family. All of you need to take up your wands, sachets and elixirs and cast your most powerful enchantments, if you all hope to live through this war."

"I agree with Katie," Gabriella and Arianna replied.

Azzurra placed her elbows upon the table. "All right, Basil. I wish you would have said something but I understand. Now, let's not fight. According to the Vicar, Deveroy and Achar think that he was investigating that spell that I can't remember the damn name of. We have time, but we need to act fast. I think we are all in agreement that we need to break the vow and teach our kids how to defend themselves."

"We are not in agreement!" Father Bernardo slammed a hand on the table. "If you break that vow, you'll be punished! Using Magick will bring evil into this family. I won't have it!"

Gabriella's voice rose. "We don't have a choice Father. Magick isn't evil. It's the people that are evil!"

Katie looked to the Father. "The Higher Spirits have given permission for us to break the vow and the Vicar thinks we should take up Magick and defend ourselves. Basil is right. We need to listen to him Father."

"The Higher Spirits?" Father Bernardo shook his head. "We are all in grave danger. Something evil is coming for this family." He made the sign of the cross.

Azzurra spoke. "Father, don't be upset. We're strong. We can defend the kids and teach them how to protect themselves." She patted his hand.

"I won't do it Azzurra. I won't use Magick." Father Bernardo looked down.

"We don't expect you to Father…but your words of prayer will mean a lot to us. You'll do that for us, won't you?" Arianna asked.

Everyone looked to her and then to the priest.

"I will. I will say many prayers and ask for guidance." Father responded.

"I'm worried about Nathan." Everyone's eyes turned to Nicolai. "Think about it. I even know that Achar isn't powerful enough to have cast that spell. Nathan will figure the same. He will wonder what happened to Katie, and what will she think about being attacked outside her daughter's house." Nicolai looked to Azzurra.

"Well, Nicolai, we have to have faith that things will be stalled enough to get us ready for the war," Azzurra replied.

"What about her?" Augusto nodded to Gabriella.

Katie's eyes narrowed as she looked to her brother. "What do you mean, what about her?"

"Miss big mouth over here caused a mess in the last Witches War because she couldn't keep her damn mouth shut." Augusto grunted.

Gabriella began swearing but was interrupted by her husband.

"…enough!" Azzurra slammed a hand on the table. "Gabriella, honey, I love you but Augusto has a point. Do you give your word not to speak to Contessa?"

"I'm about to turn your head into a boil, Augusto!" Katie threatened.

"Shush, Katie. Gabriella honey, do you swear?" Azzurra looked to Nicolai, then back to Gabriella.

"Of course I do. You know, Augusto, I didn't mean to cause…" Gabriella began.

"…good that settles it. Augusto, if you say one more word about Gabriella, I'll let Katie do whatever she wants to you." Azzurra waved a finger at her brother. Augusto rolled his eyes and looked to Father Bernardo.

Basil spoke. "Very well then, Nicco, Marta and Marie will be over this evening to get a crash course on Magick. Mateo, you'll need to tell your son,

Scott. Nicolai, you'll need to speak with your daughter, Eva. We should call Kimberly and Drago. The San Francisco and New York families need to be called as well."

Mateo and Nicolai nodded.

Gabriella looked to Father Bernardo then to Basil. "Arianna and I have agreed to help train Nicco, Marie and Marta since we feel they are in the most danger. We'll be doing it this evening. Our husbands will take care of the kids. Father, I think you should call the family."

Father Bernardo nodded.

Arianna spoke. "Katie, I think you should go to Olivia and Carlotta. They've already attacked Olivia once."

Azzurra added. "The Vicar has agreed to be Olivia's and Walter's Guardian. Her family will be fine. You should focus on Carlotta...although I don't think she's in danger."

Father Bernardo whispered the word Guardian and shook his head.

Katie looked under the table and then up to the family. "I agree, I'll go to Carlotta, but not until we train Azzurra's kids. Olivia is safe; the Vicar will be with her. Nathan knows that I would go straight to Azzurra if I found out that Olivia was being haunted. Her kids are in the most danger. Father Bernardo, *I* should go to New York and San Francisco. This is not the kind of news to deliver over the phone." She looked into the living room and then over her shoulder. "Blackie? Where the hell are you?"

"Very well, Basil, I want you to look in on Carlotta. Make sure there is nothing funny going on." Azzurra took a sip of coffee. "Have you found some Spirits to assist us? What about the spell to bring Anna back?"

"I have four comrades, two of which I need to speak with. The rest are gathering some things and will be here by late this eve or early morning... very trustworthy. I'd give my soul for them." Basil looked to the priest, then back to Azzurra. "I think I may have found a spell. Augusto?" Basil made a hand movement toward him. "I've place the spell in your front pocket, read it and cast it the next time you hear Anna's voice."

Augusto looked up and spoke with a cracked voice. "Thank you my boy."

"Thank you Basil." Azzurra smiled.

Blackie bolted into the room and growled toward the kitchen window.

"Something is approaching. Everyone, protect yourselves!" Basil shouted.

223

An Army of Demons

Medeia moaned, smeared her dark locks away from her face and lifted her head. A sandy beach lay before her. Palms, willows, white pines, red cedars and fig trees created a peninsula. The crash of a large wave turned her attention to the lagoon. Markus swam in her direction. She pushed herself up, feeling the pain of being slammed into the earth. After wetting her lips, she lowered the zipper of her jumpsuit several inches and then shielded her eyes from the sun. The heat beat against the red leather. Dabbing her brow with the back of her palm, she pivoted to the right. Her long-time companion, Dormava, trudged across the sand in her direction. Medeia's eyes scanned the other side of the beach. She spotted Damiano, striping off his black leather jacket and flinging it over a shoulder. After noticing her, he plodded his way through the sand in her direction. A snapping of a branch swayed her attention toward the trees. Deveroy and Achar lumbered their way toward her. Darting her eyes over the lagoon, her heart calmed, Lamia was nowhere in sight.

"Are you all right?" Dormava's voice carried over the heated breeze.

"I'm fine...exhausted, but all right." Medeia replied. "Dormava, you're unbuckled."

Dormava looked down and snapped a large buckle that revealed two inches of skin near her mid-drift. She carried her black spike heels in one hand and began to brush the sand from her black leather jumpsuit with the other. She winced in pain and placed the free hand to her head.

"Is everyone alright?" Damiano's eyes squinted as he fought to catch his breath. His hands braced against his knees.

Their attention arced to the lagoon. Marcus forced his way through the shallow water and then jogged over to the women and Damiano. "Damn it!" He took in a breath, looked toward the boys and then took off his t-shirt and wrung out the water. "Can anyone go to Spirit form?" He kicked off his shoes and began to remove a sock.

Medeia examined a wound on Dormava's forehead and shook her head in response to Marcus. "Stay still and let me look!"

"I can't turn to Spirit or cast a damn spell!" Dormava yelled. A gust of wind knocked her back, Media caught her. Marcus swore as he fell over into the sand. The skies darkened and wind whipped at the trees and Lamia's minions.

The boys approached, shielding their eyes as the sand pelted across the beach. Achar shook his head and grabbed his chest, trying to breath. Damiano shielded his eyes and made his way to Deveroy. "It's a bit breezy! White Pines with palm trees and even cactus…what a cool idea! At least she's creative!"

Deveroy grabbed his hair and twisted it behind his head. With his thighs and feet, he dug into the beach trying to stabilize. He nodded to Damiano. "Where is she? Where's Lamia?" He looked to Dormava. "Dormava are you all right?" He began to traipse toward her.

Medeia slapped Dormava's hand away and twisted toward Deveroy. "She's fine! Stay there! Save your energy!"

Damiano took Deveroy by the shoulder to halt him.

Medeia yelled to Marcus. "Lamia forced us in solid form most of the day! It's draining us!"

Dormava slapped Medeia's hand and covered the wound. "I don't want sand blowing in it! It hurts like hell! Let me cover it!" She felt the blood trickle through her palm. "Is it bad!?"

"Yes!" Medeia screamed over the wind.

Marcus stood strong against the wind. "Lamia told us…it's to make us stronger! Being in solid form for long periods of time will give us more control when we need it. Medeia is right, don't move! Conserve your energy."

"Where is she!?" Deveroy screamed.

"I think you'll be glad that she's not here!" Damiano scanned the peninsula.

Achar shielded his eyes and looked to Deveroy. "Keep your mouth shut! She's pissed!"

Damiano turned to Achar, eyes narrowing. "No thanks to you! Nice to save your own ass back there!" His voice rose. "Getting Contessa to forget about the question…real nice!" He pushed Achar back! "Now she'll focus on Deveroy!"

Achar stumbled back, cracked his neck and balled his fist. "I did it for all of us!"

Damiano retorted with a vulgar analogy of what Achar could do with his fist and martyrdom.

Dormava screamed over Damiano's voice. "Medeia, you need to keep your mouth shut! She'll lose patience with you!"

Marcus pulled his black t-shirt over his head and stretched it across his chest and torso. "Dormava is right! Keep quiet, Medeia! The boys will have to deal with her wrath!"

Damiano struggled to catch his breath. He grabbed Deveroy by the shoulders. "Listen to me! Her fury is fierce! When she gets here, don't say a word!"

"What is she going to do to us!?" Achar yelled.

Sand rose in a whirl wind, twisting and growing. The winds swirled and the temperature dropped as a large force of sand struck the two women in leather, throwing their bodies thirty feet into the lagoon. Marcus covered his face. The howling wind drowned his commands. A giant mound of sand struck him, flinging him across the beach. Damiano was thrown back from the next blow. Sand spiraled and twisted in front of the boys, heavy winds lashed at them. They covered their eyes and mouth and knelt to the beach. As the wind died down, the skies grew clear, Lamia appeared before them.

"How dare you speak to a Vicar!" Her hand stuck Deveroy's face. "Do you have any idea what you've done? Lamia began to circle the boys.

"Achar, you may have been a fool to cast such a spell, but you distracted Contessa for me and I am grateful. She would have forced me to tell her about The Man. However, because of you, she did not." Her eyes focused on Deveroy.

"Lamia, are you all right?" Damiano rushed to her side.

Her hand raised toward him, a ball of green energy blasted him back. "I will not be beguiled by you, Damiano." Lamia grabbed Deveroy's hair and forced him to his knees. Achar stood still.

Water splashed as the ladies in leather waded through the shallow part of the shore. Marcus walked to Lamia's side. "Did you speak with him? Did he grant you more power to resist Contessa?"

"He refused me and said that I shall get nothing until the job is done. My not being able to resist Contessa is my problem." She flicked a finger toward Achar. He flew into the air and splashed into the lagoon. "Deveroy, however, I have no use for. Once a Vicar gets into your soul, once a Vicar touches your heart — you are never the same." Another swish smacked Deveroy backward. He landed on his back in the sand near Damiano.

Damiano reached down and helped him to his feet. He was rough with Deveroy's arm as he spoke without moving his lips. "Did the Vicar tell you if you needed him, that you should call for him?"

Deveroy nodded, writhing in pain as Damiano twisted his arm. "Call for him now. Use your mind and call for him." He shoved Deveroy toward Lamia.

"Thank you, Damiano." Her eyes sparkled as she waited for everyone to gather around. Several moments later, and complaints from Achar about being cold, Lamia raised a hand and splayed her fingers, then spoke the incantation.

"Esplodi oltre spazio e tempo"
(Disburse across space and time)

A flash of red light hit Deveroy, an explosion of crimson flared. Everyone covered their eyes. When the flare dissipated, Deveroy was gone. "That's how a Disbursement Charm is done!"

Marcus spoke. "Everything will be all right." He placed a hand upon Lamia's shoulder. Her eyes moved to Damiano, a smirk slid across her face. "Will everything be all right, my Damiano?"

Marcus tightened as Damiano moved to Lamia. "You will be fine as always."

Lamia plopped to her knees. "I don't know how to fight her. What do I do?" She looked to the ladies in leather.

"We'll help. We'll do whatever we can." Dormava spoke.

"What can I do?" Achar added, shivering.

Lamia looked into Damiano's eyes. "She is too powerful. If I can't fight Contessa, I have no hope for Azzurra or Katie."

Marcus spoke. "There is a way. Azzurra may be the most powerful of the Degeli's, however her family is not. We kill them all. Start with Nicco, Marta and Marie. If she doesn't relinquish her power, then we'll kill her granddaughter, Katherine and then Carlotta's children, Elizabeth and Dino. The ladies that she plays pinochle with, her daughter's co-workers: Tony, Barbra and JoAnn. Every person she knows will parish." Marcus knelt in the sand and placed a hand through Lamia's hair. "Once she realizes that everyone she knows is dead, it will break her spirit. She won't be able to fight."

Lamia's eyes widened with a glint that sparkled. "Oh Marcus, you know them all, don't you? What of Basil? What if she called him back into service? How strong is Basil?"

"He's pretty damn strong, but I think you and Marcus can destroy him." Damiano added as he helped Lamia to her feet.

"What of her sisters...the brother." Dormava asked. She nudged Medeia.

Lamia spoke. "Gabriella is the weakest. She should not be a problem. Arianna is the next most powerful. Marcus and a few of us should be able to kill her. As for her brother Augusto, he's too old and feeble. He won't be an issue."

"What of Katie?" Medeia asked, "Contessa?"

Dormava responded. "We kill Katie's daughters, Olivia and Carlotta. With her family gone, she'll be devastated, like Marcus said."

"I would think that would make her really mad." Achar said.

Everyone glared at him. Lamia placed a finger upon her lower lip and smirked. "Katie will be weakened all ready at the loss of Azzurra's family. Olivia is a mess and leave Carlotta be. We torture the others, make sure it last a while. The thought of her loved ones dying such gruesome deaths will be devastating. As for Contessa, that will be Celia's job." Her hands dropped to her sides. "What of the husbands...Gabriella's husband, Nicolai? What's the other husband's name, Mateo? He's the spouse of Arianna, right? Are they very powerful?"

Marcus answered. "Both come from very powerful families, but the Degelis are the strongest. Again, killing their children and grandchildren should weaken them."

"We wait. We will not rush into anything. That's when mistakes happen. Damiano, what should I do?" Lamia rested a hand upon his chest.

Damiano spoke. "We wait for Stephan to tell us if Katie and Basil are back. We should send someone to Olivia's house to see if a guardian has been placed."

"Is there anyone else? Drago and Kimberly, the families from New York and San Francisco will need to be killed." Lamia turned to Marcus.

"Yes, they will. However, there is someone else we need to worry about." Marcus looked to the ladies, Damiano, then back to Lamia. "Father Bernardo."

"Father Bernardo? He doesn't even practice Magick." Lamia laughed. "Stupid old priest."

"He is powerful without using Magick." Marcus said. "His prayers are answered. I've watched him closely over the years. The heavens listen to him. He has power beyond Magick."

Lamia shook her head with tiny trembles. "Kill him. Sabino and Stella will understand that their son was a threat. Is there anything else?"

No one said a word. "Very well, then we wait for Stephan to return. If there is no sign of Katie or Basil, if things seem normal, then we stay with our original plan. However, if they are there, if they know another Witches War is in the making, then we start killing off the family. The Man will understand why we had to move ahead of schedule. Damiano, go to Olivia's and see about that Vicar." She waved a hand and he vanished. "You two ladies, go to Celia. Fill her in on what is happening." Another swish and Dormava and Medeia disappeared. "And as for you Achar...out of my sight!" A flick toward Achar and he dissolved.

"Marcus, calm my nerves and have a stroll with me down the beach." She took Marcus by the arm and began a pleasant walk.

"Do you think we're strong enough to kill them all?" Marcus asked.

"Oh, Marcus, of course not — however, The Man did give me one thing at my disposal...an army of demons."

* * * *

Oh My Stars!

Azzurra rose to her feet and motioned for everyone to be still. Basil's warnings were shushed. Step by step she made her way toward the window. Blackie barked then remained silent from his mother's command. Azzurra raised a hand and said the spell.

"Rivela ciò che non può essere visto!"
(Reveal what cannot be seen!)

A man appeared just outside the window. He stood upon his tiptoes and peered into the kitchen. Azzurra tilted her head as she took in his appearance. He wore ancient Egyptian attire and a camel stood behind him. Stephan's eyes widened as he realized that he could be seen.

Gabriella stood and shouted, "It's Stephan — he's one of Nathan's Spirits."

Stephan screamed, floated up a foot and cast a ball of light toward Azzurra. Basil cast a protective charm around her, exploding the ball of light. At the same time, the angel pendant Azzurra wore, released two beams of light, hitting the ball in tandem with Basil's shield. Trumpets sounded from the Cherubs in Azzurra bedroom. A flash of white light came through the walls and shot toward Stephan from the Cherubs clock. Katie cast a spell toward Stephan. Making a quick hand movement toward the room, she pulled the Egyptian into the house.

Stephan screamed again and shouted that it was an ambush, that there was a miss-understanding. A water bird spiraled up from a vase and flew in front of Azzurra. Stephan cast several energy balls into the room. One hit Katie and she was thrown into the far wall. Two were absorbed by the water bird and one was blocked by a panther that leapt from the sink. Blackie yelped and darted through the wall. Another blast hit the wall behind the family, exploding a painting. Everyone screamed and dropped to the floor. One of the energy balls struck Basil, sending him into the entertainment center. The panther roared, turned to Spirit form and dove upon the screaming Egyptian. A bubble oozed from the soap dispenser and floated near Azzurra. Several energy blasts were absorbed into the bubble, which squirmed and changed shapes. More bubbles were released and began sending streams of bubbles toward Basil and Katie. Flashes of electricity burst from a bubble near Stephan and struck him in the chest. He screamed. Basil turned to Spirit form as the bubble floated nearby, crimson red. One by one, energy blasts shot from his hand toward Stephan. Stephan repelled each of the blast as he struggled with the panther, the bubble, cherub clock, angel and the water bird. Katie cast another spell, turning Stephan solid as she herself turned to Spirit form. Stephan screamed. Another blast of light threw the panther into the wall. The water bird morphed into an octopus and wrapped its legs around the struggling man. Three beams of white light attached themselves to Stephan, two from the angel pendent and one from the cherub clock. Stephan's body slumped. He stopped casting balls of energy and fell to the floor.

"Oh My Stars, this is Fort Knox! I've been set up! Please stop I surrender!" He produced a white flag and feebly waved it in the air.

"Release him," Azzurra commanded of the water bird. She raised a hand to keep the panther at bay. She placed a hand over the pendant and the beams of lights vanished. She raised her other hand toward the back bedroom and the one large beam of light, from the cherub clock, released Stephan. A huge roar sounded in the room. "Shush, Sammy." Azzurra looked toward the kitchen table. Everyone began rising to their feet.

"Stephan, why have you come to my home? Why have you attacked us?" Azzurra demanded.

"I've been bamboozled! Set up! Oh, it's awful. Nathan said I was to check and see if Katie or Basil were near the house and let him know if I saw anything strange. I've been set up. He said there would be no danger. He promised me!" Stephan placed his hands over his face and began to cry.

Katie knelt down to face the man. "Oh, will you stop that! Why does Nathan want to know if Basil or I are here?"

Stephan lowered his hands and looked to Katie. "Oh Katie, you look marvelous! I'm glad they chose blue. That dress is fabulous on you…and you must be Basil. You looked so handsome when you were casting all those energy balls — very powerful, rugged and sexy."

"Stephan, quiet, and answer my sister." The floating bubble released a stream of purple that doused the pain in Azzurra's lower back. She sighed with relief.

"Oh my stars, the president should have this much protection. Between that awful kitty, that octopus water thing and those beams of white light and bubbles everywhere, I was so confused. Oh, it was simply…"

Basil, Katie and Azzurra all called his name and demanded that he answer. "Oh all right. My poor camel is probably terrified." He raised his head toward the window. "Daddy's in here. I'm all right sweetheart." He turned to Azzurra. "I know nothing else…not a thing…except that you look stunning my dear. Where did you get that incredibly classy, black pant suit?" Stephan waved to Gabriella.

Gabriella beamed and began to answer when her husband Nicolai shook his head and asked her to be quiet.

Basil took a few steps toward him. "So you know not a thing as to why Nathan has sent you here, of why he wanted to know about Miss Katie or me?"

"Nope, not a thing, I mean we went on that hunting trip to save all the deer, came home and suddenly I get a summons from Contessa demanding that I come to the house immediately. When I showed up, she upset me so much I cried and then Nathan said that Lamia should be there any minute and that I should listen up to what he needed. Then he explained that I should check to see if you two were here. I wasn't supposed to speak with you by the way." He nodded to Katie. "I think she's jealous. Anyway, they also said to be on the lookout for a Vicar. That Achar cast a Disbursement Charm…at you." He pointed to Katie. "I'm glad to see you're OK." He looked to the rest of the room and whispered. "Does she know that part of her arm is missing? Anyway, couldn't believe that cute little Achar would cast such a nasty spell. Nathan was very upset because he knew that Achar didn't have the power to cast such a spell and I agreed. Then he sent me on a mission…a mission of doom!" He placed the back of his hand on his forehead and fell to the floor.

Katie looked to Azzurra. "Stephan, did you see Lamia? Did you see any other Spirits?"

"No dear. I wanted to be gone by the time that nasty thing arrived. She may be one of the most beautiful women I've ever seen but her heart is like coal. What's that song about the Grinch?" He sang loudly. "You're a foul one, Miss Lamia. You have termites in your smile..."

"...Stephan! What else do you know?" Basil knelt down to look him in the eye.

"Well...something about Deveroy and Achar. I think Nathan wanted them to stop the haunting of Katie's daughter. Oh, look at me! I'm just spilling the beans! Anyway, I told them years ago that it was wrong, but I don't get involved in things like that. Oh wait, something is coming. Oh that's right. They were asking if I saw either of the boys. I remember, I was crying because Tessa told me I looked like a large potato in a lace sack and she asked if I've seen Achar or Deveroy and that the family was in horrible danger. I told them that they should have gone after Basil. After all, he's..."

Basil swished a hand over Stephan that made him glow white for a moment. Stephan sighed with relief.

"So the boys are missing?" Basil turned solid and rested a hand upon Stephan's shoulder.

Stephan took in a few breaths, smiled and thanked Basil. "Thank you, sweetheart. That feels so much better. Besides, I'm not sure if I believe it anyway, but I told them that I had not seen the boys. Nathan promised that I would be safe and now look at me."

"He's not going to cry again is he?" Augusto shouted.

Basil turned and spoke with a bit of anger. "You all be quiet over there. I'll deal with the lot of you in a moment." He looked to Azzurra. "Well, now we know that they are aware of the attack on Miss Katie and the spell didn't work. However, they don't know that you've summoned Katie. They are also unaware that I'm back and that you broke the vow. For all we know, they think the Vicar is at Olivia's because he's investigating the spell. I don't think there is reason to panic."

"But Stephan said they thought the family was in danger," Katie spoke.

Basil looked to Katie. "Yes, they'll be a bit paranoid, but once they realize the Vicar is only looking after Olivia, they may not feel the need to do anything. Only if they think that Azzurra summoned Miss Katie will they think to attack."

"Stephan, is there anything else you remember?" Katie asked.

"Not a thing. I just can't believe Nathan betrayed me. We always got a long wonderfully." He pretended to blow his nose in the surrender flag.

"Maybe we should compel him to go back there and see what he can find out." Augusto called over the table.

Basil turned his head toward Augusto and snapped. "I asked you to be quiet. Now, do as I say. We cannot send Stephan back there. Lamia would realize that he was compelled and harm him." He took Stephan's hand. "You seem like a good lad, just mixed up with the wrong people, but I'm afraid I just can't let you go. You see, we are in a delicate situation." He looked up to Azzurra. "Let the Cherubs hold him and his camel until we can figure things out." He spoke to Stephan. "Not to worry. You'll be comfortable and I'll come get you as soon as I can."

Stephan took Basil by his shoulders, as he began to sob once more. Azzurra and Katie looked to each other and rolled their eyes. With a swish of a hand, one large beam of light expelled from the cherub clock from the back bedroom. The beam hit Stephan, who turned to Spirit form. He floated in the air and began to drift toward the back hall. "I'm innocent. I'm innocent I tell you! Come and visit any time. Again, I just love that black blazer...simply stunning." He looked to Arianna. "You should have worn more cheerful colors. What is this...a funeral?" He flung his head backward. "You sure I'll be safe, Basil?"

Basil made a gesture toward the window and a camel began to float into the room. "I'll make sure you are. No need to worry, dear Stephan." Basil escorted the camel and Stephan to the cherub clock.

Katie and Azzurra looked at each other, then to the mess around the house. The entertainment center was in ruins. The painting above the table was in pieces and burn marks covered the floors, walls and ceiling.

"Oh, everything's a mess." Azzurra placed her palms over her mouth. Blackie peeked through a wall and gave a slight bark.

Katie rolled her eyes. "Beee, if you don't start thinking like a Witch!" She looked to Blackie. "There you are! Get back in here and lie down." Katie looked to the entertainment center, raised a hand but was interrupted by a loud voice. Basil returned to the room and shouted for Katie to do nothing.

"You'll do nothing Miss Katie! Let this sorry lot of Witches fix things up. He turned to face the table. "Not one of you did a damned thing! You hid under the table like silly rodents! Miss Katie and I were the only ones who had enough brains to react. Thank the Heavens for all the enchantments Miss Katie, Mum and I made. I cannot say the same for the lot of you! To not have cast a single shield, to have not thrown a single energy ball...it's pathetic it is. Gabriella? Do you have one sachet or elixir in your purse? And where is your purse…in the other room? Nicolai? Did you bother to make any elixirs or sachets either? What about you two…Mateo and Augusto? Did you have any brains to bring a wand? I understand that Olivia did not need a wand to protect her from the demon. You two, however, may have needed your wands! Your Wand Spirits may no longer be with us, but you still have basic attack and protective spells that you could have used." He turned to Arianna. "And you, Miss Arianna…of all the things in this house — you couldn't think to enchant one object to assist us? I love you Miss Arianna, but I'm really annoyed with you right now. The Father is the only one that I heard saying a prayer, like he had promised. Now, I'm disgusted with the lot of you! How do you expect to protect your loved ones? Stephan is a very powerful Spirit, as you well saw. We could have used a bit of help!" His voice rose. "Maybe you should go home and kill off your loved ones yourself! Go on! Go home and kill your children and grandchildren. Better they be killed…"

"…enough, Basil!" Azzurra voice rose as she stepped forward. "Stop yelling. I won't have us turning on each other." She looked to the table of ashamed family members. "Now he has a point, doesn't he? Not one of you, including myself cast a single spell."

"But Mum, you did. You cast the powerful enchantments. Stephan was weakened tremendously because of the angel pendant and the cherub clock." Basil retorted. "And you, Miss Arianna, what about your pendant? Were you not supposed to cast a protective enchantment?"

Arianna's eyes welled with tears. "It's on my dresser."

Basils voice rose and he slammed a hand on the counter. "Now that's a grand place for it, eh! And the rest of you sorry lot, where are your pendants, rings and other enchantments! Where are your wands?" Blackie yelped and disappeared through a wall.

"Basil! Stop this!" Azzurra took him by the arm and ushered him away from the table. Katie took his other arm and asked him to calm down.

"In my armoire…my wand is in my Armoire." Augusto held his head down. The rest of the family fixated on a cookie, a carrot or cup of coffee. All avoided eye contact with Basil.

"Basil, I know you're upset, but I will handle this." Azzurra looked to Katie and then to her family. "I know you all feel as though you're up in age and the idea of fighting a Witches War is exhausting. However, we are no ordinary family. For forty-one years we have not used Magick. Well, now it's time. You two gentleman will take up your wands. Gabriella and Nicolai, you will begin mixing your sachets and elixirs, and you, Arianna will begin to enchant objects. We are not too old to practice our craft. We are simply out of touch. Simply not used to casting spells and taking up our natural powers.

235

From this point on, we shall use Magick for everything. To start the dish-washer, you will use Magick. To cook dinner, you will use Magick. When you clean the house, it will be done by Magick. Everything we do, we use Magick.

Gabriella, Arianna, Basil and I will train the kids this evening. It will not be easy, but you have the memories of what it was like and we will pre-vail. We shall protect our loved ones, because we are the Degeli's. The most powerful family of Witches and Warlocks this century has ever seen. We don't know how powerful we'll be. No one knows the strength we possess. We must not lose hope. We must not let one failed attack scare us into believing that because of our age, we don't stand a chance. We have Basil and his comrades. We have Katie and you have me. I alone, carry the power of every Witch that has lived and died before me. It is I who carry the lin-eage of this family. It is I…The Matriarch that will not die without a fight."

* * * *

Milky White Spheres

The dark room's silence was interrupted by the soft crunch of packages that were placed on the floor. A voice spoke the words *Puszczać będzie światło*. The secret room illuminated, revealing the hutches, apothecary, the ornate round table and the Wooton desk. The man's eyes focused on the maple hutch. He recognized the enchanted watch that had belonged to Franco and tried to recall if Azzurra had told him if she intended to re-cast the spell. He didn't think so. The mannequin hand displayed rings and bracelets. The oval antique mirror, a jewelry box and the quills all remained in the places where he had seen them last. He noticed the absence of Azzurra's wand.

None of these items concerned him, with the exception of the wooden box lined with velvet that contained swirling, milky white spheres. Nine spheres lay in their egg shaped cradles. Three were missing. His lips curled slightly as he reached for one. Once in his hand, the soft twists and turns of the mysterious liquid began to react, swirling faster, with sparks of eruptions. Merek Kroll slipped a sphere into his pocket. If these spheres held the power he suspected, they were going to be invaluable. *Niech zgasnie swiatlo.* The lights went out.

Azzurra and Katie greeted the Witches Vendor as he appeared before them and explained that he had placed the packages in the secret room near the maple hutch. "Damn it to hell, what happened here? The place is a disaster."

Azzurra began to explain the encounter with Stephan. Basil looked to the Vendor. "Merek Kroll! It's grand to see you. Don't think them rude. They're concentrating." Basil looked to the family who had been using Magick to repair Azzurra's house.

A moment later, the family noticed Merek and greeted him. Hugs and handshakes were exchanged with words of kindness. Several minutes later, they returned to their spells; a painting mended and plates, cups and saucers floated to the kitchen sink.

Azzurra thanked Merek for bringing the rest of the supplies for the kids.

Merek hesitated and then spoke. "Not that it's any of my business…but I'm glad the kids will be trained…very shaky times." He gave a slight pause. "Might I ask, has anyone heard from Franco yet?"

"He's probably still with my husband, Dante. The last I heard, they were out of the earth's realm. See, I'm trying not to swear." Katie nudged Azzurra who rolled her eyes. "The Higher Spirits have placed a beacon to inform them of the situation as soon as they re-enter, so the Lord only knows when they'll be back." She shrugged her shoulders.

"Very well, very well, Madam, if I may, there is talk in the Spirit world… talk about an extremely powerful force that is compelling the Higher Spirits to send Vicars where they should not be. From what I can tell, no one knows what the force is or who is involved."

Katie looked to Azzurra, but said nothing.

"Thank you Merek dear." Azzurra took his hand and held it for a moment.

"You are welcome dear lady. I shall now bid you adieu." He turned to the room. "Everyone…be safe and I will see you all again very soon." He bowed and vanished.

"Did you notice anything odd about him? He didn't stay very long, now did he?" Basil asked.

"Not a thing, Basil. I trust Merek Kroll with my life. He's been a dear family friend and has our best interest in mind. We can always use another ally and what better ally than Merek Kroll." Azzurra nodded once, quick and short.

"I agree with Azzurra," Katie added.

"Very well Mum. A few things if I may, Miss Katie?" He addressed the lady in blue.

"Of course Basil, I'm all ears." Katie replied.

"I think those Bubbles may have been too distracting during the attack. Perhaps we should have them appear only on command and concentrate on healing," Basil advised.

Azzurra and Katie agreed.

"And the panther, I think he needs a wee bit of a boost. No offense, but perhaps Mum should re-cast the spell…make him more powerful. Stephan was able to throw him off with ease, now wasn't he?"

Azzurra and Katie nodded.

"And Mum…your Angel Pendant and the Cherubs did not sound their alarms until a threat actually entered the house. I think we need a protective enchantment to include the perimeter of the property itself. We need a stronghold, should anything happen. We need a safe place for everyone to be. I'd also like to go over some defensive and attack spells with you." Basil looked over to the family. They were almost finished repairing the rooms. Father Bernardo made the sign of the cross, giving thanks to the Lord and asking forgiveness for their use of Magick.

"I agree Basil. I'll work on something this afternoon." Azzurra's eyes widened. "Oh Katie, will you help before you leave for California and New York?"

"Of course I will." Katie looked around. "Now, where is that silly dog of mine?"

Basil turned to the family and began giving instructions. They were to produce as many sachets and elixirs as possible and retrieve their wands and enchant objects. "When you ladies arrive at 6:00 to train the kids, I expect a full arsenal, I do." With very short goodbyes and lots of complaining, he ushered everyone out of the house.

A soft bark caused them to look toward the fountain in the living room. "There you are! Where have you been?" Katie scolded him. "Azzurra, what's the matter with your fountain?"

"It hasn't worked since this mess started. I don't know what's wrong with it. Now be nice to Blackie. All that commotion terrified him." Azzurra walked to the little dog. He turned solid and grunted as Azzurra picked him up. "You poor thing, Aunty Azzurra is here."

"Poor thing, my ass…you need to toughen up Blackie, because this is just the beginning. You heard Merek Kroll. Something very dangerous is brewing and we have to be ready."

* * * *

Another Chance

Cacti and other plants of the desert seemed at home, unaffected by the sun's heat. He, however, felt the desert's strength. His sharp intake of breath felt heavy, dry and painful. Clothes were a protective shield, yet cumbersome. Tiny granules of sand flew past him, forming swirls of thin, ghostlike shapes created by Mother Nature. Shielding his eyes and mouth, Deveroy searched the dunes. Nothing but thin ghosts of sand appeared. The last thing he remembered is Damiano telling him to call for the Vicar, and Lamia casting the Disbursement Charm.

Trudging through the thick, soft mounds of the desert exhausted him. His bones ached and muscles tightened. Shapes morphed within his mind: people...people he hurt, their faces, screams and their fear. He fell to his knees, sinking deep into the sand. Once again, he felt mortal...alive and it was awful. For years, the thought of being alive fueled the bitterness within him...to taste food...to feel passionate sex...ah the excitement of flesh! Exhaustion, dehydration and pain were feelings he had not missed. Pale blue eyes tried to focus on the sun. He felt the stinging pain. Pelts of sand tried to force their way into his nose, his mouth. Lips held tight as he began to do something he had never done before. He prayed to the man he knew had saved him, to the man in white who had brought him to the desert once before with Achar. To the man who made him mortal, not to feel the pleasures of life, but to feel the pain and agony of what it's like to be alive.

The words in his mind were confusing, random and childlike. Not knowing where or what to say, he asked for forgiveness. He asked those souls who he had tormented, to forgive him. His mind swept to the raging animal inside that always tempted him, urged him and roared with an annoying guttural purr, yearning for the quick release of stress, release of anxiety and dousing of pain — if only for a few moments. He convinced himself that the animal gave him what he needed, what he desired and that there had been nothing else in life that he needed more than to please the purring hunger of that animal. He didn't need his father or his mother. He didn't need money or someone to love or to love him in return. A tear ran down his cheek as something inside him told him, that what he needed all along was faith and patience and to stop listening to that persistent purr.

Words flowed through his mind in silent prayers. He spoke aloud of making amends to Katie for the haunting of Olivia and her family. He swore to help the Degeli's and do as they asked of him. He would follow Basil's instruction. He would admit his despicable actions, to keep away from those who cause influence and to put to sleep that raging animal inside.

Another hour of prayer: randomly speaking of acts from childhood, acts of adulthood and his deeds in the afterlife. Lips cracked and seeped blood. He looked up to the heavens and spoke aloud, "I'm sorry. Please, forgive me for what I have done."

The sky began to move. The wisps of sand ghosts took the shape of people he knew, Achar...Contessa...Damiano. His eyes became heavy. His vision faltered and swayed. His focus of the cacti, the mounds of wispy sand and the windswept ghostly figures all faded into black as his body became limp and plopped into the sand.

A voice spoke to him. The man in white stood beside him telling him to go to Azzurra, listen to Basil's instructions and follow his heart. It warned that this was his second chance and there would be no third. His shoulders were lifted as he faced the man in white. A feeling of love washed over him. The man placed a feather plume in his hand. Deveroy looked to the plume...soft and white, blowing in the breeze. All of his questions were answered before he asked. He would be returned to Spirit form. He would go to Azzurra and explain himself, ask for forgiveness and give the white plume to her. The Vicar explained that Azzurra would know the plume came from the Vicar Aiden Sinclair. The Vicar's deep voice whispered to Deveroy that he would know his heart, know his desires and know the moment he failed to keep his word.

* * * *

242

The Plume

"The lasagna is in the oven and the salad is made. I went with a Greek salad, thought the kids might like it. Olives and garlic butter are set. I'll warm the bread just before they get here." Katie took off the apron and hung it in the cabinet. "How did things go with you and Basil?"

Azzurra shut the door to the basement and looked to her sister. "It went well Katie. It felt good to pick up my wand again. Basil entered my wand and well, it was strange. I became more focused. It was though our minds melded. Very odd, I don't remember feeling that before. He said I should use my wand, even if I don't need it. It helps to focus energy into something with a tip. Anyway, I practiced a lot of defense and attack spells. We adjusted Sammy and the Bubbles, but I feel as though I'm missing something."

"I don't think so. You and I already adjusted the clock and the pendant, so what else is there?"

"You're right. I guess I'm just tired." Azzurra placed a hand on her lower back. "Oh Katie, I can't believe how much my powers have grown." She opened the refrigerator and pulled out some scallions. "Thank you so much for your help with dinner. I couldn't have done it without you. I'm thinking some chopped scallions sprinkled on the lasagna. I know Gabriella likes them." Azzurra pulled out a large knife from one of the drawers. She took the cutting board out from another cabinet and began to chop them.

"Where's Basil?" Katie asked as she headed for the dining room. "I figure we can eat in the dining room again, that was so nice last night." She stood in front of the entrance and made a hand movement. "There…the dining room looks beautiful. I went with the *Blue Italian by Spode*."

"Beee, I forgot how nice it is to use Magick." Azzurra swished a hand through the air. "Basil will be back in a while. He went to Japan to secure a good friend. Oh, I like the *Spode*. Thank you Katie."

Katie called for Blackie. Nothing appeared. "Now where is he?"

"He's with Basil," Azzurra said as she transferred the scallions into a bowl.

"My little Blackie went to Japan!" Katie placed a hand over her mouth.

"What are you worried about? He's with Basil. Basil asked if he wanted to go and he got real excited."

Katie swished a hand toward her sister. "He probably though Japan was food!"

"Oh, Katie let's sit and have a cup of coffee before everyone arrives." Azzurra placed the scallions in the refrigerator. She took up her wand, looked to the kitchen table, made a tiny swish and two cups of steaming coffee appeared in Katie's antique cups.

"That sounds wonderful." The sisters sat together at the table. Azzurra took a sip of coffee and looked up to Katie. "Oh, Katie that's right. You can't drink. I'm so silly."

"It's all right, I'll pretend." She picked up the cup and placed it to her lips. "See…I still can't believe after all these years, you use my cups."

"Well of course Katie, almost every morning, unless I'm doing some work around the house. You know, in case it should break."

Katie laughed. "Does Arianna use my cups?"

Azzurra shook her head. "Oh Katie, she wants to but she's afraid she'll break them, so once a month she has Mateo make the coffee, pour it into the cup and fix it nice, then he sits next to her as she drinks"

Katie placed a hand over her face and turned beat red.

"I know it's silly, but she doesn't trust herself and she hasn't broken that cup in all these years. It means a lot to her." Azzurra placed her hands over her face and began to laugh.

Twenty minutes later, Katie instructed the soap dispenser to heal Azzurra's back. A tiny bubble emerged from the dispenser, morphed into several shapes as it grew in size and then turned purple. Tiny strands of weightless ooze crawled up Azzurra's arm, another one inched to her back while two more slithered down her legs. Azzurra sighed with relief. "Thank you, sweetheart." The Bubble morphed again and then popped into tiny bubbles which whizzed in tiny swirls back into the dispenser.

Down from the ceiling four wriggling legs appeared, followed by a body, a tail and a head.

"There you are! How dare you leave for Japan without telling Muma? What has gotten into you? You could have gotten lost. Basil does not keep an eye on you the way he should." Blackie turned solid and dropped into Katie's arms, wagged his tail, barked and began licking her face. "Oh enough, OK, OK you can go to Japan with Basil whenever you want. Isn't he cute?"

Basil appeared next to Azzurra. "I've secured another Spirit. That makes four and I trust them with my life, I do. But then again, I guess that doesn't mean so much, now does it." He walked to a chair, pulled it out and rested a foot on the seat. "I showed Mum several defense spells and unfortunately attack spells, but sometimes you have to learn to be aggressive to stop the threat." He adjusted a belt buckle on his boot, stood and then plunged his hands into the pockets of his trench coat, leaning his buttocks against the counter. "You should have seen her Miss Katie. Your sister was fantastic down in the cellar. I couldn't believe the things that just came natural..." Basil stopped mid-sentence and bolted upright. A young man appeared before them. He had long blonde hair, blue eyes, faded jeans and a red thick ribbed turtle neck sweater with scuffed tennis shoes. A large white feather plume rested in his hand.

Azzurra stood and cast a spell that brought her wand to her. Katie let Blackie down and told him to hide as she put her hands in the air ready to defend. She and Basil turned to Spirit form.

"Become solid and state your purpose," Basil ordered him. Azzurra looked down to her angel pendent, nothing happened. Katie tilted her head to listen to the tiny trumpets of the Cherubs...nothing sounded. The panther sat still while Merlin remained in his vase.

"I am sent here from the Vicar. He asks that you not harm me, treat me with kindness and to forgive me." Deveroy became solid, looked away from Katie and focused on Azzurra.

"What Vicar...what Vicar sent you?" Azzurra raised a wand toward the man.

"I forgot his name. Oh wait...I think he said it was Vicar Aiden St. or Sinclair? He wore all white, with an odd tie made of gem stones. He said that you shouldn't destroy me and I have a message for you. I'm to listen to Basil and do whatever I can to assist Azzurra and her family. He also said that Katie should forgive me." He looked to the floor.

"Would you be one of Tessa's Spirits?" Basil walked toward him and became solid.

"Yes...I mean I was...I mean I am...the Vicar has promised to help me. I am Deveroy. Katie, I'm sorry for my friend Achar's attempt at disbursing you earlier this week." He knelt down in front of Katie and held his head low.

Katie's chest welled and voice rose. She turned solid and spoke. "I thought you looked familiar, you dirty little bastard, filthy little freak." She began to raise her hands and speak an incantation. Deveroy looked up and squinted.

Blackie yelped a tiny cry from under the couch.

"Stop!" Basil yelled. "Miss Katie, I know you are upset, but if what he says is true then the Vicar has seen something in him worthwhile. All must be forgiven if he is telling the truth." He turned to face the young man. "You there...Deveroy...stand up and prove to us that you come from the Vicar."

Deveroy quickly stood and addressed Azzurra. He held out the white plume. "The Vicar said I was to give this feather to you. He said that you would know that it came from him."

Basil stepped in front of Azzurra. He placed a hand around Deveroy's throat and lifted him slightly off the ground. "If that feather hurts her, I will tear you apart and make you regret the day you died." He touched the plume lightly and then released Deveroy. "It's from the Vicar. I sense the Vicar's effects on the plume. It's all right Mum, take the feather."

Azzurra placed her wand on the counter and took the feather from Deveroy. The moment she touched it, she felt what Basil had meant. The same comfort and protection filled her soul. "It's an old feather pen...you know, an old quill."

Without warning, the feather shot out of her hand and began to write in the air — specs of blue and white light sparked like a welder's arc as the plume wrote its message.

The young man before you is Deveroy. He has been given a second chance — as his heart is sincere. I ask that you trust him and be kind and patient. He is to tell you everything he knows about Tessa's Spirits and is to assist in any way possible. Basil, I would like you to take him in your charge. I will ask that Katie set aside her anger and have faith, that I, as a Vicar, am doing what is best for all. Make sure Deveroy is kept out of sight as they think he has been destroyed. I shall be with Olivia. You are to release Stephan, appeal to his heart and you may find your-self another ally. Keep the plume nearby, it may come in useful.

Vicar Aiden Sinclair

Azzurra took the feather. "Well if the Vicar says that your heart is in the right place, how can we argue? Welcome to our side Deveroy, the better side." Azzurra nodded and smiled at Deveroy.

"Bullshit! He haunted my daughter for how many years and I'm supposed to..." Katie was interrupted by Deveroy.

"...I am sorry. I will do anything to make up for the bad things I've done." Deveroy hung his head down.

"Don't you dare cut me off, you little snake! The Vicar may trust you because he has powers and can see things I can't. But since I don't have those powers...I don't!" She folded her arms across her chest. "Besides, just this week you tried to discombobulate me."

"It's called a Disbursement Charm and it wasn't me, I wasn't sure what Achar was doing..."

"...don't you dare correct me, you skinny little brat! I should pull each and every hair out of that head of yours...you good for nothing, long hair, useless, nasty, rotten...haunt my daughter will you...filthy little..."

"...Miss Katie! The Vicar has asked us to trust him. Just because you don't have his power of sense doesn't mean he doesn't know what he's doing. We need to have faith in him. I trust the Vicar and so should you." Basil looked between Katie and Deveroy.

"I don't know why I can't remember the name of that stupid spell." Katie turned her back to Deveroy. "It will take some time. I'm sorry Devehoy or whatever the hell your name is. Why can't they have names like Daniel or James, for the Love of God? Anyway, it will just have to take time." Katie looked up to the ceiling.

"I know Ma'am. I don't expect forgiveness right away." He paused and then took several steps toward Katie. "I was lost in life and in death, never felt as though anyone cared if I was alive or even noticed the day I died. I did horrible things. I'm sorry. I am lucky enough to have come across the Vicar. He gave me a second chance. I have the chance not to be condemned for what I've done. I have sworn to him my loyalty to the family. He said he would know the moment my heart wasn't sincere."

"Tell us what you know, Deveroy." Basil pushed the trench coat back, plunged his hands into his pants pockets and leaned against the counter, waiting for an answer.

* * * *

Trust in the Vicar

$\mathcal{D}$everoy explained. "I became a Spirit for Contessa a few years before the first Witches War. Achar was my friend. He's the one with long dark hair. I introduced him to Contessa, but she never liked him much, refused to make him a household Spirit, but for me she let him stay."

Deveroy looked to Katie then to Azzurra. "I remember meeting you. You had come to pay a visit with Contessa and sat and had coffee with Katie, Gabriella and Arianna. It was shortly after the Witches War began. I remember hearing strange things. They never told me much, nor Achar. Stephan was kept in the dark as well. Anyway, it was forty-one years ago that Vincent was killed. I remember how devastated Contessa was…to lose her only son. I comforted her as best I could. It was the first time my heart ached for someone else. Shorty thereafter, Nathan and Contessa asked Achar and I to do a minor haunting of Olivia and her family. We were only to open doors and slam them…turn the lights on and off…whisper awful things in their ears. A few months in, Lamia told us that it made Contessa stressed to think about Olivia, that she herself was going to take over the haunting. She placed the Culls that leached themselves onto Walter and Olivia. There was something from Olivia that she wanted. I'm not sure if she ever got what she was looking for. Anyway, Stephan would have nothing to do with the haunting and said we were all crazy for following orders from Lamia."

Deveroy looked to Katie who still had her arms folded, glaring at him. He turned to face Basil.

"After several months, I think Lamia became frustrated. Tessa refused to let her kill Olivia or any member of the family. She never knew the Culls had been placed and Lamia told us to keep our mouths shut about them. Lamia can be really nasty. That's one of the reasons why we tend to listen to her. Stephan's the only one that's not afraid of her."

Katie exchanged looks with Azzurra.

"Now, I don't know much about the first war...like I said...but I heard things. I know that Tessa believed that Katie sent a Spirit to kill Vincent, to teach her a lesson about the use of Spirits. That evil could be brought to the family by communicating with the dead. I also know that her cousin Debra told her that the Spirit snuck into his room and suffocated Vincent. He did it on Katie's orders. Your other cousin, Dorthea, also tried to convince Contessa that Katie sent the Spirit, something she heard Katie say at the funeral parlor. I remember Contessa crying, telling me that she couldn't believe Katie would do such a thing. Carlo, Debra's husband, cast some weird spell that I never heard of. It showed the Spirit that killed Vincent...showed him in the room that very night. The Spirit who killed Vincent..." Deveroy stopped and looked to Basil. "...the Spirit was him." He nodded to Basil.

Azzurra took in a breath and looked to Katie. "That's ridiculous. Basil and Katie would never harm Vincent!" She looked to Basil "Did you know about this? I knew she suspected Katie of doing something, but I never heard anything about you."

Basil stood, looked to Katie and then to Deveroy, cracking his knuckles. He then turned to Azzurra. "Mum...I didn't want to say anything because I knew it would upset you. It's like you said. It's ridiculous...even Miss Katie laughed at the notion."

Azzurra's face turned red. Her eyes narrowed as she slammed a hand on the counter top. "You knew about this Katie! You knew that Contessa thought Basil killed Vincent and never told me!"

"Now don't start slamming counter tops. I only knew after my death. I wanted to talk to you about it after Stephan mentioned it and I forgot. Now don't get upset...better off not listening to such nonsense. That's why Arianna and Gabriella never told you either." Katie rolled her eyes at the reaction of her sister. "Now don't be upset with them...Azzurra, please listen..."

"…I never understood why Contessa was so awful to Basil. Why she hated him so much. Basil, I'm mad at you! You should have told me! I would have understood my sister a little better. Maybe I could have spoken to her, convinced her that you and Katie had nothing to do with Vincent's death. That also explains why she was so angry with me, now doesn't it." Her hand slammed the counter top again.

"There she goes again," Katie took a few steps toward Deveroy. "You, you shouldn't have opened your mouth. Now look what you've done!"

"Mum please…I thought about it, I did. It would have made a difference. You didn't seem so upset when Miss Katie was accused." Basil's eyes darted to Katie and then back to Azzurra. "Mum please, I was so upset and the thought of you believing her for one moment, it would have devastated me so, to think that you didn't trust me."

"Believe her? Believing that you had something to do with Vincent's death?" Azzurra's energy simmered. "Basil honey, not for one moment…not even for a second would I consider you would have brought harm to Vincent. I can't tell you why, but it's different than Katie. I was there at the funeral home when Dorthea overheard what Katie had said. But I had no idea that she thought you were involved. Not my Basil. I don't know why I feel it's different, but I do."

"I'm sorry Mum. I should have told you." Basil held his head down.

"Azzurra, you and your temper, now look at Basil — you hurt his feelings." Katie nudged Deveroy out of the way and placed a hand on Basil's shoulder. "I told you years ago that she would have never doubted you. That you had nothing to worry about."

"Basil honey…I'm sorry for yelling. This is all Katie's fault!" She rounded on her sister as Katie arms flew in the air. "You should have told me!"

"I was dead, Azzurra." Katie said.

"You could have come to me in my dreams and told me! Maybe I would have tried to explain to Contessa…maybe…."

"…maybe my ass! Contessa would not have listened to you with Debra, Carlo and that Dorthea chanting in her ears! She thought I had something to do with his death. It wasn't going to be different with Basil." After a slight pause she added. "Azzurra let's not fight, I love you and I'm sorry." Blackie crept out from behind the sofa.

"Alright, let's not fight. Wait till I get a hold of Arianna and Gabriella. They could have told me…they're not dead." Azzurra waved a hand in the air. "Basil, honey…don't be upset."

251

"Thank you Mum. I'm fine." Basil moved toward Deveroy. "You and your big mouth...I should rip out your tongue, I should."

Azzurra took his arm and told him that was enough. With one last glare, Basil released his hostility.

Katie turned to Azzurra. "Well at least we know that Carlo, Debra and Dorthea had a hand in all this."

Azzurra turned to Deveroy. "Does Lamia speak much with Debra and Carlo? What about Dorthea?"

Deveroy nodded. "Yes, she sees Debra and Carlo all the time, along with Celia. Dorthea lives in New Orleans but yea, they speak. She is also close with Sabino and Stella. I think other members of the family as well, but I never heard names."

Azzurra looked to Katie, then Basil. She spoke. "Basil, we need to know who is involved. I'm beginning to think that Contessa has very little to do with what's really going on."

"I would agree Mum. As soon as my comrades arrive, I'll take care of the matter."

Katie looked to Deveroy. "You there...what else can you tell us?"

"I can't think of anything else," Deveroy said. "Like I said, we were kept out of the details."

Basil spoke. "Thank you, Deveroy. You've been very helpful indeed, but I feel you need to be away from Miss Katie for a while. I'm not sure I trust her being around you. I'll have you wait for my comrades at the theatre."

"Thanks." Deveroy nodded rapidly "Wait, there is one more thing. The Man...The Man seems to pull the strings. Even Lamia's afraid of him."

Katie, Azzurra and Basil focused on Deveroy. "Who's The Man?" Azzurra asked.

"I don't know. He's referred to as The Man, never met him. I saw him from a distance years ago. Older gentleman, long grey hair, kinda nice looking in a creepy way and I hear has a wild temper. Dormava, Medeia, Damiano and Marcus are kinda creeped-out by him too," Deveroy answered.

"The Man?" Basil whispered to himself.

Deveroy looked down to see Blackie at his heels. "Hey there little guy?" He went to reach for Blackie but was slapped on the shoulder by Katie.

"I shall send you to the theatre. Fill my comrades in on everything once everyone arrives, then bring them back here to the house." Basil made a hand movement and Deveroy vanished.

"We need to release Stephan." Basil said.

"Stephan? But he'll tell them that I'm here! He'll report back to Nathan." Katie turned to Basil and put her hands on her hips. "We can't release him, Basil."

"We will always do what the Vicar asks, Miss Katie. He won't lead us wrong. You must have trust in the Vicar," Basil said.

He waved a hand and a camel and round man wearing a black and white stripped suite with a ball and chain attached to his foot, appeared.

"Oh my stars, that was fast! I almost got dizzy. I'm out! I'm free! See, I told you I was framed I tell you...framed...just like that rabbit!" Stephan made an elegant swish of his arm and his clothes changed to safari shorts and jacket with a hat. His camel changed into a donkey. He held in his hand a large whip and began waving it madly in the air. "Ok....where's that horrible kitty and that water freak? I'm ready!"

"There will be no kitty or water creature." Basil walked toward him and smiled. "We are sorry for your incarceration dear sir, and beg that you forgive us. We had no intention of harming you. We thought you meant a great danger and were spying on us. That is why the alarms went off. But as you see, all is quiet. You are free to go and tell whoever, whatever you like." Basil took a great bow to him, throwing his trench coat to the rear. Then with his body still in a bow, he jerked his head up and smiled once again, green eyes piercing.

"My dear, oh dear, oh dear...well I did mean to spy. That was wrong. I mean that's what I was sent to do...find out if she was here and if you were around." He pointed to Katie and then looked to Basil once more. "But it was a trap. They said I would be in no danger, yet I was attacked by screaming angels, flashing lights, a water monster and a big black kitty and those Bubbles hurt, they were everywhere...oozing and morphing into horrifying beings."

Basil straightened into a strong stance. "No hard feelings, I hope." He made an elegant hand gesture to Azzurra and Katie. "This is Azzurra Stephani and Katie Marinacci...and that's Blackie." Blackie put his ears flat against his head.

"Well, nice to meet you all. I've heard so much about you. To tell you the truth, you all don't look that evil to me. My Lord, I was expecting pointed ears and long tails, with the way they talked." He made another hand movement and his donkey turned back into a camel. "I missed my camel." He smiled brightly at Basil. "I know that was a lie…about you doing something to Vincent. I never believed that line of drama. I don't care what that spell showed."

"I did not a thing to harm Vincent. Let me introduce myself properly. I am Basil O'Bryan…from the theatre!"

Stephan screamed so loud that everyone jumped. Blackie put his head under Katie's dress and tried to hide.

"The theatre, Oh my stars, I knew we had things in common! Oh, I was in all sorts of productions…"

"…yes, I as well, however, we shall chat about it another time. For now, we have to get ready for battle. A Witches War has been waged against us and we need to begin training the children, for none of them know that they are Witches and know nothing about Magick." Basil turned his back and smiled at Katie and Azzurra whose mouths were slightly ajar.

"Witches War? Children who don't know they are Witches? Oh for heaven's sake, you're dealing with some real powerful entities! The poor children!" He waved a hand in the air. "But have no fear, Stephan is here! To aide and protect!" His whip turned to a sword and his outfit changed back into the Egyptian warrior.

Basil turned toward Stephan and smiled widely. "As you are very welcome to join us, I would be delighted to work beside you, dear Stephan! However, I cannot promise there won't be danger. So with that said, may I call upon thee for help when we are in peril?"

"Oh my stars…you can call me anytime! He's too damn cute this one. It was nice to meet you ladies and Blackie too!" He appeared upon his camel. "Danger is my middle name. Until we meet again, may the force be with you! Hi ho Silver, away!" He rode out through the living room sliding glass door and vanished. Blackie peeked out from under Katie's dress.

"I told you, we should always have trust in the Vicar!" Basil proclaimed.

Azzurra and Katie beamed. "You are so dashing, my Basil." Azzurra pinched his cheeks.

Katie pinched his cheeks too. He blushed.

Azzurra looked to Katie. "Now Katie, don't you worry about us. You have to go to New York and San Francisco. You need to talk to Bella and Thom and then you should see Carlotta and Olivia. Basil and I will be fine with the kids."

Katie began to protest, saying that she was worried, that her feelings told her to stay. Basil and Azzurra assured her that they would be fine. Katie told them she should be back near 2:00am.

"I don't like this, but I'll go. Come on Blackie, you and Mommy have some work to do. It's not going to be Japan however, they are very nice cities." She reached down and picked up Blackie, took hold of his paw and waved as they vanished.

* * *

A Dream

"Michael are you gonna be home tonight?" Olivia asked her son as he walked into the kitchen.

"Yeah Ma, it's either home, studying, at work or on campus. What a life!" He paused and then continued, "Why do you want to know?"

Olivia replied. "I made lasagna for dinner. I've been craving lasagna for the longest time."

Michael turned to address his mother who stood near the stove. His eyes widened, jaw dropped and head jerked back. His mother wore a light-weight black blouse with a small scattering of gold, deep red and plum geometric shapes about the front. The blouse fit her loosely. Black slacks and tiny black slippers completed her attire. Olivia's dark hair had been washed and styled toward her face. A tad bit of makeup had been applied, accentuating her hazel eyes and high cheekbones.

Her eyes reflected something he couldn't quite put a finger on. There had been something about the way they contrasted with her olive skin tone…but there was something more…a flicker of something.

His mother took a sip of coffee from an old antique cup and saucer. He hadn't seen her use those in years. "Ma, you're dressed! You're hair looks nice and you're smiling. I'm in shock." Michael said.

"Beee, you act like you've never seen me before." She swished a hand at her son.

Michael sat down at the kitchen table. "Hey, I'm not complaining. It's actually nice to see you in something other than a housecoat. My God, Rose will fall over dead when she gets home." Michael cocked his head and leaned back in the chair. "What happened?"

Olivia joined him at the table. "You know Michael, I woke up this morning and I felt…well, I felt happy." She took a sip of coffee. "I felt happy and grateful that I have three healthy kids and I even felt happy to have your father, if you can believe that."

She placed the saucer and cup gently on the table. "After all those horrible dreams last night, I would have thought I'd be tired today — but I feel rested. I washed my hair and sat under the dryer and then I did laundry, cleaned the bathrooms and vacuumed. I washed down the counter tops and cleaned the kitchen floor too. I don't know why, but I seem to be full of energy today."

"I had a really weird dream last night too." Michael said. "I dreamt I heard you screaming and for some reason in my dream. I knew that Dad was dead — don't ask me how I knew, I just knew. Anyway, I went to run to your room, but then I heard Rose screaming and my door was thrown open. Everything else is kind of foggy but I thought I remembered seeing this blonde guy in my room. I knew he meant me harm. I think he was a ghost or something, but he never attacked me. It was a really freaky dream."

Michael pulled his legs up to his chest and rested his stocking feet on the chair. He flung his dark blonde hair out of his face as he hugged his legs against his slim body.

Olivia's eyes widened. "I can't believe you had a weird dream too. I'm not sure if I should tell you mine. You might have nightmares then you'll be up all night. You kids are all afraid of your own shadows."

Michael's hazel eyes widened. "Tell me. I'll be fine."

"Well, in my dream, I had woken up and that damn thing had come back. You know that thing that sits at the end of my bed. I felt the mattress sink down like someone was sitting there. Oh, I hate that! It scares the hell out me." Her eyes searched the kitchen for a moment.

"The next thing I remember is that I looked over to your father and this horrifying thing was on top of him. I remember my heart beating so fast. I could see this beast thing in the moonlight. Oh Michael, it was horrible. It had long hair all over its body, huge paws and it was inches away from your father's face." Olivia shuddered. "I screamed for your father to wake up, but he didn't move." She glanced toward the hallway that led to the bedrooms and then back to her son.

"I remember running for the bedroom door and that thing...oh God Michael; I think it was a demon or something. The thing leapt to its feet and threw me back across the room into my jewelry box. I felt pain everywhere. It had these ugly yellow eyes and it squealed like a pig. Oh, it was so real." Olivia placed a hand over her mouth, and then released it after a moment.

"I got up and I told it to get away from your father. I raised my arms to block something...I think, then it squealed in pain. I don't know what I did, but it was thrown off your father or maybe it jumped. I don't know. Anyway, I remember a man appeared...this handsome man and I knew that I was safe. He made me feel so protected...happy. Anyway, there was a red light and the demon thing vanished." Olivia's eyes glazed over for a moment. "It was so real."

Michael grimaced, lowered his legs to the floor and leaned toward his mother. "Was he in a white suit?"

Olivia took a deep breath and placed a hand over her chest. "Yes! All white and he had dark hair. How did you know?"

"I don't know. I just knew it was a man in a white suit and he had a tie. A strange tie made of gemstones." Michael stood and walked toward one of the kitchen cabinets. "That's weird Ma. I'm getting chills!"

"Yes, there was a tie with gemstones. Oh Michael, remember all the strange things that used to happen when Caesar was alive? Oh that dog used to scare the hell out of me. He'd always stare off into the air and growl. His fur would stand on edge and he'd follow something that I never saw." Olivia rose to her feet. "I don't know what it could mean...with this guy in a white suite. Maybe he's an angel looking over us." She walked to Michael, who began fixing himself a cup of coffee.

"I used to freak out when Caesar did that. He used to do that in my room and then stand near me like he was protecting me or something." Michael walked back to the table and took his seat again. "Maybe we should get another dog?" He raised he legs to his chest. "I miss Caesar. He was my little buddy." Michael began to nibble on the sleeve of his black sweatshirt.

Olivia took a seat at the table. "Little? That dog was huge. Michael, stop that! That's so disgusting. You're nineteen, not four and you need a haircut. Your hair looks like hell. Did you lose weight…those jeans are too baggy on you." She swished a hand at her son. "I miss Caesar too. It's not the same without him. Maybe we should get another dog, maybe not a German shepherd/wolf mix. Maybe we should get a golden retriever or collie, or even a shepherd without the wolf."

"There is nothing wrong with wolves." Michael said. They looked toward the front door as they heard it open. A couple of seconds later, Rose entered. She dropped a bag to the floor and began a cheer. Her vocal cords rang through the house. A full cheer later, she adjusted her orange sweats and sat at the table. Michael narrowed his eyes as he focused on two large blonde pigtails that hung down the sides of her head.

"I have had the best day ever! That was a new cheer for next Saturday's game…we just learned it today. Man! I could run around the world!" She smiled at Michael and then to her mother. "Oh I know, pigtails, haven't worn them in years! Just felt kind of crazy today." She bounced her head back and forth as Michael rolled his eyes. "My God, Mom! No housecoat? You look cute and your hair is washed and decent looking. I guess you had a good day too, eh." She removed both orange scrunches' and flung her head all around. Once the flinging had stopped, she began to run her fingers through the mass of light brown waves.

Olivia swished a hand toward her daughter. "Beee, Michael said the same thing." She shook her head. "I made lasagna for dinner."

"Awesome, I'm starving." Rose looked to her brother and then back to her mother. "I don't know what it was, but I woke up feeling so happy."

Michael and Olivia looked at each other, then back to Rose.

Rose rambled on. "I had a really cool dream last night. I remember sleeping and something happened to wake me up. Have no clue what that was, but I remember being awake in my dream. You know, when you dream you're waking up from a dream? Anyway, I felt so protected, warm and loved." A smile slid into place as she shivered with delight.

"Why do I get nightmares and she gets warm and protected?" Michael lifted the coffee mug and held it in his palms.

Rose continued. "There was this beautiful, handsome man. Oh Ma, he was so handsome! He wore this immaculate white suit, kind of like a tuxedo. It had tails but he didn't have a bow tie. Instead, it had this really cool tie made of gemstones."

Michael spit his coffee over his sweatshirt as his mother gasped.

"What the hell is the matter with you two?" Rose put her hand to her chest. "What?"

They began to share their dreams with Rose, whose mouth dropped as she listened to their description of what they had dreamt.

"Remember how Caesar used to creep us all out, staring into space at some Spirit or something?" Rose got to her feet and headed for the coffee.

Olivia spoke. "You know what else is weird? I've had your Aunty Azzurra and my sister on my mind all day today. And I don't have good feelings either. I've got to call them. Carlotta said she was taking me to lunch Saturday, but something is wrong. I need to call her. I also feel that my mother...never mind." She looked to Rose, then Michael and continued. "I feel her near."

"I haven't seen Aunty Azzurra since Uncle Franco's funeral or Aunt Carlotta for that matter." Michael started to nibble on his sleeve again.

"I know, I miss them...poor Aunty Azzurra. I called her about three weeks ago and asked her how she's doing without Uncle Franco. She said she's a tough old lady. We are supposed to have lunch soon. I need to call her. Ma, we have to see her. It's been three months." Rose looked toward her brother. "You are a gross pig! Stop nibbling your shirt! You're like a deranged rabbit."

All of their eyes looked toward the front door as they heard it open. A few seconds later, Walter entered. "Hey there gang, got out of work a bit early today."

"Let me guess. You're having an awesome day, right Dad?" Michael spoke rather reluctantly. Normally the energy would turn cold and bitter, defenses would rise and everyone would leave the room when Walter entered.

"Yes, I am." He kissed Olivia and Rose and flicked a piece of Michael's hair, proclaiming that a haircut was in order. "I smell lasagna!" He broke into a sideward smirk and winked at Olivia.

Three pairs of eyes widened as they watched the man before them. His blonde hair had been combed neatly to the side. Deep blue eyes sparkled. Slight in build, he looked neat and pressed in his charcoal grey suit with a blue and grey swirled tie that David, his eldest son, gave him years ago.

Olivia spoke with care. "Have any weird dreams?"

"Not that I can remember." He poured himself the last of the coffee and turned off the warmer. He faced his family, leaned against the counter and took a sip of black coffee. "You two going to be home for dinner? It would be nice to have everyone sit at the table together. We should call David; see what he's up too?"

The Vicar lowered his hand that had been raised toward Walter. He knew that Olivia and Michael would retain more of their dreams than Rose. He also knew that Walter would remember nothing. Michael was the next in line to inherit the linage of the Degeli power. He would need to be protected, as he knew that they would eventually come after him. The family indeed had become too powerful. It was no wonder why evil was so interested in the Degelis.

It had surprised him when Olivia threw the demon from Walter. To use that kind of power without the assistance of a wand or Spirit was beyond expectations. It had also surprised him that she was able to remember the event so clearly. They indeed have grown too strong...too strong for their own good. Olivia's other power was developing, the power of precognition. She's sensing the danger already, only after a day of being in his presence.

The Vicar's heart ached for a split second. He knew they had free will to do as they pleased. He also knew that the Higher Spirits would not tolerate a Witches' family with such power. When would they decide? Or could they? After all, it is their own laws to let those live and carry out their Free Will. He would continue to heal the family and support them. He would pay a visit to David, Olivia's eldest son, and open his mind so that he may begin to heal from the emotional scars. He would continue to do as he was told...to support the Degelis, to protect them with the least amount of interference. He would do this until the threat to them dissolved or until the day when their lives must be sacrificed for the greater good of mankind.

* * * *

Lamia's Lament

For the past two hours Marcus sat patiently. He listened to the most beautiful woman he had ever met threaten to rip the heads off any mortal that stood in her way. *Why was everyone so incompetent!?* The words rang in his brain. His eyes followed her as she paced back and forth — muttering horrid threats. She writhed with anger and swore incessantly. Lamia stopped abruptly, turned toward Marcus and asked the question that she had asked several times that evening.

"Where is that stupid, oversized queen!? He should have returned hours ago! It's near 7 and that fool is nowhere in sight. Try that summoning spell again! Force him here!"

Marcus stood, rubbed his jeans and said the incantation.

"How powerful can that pansy be? Bring him to me!" Lamia screamed and threw a lamp across the room.

"We know very little about Stephan, with the exception of his theatre background. He must know of an incantation to block the summoning spell or be in the presence of someone who does."

Lamia looked up to the ceiling and then scanned the room for a sign of Stephan. She made a deep guttural sound and threw a picture frame in the blazing fire place. "Where is Damiano!? It takes all evening to find out if a Vicar is with Olivia!?"

Marcus took his seat in a high-back leather armchair and answered. "Damiano should be here soon. If the Vicar is with Olivia, he will need to be careful."

"Idiots!" Lamia shouted. "Where are those tramps? Dormava and Medeia had better done what I asked. Celia needs to know we can no longer trust Contessa!"

Marcus sighed and answered. "I'm sure Dormava and Medeia have informed Celia of your distrust in her mother. Please, my dear, calm down and sit. They will be here shortly." He focused on a painting of a weeping willow and inhaled a large breath. After a sigh, he continued. "Stephan often gets distracted. Maybe he has gone to the *FOX Theatre* again."

"Distracted?" A figurine of an old British soldier went across the room and hit the wall. "I need him to tell me if he has seen Basil or Katie at Azzurra's house! I've been waiting for hours and you tell me he may be at the theatre!" A vase smashed into an end table. She turned and pointed at Marcus. "I want you to check with Nathan and Contessa once more! Ask them if they heard from Stephan."

"Lamia, I just got back ten…"

"…do it!" She commanded.

Marcus vanished, leaving the beautiful woman to herself. She cursed under her breath and paced. After several minutes, Lamia caught her reflection in the full-length mirror and paused. Long tresses of black hair cascaded over her shoulders and down her back. She smiled at her appearance. Soon she would have what she desired, to stay in corporeal form for as long as she wished.

Marcus appeared before her. "Contessa has not heard from him. She asked about Deveroy."

"Damn!" A painting was ripped off the wall and flung into the baby grand piano. "I'll tell her Deveroy is with Achar. Let me go to Azzurra's, after which I shall go to Contessa's. I shall calm her and engage her trust. If Contessa gets nervous, she may try and control me." She sighed then turned away from Marcus. "The Man has not yet given me the power to resist her." She turned to Marcus. "I simply want to see her eyes when she answers. Her eyes will tell me if she is lying." Lamia strode up to Marcus, placed a finger upon his cheek and traced down to his chest. "Although, if The Man feels something is wrong…if he feels that Azzurra has the upper edge…he may just grant my powers early."

* * * *

Enchanted Objects, Sachets & Elixirs and Wands

The clock chimed seven times. With a last gulp of wine, Marta joined Marie and Nicco who stood by dining room entrance. She paused, turned and reached for the bottle of cabernet. Nicco took hold of one arm and began to drag her toward the exit. Marie wrestled the bottle from her firm grip. "Let go Marta! We have to be focused! It's probably not a good idea to cast spells drunk!"

Several minutes later they entered the kitchen. Marta looked down at her stained sweater. "Marie, this had better come out."

"Do you really think a stain matters, Marta? Maybe Magick can get it out." Nicco retorted in a snap.

"Can we stop saying that word? It sounds so ridiculous." Marta brushed Maries hand away.

Nicco shrugged his shoulders as they past his aunts and mother. "Where's Aunty Katie?"

"I told you at dinner, Nicco. Your Aunty Katie went to see Uncle Thom and Aunt Bella. You don't listen, Nicco," Azzurra scolded.

"Sorry Ma. My attention was on the lasagna."

Arianna laughed while Azzurra continued to remind him how inconsiderate and rude it was not to listen when someone speaks to you.

The six of them rounded the corner of the cellar and watched as their little Italian mother stood near an opening in the floor that they had never seen before. Azzurra flicked a switch on the wall and light illuminated the old steps.

"Be careful going down." Azzurra glanced over her shoulder." Marta, don't worry about the stain. I'll get it out later." She disappeared down the old stone steps.

One by one, they made their way down to the secret room. Marie held onto Nicco's shoulder as they walked down the steps. They marveled at the apothecary and the old hutches full of items and books. It was real...they were really Witches. Nicco glanced down onto the maple hutch. He picked up one of the spheres that held a milky white liquid. He raised it up to his eyes and watched the liquid explode into gyrating swirls within the egg. "This is cool."

Arianna took the sphere from him and placed it back in the wooden egg carton. "We don't know what that is and God forbid if you should drop it." Arianna pinched Nicco's cheeks. "Don't touch anything else."

Gabriella noticed a watch that once belonged to Franco. She knew of the powers it possessed. "Azzurra, did you decide if you're going to re-cast the spell on the watch and bind it to Nicco?"

"Yes, I have Arianna, I mean Gabriella and that would be no, I am not. I've decided it's far too powerful of an enchantment to give to someone who could accidently kill us all if he used it at the wrong moment."

"Good thinking," Gabriella said.

Arianna patted Nicco's cheek and smiled. "What are you gonna do? You could kill us all."

Azzurra continued as she stood near the Wooton desk. "Remember to thank your Aunty Katie for the wonderful dinner when she gets back." She cleared her throat to get Nicco and Marie's attention. "We have to concentrate…no fooling around! I cannot tell you the importance of knowing how to defend yourselves. Here are your supplies." She glanced down to three large boxes, each labeled with their names.

Her eyes narrowed at Marta who was muttering to herself. Marta apologized. Azzurra took a deep breath then spoke. "Basil will be here in a moment and will be instructing you during your training. You are to listen to anything he tells you. Now, Arianna has the power of Enchanted Objects. She'll be with you, Nicco. Marie, you will be with your Aunt Gabriella, as she has the power of Sachets and Elixirs. Marta dear, you'll be with me. We have power of Wands."

Several comments of delight were made about the power of Sachet and Elixirs from Marie. Marta complained about having Wands. It seemed boring. While Nicco made a lude comment about enchanting something on his person. Gabriella slapped him upside his head as she took Marie to one of the boxes.

Azzurra narrowed her eyes. "Thank you Gabriella. Nicco, one more comment like that and Tracy will think she's dating a woman!"

"Ma, I made a joke. I'm sorry. Gee!" He picked up the box labeled with his name and stood near Arianna.

"Marta, you and I will practice right here. Slide that box over this way. Oh and by the way, Wands are anything but boring, I'll have you know." Azzurra said.

Marta bent down and slid the box over toward the Wooton desk.

Basil appeared next to Marie. "Sorry Mum. I was checking on Deveroy. Two of my comrades have arrived, still waiting on one from Japan and another from England."

"They'll be here soon, I'm sure." Azzurra eyed Marta once again then turned to her Wand Spirit. "Basil honey, I want you watch us as we go through the training and assist in any manner you see fit."

"Of course, Mum." Basil rubbed his palms together. "Now let us get started, shall we?"

* * * *

Sachets & Elixirs

Gabriella's charm floated Marie's box in the air and glided it up the stone steps. She winked at her niece as Marie's eyes widen with excitement. "Back in the day, I would have needed my wand for that charm."

As they passed Nicco, Marie slapped him on his shoulder for advising her not to blow anything to smithereens.

The downstairs had a full service kitchen, complete with sink, refrigerator, and stove. It had all the kitchen supplies that anyone would need: pots, pans, measuring utensils, appliances and a large table just outside the main kitchen area that seated eight.

Marie began to arrange the items from the box onto the countertop.

"Sachets and Elixirs is your strength Marie." Gabriella began. "What that means, is that you have an instinct in the mixing of ingredients that will bring the effect you desire."

Marie smiled. "It's like cooking?"

"Yes honey, it is very much like cooking." Gabriella helped organize the contents of the box onto the counter. "This calling can be useful in the unfortunate situation in which you must defend yourself or a loved one. We never attack...we defend. Always remember that." She winked at Marie. "Although, sometimes you need to attack to defend."

Marie nodded.

"You see, each Witch or Warlock has a concentration...one power that they excel in. However, we all have a secondary power as well. I am double Sachet and Elixirs."

"Double?" Marie questioned

"Yes, double. That makes me very powerful in creating sachets and elixirs. People under estimate my powers because of that too. It's like only including your sun sign and never considering your moon sign. Double, means I don't have another concentration to weaken my first concentration. Not many Witches are double anything. Your Uncle Nicolai is also Sachets and Elixirs, but he has a secondary power of Enchanted Objects. We all have the ability to use one of the four concentrations, but we are limited to the extent of its effect. I could use a wand to do simple tasks, but could never use a wand the way your mother does. Your Aunty Arianna is very good with Enchanted Objects, while my enchantments would fizzle and fade. She also has a secondary power of Sachets and Elixirs, which I don't have to tell you, she never honed. You see, Sachets and Elixirs are pretty common, but double concentration is not."

"I see. What's my secondary power?" Marie asked.

"Oh honey, I have no idea. We'll find out though." Gabriella read a bottle of one of the ingredients and looked up to her niece. "Ingredients are simply ingredients. It is a good chef that will morph them into the most explosive sachet you'll every toss at your enemy."

Gabriella opened a long cabinet and took out two white aprons. She gave one of the aprons to her niece. Marie glanced at the writing. It had large red letters in a script font that said: *Brewing Something Delicious!* She glanced down at her own apron which had bright red letters in the same font — *A Cauldron of Love.*

Gabriella finished tying the strings tightly around her waist and then began to explain. "The downfall of elixirs is in the event of an attack. Think about it...who is going to be willing to drink an elixir from an enemy during a battle? Therefore, they have little use in battle, with the exception of healing the wounded." She smoothed her apron.

"Now, there are some elixirs that you can throw at your enemy. They have a kind of exploding effect, which can be very useful in defending." She saw the look on Marie's face and spoke quickly. "But I think explosives will be far too advanced for the beginner Witch."

Marie wished she had drunk a bit more wine at dinner. "What can they do? I mean if you throw them or drink them?"

Gabriella began to line up several small vials on the counter. "Well honey, you can drink an elixir to heal yourself or someone else. Sometimes, you just have to pour it over the wound. This can be effective even if they are moments from death, or just minutes after death. You can give elixirs to animals and plants as well. There are elixirs to compel you to speak the truth, ones that make you appear dead, alter memories and even ones that can place you into a catatonic state."

Marie nodded as Basil approached and greeted them.

Gabriella waved at Basil and then spoke. "I think what makes a Witch exceptional at Sachets and Elixirs, is the ability to be creative with how you use them. I don't mean in mixing them. Most people can mix ingredients. What I mean, is how you disguise them. Now, think about it. You are a creative woman. You sew and cook. You can do pottery and all that crafty stuff. I wasn't good at those things. But you, you have an advantage. Be as creative as you like. A sachet doesn't have to be wrapped in a cloth. It could be sewn into a hair ribbon. The same is true with elixirs." She placed several bags of herbs on the counter.

Marie's mind swirled with ideas on where she could place elixirs and sachets: blown glass, vases, stained glass, ceramics and clothes. The possibilities were endless.

Marie looked at the book, *Basic Elixirs for the Starting Witch,* which was left open to a healing elixir called *Renew.* She read through some of the ingredients and then flipped several pages ahead. All the ingredients sounded like herbs and spices. They usually had some sort of root of a plant or a hair of some animal.

Gabriella asked Basil to place a large cauldron on the stove. After lighting the burner, she turned the valve and set the flame to low. "You just don't want to use any pot or pan. You should use cast iron. Not necessarily a cauldron either, but cauldrons tend to hold heat evenly."

"Sachets are more popular than elixirs in battle for the simple fact that most of them you can just toss at your opponent. There are four main categories of sachets: smell, taste, touch and speech."

"Now, smell is the first type of sachet. Not as tricky as you may think. It's very hard to block a smell, especially if you're not expecting it." She nodded to herself in agreement. "There are plenty of things you can do with sachets that smell. You can make an enemy hallucinate, vomit and levitate. Oh let's see, you can make them faint or put them in a deep sleep for a specified time. I liked that one when I couldn't seem to get a good night's rest. Oh, it's been years since I've done that."

"The victim can become giddy and light headed, fall in love with the first person they see for a specified time, which can be very helpful in distracting them. You can even transform someone into an object of some sort. That's very difficult by the way and can go horribly wrong."

Marie's eyes widened as she continued to listen to her aunt.

"Taste has the difficulty liken to that of elixirs. You must have them taste it. But that doesn't necessarily mean drink it, as with an elixir. So, it's much easier. It just has to touch their taste buds. So if they are not expecting it, it could be quite easy." Gabriella opened a couple of cabinets until she found a pitcher and then brought it to the sink and began to fill it with water.

"All of these will do nothing or backfire if you don't do them properly or have enough power behind you. Anyway, taste sachets can lock up every muscle in your body and freeze you. You can make a person go blind, lose their voice and even morph them or yourself into an animal. But that's really tricky and far too advanced." Gabriella poured the water into the cauldron then took the book, *Basic Elixirs for the Starting Witch*.

Basil interjected. "Visualization is the key. If you let you mind wander just a wee bit during the process, your outcome could be quite different."

"Basil's right, seen it a dozen times myself. You'll learn the proper way to concentrate…it's very important. Anybody can mix ingredients, but the concentration and visualization is vital. Anyway, touch is the third type of sachet. These can be wonderful for protection. It's all in the Witches' creativity. They can be reused over and over too, without having to remix the ingredients and cast another incantation. Normally this is used in objects. You can blast people across the room, make them feel as though bugs are crawling over them, or capture them inside the object. That can be tricky though, I once turned someone into the object. Muma was so mad that time." She swished a hand. "What are gonna do? Anyway, touch can be very simple to inflict upon an enemy. The ingredients just have to touch them and it doesn't have to be the actual ingredients either. The container will act as a conduit and give the same effect." She skimmed to a particular page in the book.

"The last type of sachet is speech. This sachet must accompany an incantation. Speech is a very powerful category and takes time to learn. Now, with these types of sachets a person can speak to the dead, raise bodies from the grave...zombies, pretty awful stuff to fool around with. You can cast the evil eye, placed hexes on people, bewitch objects and produce fire and ice. Evil Witches use this sachet quite often, but it can be useful for us good Witches too." She pinched Marie's cheek.

"They can cause explosions, the freezing of air or water, or enchant an object. Speech sachets are the most powerful. However, you have to be able to say the incantation." She placed a hand to the side of the cauldron and continued. "Sachets and Elixirs don't have to be so scary. Some can produce wonderful things. It just depends on how you mix them and what you visualize. Since we're preparing to defend ourselves, I thought I'd stick to the more basic spells."

She began to read one of the recipes and then looked up to her niece. "For this evening, I think we should stick with healing elixirs and some defensive sachets." Gabriella sorted squares of felt and other fabrics and placed them on the counter.

Marie looked to her aunt and then took a deep breath. "OK Aunt Gabriella. Elixirs are good for healing & exploding and sachets have four elements: smell, taste, touch and speech, with speech being the most powerful because it needs a vocal incantation." She nodded to herself. Basil smiled.

Gabriella took a breath and then spoke. "I don't mean to scare you, but remember you must concentrate on the effect you wish to have during the process of making the sachet or elixir. Otherwise, instead of creating a bolt of ice...you'll just get a squirt of water. Now, lets' make some healing elixirs. Remember to visualize the effect or it could be disastrous."

* * * *

Wands

*A*zzurra pulled a drawer from the Wooton desk and removed a rather ornate wand. It was seven and a half inches long, spiraled with oak, ash, cedar and maple. She held the wand up to her daughter. "Marta, you have the Magickal power of Wands. This was your grandmothers. I'm bequeathing it to you."

Marta took the wand and smirked. "Ma, this is so silly…a wand? What is this supposed to do?" She made a large letter Z in the air.

"Marta! Don't do that!" Azzurra took Marta's arm and held it still. "We all have natural abilities that can do things even without the use of a Spirit. It can be very dangerous waving a wand around."

"Sorry Ma. This is all kind of weird. I mean a wand? That's fantasy." She made a quick flick with the wand. A tiny light expelled from the tip, followed by a swishing noise. A bottle exploded on the pine hutch. Nicco, Basil and Arianna turned to look. Marta screamed and dropped the wand.

"Are you blowing things up already, Marta?" Nicco called out.

273

"Marta!" Azzurra bent down and retrieved the wand. She took her daughter's hand and placed the wand back into her daughter's palm. "Marta, I'm going to get mad. Now, are you going to listen to me or not? This is not fantasy! Once you take a wand in your possession, it immediately has power through the Witch herself. Because this wand was my mother's, it reacts to what it recognizes. The wand will know the power of a Degeli."

Marta took a large breath. "I'm sorry Ma. I just didn't think anything would happen."

Basil walked over. "Marta, you need to take this more seriously. Your mum's trying to teach you something and you're saying it's weird and silly. Now you need to grow up and be respectful."

"Grow up? I need to be a child to believe in all this," Marta laughed.

Basil's voice raised, face reddened and eyes narrowed. "It wasn't silly when your Uncle Gilbert had a cross speared through his chest at little Vincent's funeral. Nor when your Aunt Angelica had seven knives thrust into her while standing in her very own kitchen and your poor Aunt Francine was forced off the road by a demon." Basil's voice rose louder. "They were accomplished Witches that thought nothing silly of Magick, and look what happened to them. I will tell you this one time and one time only…you listen to your mother, because if I have to come over here again, I'll show you what *I* can do with a wand!"

Marta's eyes flooded with tears. She swallowed hard and with a barely audible voice, said that she was sorry. Basil turned and strode back to Arianna and Nicco and began to scold them for not working.

"Now, I tried to tell you, didn't I? Here take this tissue. Don't let him see you cry or he'll come back." Azzurra shifted to the right and blocked Basil's view. "I hope you're ready to listen."

Marta nodded and dabbed her eyes. A moment later, her voice broke as tears streamed down her cheeks. "He didn't have to be so mean."

Azzurra placed her palms upon her daughter's cheeks and spoke firmly. "If I thought he was being mean I would have stopped him. He knows what he is doing. He loves you and wants to make sure you survive this Witches' War. Now, pull yourself together while I tell you a few things."

Azzurra turned to look at Basil and mouthed that they were fine. "Honey, I know that this is all new, and I understand it must come as a shock to you. However, once you understand and let it all sink you, you'll feel better."

Azzurra gave Marta several more tissues and continued. "Let me explain a few things. A Witch with the power of Wands does not necessarily need a

274

wand. Anything with a tip will do. This helps to focus the energy. Basil just told me that this afternoon. Anyway, if you should lose your wand in battle, remember, anything with a tip will suffice. The power it will produce will not be the same, but it may just mean the difference between life and death. The moment a Witch picks up an object, something with a tip, she can perform Magick. Now, the wand is more traditional because if you use the same object, the power begins to reside within the wand, producing more power." Azzurra nodded to her daughter and smiled as Marta nodded and dabbed her eyes.

"Now, Wands are more the trend of Warlocks. However, it doesn't mean that men are more powerful at Wands than women. It's all in the genes, the Witch herself and the knowledge she possesses." Azzurra reached into Marta's box of supplies and retrieved a book. She handed it to Marta.

"I want you to read this. It's a very good book. I read it when I was little girl. It may be old, but I think the generation nowadays, forgets how powerful old Magick can be. Now, don't get discouraged if things don't go well right off the bat. Wands can be tricky and can take a very long time to master. The most important thing any Witch can do is to have the confidence that she can do the spell and the act of visualization. Without that, you're just a woman carrying a pretty stick."

Marta read the title of the book her mother gave her: *Getting to Know Your Wand.*

"Oh how cute Ma…*Getting to Know Your Wand.*" She cleared her throat. "Should I name my wand?" Her eyes widened as she began to shake her head. "No, never mind. Sorry Ma. I'm just that way. It's how I handle stress." She quickly turned around to see if Basil had heard her. "I'll read it tonight."

"I know sweetheart. We will all laugh about this one day. Unfortunately, today is not that day." Azzurra noticed that Basil was heading up the stone steps and out of the secret room. He must be going to check on Marie, she thought.

Azzurra pulled her own wand from the desktop and continued to explain. "All Warlocks and Witches have native, instinctive powers that can be used without a wand. For instance, we just have to raise our hand and we can block flying objects from hitting us. Boil and freeze water, and send objects across the room. We have the innate ability to communicate with plants and animals and have a keen insight to people, both Magickal and non-Magickal. We also have the ability…well some of us, have the ability to see from our loved ones eyes in times of stress or danger. That's how I knew it was a fluffy squirrel at the cemetery and not some rabid monster." She swished a hand toward daughter. "Some Witches even develop the power of premonition."

Azzurra looked over to Nicco and Arianna, then back to Marta. "You have Wands as your power. That means that all of your natural abilities are increased tenfold. By using a wand, you focus the energy. Now recently, we discovered that the use of wands may be fading out completely. Although, Basil still believes that using something with a tip is beneficial...producing more powerful Magick. We are not quite sure why your cousin Olivia could fight a demon without the use of a wand. However, until we understand what has happened to our powers and see how they have developed, I'd like you to use a wand." Azzurra nodded.

Marta acknowledged her mother with a short nod of her own.

"You can do many things with a wand beyond your natural abilities, but that's where it can get dangerous for a Witch." Azzurra pulled the chair from the Wooton desk and sat. "That is, because very powerful defensive and attack spells require the use of a Spirit to enter the wand and do your bidding. When a Spirit enters your wand, both of your powers are combined to create a force even more powerful than if separate. When Basil entered my wand earlier today, something was different. It was as though our minds melded. Normally, our powers would meld but not our minds. Anyway, the Spirit has to be willing to enter your wand, unlike that of a Witch with the power of Spirits. These Witches can force a weaker Spirit to do her bidding, without his or her consent. Your Aunt Tessa has the power of Spirits." She shook her head slightly.

"The risky thing about Spirits is that they can abandon you at anytime. Spirits can be fickle and have been known to let their Witch die in battle if she does not say the proper incantation or simply for a laugh. I have never had that problem, as Basil has always been my Wand Spirit."

"Ma, that's horrible! I can be in the middle of a fight and the Spirit can just leave? I don't like this whole thing with using a Spirit. It sounds scary to me. Who's my Spirit? What if I get a mean Spirit?" Marta looked around for a chair.

"Well honey, I don't think we will have to worry about that right now. I don't want you using your wand with a Spirit just yet. It's too dangerous. Basil has some friends. Maybe one of them will want to become your wand Spirit?"

Azzurra stood up. "Here honey, sit down." Marta sat.

"One of the main reasons why the family gave up Magick was because of Spirits. Oh Marta, you have no idea what can be out there. The evil you can invite into your home, when calling upon Spirits. You don't know them from Adam. They could be demons or other celestials that are more horrifying than you can imagine. Basil knows a lot about what is out there — beyond the living. That's why he gets so upset. He knows what can happen." Azzurra looked down for a moment.

"They can physically hurt you, torture and even kill you. They can be horrible looking creatures with powers beyond us simple Witches. Witches should have never invoked the power of Spirits. You can be dealing with the devil himself." Her eyes flickered and lips tightened.

"But why does Aunt Tessa use Spirits? How did you get Basil?" Marta asked carefully.

"That question is what began the first Witches War. Your Aunty Katie felt that the use of Spirits were far too dangerous and should be banned. But my father didn't agree. You see, my father knew Basil for a very long time and he bequeathed him to me. That's how I met Basil. It was through my dad." Azzurra looked to Arianna and Nicco and then focused back on Marta.

"Even though I agree with Katie that the use of Spirits can be very dangerous, we have to use Spirits because your Aunt Tessa is using Spirits…and you must use Spirits to fight Spirits."

Azzurra began to pace a bit in front of the pine hutch. "But not to worry, you will not be using Spirits any time soon. We have enough Spirits to help us. Basil has recruited some of his friends from the theatre. We have Deveroy and Stephan and of course, Basil himself and your Aunty Katie, who we know we can trust."

Marta nodded.

"Enough about Spirits, I want you to practice the basics." Azzurra flipped through a couple of pages of the book and turned to a chapter called *Protective Charms*. "I want you to read this tonight."

"OK, it sounds charming." Marta quickly looked over her shoulder.

"Remember, the key is to visualize the effect you desire and have the confidence that you can do the spell." Azzurra smiled. "Read anything else in regards to protection.

Azzurra took Marta's hand and touched the ring that she had given her the night before. "Now, I did an enchantment to bind this ring to you the other day. It works very much like my pendant, with the exception that it will strike the Spirit or entity with such force, it should make it flee. Never take this off."

"Do I have to do anything to make it work?" Marta asked.

"Here's a note. Three simple incantations depending on what type of threat there is. I've accounted for mortal Witches from the evil side of the family, Spirits and well…Demons. Other than a few simple words for the correct entity, there is nothing you need to do. A loud hum will sound if you're sleeping to alert you. It will vibrate if you're awake or asleep. Check to see what color it is and simply point the ring at the target and say the corresponding incantation. I thought of giving the ring an automatic response but with an incantation, the spell becomes more powerful. I want you to sleep with your wand under your pillow."

"Thanks Ma, for the ring, and Grandma's wand. I won't take it off and I'll read through this book tonight and learn the incantations for the ring." Marta rose to her feet.

She watched as her mother opened one of the drawers of the Wooton desk and pulled out a rubber ball. "I used to practice my levitation and wand control with this little rubber ball. We shall do the same." Azzurra smiled. She picked up her own wand from the desk and asked Marta to hold up her wand and concentrate on controlling the ball.

* * * *

Enchanted Objects

$\mathcal{N}$icco smirked and watched the box of Marie's items float up the stairs. "Don't blow anything to smithereens, eh sis." Marie slapped his arm and followed her Aunt Gabriella up the stone steps.

"Leave your sister alone or I'll turn you into a toad." Arianna pinched his cheeks.

"The cheeks Aunty...the cheeks." Nicco blushed.

Basil spoke. "I'd watch what you say Nicco, you're sister is wonderful in the Kitchen and that will make her very powerful with Sachets and Elixirs. You on the other hand, may have some difficulty. So don't make fun of her until you see what you'll be like."

"Difficulty?" Nicco folded his arms. "Not a chance."

Basil placed his hands into his trench coat and arched a brow. "Enchanted Objects can be useless if you lack the ability to focus, and if you have not a creative tongue."

"He's right Nicco." Arianna added. "Enchanted Objects are tricky. You have to think fast and really visualize what you want to have happen, and if you don't vocalize it with the exact words that meet your intent…well nothing will happen…if you're lucky. If you're not lucky, well you could blow your own head off." Arianna looked to Basil.

Nicco rubbed his hands together. "Yea yea…how does it work?"

They heard a sudden crash as a bottle flew off the pine hutch and smashed to the floor. Marta had dropped her wand. Nicco laughed and made a joke.

Basil's voice lowered as he took Nicco by the shoulder. "You need to be more supportive Nicco, I won't say it again. I'll be right back." Basil walked toward Marta and Azzurra.

"Now I've always thanked my lucky stars that I had Enchanted Objects. I would have blown up the house if I had Sachets and Elixirs!" Arianna waved a hand at her nephew and then noticed Basil having heated words with Marta. "Oh dear…poor Marta, I feel bad." She turned to Nicco. "He's not going to tell you again…be supportive to your sisters." She slapped him lightly on the cheek.

Nicco and his Aunt stood for a moment as Basil raised his voice to Marta.

"Wow, he has a temper." Nicco added. "Marta's gonna be upset."

They watched as Basil turned and walk toward them. He raised his voice as he addressed them. "Why are the two of you just standing there…what I said to your sister is none of your concern…unless you think this is nothing but silly nonsense too."

They shook their heads quickly.

Basil tone became light once again. "Your Aunt Arianna is pretty scary with Enchanted Objects, she is. You'll learn plenty from her."

Nicco looked to his Aunt. He just couldn't image her being in a fight. She had to be one of the sweetest, most gentle persons he had ever known.

Basil excused himself and said that he was going to check on Marie.

"Marta's crying. He shouldn't have yelled at her like that." Nicco whispered. "He's scary when he's mad."

"When your mother tells him to do something, he takes it to heart. It's only for your own good. He knows there may not be much time." Arianna glanced up the stairs to make sure Basil was gone. "Oh I used to cry when he tried to teach me things. I would act silly and then his temper would ignite…

beee, then I'd cry like Marta." She swished a hand. "He's a sweetie, all out of love."

"Marie will gain 400 pounds if he yells at her like that." Nicco said.

Arianna slapped his arm. "Marie will take things serious. She doesn't have the silliness like Marta and I." She glanced to Marta and Azzurra and then focused back to Nicco.

"Now, any object can be enchanted. You have to visualize what you want the object to do; this will bring life to the object and give it a means by which it can act on its own accord. Some Witches and Wizards lack the concentration and the power — their enchanted objects simply fizzle out half way through. Gabriella is so-so with Enchanted Objects. You're mother does very well with them, Augusto is awful…but you didn't hear that from me." Arianna began to rummage through Nicco's box.

"So how does it work?" Nicco asked.

"Well, you say an incantation that can transform an object or give it specific instructions on how to behave. Now, you can do it without all the fuss of gathering ingredients and smudging and all of those things. However, the enchantment will only last a few seconds…which could save your life. If you want the enchantments to stick, well, then you have to do all the fussing: make sure you face the correct direction, a pinch of this and a dab of that."

Arianna retrieved a book and placed it on the cherry hutch…*The Art of Enchanting Objects*. Several ornate vases: a necklace, a couple of rings, a feather and some articles of clothing were also placed on the hutch. "I should move these. Here honey, put these on the top shelf." Arianna handed Nicco the egg carton of milky white spheres. Nicco took the carton and placed it upon the top shelf.

"OK Aunty Arianna, if I want to enchant an object for that one instance I can, but if I want it to be available all the time, I have to go through some type of ritual…the facing this way or that way and gathering all the ingredients?" Nicco confirmed.

"Precisely." Arianna replied. "The bracelet your mother gave you, the plants she gave Marie, the necklace she wears…all of those are enchanted objects and their power does not go away after one use, they continue until the Witch cancels them or she dies. The trick when you enchant an object is to make sure you give the object thinking power and the ability to act on its own accord." She looked up to Nicco and elbowed him in the stomach. "Not too much thinking power…you don't want it smarter than you."

Nicco laughed as his aunt continued. "The benefit you have is that you inherit your mother's power to a certain extent. She of course, it the most power Witch in the family. Your inherited Warlock powers should not have much issue with giving it thinking power...your issue will be the visualization and the use of words. Now, your mother made a necklace of protection that you should have given to Tracy. How is she, by the way? Are you going to ask her to marry you? You two have been together forever, why not marry?" Arianna waved a small finger.

Nicco rolled his eyes. "She's doing just fine."

"Did you give her the necklace?"

"Umm, yea of course." Nicco said.

Arianna looked at the contents laid out on the hutch and placed her hands on her hips. "One downfall about enchanting objects for immediate use is that you have to say an incantation. I'm actually very good at this...better than the fussing with incantation that stick. This can be difficult...you don't always have time. Another issue can arise if you can't think of the right words to say. The words are literal and you won't have but a few seconds to think of the proper incantation for Immediate Enchantments. This, unfortunately, can take years of practice...which we don't have." She shrugged her shoulders.

"You mean I have to make up rhymes or riddles on the spur of the moment." Nicco's mouth contorted and eyebrows furrowed.

"Well maybe not riddles dear, but short incantations. They can be two or six lines...whatever it takes. I told you it was a downfall, but what are you gonna do?"

"Great, why did I get Enchanted Objects? Marta's good at coming up with stuff off the top of her head...even Marie is better..."

"...because it's your calling. Now, hush and listen. I may have the power of Enchanted Objects, but because your mother is the Matriarch, her enchantments are very good too. By the way, her second power is Enchanted Objects, her primary power is Wands." Arianna took Nicco's wrist and examined the Dragon bracelet.

"Second power?" Nicco asked.

"Yes, your primary power is Enchanted Objects, don't know what your secondary power is yet, but we all have a secondary power...a power that is best suited to us. You see there are four powers of Witches and Warlocks: Sachets and Elixirs, very common, Wands and Enchanted Objects, they can be very powerful. However, the most uncommon of the powers is the most deadly and tricky to use. That is the power of Spirits. Your Aunt Contessa has that rare power. Anyway, we all have the ability to use every power, but we each have our main power and then a secondary power which is, well your secondary power." Arianna swished a hand. "My secondary power is Sachets and Elixirs, which means nothing to me because I'm awful at them. Sometimes a Witch doesn't develop certain inclinations."

"Are we sure I'm Enchanted Objects? What are Spirits?" Nicco asked.

"Well your mother seems to be sure. My gut tells me you're Enchanted Objects as well. Spirits...allow one to force the dead to do their bidding. Very dangerous stuff to get into, anything can go wrong when controlling the dead."

Nicco's eyes widened and mouth frowned. "You mean people control the dead?"

"Yes, now shush and be thankful you don't have that power. Don't know why your Aunt Contessa was so proud to have that power...very creepy if you ask me." Arianna waved a hand toward her nephew.

"Maybe it won't be that difficult...I mean, so I have to make up rhymes... what kind of stuff can I enchant?"

"Well honey almost anything can be enchanted." She picked up one of the vases and held it up to Nicco. "I could enchant this vase to swallow you whole and hold you prisoner or I could enchant it to always contain fresh water. Possibilities are endless. It is the most flexible and varied of the powers...and don't get too comfortable...it won't be easy to say an incantation off the top of your head. The words you use are exact and you must visualize."

"I can't be that hard." Nicco shrugged his shoulders and rolled his eyes. His heart thudded and forehead began to break into a sweat.

"It is very difficult. The trick with Enchanted Objects is that you must think of how you want the enchantment to behave...what the enchantment should be thinking. For example, your Aunty Katie enchanted the panther on your mother's kitchen sink. He's always working...any signs of danger or ill intent and he springs into action. It's like telling the enchantment what to look out for. To enchant an object so that it continues to be enchanted is far easier than to enchanting something in the moment...that's called Immediate Enchantment. Very powerful either way, although Immediate Enchantments are less useful at times...they can't protect a Witch when she sleeps, like your mother's cherubs on Grandma's clock. They watch over her while she sleeps. The cherubs are enchanted objects that continue to work. Now your mother was going to enchant a very power spell upon your father's watch and bequeath it to you, but it's far too powerful to be in the hands of a beginner."

"She should have enchanted it." Nicco picked up a mirror and turned it over.

Arianna placed her hands upon her hips. "Nicco, I'm going to get mad! Now you don't even know what the enchantment is, that kind of careless attitude will get you in trouble…mark my words."

"All right, all right…sorry Aunty Arianna." He pulled Tracy's necklace from his pocket. "Can we enchant this to be pretty?"

"See, you lied to me. You give that necklace to Tracy, Nicco." Arianna picked up one of the old vases and placed it in front of Nicco's face. Her voice softened as she began giving instructions. "I want you to visualize the vase filling with water when flowers are placed inside. See the flowers placed in the vase; see the type of flowers…the color…the texture…see the water fill the vase."

* * * *

Practice Makes Perfect

*M*arie had done splendid. Basil knew that she would. It would not surprise him if she has a double calling in Sachets and Elixirs. Her cloud of smoke blinded him and Gabriella. She, however, saw right through the thick grey swirls. She also successfully created a sachet that produced an energy ball around her and Gabriella. When Basil cast a medium energy blast, the shield of the energy held strong.

When Marie had accidently cut herself, she concocted a *Renew* elixir and with a single drop, healed the wound. Basil left her in the competent hands of her Aunt Gabriella.

He made his way down the old stone steps to the secret room. Arianna had just let a feather drop in front of Nicco. His objective was to make it levitate.

Nicco cast a spell of Immediate Enchantment.

"Feather of light, feather flight, give you wings to go...tonight?"

He swore loudly as he watched the feather fall to the ground without as much of a flutter.

Arianna rolled her eyes and placed a hand upon her forehead.

Basil looked over to Marta who stood in front of the apothecary with her wand held out; a tiny rubber ball floated at the tip of her wand. The ball began to float toward Azzurra, when it reached her mother, it was sent back her way. Marta did a quick twisting motion with her arm; the ball rose up and then swirled with the motion of the wand. A moment later the ball dropped.

"Oh Marta, that was wonderful! I was waiting for you to get creative. I knew you could do it sweetheart." Azzurra's eyes widened with excitement. "Now, block yourself!" She made a movement with her wand and sent one of the hats from the armoire toward her daughter.

Marta turned quickly and made a flinging movement with her wand over her left shoulder. The hat scurried past, hitting Nicco behind the head.

Nicco turned and swore. "Watch what the hell your doing Marta, dam it!" He picked the hat up and threw it at his sister. She made a lazy movement of her wand and floated it back to its original place.

"I'm sorry Nicco…I didn't…" Marta began.

"Nicco Stephani!" Azzurra called out.

"Nicco, don't get upset honey!" Arianna said softly.

Nicco slammed his fist on the maple hutch and swore again. Basil stepped up to him and crossed his arms.

"Now it's no laughing matter is it Nicco!" Basil voice rose." You can't even make a feather float and your angry with your sister, are you? I heard your snide remark to Marie earlier and you making fun of Marta when she blew up the bottle. I told you that it may be difficult now, didn't I. I told you because Enchanted Objects is the most difficult to learn…but did you heed my advice?" Basil paused for a brief moment. "Now you lose your temper because you can't so much as make a feather float! You think your temper will save you eh…well it dam well won't!" Basil turned red in the face and yelled. "I will not have you fight with your sister. You made fun of everyone, made light of the craft and now you're mad because you can't do a damn thing. Well I'll tell you something Nicco, defending yourself against a flying hat is the least of your worries. Now I need you to be supportive to your sisters and listen to what Miss Arianna tells you. Losing your temper…it only shows weakness in a man."

Nicco shouted to Basil. "What the hell are you doing? You've been losing your temper with us all night!"

"I am training you! I'm yelling to make a point; to force you to listen! I've not lost my temper once this eve. I spoke harshly with Marta because she wasn't taking it serious. It's what a good trainer does. I'm speaking harshly with you because you've let your frustration hinder your abilities all night, now haven't you? If you want to see me get riled up...continue with your stupidity. You did the same thing when you tried out for football Nicco. You walked in there with a cocky, no-it-all attitude and didn't listen to the coach and I don't need to tell you what happened, now do I? You've been frustrated all night! It only makes you stutter and the incantation won't work. You need to be calm. It doesn't matter that the feather didn't float...it only matters that you try again."

Basil turned to Arianna. "Work the mind Arianna, force him to let go. Tell him to drop off the mind and say what comes to his head. I'm going upstairs to see if Marie can brew him a calming draft." Basil walked up the stone steps, two at a time.

Nicco breathed heavy. His face flushed when Azzurra walked up to him and put a finger to his face.

"I'm going to tell you something Nicco Stephani. I'm two seconds from conjuring a pan and hitting you over the head with it! How dare you not be disciplined! Basil is trying to help save our lives! And I will tell you this much, he is always in control. You may think it's funny to tease your sisters and then get angry when you haven't enchanted a single damn object, but when you're alone with Tracy and some demon or celestial being attacks you; you had better focus and not lose your temper. I will tell you another thing Nicco...you are to apologize to Basil and Marta and work with your Aunt. You don't go home until you enchant something." She looked to Marta. "Let's go upstairs, I'm too mad to be in the same room with him."

Nicco breathed heavy. "Ma...I'm sorry." Nicco paused. "How did he know about the football?" He tightened his mouth.

"Because, I know Basil...he was most likely at every football game and practice." Azzurra walked up the stone steps.

Nicco pulled Marta into a hug as she passed. "That was great work with the ball...keep it up...I'm sorry, Marta." His voice was low.

"No worries Nicco. I'm a tough old broad. When you get really good at this, you'll have to show me how to enchant my mirror to always make me look fabulous." Marta winked at him as she too, headed up the stone steps.

* * * *

Katie in Her Blue Dress

The woman's eyes focused upon the two cars parked in Azzurra's driveway. She had seen them before…they belong to Gabriella and Arianna. Nicco, Marie and Marta's cars were also in front of the house…something told her that it wasn't a family celebration. When she asked Contessa the reason for the family get-together on a Thursday evening…Contessa said that they may have been getting together for Marta's birthday. Lamia contemplated and couldn't remember if Marta's birthday was indeed in September. She thought of Contessa's response to Stephan's report about Katie and Basil and wasn't confident that the story wasn't a downright lie. There had been a glint of something odd in Contessa's eyes.

She lazily sat upon the swing on Eleanor's front porch, pondering her next move. If she went any closer to the house…an enchantment may execute. That, she couldn't risk. To sit and do nothing was not an option. If she attacked early…much earlier than she had planned…The Man would be furious if it was for nothing. What would she tell him? Would a look in Contessa's eyes be sufficient? She thought not. Lamia rocked gently upon the swing, tossed her locks of dark hair over her shoulder and thought some more. The question was not about Marta's birthday, but whether or not Azzurra had broken the vow and summoned Katie from the dead and whether or not her faithful Spirit, Basil had returned.

For two hours she had sat upon that swing. It was now near the Witching Hour and something had to be done. A phone rang in the distance. Eleanor was receiving a phone call near Midnight on a Thursday evening? Something told her to go inside. Through the walls she floated and sat upon a sofa near Azzurra's pinochle lady friend.

"Mary? Oh thank goodness you called! I've been waiting…I couldn't sleep a wink! Wait till you hear what happened."

Lamia waved a hand and could now hear both ends of the conversation.

"I've been at the Theatre…remember I told you…what happened I was so surprised to get your message? Is everything all right? Is Azzurra OK?" Mary asked.

"Yes, I think she's fine. It's me…I think I'm going insane. Oh Mary, my heart is still beating! I was pruning the mum's earlier today when Arianna and Mateo stopped by Azzurra's. We exchanged hello's…I didn't think anything of it…but when I heard Arianna call out Katie's name and looked up… oh my word…I saw her…I saw Katie! I saw Katie in the blue dress she was buried in!"

Lamia stood, smiled and vanished.

* * * *

We Were Wrong!

Nathan entered the kitchen, paused at the entrance and cleared his throat. Contessa dipped a teabag into one of Katie's antique cups and looked up to her husband and yawned. "I couldn't sleep."

"Couldn't sleep? It's near two am...you look exhausted...what's the matter?" Nathan went to the stove, placed the kettle on a burner and turned up the gas. "Has Stephan showed up? Lamia?"

"No and Yes." Contessa placed her face in the palms of her hands.

"Contessa what happened? Talk to me." Nathan took a seat next to his wife.

"I summoned Stephan and he never responded...not sure where he is. I do hope he's all right. He tries my nerves...but I do like him." She looked down to her cup and glided an aged finger around the gold rim. "I've been trying to summon Deveroy. Nothing, I know something has happened to him...I feel it in my bones."

Nathan arched an eyebrow. "We're aging...we feel a lot of things in our bones." He winked and nudged her.

Contessa made tiny shakes of her head. "No, Nathan...not this time. I feel it so strong. Something's happened to him" A finger traced the rim of the saucer and into one of the roses. With a slow raise of her head, she looked up to her husband. "Marcus stopped in, been popping in for hours. I knew something was wrong...he kept fidgeting, rubbing his jeans. Shorty after his tenth visit, Lamia made a memorable appearance. She wanted to know if I heard from Stephan and also asked why Gabriella, Arianna, and all the kids were at Azzurra's." Contessa looked down to the cup and began tracing a stem. She took in a deep breath. "Something's not right. Why did Lamia go to Azzurra's?" Contessa shook her head with quick, sharp movements. "Oh, Nathan, I think she means to attack Azzurra! The kids are there... Gabriella...Arianna. What if she hurts them?"

Nathan leaned forward in the chair. "She has no reason to attack them. However, something's up if everyone's at Azzurra's on a Thursday evening. What did you tell Lamia? What did Marcus want?"

"Marcus wanted to know the same thing...have I spoken with Stephan. I told them that Stephan appeared and told us that he saw no sign of Basil or Katie and decided to take a vacation to Egypt...that he missed the pyramids." Her eyes watered. "I also told her that it was Marta's birthday and that's why the family must be there." Contessa looked up to the light fixture and smeared the tears from her cheeks with the back of her hand.

Nathan stood. "You lied to Lamia! Why? Why would you lie to Lamia? If she's asking the same questions that Marcus asked it means she doesn't trust you. Damn it Contessa! She'll know your lying."

"Nathan she's done something to Deveroy! I feel it in my bones! He's not answering my summons and she said that he was with Achar. I...I don't believe her. Achar won't answer my summons either. I didn't want to challenge her again. Something about her was different." She paused. "Nathan, I've been thinking so much lately." Her breath became shallow. "Nathan, we...were...wrong. Katie had nothing to do with Vincent's death, neither did Basil." She stood and wrapped her arms around herself. "Something happened earlier today...I was sitting in my chair, reading. I was chilly...but just as I was ready to adjust the heat...this warmth came over me." Contessa covered her mouth and then released her hand. "Nathan...it was as though Dad were with me. It was as though he put his strong arms around me... and nothing...I mean nothing could harm me. I felt so protected...happy, so content...loved...I felt so loved." Contessa searched the room randomly. "I sat there for a few minutes. I could have sworn I saw a man in a white suite standing in the kitchen. He wore a tie made of gemstones. I think he was a Vicar. A moment later he vanished. I closed my eyes and absorbed this wonderful feeling...and suddenly everything in my soul told me that

I should love Katie. That there was no need for anger…or pain. That she never harmed Vincent. She's my sister…and she wouldn't do such a thing." Contessa began to pace, her voice cracking and tense. "Nathan…Katie never did it. I am telling you with all my heart…Katie and Basil had nothing to do with Vincent's death." Her eyes searched the ceiling, the floor, the counter… tears streamed down her cheeks. "We were wrong Nathan. We…were… wrong." Her voice strengthened as she began to pace back and forth. "Debra and Lamia showed us that spell. We saw Basil in the room the night Vincent died…but he didn't do anything! I don't know how I know, I just know it!" She shook her head frantically, hurried to her husband and grabbed his shoulders. "Nathan he didn't touch Vincent! Every inch of my being tells me that he didn't touch him!" She turned away. "Oh dear God, Nathan…we were wrong!" Her voice lowered as she slammed an arm against her thigh "We haunted Olivia…my niece…Katie's daughter…for what?" She placed a hand on her forehead. "Oh dear God, Nathan we were wrong…we were wrong, we were wrong!" The tea kettles piercing call exploded. Contessa turned to the stove, grabbed the kettle and threw it into the sink. She screamed and fell to floor, gasping and crying. "We were wrong Nathan! God forgive us. God forgive us. We…were…wrong!"

Nathan cradled her. "Shhhh, shhh don't cry sweetheart. I'm here…It's alright. God will forgive us — he forgives all. We were crushed, lost and in pain." Nathan's voice cracked. "We thought that Katie and Basil killed him. It hurt so bad to lose our son…God will understand. They too will forgive us — someday"

Contessa looked up to Nathan and whispered. "You believe me?"

"It was dream…but I felt the same way. I knew something…or someone must be trying to tell us the truth." Nathan rocked his wife back and forth.

Contessa screamed. She pushed her husband away and rose to her feet, staggering slightly then stabilizing, grabbing her thigh. "I have to call Azzurra!   ! I have to call my sister!" She ran toward the phone. "Dear God…I have to warn her! Nathan! I have to warn her!"

* * * *

In The Moonlight

*B*asil stood, raised a crystal wine goblet and toasted the three ladies.

May God give you…
For every storm, a rainbow
For every tear, a smile
For every care, a promise
And a blessing in each trial

"For every problem life sends
A faithful friend to share
For every sigh, a sweet song
And an answer for each prayer"

The sisters toasted him. "Basil honey, that was very sweet." Azzurra took a sip of wine as Basil placed his glass upon the table, without drinking.

"That was very nice Basil…an old Irish prayer?"

"Yes Gabriella and you are very welcome, indeed." Basil gave a sharp nod and sat.

"Thank you Basil sweetheart." Arianna patted his hand.

Gabriella set her glass on the table and looked to Azzurra. "I think Marie did wonderful. As a matter of fact...I think she's double Sachet's and Elixirs."

"That's nice." Azzurra focused on the rim of her wine glass. The room remained silent for several minutes.

"What's the matter Azzurra?" Arianna twirled the stem of her glass between two fingers.

"It's Nicco...I'm worried about Nicco." She looked up from her glass.

"It's a difficult craft Mum. He'll just need some time, that's all. You'll see...he'll be grand before you know it." Basil said. "He finally enchanted the vase and he even made the feather float...it's a lot for the first time ever doing Magick."

"He's right, Azzurra. I think he felt more positive when he left. He'll be fine honey." Arianna glanced to her watch. "It's almost 1:30 I better get going." She dabbed her mouth with a napkin. "Scott said he'd wait for me to get home...he called Gracie and told her there was a family emergency. He said that Merek Kroll dropped off an arsenal of supplies. Seemed to like Merek, went on about the trolley cart. Anyway, he's been practicing Wands with his father all night. Mateo said he did very well and displayed a lot of power for a beginner."

"I'm glad Arianna. I had a feeling Scott would be Wands...just like his Father." Azzurra looked to her wine glass once more. "I just...I just don't feel right. Katie said she didn't have a good feeling either. I can't put my finger on it...but something's wrong."

"Oh no...you and Katie both have bad feelings?" Gabriella asked.

"It's probably nothing...don't worry. You two should go home...it's late." Azzurra rose from the table.

Gabriella rose and spoke. "You know, Nicolai said Eva acted really strange when he told her about being a Witch. Told him that she couldn't make it over to the house...said she had things going on but she would try. He said Merek Kroll had dropped off dozens of items...so he's been busy. He's been making plenty of Sachets and Elixirs, but Eva never showed."

"Well I hate to say it, but that daughter of yours has always been strange." Arianna rose to her feet.

Gabriella slapped the table. "How can you say that about my daughter?"

"Because it's true," Azzurra said. "Now don't get upset. Eva's very private and has always acted strange when it came to issues with the family."

Arianna hugged Gabriella "I love you Gabby, but I'm telling you now there is something wrong with that girl. Her Father tells her that there is a family emergency…that she's a Witch…and she's too busy?" Arianna swished a hand through the air. "Beee that girl's up to something. I don't like it and if you ask me…it was no surprise to her that she was a Witch. You need to speak with your daughter."

Gabriella began to respond when Azzurra cut her off. "It's too late to fight…now be careful driving home." She turned to Basil. "Basil honey, can you make some moonlight so they can see their way to their cars."

"It's a full moon…I won't need to do much at all, maybe a wee bit of re-direction." Basil walked to the front door, turned to Spirit form and stepped through the door.

Arianna hugged Azzurra and whispered. "Something's not right with Eva…we'll chat tomorrow. *I'll* call *you*." Arianna tightened her shawl and headed to the front door.

Azzurra nodded and hugged Gabriella. "Her son is wonderful and there is something wrong with my daughter?"

"Well honey…we both know that Eva is secretive and she's very close to Celia…now am I right?" Azzurra fixed a strand of hair on her sister's forehead.

Gabriella inhaled a large breath of air. "You're both right. I'll talk with Nicolai when I get home. I'll call you tomorrow…I promise." She kissed Azzurra on the check and headed for the door.

"Arianna do you have your enchanted pendant?" Azzurra asked. She and Gabriella stepped onto the porch.

The moonlight lit the driveway; Arianna turned and pulled out a chain from under her blouse. "Of course I do." She looked up. "Thank you Basil." She unlocked her car and opened the door.

"Do you have sachets and elixirs?" Azzurra asked Gabriella.

"Let's just say if I bump my purse I think I'll explode." Gabriella hugged and kissed Arianna and then walked to her own vehicle. She opened the car door and laughed.

Arianna rolled down her window and looked up to the stars. "It's a beautiful night ladies."

The full moon cast it's radiance upon the three sisters. Azzurra's mind raced as Arianna backed out of the driveway. Time…time can change everything. Memories of holding hands with Franco filled her heart. A few months back and they walked in the pale moonlight on an evening just like this. What a difference three months can make. With time, comes change, and with change brings the beauty and sorrows of life. The moonlight landed softly upon the car window at just the right angle to produce an elegant lighting effect upon Arianna. Azzurra waved, Arianna waved back. "I love you Azzurra…and thanks for being there for me."

Azzurra placed her arms around her shoulders and shivered. "I will always be there for you…and thank you for being there for me. I love you too." A hand waved as Arianna pulled away flashing her headlights.

Gabriella backed out of the driveway, waved and called out the window. "I love you, my sister."

"I love you too." Azzurra stood upon the softness of the grass and watched as Arianna turned right and Gabriella turned left off of Cedar Grove Court. In the pale moonlight, Azzurra lowered her arm, placed a hand upon a thudding heart and took a deep breath as a single tear ran down her cheek.

* * * *

Basil's Comrades

"Mum is there something the matter — why all the tears?" Basil asked, remaining invisible as Azzurra stood upon the lawn.

"I can never tell what my feelings are about. Katie couldn't either. We just know when something awful is about to happen. Augusto could target his feelings better." Azzurra rubbed her shoulders and headed for the front door.

"I understand Mum...but with all the trouble that's going on...it could just be your worried that another Witches War is about to begin."

Basil appeared solid and sat at the kitchen table with Azzurra. A cup of coffee appeared before his Mum. "I made it decaf Mum...I know it's late."

Five Spirits appeared before them. Azzurra gave a slight jump and Basil stood. "It's all right Mum...my comrades are here." He focused his attention on the five Spirits. "It's about time my dear friends. It's near 2 am."

Four of them turned solid and greeted Basil with warm handshakes and tight hugs. Deveroy stood in Spirit form by the counter.

"Deveroy, come here honey." Azzurra waved him over. "Turn solid and let me give you a hug for helping us." Deveroy did as she asked.

Azzurra stood and waited for introductions. Basil smiled wide, ran his hand through his dark hair and spoke. "Mum this is Michale."

A young man with dark hair extended his hand. He shook it enthusiastically. He wore black jeans, a black thick ribbed turtle neck sweater that hung loosely over a thin frame. "Good to meet you finally." Michale said as piece of dark, curly, hair, flopped over an eye.

Azzurra fought the urge to reach out and pinch his cheeks. "It's nice to meet you sweetheart and thank you for your help. You have the most adorable dark brown eyes; you're so cute I have to fight not to pinch your cheeks." Michale's full lips curved into a dazzling white smile as his cheeks blushed red.

"And this is Ritsuko." Basil motioned toward a beautiful young woman with long, straight dark hair.

"It's nice to meet you, Ritsuko." Azzurra spoke. "Isn't that a lovely name...is it Japanese?"

"It is. Thank You. It's very nice to meet you as well." Ritsuko responded.

"Hope you don't mind me saying, but you look strong...very toned. I'd be afraid of this one." Azzurra noticed the Ritsuko wore all black as well.

Ritsuko bowed.

"This crazy guy likes to go by the name of Pip." Basil smiled widely and brought Pip forward.

"Hello Mum...nice to meet you." Pip spoke with a thick Australian accent. He brushed a clump of wavy blonde hair away from his face and stepped forward to take a deep bow. He had a muscular frame and wore black.

"Nice to meet you Pip...a very fun name. I like that." Azzurra winked at him. Azzurra thought to herself that all of Basil's friends were young with the exception of the woman who awaited an introduction. Basil was 23 when he died, Michale must have been in his late teens, Ritsuko was in her mid twenties and Pip must have been no older than 28. The theatre life back then must have been rough to have all died at such young ages. Azzurra almost said something but thought it better not to mention their death ages.

"And this is Violetta." He gestured toward a beautiful older woman with silver hair.

"Nice to finally meet you, Azzurra, I've heard so much about you." Violetta spoke in a soft French accent, she bowed her head slightly.

"It's very nice to meet you too. I love the name Violetta…very pretty and what a beautiful shawl, my sister Arianna loves shawls." Azzurra added, as they shook hands.

Violetta smiled and nodded, she too wore all black.

Everyone took their seats at the kitchen table. Stories began to be told about Basil's theatre days. Azzurra nodded politely, as the words went in one ear and out the other. She wished Franco were there. A long sigh escaped…a moment later she gasped. The stories stopped as eyes focused upon Azzurra. The feeling she had earlier…the feeling of something awful about to happen, plunged into her like a dagger.

* * * *

Tonight, We Attack!

Lamia slammed a hand upon the sofa's arm and stood. "It's about time! Where the hell have you been?"

Damiano glanced toward Marcus, who nodded with a slight, crisp tilt of the head. "There is a Vicar at Olivia's. However, we cannot be sure of why he has positioned himself there. It is most likely because of Achar's Disbursement Charm. Casting spells of that nature will always bring a Vicar…

"…and it took you until nearly 1:00 in the morning to find this out." Lamia took a picture frame and threw it at him. "I've been pacing around like a manic Cheetah and that's all you have to say!"

Dodging the frame, Damiano looked toward Dormava and Medeia, then back to Lamia.

"I…"

"…why does everyone look to Dormava and Medeia? I am the one in charge! You will look to me!"

Damiano nodded once. "I could hardly walk into her house and say, 'hi, is there Vicar among thee?' I had to wait and sense what type of energy emitted. There was a strong presence from inside but it was inconsistent, so there was no way in hell I was going inside. So I hung out and played with a stray..." Lamia's eyes narrowed. "I saw a random Spirit a few hours later. I asked the guy to enter the house and tell me what he saw. He did as I asked and said that there were no Spirits of any kind. There was just a woman with dark hair, a man with blonde hair, a young man and a girl. I figured it was Olivia, Walter, Michael and Rose. That's when the good looking guy in the white suit showed. He was near the back yard looking toward the neighbors. I asked the Spirit, his name was Vincent by the way...which I thought was a bit creepy. Anyway, I asked Vincent if he could stick around and that I'd be back in an hour. I asked him to try and engage with the man, see what he could find out. I left and then came back. Vincent said the guy was a Vicar, asked about a Disbursement Charm that had been cast. The Vicar told Vincent that he should move away as the area wasn't safe." Damiano shrugged his shoulders. "Did it as fast as I could, effective without being caught. Things take time...you need to learn to chill."

Lamia's eyes widened. "Very well...I guess I need to chill! She threw an antique statue of a Spanish soldier across the room. She composed herself, took a moment and then spoke. "I bet that Vicar would have known who you were if you entered. I am glad you stood out of sight. Smart thinking Damiano, I forgive you. Marcus what do you think it means?" She strode past Damiano.

Marcus looked to Damiano then to Lamia. "He could have been placed by the Higher Spirits? The Disbursement Charm would have brought an investigation. However, the Vicar would have scanned the area and have picked up on the Culls in Olivia's house. He would have destroyed them; alerted the Higher Spirits of the situation and would have launched a further investigation as to who sent the demons. The Vicar would have been placed acting as a Guardian to the household."

Lamia placed her hands upon her hips. "What does that mean? Does the Vicar know about the demons we sent to Olivia? The energy Damiano sensed had been inconsistent...would he not be there around the clock if he acted as a Guardian to them?" Lamia shook her head, "Well it does not matter if he is there. I guess the world will be down a few demons. On to other things...Medeia and Dormava informed me that Celia and Eva understand what needs to be done. We shall see how they succeed. Am I missing anything?"

She strode across the room and looked in the mirror. After adjusting several tussles of hair, she addressed the room. Nobody spoke.

"We cannot wait." She sauntered over to Damiano and rested a hand upon his chest. "Katie is back...and most likely Basil." A hand traced his cheek. "Contessa grows weary and suspicious about Deveroy, which brought distrust in me. I guess I shouldn't have destroyed him...well no matter. Then there is Stephan...who never showed. You wait till I get my hands on him." A hand slid down Damiano's shoulder and once again rested upon his strong chest. "However, I did some investigating of my own. Azzurra's neighbors told me what I needed to know" She pushed a hand against Damiano's chest, forcing him backward. Lamia strode past him and focused on the ladies. "It looks like if you need something done correctly...don't send a man, I should have sent the two of you."

Medeia and Dormava shifted positions and gave a slight nod.

"What should we do?" Marcus asked.

"I'll tell you what we are going to do," Lamia responded. "Azzurra knows about Olivia and Katie is back. Gabriella, Arianna and the kids were all attending Marta's so called birthday party. Birthday party my ass! They know exactly what happened and are trying to plan their next move. They won't have time, because tonight...we attack. I am sending an army of demons to kill them all. We shall meet the Hags at Arianna's, since she is the most powerful next to Azzurra. I will send a message to Phillip to meet us there. It's about time to enlist the aid of another family Spirit." Lamia extracted visible thoughts from her temple and spoke a command. The mist of thoughts hovered for a moment and then vanished through the brick walls. "Then it's Azzurra's son Nicco...oh, when a mother loses her only son...such heartbreak. Gabriella, Father Bernardo and Augusto should be easy — one has average powers...one's a silly priest and one's a crabby old man. Marie and Marta don't know Magick and if they do, it won't be enough to save them. If Olivia is protected by the Guardian...so be it! Olivia is a mess anyway. After it's done we shall attack the New York and San Francisco Cousins and their families. The last to kill will be Drago and Kimberly. I have not instructed anything to attack Carlotta. We will leave her out of this." She remained silent for a brief moment and then continued. "Basil and Katie can't be everywhere and Azzurra is mortal and hasn't used her powers in forty years. Besides, she's been in mourning over her beloved Franco."

Lamia made a hand movement that traced a circle around her. Damiano, Marcus, Dormava and Medeia all came closer and took their positions. "The five of us shall play our own role in their destruction. To place all my trust in Demons would be foolish." She looked to each one of her followers. "Stay focused...stay calm and be vigilant, because this won't be easy."

* * * *

302

A Witches War!

Candles lit the room. Flickering shimmers of light danced against the walls, ceilings and carpet. Turrets of a castle, belonging to an animated clock, flickered in quick, diffused movements. Several silhouettes of zebras appeared and disappeared, forced to mingle and glimmer amongst the glass vases, picture frames and plants. The woman sat curled upon the plush, quarry red sofa. A small lamp joined the ambiance of the room. She placed a bookmark and then set the copy of *A Modern Day Witch* on the cushion. After a slight yawn and a glance to the castle clock's display, she reached for the note on the end-table and began to read it once again.

Hi Sweetheart

About your ring...the enchantment goes way back to my great grandmother's days. It's very powerful. Here's how it works. The ring will stay an amethyst if there is no threat. If the ring senses danger from a Spirit, Demon or Witch, it will vibrate & hum to alert you. A threat from a Spirit will turn the ring a bright citrine. If the threat is from a Mortal, the ring will turn a sapphire and, I don't mean to scare you...but if there is a threat from a Demon, the ring will turn a ruby red. Since you have the power of Wands, casting a spell is more powerful. If you are asleep, it will vibrate and hum. Depending on the color, you should use the following incantations.

Red (Demon) Protezione da Demonio (Protection from Demon) Try to use the Italian honey it works better, and don't roll your eyes. A bright red circle of energy will shoot from your ring...hitting the demon. Repeat the incantation until it flees or is destroyed.

Blue (A Mortal/Witch or Warlock) Protezione da Mortale (Protection from Mortal) A ball of blue energy will expel from the ring...blasting the Witch away from you. Remember to visualize the effect.

Yellow (Spirit) Protezione da Spirito (Protection from Spirit) A powerful golden bolt of energy will expel from your ring...it should result in damage to the Spirit...repeat if necessary.

Now remember Marta, visualize and have the confidence that you can produce the effect. Simply point your ring at the target and say the proper incantation.

Sleep well, honey

Love Ma
XOXOXO

Marta rolled her eyes and took a in a deep breath. The contemplation of lighting a cigarette entered her mind and then quickly vanished. She had not a single cigarette since Sunday's fiasco at the cemetery.

Sleep could no longer wait. After folding the note and placing her glasses on the end-table, she clicked off the lamp. One by one, each candle's flame disappeared. Upon blowing out the last candle, she noticed her wand...it lay upon the cushion. "I can't go to bed without you." She spoke out loud.

In the dark she reached for the wand...found it and grasped its handle. The clock's animation began as she entered the kitchen. With a bit of moonlight, Marta found the switch and flicked it up. The hallway illuminated. Two soft strums of a harp, sounded from the ornate clock. The time was 2:00am. Another yawn escaped. She covered her mouth and turned on the bathroom light.

Marta placed the wand on the counter, slid off her rings and began to wash. Several minutes later, she blotted her face with a towel and jumped at the sound of the land line.

Her heart leapt...*something's happened to Ma?* She set the towel on the counter and hurried down the hall to the kitchen phone.

"Ma...is everything alright!?"

Static erupted. Marta held the receiver away and then repeated the question. When the static subsided, the voice that spoke did not belong to her mother. It was guttural and deep. *"Your ring turned a vibrant red. Can you get to it fast enough?"*

***

Marie stirred the contents of the cauldron, her mind plagued on the evening's events. Sachets & Elixirs had been her calling...Marta had the power of Wands and poor Nicco got stuck with Enchanted Objects. Nicco's face entered her mind's eye. Shaking her head, she convinced herself that Nicco would learn his craft in time. Thoughts jumped to her daughter and husband. Steven and Katherine still knew nothing about her being a Witch. A large breath exhaled. *How in the world am I going to tell them?*

When she entered the house, slightly after 10:00, Steven asked how the emergency meeting had gone and demanded to be filled in on the recent events. All Marie could muster were the words..."I'm too tired and I am not a dog to be commanded upon. I will explain everything tomorrow. I promise." She felt a bit of guilt at her sharp tongue but he would understand soon enough.

After several unsuccessful protests, they went to bed. About an hour later, Marie tip-toed to the kitchen and organized the box of supplies on the countertop. She once again checked on the Ivy and Cactus that her mother had given her. Nothing changed...so the enchantments must be working. Her mother's note didn't explain all the details of what the plants did. The only information offered had been short and brief. *Keep them in the kitchen...* and that's exactly where they sat.

Marie now stood at the stove, stirring one last time, counterclockwise, to complete the potion. After turning the burner to off and transferring the contents to a bowl, she placed it aside, letting it cool. Flipping the silk scarf over a shoulder, she placed the cauldron in the sink. Through the kitchen window, the moonlight shined...it was a full moon.

A glance down at the scarf every few minutes calmed Marie. The scarf remained white. From what her mother's note read...white meant no threat of evil. It would change colors the moment it sensed danger. Not only did the scarf provide an alert, it could hide anyone from dark forces and provide a powerful protection. An incantation would activate the spell.

Marie gave a sigh and took in the sight upon the counter, ten elixirs and fourteen sachets lined the surface. Yellow sachets meant healing, while blue meant some type of defensive counter-attack. The elixirs produced sleep; healing and revival powers. The one marked with a red label…caused an explosion. Marie grimaced. Aunt Gabriella had said that explosions were far beyond the powers of a beginning Witch…however, after looking over the spell it didn't seem that difficult. So, she made an explosive elixir. Marie jumped at the sound of her husband's voice.

"What are you doing?" Steven pulled a tee shirt over his slim torso.

"Um, nothing, did I wake you?"

"Wake me?" Steven dropped his head, keeping his eyes upon his wife. "I've been up for an hour. I thought you were baking or cooking to calm your nerves. I didn't want to bother you." He glanced up at the clock and smeared a hand through his thick dark hair. "For the love of God it's two in the morning." He padded barefoot over to the sink. "Is that a cauldron? A Bunsen burner…what's with the vials? What are these?" Steven picked up a blue sachet and tossed it in his hand.

Marie's eyes widened. "Put that down!" She grabbed the sachet and placed it gently next to the others.

"Marie, have you gone nuts?" He crossed arms as a piece of dark, wavy hair, fell over his forehead, obscuring a dark brown eye.

"No I am not nuts. Steven, listen honey …it's nothing really. Um…it's for the ladies from my book club. It's for tomorrow and I got so tied up with Ma…I forgot, so I'm doing it now?

Steven looked to the candles that were lit throughout the room. He adjusted his pajama bottoms and scratched his thigh. "Who's in your book club…a bunch of Witches?" He picked up a book and turned it over. Marie cupped her mouth as he read the title aloud. "What Every Good Witch Should Know. Dear God! Marie! You're practicing Witchcraft!"

"Shush, you'll wake Katherine. It's not like that…well it is." She hissed. "Oh, I'm sorry for lying. I shouldn't have lied. It's just that Ma…well Marta and Nicco…" Marie looked toward the back bedroom. After a large sigh she whispered. "Yes, I'm practicing Witchcraft! We are all Witches!" She lost the whisper. "The entire damn family: Marta, Nicco, Ma, Aunty Arianna and Aunt Gabriella…are all Witches! I even saw Aunty Katie! Ma summoned her from the dead. And there is a Spirit named Basil…you know, Mousy when I was a little girl…anyway we think another Witches War…"

"…are you frickin' kidding me!?" Steven's brown eyes widened and voice rose.

"Will you two please be quiet? I have two exams in the morning." Katherine walked groggily and stood next to her father in a rumpled blue night shirt and long brown hair that stuck out at odd angles.

"Great Steven, now you woke our daughter!" She spoke to Katherine. "Go back to bed honey. Daddy and I will keep it down."

Steven and Katherine titled their heads and stared at Marie's chest. Steven pointed. "What's going on with that?" Marie looked down; her scarf began turning a blood red.

Marie gasped; a hand flew to her mouth and heart thudded. Hazel eyes grew and darted to the ivy. It was growing rapidly and slithering. A small buzzing came from the cactus which began to produce puffs of smoke from its flowers.

Katherine and Steven followed her gaze. Katherine screamed when she saw the vine. Steven pulled his daughter against his body. "Marie what the hell is happening!?"

"God protect you both!" Marie took off the scarf and threw it toward her daughter and husband as she spoke the incantation.

"Attiva il tuo potere"
(Activate your power)

The scarf expanded in size and wrapped its blood red, silky material around Katherine and Steven. Marie watched as her daughter and husband disappeared from sight.

A loud gurgling sound forced Marie to turn toward the kitchen window. Moonlight revealed something large and white beyond the glass. It floated through the window and into the kitchen. It turned solid. Marie's heart skipped a beat. A thudding…a powerful, rapid thud beat against her chest. Sweat broke out upon her forehead. Palms moistened, and eyes widened. The sachets and elixirs were behind the creature. Her throat tightened and legs weakened with every backward step. It stood from floor to ceiling with an arched back. Arms dangled from its sides. Thin material flowed loosely around its gangly body. Its head wrapped in the same damp cloth… stretching tightly around its face. A large oblong mouth opened and expelled a foul scent.

Marie could hear the rustling of the leaves from the ivy and the loud humming from the cactus. Marie bumped against the kitchen table, unable to scream. It methodically angled its head, large black holes for eyes stared into her. A sickening rattle made her heart leap with fear. The creature lunged its' head downward an inch from Marie's face. Foul breath, dank and moist invaded her nostrils. Marie found her voice, covered her mouth and screamed.

Father Bernardo knelt at the altar and began the Hail Mary. A beautiful ivory rosary twisted within his hands. Something ate at his insides…gnawed and gnawed at him. Two dim lights cast a glow over the altar. Several candles lit for loved ones, flickered behind and to the left of the priest. Father Bernardo prayed alone…but in his gut he knew that something lingered just beyond the churches walls.

His voice broke the silence. "You have no place here. Nor do you have power over me and the kingdom of God. I serve the Lord and I am in his protection. Be gone, fowl things!" He rose to his feet and looked to the pews. With his back to the Altar, he stepped forward. The great wooden doors remained closed. His eyes scanned the ceiling, moonlight shown through the stained glass windows.

Father Bernardo glanced down to his watch. It was near 2:00 am. He had prayed for the safety of everyone's children and their families. He had prayed that Azzurra be guided and protected. That Arianna, Gabriella, Augusto and Contessa…all be guided. He asked the Lord to forgive them… forgive them for using Magick. Over and over that evening, he prayed for the protection of his cousins families. "It is not in their knowing that they are Witches. God Protect them. Let my cousins do battle if they must…but protect their family."

His eyes darted once again to the ceiling. Beyond the windows, large shadows contrasted the moonlight. Winged demons hovered and gathered around his parish.

"You cannot enter where a servant of the Lord dwells. I am in this church and with the power of God…I command you to leave!" He turned and hurried to the Altar and knelt before the Lord. "Dear God, my loving Lord…rid me of these demons. Do not allow such fowl things to enter your house. The Lord…who is all loving and forgiving, you know my cousins are good people and have not sought to use Magick in years. Now, it is only in the protection of their loved ones that they use such powers. They are your children. Do not forsake them. Though their faith may be weak…they do not know what I know." Father Bernardo wrapped the rosary tighter in his hands and kissed the Holy cross. "Our Father, who art in heaven…" The shattering of glass interrupted the priest prayers.

***

"I told them my presence would aid them!" The Vicar insisted.

"I am sorry Aiden. The Higher Spirits feel that your place is to protect Olivia and her family. Walter is a mortal man who knows nothing of Witchcraft. Their children, Michael and Rose reside within these walls. Their other son, David lives in a nearby apartment. You are not to interfere

308

with the attack upon the family. They will not allow you." Vicar Thomas O'Connell spoke, his eyes level with those of the Vicar's.

Vicar Aiden Sinclair began to pace Olivia's kitchen. "Is there nothing we can do?" He turned to face his long time friend. "Thomas, they are good people! I must guide them!"

"Aiden, I am sorry. The Higher Spirits are aware of what is happening and certain events must occur. Neither you, nor I, may interfere." Vicar Thomas looked to the floor, red hair falling slightly forward.

"Thomas, Lamia has sent Demons — Demons given to her by him. He unleashed celestials that have not been seen in centuries. Why should we sit and do nothing if the card has been played? Lamia herself has no idea who she is in alliance with."

"They know of his involvement with Lamia. They know The Man gave her an army of demons. It is how the Degeli's react tonight that will set the tone for the future. They must fight. They must strengthen themselves. It is not in the concern of the Higher Spirits that Lamia does not know The Man's identity. She has made a choice." Vicar Thomas walked closer to Aiden. "It is not his card that he plays. It is a sly and clever rouse and Lamia is his puppet. As long as The Man does nothing himself...we cannot interfere."

Aiden lowered his voice. "These are powerful demons. They don't deserve this, Thomas. They trusted me to be there for them...I have failed them."

Thomas placed a hand upon the Vicar's shoulder. "You are too close my dear friend."

They turned their heads at the sound Olivia and Walter entering the kitchen.

"Walter I know it's late...but I have to go! I have to see Carlotta now!" Olivia slid a chair out and sat. She jammed a foot into a tennis shoe.

"For God sakes Olivia...she'll be sleeping. It's nearly 2 am! What's so important that you have to go now?" Walter brushed a hand through his blonde hair...feeling an odd sense of calm. "I'm coming with you."

"No! You are not leaving Rose and Michael alone!" Olivia stood.

"They're old enough. They'll be fine."

"Walter! You...are staying...here! Don't argue with me! It is between me and my sister!" Olivia's eyes narrowed as she slammed a hand upon the table. "I have to see Carlotta...alone!"

Walter nodded quickly and spoke, his temper keeping at bay. "I understand...go."

Olivia went to the hall closet and grabbed a light jacket.

"Does this have something to do with the dreams? The dreams of you and Carlotta...the night Angelo died?" Walter asked.

She punched her fist through the sleeve. "You bet it does. Carlotta knows what happened that night...and tonight...she's going to tell me everything." Olivia snatched her purse and walked out the front door. Walter put a hand through his hair, staring out the front window. He watched his wife get into the car, back out of the drive way and screeched the tires in the direction of her sister.

Vicar Thomas spoke with an even tone. "You must stay here with Walter and the kids. I shall follow her. A Guardian is at David's apartment. He will be fine." He looked to his right then back to Vicar Aiden Sinclair. "The Higher Spirits have just received a prayer from Father Bernardo. I have to leave. Be well Aiden." He vanished.

Walter entered the room, walked through the Vicar and began to brew some coffee. Through the kitchen floor, three demons rose and moved toward Walter. Vicar Aiden Sinclair stood motionless as his tie of gemstones lit up and sucked the three into captivity. Six more demons floated into his tie from the back bedrooms. Walter poured the water into the coffee machine and yawed.

***

Basil stopped in mid-sentence and looked to Azzurra. "What is it Mum?"

"I'm not sure. I didn't like the way I said goodbye to Arianna and Gabriella... something isn't right." She shook her head and tried to rid the thoughts.

"I'm not sure what you mean, Mum. I thought it was very decent. You all said you loved each other. How bad could that be?" Basil leaned closer to Azzurra and placed a hand upon hers. His comrades remained silent.

"No, no Basil...that's not it, honey. It's just that...I felt as though, that was the last time I would see them. The last goodbye....the last I love you." She rubbed her eyes. "It's almost two in the morning. Maybe I'm just tired. I think it's time for bed." She smiled at Basil and the others and stood.

"Mum we shall check in on them. They should be arriving home shortly." Basil stood.

Everyone turned their heads as the phone on the wall rang. Azzurra glanced up to the clock once more — 1:58 am.

"I told them to ring once when they got in." Azzurra eyes bolted toward the phone as it rang a second time. She glanced toward Basil and made to answer the phone.

"Hello?"

"Azzurra, she's attacking! Protect the kids!" Contessa screamed into the phone.

"Tessa what are you talking about!? Who's attacking?" Azzurra clutched her chest and quickly turned to Basil, eyes wide.

Tessa yelled into the phone. "Lamia is out of control. Nathan and I think she's going to attack the family! Azzurra the kids! Protect…" The line crackled and went dead.

***

Augusto sat in a *La Z-Boy*, with the dim glow of the lamp beside him. An ill feeling couldn't be shook. The family…something didn't sit right about the family. Anna entered his mind. He hadn't heard her voice in over twenty-four hours.

He glanced to his wand that sat on the end-table. After practicing several spells, he felt confident that everything would come back to him.

The television sat in darkness; the clock from the cable box said 1:53 am. Maybe he'd be able to sleep…perhaps a little reading before bed?

"I don't like it." Augusto spoke aloud. "Something isn't right. Tessa wouldn't go to these lengths."

Augusto's thoughts turned to his conversation with Father Bernardo on the way home from Azzurra's that afternoon. It had been about the Vicar. Both he and the priest had the same question — *Why was a Vicar involved with a family of Witches?*

He picked up his wand and stood with care. A yawn escaped as he reached to turn the lamp off. The room plunged into darkness. In the faint distance, he heard a voice…it was Anna. He froze. "Anna?"

"Augusto! Augusto!" Anna's voice cried out to him.

You can't save her. She is lost forever. The family is safe. You're being paranoid. Augusto heard the voice in his head. *The Spell will not work. She is lost. Just get some sleep.* He rubbed his hands over his face and yawned once more, shaking his head.

After entering the bathroom, he stared at his reflection. *They hate you. They think you're an old, crabby bastard and should die. Mateo, Nicolai…your sisters, they all hate you. Tessa hates you too. She only tolerates you. Anna will never be free!* Augusto pounded the counter top. "No stop it! Get out of my head!" He screamed at the mirror, letting his wand drop in the sink.

Go to bed and get some rest. You cannot save her. It's been too long. His eyelids closed and then forced back open. But he heard it again...this time it was stronger. "Augusto! Help me Augusto!" He shook his head once again

No, no it's what you wish. That is not Anna's voice. It is the memory of someone long dead. You are old and only hearing what you wish...what you have wished for so long. In death and only in death will you see her again?

Augusto raised an eyebrow. "Get out of my head?" he questioned.

Augusto grabbed the wand from the sink and pointed the tip to his throat. He spoke the spell.

"Rivela ciò che non può essere visto!"
(Reveal what cannot be seen)

In the mirror it revealed itself — a Cull clutched to his throat. Augusto's eyes widened as the creatures bony hand knocked his wand to the floor and screeched in his face.

***

Gabriella turned onto W. Abbey Street near downtown Ferndale. She smiled to herself, feeling proud of Marie. Her niece was a natural. The smile faded as thoughts shifted to her daughter, Eva. Was Arianna right? Nicolai and she will need to speak to their daughter.

The voice from the radio announced the time to be 2:00am.

She turned the wheel and pulled the *Lincoln Towncar* into the driveway and pressed the brake. Her headlamps shown on the garage door as she reached for the remote. A glimpse of light flickered in the front bay window. Her eyes narrowed toward the window...another flicker. Gabriella pressed harder on the break, finger frozen on the remote...eyes mesmerized on the bay window. There it was again. A bright light flashed inside the house. For a split second a shadow appeared behind the light. Another flash of light, this time it revealed the source of the shadow— Nicolai. The light came from her husband.

Transfixed by the shadow of her husband, the flashes of light became longer and brighter. Her pulse quickened as a large circular shape of light appeared. She knew that shape...knew that light! It is cause by the *Protezione* spell.

The DJ's voice broke into static.

Gabriella slammed the car into park and grabbed her purse. A crashing sound of garbage cans forced her body to constrict. Through the front windshield, the cause of the ruckus displayed itself. The headlights revealed something on all fours...large...brown with thick gnarly fur. Its eyes were shimmering red off the head lamps. It snarled and then looked up to the pale moonlight and howled. Three times the size of a normal wolf, it lowered its head, roared and leapt forward.

The crunch and bending of metal forced Gabriella to scream. The beast jumped up and down upon the windshield. The moonlight shone brightly into the cabin. Gabriella fumbled in her purse. Her eyes darted to front bay window, Nicolai's shield remained vibrant. Another scream escaped as the paws barreled down upon the windshield. She looked down into her purse... rummaging for a red sachet. The moonlight revealed a blue one. Head up...Nicolai's shield held. Head down...the red one? Up...shield still there. Down...red...Red, RED! The wolf pounced again and again. The cracking and splintering of the windshield forced her focus to raise her head. Eyes flitted to the window, the protection shield flicker and then collapsed. "Nicolai!" She screamed. The wolf reared up once again and pounced, collapsing the windshield into millions of tiny fragments.

**

"Mum, what is the matter? What did Contessa say?" Basil spoke rapidly.

Azzurra hung up the phone. "The line went dead. Tessa said that Lamia may be attacking." Azzurra took her wand from the kitchen table and then spoke to her beloved Spirit. "Basil, the Witches War has begun."

"Listen up my comrades. We must separate and protect the family. Everyone come back here. This will be the stronghold!" He turned to Pip. "Pip I need you to go to Nicco." Pip muttered something then vanished. "Violetta protect Marie and her family!" Violetta looked up, whispered something and disappeared. "Michale go to Father Bernardo, Ritsuko to Gabriella." They said something...looked up, and then vanished. He turned quickly to Azzurra. "I'll go to Marta. Mum you should go to Arianna...they will attack her with full force."

Basil turned to Deveroy. "Deveroy, stay here and try to contact Stephan, send him to Nicco."

"I will. Once I reach Stephan, I'll assist you at Marta's." Deveroy answered.

"Basil, when you know Marta is safe...leave Deveroy with her and come to me." Azzurra staggered and then regained composure. "Maybe I should go to Nicco?"

"Pip is very powerful, as is Stephan. You are closest to Marta and Arianna...Nicco has the dragon bracelet. He should be fine." Basil answered.

Azzurra nodded, took her keys from her purse and headed to the garage.

"No Mum! Don't drive. We don't have time for such things." He turned to the kitchen counter. "Merlin…we need you." He spoke to Azzurra. "Mum, let the Merlin take you."

A splash and surge of water rose from a vase upon the counter. Wings flapped as the bird flew over Deveroy, around Basil, past Azzurra and through the wall. Water splashed the surface and then retracted back into the bird.

"I've traveled upon them before. He will turn to ice for you sit. It won't be cold." Deveroy offered

"The Merlin will wait for you outside." Basil said

Azzurra rushed to the front door, stopped and faced Basil. "Basil we forgot Augusto! What about Augusto?"

Basil spoke toward the kitchen sink. "Sammy!" The pewter cat began to grow and morph into a full grown black panther. It leapt from the sink and roared.

"Sammy, go to Augusto Degeli. Protect him and keep out of sight from mortals—hurry!" Basil ordered.

The black cat roared once again and then leapt through the back sliding glass door and into the night.

"Basil did we get everyone? Is everyone protected? I can't think!" Azzurra yelled.

"Olivia and her family should be protected! The Vicar is with them! We should warn Drago and Kimberly…Thom in San Francisco and Bella in New York. However, Mum, there is not the time. I must go!"

"Go Basil! Go to Marta!"

Basil nodded and disappeared. Azzurra rushed to the front door, paused and headed back to the kitchen table. Grabbing the plume that the Vicar sent, she closed her eyes and spoke to the feather.

"Protect yourselves. We are under attack. The Witches War has begun." She waved a hand over the plume. Somehow she knew the only thing needed was to tell the plume where to go. Azzurra spoke the names of Thom Stryker, Bella von Eisenberg, and Drago & Kimberly Degeli. After a slight pause… she added Carlotta O'Reilly."

She let the plume go as it began to vibrate and quiver, and then vanish. Azzurra rushed past Deveroy. "Send a messenger to Katie! Tell her what has happened!"

"I will!" Deveroy replied. He knelt to the ground and raised a hand to begin the spell.

Azzurra rushed into the chill of the night, tightened her sweater and dashed across the lawn to a gigantic water bird.

***

Nicco sat on the sofa, hands thrust into his hair as he stared down to his bare feet. His mind whirled with thoughts...*I should have told Tracy...I should have given her the necklace.*

He lifted his head and looked up to the brick wall that displayed the family portrait. A soft whisper came from his lips. "Dad...I don't know how to tell her. I need you. Please Dad, I need you." He slid a hand into his pajama bottoms pocket and pulled out a rather large silver herringbone necklace. *It's not that ugly...so it's a bit manly. She'll have to wear it until I enchant something else.*

Something pulled at the hair upon his wrist. He shook his hand and loosened the enchanted dragon bracelet. He stared at the bracelet, unable to comprehend the evening's events. A soft purr broke his trance. "Hey Charlie...what are you doing up so late?" He rolled his eyes. "Dam it, she's up." The chinchilla/tiffany cat, made a soft coo, and rolled onto his back, green eyes darting out from his black fur.

"Nicco, would you please tell me what's going on?" Groggy green eyes looked down to Charlie and then back to Nicco. Tracy ran her fingers through long dark hair. "It's after 2:00 in the morning and I have to work in a few hours. However, I will stay up all night if you need me. Is it your mother? Is she OK?"

Nicco stood; his mouth went dry as he forced some words. "I don't...I don't know how...how to tell you."

Tracy's eyes narrowed. "Nicco what happened Wednesday night? You went to dinner and came home and have not been the same since." She shook her head slightly. "You know I love your mother, but she has never once, in all these years, not invited me to dinner. I know she's not mad at me." Moonlight shown through the skylights, Charlie looked up to the beams of white and purred.

Nicco dropped his shoulders, plopped back down on the sofa and looked up to his long-time girlfriend. "No, that's not it. She didn't invite you...because she...because she...had to tell me about it first. Then I could be the one...be the one to

315

tell you. I just don't know how." He searched her eyes for a way of communicating without words. He tugged at the collar of his t-shirt. "Tracy..."

A hiss interrupted Nicco. Charlie hunched and arched his back, fangs bared. Another hiss, escaped. His eyes focused upon the fireplace. "What's the matter with you? Charlie, come here? Maybe we have bats?" Tracy knelt down and wiggled her fingers toward Charlie.

Charlie's fur stood on end as he backed away from the fireplace toward Tracy.

"Oh, dear God, it's happening! Tracy put this on!" Nicco fumbled for a moment and tossed Tracy the necklace.

A clang came from the fireplace as ash and soot blew low to the ground and into the room.

"Nicco what is this? What's happening?" She caught the necklace and examined the weight of the herringbone.

Nicco's eyes widened and looked to Tracy. His skin became pallor and voice dropped. He shouted to Tracy. "Put the damn necklace on, now!"

Charlie hissed once again as a whitish glow appeared in front of the fireplace. The shape morphed into the shape of a young man with blonde hair.

"It's begun. The Witches War has begun. Basil sent me to help. I'm Pip." The Spirit blurted.

Tracy looked toward Pip. Charlie leapt up onto her chest and burrowed his head. "Shhhh it's alright Charlie. Nicco, listen to me..."

"...Pip, what do we do?" Nicco yelled.

"We set up a..." Another clang echoed from the fireplace along with more soot and ash. Charlie hissed again as Pip screamed. He struggled for a brief moment, his Spirit form flickering in and out existence... and then he disappeared...sucked into the fireplace.

A tingle of something warm, twitched Nicco's wrist. He looked down to the dragon bracelet. It glowed white...then faded...sparked, and then burned his wrist. Nicco yelled and tried to remove the bracelet.

"Nicco, get back!" Tracy dropped Charlie. "Charlie, stay!" She clasped the necklace around her neck and as soon as it snapped, a bright, swirling light encompassed her and Charlie. Charlie twirled in a tight ball near her feet.

Nicco stepped away from the fireplace, the bracelet still burning his wrist. Ice cold air crept over his feet. A plume of soot and ash rose, blocking his view. Tracy screamed again. Nicco stepped backward as he pulled at the clasp of the bracelet. "I won't come off! It's burning me!"

Tracy swore. A large creature appeared out of the plume of soot. Nicco saw the large black arm, just before it struck. He left the ground, feeling the bone snap in his arm. His body flew through the air, into the kitchen, onto the table and slid to the floor. The crashing sound of glass, stones, a body and candles, collided with the walls.

Tracy yelled for Nicco. Charlie hissed as the electric energy flickered around them. Tracy tried to remove the necklace, but the clasp would not release. Nicco opened his eyes. He saw the thing banging on the sides of Tracy's barrier. Charlie snarled. The white swirling light flickered with each pound. It opened its mouth wide and began sucking in the energy from the shield.

The creature resembled a human figure, three times the size of a normal man. Its body was thick, wide and held a glossy sheen as though it were wet. A sickening breathing expelled from its mouth. A man screamed. Tracy crouched on the floor with Charlie. She repeated something over and over. The shield swirled white as the creature continued to pound and grasp at the walls.

"Leave her alone!" Nicco scrambled to his feet...left arm dangling to his side. He grabbed a large candle with the right and threw it at the creature. It absorbed into the black, shinning skin.

The creature turned to Nicco. It had no face, no eyes nor nose...but its mouth was as big as its head. It opened to reveal more blackness. A man's screamed again. A sound gurgled from its mouth... sucking in air as it opened and closed its mouth like a fish.

Nicco felt his lungs tighten. His body became weak. Lightheaded and dizzy, he began to step backward as the creature move toward him. A sharp pain echoed from his foot as a piece of glass pierced the skin.

"Shards of glass, on the floor....protect me now!" He fumbled the incantation.

***

Arianna hit the key fob and waited for a split second as the *Chevy Traverse* beeped. Scott's *Ford F-150* sat next to hers. She smiled, knowing that her son waited for her.

She looked up into the night's sky. The moon showed bright.

A rumble of thunder rolled. Arianna looked around and could not see many clouds. She narrowed her eyes, *maybe it wasn't thunder.* Tiny feet took her up the stone steps of the porch. After opening the screen door, she placed the key into the lock and opened the large oak door.

She gasped. Scott was pinned against the wall; icy blue eyes darted toward the door, wide with fear. The hand that held him possessed long nails and skin lesions. Straggly, long dark hair flung to the side as it turned its head toward the intruder. Its face was hideous…long nose, grey skin, and bulging eyes. It wore shredded clothes layered in frayed material. It opened its mouth and displayed its fangs. With a bony index finger, it traced the blood that trickling down Scott's forehead. A long tongue lapped at her finger as its eyes met Arianna's. A loud hum came from Arianna's necklace. The Hag's high pitch call pierced the night.

* * * *

Carlotta

$\mathcal{C}$arlotta woke from a dead sleep, pushed dark hair away from her face and listened. Someone pounded on the front door. A quick glance at the clock told her it was 2:20 am.

It's been quite a while since her son Dino had been in trouble…almost four years. Maybe it's her ex-husband…begging for forgiveness once again. The various thoughts raced through her mind. In the hall mirror she stopped, fixed her robe around a large bosom and fussed her hair.

The pounding persisted on the door.

"Who's there?" She looked through the glass of the front window and saw a woman standing on her porch. "Olivia?"

"Carlotta! It's me…Olivia. We have to talk!"

Carlotta rushed to open the door and ushered her sister into her home. "Dear God! Olivia, you gave me a heart attack! I thought maybe Dino was in trouble. I don't know why he's been... What's wrong? Are the kids OK? Is it Walter? Did he hit you? I'll teach that son of bitch...I'll get my gun."

"What do you think you're going to do with a gun? Beee it's nothing like that! You and your gun...I need to talk to you." Olivia said.

Carlotta shut the door, turned the lock and slid the deadbolt. She waved her sister into the kitchen. "Sit down. I'll start some coffee. Oh my heart is racing Olivia. You scared the hell out of me."

"I know — I'm sorry Carlotta. Walter begged me not to go...but I had to. I've had the dream again." Olivia stood by the kitchen table.

Carlotta froze from opening the cabinet. After a slight pause she reached in and pulled down the coffee. "There is nothing more to discuss. Now it's just a bad dream. For the Love of God Olivia, it's almost 2:30 in the morning."

Olivia crossed her arms and took a few steps forward. "Oh there is a lot to talk about. You know something you're not telling me. You know exactly what happened the night Angelo died and I have to know the truth...did I...did I kill Angelo?"

* * * *

A Test of Powers

"Marta's heart skipped a beat as a lump appeared in her throat steeling her voice. Panic, shear panic consumed her. Fingers splayed as her eyes darted to the back hall. The phone crashed to the floor. *It's a demon! The pounding of her heart* exploded with fear. Not knowing that legs could move without a command, she entered the hallway — toward the ring. A bright cast of moonlight came from the spare bedroom, igniting the hallway. A tiny black figure rose from the floor. If it had not been for the moonlight, they would have collided.

Marta came to a halt...eyes wide in fear. A shadow...it was a shadow of small person: two arms, two legs, a body and a head...no visible face. The three-foot shadow splayed its arms, wriggled its fingers and giggled. Marta's mouth contorted as she tried to inhale the air that was needed to scream. Giggling, a child-like giggle, taunted her ears.

The shadow screeched and lunged itself towards Marta.

"Protezione!" A bright white shield of light exploded from her palm. When the shadow hit the shield, it bounced backward, rolled to the ground

and giggled. There were other giggles. Marta's eyes darted to her left, then the right. Freezing cool air touched her toes. Looking down she saw more Shadow People. Tiny hands and tops of heads appeared through the floor.

Marta lost her concentration...the shield collapsed. The three shadows pawed her legs, and then took a hold of them, as they began to drag themselves up her body.

The shadow, to her front, laughed and then leapt upon Marta. Its tiny hands clutched her throat as it screamed hysterically into her face.

Marta crashed to the floor in a silent scream. Bright lights of reds and purples dashed before her eyes as the back of her head smacked the floor.

Tiny hands clasped her body. Tugging and pulling...pawing and patting.

Never before had Marta's lungs produced such a sound of horror when she finally released a scream. Her body became limp. Something was eating at her energy. Sleep, sleep was all she could think about as she closed her eyes. They dragged her down the hallway, around the corner and into the kitchen. Giggling and laughing, pawing and patting, sucking the energy. They feasted upon their newest playmate. A cacophony of laughter and cheers came from a dozen more Shadow People, who jumped up and down upon the kitchen floor.

A tingling feeling pierced her skin...bones and nerves. Everywhere the Shadow People groped, a sharp tingle coursed through her body. *Sleep, I must sleep.*

Threw the slits of her eyes, Marta saw the tiny black shadows — dashing in and out view —shadows shoving others out of their way to have a turn. Hushing each other when one giggled too loud. The tingles sharpened, consciousness was losing the battle.

Marta's head lulled to the left, then the right — *nothing but black shadows and hushing of giggles. P*ain, she knew it was pain, but could hardly feel the effect of her head smacking against the kitchen tables leg. The feeling of nothing almost seemed to comfort her. Sleep tried to prevail. A plop of her head to the left and then the blurred vision of the stove came into a view... then a wall. A door opened. Sleep...all she could think of was sleep. The basement door...it was the basement door that made the soft, relaxing creek.

A slight whimper released itself from Marta's lips as her legs began the decent into the basement.

A far away scream of frustration seeped into her ears. The Shadow People released their pawing and patting. The giggling ceased, tingling subsided. Marta began to feel a sense of self, as her strength began to resurface. Her

322

eyes flung open. Bright blue lights flashed over head. She scuttled toward the top of the stairs.

Hisses erupted from the Shadow People. One by one they screeched in pain and tumbled down the steps.

Marta felt herself being lifted to her feet as more blue lights sped past her shoulder and around her head. A man took Marta's shoulders and forced her to look at him. "Go Marta! Get to your wand and ring. I'll hold them off!" Relief filled her soul at the sight of Basil.

Marat ran through the kitchen, around the corner and into the dark hall.

Basil changed to Spirit form. Flashes of blue lights flew in all directions as the shadows rose from the floor and attacked him from all sides.

Halfway down the hallway, Marta saw a stream of moonlight appear through the spare bedroom. Three Shadow People rose from the floor and into the moonlight. They hissed and lunged.

Marta stumbled backward, screamed and raised her palms. "*Pro...*"

A bright red ball of flame interrupted her spell. It shot from the spare bedroom and hit the Shadow People. They exploded.

A young man, with long blonde hair, rushed through the entrance and faced Marta. "Don't panic...I'm Dev..." The young man yelped as six Shadow People leapt from the spare bedroom and took him.

Marta swore, bolted past the bedroom and into the bathroom. She grabbed the ring, placed it on her finger and felt the warning vibration...it hummed and gleamed red. After grasping the wand, she darted to the spare bedroom. A black lump of tiny bodies heaped over the man.

Marta pointed the ring toward the shadows.

"Protezione da Demone!"

A bright red circle struck the tiny black figures. The top layer exploded.

The remainder of the Shadow People leapt to their feet and rushed toward the intruder.

"Protezione da Demone!"

Three shadows exploded into tiny black particles.

"Protezione da Demone! Protezione da Demone! Protezione da Demone!"

Tiny dark granules of Shadow People mingled with the air. Two Shadow People looked to each other, hissed and fled into floor.

The man looked up to Marta, his blond hair falling over the side of his face. He collapsed backward, against the wall. Flickering into solid form and then back Spirit, the man vanished and reappeared.

"What can I do? I don't know how to heal you!" Marta screamed.

"Help Basil, don't let them touch him!" The man closed his eyes and leaned against a wall. A bright blue light began to emanate from his body.

Marta rushed out of the spare bedroom and into the kitchen. Basil had a dozen of Shadow People clinging to him: clawing and pawing, patting and gnawing, giggling louder and laughing. A second latter, Basil disappeared into the floorboards.

Marta swore, rushed to the end table and took the book she had been reading. Panic coursed through every vein and artery. She flicked through the pages and found what she was looking for — a spell to summon a Spirit. Her eyes tried to focus as she reached for the lamp, fumbled and heard it crash to the floor. She swore again just as a beam of moonlight shown through the glass blocks above the door wall. The page lit up and the words were revealed. She spoke the incantation.

"Across the skies I beckon thee
Come across you cannot flee
I command to thee, with the power that be
To force you now to come to me!
BASIL!"

Basil appeared before her. He was in Spirit form, then vanished and reappeared. His trench coat slid off his face as his eyes moved upward. "Behind you!"

Marta reeled around, and for the first time, she pointed her wand to the Shadows People and screamed the spell.

"Protezione!"

An enormous white shied exploded from the tip of her wand, exploding ten or more of the Shadow People. Tiny partials of their remains descended to the carpet.

Breathing, deep heavy breathing, a static noise and the flashing appearance of Basil through the black dust, filled her senses. She knew that the breathing came from her. Heart pounding and blood coursing through her body consumed her. Marta raised her hand and looked at the ring. It was purple…the humming and vibration stopped…they were safe.

Shaking, uncontrolled shaking took control of her limbs. Tears began to stream down her cheeks. The blonde man, who helped her, stumbled to Basil's side and collapsed.

"Thank you." She said through tears and heavy breathing.

"You're welcome and thank you. I'm Deveroy."

Marta smudged a hand over her cheek and turned to Basil.

"Basil?" Her chest rose and fell in heaves. "How did I do?"

Basil grinned. "You were grand, Marta, simply grand."

***

Azzurra felt the water from the Merlin Falcon spatter against her. The droplets zoomed back to whence they came. A strange crackling, gurgling sound guided her attention to the rear of the gigantic bird. Water bubbled and morphed into steps, then froze solid. Merlin arched his head around and motioned that Azzurra should climb upon him. "Oh dear Lord...let Eleanor and Mary be sleeping."

A thirty foot wing span began to flap as Azzurra took the first steps. Merlin's back morphed and bubbled and then turned solid. Once upon his back, thin ropes transformed before her eyes. The solid ice felt cool to the touch, but nothing like it should have.

A crack of thunder rolled over head...clouds began swirling and colliding above. "Merlin...I need you to go to my sister's house...Arianna Valente!"

Azzurra let out a slight scream as they left the ground

***

Shards of stained glass descended toward Father Bernardo. "You will not harm me!" He stood with arms at his sides as glass shattered to the floor, the pews, and upon the altar. Unscathed by the glass, the priest kissed the rosary. The Winged Demons hovered over the opening.

Smatterings of rain pelt against the priest's body. Wind whipped through the church, pamphlets and bibles pages scurried through the pews. "You cannot enter in the house of the Lord! Be gone!" Father Bernardo looked to the statue of Jesus and wrapped the rosary around his wrist. "If it is in you will that I may perish...take me into your kingdom..."

"...Father Bernardo!" A voice came from behind.

Father Bernardo turned around and shielded his eyes from the rain and wind. A young, dark haired, man stood near the wooden doors. "I am Michale...Basil sent me to help." Michale raised a hand toward the ceiling. A bright blue shield expelled from his palm. A dome covered the priest.

325

"I thank you Michale, but I am in no need of your help. I beg that you go to Augusto. Assist him in any way you can. I have the Lord to protect me."

"But Father, they are Winged Demons! They may not be able to enter the church but you are not safe. Glass and shards of wood are falling!" Michale took a few steps forward.

"I am safe! The Lord is with me!" He turned to the altar and faced once again the statue of Jesus. "I ask that you remove these demons. I call upon the Angels...I call upon Michael! Gabriel! And Uriel! Destroy these demons!"

Father Bernardo looked up to the Winged Demons. "Go Michale! Protect Augusto...Augusto Degeli!"

"If you are sure you will be protected?" He waited for the priest to nod. Michale released the shield and opened his arms and spoke. "Augusto Degeli." He rose and vanished through the ceiling.

Father Bernardo felt the rain and wind pelt against him. He shouted at the Winged Demons. "Leave this church! I am in the protection of God and you have no power over me!" He held the rosary up to the ceiling and yelled again. "Be gone! You cannot enter where the Lord does not permit!" Glass and metal grinded and shattered as two of the Winged Demons entered the church. They screeched, fangs barred, as they flew toward the old priest.

"You will not harm me!" Father Bernardo screamed as he raised the rosary to his lips and then held it up high. The demons dove upon the aged priest...within a second of impact, a bright white light flashed throughout the church. Father Bernardo covered his eyes and fell to the floor. His fist pounded upon the wet carpet as he began the *Our Father*.

Several minutes later the priest grabbed the side of a pew and pulled himself to his feet. The moonlight showed strong through the opening of the ceiling. Candles had been snuffed by the wind and rain. Each step took him closer to the altar. He paused and looked up to the ceiling; massive clouds rushed the skies. Father Bernardo searched the church, incredulously inspecting the moonlight that guided his way. Once to the altar, he brushed the shards of glass aside and knelt. He kissed the Rosary and whispered, "Thank you Lord."

***

Marie screamed again as the White Demon opened its mouth and screeched. Thick strings of milky, slimy, wet skin, stretched across its opened mouth. Green leaves and vines appeared before her eyes forcing the demon to stagger backward. The English ivy grew and slithered across the floor, rising up to form a barrier between Marie and the demon.

Smoke began to fill the room from the cactus. The demon ripped and shredded the ivy, only to be replaced by more vines. It screeched and then opened its mouth wide. A thick mist expelled and covered the vines…they crystallized. A sheath of ice encased the ivy's leaves and stems. A crackled filled the room and a moment later, part of the English ivy shattered to pieces.

The demon brought its arm across its chest and then outward, striking Marie. She flew against the opposite wall and felt the pain rupture through her body. Blood trickled from the side of her head as she hit the floor. Her eyes lost focus and then blurred shapes of smoke filled her vision. The ivy's rustling vines darted in every direction around the demon — a screech, another crackle and then shattering.

Dark, thick mist floated about the room. Marie couldn't see the kitchen, the demon or the walls. She tried to pull herself to her feet. Her arm collapsed with pain, blood continued to run down her head, a moist heat covered her thigh. A sharp prick struck her arm, immediately revealing the room. The White Demon appeared through the fog. She could see the kitchen…the elixirs and sachets, candles flickering within the smoke. The demon groped the air, smashing the refrigerator…ripping the door off its hinges and hurled it to the living room. At every attempt, the vine circled the demon. It screeched again as the vine froze, crystallized and shattered.

"Marie, where are you?" A woman with a French accent demanded. "I cannot see!"

"Over here!" Marie screamed again. She tried to move but the pain shot through her once again.

Violetta turned toward Marie's voice and spoke over the smashing of the china cabinet. "I cannot see! This thick smoke has blinded me! Is it the demon that makes this smoke? Are you hurt?" Her voice was calm and strong.

"I can't stand! I think my arm is broke too!" Marie shouted in Violetta's direction. "The smoke is from the cactus, it pricked me with a thorn, only I can see through it!"

"Do not move, Marie." Violetta's commands were sharp and focused. "I will destroy this demon."

"Don't let it get near the elixirs and sachets! The whole house will explode!" Marie grabbed her thigh, blood seeped through her hand.

"I have no intentions of letting that demon do any such thing." Her voice spoke with a deadly threat. "I cannot see the demon, but no matter, just stay where you are." She cast a spell to clear the smoke.

""*Fumee Effacer*"

A large ball of light vanished in the thick clouds. Everything remained hidden.

"My spell has vanished into the blackness! Where is this demon? It has gone quiet?" Violetta asked in a low, deadly tone.

"He's coming toward you! Protect yourself!" Marie screamed. Vines once again shattered in millions of tiny particles.

"Moulinet"

An enormous rainbow of bright lights formed a ring and a jet of red exploded from the center. It struck the demon and threw it into the wall.

Marie screamed and began to crawl toward Violetta. "Behind you, the sachets are behind you! Blue are for defense…yellow heals!"

The demon grabbed Marie's leg; vines came between them, followed by a screech and tiny droplets of ice. She screeched and kicked at the White Demon with the other leg.

"Protezione! Say it Marie!" Violetta ordered.

Marie said the spell; a bright light encompassed her and knocked the White Demon back. It regained composure and tossed the kitchen table into the living room. Marie screamed as the demon pounded upon the shield.

"Stay low! Maintain your shield!" Violetta cast another circle of protection. A red flash flared above Marie as the demon howled in pain, flipping over Marie's shield and crashed into the wall.

"Do not speak Marie. I will handle this demon!" Violetta spoke with a deep guttural command. She cast three more spells toward the demon. Marie felt the impact of the spell blast against the shield and heard the demon squeal. Her shield held. The vines crept over Marie's shield and then tentacles grasp at the demon. Marie saw the demon inhale a large breath, rip away the vines and face Violetta.

"He's going to blow freezing air at you! Protect yourself!" Marie cried.

Violetta cast a blue shield around her as the mist struck her shield of protection and formed a covering of ice. Violetta disappeared.

A second later, the ice exploded outward. Violetta cast several spells; some missed the White Demon, while others struck it and tossed it through the wall.

Marie could see that Violetta stood just a few feet in front of the sachets. "Behind you, there are blue sachets! Grab one and toss it at him. It's coming back through the wall!"

Violetta spoke an incantation.

"Red and yellow, orange and teal
Bring the sachet of blue appeal"

Violetta's spell brought the blue sachet to her.

"The demon is directly in front of you! Throw it!" Marie screamed.

Violetta threw the blue sachet...hitting the demon. It howled as black dust surrounded it. Violetta cast another protective shield that glowed around her.

Marie saw the demon stumble backward through the slithering ivy. She saw Violetta cast a spell behind her to cover the entire counter of elixirs and sachets.

The repercussion of the explosion smashed through the cabinets. Flames erupted in the living room, crawled to the ceiling and walls of the kitchen and ate at the vines. Every appliance evaporated or flew to pieces. The White Demon staggered as it looked to Violetta and then Marie. It was no longer white, but seared in black, torn and frayed. It screeched and then broke through the kitchen window; smoke billowed after its exit. Voices screamed for Marie and Steve from outside the walls. Sirens blasted in the distance.

Immediately the smoke from the cactus began to dissipate and the ivy slithered off Marie's body. The cactus began sucking in the smoke from the flames. Marie's shield had collapsed. A shard of wood stuck into her chest.

Violetta withdrew her shield, took a yellow sachet and rushed toward Marie through the flames. An enormous silk scarf slid to the floor and revealed a man hugging a younger woman.

Katherine screamed as her father moved her away from the flames and hollered for his wife.

Violetta knelt and withdrew the shard from Marie, stood and threw the yellow sachet upon her...demanding that the girl and man stay back.

At impact...the sachet exploded. Tiny lights of blue speckled into the air above. Dancing sparks of white interspersed with blue. They hummed and clumped over Marie's leg, arm, chest and head. Yellow and orange lights shot in and out of the wounds, while a mist of rose, expelled softy from her mouth. After a moment, a large display of green illuminated her entire body and then vanished. Marie gasped and took in air and began to cough.

Violetta raised a hand and produced a blast of freezing air. The fire snuffed in all directions. A moment later, she turned to see Marie crying in a man's chest and a young lady staring at her.

"I am Violetta and I have forced the White Demon to flee. Do not be afraid. Basil has sent me. Ah, but I am sure you know nothing about a man named Basil, now do you?"

Katherine coughed from the smoke and shook her head, tears streaming her cheeks. Violetta made a sweeping hand gesture and swished the smoke out through the kitchen window, into the bright moonlight. Voices and pounding upon the front door, interrupted them.

***

The Cull screeched once more into Augusto's face.

"Distruggi un demone o caccialo via!"

Augusto cast the spell. A bright yellow streak emitted from the palm of his hand, blasting the Cull into the mirror. The mirror shattered as tiny plumes of the Cull floated in the air.

"I hate those damn things!"

Augusto knelt to the floor, placing a hand on the lower part of his back. He picked up the wand and stood…wincing in pain. His eyes focused down the dim hallway. There were forms of people…humans…demons?

"Palla di luce!"

A ball of light burst from Augusto's wand and streamed down the hall, revealing three men. The light briefly revealed colorless faces and red veined eyes…demons. They shielded their eyes as they caterwauled. A moment later, Augusto's spell faded. The three men leapt toward the old man.

Augusto flung his hand toward the demons, made a quick sharp twist and jabbed with the wand.

"Distruggi un demone o caccialo via!"

Red, green and orange circles shot from the tip of the wand. One of the demons caught Augusto's spell full blast in the middle of its leap. Green globs of goo spattered the walls. The other male demons were forced ten feet back, smashing threw the hall closet and wall.

Augusto cast another light spell. He could see two demons struggling on the ground…one reaching for its arm several feet away. He pointed the wand and repeated the spell of light…walking past the green glop's of goo. Around the corner three female demons entered the hall, same colorless faces and blood red eyes. They shielded their eyes from the bright light and staggered backward.

"Palla di fuco!"

A ball of red swirling fire erupted from Augusto's wand, exploding one female while knocking the others to the floor.

Only the pale moonlight remained. A rumble of thunder rolled overhead.

A scuffle came from behind Augusto's left ear. The male that had been green glop's of goo...reformed and stood behind him. Two females ran toward Augusto, while the third female began to reform from goop.

"Raffica energetica!"

A blast of white emitted from every inch of Augusto's body, sending his assailants backward several feet...crashing through walls, doors and into the spare bedroom. The male that had re-attached its arm, reeled in anger and walked past the female that was still trying to re-form from goop.

A roar came from the bathroom. Augusto turned to see an enormous black panther. It ran past Augusto and leapt onto the male demon just before it reached Augusto.

"Palla di luce!"

A ball of light filled the room. One male came from the spare bedroom as the female rushed toward the old man. Another female appeared from hole in the wall. They shielded their eyes and continued forward.

"Pietrifica!"
"Scolo di energia!"
"Trasferisci l'energia verso di me!"

Augusto cast one spell after the other. One female froze solid in its tracks; the male howled, fell to its knees and crumpled. While a mist of white flew from the other female and into Augusto. It collapsed to the floor, drained of all energy.

Augusto turned to the panther who sat next to a swirl of smoke. "Protect me, Sammy. I have to cast the spell to bring back Anna!"

He turned to face the hall, lightning flashed to reveal all six of the demons, some reforming from green goop. The panther leapt into the crowd of demons.

"Augusto?" Anna's voice came loud and strong. "Augusto, help me!"

The panther ripped apart demon after demon and sunk his teeth into another while draining its energy. Green goop flew in all directions...howls and screams filled the hall.

"Anna! I'm going to cast a spell to try and bring you back. Concentrate on my voice!" Augusto yelled over the cacophony of Sammy and the demons screams.

"Palla di luce!"

A ball of light appeared. One of the males broke free and leapt toward Augusto. A flash of white shot past his right shoulder, the demon flew backward and into the wall.

Augusto switched focus to behind him. A teenage male Spirit with dark wavy hair stood in the bathroom. "My name is Michale…A friend of Basil's. Father Bernardo wished me to come to you. Are they Vetala?" A loud roar erupted from Sammy, forcing their attention to the fight. Two of the females broke in half, spewing green ooze to the floor. A paw swatted across another, removing its legs. Sammy grabbed another into his jaws, shook his head and then smashed it into the wall…exploding it into green goop.

"Yes! I think they are! They've regenerated several times, they should be weakening." Augusto glanced down at the piece of paper, glasses sliding down his nose.

"Palla di luce!"

A ball of light appeared. "I must cast it now! I have to free Anna!"

"Do it! The panther and I will handle the Vetala." Michale turned toward the demons and began casting spells. Red, purple and silver light hit the Vetala. They were generating faster and faster. Green goo flew in all directions forming back into the shapes of males and females.

Michale fell backward as a male leapt upon him. Fangs bared as it lashed at him. Michale twisted his legs around the Vetala and struck his face. With his other hand, he cast a spell. Black mist exploded outward and coiled around the males face. It screamed as its face melted. Globs of green spattered Michale's jaw and cheeks. Michale rolled to his feet and faced two females as Sammy ripped apart the third female. A male plunged its fangs into Michale's neck from behind. Michale swore, flipped the male over his shoulders and blasted him with the same black spell.

Michael felt his energy drain from the bite. He began to flicker in and out and then stabilized. Sammy continued to swat and bite down on the Vetala. Michale cast spell after spell, dodging the green goop.

"Augusto!" Anna's voice came through the ruckus. Augusto pointed his wand toward the ceiling and cast the summoning charm.

"Attraverso tempo e spazio io ti chiamo
Io ordino la tua anima di essere libera
Lontano dai turbinii dell'oscurità
ti ordino di donarmi il tuo spirito!"

(Through time and space I call thee
I beckon the soul to be set free

332

Away from swirls of darkness flee
I command you now to release your spirit to me!)
Anna Degeli)

"We must leave! I cannot regenerate again!" A female Vetala shouted in an Italian accent.

Three Vetala rose from the ground and fled. The female who gave the order followed suit. Two males remained; Sammy stood in front of Michale and Augusto.

"You will not win this battle! Leave!" Michale cast another blast of black toward the Vetala. The two males were knocked to the ground, their bodies melting. They scurried to their feet and fled, green goop, following them. Sammy turned to Michale and licked his teeth clean.

Augusto looked toward the ceiling. A tiny swirl of white light began to form. It grew and expanded into a whirlpool of opal. Michale and Augusto became mesmerized by the swirls. It began to crackle and sparks of white shot from the center. After several minutes, a wispy orb expelled from the middle of the swirls. Michale and Augusto covered their eyes as the panther roared and turned his head.

When Augusto lowered his hands, he saw a woman hovering just above the floor. "Anna?" He hurried to her side, wincing as he knelt. Michale placed his hands over the body and began to transfer energy. Anna lifted her head, disappeared, reappeared and flickered from sold to Spirit form. Her coloring was grayish, clothes torn and eyes sunk deep into her skull. "Augusto…" Anna's eyes closed, her head fell back and lay level with the rest of her body.

Augusto produced a soft white light from the palm of his hand as Michale continued to transfer energy.

***

Azzurra saw her sister's house below as the Merlin descended through the clouds. A sudden feeling came over her that Nicco was in grave danger. It harpooned into her gut. "Merlin, go to Nicco's…Nicco Stephani." The Merlin swooped over the roof of Arianna's house and headed east. "Be safe Arianna." Azzurra whispered.

***

You have to visualize what you want the object to do; this will bring life to the object and give it a means by which it can act on its own accord. You had better focus and not lose your temper! Nicco heard a combination of his mother's voice and Aunty Arianna's in his head as he slid down the wall and to the floor. Everything lost focus. The black creature's body turned fuzzy. A second later, his eyes closed.

A man's voice…he heard a man's voice and then a large thud…followed by a howl. Something went into him. He saw a bright light through his eyelids. Whatever it was…it gave him energy. Nicco's eyes flew open to see something not expected.

A camel…a small camel flew across the room and down the creature's throat. A large man, in what looked like an Egyptian costume, covered his mouth and screamed. "My camel, how dare you! Give him back!" A red blast came from his sword, knocking the creature off its feet and back against the far wall. The creature swelled in size.

Stephan turned to Nicco. "Listen honey, I gave you a huge energy surge, my camel is in deep trouble and that ugly no-face creature is really mad at me! So you better do something fast." Stephan blasted the creature with another spell, which it seemed to swallow.

Nicco glanced to Tracy, who cowered at the bottom of her encasement with her cat, Charlie.

Another red blast hit the creature. It smashed through the entertainment center then rose to its feet and began to wretch.

"Oh dear…is it going to be sick? Stephan asked.

Out from the creatures mouth plopped a camel and a young man with short wavy blonde hair.

"That was repulsive!" Pip rolled away from the creature and cast a protective shield.

"Oh Darling…you're OK!" Stephan rushed toward his camel, giving it a hug.

The Black Demon sucked in hard…lamps, chairs; cushions, pictures and objects flew toward the creature. Pip's shield expanded and stretched. The camel and Egyptian hung to the ground…sliding toward the creatures opened mouth.

"Nicco, do something!" Tracy screamed from inside her cage of light.

Nicco raised his hands toward the broken glass on the floor; he envisioned the glass forming a shield around them. The shield would protect them from being sucked into the creature's mouth.

"Shards of glass here my calls, give us now protective walls."

Pieces of glass flew from the floor, multiplied and formed bubble shapes that sealed himself, Pip & his camel and Stephan. Chairs, end-tables and pictures disappeared into the creature's mouth.

"Oh thank the heavens! If I got swallowed by that ugly beast I'd need therapy for an eternity. Stay down honey, Daddy will handle the bad ole demon." The camel buried his head under Stephan's gown as he wielded his sword behind the wall of glass.

"They feed off energy. I don't think our spells are doing anything but strengthening the demon!" Pip yelled over the angry howl of the creature.

Stephan made a large hand gesture with his sword. "If' its energy it wants…let's give ugly all the energy we can!" Tiny birds flew from his sword and zoomed toward the demon. The demon began to swallow each bird. "I think that's why he couldn't hold down my camel and that adorable young man. He's an over eater and purged!"

Pip produced large diamonds full of energy and hurled them toward the demon.

Nicco looked around the kitchen. He shook his wrist trying to loosen the dragon bracelet that still burned his skin, blisters formed over his wrist. Blood smeared the floor as he limped toward the kitchen counter. Nicco saw the salt and pepper, a microwave, cabinets, dishtowels, Tracy's tiny butler holding a tray of fruits, magnets? His eyes darted in every direction, trying to think of what to enchant. Voices urged him to act. Nicco closed his eyes and envisioned the butler tray being filled with massive amounts of energy. The butler would whip a tray of energy at the demon, producing as many trays as he needed.

> *"Tracy's butler dressed in black*
> *Throw your tray at the demon in black!"*

Nothing happened.

> *"Tracy's butler, come to me*
> *Fling your trays at the demon to be!"*

The butler leapt off the kitchen counter, ran to Nicco and began to fling tray after tray at the Black Demon.

Nicco turned to the kitchen once again.

> *"Kitchen towel on the stove*
> *Move over the demon to stop his moave?"*

Nothing happened, Nicco swore.

> *"Kitchen towel of baker and cheese*
> *Cover its mouth so it cannot breath!"*

Nothing happened. Nicco envisioned what the towel would do. He envisioned the baker throwing hunks of cheese filled with energy at the demon. The towel would cover the demons mouth, not letting anything inside.

Once again he said the incantation.

"Kitchen towel of baker and cheese
Cover its mouth so it cannot breath!"

The baker leapt off the towel and began tossing hunks of cheese from his apron at the demon. Stephan's birds, Pips diamonds and the trays of energy began to force the demon to swell in size

The towel flew over Nicco, around the Egyptian and covered the demons mouth. The creature roared and struggled to remove the towel.

"Good one honey! Oh that was wonderful! Bravo!" Stephan yelled. "Good for you! Ruff ruff ruff!"

A moment later the Black Demon writhed and then stretched and moaned as another creature split from him…and then another.

"Oh dear…that's not good. That is so not what I expected." Stephan grimaced.

One of the creatures swallowed the baker…the demon exploded. The other two creatures roared. One lunged toward Pip and his camel, while the other lunged toward Nicco, mouth still covered by the towel.

The walls of glass began to crumble around Pip and Nicco as the creatures banged on the outer walls.

"Air inside the living room; sweep these creatures…from us soon!"

Nicco shouted the incantation. Air swooped over the creatures and threw them against the far wall. The butler hung onto the carpet as one of the demons reached to grab him. The butler rolled out of the way and flung a tray into the demon's mouth. The tray produced such an enormous amount of energy, the demon exploded. The butler hurled into the air and clinked against Stephan's glass wall.

Three more demons appeared from the floor. One attacked Stephan and his camel, the other Pip and the last attacked Nicco. The original one, tried to pull the towel from its mouth, gave up, and began to pound on the walls of Tracy's encasement. Tracy screamed as Charlie gave a guttural cry.

Nicco's wall cracked, but held. Pips' wall shattered to the floor as he and Stephan attempted shield charms, which quickly evaporated into the demon. The butler flung a tray at Stephan's wall. The wall absorbed the energy and repaired itself.

Tracy's wall flickered but held against the beast. Nicco's wall of glass crumpled to the floor as the butler rushed to his side, flinging trays of energy at the demon.

A large crash forced Nicco and the butler to turn toward the front door. The door flew into the hallway and slid to the floor. A small woman entered the kitchen, a bright light shinning from her chest. A high pitched call pierced their ears.

"Torna all'Inferno!"
(Return to Hell)

The demon staggered backward. It was a moment away from reaching Nicco when Azzurra's spell struck. The Black Demon exploded to a cloud of grey smoke. Azzurra covered her Angel pendant, the light from the Angel, vanished. She pointed her wand to the demon who struggled to get Pip down its throat. Stephan screamed.

"Torna all'Inferno!"
(Return to Hell)

The demon exploded with a gray poof. Azzurra hit the other demon that attacked Tracy's wall and more grey smoke filled the room.

Azzurra rushed to Nicco. "Nicco, are you all right?" She examined his wrist to see the burnt skin under the Dragon bracelet.

"My Stars, aren't you the powerful one?" Stephan fanned himself as the wall collapsed and his camel's head emerged from under his garments.

"It didn't work. My enchantment didn't work!" Azzurra pointed her wand tip at the bracelet.

"Poni fine a questo incanto!"
(End this incantation)

The bracelet released from Nicco's wrist. "I'll recast it later."

Stephan helped Pip to his feet as the butler plopped down, dropped his trays and collapsed onto his back.

Azzurra examined her son, raised her wand and spoke an incantation.

"Through the body, through the soul
Mend what's broken, heal him whole."

A large white blast encompassed Nicco. He staggered backward and then regained himself. The wounds upon his body healed.

Tracy curled up with Charlie on the floor, her protective encasement gone. She cried softly.

"Ma, is everyone else all right?" Nicco yelled.

"I need to get to Arianna! Go to the house. We'll meet you there! Cover things up as much as you can!" Azzurra rushed down the hallway and outside to the Merlin bird.

The Hag dropped Scott and flew toward Arianna. A beam of bright light shot from Arianna's pendant and hit the demon in the chest. It squealed and flew back, past Scott and into the kitchen cabinets.

Arianna hurried to her son. Shouts of spells came from upstairs. "Dads upstairs, he's fighting them. You need to help him!"

Another beam of light shot from his mother's chest, striking the same Hag again, throwing it back into the kitchen.

Arianna took off her necklace and placed it around her son's neck. She whispered as spell.

Scott's wavy dark hair, matted in clumps of blood. "Mom, no, you need this!"

"A mother only needs to protect her child. I'll be fine. Stay here, let the necklace protect you. There is a spell…" Another beam shot from her pendant and hit a second Hag. "…a spell called *Protezione*! Simply point your wand toward the Hag and shout the spell. The pendant should protect you."

"I forgot! Dad told me the spell! We've been practicing all night…I @#!%ing forgot Mom, I forgot…I forgot the spell, I panicked!"

Arianna kissed her son upon his forehead. "It's all right…I love you Scott. Just say the spell, remain calm."

Two more Hags were thrown back from the pendent. Arianna turned and headed up the stairs. She stopped near the top; Mateo could be heard shouting incantations. A woman in white appeared, peering down at Arianna.

Lamia raised her hands.

Arianna threw a hand up and called *Protezione*! With her other arm she made a low swooping movement from her waist and jabbed toward Lamia.

"Lontano da me!"
(Away from me!)

Lamia was thrown back and into the wall and swore loudly. Arianna rushed down the stairs, past Scott who shouted Protezione as three Hags were blasted away from him.

Arianna ran into the formal room where Lamia appeared.

"Organ keys I call to thee form a wall so she cannot flee!"

The organ keys flew from their resting place and formed a wall around Lamia, duplicating until she was covered by black and white ivory.

Arianna turned quickly around; she stabilized against the chair, feeling dizzy.

Two Hags rushed toward her, "Protezione!" The Hags flew against the far wall. Once again she heard Mateo's voice, Scott shouting spell after spell, items smashing and explosions against walls and furnishings. Arianna rushed past Scott and up the stairs to Mateo.

* * *

Gabriella spayed her fingers and shouted Protezione! The windshield's pieces flew toward the beast as it slid down the hood of the car.

A burst of moonlight shined into the car as raindrops began to fall. Her eyes darted up to the wolf. It began to regain its composure, shaking its head. She looked down into her purse...then back up...down...then up... red she need the red one! Down...up...I need the red sachet! The red sachet came into view. She grabbed the sachet, looked up and saw the wolf's head enter through the broken windshield. It growled and opened its mouth. Into its mouth the sachet went. "Protezione!" She yelled once again.

The beast tumbled back down the hood of the car and slid onto the cement. It shook its head violently and coughed. Rising to its feet, it continued to cough. Gabriella gathered her purse and opened the car door, casting another shield of protection that surrounded her. Her eyes glanced to the front bay window...then to the creature who stumbled upon the driveway. It howled, shook its head once more and then focused on its prey.

"Gabriella? Are you alright?" An older woman rushed across the lawn in a housecoat and approached Gabriella. The growl made her stop halfway through.

"Go back inside! Hurry Shirley! Go back inside...it's a wolf!" Gabriella ordered.

Shirley looked toward the garage door and screamed at the sight of the wolf. Moonlight shone brightly. The beast growled, moaned...shook its head and stumbled, a soft cry escaped from its mouth as a moment later it exploded. Shirley flew backward and hit the ground. Gabriella's shield collapsed. Tuffs of fur floated down to the earth. Another snarl came from behind. Gabriella reeled behind to see three more wolves approaching

Neighbor's porch lights illuminated the front yards. A woman from next door called out. A young man wearing night pants ran toward Gabriella from across the street. Moonlight lit the driveway. It revealed the three wolves that approached. Shirley screamed from the grass. The young man stopped in the middle of the street. He looked to Gabriella. "What the fu..."

"Derek, go back inside!" Gabriella's voice carried a command that she had not known in decades. "Protezione!" Two wolves leapt toward Gabriella, while the other leapt toward Derek.

339

Thunder rolled above as trickles of rain began to fall.

The first two wolves howled in pain as they hit Gabriella's shield and flew back twenty feet.

"Protezione, Derek!"

A ball of white shot from her hand and surrounded Derek. He fell to the ground as the Wolf hit the shield and flew back. Derek hit his head and lay still, the shield protecting him. An elderly man from across the street shouted that he was getting his gun...a woman screamed and ran back inside her house. Gabriella pushed Shirley toward a couple that approached. "Go back inside!"

Shirley turned to the couple and screamed that it was wild wolves.

"Palla di fuco!"

A ball of fire burst through the air...blasting the wolf into an inferno. It howled and ran across the lawn, then smashed against the garage door and fell. Shirley and the couple cowered from the flames.

Three wolves jumped toward Gabriella. She screamed as two wolves burst into flames and one flew thirty feet in the air over her head. Gabriella searched the perimeter and saw no one that could have cast that spell. She cast a spell to reveal who attacked the wolves.

"Rivela ciò che non può essere visto!"

A woman appeared with long dark hair, black slacks and a button down black shirt. She flipped her head back, throwing the long mane of dark hair away from her face. The woman sent a message to Gabriella. "I am here to help. I am Ritsuko. Basil sent me. I cannot be seen." Ritsuko spoke something in Japanese that produced a large yellow whip that appeared from her hand. She began to attack the wolves that leapt upon Derek's globe of protection. Derek began to regain consciousness.

Gabriella rushed around the car...past the burning bodies of wolves and toward the porch.

Derek's shield collapsed, the wolves that attacked him were fighting something in the air. "Wolves...they are frickin' giant wolves?" Derek ran to join the others on the front lawn.

Sirens blared in the near distance. Lightning flashed across the sky as thunder rumbled above. Shirley looked around. "Where's Gabby?" Shirley yelled. "Where's Gabby!"

Two more neighbors joined the group on the lawn. Lightning flashed again as buckets of rain began to pelt the earth. Derek ran toward Gabriella's front door, stopped, shook his head and followed the command that told him to run under Shirley's porch with the others. They watched in horror as the wolves leapt at the air, snarled and growled at something unseen.

"Raffica energetica!"

The front door blasted off its hinges as Gabriella walked through the threshold.

A creature stood above Nicolai. A stream of orange light expelled from its large softball eyes. It was hairless with a large watermelon shaped head… no mouth or nose. Near eight feet tall…its limbs were gangly and hung to its sides, scraping the floor. Grayish skin hung loosely upon its body. The demon took no notice of Gabriella as it fed upon her husband.

Protezione Nicolai! Gabriella shouted. A ball of white light shot from her hand. The demon absorbed the light casually with its palm. The shield dissolved.

A growl and bark erupted to Gabriella's left. Her dog leapt upon a wolf entering the house. Snarling and growling and finally a yelp ended the struggle. Gabriella stumbled backward, twisted on her ankle and fell…her purse's contents scattering.

"Energia Raffica!"

Gabriella shouted. The wolf flew back, burst into flames and ran through the door. Her black Labrador's bloodied body lay motionless. Several sachets and elixirs lay to her right. She grabbed a sachet and tossed it at the demon. The demon caught the sachet in its hand. The orange glow from its eyes dissolved as the Dover Demon slowly moved its large eyes to stare at the sachet. It looked up to Gabriella just as the sachet erupted. A horrific squeal filled the room followed by a gust of wind. The demon vanished.

The front bay window blew outward. Gabriella's body spun in the air and smacked into the wall. She rolled to the ground and came to a halt next to the dog. Another two sachets exploded…immediately redirected by Ritsuko. The explosion ripped through the second floor.

"Gabriella!" Ritsuko knelt and cast a healing spell. Several reds, blue and oranges twirled around her body. A lime green mist floated from her mouth. A second later her eyes flung open. "Nicolai!"

"He is there." Ritsuko helped Gabriella to her feet. Gabriella rummaged through the spilled contents, took a vial and crawled to Nicolai.

"It's too late! It's too late!" Gabriella sobbed.

"Do not say such a thing. You are very powerful. I have never seen a Dover Demon flee from a Witch before. I shall give your husband energy. You will pour the elixir." Ritsuko began exchanging energy to Nicolai.

Gabriella took the vial and poured it down her husband's throat. Purple's, Violets, Lime Greens and Sapphires leapt from his chest and shot out to the ceiling. Several seconds later, Nicolai coughed and opened his eyes. Gabriella kissed him all over his face…tears streaming down her cheeks. "My Nicolai…I thought I lost you. I'll be right back."

She crawled to her dog and poured an elixir into his mouth. "Come on Rex…you fought to save me…now it's my turn." Lights illuminated from his throat. A green mist expelled from his mouth as his wounds healed. A moment later he rolled to his feet. Rex cried and began to lick Gabriella. Nicolai crawled to his wife and hugged her close.

Lightning flashed, rain began seeping into the family room. Thunder cracked and mixed with voices shouting for Gabriella and Nicolai. Three police cars came to screeching halt as a fire truck's horn blasted through the night's sky.

**

Arianna saw two more Hags at the top of the stairs. The Hags gave a high pitched screech and rushed toward her.

Protezione! The Hags were blasted back.

Arianna rushed past Scot and into the living room. She shouted. "You keep that necklace on, no matter what!" She flung back sliding glass door.

"Across the skies…through the night…I call for help from those with flight!"

The Hags rose to their feet and snarled at Arianna. A whoosh of black feathers rushed past her…flapping and squawking. She waved a hand and motioned for the birds to assist Mateo upstairs. Dozens of birds of every type flew around her, past Scott and up the stairs.

"Protezione Scott, don't forget!"

Arianna fled to the dining room, opened a drawer from one of the China hutches and pulled out a shoebox that Gabriella had given her in the first Witches War. After placing it on the dining room table, she opened the lid and took a blue sachet in her aged hand. Mateo, the birds and the high pitch screeches of Hags could be heard from upstairs. A sixth sense told her to look up — nothing but a wall of organ keys.

The lights flickered, followed by a loud crackle of thunder. Scott's frantic voice screamed Protezione!

A loud crack and the lights went out.

"Eyes in head let me see, through the night not meant to be!"

Five Spirits came into focus. They were looking at the wall of organ keys. "I'll work on getting Lamia out of this...kill her!" Marcus ordered as he gestured toward Arianna.

Arianna recognized the Spirits, two were Celia's; Dormava and Medeia and two were Tessa's; Marcus and Damiano. The other Spirit came from her cousin Debra...his name was Phillip.

Arianna threw the sachet toward the group. The five dispersed threw various walls and windows. Marcus reappeared almost instantly...turned to Spirit form, raised his hands and cast a spell. Arianna countered.

"Rifletti questa parola Magicka!"
(Reflect this spell)

Marcus flew through another wall and into the study.

Medeia and Dormava appeared and cast several spells in an attempt to release Lamia. Phillip and Damiano rushed toward Arianna.

Arianna spoke an incantation.

"Wall of art I command to take, these Spirits who mean to set my fate!"

Damiano and Phillip struggled for a split moment before they were sucked into a painting.

Arianna turned to the ladies.

"Let these Spirits, two that be
Make them mortal, just like me."

Dormava and Medeia turned solid. They rushed to Arianna, one grabbed a lamp the other a vase.

"Like fairy tales and stories told...make them both grow very old."

Both ladies fell to the floor, ageing hideously. The lamp broke and the vase rolled against the carpet and hit the organ keys.

Through the wall, Marcus appeared. Looked to the floor and raised a hand toward Arianna. *Protezione* blocked his spell. She retaliated.

"Rug in hall I call to thee, wrap this man so he cannot flee!"

The rug rose and surrounded Marcus so fast, he had no time to react.

Scott saw constant flashes of white light shooting out from his chest. Lights revealed the Hags and then everything plunged back into darkness...save for the dim moonlight. The squawking of birds and screeches from the Hags pierced the room from the second floor. There were too many Hags...the spells were not shooting fast enough. They tore at Scott's legs as he shouted *Protezione*…three more took their place. He screamed as a Hag bit into his leg. Another Hag bit the side of his face.

A flash of bright light exploded, a half dozen Hags flew away from Scott. Mateo stood at the bottom of the stairs…wand in hand. Moonlight shone brightly.

"Are you all right?" Mateo shouted. Birds and Hags screeched from upstairs.

"Mom! She's fighting them in there, hurry!" He pointed to the dining room.

Mateo turned toward the dining room just before his feet left the ground. Three Hags pulled him from behind, biting and shredding his skin with their long nails. One Hag was blasted off by the pendant. *"Protezione Dad!"* A ball of light shot from Scott's wand…the Hags were thrown away.

Mateo staggered…grabbed his neck and pressed down hard. Blood seeped through his fingers. He turned and began fighting four Hags. Scott's pendant never stopped. *Protezione!* Six rushed him at once; *Protezione!* Three were thrown back…one blasted away and two bit down into his legs. Scott's howled as long nails began tearing into his leg muscles. The Hags lapped at the blood.

A bright blue light filled the room. A small dog bark followed by a growl. A woman stood in a blue dress, next to a small black and white Terrier. The Hags turned to see the woman. The pendant blasted another Hag.

"You filthy bitches! Get off my Nephew!" Katie waved an arm and four Hags burst into flames. The rest of Hags emitted a high pitch and then rushed toward Katie. Katie threw out both hands…all the Hags burst into flames and evaporated.

"Nasty, ugly little demons, take that and that!" The Hags turned to Scott and leapt toward him. Scott yelled Protezione. Blackie leapt on a Hag that was about to bite Scotts arm. It screamed as it struggled to release the dog. "Take that and that, you filthy Hags!"

Mateo staggered past Katie and Scott in an attempt to get to the dining room…to his wife. The room swayed and became fuzzy. He turned at the sound of Scotts voice, clinging onto the wall. Dozens of Hags floated into the room, from the ceiling, the walls and the floor. Katie cast spell after spell. The pendant continued to shoot its blasts. Blackie leapt upon another Hag that approached Katie from behind. Scott yelled over and over Protezione as he pointed his wand to the Hags.

Mateo cast several spells. Two Hags flew away from his son…three more blasted away from Katie. The last thing he saw was Blackie being attacked by two Hags. He slid down the wall and to the kitchen floor as everything went dark.

Arianna looked over her shoulder. Scott's voice continued to shout the protection spell. She heard Katie's voice! "Oh thank the Lord Katie's here!" she spoke out loud. She had heard Mateo's voice too. She was thankful that he was downstairs.

Lamia's voice came from inside the wall of organ keys. "Marcus! Get me the hell out of here!" She pounded on the walls...casting spell after spell. She even called for The Man. Nothing happened. She opened a palm and produced a bright light. Her eyes focused above...organ keys...on all four sides...organ keys...then she looked to the floor and saw the carpet. Lips tightened for a brief moment and then slid into a smile.

Arianna rummaged through the box...looking for another sachet. Another shout from her son, Katie screamed...Blackie yelped. A red sachet...she found a red sachet! Into her tiny hands she clasped the sachet and headed out of the dining room...to her husband and son.

"Arianna, are you OK?" Mateo's voice came from behind.

"Mate..."Arianna turned to see a woman in a white dress...grinning. A blast of red light filled her view just as she tossed the red sachet toward Lamia. "Prot..." Her body lifted off the ground...arms flew out to her sides...head forward. She crashed through the curio cabinet ...through the Lladro figurines...the vases and the collectible plates. Glass shelves smashed as her body slid to the bottom of the cabinet, faltered and then slumped to the right. The figurines, broken glass and shards of china settled over the small body.

Lamia could do nothing...the sachet struck her, forcing her to turn solid. She would feel all the pain a mortal would feel. Through the air...over Marcus that crawled out of the rug...over the young women who lay on the ground and past two men that appeared in front of a painting. Splinters of glass...blast of pain shot through every ounce of her body. Her dress tore... hair ripped from her skull and skin sliced opened as her body catapulted through the front window.

Katie blinked in and out of view...another blast of blue lights shot from her hands toward Scott and then over Mateo. The pendant made a funny sound...like fritzing and then stopped. Katie looked toward the dining room. Several Hags leapt at her. Scott made a guttural sound of anguish.

A sound of water...splashing water entered the room. Several Hags were swallowed by Merlin. Through the opened sliding glass door, Azzurra entered. Lights flashed in every direction. Screeches and howls filled the room. The Angels' high pitch, then two blast of white struck several Hags. They exploded. Water splashed everywhere and then contracted back into the falcon. He squawked and blasted a fire hose of water at several Hags, pushing them against the walls. Several Hags fled.

"Distruggi un demone!"

Azzurra shouted the spell over and over. The Hags coiled and screeched as they watched each other explode into grey poufs of dust. More Hags fled through the walls until none remained.

"Katie, help Scott and Mateo! Where's Arianna?" Azzurra commanded.

Katie stabilized and then spoke. "The pendant stopped working. She..." Katie pointed to through the dining room doors.

Azzurra rushed through the entrance of the dining room, moonlight shown through the front window. Azzurra's pendant cast out two bright lights into the darkness. The Angel's voice sang through the dining room in warning.

"Rivela ciò che non può essere visto!"

The five Spirits came into view. Marcus fled before the others noticed. Azzurra covered the Angel with her hand, raised her wand and spoke.

"Disturba l'energia!"
(Disrupt energy)

The four Spirits wailed and writhed...then flickered...stopped moving and floated through the ceiling.

Azzurra saw Marcus appear on the front lawn. Moonlight shined brightly upon him and a woman in white spattered with red. He helped her to her feet. They looked up and then disappeared.

Basil appeared next to Azzurra. *"Mum, are you all right?"* He flickered once and then stabilized.

"Yes! I need to find Arianna!" Azzurra eyes widened as she saw a look of pain upon Basil's face. He was looking past her, onto the floor. Azzurra turned and said a spell.

"Palla di luce"

A soft glow of light revealed a crumpled green shawl and small amounts of a flowered patterned dress. Arianna's head tilted to the side...blood ran from her ears and nose.

Azzurra covered her mouth and screamed, raised her wand and then cast a spell.

"Through the body, through the soul
Mend what's broken, heal her whole."

Nothing happened. She repeated the spell. No lights...no streams of energy...nothing happened. Azzurra turned to Basil as he brought her to his chest. They sank to the floor as she sobbed.

"Azzurra, Azzurra?" Soft words were spoken by Katie. "Azzurra honey… I have to go look for her. She'll be lost…she'll be disorientated. Blackie should be able to find her quickly. Mateo and Scott…I can't do anything more…we need healing elixirs. They lost too much blood. Scott is a mess."

Azzurra looked up from Basil's chest and took in a breath. "Go Katie… find Arianna and bring her back to the house. We will meet you there. Basil? Go to Marie…she has elixirs…hurry Basil go!"

Basil helped her to her feet and vanished.

"Blackie?" Katie called.

A tiny dog entered through the wall…blinking in and out of view.

"I know we are all drained…listen to me…I need to you find Aunty Arianna…hurry…find her." Blackie barked and leapt through the wall.

Sirens blasted the night air as the rain and wind pelted the trees and ground. Azzurra took in a deep breath. "Katie they can't find her like this. I need to fix the house. Stay with Mateo and Scott, help them as much as you can and then help Blackie find our sister." Katie nodded and headed through the dining room and into the kitchen.

Azzurra took tiny steps toward the front window. Moonlight shown upon Arianna's broken house. Out the window clouds rolled over, lightning flashed. Her eyes examined the moonlight…then the night sky. She shook her head, and then looked over her shoulder toward her sister. The glow of the spell of light, shined upon the body. Azzurra felt more tears run down her cheeks as she rose her hands…closed her eyes and spoke.

> *"Through time and space of what used to be*
> *Mend what's broke for the eye to see*
> *Put items back the way they were*
> *To a time before the attack occurred."*

Rugs…vases…paintings…glass, metal…wood and cloth…all flew about the house and returned to the original state. Arianna's body floated, still surrounded by the light. Azzurra guided the body to the front room and let it rest upon the floor.

> *"Winds of warm and winds of cool*
> *Begin a funnel of strength to rule*
> *Toss the cars and topple trees*
> *Bring the cyclone of destruction to see."*

Several trees limbs smashed to the street…causing a police car to swerve up the curb. A fire truck and ambulance stopped as a car rolled before them.

Basil appeared. "I have the elixirs! Marie's OK. I'll go to Mateo and Scott." He left the room.

"Hurry Basil people are here." Azzurra looked outside and the called for the Merlin

A splash came through the wall. The falcon flapped its wings in front of its castor. "I need you to stall them...don't be obvious of what you are. Make sure no one gets hurt."

The Merlin nodded once and splashed through the window. Azzurra could see what looked like a hurricane. People rushed back inside their homes...paramedics and police stayed within their vehicles.

Azzurra began to shake, tears streamed down her cheeks as she brushed her sisters hair away from her face. She screamed for Basil.

"Mum?" Basil appeared next to her. "What is it Mum? Mateo and Scott will be fine. They are waking now."

"You have to do it Basil...I can't...I can't!" Azzurra began to sob.

"Mum, do what? By what do you mean, Mum?" Basil said gently.

"Her wounds are all wrong. We have little time. I've produced the effects of a tornado. The Merlin is protecting everyone. We need to make it look as though a tree branch broke and was thrown into her while she was on the porch. Break the window to be broken inward. Arrange her body for me I can't." Basil knelt down and reached for Arianna's arm. "Basil wait, no I'll do it!" Azzurra began to arrange the body, after a moment she nodded to Basil.

She stood aside as Basil conjured a tree branch from outside, placed it near the body and gently broke the glass to appear within the house. He knelt beside Arianna...examined the tree branch, waved his arm and produced an injury upon her chest. "It is done Mum."

"Arianna?" Mateo called.

"Mom?" Scott and Mateo entered the room. Scott's clothes were shredded and stained, but his body was healed. Basil waved a hand over Scott and Mateo and repaired their clothes.

Azzurra approached them and stood. The glow from the spell revealed the body. "There was nothing we could do. Katie and Blackie are searching for her soul. Get to my house as soon as you can. We are going with a tornado."

Mateo nodded. Scott rushed past his aunt to his mother. Mateo grabbed Azzurra and hugged her tight. "I know you did all you could." He swallowed hard, tears streaming down his cheeks. He then went to his wife's body… spoke her name over and over and began to sob.

"Poni fine a questo incanto"
(End this incantation)

Azzurra's words doused the glow of light. Mateo, Arianna and Scott fell into darkness.

"Basil, can you please call the Merlin to the back yard. I need to be home. Is Marta all right?"

Basil flayed his fingers toward the outside. "Marta is fine Mum. The Merlin will meet you in the back yard."

Azzurra spoke to her beloved Spirit. "Thank you my Basil."

"You're welcome Mum." Basil looked to Mateo and Scott and then vanished.

Azzurra hurried through the hallway, into the living room and stood at the sliding door. A rush of birds flew past her and out into the night.

The Merlin produced stairs and morphed its back solid. The night sky disappeared in pitch black. Not a single drop of moonlight could be seen. Tears ran down Azzurra's cheeks as she gave a slight scream when the Merlin lifted from the ground.

* * * *

Carlotta's Secret

Carlotta's pulled the coffee container from its shelf and set it upon the counter.

"Did I kill Angelo?" Olivia whispered.

She opened the coffee container and scooped out several heaps of grounds into the filter. She closed the container and replaced it, gently closing the cabinet. Her hand lingered upon the wood.

"Angelo? Did I kill Angelo?" Olivia asked once more.

Carlotta took the coffee carafe to the sink, filled it and emptied the water into the machine. Her eyes closed then opened as she pushed start.

"Carlotta, answer me!" Olivia slammed a hand upon the counter.

Carlotta flinched. The rumbles of the coffee brewing gently filled the room. "I will...I will tell you everything." She pulled a dish from the cabinet and placed cookies and a couple of pastries around stoneware. Carlotta then retrieved two antique cups that had once belonged to her mother. After a slight pause, she set them on the table an angled their handles just so. Cream, Sugar, and a few napkins were placed between the cups.

Olivia sat at the table. "Maybe you shouldn't tell me?"

Carlotta moved to the coffee machine, placed her hands upon the counter and spoke. "It's alright...you should know."

Aunty Arianna entered her home...she wore a green shawl...a horrifying creature held her cousin Scott against the wall...it licked the blood from its finger. Marta screamed as tiny black shadows pulled her across her kitchen floor...her head smacking a chair. A wolf...a giant wolf jumping up and down on Aunt Gabriella's car...she screamed as the windshield shattered.

Olivia rose to her feet in a sudden jolt.

Nicco was struck by something huge...he slid across the kitchen table and struck the wall.

Olivia's eyes widened. Her hand rose to her mouth.

Carlotta grasped the handle of the coffee carafe and waited...staring at the tiny green light.

Uncle Nicolai raised his hand and shouted something...a large white cylinder expelled from his palm...he shouted other words...Rex barked and growled. A man in white stood in her house...his tie lit up...things...flashes of things...flew into the gemstones of his tie. Uncle Mateo held a Wand...shouting at hideous creatures that held Scott. Aunty Azzurra loomed in the air...she sat upon what looked like a large glass bird.

"Carlotta?" Olivia whispered.

Almost...the drip almost subsided.

Marie's kitchen table flew across the room, a vine...smoke...screams. Uncle Augusto pointing a wand...rings of color shot down the hallway...stained glass ceiling smashing...two winged creatures zoomed toward Father Bernardo. A bright red light...

"...Carlotta?" Olivia balanced herself on the table.

A bright ball of light struck her Aunty Arianna...her tiny body limp, bloodied and lying under the debris of her curio cabinet.

"Carlotta!" Olivia screamed.

Carlotta spun around. "I am organizing my thoughts...give me a..."

"...I saw them...I saw them all...oh dear Lord something's happened. I saw them being attacked...creatures...Aunty Arianna...I saw Nicco, Uncle Augusto...Marie, Marta...I think Aunty Arianna is...is dead."

Carlotta's eyes widened. "Olivia, are you sure that's what you saw?"

A white feather plume appeared before them...it drifted toward the living room. Olivia jumped and stabilized herself against a kitchen chair. Carlotta took a step toward the plume. It began to write. Sparks flared from its tip as it spelled the words, Protect yourselves...we are under attack...the Witches War has begun!

Carlotta raised her hands a spoke loud and strong.

"Attiva i miei incantesimi!"
(Activate my enchantments)

Lights flashed from Carlotta's hands...a yellow energy wave blasted through the room and up the walls...over the ceiling and across the floors. Clocks began to chime...a voice came from a painting within the clocks backdrop. "Ready for battle, my lady!"

A nutcracker yielded its sword and took several steps out from the under the mantel. Olivia backed against the table and screamed. A clanking sound turned her focus to the coffee table. Two glass birds sprung to life, stretched their wings, they looked to Carlotta...tiny eyes blinking.

"Circle the perimeter of the house, engage in anything hostile. Do not harm mortals...only celestials or Spirits with evil intentions." Carlotta commanded. The birds flew from the coffee table and darted through the wall. Olivia shrieked and covered her mouth. "Clancy secure the front entrance." The nutcracker saluted and darted through the kitchen and took up guard at the front door. "Captain Morgan...you and your men take the back bedrooms and basement...block anything with evil intentions...let any messages come through." Olivia's eyes darted toward Carlotta's command. A Spirit of an older gentleman and stunning black Andalusian horse leapt from a grandfather clock. Olivia screamed again. "Have no fear Madam Carlotta...my men and I shall secure the premises." Several Spirits leapt from the clock; two rushed to the basement while the rest rushed to the back hallway.

"Olivia, don't be afraid. Olivia, look at me...look at me Olivia. Listen, I know it's a lot to comprehend, but listen to me...if the plume and what you saw are correct, it means another Witches War has begun."

"I can't believe what I just...the nutcracker...I bought you him years ago... he came to life...the birds...Dad gave you those...they were Muma's. What are you!? What's happening?" A second later a rush of calm entered her...protection... strength...a need to sit. Olivia pulled out a chair and waited for an answer.

Carlotta breathed a heavy sigh, turned to the coffee maker, took the pot and poured the steaming liquid into both cups. She returned the carafe to the burner and took a seat at the table.

After placing both hands flat upon the table, she spoke. "I will explain everything...Angelo...the nutcracker...the visions you saw...give me a moment." Carlotta looked down to the cup. Several moments later she looked up to her sister. "Are you going to scream again?"

"No, I am not going to scream. I am fine. I feel calm and serene." Olivia took a sip of coffee.

"Are you OK?"Carlotta asked.

Olivia nodded.

A thick Cockney ancient filled the room. "It's the Vicar, Madam...he's standing next to her...a dashing young lad in white with red hair...whoops he didn't want me to say he was there. Sorry Mr. Vicar. I'll say not another word." Clancy, the nutcracker, darted back to the front door.

Carlotta sighed with relief. "We are safe. A Vicar is one of the most powerful beings next to that of the Higher Spirits themselves. You see Olivia... you and I...are Witches. I've known this for a very long time...since before Angelo died. I should have told you...I should have said something. I didn't know how. I wanted to protect you. The dreams you have, the visions... they are placed there by a Spirit. You should not have remembered anything from the night Angelo died...you were too young. You shouldn't remember Muma the way you do...again you were too little to remember her. I don't know how you know the things you know, but I think it's because of your power. You have a gift of precognition and I believe you have the power of Spirits. This allows Spirits to communicate with you very easily... through your dreams. It is this communication that has purposely led you to believe that you killed your brother. That's why I insisted that they were just dreams...to block them out...to ignore them."

Olivia covered her mouth and shook her head. "Carlotta, why didn't you tell me?"

"I ask myself the same question. But I prayed, and this is the answer I was given. That it was safer for you not to know." Carlotta took her sisters hand.

Olivia inhaled three deep breathes, a shiver rushed through her body. "So my dreams...I didn't kill Angelo?"

"No. You did not kill Angelo. If anyone is to blame...it would be me. I knew the Spirit. I knew her before you met her...before that night. I thought she was an Angel."

* * * *

An Angel?

*T*he soft patters of rain upon the rooftop were the only sounds in Carlotta's kitchen.

Olivia waited...feeling calm, warm and protected. Carlotta took a sip of coffee, traced the rim of the cup and began to speak.

"I met her two years prior to the night Angelo died. I had been sleeping... it was October. I remember it was windy and cool. There was a brisk chill in the air that woke me...so I got up and shut the window. When I turned, she appeared." Carlotta looked up to the ceiling and then back to her sister. "Oh Olivia, she was so beautiful. I remember her as though it were yesterday. I was nine years old." Carlotta eyes appeared heavy; her voice was low but soft. "She had long flowing black hair...I remember her hair so well. It had thick, shinny waves that fell over her shoulders...it was so beautiful." Carlotta traced the cup's rim absentmindedly as she continued to describe the woman. "Large brown eyes looked gently down upon me. I remember feeling so safe... so happy. Her cheekbones were high and she wore red lipstick. It was as though she popped out of one of my books...the fairy princess. Diamonds...oh I remember them sparkling everywhere. They were embroidered with beautiful swirls all throughout the bodice. The neckline plunged low over a rather large bosom. The dress came tight at the waistline, revealing a sharp figure. Oh she was so pretty. It wasn't full and poufy...it was slim and fitting, elegant and classy and one of the most beautiful dresses

I had ever seen. Of course I thought she was a princess or an Angel. I can just see her beautiful white, satin shoes." Carlotta closed her eyes, shook her head with several small shakes and looked up to her sister. A tear welled over her lid and slid down a cheek. "I thought if she clicked her heals, together we'd disappear into fairy land."

Carlotta tightened her lips and made a tiny fist. "She told me not to be afraid...that I was a very special girl to be visited by her. She told me that she was an Angel...that we would be friends. She said Mom and Dad couldn't know. That they didn't believe in Angels that talked to people and would think I was lying...making things up." Carlotta paused for several seconds. "I would get into trouble." She smeared a cheek with the back of her hand. "We chatted for a short while and then she said that she would be back the very next night and we'd chat some more. I asked her what her name was. She told me that her name was Lamia. I thought it was a princess's name. What a beautiful name...Lamia."

Carlotta paused for a moment, closed her eyes and continued with them shut, shaking her head once more with tiny movements. "Lamia visited me the next night, like she had promised." Carlotta opened her eyes. "We talked for hours. We grew to be such good friends. Every night we'd have our conversation. I'd tell her my thoughts and feelings. She asked all sorts of questions and everything I said was so exciting and interesting to her. She said how wonderful it was to have such parents as mine. She told me that I was lucky to have been born into such a good family — a perfect family." Carlotta smeared a cheek. "She said that I made her laugh...I could always make her laugh." Carlotta smeared the other cheek with a force stronger than before. "She said that I reminded her of herself when she was my age."

Carlotta took a napkin and dabbed the sides of her eyes. "I was so stupid." Her voice rose. "I was so stupid!" She slammed a hand down upon the table. "I knew...I knew what we were! I overheard Mom and Dad talking about Aunt Tessa. They thought that Vincent was killed by an evil Spirit. I heard Ma talking with Aunty Azzurra and how they would defend themselves against the attack. I knew something was wrong. I knew they believed in Spirits and things. Why didn't I say anything about her...about Lamia?" Carlotta placed her face into a napkin and cried. A moment later she bolted her head up, stretched her neck and took in a breath. She felt calm, strong and secure. Olivia squeezed her sister's hand.

"Lamia visited me twice a week for almost two years." Carlotta struggled to fight back another burst of tears, shook her head back and forth several times, tightened her lips and then continued. "One night she didn't visit me when she said she would. I didn't understand why. I was afraid I had done something to upset her. I called for her but nothing happened. I went to bed...and I cried." She smeared away more tears. "It was near two in the morning when I heard your voice. I crawled out of bed and saw a white glow coming from Angelo's room. I peeked through the crack in the door and saw you standing there…you were talking with Lamia. She wanted the necklace that Angelo wore. Grandma gave Angelo the Patron of Saint Ann. I overheard Ma talking to Aunty Arianna over the phone months before. Mom said that Angelo was safe and that the spell didn't die after Grandma's Luciana's death. She purchased it from a Witches Vendor and he bound the necklace to Angelo. Whoever wore the necklace…would be protected. Lamia must have known I knew what the necklace did…that's why she didn't ask me." Carlotta tried to catch her breath after several attempts; she calmed and spoke once more. "I would have never taken the necklace from him. You didn't know what the necklace did. You were four and you loved angels. I watched you hand the necklace to her but she refused to hold it." Tears streamed down Carlotta's cheeks and once again she tried to catch her breath, shivered and then continued. "Lamia leaned over Angelo and said something to him. I didn't think she would harm him. I would have stopped her. When she asked you to put the necklace back on Angelo…I pushed the door open. You were holding the necklace. Lamia smiled at me…told me to go back to my room. That she wanted to say hi to my brother and sister before we had our chat. I looked to Angelo and I knew." Carlotta sucked in a deep breath and then regained composure. Olivia knelt down and took her sisters hands into hers. Carlotta looked to her sister, searched the ceiling, the floor and then her sister's eyes. "I knew he was dead. I looked up to Lamia and she began to speak in a quick, gentle tone. She asked me to forgive her… that it was for the best…and that it had to be done. She said we could still be friends." Carlotta choked and squeezed Olivia's hands, then stood abruptly and placed her hands over her mouth. After a second or two, she faced her sister and dropped her hands to her sides. She spoke through quick, deep breaths. "I told her to leave. You began to cry. Lamia left. I took the necklace from you and placed it on Angelo. I told you to be quiet. I wanted to explain what happened. That Angelo was dead — that you should be quiet about seeing an angel or removing the necklace. That's when Mom opened the door and asked us why we were up so late. Why were we in Angelo's room?" Carlotta let herself fall against the refrigerator and slid down its door. Olivia knelt beside her. "I'll never…forget…that scream." Through deep heaves she cried. "Never…never!" Carlotta collapsed into Olivia's arms and sobbed.

Olivia hugged Carlotta and stroked her hair. She whispered, "I know who she is. She's been in my dreams. She tells me that I killed him…that I killed Angelo."

Carlotta stood and pointed to her sister, her voice was strong. "You did nothing to kill Angelo! You would have never known not to take that necklace from him! It's my fault! She is lying to you! She wants you insane!" She rushed to the counter and searched the living room. She flung herself around and faced Olivia. "You did nothing Olivia!" Carlotta stammered to a chair and fell into the seat. After several moments of silence, Carlotta spoke. "Lamia tried to explain. She came back the next night and tried to comfort me. I told her to leave and that I never wanted to see her again. I was afraid if Mom ever found out the truth…that she'd hate me…that she would hate us both. I screamed at Lamia to leave. Mom came in and asked what I was screaming about. I looked to Lamia and she shook her head. I told Mom that it was just a bad dream. When she left the room, Lamia leaned down and said that I was too young to understand. That she would look in on me from time to time. She kissed my forehead. I saw a tear fall from Lamia's eye as she vanished. I never saw again."

* * * *

Breaking News!

$\mathscr{A}$zzurra set the empty glass of the Renew elixir aside, dabbed her mouth with a napkin and listened intently.

> *"Good Morning I'm Tasha Delasandro…"*

> *"…And I'm Dirk Waignright."*

> *"Tragedy strikes near downtown Ferndale, leaving one woman dead…"*

> *"…thousands of dollars in damage at a local church…"*

> *"…and wolves terrorize a neighborhood."*

> *"The time is six O'clock, your local sports, weather and morning traffic is coming up next."*

Azzurra placed a hand to her mouth and shook her head. Gabriella sat next to her sister and sipped on the Renew elixir. "Are you OK Azzurra?"

"I'm fine. I just wanted to see what the news has to say about all this. Have you heard from Eva?"

"Not a word. I left three messages and nothing. Arianna was right…my daughter is up to something."

Gabriella stood and walked over to Nicolai who spoke on his cell phone near the counter. The news cast continued.

> *"Severe weather struck last night leaving one woman dead on W. Oakridge Street in Ferndale. A freak tornado whipped through the neighborhood just after two in the morning leaving 62 year old Arianna Valente, dead. Investigators report that debris from the tornado hit Valente as she stood upon her porch, throwing her through the front window…killing her instantly. The tornado tumbled cars, uprooted trees and damaged several homes. Miraculously, no one else was injured in the incident. Arianna Valente is survived by her husband Mateo — her only son Scott, a daughter-in-law Gracie and three grandchildren."*

Marie hugged her mother and asked if she needed another Renew elixir. "No, no I'm fine honey. I feel as though I've had a full nights rest. Thank you, sweetheart."

Marie smiled and walked toward Steven, Katherine and Marta. Marta waved her arms dramatically and raised her voice as she explained to Steven and Katherine the events of the Shadow People.

Nicco sat with Tracy at the opposite side of the kitchen table…informing her of the events of the dinner on Wednesday evening and how his mother broke the news of being Witches & Warlocks. Tracy took continuous sips of wine.

"Are we OK Mum, anything on the telly?" Basil appeared and pulled up a chair next to Azzurra.

"So far we're safe…they'll explain every supernatural event with logic." Azzurra nodded and turned back to the TV.

> *"…A pack of wolves terrorized W. Abby Street in Pleasant Hills early this morning. Gabriella Pavalak was lucky to make…"*

"Azzurra?" Father Bernardo took up a seat opposite Basil.

"Oh, yes Father." Azzurra looked to her cousin.

"Mateo and Scott are resting in the basement. I've spoken with Gracie. She knows everything. As soon as Scott is up to it, we'll get him home. She's worried and frightened."

"Gracie's strong Father. He married a woman just like his mother." Azzurra replied.

Basil interjected. "I hate to ask this...but I feel I must...Anna is back now." He jerked his head toward the front room. Azzurra could see Augusto talking with the Spirit form of Anna on the sofa. "Shouldn't we ask her what happened the night she vanished...if she knows anything?"

Azzurra looked to the TV.

"...Father Bernardo Degeli was the only priest inside the church when lightning struck ..."

Basil cleared his throat. "Mum, Miss Katie should be back anytime with Arianna."

"I'm sorry Basil. I didn't mean to ignore you...yes we will let her regain some strength, spend some time with Augusto. She still looks stressed and depleted...no coloring. When she's stronger, then we will ask her questions about that night." Azzurra took Father Bernardo's hand. "Father...Tessa is not the one making the decisions...it is Lamia. Tessa called and warned me to protect the kids."

Father Bernardo nodded.

"Father, a Witch must be working with Lamia. I think Debra and your brother Carlo are helping her." Azzurra placed another hand upon the priest's hand.

Father Bernardo nodded once again.

"I believe that someone has made it appear that Contessa and Nathan are to blame. Celia knows who is behind this and I believe Eva does as well."

Father Bernardo looked down and then squeezed Azzurra's hand.

Basil spoke. "Father, you are the talk of the Higher Spirits. I heard your faith was tested."

"We are tested everyday Basil." Father looked to Azzurra and then back to Basil. He removed his glasses and pulled out a hanky and began to clean them.

"Yes, but when the Lord let the demons enter the church...you stood ready to die." Basil raised an eyebrow.

"I knew that the Lord had let the demons enter the church, so I knew it was the Lords will." Father Bernardo returned his glasses securely behind his ears and replaced the hanky.

"Your faith saved you Father, with not a drop of Magick." Azzurra squeezed her cousin's hand. She then turned to face the TV.

"...*a gas explosion rocked the neighborhood in Pine Hills early this morning when Marie and Steven Giordano...*"

"Azzurra?" Katie appeared in front of her sister. Everyone gathered. Augusto and Anna entered the kitchen.

"Katie...did you find her? Where's Arianna?" Azzurra stood.

"She's in the basement. She hasn't taken into Spirit form yet. She's disoriented, you know, most Spirits are at first. She's spending some time with Scott and Mateo. They drank calming potions, they were a mess... poor things have been through a lot tonight. Blackie will guide her upstairs when she's ready. I want no fussing...it will only upset her further...she's embarrassed."

"Embarrassed about what?" A gruff voice called out.

"Augusto...she lost the battle! Lamia fooled her by mimicking Mateo's voice. Of course she's embarrassed." Katie replied.

"From what I understand it sounds as though she put up a damn good fight. An army of demons and powerful Spirits attacked her and she would have destroyed them all if..." Augusto trailed off as a small bark entered the room followed by a bright ball of light. The orb floated toward Azzurra and rested near her shoulder. Gabriella turned into Nicolai's chest.

Azzurra's eyes filled with tears. "Arianna honey...it's good to see you. Don't be upset...we are all here." The orb buzzed.

"She's crying." Katie said.

"We all know you put up a grand fight." Basil said.

"She said to say thank you, Basil." Katie replied.

"I know Miss Katie...I can hear her just fine." Basil smirked.

"Oh that's right....sorry honey." Katie swished a hand.

"Arianna laughed." Basil said. "She wants to know about the news. Did they report anything strange?"

"Well so far honey…it's all been explained. They don't know where the wolves came from so of course that led into a story about illegal pets." Azzurra answered. "Too many neighbors heard the commotion at Marie's; thank goodness Basil made it look like a gas explosion. Ritsuko repaired Gabriella's house before the police entered, no one seemed to think anything of the explosions from within the house. They were too focused on the wolves and Ritsuko cast a spell to make sure no followed Gabriella inside. They blamed the church on the storm and thank goodness Augusto lives in a condominium with senior citizens, no one heard a thing. Augusto and Michale fixed the damage."

"Arianna's laughing, says that Magick could be performed on stage and everyone would think it was part of the show." Katie nodded.

A bark forced everyone to look down.

"And you! Have I told you how proud Muma is of you? You fought those nasty bitches right alongside me! I don't know what got into him? But you should have seen him! He was so brave!" Katie picked up Blackie and raised a paw in triumph. Everyone applauded him as he wagged his tail and barked.

Blackie looked toward the front door and barked once again…the doorbell rang. Azzurra looked down to her pendent…nothing. Augusto headed to the front door, Anna, flickered once and then followed.

"It's the Shadow People…I know it's the shadows!" Marta took Tracy's wine and gulped it down.

"Yea, and they are knocking on the front door!" Nicco poured Tracy more wine.

Tracy looked around, eyes darting everywhere. "Shadow People?"

"It's alright Marta…no shadows. Tracy, ignore her and Nicco, don't be mean!" Marie scolded.

Augusto peaked through the hole and shook his head. "Everyone be nice…our sister is here."

"He has the nerve to tell us to be nice." Nicolai muttered.

"Shush." Gabriella nudged her husband.

Contessa and Nathan entered Azzurra's home. Basil stood quickly and appeared before them. "Basil, be nice." Azzurra instructed.

"Is everyone alright?" Contessa looked to Azzurra and then Gabriella as she entered the kitchen.

"Are you alright?" Azzurra asked. "The phone went dead...I've been worried about you...and thank you for calling. If it had not been for your phone call, I think Father Bernardo would have been the only one to survive."

Contessa spoke. "I'm glad and we are fine...not sure what happened to the phone. I heard the static too." She smiled toward Nicco, Nicco did not smile back. "We've been waiting for someone to call and we couldn't wait any longer." Her eyes rested on the orb and tears welled. "Arianna!"

Nathan closed his eyes and shook his head. Contessa rushed to the orb. "It's Lamia...she's out of control! I had nothing to do with this. I swear! Neither did Nathan. I never knew about the Cull on Olivia. Achar said something about a Cull. I would have never done that...I hate Culls."

Tracy gulped more wine.

"See, I told you she hates Culls." Katie let Blackie to the floor and folded her arms.

"And the reason you sent demons to Olivia's house?" Father Bernardo stood and walked a few steps toward his cousin.

"I didn't send demons Father. I sent Achar and Deveroy. They were to do a light haunting...you know, scare them. Make them pay for my Vincent's death. But I was wrong." Contessa turned to her husband.

"You put your trust in the dead! It is sin to communicate with the dead!" Father Bernardo slammed a hand on the table.

"You're right Father." Basil winked at the priest.

"Thank you Basil." Father replied.

Gabriella stifled a laugh; Azzurra shook her head to Basil, who smirked.

Nathan turned to Katie. "We never sent demons to Olivia and never sent the Cull. We called off Achar and Deveroy" He turned to address the room. "Last night it was revealed to us that Basil and Katie had nothing to do with Vincent's death. We were wrong." He turned to Katie. "Katie we are so sorry, please find it in your heart to forgive us someday."

Katie turned her back to him and began swearing.

"What the hell is everyone talking about?" Steven looked to his wife, Marie.

"Shush Honey. I'll explain later." Marie put her arm around her daughter, Katherine, who still had not regained coloring.

"What do you mean revealed to you?" Nicolai asked.

"We don't know…it came to us both. I had a dream…she had a feeling come over her and then a man in white appeared to us. After that…we knew… we knew when Lamia and Debra showed us that Basil killed Vincent…we knew it was a lie." Nathan rubbed his wife's shoulders.

"What are you talking about?" Gabriella took a step forward.

"Showed you that Basil killed Vincent?" Augusto asked.

"I did no such thing." Basil turned to face Azzurra.

"What do you mean Nathan?" Azzurra raised a hand toward Basil. "I have complete faith in you Basil…do not doubt that."

"Lamia cast a spell." Contessa spoke. "She cast a spell that showed Basil entering his room that night…that showed Basil raising his hand. Oh, it was so real. I thought all these years…I would have given my life…that he did it…he killed my Vincent and you protected him…sided with him over me."

Father Bernardo shook his head and made a slight noise.

Anna raised her voice. "They lied to you! That spell was nothing but trickery." Anna stood in front of Contessa and Nathan and folded her arms. A piece of disheveled hair flopped over her forehead. She appeared in grays… like a black and white photo. Augusto stepped beside her.

"Anna? My Lord I hardly recognized you…you're free?" Contessa asked. She examined the haggard look of Anna…torn dress…ripped boots…tattered head ban. Anna flickered once and then reappeared.

"Yes I'm free, thanks to my husband and Basil. But the both of you've been totally duped by Lamia, Debra, Carlo, Sabino and Stella." She turned to face the priest. "I am sorry Father Bernardo…but it looks as though your family is responsible." She turned to face Contessa and Nathan. "Vincent did not die at the hands of Basil…and I know that for sure!"

Azzurra stepped forward. "Anna, tell us what happened that night. Who banished you and why?"

* * * *

The Higher Spirits

Wisp of sand blew across the deserts floor as two men in white suites stood before an elegant table made of mahogany. Twelve members, that formed the council of the Higher Spirits, sat upon cushioned, high-backed 1920's oak chairs, facing the two men. All the members wore white robes, with the exception of a woman who sat between them; she alone wore a dress with an embroider bodice elegantly adorned with lace and various precious stones. Six members sat to her right and six to her left. The woman in the center remained silent as the members of the Higher Spirits responded to the Vicar's guilty reply.

A Chinese woman raised her voice and demanded that the two gentlemen explain why they had broken a law, forbidding them to interfere with the attack upon the Degelis.

An aged American male stood and questioned the gentlemen's loyalty to the wishes and demands of the Higher Spirits and their laws. A German woman asked the American to be seated, that these were Vicars and should be treated with respect...not like common criminals.

The Chinese woman made a sound of disgust and then raised her voice and demanded the gentlemen answer their questions.

Vicar Aiden Sinclair and Vicar Thomas O'Connell remained silent. Neither Vicar's responded to the Asian woman's request, nor to the Americans. The female in the middle watched and listened intently.

A fair skinned British woman shushed the Chinese Spirit, asking her to please be patient and have understanding…to let the gentlemen explain themselves.

The scorching heat from the desert, blazed upon the two gentlemen and those seated at the large ornate table, though they felt not the heats intent. Crashes of nearby waves soothed the gentleman.

An Indian woman stood and spoke with a thick accent, she suggested that the two gentlemen be relieved of their duties and stripped of all powers. That these two gentlemen, having known the wishes and laws of the Higher Spirits, neglected their duties and disrespected the members of the council that oversaw that region of North America.

An Ethiopian male stood and rounded on the Indian woman, demanding that her statement be retracted. That it had been unloving and non-compassionate. He reminded her that Vicar Aiden Sinclair had been with family for over forty years. That if she did not understand why he interfered with the attack upon the family…than she should re-examine her soul and purpose of the Higher Spirits.

Vicar Aiden Sinclair closed his eyes and then re-opened them. He knew each member of the Higher Spirits, with the exception of the woman who remained silent at the center of the table.

"Do not tell me that I am neither compassionate nor lacking the understanding of love." The Indian woman retorted. "It is because I respect the wishes of the Creator and Free Will that these gentlemen must be punished."

"Punished for what?" The British woman stood. Her robes billowed in the wind. "So they interfered slightly with the attack upon the family. I see no reason why we should not show them compassion?"

"Here, here! I agree with you. We are a council of Higher Spirits, not a committee of den Mothers!" An older woman with a thick Jamaican accent replied.

"Perhaps you do not understand why the laws are in place? Perhaps you do not understand that the Creator himself made these laws!" The American male looked to the Chinese woman for support.

"I agree! Why are we discussing the blatant disregard of our laws? All in favor of stripping their powers and..." The Chinese woman was forced to silence as the woman in the center of the table rose to her feet.

Everyone took their seats and remained silent. Aiden Sinclair's attention turned to his left, as a large wave crashed against the beaches' shoreline. His eyes softened and then examined a nearby cactus growing happily in the deserts heat. Thomas O'Connell nudged his long time friend to focus upon the woman who remained standing. Aiden turned to his friend, and then examined the lush jungle in the far distance. He smiled and looked into his friends eyes. "A desert, a jungle and a beach...it is beautiful."

Vicar Thomas looked over his shoulder, to the jungle. After several minutes of silence, both gentlemen turned to face the council.

The woman who stood at the center of the table had the most beautiful black skin Aiden have ever seen. Elegant laced adorned her white attire, shimmers of rubies, sapphires and diamonds caught the bright rays of the sun, casting a rainbow of color. A wavy pixie hairstyle, framed beautifully high cheekbones, large black eyes and full lips.

As the gentlemen stood at attention, the woman from the center of the table addressed them. "I am Ashima. I oversee the Higher Spirits of the Earth. I am well informed of the situation in Metropolitan Detroit, Michigan within the United States of America." She spoke every word with care and enunciated with a slightest bit of contempt. "I have listened to several viewpoints of the council and with great disappointment."

Ashima's eyes focused on the Indian female. "Chandni, what is the purpose of the Higher Spirits?" Chandni began to speak when Ashima raised a hand to silence her. "You have not an intelligent answer. So do not speak." She turned to the Ethiopian gentlemen. "Bohlale, I am pleased with you." She looked again to Chandni. "You will apologize."

"I apologize, Your Grace. I thought..." Chandni began.

"...you thought wrong. It is not to me you should speak."

Chandni apologized to Bohlale. Ashima turned to face the Chinese woman. "Lan Lee, you will never again raise your voice when seated in the company of the Higher Spirits. Learn to control your flaws." She addressed the American male. "Samuel, you do not seem to grasp the wishes of the creator and perhaps next time you should use wisdom before speaking." The American lowered his head.

Ashima nodded to the British, German and the Jamaican women and curled her lips upward in smile. "I am please with the three of you." Her smile vanished as she looked upon those who had not spoken. "Those of you who felt the need not to voice your thoughts…perhaps you do not know your own convictions. I will speak to each of you in due course."

A Japanese male apologized to Ashima. She gave a slight nod and spoke softly. "Hisoka, I understand your reason." He lowered his eyes. The Russian, Brazilian, Canadian & Spaniard also lowered their eyes and spoke words of forgiveness.

Lan Lee raised her voice and began to speak, after a glance from Ashima, she became silent. Step by step, Ashima rounded the table, hands clasped to her front, resting upon the white dress of silk. After several moments of eye contact with Lan Lee she spoke. "Your services as a Higher Spirit are no longer required." With a wave a hand, Lan Lee vanished.

Ashima turned to the Vicars…the ambassadors between those who reside within the Earths realms and those that interfere with mortals. The two men knelt into the sand.

"You have been brought before the Higher Spirits to be punished…to be berated…judged and belittled as Vicar's. I, however, do not see the purpose. I am aware of Azzurra and her family. I am aware that you, Vicar Aiden Sinclair, have been assigned to the family for over forty years. Bohlale knew what this meant and understood your compassion. It is with these thoughts and knowledge that Alyse, Robaire and Brigitte spoke in your defense. I am also aware of Lamia's involvement with the family and of her relationship with the being known to her as The Man."

Ashima glided around the table and hovered and inch above the sand. Her eyes focused upon the gentleman that knelt before her. "The attack upon the family tonight is known throughout the Higher Spirits of the Earth. I, on the behalf of all Higher Spirits…do sincerely offer my deepest apologies. It appears that some of the Higher Spirits behaved like Pharisees, whose' arrogance, ignorance and self indulgence has betrayed the very essence of what it is to be a Vicar or a Higher Spirit." She looked to Thomas and then Aiden and then back to Thomas. "I understand that you were sent to inform Vicar Aiden Sinclair that he was not to interfere with the attack upon the family. Am I correct?"

"That is correct." Thomas replied.

"And you conveyed the message?"

"Yes." His light grey eyes met hers.

She then spoke to Vicar Aiden Sinclair. "Did you understand what Vicar Thomas O'Connell's words meant?"

Aiden paused for the slightest moment and spoke. "I did."

"And yet you interfered with the attack." Ashima lowered her hand beneath his chin and raised his head. "Why?"

Aiden answered. "Because I love them."

Ashima searched his deep brown eyes. "I thought so."

She then turned to Vicar Thomas O'Connell. "And you knew that he had no intention of following these orders and yet you did nothing? Why?"

Thomas focused upon a flower of a nearby cactus and then looked into her eyes. "I have faith in Aiden's judgment — faith that he made the right decision."

Ashima gently guided a piece of red hair from Thomas's forehead. "I know."

She addressed the Higher Spirits. "Faith and love — do you not understand these words?" Several members lowered their heads. "You will look me in the eye when I address you." Immediately, they focused upon her. A few more steps took her closer to the council.

"Vicar Aiden Sinclair redirected the moonlight to assist a family that he loves — a family of Witches from whom we have had interest in for over a hundred years. Vicar Thomas O'Connell placed his trust and compassion within a dear friend, trusting his instinct. Am I pleased with this disobedience? I am not. Do I understand what it is to have emotions…to love…to feel compassion? Yes, I do. It is because of those traits…those human traits…that you should have understood and shown forgiveness. I will speak with those of you who do not understand this concept. Perhaps you have forgotten what it is like to be human? Perhaps you have forgotten why the Higher Spirits are involved with a family of Witches? They are good people…Witches or not. Vicar Aiden Sinclair knows this. He has known it from the beginning. The practice of Witchcraft should not be construed as negative. It is the person that produces a negative effect, not the craft." Ashima looked to the ocean and then to the long mahogany table. "Humanity is at risk. The one who calls himself The Man has waited many years to find a family of Witches with this kind of power. Azzurra failing…is not an option. We shall let those involved have Free Will. However, if it means that we redirect a bit of moonlight…or appear in a dream…or send a feather plume to communicate — so let it be." Deep black eyes focused upon the two gentlemen.

"Continue to have love and faith. That is what I ask of you both. Now go."

* * * *

Anna

The Grandfather's clocks ticking passed with each second as Anna took a moment to comprehend Azzurra's question — *Anna, tell us what happened that night. Who banished you and why?"*

An animated black and white human looked at each family member. Anna's eyes were sunk into her skull. She looked upon her grayscale hand, torn dress and tattered boots. Her eyes met her husband's.

Augusto whispered. "Anna?"

She raised a palm to her husband, vanished, and then reappeared with a crackle of electricity. Basil and Azzurra raised a palm and released a thick mist of white that surrounded her. Anna thanked them and stabilized into Spirit form. Her eyes scanned the room and then rested upon Contessa.

Her voice was uneven and crackling into sparks of words, weak and frail. "It's was a set up. Basil and Katie had nothing to do with Vincent's death. That's just bogus. I know what I saw...I know what I heard." She turned to Nathan and then back to Contessa. "It was a like a week after your mother passed away that Azzurra, Arianna and I, were shooting the breeze, trying to chill out, you know. We wanted to know if Luciana's death was caused by nature or if something had interfered. What a nightmare. Your mother was the last hope to prevent an all out Witches War." Anna's Spirit flared and sparked. She vanished and then reappeared. After a moan she clutched her stomach. The older generation sent a stream of white into her. She stabilized and then spoke again.

"I'm fine…I'm fine. Thank you." After a pause she continued. "Arianna, Azzurra and I had a confab. We knew Luciana had a weak heart, you know. Your mother was a complete basket-case over this Witches War mess. Luciana never liked to fight…she was a sweetheart. I remember Katie said that she thought Luciana freaked-out about the Witches War and that's what gave her the heart attack. Azzurra was so-so about it all, but I leaned toward something funky. I, mean I felt something was kooky. I felt it in the pit of my stomach. So, you know, I wanted to do something. So, I thought to Astral Project." She turned to a young girl she didn't recognize. "You know, that's when your soul leaves your body."

Katherine, Marie's daughter, nodded several times.

"You know" Anna continued. "I wanted to hear the scoop on Carlo and Debra. I knew that that nasty Dorthea was involved. Then there's Stella and Sabino, two of the most evil looking things I've ever known. I wanted to get the skinny on what was happening." Basil's and Katie's stream of vapor evaporated. Anna began to fizzle in and out of visual perception. Her voice became static and could no longer be understood. Anna collapsed. Augusto held on to her while Gabriella tossed a sachet at her. Sprinkles of reds, oranges and lavender encompassed her, swirling in and around her body.

After several seconds, a crackle of static filled the room and she continued to recall the event. "Azzurra and Katie shot me down, saying it…it's not cool to Astroproject. I could get severed from my body…it was too dangerous." Anna paused, flickered and disappeared. After a few seconds, she reappeared.

Father Bernardo shook his head and spoke with a low tone. "It is sinful to have your soul to leave your body!" He seated himself at the table. Anna held her stomach, moaned, disappeared and then reappeared with an array of static. The sparkles of energy from Gabriella's sachet zoomed faster and faster, in and out of her body.

Katherine, Marie's daughter whispered to her Aunt Gabriella. "I'm having trouble following her. She talks weird."

"Your Aunt Anna knew all the slang of the 60's and 70'. She was the cool one." She winked to her niece and then turned to Father Bernardo. "What good is saying something like that, Father? It's over and done with. No need to throw out your guilt trips"

"Please, not now Gabriella let's just hear what she has to say." Nicolai said.

Azzurra and Katie's eyes' widened at Gabriella's response.

Father Bernardo made the sign of the cross.

Anna looked to Azzurra. "How long...have I...gone?"

Azzurra took a few steps forward. "Now, Anna things are different, don't panic. It's been about 40 years."

Ann clasped a hand over her mouth and shook her head. Several minutes later she spoke. "OK, 40 years. Things look so different, the Television, the appliances, the cars...it's OK...OK...I'm cool...I'm cool with that." Augusto asked her to sit and take a few minutes.

"Leave me be, Augusto. I'm fine." Anna spoke to Katie. "Katie begged me not to Astral Project, that it was too dangerous." Oranges and lavenders zoomed and sparkled in and out of her body. Anna gained a bit of strength. "Azzurra suggested that I come clean with Augusto first — ask him what he thought." Anna looked to Augusto.

"Anna? Why? Why didn't you speak with me before you...?"

"...please Augusto. Chill out, it's all copasetic now, no need to go in rewind." She paused then continued. "I'm back, forty years later, but I am back." She shook her head several times and spoke. "I'm sorry, Augusto...I'm sorry, I should have, I didn't and I died. Do we want to hash up all the things you've done without asking my permission?"

Augusto spoke. "You're right, go on honey. I'm sorry."

Nicolai whispered in Gabriella's ear. "It's so weird to see him kind and gentle."

Gabriella stifled a chuckle and told him to hush and gave him a wink.

"Thank you, Augusto. Ok so, I shot down Azzurra's idea of telling Augusto." Her voice picked up in volume. "I am my own woman and can make decisions without asking permission from my husband." She eyed him again. "I didn't want to hear Katie's warnings about losing contact with my body. I wanted to know if they killed my mother-in-law. I loved Luciana. I told Katie and Azzurra that I would sleep on it. However, I couldn't sleep. Luciana was always so nice to me and loved me like her own daughter, so I decided to Astroproject. I remember seeing my body lying on the bed and then I floated through the ceiling. I went to Debra and Carlo's first, you know." Anna paused as she flickered once more and then vanished. Augusto looked to Azzurra and then to Katie. His eyes were searching for something in their faces.

Contessa spoke while waiting for Anna to reappear. "Augusto blamed the both of you. He thought you encouraged Anna to Astral Project that night. He believed her death to be your faults."

"Dam it, Contessa!" Augusto retorted as Anna reappeared.

Azzurra took in a breath, while Katie spoke. "Augusto! You thought that Azzurra and I would put Anna in danger?" Her hands flew to her hips. "You know what Augusto…you're nothing but a mean…"

"…enough!" Father Bernardo yelled. He stood.

The room became silent, save for the ticking sound of the grandfather clock and the whizzing of energy around Anna's body. Marie stepped forward "Let's not fight! We've all been through a lot this evening. Uncle Augusto…you've been bitter with my mother long enough, now can we please put aside our feelings and listen."

Augusto apologized to Contessa and nodded to Marie. Katie whispered a sorry to her brother, although it sounded as though a swear word was muffled. Blackie barked and then placed his tail between his legs and darted near Basil.

"Shadows, they were everywhere!" Marta grabbed Tracy's wine and took another gulp. Nicco rolled his eyes. Tracy stood, grabbed the bottle and refilled her own glass. "Sorry, she's still loopy. Go on, Aunt Anna, tell your story." Nicco said.

"Marta honey, be quiet. There are no Shadow People. The house is protected, they cannot get in, so please let Anna finish." Azzurra patted Father Bernardo's arm and asked him to sit. "We can never stay on track and let anyone finish speaking! Now I won't have this. Katie, calm down and stop swearing under your breath." She turned to face her brother. "Augusto honey we are sorry you felt that Katie and I caused Anna's death. Believe it or not, we did try and talk her out of the idea. But she is her own woman, as you very well know. Now, you have harbored resentment for years toward Katie and me. Am I right?"

Augusto looked down to Blackie.

"Harbored resentment for over forty years…and for what?" She took a few steps closer to her brother. "Look at me!"Augusto raised his head and looked to his sister. Blackie squirmed between Basil's feet. "Isn't that a shame Augusto? No brains to come and ask Katie and me ourselves? Instead, you assumed something that you did not know. Now didn't you?" She pointed a finger at her brother. "Years wasted on bitterness and misunderstanding. Years of anger and resentment that should have never existed." Her voice rose after a slight intake of breath. "Maybe next time you could come and talk to us like an adult!" Azzurra slammed a hand on the table.

Father Bernardo threw his hands in the air and sat. Basil rolled his eyes as Blackie wined and tried to get even closer to Basil.

"Azzurra don't get upset, sweetheart." Gabriella said.

"Can we please hear Anna's story. Maybe you should give your mother another elixir" Steven looked to his wife, Marie.

"Shush honey!" Marie waved a hand.

Steven raised his voice. "Do not tell me to shush! I have had it with the…"

"…will you two stop fighting? Let's listen to what Aunt Anna has to say!" Katherine abruptly turned to her Aunt Anna, dark, wavy hair falling over a shoulder. "I'm Katherine. Azzurra is my grandmother and my mother, is Marie. This is my father, Steve. I'm still tired and would really like to hear your story sometime today."

Marie poured her daughter another glass of Renew elixir. "Drink honey. She's right. Now if one more person interrupts Anna, I'm going to reach in my purse and toss the first sachet I grab!"

"Ma she can't do that." Nicco said.

"Nicco, I'm gonna pull my Wand out if everyone doesn't shut up. Go on Anna sweetheart." Azzurra said.

"Everyone chill. Marie, honey, I'm fine. I can use the slight breaks. Gabby, your sachet is really doing a job on me, thanks." Anna turned to Katherine. "It's groovy to meet you." She faced Azzurra. "OK, so I Astral Projected and went to Debra and Carlo's first, you know. Nothing was freaky so I went to Stella's & Sabino's. Sabino was home and chatting up the breeze with a woman in white. She was a Spirit, very pretty. I thought I recognized her as one of Contessa's Spirits. I think her name was Latima?"

"Lamia, the bitches' name is Lamia." Katie offered.

"Lamia, I knew it was something like that. Well, anyway, I heard Lamia speaking with Sabino, and then Stella entered the room and asked if Contessa believe Lamia's story? I was in the fog as to what Stella meant. Lamia turned and explained to Stella that she had cast a spell for Contessa. The Spell revealed that Basil killed Vincent. The spell showed him in Vincent's bedroom and how he killed him. She also said she told Contessa it was upon Katie's orders that Basil kill her son. That it was a lesson to be learned in practicing the Magick of controlling Spirits. I snuck a bit closer.

Lamia laughed and said that Contessa had no idea that his death was caused by a deformed heart valve and Vincent's death could not have come at a more opportune moment. She said that the Witches War must separate the family. Stella laughed. Damn that woman looks evil, gives me the willies. Stella then said something about your father, Pasquale." Anna looked to Azzurra and then back to Contessa. "She said that Pasquale was a fool to insist that the family take the vow never to use Magick again. Then a man stood from a high-backed leather chair. I didn't know that crazy cat was there. He was an older dude, long grey hair...bright amber eyes, very handsome; but at the same time there was something way too creepy about him. Sabino asked the grey haired guy if he thought they were ready. Again, I was in the fog as to what "ready" meant. Anyway, the man spoke calmly and said: *That the time was not right. That they should be patient...let the power build.* I don't know what he meant by let the power build. That's when it happened. The grey haired guy turned and looked in my direction. He told the others that I was there. He waved a hand and I became visible. Stella said, kill her. I tried to move, but couldn't. I was frozen or something. Lamia cast a spell and then there was blackness...I was Banished."

* * * *

Katie's Daughters

*A*fter several hours, Carlotta finished explaining to Olivia the different enchantments, how she made them and the years that it took learning Magick. When she found out about being a Witch and how she learned the most after their father's death. She told of Captain Morgan from the grandfather clock and of the two doves from the coffee table and of Clancy the nutcracker. Olivia sipped on a renew elixir.

Clancy's voice interrupted. "Step away lady! State yourself and what business do you have here?"

"How dare you swing that sword at me, you little bastard…I'm their mother!"

"Well now, you don't have to get nasty there lady. I'm following orders, I am." Clancy replied.

Carlotta and Olivia sprung from the table and rushed toward the hallway. The tiny nutcracker had grown to a man's height and sheathed his sword. A woman in a blue dress stood just beyond him. Clancy turned to face his castor. "You're foul-mouthed mother is requesting an audience with thee."

Katie turned to Clancy and placed her hands, for the thousandth time, upon her hips. "How dare you! Carlotta, call him off please!" She then pointed to Clancy. "Foul-mouthed...I'll give you foul-mouthed!"

Olivia leaned against the wall, eyes wide.

"Clancy, be nice and let my mother through." Clancy grimaced, shrunk down in size and marched toward the front window.

Carlotta's eyes filled with tears. "Mom?" She ran toward the woman in blue. Katie turned solid and hugged her daughter. Tears flowed down their cheeks.

"Now don't get used to this. I am only here for a short while...until this mess is over." A tiny bark entered the room. Carlotta spotted Blackie and called his name in surprise. Blackie wagged his tail, barked and then greeted his long time friend.

"You did a good job with your enchantments. I'm proud sweetheart. Maybe you should make an adjustment to that nutcracker's attitude, however, very nice honey." Katie crossed her arms. "So you knew you were a Witch?"

"Ma, I've known since I was a little girl. I found all of Dad's books when he died too. That's when I learned the most."

"Your father should have never left those books around! Speaking of that bastard, I've been fighting demons and going through hell and back and he is nowhere to be found." Katie said.

"Mom?" Olivia stepped forward.

"Is she going to scream?" Katie asked.

Carlotta looked toward Clancy. "The Vicar is gone. So yes, she may scream, my lady." He folded his arms and sank to the floor.

"Olivia...it's really Mom. Don't be afraid." Carlotta said.

After several tears and hugs the three women settled around the kitchen table. Olivia sat oddly quiet. Katie informed her daughters of their Aunty Arianna's death and that the family expected them at Aunty Azzurra's soon. Carlotta told her mother about the plume appearing and how it scrolled the message of another Witches War.

Carlotta began to tell her mother the story that she hid from Olivia for almost forty years. Silence filled the room after the story had been told. Two birds fluttered near the coffee table...looking back and forth between Olivia and the woman in blue. Clancy sat upon the floor, between the kitchen and the front room. Several men peeked in from the hallway, over Clancy's head and a horse made a sound near the basement steps.

"Shouldn't you be protecting the house?" Carlotta questioned her enchantments.

The birds chirped and then flew through the wall. The men returned to their post and Clancy stood and then sat back down, folding his arms in a huff.

Katie rose from the chair and took a few steps toward the living room. Blackie let out a small cry and laid flat to the floor.

Olivia and Carlotta watched as their mother turned to face them several moments later.

"I'm sorry." Katie said. "I'm sorry you had to keep that secret for all these years. But I think it was best. I am not sure how I would have reacted if I had known back then. I'm different now. Death changed me. I see things in a new light. It is neither of your faults that Angelo died. It is not your fault Olivia for taking the necklace off him and it is not your fault, Carlotta, for befriending someone you thought to be an Angel. If anyone is to blame, it is the Degeli family. It is my grandparents who brought Magick over from Italy. It is my parent's fault, who taught us about being Witches. They taught us to be good Witches because we are good people. Witches attract things… entities that never breathed upon this planet. Foul creatures are drawn to our power. Witches are misunderstood. If we would have never learned Magick…evil would never have had a place in our homes. They would not have been attracted to our power. Could it have been avoided? Probably not, it is our destiny. It is who we are. I tried to shield you girls from the truth. We thought Spirits may be trying to start a war between the families. Spirits do that, you see. They have been known to kill someone in a Witches family, just to begin a feud. However, something is different about our family. Should I have told you girls when you were little? If I did maybe Angelo would still be alive? If I didn't, would you have been safe from evil? I guess it doesn't matter…evil came anyway." She turned to her eldest daughter. "Carlotta, you did what you thought was right by keeping it from Olivia. It also explains why the attacks were focused on her. It was payback for me asking Dad to ban Spirits and to help divide the family. Lamia did not want to harm you. I'm not sure how your Aunty Azzurra knew this, but she did." She took a few steps closer to her daughters. "I am sorry girls. I am sorry that you were born into a family of Witches of such power that it has attracted evil. I am sorry that certain members of the family are beguiled by power and wealth. I am, however, not sorry that we are good Witches. We are good people and we shall prevail." She took a hand of each of her daughters into her own. "Now, your enchantments will guard the house. Carlotta, drive your sister to your Aunty Azzurra's and I will meet you there. We need to keep the family together."

* * * *

Forgive & Forget

"That dirty little bitch killed my Angelo!" Katie appeared in Azzurra's kitchen moments after leaving Carlotta and Olivia. She let Blackie down who scurried over to his Aunty Azzurra and leapt on her lap.

"What are you talking about Katie? Are the girls OK?" Azzurra asked.

"Yes, the girls are fine! Olivia was with Carlotta, they're on their way." She placed her hands to her mouth and then released them to speak. "They know everything. Carlotta apparently knew she was a Witch and had powerful enchantments protecting the house. They all had full personalities, very detailed. I was very impressed." After a pause, she continued. "Carlotta told me how Angelo died. She knew all these years and kept it from Olivia to protect her. She kept it from me and never told a soul." Shaking her head, she placed a palm over her mouth. After several seconds she continued through tears. "It was Lamia! That bitch, killed my Angelo." Katie turned to Basil and hugged him.

Contessa sank into the kitchen chair next to Tracy and put her face into the palm of her hands. Nathan placed a hand upon her shoulder.

379

Katie pushed Basil away and rounded on Contessa. "Did I not tell you that we should not have Spirits in the family? Did I not make everyone uphold Dad's vow not to introduce any new Spirits to the family? Your Spirit killed my son and made it look as though Basil and I killed Vincent!" She took a few steps toward her sister. "Its' because of you, because you didn't listen to Dad or I…that my son is dead!" Katie slammed a fist upon the table.

Tracy grabbed her wine glass, Nicco jumped, while Contessa burst into tears.

Katie continued. "I will tell you another thing. I am told that I should forgive and forget — to be kind and understanding. But you know what Contessa? That's Bullshit!" She raised both arms toward her sister. Basil shouted. Nathan shielded his wife. Marie and Katherine screamed.

Azzurra's voice forced silence. "Stop it! Katie you will not harm her! Now, sit!" Azzurra turned to Basil. "Basil?"

"I understand where she is coming from, Mum" Basil replied

Azzurra threw her arms in the air.

"Katie, you may harm your sister. You may kill Nathan if you wish. If it makes you feel any better." Everyone turned to stare at Father Bernardo, including Katie. "However, you will fall in God's grace. You will become one of them."

"And that won't help anyone." All eyes turned to the living room. The Vicar Sinclair stood at attention, white suit immaculate wearing his gem-stone tie. "Katie, lower your arms and find peace within you."

Katie began to cry and shielded her eyes. "Vicar…there is no peace."

The Vicar looked up and to the right and then spoke. "There is peace. Faith will bring you peace. Peace will bring you love."

"Katie you need to find God…" Father Bernardo began.

"…and you need to shut up." Gabriella turned to him. "Let the Vicar handle this! Sometimes you just don't know when to keep quiet, Father."

Nicolai put an arm around her shoulder and squeeze. The Vicar looked toward the priest.

Father Bernardo continued. "Gabriella, if you had faith in God, we wouldn't be in this mess. If you had given up Magick, stuck to the vow that your father wanted…"

"…Father please." Azzurra said.

"…we'd all be dead!" Augusto shouted at the priest

Father Bernardo stood. "If you had the faith…"

"…Shut up! Shut Up!" Gabriella pushed her husband away and stood in front of the priest. "Father I love you, but if you cannot understand Katie's hurt and frustration. If you can't understand what this family is going through without spouting off about God every two minutes, well then maybe you should keep your damn mouth shut!"

"Honey, please!" Nicolai tried.

Azzurra shook her head and began to speak when Father Bernardo shouted. "When God is your life…"

"…Shut up and sit down or so help me…I will knock you down!" Gabriella screamed.

Anna gasped. Augusto grunted. Tracy gulped more wine, while Nicco stood. Marta grabbed the bottle and took a swig, as Marie tried to wrestle the bottle away from her. Katherine stepped back as Steven told Marie to let Marta drink for the love of God. She shushed him as he began to yell at her about the shushing.

The Vicar's voice forced silence. "This is what you want? You wish to fight with each other?" He raised his hands toward the room and released a large plume of white that seeped into everyone…even Blackie.

The Vicar faced Anna and a stream of white emanated from one of the diamonds of his tie. It struck Anna, encompassed her body. A think black plume of energy whizzed out of her body and into his gemstone.

Anna's bubble drifted back to the dispenser as she regained full color. The short mini dress mended and appeared in full lime green. Her large lime green headband appeared in thick black short hair, styled with two little curls toward the face. High black leather boots appeared shinny and new as two large hooped lime green earrings dangled from her ear lobes.

Anna thanked him as did Augusto. The Vicar nodded once and then spoke. "Now be calm." He focused on the priest. "Father, I suggest that if you don't think before you speak than perhaps you should not speak. Learn compassion for those who have not your faith and learn to be quiet when you should. You only alienate people away from the creator."

Father Bernardo looked to the floor and met Blackie's eyes. Not a single sound could be heard, save for the tick-tocks of the clock. The priest looked up to Gabriella. "He is right. I am sorry Gabby."

Gabriella wiped away a few tears and accepted his apology.

"Oh my stars…did someone else die?" Stephan appeared with Deveroy, Violetta, Ritsuko, Michale, and Pip. He turned solid and opened his arms to Azzurra.

"No, we're OK." Azzurra hugged Stephan.

Contessa ran toward Deveroy and hugged him tightly, telling him how glad she was to know he was all right.

The Vicar spoke and silenced the room. "I have found two souls that are eager to speak with you."

To everyone's surprise two men appeared in the living room…Dante and Franco.

* * * *

Franco & Dante

Dante placed his hands upon Katie's cheeks and looked into her face — searching her eyes. "Katie! Are you alright?"

Katie shrugged away from him and turned her back.

Dante lowered his gaze to floor for a couple of seconds. "Katie, you have every right to be mad. From what I heard, you've been through hell and back." He looked up. "You fought dozens of Hags, lost your sister...and where was I? I was out gallivanting with Franco!" Dante removed his pub cap, revealing dark waves of thick hair. "Can you forgive me sweetheart?"

Katie turned and looked to her husband. "It's been very difficult...and I needed you, Dante."

"I know you did. I'm sorry Katie." Dante took her hands. "I'm here and I promise I'll always be here for you."

Katie's hesitated, looked into his eyes, squinted and then relaxed." I'm told I'm to forgive and forget. Thank you for saying that...even though I know it will happen again." She leaned into him and kissed his cheek. "I've been around a Vicar a lot lately."

They embraced, as Blackie barked and did circles.

Olivia and Carlotta arrived. Carlotta screamed and hugged her father. Dante squeezed his daughter tightly as Katie joined in the hug.

Olivia stood back and took a few moments. Dante carefully approached her and nodded his head. Tears welled in his eyes. Olivia turned to mush and fell into his arms. The four of them huddled in a hug.

After a moment, they separated. Katie placed her hands on her hips and addressed her daughters. "You couldn't bury your father in a nice suit, could you? You picked old black corduroys and a black sweater with loafers? Out of all the nice suits? You even put that damn black pub cap on him?"

Azzurra broke from Franco's hug and spoke to her nieces. "Don't you let her do that to you? She told me, just the other day that she wanted to be buried in a housecoat! Shame on you Katie, that's what Dante liked."

Katie looked to Azzurra and narrowed her eyes. "Then why am in this blue dress?"

Azzurra quickly turned to Franco. "Oh Franco, my Franco."

Katie rolled her eyes and fluffed her dress. She leaned to Contessa and Gabriella. "A housecoat would have been nice. But it is beautiful."

Contessa placed her cup on the saucer. "For heaven's sakes Katie, Stephan changes his outfits a thousand times a day. Wear a housecoat if that's what you want?"

"No." Katie looked down at her dress. She recalled seeing Azzurra giving the beautiful Satin dress to the mortician along with a pearl necklace with matching earrings and satin slippers. "Until she passes…I will always wear this dress." She looked to Azzurra and smiled and whispered. "I love my dress."

After lots of hugs, kisses and tears from Nicco, Marie and Marta, Azzurra and Franco sat upon the living room sofa. She brushed a hand through his thick grey hair. "I don't even have the words to tell you how I feel. I need you Franco."

Franco took her hand. "It is I who always needed you." He kissed his wife.

"I miss you Franco. I'm lost and scared." Azzurra placed a hand upon his.

"You, my dear, are neither. It is the change that you must adjust to. That's all. You will be fine...trust your instincts."

Franco brought Azzurra to her feet and together they entered the kitchen. Azzurra hurried to the counter to brew more coffee, stopped, and swished a hand. Everyone had steaming cups of coffee at their setting.

Franco met Tracy's eyes and winked. "Tracy? Had a rough night eh? Everything OK?"

Tracy smiled and toasted her elixir. "Never better, Mr. Stephanie." She looked to Nicco, then back to Franco.

Augusto shouted. "What the hell finally made the two you two come back? We've been going through hell here!"

Franco faced the room. "I heard Nicco. I heard him calling for me, asking for help. I told Dante that something horrible was wrong, and we rushed back. Once we re-entered the Earth's realm, a beacon of light collided with us and told us everything."

The family began to chatter in different groups that interacted with other groups.

The Vicar stood back and watched the family interact. After a few moments, he vanished.

Tracy and Marta sat together at the table and sipped on the blood cleansing elixir. Marta pulled Marie away from Katherine and leaned into her sister and Tracy. "Tom called me. Oh God Tracy, you don't know what the hell I'm talking about. You know, Mr. Tom Buchman, my boss. He called me and he's coming over tonight, bringing me dinner. I'm so excited but kind of feel weird being excited after all we've been through." She swished a hand. "Oh listen to me. I sound like dumb school girl. But I am excited."

The mood of the room plummeted into tears when Mateo and Scott came up from the basement.

* * * *

You Have to Laugh a Little

$\mathcal{S}$tephan interrupted. "Oh my stars, I have had enough of this depressing crying. Arianna, honey, no offense, but I think we could use a bit of entertainment." Stephan raised an arm and made a dramatic sweeping gesture. Azzurra's living room furniture vanished and several instruments, a small stage with theatre lighting appeared. "Take your places everyone!"

Pip sat behind the drums, tapped the base drum with his right foot and did several shank tips on the hi-hat. Ritsuko took her seat upon a bench, flipped her dark hair over her shoulders and played a few notes from the baby grand piano. Michale tuned the acoustic guitar while Violetta found her pitch on the saxophone and adjusted the reed to the top of the mouth piece. Deveroy connected the strap to the bass around his shoulders and plucked a few cords.

Stephan blew the trumpet to get everyone's attention, screamed at the burst of sound, and laughed. He then explained to his camel that he should sit still and watch Daddy perform.

The family produced more chairs and faced the band. Basil produced a Microphone, stepped onto the stage and dedicated the show to Arianna Valente. The orb expanded and glowed.

Basil introduced the band members. Each acknowledged him by inclining their head or a slight bow. He gave hushed instructions to the band and faced his audience. After a smirk Basil pushed back his trench coat, looked down at himself and waved a hand. A black tuxedo replaced his attire. He flipped his hair away from his forehead, green eyes sparkling. The first notes were hit and Basil began to sing, *Luck Be a Lady Tonight, from Guys & Dolls*.

Everyone applauded at his conclusion. Stephan batted his eyes and sat upon the bench next to Ritsuko, dabbing his eyes dramatically with a large polka dotted handkerchief. Basil introduced his next song *as Being Alive* from the play *Company*. Azzurra interrupted and said that singing "Being Alive" would be in bad taste, making eyes toward the orb. Basil apologized, but Arianna insisted that he should sing it anyway. So he did.

Mateo watched the orb and smiled as it bounced up and down. He nudged his son Scott and nodded toward his mother. Scott's deep blue eyes sparkled just a bit, and for a slight second, his devilish grin slid into a smile. "She's happy, Dad."

Stephan requested the microphone from Basil, made a hand gesture and changed his Egyptian outfit to a sequenced plum tux with tails. With a gentle voice, he sang *Moon River by Henry Mancini*. The lights went up and everyone applauded as he took his dramatic bow. The camel grunted loudly.

Nicolai coaxed Marie's husband, Steven and Mateo to join him as he took the stage. Mateo refused. However, Arianna's orb dimmed. Basil then said, "She'd like you to sing for her." He squeezed Scott into a hug and then headed to the stage. Basil released a cool blue mist that spiraled around him. Mateo smiled and felt happy to be singing for his wife. Nicolai, Steven and Mateo sang, in harmony, *"Going out of my Head, by Teddy Randazzo & Bobby Weinstein.* Everyone applauded, commenting on the harmony.

Father Bernardo took center stage. He sang a heartfelt song from 1967 — *What a Wonderful World, by George David Weiss*. More applause and dabbing of the eyes from the women as he sung the last words:

"Yes, I think to myself….what a wonderful world."

Carlotta took Olivia's hand and brought her sister to the stage. Together they sang a duet of *Irving Berlin's, Sisters*. Once again, everyone applauded.

Olivia handed her microphone to Augusto and grimaced to Carlotta. He took to the stage and sung a surprisingly powerful version of *To Dream the Impossible Dream by Mitch Leigh*. Halfway through, his voice began to fail. However, the family helped him finish the song. Anna hugged and kissed her husband as he left the stage to a thunderous applause.

Franco and Dante serenaded Katie and Azzurra with *Let Me Call You Sweetheart, by Leo Friedman*. Both women hugged their husbands.

"Slow dance, one more time!" Nicco yelled.

Everyone in the room, including, Ritsuko, Michale, Pip and Deveroy, *sung Let Me Call You Sweetheart*. Katie & Dante, Azzurra & Franco — slowed danced.

Katie kissed Dante and then took Gabriella by the hand and motioned to Anna to take the stage. Azzurra, Franco and Dante took their seats.

Katie made a large swish with her hand. Anna, Gabriella and she appeared in 1940's army attire. They wore khaki button down shirts with matching ties, under a dark olive drab jacket, skirt and garrison cap. They huddled for a few minutes and then Katie whispered to Basil. He in turn, informed the band of the song. Katie produced three standing microphones. The lights dimmed, as three spotlights appeared on each of the ladies and the first cords were struck.

Anna, Katie and Gabriella sung a fast paced tune of *Don Raye & Hugie Prince's, Boogie Woogie Bugle Boy* to a round of applause and excited barking from Blackie. The camel grunted. After taking several bows and blowing kisses to the audience, Katie changed their outfits to 1950's blouses, sweaters and poodle skirts of reds, violet's and blue's. Together they sung an upbeat rendition of *Pat Ballard's, Mr. Sandman*. Katie and Gabriella did backup while Anna took the lead.

At the last note everyone cheered. Contessa applauded with her husband Nathan beside her.

Marta took a large swig of elixir and then shouted that she wanted to sing a song. She whispered something in her Aunty Katie's ear. Katie blushed and waved a hand toward her niece. She then took both hands and made a large circular gesture toward her niece and then over the stage. The stage sank into darkness. After a few seconds, a soft spotlight flooded over Marta as mist drifted over the floor. It swirled over the bottom of her sequenced, royal blue gown, with a plunging neckline. Basil hoisted her upon the baby grand piano. She crossed her legs that revealed a slit in her dress up to her thigh and six inch, royal blue, velvet stilettos. Whistles sounded over the room from the men. Azzurra turned red as she laughed with Gabriella and Contessa. Marta flung a mane of straight brunette hair over her shoulder and half closed her blue eyes. She batted her long lashes and licked her hot red lips. To the audience, her raspy voice filled the room as she sung *Fever, by Otis Blackwell.*

"Never know how much I love you,
Never know how much I care,
When you put your arms around me,
I get fever that's hard to bear....you give me Fever!"

She received a standing ovation and a burst of tears and a hug from Stephan.

Scott gave another grin. He had noticed Basil and Katie laughing with his mother.

Marie belted a powerful rendition of *"Don't Rain on my Parade", by Jule Styne* with hoots and whistles from the crowd. Half way through the song, she waved Katherine to the stage, and together they belted the song with such power, that the audience rose and screamed with delight.

Mateo asked the orb what she wanted to hear next. Basil and Katie smiled to Azzurra. Azzurra shook her red face and hugged Franco. "I can't...I'm too old."

A round of boo's filled the room. Azzurra shushed them but had no choice, as Franco took her by the hand and led her to the stage. "Beee, what does she want me to sing?"

Basil smiled. "Well mum...it is your sister's request that you sing, *The Glory of Love, by William Joseph Hill.*" Everyone applauded. The band took their cues and the beat began. A soft, blue spotlight cast upon her.

"You've got to give a little, take a little,
And let your poor heart break a little.
That's the story of, that's the glory of love.

You've got to laugh a little, cry a little,
Until the clouds roll by a little.
That's the story of, that's the glory of love.

As long as there's the two of us,
We've got the world and all it' charms.
And when the world is through with us,
We've got each other's arms.

You've got to win a little, lose a little,
Yes, and always have the blues a little."

Azzurra asked everyone to join and repeat the last verse. The Degelis, the Spirits and Tracy all sang.

> *"You've got to win a little, lose a little,*
> *Yes, and always have the blues a little.*
> *That's the story of, that's the glory of love.*
> *That's the story of, that's the glory of love."*

* * * *

The Man

Cursing and screams of frustration accompanied the sound of objects smashing against the plastered walls. Medeia hovered just above the floor, crossed legged and arms rested upon her thighs, palms up…eyes closed. Her long dark hair floated without gravity. An object flew through her and smashed into the grandfather clock, sounds of glass breaking joined the cacophony. Dormava held her stomach and flickered in and out of focus near Medeia. Her dark, short hair was singed at the ends. Another vase flew bye, followed by a picture frame.

Damiano's Spirit hovered near the ceiling, concentrating on not floating through the chandelier. His eyes were closed. Marcus sat with his legs crossed, solid form and arms resting upon an enormous high-backed purple velvet chair from the 1920's, with large diamond divots. He casually watched as objects flew across the room and obliterated into the walls.

Lamia took an elegant laced pillow and began the attempt at ripping it to shreds…she failed, threw the pillow and grabbed her stomach. After collapsing to the floor, in a rumpled mess, she flickered in and out of being transparent. Several moments later, she remained in solid form. She smeared the matted hair away from her face and then found a cool spot to rest her skin upon the cold stone floor. Her dress was soiled, torn and blood stained. "Will I ever heal? Am I doomed to be a mess of a soul?" Her eyes darted up to Damiano, who did not move or flutter, then to Marcus, who sat comfortably in the cozy chair.

"You will recover, have patients." Marcus said. "That was a very powerful sachet." His voice had no emotion, sympathy or kindness, nor did it contain contempt.

"A stupid sachet…a sachet! How could a sachet be that powerful? Why did everything go so horribly wrong? Have I not done all that he asked? Have I not followed his instructions faithfully? Placed all of my trust within his words?"

"For the same reason why he wants the family's powers to be inherited to Stella's side of the family…power." Marcus cast a glance up toward Damiano, and then focused his attention back upon the torn and shredded woman. Bruises, lesions and blood shown through the rips and tears in the once beautiful dress.

Lamia sat up, violently brushing her tangled, bloodied hair away. "How does that answer my question, you fool?' She wretched in pain upon the floor and then began to crawl toward Marcus. "Oh Marcus…hold me."

Marcus tilted his head toward the woman. "I did answer your question… the power Azzurra and her siblings have is unparalleled to any Witch or Warlock in the United States of America. That sachet must have been made by Gabriella. She must be double Sachet's and Elixirs. From what the Dover Demon tells me, he has never seen a Witch produce a more powerful sachet. He would have killed Nicolai if it had not been for her. That is why the attack of the wolves failed as well."

Lamia dropped to the floor, eyes gazing toward the man who sat so comfortably upon the plush velvet cushion of such an elegant chair. "What about Marie? That little Miss Suzie Homemaker can't be that strong? She fought the White Demon! She is only Sachet's and Elixirs! How Marcus! How could she have survived?" Once again her face touched the floor; a sigh of relief escaped her cracked lips.

"You do not understand Sachet's and Elixirs, nor do understand the power that has been bequeathed to Azzurra's children. Just because it is the most common of the powers does not mean it is a simple, weak power. For having double strength in any of the powers and being a successful maker of them…gives them extraordinary possibilities. Marie would have been killed if not for her powerful healing sachet and help from a French female." He moved his foot slightly to the left to avoid her reach.

"Help…why does everyone receive help? Does no one fight their own battles anymore?" She grunted. "Marcus, comfort me!" She sat up quickly, grabbed the remains of the glass clock from the floor and threw at him. "Comfort me!"

He waved a hand to redirect the clock. "I cannot touch you. I do not know the strength of the sachet, nor do I know its effects. The others are in grave condition from Azzurra's spell."

Lamia looked upon the blood streaming over her thumb, a cut from the clock. A moan escaped her lips as she collapsed to the floor. "I don't care about the others! It's me I'm concerned about! Oh Marcus…why did that crabby old Augusto survive? Surely we should have killed him?"

"You simply under estimated his power. He is the eldest. Because of his age, his power has grown and he is of solid mind. He is also the descendant of the Degeli line which produced Azzurra. Vetala were not strong enough. Someone also came to his aid as well, a young man with dark hair. They said a powerful enchanted panther thwarted their efforts as well. He succeeded in releasing Anna from your Banishment."

"Damn it! That meddlesome woman is back! The Man will be furious with me! I failed." Her eyes darted to Marcus. "You made me fail!"

"You commanded us, not I. However, he may not be angry with you at all." Marcus switched legs and adjusted his comfort.

"Why do you say that? Of course he'll be angry, they all survived except for Arianna. Even that damn priest survived! The Winged Demons said they could not touch him. He was protected by his stupid prayers." Lamia pounded upon the stone floor and then whimpered in pain, holding her right hand.

"Do not be upset until The Man is upset. You would have succeeded with Nicco had his mother not rescued him. Marta would be dead if not for Basil and…well if not for Basil. The Shadow People said once Basil allowed her to get to the ring and her Wand…it was impossible. They were being destroyed with ease. It seems several family members had assistance from Spirits. I think Basil recruited them." Marcus looked to Medeia then over to Dormava.

"I am so upset…so terribly upset. I have only done what was right…what was good for him and now he leaves me to suffer like a dog." Lamia closed her eyes and gently rubbed a cheek against the cool floor. "We didn't even destroy Katie's dog, did we?" She sobbed.

"I would stay away from the Hags for a while — they are not happy. Katie destroyed dozens of them. Mateo and Scott were mortally wounded but they were healed in time. And the Vicar assisted each family member in providing moonlight at just the right moment."

"The Vicar!" Lamia bolted upright. "How, how could a Vicar interfere?" She collapsed back to the floor. "It is not fair!"

A deep voice penetrated the room. "Neither life nor death is fair, Lamia."

Marcus rose to his feet; Damiano opened his eyes as did Medeia. Dormava looked up and took in the sight of the older man…handsome, long, thick grey hair, deep crow's feet and beautiful amber eyes.

Lamia struggled and pulled herself upright; she looked up to the man in a classic suit. "They were too powerful. Arianna is the only one dead."

"I know what has happened. I expected as much. I am pleased that you have killed Arianna…she was too powerful. Her power now resides with Azzurra or Gabriella. I do not know which yet. I was hoping that it would have gone to Carlo or Dorthea." He gently guided Marcus out of the way and took a seat, sinking into the plush velvet chair.

"You expected as much?" Lamia fell forward. Marcus stepped out of the way and let her fall on her face. She swore.

"Lamia darling…of course I knew that they would be too powerful. I have spoken to the Wolves…the Dover Demon…the White Demon…the Black things you sent to Nicco — very powerful but yet disturbing creatures. I also have spoken to the Vetala, the Shadows and the Hags; the only report that startled me is the one from the Winged Demons. I do not like what they had to say…but then again we can't like everything, now can we? I had a feeling the priest may give us grief." He rolled his eyes, and then smiled upon Marcus.

"What do you we next?" Marcus asked.

"We are ready. You all know what you are up against and the power is in its prime. Perhaps more of the family Witches are needed? I understand you recruited Phillip…it may have been wise to call upon Patrick, Maleagant, Vida and your sister, Marguerite. Demons do not possess the intelligence that humans do. I am sure your sister would forgive you and come to your aid if you only ask. I am suggesting that you do as such." He adjusted his position, sighed and then spoke again. "This is the best opportunity we have. Oh sure, the family is strong, there are Vicar's watching over Olivia and unfortunately Michael as well…but we need to press on. So what do we do? We call upon the assistance of those that can match their power. I believe that the assistance of those I have mentioned will aid us; however, they do not match their powers, with the exception of Marguerite. No, we shall need to call upon members of their own family. We shall call upon Dorthea,

Theodor, Stella, Sabino, Carlo and Debra. We are now ready to pit one family's powers against the others. They come from the same linage. It will be grand. I shall also call upon the help of my angles. I am not sure about the Hags — they are really upset. Anyway, my angels shall assist the family and then the power shall be transferred. I'll make my move after everything is settled. I do not wish to be tacky."

"How are we to assist? Look at us; we are all damaged, powers unstable, feeling pain and misery. Besides, Marguerite is furious with me...I don't think she'll help." Lamia coughed and rested her face once again upon the cool surface of the floor.

The Man stood. "That is why I will call in a favor that she owes me. Marguerite will assist you; you need to only ask for forgiveness." His eyes squinted as he noticed the mess of a woman who lay before him. "Lamia darling...do forgive me, sometimes I just don't pay attention to the obvious. Please accept my deepest apologies." He waved a hand. Dormava straighten and unclenched her stomach, Damiano fell to the floor with a thud, while Medeia opened her eyes, glided to the floor and smiled. Lamia healed.

"You see, as wonderful as your intentions were, Lamia...you need help from the Degeli family. Celia and Eva will be our best allies, as they are closest in inheriting the linage as direct descendants from Gabriella and Contessa. Carlo and the rest of the cousins will be extraordinary allies as well. I would expect Thom from San Francisco and Bella from New York will attend the funeral. So we'll have more opposition. Then there is Kimberly and Drago. However, there is nothing we can do. They will attempt to defend their cousins. We, on the other hand, shall do what no other Witches War has done. We shall break an old tradition and take them when they least expect." The Man stood and helped Lamia to her feet. Dormava narrowed her eyes, as did Damiano.

"Thank you...but how do we catch them by surprise? We've already attacked." Lamia ran her fingers through her hair and examined the beautiful dress within a full length mirror. "Of course, we shall do whatever you wish. Gather around, The Man will tell us what needs to be done."

"It is common knowledge that families show respect during funeral proceedings, an old tradition but very helpful. It's about time we break that tradition. I will speak with Sabino and Stella. They will set the stage." He angled his head toward Lamia. "I think it's about time you call me by my proper name. After a slight pause he spoke his name."

Dormava stopped in her tracks. Medeia quickly glanced to Damiano who also froze. Marcus remained focused upon the elderly man that stood before him.

Lamia stumbled a bit backward and looked to Marcus. Marcus shook his head ever so slightly.

"Oh now come, come…do not make such harsh judgments. Have I not kept my word? Treated you all with kindness and compassion?" He reached out and touched Lamia's cheek. She did nothing, no eye movement, and no flitter…her cheek felt like stone. His eyes narrowed and darted to Marcus, his body hard and unmoving. The Man's eyebrows furrowed. He looked to Damiano, who stood as a statue, as did Dormava. Medeia remained motionless, halfway upon getting to her feet. After searching the room; he stepped away from his minions. "Who is there? You have no idea who you are up against? Release them!"

"I know exactly who I am up against." Ashima appeared before The Man

He smiled. "Ashima, the master and guide to all of the Higher Spirits within the Earth's realm, to what do I owe the pleasure?"

* * * *

Friends & Foes

Ashima took a few steps toward the man wearing a black pinstripe suit, a deep crimson necktie and a white silk shirt. He took her hands into his. Ashima leaned into him and displayed her right cheek. After a gentle kiss, she displayed her left. She squeezed his hands and then released them. "You look very dashing. Although, I must say there is a creepy element to you. Perhaps it's the long hair?"

"You may be right, my dear. You, on the other hand, look simply fabulous." He strode over to Lamia, who was turned solid as a statue by Ashima's spell. He examined her. "Lamia really is beautiful. Too bad her temper is uncontrolled."

Ashima took a few steps forward. "You know the reason for my visit. Is there any possibility that I may talk you out of this?"

He took in a deep breath and then made his way to another statue. He gently placed a hand upon Marcus's cheek and smiled. "He is a fine young man, handsome...so handsome. Yet, he is cunning and devious...a wonderful, different kind of sociopath."

"I asked you a question and I expect you to be polite enough to answer." Ashima said.

"Do not be impatient Ashima. Perhaps I linger to keep your company. Perhaps I am lonely and I have missed you." He clasped his hands behind his back. "So, how do you like overseeing the Higher Spirits? Do you enjoy your post?" He turned to face her. "I heard you have dismissed Lan Lee from the council of the Americas?"

"She was not suited for the post." Ashima clasped both hands behind her back. "I have missed you. I miss how close we once were."

He smiled and strode over to Damiano. He placed a hand upon the young man's' chest and closed his eyes. "Do you, Ashima? Do you miss me?"

"Enough. Now answer my question." Ashima said.

"Damiano is so handsome, and he is kind and caring. Ah, but easily influenced." He gestured to Dormava and Medeia. "And these two creatures are simply beautiful, deadly, but beautiful."

Ashima vanished.

"Don't leave! I am sorry!" He spoke rapidly. "I shall answer your question."

Ashima reappeared. "Thank you."

"Witches, created by the Universe, and they are made to feel as though they cannot use their powers. Judged by others to be evil for using what they have crafted." He looked up to a large painting of a man upon a horse.

"If I leave again, I shall not return." Ashima joined him in front of the painting.

"I don't like the way the Universe has designed Free Will. Never have, never will. I think that was a flaw in the creation of the Universal Laws." He leaned in, to examine the horse.

"You are going to stand there and be so arrogant as to say that you know better than the creator of the Universe? We understand the Universe more than you. We understand its consequences for interference when not necessary." Ashima said.

"And who decides what is necessary and what is not!" He slammed his fist into the wall, busting through the plaster.

"If you are going to lose your temper..." Ashima warned.

"I am sorry. You know how I feel about the decision that you follow. I feel the laws of the Universe are designed to do whatever must be done, to assist in the survival of a species." He said.

Ashima tightened her lips, paused for a moment, and then spoke. "It is in the nature of the Universe to be violent, to let each species decide if they wish to exist. It is in nature, that actions of humans, will allow the Universe to react. We are upholding what is only natural without destroying more than half the species in order to guarantee their survival. It is wrong to kill. It breeds such negative energy into the Universe and its outcome is still in discussion." Ashima walked over to a painting of a German shepherd sitting next to a Ragdoll cat.

He took a few steps and stood beside his long time friend. "Some of these humans are mentally ill because they have been raised in such horrid conditions. Governments are corrupt and nobody seems to want to come together as a species and do something that will prevent these ill individuals from existing in the first place? Their minds are damaged. They are not evolving in a direction in which survival is a guarantee."

"And you should decide if the species should survive? It is in the design of nature that a species should evolve through higher levels. It will be the Universe, which will decide their future. The species that we know, the human species, may evolve into a different type of species from us. It is in nature that a species lives or dies. Sometimes that species has a choice... sometimes they are overpowered." Ashima leaned in to the Ragdoll.

"And why do you decide that we should not intervene? In nature it is common to have something change from the norm — a spark of energy in an unexpected place, a freak of nature. Who is to say what is the freak of nature, and what is the proper direction of evolution. People that seem different are deemed an abnormality. It is difficult to survive if you are so misunderstood. They need help. The humans that understand what must be done are far outnumbered by those that deem them freaks. Is it nature? You and I were human, were we not? Should we not assist our own kind?"

Ashima raised her voice. "You speak in riddles and do not make any sense of your actions. You influence people to kill each other, to create these mentally ill people. You encourage governments to be corrupt and the destruction among religions! You say that you are trying to save them, yet you help the species die."

"It is because we wish to change the laws of Free Will. Let us intervene in the manner in which we desire and there would be peace. There would be a guarantee of survival. You insist that we stand down and force our hand because we are outnumbered. I would say...over powered." He leaned into the Shepherd.

"You imply contradictory. I will never understand why we are friends and yet we are foes. We want the same thing. Yet, you are too narrow-minded to have trust in the Universe. There are incidents happening all over the Earth, that give us signs that people are standing up to corrupt powers and those that have not evolved toward love. This is a small percentage, but a start. It always begins with a flick of energy…a break in the common law. Then it happens and spreads like wildfire. People pray to their Gods, their deities… and they are being heard. The percentage is growing. You must be patient and have trust in the Universe." Ashima took in a breath and walked to a painting of a woman in a cotton field.

He stepped next to Ashima and gazed upon a painting of a little girl running through a cotton field. "The other day I watched as two brothers spoke upon their sofa. They were smoking and enjoying their herbal high… laughing and loving life. They began to speak of their lives. Both of their energies began to change. You see, their parents divorced and remained in their own hell. Unfortunately they could not guide their children properly so that they may succeed in comfort. These boys have moved homes more times than their years in age. Their self esteem, patients for ignorance and lesser evolved humans, flabbergasts them. They struggle in adulthood in a society that calls them defects from the normal, in which I agree. Normal is the most popular, not the most intelligent. They cannot maintain relationships and seem to roam the United States. The one brother second guesses everything he does trying to make logic that the rest of the world lives horrible lives. He finds it difficult to communicate in the most simple of conversations. He is like a gazelle in the wild…afraid of his surrounds and runs away from who he is. He does nothing but wallows in torment over his decisions and refuses assistance with logical examination of the world. The other brother is prone to violence. He alienates people and is a loner. He is sad and terrified. He tries to make a life for himself and then sits and does nothing to establish his desires." The Man looked to Ashima. "They argued this morning, both in mind sets that should have told them to walk away. If it had not been for their herbal high, their love for each other, the need to not lose a good mood, and a slightest bit of interference from an outside source, I fear they would have killed each other."

"So you assisted them. Like the Vicar's, Guardians and Angels." Ashima strolled behind him to the baby grand piano. "Why can't you do that for everyone? Just like us. We wouldn't be in this constant flux."

"We will continue to influence the negative because there are too few of us that believe as I. If we come together, there would be no need to be foes. We could become friends once more." He continued to look upon the painting.

"By killing eighty percent of the population, we can be friends. I see." Ashima shook her head. "We could argue all day." Ashima placed the tip of a finger on an ivory key and pushed. A note sounded from the piano. "I ask you this, as old friends, leave the Degeli's alone. The power you will unleash will destroy an entire city in days. Once the greedy and reckless side of the family receives that power, it will only spread to the entire state of Michigan, then to the rest of the Midwest, the United States of America and spread across the globe. You are creating a condition of which you say you do not wish."

He smiled. "Then join me, and do what we must to guarantee their survival."

"You are playing Russian Roulette. The Higher Spirits are not foolish. They will understand that you will expect them intervene and end up saving the human race. It is not in the design of the Universe to do so. We do not understand the outcome of such violence!" She pushed hard on a high C of the piano and walked away.

"We are a part of that species! We, have the power to stop them from becoming extinct." He rushed over to Ashima and stood in her path.

"We have evolved into a different level of being! It is up to them to decide if they want to continue!" She took a forward step to her right.

He countered. She crossed her arms and sighed. "Let us not fight." He said.

She paused for several seconds, looked down and then into his eyes. "You know of Vicar Aiden Sinclair and Vicar Thomas O'Connell?"

He nodded.

"There are others, just like them. Others that feel they should interfere to save people. Save them in the name of love, compassion and of understanding. They have faith that the species will do the correct thing...eventually. They, of course, do not see the entire outcome of their tiny, almost romantic, intervention. They do not know as I. They do not know it is helping to save the species, quicker than what the Higher Spirits are expecting." She lowered her arms. "We are doing the same thing, guided by different perspectives. In my way, there is no war between our species. We could be friends. I am on your side." Ashima turned on her heal, and walked away from him, up to the piano and sat upon the bench. She began to play *Clair de lune*. After several minutes she stopped, and stood to face him. When she spoke, her voice was gentle. "However, if you should intervene, if you make a physical move to alter the course of what the Universe has or has not decided...the Vicars, Guardians...the Angels and I, will stop you. There will be a new war waged between us. Is that what you wish?"

"If it brings the results that I desire, then yes." He sat at the bench and hit a few cords, of *Clair de lune*.

After several cords, she sat beside him. "You are enlisting such foul creatures, things that can devour the human race."

He shrugged his shoulders and continued to play.

"I see. It is once again that we part as foes."

He stood and bowed, then took her hands into his. "I know."

Ashima leaned in and kissed him on both cheeks. Before she could pull away, he held her close, and whispered in her ear. "I love you Ashima."

"And I...love you." She smiled and vanished.

* * * *

Debra & Carlo

A woman of short stature, hazel eyes and graying dark hair sat at the writing desk. Tips of her fingers slowly massaging her temples as her husband's voice rose once again into the phone. She shook her head and rolled her eyes. The rustle of the bird in its cage, caused her to change focus. "Stop it, you're scaring Pookins! He'll be a wreck for days."

Carlo pushed a button on his cell phone and turned to his wife. "I'm sorry. Kimberly and Drago really piss me off!"

"Kimberly and Drago, I thought you were speaking with Father Bernardo?"

"I was. They called as I was telling him goodbye." Carlo punched his forehead. "Dam it! I should have never spoken to him."

Debra rose from her chair and walked to her husband. "Stop hitting yourself, you look ridiculous. What did your brother have to say…Bernardo?"

"Oh…God this and God that and how we will all perish in hell." He adjusted his black sweater over the belt of his black slacks and swore.

"Well, did you expect anything less? What did your other brother want... Drago?" She took a few steps toward her husband, hazel eyes narrowing.

"He said that if we attacked Azzurra's kids once more, he'd kill me himself. Kimberly was on the other line. She said if we want a Witches War, we've got one." He swore again and punched the wall. Pookins screeched and fluttered in his cage.

"Just ignore her! Ignore them all. Soon, it will all be over." Debra gently stroked her husband's arm.

"Who were speaking with before Father? Before Bernardo called?" Carlo asked.

"Eva. She said that Mateo wanted to get the funeral over with as quick as possible. The viewing is this evening. The funeral will be tomorrow. I guess Gabriella is very upset with her, Nicolai as well. Eva said that she and Celia would be taking care of things by tomorrow's funeral. She told her mother that her cell phone was dead and she forgot her charger. That she spent the night at her boyfriends. I don't think they believed her."

"Eva should have gone to her parents the moment they called and said that their Aunt Arianna was dead! Now, they have suspicions...no-doubt, planted by Azzurra." Carlo shook his head and then smeared thick fingers through his dark hair. "They better succeed. How's Philip?" His blue eyes darted to his wife's.

"He's in bad shape. He's still recovering from Azzurra's spell after killing Arianna. Apparently Lamia suffered an awful blow as well. Arianna managed to throw a sachet at her just before she died. Damiano, Dormava and Medeia are a mess too. Marcus was the only one to make it out unscathed." Debra walked over to the frightened bird and began to calm him.

"Will he be alright? Philip?" He turned to face his wife.

"Eventually, I told him to go to your parents. Stella is good with healing things. I wonder what The Man thinks of all this, if he's angry with Lamia?" She reached in the cage and stroked the feathers of the colorful parakeet.

"What time do we have to pick up Dorthea?" Carlo asked.

"She should be arriving near three. It's almost two so we should head to the airport now." Debra walked toward the back hallway. Carlo stopped her.

"Do you think Eva and Celia will succeed?" His bright blue eyes searched his wife's eyes.

"I hope so." Debra gently took her husband's hand. "I hope so."

* * * *
404

Wine & Pizza

Marta placed her spell book down on the sofa and went to answer the door. After a quick glance at the ring, she sighed with relief. It had shown purple.

The hall mirror displayed a well rested woman with just the slightest hint of stress in the eyes. It would be him. Her heart did something she didn't think it knew how to do...it skipped a beat and began to thud. Mr. Buchman...Tom, stood on her doorstep holding a large pizza and a bottle of red wine.

"I figure we could eat something before going to the parlor. I would like to come with you if you don't mind. But I totally understand if you don't."

"I...I don't mind at all." Marta smiled. Tom walked over the threshold as she closed the door.

* * * *

Celia

Contessa gazed through the sliding glass door to the ash tree. Deep in thoughts she leaned against the glass, crossing her arms. A blue bird darted from under one of the branches and flew to a nearby pine.

"Are you alright, Contessa?" Nathan approached.

Contessa turned to her husband. "You look very handsome, Nathan. I can't remember the last time I saw you in a suit."

"Thank you Tess and you look beautiful. I figured I'll save my black suite for the morning."

Contessa returned her gaze to the blue bird...fluttering among the branches. "Will they ever forgive us? Katie...Azzurra?"

Nathan took in a deep breath and pulled his wife against him. "Give it time, Tess."

They looked into each other's eyes, they didn't have to speak the words...
but they both knew...they both knew they were fools.

"It was so good to be around them." Contessa sighed. "They are so different than Debra and Carlo. I enjoyed listening to them sing. I forgot how much fun the family could be...even in stressful times."

"Has Lamia answered your summons?" Nathan asked.

"No. By now she knows that I know everything. When we get back from the funeral parlor, we really need to set up some protective enchantments to the house." Contessa leaned against the glass once more and stared out to her tree. "I tried the rest of the Spirits...no one answered except Achar. He appeared while you were in the shower. He said he would never speak to Lamia again and asked if I needed anything. I didn't tell him Deveroy was OK. He is very distressed over the thought of Deveroy's atoms spread across the universe. I simply thanked him and he left."

The front door handle sounded, a key entered the lock and the door opened. Contessa and Nathan turned to the hallway. Celia called out for her mother and father, announcing her entrance.

"Remind me to change the locks." Nathan whispered. Contessa hushed him.

Celia entered the kitchen and smiled at her parents across the room. "I am so sorry about Aunt Arianna. I still can't believe all that's happened."

"Did you think you were going to a funeral home this evening? Or out to a night club?" Nathan placed a hand upon his black tie.

"Dad, don't start, I lived forty years without your advice and I certainly don't need it now." She snapped. Her voice relaxed as she spoke her next words. "I figured we could all go to the funeral home together."

Contessa looked her daughter up and down. Tight, black jeans, scarlet blouse and animal print boots, hair styled with a spiky new hair cut.

"Your father is right. You don't know how to dress and your father does not deserve that tone." Contessa reached a hand around her back and grasped her wand. "A new hair cut? Are you celebrating?"

"What is the matter with the two of you?" Celia took a few steps forward, a single hand in a large purse. "Now are we going to the funeral home or not?"

"Where are Alfonso, Fredrick and Felicia?" Nathan asked.

"He's not feeling well, Fredrick had to work and Felicia is out of town. They will be there tomorrow." Celia looked away from her parents.

Contessa and Nathan eyed each other. Nathan wrapped a palm around his tie as Contessa pulled her wand and let it rest to her side. Contessa whispered a spell. She could see Dormava and Medeia standing behind Celia… staying transparent.

"You two are acting very strange. What's with the wand?" Celia asked.

"Why are Dormava and Medeia hiding? Why don't they reveal themselves?" Contessa asked. Nathan narrowed his eyes and reached into his pocket with the other hand.

Celia laughed and looked to her left and then right — a hand still in her purse. "Oh…they are conserving energy. Mom…Dad…are you alright?"

Contessa looked to Nathan. "We are fine." Nathan spoke.

"Are you sure? You are both acting very strange. I mean…

"Ferma il cu …"
(Stop the hea…)

Celia shouted

"Protezione!"
"Rivela ciò che non può essere visto!"

Contessa countered.

Medeia and Dormava were forced to reveal themselves to all. Celia and her Spirits were blasted back by the Protezione spell.

Nathan pulled a hand from his pocket and threw a coin at Celia.

Celia scuttled across the floor to her wand. The coin rolled and plunked against her thigh. It expelled an energy wall that enclosed her. Streaks of red light caressed his daughter. Celia swore.

Medeia rolled to her feet and raised both arms. Dormava shouted a spell that was blocked by Nathan.

Contessa yelled.

"Vieni a me, nella mia bacchetta, io ti comando!"
(Come to me, Into my wand, I command!)

Medeia struggled for a brief moment, screeched and entered Contessa's wand.

Nathan pulled his tie and threw it toward Dormava. The tie expanded in size and coiled around her. Sparks of white, red and orange flickered from the coils, twisting and winding throughout the Spirit. Dormava writhed in agony, fell to the floor and began chanting a counter curse.

A few seconds later, the coils exploded outward, knocking Contessa and Nathan to the floor.

Contessa kept focus, forcing Medeia in stay within her wand and do her bidding. She rolled to her side and pointed her wand to Dormava.

Dormava struggled, swore and was forced to do the bidding of this Witch.

Celia broke free of Nathan's energy encasement. She pointed her wand to her mother.

Dormava attacked Celia with a ball of green that expelled from her hand. Celia blocked the spell.

"Nathan, do something!" Contessa shouted; concentrating on controlling Dormava who cast another green ball of energy toward Celia and Medeia. Celia rolled out of the way as it exploded into the family room. She aimed her wand at her father.

"Fulmine luminoso!"
(Lightning bolt)

Celia screamed.

Nathan tossed a button toward his daughter. It collided with Celia's spell and exploded, throwing her backward, through the hallway. Nathan flew against the wall and rolled to the floor.

Contessa began to stand, still forcing Dormava to attack Celia and keeping Medeia.

Celia countered Dormava's curse.

Contessa winced at a stabbing pain in her thigh. In that split second — she lost the concentration.

Nathan stood and began an Immediate Enchantment.

"Second hand of the clock, force…"

Medeia rose from the tip of Contessa's wand and struck Nathan just before he finished the incantation. He flew over a sofa and to the floor. Dormava disappeared.

Medeia threw Contessa over her shoulder. Contessa slid across the kitchen table, striking the far cabinet. Shards of glass falling upon her she plopped to the floor.

Nathan pushed himself up by the sofa's edge.

"Energy, power, strength to heal...to Contessa, from her I steal."

Medeia flickered once, turned transparent and then floated to the ceiling. Thin wisps of energy streamed from her body and gently glided toward Contessa.

Nathan rose to his feet, and rushed to Contessa. He brushed his hand over his wife, expelling energy that cleared the broken glass, china and wood cleared away from body. Contessa lay to the side as the strands of white, blue, green and red caressed her. Nathan cursed, reached for his wife and laid her within his arms. Blood trickled from her ears and nose. Her eyes remained closed. Nathan released a plume of white over his wife's head. The wounds began to heal. Instinct told him to look up. Celia stood before him, wand raised, blood dripped from her cheek.

"Ferma il cu..."
(Stop the heart)

Nathan countered,

"Protezione"

His spell forced Celia's spell to rebound into the living room, shattering a lamp. Nathan cast another spell as Celia cast the spell of Protezione.

"Palla di fuco!"
(FireBall)

Nathan's spell ripped through her shield of protection. Celia screamed as a ball of red threw her against the wall. Nathan watched as his daughter staggered forward and then crashed to the floor. She rolled to her side and lay still.

"Tessa, please be OK! Contessa, open your eyes!" Nathan cradled his wife in his arms and then felt a piercing pain in his lower back. The plume of white disappeared. Warmth...wet warmth. Dormava stood behind him with a large knife...blood dripping from its blade.

Nathan released his wife's body and fell against the cabinet. He saw Dormava cast a bright light upon Celia and then one toward Medeia.

Wedding bells, sounds of music...he in his Tuxedo, Contessa in a ball-room wedding gown. The birth of Vincent...Celia riding a bike...Vincent's funeral...Azzurra's wedding...playing cards...Angelo's funeral...hunting with Alfonso, laughing with Stephan, Azzurra singing, kissing his wife. These images flashed before him as he took his last breath.

* * * *

The Funeral Parlor

Azzurra's eyes widened at the sight of her long time friends and confidants — Kimberly and her first cousin, Drago Degeli. Her heart warmed and filled with memories. Memories of Drago, Ben, Katie and she hanging out at the shopping center or in Chandler Park came to mind. After a moment, the memory dissipated as another one bullied its way to the front...a memory of an argument between her parents and Drago's parents. Her mother forbade them from seeing Sabino and Stella Degeli, that were not good people and if she or her siblings saw them, they were to run the other way. Azzurra's mother warned that until they were of age...there would be no contact with Drago or Ben.

Memories of Katie and she sneaking phone calls to their cousins surfaced. A moment later another memory bubbled to the top...their reunion. Ben and Drago surprised them at Katie's prom. Ben announced that he was going to become a priest while Drago introduced a very pretty girl with long dark hair. Her name was Kimberly. He said he was getting married.

Azzurra's mind catapulted to the present as she stood with her pinochle lady friends. With a glance to her left, she saw Drago and Kimberly approach the casket. Mary, Eleanor and Carol, assured Azzurra that they would be there, night or day, if she should need them.

After several minutes, Azzurra felt the presence of people's eyes upon her. Drago and Kimberly had paid their respects to Arianna and now stood politely waiting their turn.

Mary placed a hand upon Azzurra's shoulder and motioned toward Drago and Kimberly. The pinochle ladies excused themselves in order to allow Azzurra the comfortable transition from one guest to the other.

A smile slid across Azzurra's face as she met eyes with her cousin. Tears welled as she held out two hands for him to take. After a tight hug and soothing words, Drago released his cousin to his wife. Kimberly hugged Azzurra, kissed her on both cheeks and then whispered in her ear. "We are here for you, Azzurra. If it's a Witches War they want…we'll give them a Witches War." She released Azzurra, smiled and winked.

Kimberly Degeli's penetrating green eyes had a glassy sheen as she looked upon Azzurra. Her gray hair was parted to the left side as it reached shoulder length in a Bob. She let go of Azzurra's hands, took a tissue from her tiny black purse and dabbed at her eyes. Azzurra complemented the color of her hunter green silk blouse, which made her eyes sparkle. Kimberly adjusted the collar and thanked her long time friend. Her black slacks draped over shapely legs and into a pair of black high heels. Silver tear-drop earrings dangled from her lobes and boasted olive green Peridots. Kimberly shook her head and looked toward the casket and then took her husband's aged hand. They were both in their seventies, but age had been kind to them. Kimberly's eyes were lined and lips thinned, however she still displayed smooth skin with very little age spots.

Drago was four years his wife's senior and showed his age a bit more. The bone structure of his face was strong, with a square jaw line and deep set eyes. Drago could look gruff or a down-right mean. However, when he smiled, he morphed into something kind and gentle with a fun soul. Crow's feet extended from his deep brown eyes, which displayed a need for sleep and decompression. Azzurra moved a tussle of grey hair from his forehead and pinched his cheek. Drago adjusted his black and green swirled tie and leaned forward to whisper into Azzurra's ear. "We know who is responsible for this and we'll make them pay for what they've done." He tugged downward upon the jacket of his black pin-striped suit.

Azzurra placed a hand upon his strong chest, smoothed the material and looked up into his eyes. "The two of you have always been beside me…and I won't ever forget that. We shall protect ourselves and our children…other than that, no violence." She lifted her hand from his chest and adjusted the collar of his black shirt. "Arianna, Basil, Katie and Anna are in the back of the parlor." She nodded her head over her right shoulder. "You should come say hi…Arianna would like that."

Azzurra stepped between them, turned around and took the right hand of Kimberly's and the left of Drago's and led them toward the rear of the parlor.

Gabriella saw him first and rushed toward the front of the parlor. Thom Stryker, from San Francisco, had entered. Thom's voice broke the tranquility of the somber room as it bellowed at the sight of Gabriella. He picked her up and twirled her around.

Gabriella let out a soft scream. "Thom, look at you! You look wonderful!"

Thom laughed loudly and patted his large stomach. His deer sized, grey eyes twinkling. "I enjoy far too much pasta, love my wine and crave the sweets to look as good as you boast. However, I shall take the complement." He pinched her nose.

Nicco rushed toward his Uncle Thom and shook his hand enthusiastically and moved aside for Tracy's greeting.

Thom looked Tracy up and down and then spoke. "Well well, look at you! Has this young man made the proposal yet or is he still leaving you dangling?" He chuckled and then nudged Nicco.

Nicco's eyes widened, followed by a laugh. "Uncle Thom, no need to go there. Besides, it's in the works…it's in the works." He winked at Tracy.

Tracy's eyes narrowed and then rolled. She kissed Uncle Thom on both cheeks and said that she heard Nicco say that a thousand times…that maybe this time he will follow through. She elbowed Nicco and said that she was content for whatever he would do. It really wasn't all that important to her.

Thom winked at Tracy and turned to Gabriella. "Gabriella, you look simply beautiful."

Gabriella reached up and brushed several fingers through his grey hair. "You have such thick hair, Thom."

"Well now I thank you." Thom leaned forward. "My Dear…I don't know how you do it…and I do hate to say it, but you look better than my daughter Claudia…and she's half your age!" Gabriella blushed.

"And it costs her a fortune!" Azzurra squeezed past her sister and hugged her long time friend. After releasing Thom, she pinched his large cheeks and tapped his nose. "You look so cute Thom!"

Thom chuckled, "Now...now Azzurra you are too kind! I like far too much of the good life to look cute. But then again, Polar Bears are cute too eh." He laughed loudly as more family and friends approached. "I have news! I have finally retired at the age of 76!"

Thom adjusted the black jacket around his large stomach and gave a boastful laugh. "If they call I'll still come in...but only in an advisory capacity...far too old to take responsibly for anything and far too dangerous to make a mistake."

Everyone began to congratulate Thom as he shook hands enthusiastically and gave plenty of hugs.

"Uncle Thom, I love your moustache...hysterical!" Nicco said.

Azzurra slapped his arm. "It is not hysterical."

"Oh no, no Azzurra, Nicco my dear boy...I love it! Couldn't boast a walrus mustache in my younger years...would have looked foolish. But now that I'm a good healthy size...notice my purposeful gesture of the word *healthy*...I can pull it off."

Thom shook hands with Nicolai and Drago as they approached and then hugged Kimberly. He gave tight hugs to Carlotta and Olivia and flung Marta into a swirl through the air.

After several minutes of greetings, Thom begged Azzurra for some privacy along with her sister, Gabriella. Everyone pardoned themselves.

"Preposterous! This whole thing is preposterous. You know, I could not allow my kids to come...couldn't tell them why, of course. They think something has gone wrong in my head, not letting them come to dear Arianna's funeral. But what was I to say? Kids, we are in the beginning of another Witches War? By God they know nothing of being Witches or Warlocks!"

Thom sat upon a large flowered patterned sofa. Azzurra and Gabriella sat across from him in high leather-backed arm chairs. Thom looked toward the back of the parlor to Scott, Arianna's son.

Scott had broken down in front of a video of his mother during Christmas somewhere in the 1970's. Gracie, Scott's wife, rushed to his side followed by Mateo and Father Bernardo. Thom faced Azzurra and Gabriella. "It's a shame...listen to me. I know my dear wife, Beatrice, was your true cousin and family. May the Lord rest her soul? But I am as good as blood, and will be by your side...through thick and thin." He once again glanced over to Scott." "Poor boy...had to find out that he was a Warlock during a war. I heard he almost lost his life too. Hags are horrifying creatures." He shook his head. "Honestly my dear ladies, I don't see how my children are going to handle the news. I mean my Paul and Harrison may accept this, but I don't see Claudia accepting any of it…not at all my dear ladies, not at all." He shook his large head and fanned an aged hand toward himself. "It's a bit warm in here."

Azzurra leaned forward and placed a hand upon his large arm. "Thank you Thom. We knew we could count on you. You have always been like family. Now, say nothing to your children, Thom. Not at this time. No need to get them involved. However, if we feel their lives are in danger…as it is with Marta, Marie and Nicco…well, then you will have to tell them for their own safety."

"She's right Thom. Say nothing at the moment." Gabriella agreed.

"This is preposterous, Nicco…Marie and Marta, all of them in danger? Simple preposterous! That attack upon them was not called for. They will pay for their mistake. I won't have it I tell you." He slammed a large fist upon the sofa and then looked around. "Where is my dear Bella? Has she arrived yet?"

"Why yes, I have Thom. Thank you for asking." Bella von Eisenberg stood behind him with her hands upon her hips. Gabriella and Azzurra rose to their feet and greeted their first cousin from New York. Thom took several extra seconds to worm his way out of the cozy, plush sofa and boasted loudly an apology for not rushing to his feet sooner…far too much of the good life.

Thom hugged Bella and kissed her once upon each cheek. He exclaimed how wonderful it was to see her and how simply beautiful she looked. Bella patted her short gray hair and batted her icy blue eyes. She then told him that she knew there was a reason she was looking so forward to seeing him.

Bella donned an elegant charcoal grey pant suit adorned with a black cashmere scarf. She held Thom's hands in hers when the pleasant reunion was interrupted with several gasp that filled the room. Bella quickly turned toward the entrance and placed a hand to her chest. Gabriella swore as Azzurra's eyes widened at the sight of the aged couple. Stella and Sabino Degeli stood at the entrance of the parlor. The other side of the family had made their appearance.

* * * *

Sabino & Stella Degeli

The antique couple stood at the entrance of the somber parlor and observed the room. Stella glanced toward the casket and then back to the audience. A smirk slid over her aged lips. Her large eyes were black and outlined in heavy eyeliner. Pasty thin lips were painted bright red as her chalky face boasted two dark patches upon her cheeks. Stella clutched a black purse against the middle of a white dress adorned with a black & white polka dotted scarf. Warm beige stockings poured into heavy black shoes. She opened her purse and took out a tissue…dabbed at the corner of a dry eye, and smiled faintly. After dabbing the other eye, she pushed the tissue under a bra strap. With a deliberate glance toward Azzurra, she looked up to her husband Sabino and nodded once.

Sabino looked over his wire framed glasses toward Azzurra. After several long seconds, he then shifted his eyes toward the rear of the room to where the Spirits of Basil, Katie, Arianna and Anna lingered — invisible to the others. He adjusted his sky blue tie against a royal blue shirt, placed a hand into navy suit and retrieved a hanky. Large pupils retracted, revealing bright amber eyes as they widened and then half closed. Sabino took obvious notice of his son Drago and daughter-in-law, Kimberly. After dabbing at the ends of dry eyes, he placed the hanky back into the jacket and then focused upon Azzurra once more, met her eyes and smiled.

He cleared his throat loudly and then motioned for his wife to move toward the casket. With slow steps, the antiques approached Arianna's body and glanced down. Stella raised her head, took the tissue from her bra and then dabbed at her dry eyes once more. A small pathetic sound escaped from her thinned lips. A smile melted over her pouty, wrinkled face for a brief moment and then sank into an over exaggerated sad expression. She searched the room, like an owl deciding on which prey to dive upon, eyes darting to Augusto, then Gabriella, followed by Father Bernardo and finally, her other son, Drago.

The room remained silent for a brief moment as everyone focused on the exchange. Father Bernardo walked swiftly past Drago and Kimberly and approached his parents. "Mom, Dad? You shouldn't have come. It is a long way for you to have traveled." Stella raised a cheek to greet her son. Father Bernardo stood before his parents; he did not lean down to give his mother a kiss.

Sabino looked toward Drago and then to Father Bernardo. "Your mother would like a kiss from her holy son." His eyes met the priest.

"Of course." Father Bernardo took in a deep breath and kissed his mother on both cheeks.

"And you, Drago? Will you not greet your mother with a kiss?" Sabino looked to his son.

"He will most certainly not!" Kimberly stepped forward. "Why have you come?"

Several murmurs flooded the room and then fell to silence. Kimberly placed her hands upon her hips and hushed Drago's request for her silence.

Stella and Sabino turned to Kimberly and stared. They said not a word nor did their eyes leave their target.

Whispers filled the room as friends, family, co-workers and neighbors observed.

"The Lord knows this is an upsetting time…don't think upon it, Kimberly is just upset. We are all very upset by last night's tragic events." Father Bernardo placed a hand upon Drago's shoulder and smiled to Kimberly, and gave a crisp nod.

Stella's aged voice shook slightly as she spoke. "Why Kimberly, my daughter-in-law, it's been such a long time. As to your question, I thought it would be obvious as to why we are here — to pay our respects on such a sad, tragic occasion." Her eyes moved to Drago. "Will you not let my son kiss me hello? It is bad enough you keep him from me." Her sunken eyes narrowed, and lips quivered.

"You have no right to be here and your son does as he wishes. It is not my fault that he sees you for what you are…two devils!" Kimberly's face turned red.

People began to murmur and scuttle across the room to gather their children and escort them from the parlor.

Father Bernardo made the sign of the cross and asked Kimberly to be silent, telling her that this is neither the time nor the place for such words.

Kimberly whispered to Father Bernardo. "I am sorry Father…she is behind all this….her and that Satan husband of hers." She rounded upon her husband. "Drago, you had better voice yourself."

Augusto moved toward his sisters. Thom blocked Azzurra from Stella and Sabino's view and stared them down.

"Devils, why Sabino, darling, did you hear what that little tramp called us? She referred to us as devils." Her lips quivered once more and an eye twitched.

Carlotta and Olivia removed their kids from the parlor and then approached their Aunt Azzurra.

Father Bernardo stepped forward. "Please this is neither the place nor the time for such words." He turned to Kimberly and Drago. "Please hold your tongues." He turned back to his parents. "You should not have come this evening…feelings are raw and there is much anger and confusion this evening. I suggest you leave."

"Why son, we have come to pay our…" Stella began.

Father Bernardo interrupted. His voice shook as he pounded a hand upon the back of a leather chair. "…You have come to gloat! You have come in your white dress and smirks to only exacerbate an already volatile situation. Do you not understand what you have done? Do you not understand… "Father Bernardo broke off and looked around the room.

Marta took Tom Buchman's hand, squeezed it and then asked him to step out, that the family needed some privacy. Tom leaned down, kissed Marta on the cheek and told her that he'd be just outside the doors. He nodded to Tony, Marta's co-worker, and the rest of her colleagues from the law firm, and ushered them through the door. Marie asked her husband, Steven, to ask those who were not family to step out in the hall for a few minutes. Gracie removed her three children from the room and then re-entered and stood next to her husband, Scott. Gabriella hugged her neighbor, Shirley and asked that she and the rest of friends step out. Carlotta once again, removed her son, Dino, from the room.

After a few moments the doors were closed. Steven, Marie's husband and Tony, stood in the hall making sure that no one entered the room. The room remained silent for several long seconds.

Father Bernardo turned to face his parents. "I have struggled...I have prayed for guidance and patience. I have prayed that this family be united, to place aside the evil temptations of the past."

"Now, son, do not get so upset. We have come to pay our respects, not gloat." Sabino said.

Father Bernardo's voice spoke in a harsh, strong whisper. "Do you not understand what has happened? Another Witches War has begun!" He took several steps forward and gently took his father by the arm and then held his mother's hand. "I beg you both. I beg you both to stop this. Please. In the name of God tell us that you had nothing to do with Arianna's death. Tell us that the Spirits are out of control. That you tried to stop them."

Stella smiled and patted her sons face. "Oh son, you are so dramatic. Perhaps the theatre should have been your calling."

Father Bernardo brushed his mother's hand away and took several steps backward.

Sabino stepped forward. "You and your God? Where was he last night my son? Did he save Arianna?" He then turned to Mateo and grinned.

"Get out! Get out of here!" Father Bernardo raised his voice.

Mateo, Arianna's husband, stepped forward, placed a hand upon the Father's shoulder and moved him aside.

"Dad?" Scott took a few steps forward, Gracie beside him.

Augusto spoke to Gracie and Scott. "Your father will handle this. The two of you stay here."

Mateo took several steps forward until he stood in front of Sabino and Stella. His eyes darted between them. "But God did intervene, didn't he? Did Lamia not tell you how the winged demons were forced to flee the church?"

Stella and Sabino's expressions harden.

Mateo's voice was steady, yet deadly. "Lamia does not tell you every-thing. Has she told you that a Vicar has been assigned to watch over Olivia, her husband Walter, and the kids? Did she not tell you how Azzurra cast a single spell that removed four Spirits from my house?"

Sabino's eyes widened narrowed. Stella's lips quivered. Her eyes darted to Azzurra.

Mateo's face reddened. He lowered his voice into a deep whisper, as veins bulged in his neck. "You will do as the Father suggested, and get the hell out of my sight. Or I'll kill the both of you right here and now." He drew a wand from within his black suit jacket and pointed at the antiques.

Father Bernardo intervened and asked Mateo to put his wand aside. Drago stepped next Mateo, and drew his wand. Nicolai approached Mateo's other side, lowered his gaze, clutching an elixir. Drago raised his wand and pointed it at his Father's heart.

Azzurra stepped forward and stood in front of the three men. "Put your wands away. Nicolai, do not think about using that." Mateo lowered his wand and placed it back inside his black suit. Drago turned at the touch of Kimberly's hand upon his shoulder…looked to Azzurra and stowed his wand. Nicolai stood there, he did not stow the vial of deadly potion.

Azzurra took Mateo's arm and ushered him toward Thom, Bella and Gabriella. Nicolai placed an arm around Mateo's shoulder and began to whisper to him.

Drago stood alone facing his parents. Kimberly moved to his right while Augusto to his left. A cold, hard expression lined his facial features. His square jaw tightened and eyes narrowed. "Get out of here!" A guttural threat escaped his lips. "Get…the hell…out of here!"

One of the double doors opened and three people walked through them.

Carlo brushed Steven's arm away. Steven raised a fist. Marie shouted for him to stop, and asked her husband to please close the doors. The three people scowled at Steven as he closed the doors, leaving them inside the parlor.

Sabino and Stella looked toward the double doors at their other son, who stood with his wife and their daughter. "They told us to leave Carlo? They accused your mother and me of being evil. And Mateo and your brother, Drago, pulled wands. Nicolai still holds something in his hands to hurt us. They threatened us."

Carlo looked around the room and then spoke. "It's a good thing we got here when we did."

"What do you plan on doing, Carlo? You don't have the guts to do anything without a backup of Spirits." Drago looked to Kimberly as she assessed the room and then nodded quickly in agreement.

Carlo looked to Debra, then at large woman who stood between them.

Father Bernardo faced his brother, Carlo. "I will not have this on an occasion which should be holy." He placed a hand threw his grey hair and adjusted his white collar. His voice rose once more. "Carlo, take your parents, your wife and that monstrosity that stands between the two of you and get out!"

Dorthea, the very large woman who stood between Debra and Carlo, puffed larger in size and turned red in the face. Her large breast heaved, expanding the bright orange embroidered dress to its limits. Cold black eyes bulged in an oddly shaped rounded head with dark curls of black short hair framing a pasty face with plumped peach lips. Heavy mascara and thick smears of rouge covered blotchy skin. She pushed Debra and Carlo out of the way, moved forward and swelled again before she spoke. "How dare you speak to me that way? I am your sister, you filthy priest!"

Gabriella placed her hands on her hips. "Do not speak to him that way. You and your rotten parents need to leave or so help me we shall do battle right here and now!" Nicolai rushed to her side. Bella and Thom flanked Azzurra. Olivia and Carlotta moved toward Gabriella as did Augusto. Marie took a few steps past Nicco and Marta and reached into her purse.

"Oh, Gabriella grew some balls did she? What are you hiding over there? Is that nasty Azzurra standing behind you? Too afraid to face me is she?" Dorthea squawked.

Carlo placed a hand upon his sister's shoulder as Debra asked her to please calm down. Dorthea brushed her brother's hand away. "Leave me alone, and don't tell me to calm down!" She took a few steps forward. "They won't attack here and now...children are just outside the doors. Now stand aside Thom and Bella, Franco's dead. She has no one to protect her now. I just want a few words with her. I want to know how it feels to lose another sister. Poor ditzy Arianna who couldn't bake a decent loaf..."

Augusto pulled his wand and pointed it at the beast. "...shut your mouth! Arianna was ten times the woman you'll ever be!" Thom and Bella took several steps forward. Marta's hand trembled as fingers grasped the wands handle within her purse and felt the vibration of the ring. Nicco's eyes darted over the room, looking for objects to enchant.

Azzurra stepped out from behind Thom and Bella. "Augusto, put your wand away." Several steps later she faced Dorthea. "Say that again." Azzurra threatened.

Dorthea's head jerked backward, eyes widened.

Stella and Sabino moved forward. Sabino reached into his suite jacket and Stella's hand unobtrusively reached into her purse.

The ghostly figure of Basil appeared next to the antique couple. He leaned down and smiled. "Just wanted to remind you of my presence, should you make a move toward Mum or anybody else I'll make sure it is the last thing you do before I kill the both of you."

Thom and Bella pulled Azzurra back several feet from Dorthea.

After taking deep breathes, the antiques removed their hands and placed them to their sides. Anna's Spirit appeared next to Carlo while Dante, Katie's husband, appeared on his other side. A bright white orb floated down through the ceiling and rested near Debra. The buzzing caused Debra to shield her ears...the bright light forced her to look away.

Dorthea's eyes widened at the sight of the Spirits. Then she turned her massive body toward Azzurra, withdrew a wand from her purse and took gigantic steps, stampeding like a rhino towards her target. Nicolai and Gabriella crossed over and stood in front of Azzurra. Gabriella pulled a blue sachet from her purse as Nicolai raised the elixir.

Katie appeared next to Nicolai, Franco alongside Gabriella. Franco folded his arms and glared at Dorthea. Dorthea stumbled backward...lost her footing and grabbed a lamp on an end table for support. She and the lamp toppled over the back of a burgundy sofa. She grunted and thudded to the floor.

Dorthea swore loudly and began cursing her brother Carlo to help her to her feet. When she righted herself, she thanked Carlo and patted Debra on the shoulder. "I'm fine...I'm fine." She breathed heavily as she took her wand from Carlo and stowed it into her purse.

"You are far from fine!" Augusto grunted.

"Fix you wig on the way out! It's lopped sided." Kimberly stepped forward and stood in front of Dorthea. "Now do as the Father suggest and get the hell out of here! All of you!"

Dorthea puffed up and raised a hand to strike Kimberly. Carlotta gasped. Olivia stopped Maria from tossing something toward the beast. Mateo pulled his wand as Drago shouted. A loud voice broke the commotion.

Sabino shouted. "Enough! We shall go if we are not wanted. That priest is correct. It is neither the time nor the place. We should uphold the respect for the dead during funeral proceedings." Sabino eyed Marie and then looked towards Azzurra.

Gabriella and Nicolai moved aside as Azzurra stepped forward and faced the old man. Katie flanked Sabino, opposite Basil.

Dorthea's hand lowered as her faced reddened.

Azzurra spoke. "You were asked to leave...and we are not going to ask you again." Azzurra looked to Stella, then to Sabino and then to Dorthea. "I am not afraid of you Dorthea and I certainly don't need my husband to protect me...and I believe all of you realize that."

Dorthea puffed in size and took in a large amount of the room's air. Stella and Sabino walked past Azzurra and approached Drago and Father Bernardo. "You are both dead to us." Sabino said.

Stella's eyes narrowed and looked to the priest. Her lips quivered. "You'll meet your God soon, my dear." Yellow teeth revealed a smile as she took her husband's hand and paused to stare at Kimberly. "You?" she whispered to Kimberly, "You, I shall take care of myself."

With tiny steps they approached the entrance, paused to look toward Katie, Basil, Arianna and Anna and then turned toward Franco and Dante. "Only six Spirits of the family, how nice."

Carlo opened the door for his parents. With a glance backward, they crossed the threshold. The Spirits turned invisible.

Dorthea's jowl shook as a sausage like finger rose toward Kimberly. "I can't wait to see you die."

A large voice boomed through the parlor. Thom had yelled and took several steps forward. He over enunciated each word as he spoke the command. "You will leave!"

Dorthea scoffed and when Thom took quick steps toward the monstrosity, she let out a quick grunt, turned on her hooves and left.

Debra shook her head, turned and walked out. Carlo approached his brothers. "You should have let them be." He glanced toward Azzurra and left.

* * * *

Why Now?

*A*zzurra squeezed Nicco's hand and told him that she was just fine, that he was not to worry. She then asked if he could find some *Advil or Tylenol* for her back. A moment later, Marta and Marie rushed up to her. "I'm fine, I'm fine. Listen to me, both of you. Marie, I want you to watch the front entrance. Marta you watch the rear. If anyone affiliated with Sabino and Stella should arrive…come find me. I'll be in the back room where the food is. Where's Gabriella?"

"She's over by the casket. I think she's talking with Aunty Arianna." Marie said.

A few minutes later, Nicco approached from behind his sisters and held out a cup of water to his mother. Marta screamed and then placed a hand to her chest.

Azzurra took the cup of water. "Marta honey, you really need to calm down. Thank you, Nicco."

"Easy there Marta. Ma, here I got some *Motrin*." Nicco handed his mother two pills. Marta and Marie took their positions, one at each entrance of the parlor.

Azzurra took the pills and then turned to her pinochle lady friends. She took Mary's hand and looked to the three of them. "I am fine. Don't worry, just a little squabble. I'll explain everything...someday." The three ladies gave their friend a hug and assured her that if she should need anything, she was to let them know. Azzurra thanked them and excused herself to approach Gabriella.

"Gabriella, can you please gather Nicolai, Mateo, Thom, Bella, Augusto, Drago, Kimberly Father Bernardo and the Spirits. Tell them to meet me in the back room, where they placed the food." Gabriella nodded, looked over Azzurra's shoulder and then gasped. "Oh my word, look who's here? Where's Carlotta?" Gabriella's eyes searched the room."

Azzurra turned around and saw what Gabriella had seen...Carlotta's X husband. He was speaking with Marta and several of her co-workers.

Carlotta's X husband, Gregory O'Riley looked as good as Azzurra remembered. His tight, black sweater hugged a full chest, and slim abdomen. He wore jeans that stretched over thick thighs and full buttocks. His face was chiseled with strong cheek bones, bright blue eyes, a squared jaw line and short dusty grey hair.

Azzurra gave a slight intake of breath. "Oh Dear, find Carlotta. She'll have a heart attack if she bumps into him without warning." Gabriella and Azzurra watched him for a moment. "Oh...Gabriella, he's so handsome." She then looked to her sister. "Tell Carlotta that I've heard that he's been sober for over a year. Not to be harsh...find Dino and Elizabeth. Tell them to give their mother some time alone with their father." Gabriella nodded and then rushed into the hallway to find Carlotta.

Azzurra walked over to Olivia, who had just noticed Greg, Carlotta's X. "I've taken care of it. Gabriella is finding Carlotta now." She then took Olivia by the hand and escorted her to a position more private. "If your sister is smart, she'll keep her temper down. He's been sober for over a year."

"How do you know that?" Olivia asked.

"Well, I tried to talk with your sister, but every time I mention his name she gets upset. So, I never said anything. But I keep in touch with his mother, you know. She and I talk. And she said he's been sober for over a year...still pines for her too."

Olivia's jaw dropped. "She'll be so upset you didn't tell her."

"Well, it's her own fault, I tried several times and she says she doesn't want to talk about him. So what was I supposed to do?"

"He's even more handsome than I remember." Olivia remarked.

Carlotta entered the room, took notice of her X husband and took in a deep breath before she approached him. Azzurra took Olivia by the shoulder and turned her around. "Never mind them. Listen to me."

"Are you alright? I can't believe Sabino and Stella showed...and Dorthea...she looks terr...

"...hush, now listen to me...I'm sorry sweetheart, I didn't mean to be rude...but there is little time. Gabriella is gathering the family for a meeting. I need you to do me a big favor."

Olivia nodded and leaned down toward her aunt.

"I need you to find someplace private. It can wait till tonight, but the sooner the better. Anyway, I need you to place yourself in a deep meditation. But concentrate on this mess, on the Witches War. If my inclining is correct you have a very unusual power. You have the power of clairvoyance." Olivia placed a hand to her head. "Olivia, this is very important honey, don't stress. Close your eyes and clear your head of everything, with the exception of the family and the Withes War during the meditation. Write down everything that you see. No matter how trivial. Do you understand?"

Olivia's eyes widened and then narrowed. "Yes. Ok yes. Yes, I do." After taking a breath she spoke again. "Aunty Azzurra...the dream I had of the attack on the kids and me the other night? That monster...demon, and Walter was dead? Then there was a man in the white..?"

Azzurra interrupted once more. "...I'm sorry dear. Don't think of that. You have a Vicar watching over you. He's the man you saw in your dreams. He's one of the most powerful beings sent to us from the Higher Spirits. He's your Guardian. Nothing can happen to you, not while he's around... or your family."

Olivia nodded quickly and then shook her head and focused. "What are you hoping I see?"

Azzurra eyes scanned the room. She then leaned in a bit closer. "I am hoping that you could find out why the evil side of the family is showing up after all these years of silence? What do they want? What do they need? Why now?"

Olivia's eyes wore dark circles under them. Without the Vicar being right beside her, the effects of forty years of living with a Cull began to resurface.

"I understand…this is so horrifying. I think that dream was real? Michael saw things…Rose saw the man in white…the Vicar." Olivia reached in her black handbag and took out a tissue. She dabbed her eyes. "This is too much." She rubbed her temple "This is really too much." Her eyes began to water.

"No time to get misty dear…be tough, like your mother, Katie. I want you to go home soon. Once your there, you'll feel the presence of the Vicar. You'll feel better. Basil and Katie promised to be with you on the way home." Azzurra's eyes searched the room. She looked back into her nieces eyes. "Honey, I know this is hard, but you must try. There must be a private room someplace. Ask the funeral director if he could find a room for you. Close your eyes and let the images come. I'll be in the room with the food if you see anything. I'll send your mother over to you after I speak with her about Sabino and Stella. She'll comfort you sweetheart. You can do this. You're a very powerful Witch. You just don't realize that yet."

Olivia nodded, smeared away a tear and walked out of the parlor. Azzurra hurried past her lady friends, towards Marta's group. She kissed Greg on the cheek and winked at Carlotta, gave Barbra, JoAnn hugs and thanked them and then took Tony by the hand and ushered him away.

"Tony, honey, listen I need you to do me a favor. There is a family meeting in the back where the food is. I will be joining my sister, cousins and brother in a moment. Would you be a dear and not let anyone in, except Olivia and Carlotta?"

"Absolutely, Mrs. A. Got it covered." Tony replied.

Azzurra patted his cheek and then looked around the plush parlor. Her cousins, Augusto and Gabriella were nowhere in sight. She walked past several people and nodded politely, Tony following.

She opened the door and entered the tiny room. After closing the door, she turned to face her family. "Why? Why did they show? Why did they attack after all these years? Why now" She looked to Basil. "And I want to know why a Vicar and the Higher Spirits are involved with a family of Witches?"

* * * *

Eva

*M*arta placed a hand into her purse. "I need a cigarette." She spoke to herself. "No…I don't. Yes I do…no I don't." Marta felt her arm twist and was face to face with her sister, Marie. "They're here."

"Who…who?" Marta's eyebrows raised into her forehead as her eyes scoured the room.

"Calm down, you sound like an owl…it's Eva and Celia. Go talk to them." Marie turned her sister to face the pair of ladies.

"Me, why me?" Marta took a few steps with Marie as they strained their heads to look past some of Gabriella's neighbors to where Eva and Celia stood, whispering to each other.

"Let's go together." Marie took Marta by the arm and ushered her toward their first cousins.

"For the love of God, you heard what Mom said…she thinks they're in league with Stella and Sabino. Should we get Ma?" Marta whispered.

"Shush let's first see what's up." Marie whispered back.

Marta stopped and stared at her sister. "You know Marie...you're a little too much with the shushing...Steven is getting annoyed and I certainly don't need to be shushed."

"Will you shush?" Marie demanded, eyes narrowing in on her target.

"Stop with the shushing!"

"Marta I'm sorry. I've been a nervous wreck, now shush...I mean be quiet...I mean oh just come on." She took Marta by the hand and after a few strides and plenty of protest from Marta, they stood before the ladies.

Eva smiled as the two approached; flinging her long straight blonde hair over her shoulder...it cascaded down her back. A black suit with a double breasted jacket revealed a curvaceous, voluptuous body and large breast with a tasteful amount of cleavage. She had rested her weight on one hip upon the greeting, letting black slacks billow away from her very attractive high heel shoes. They were black with a hint of dusty silver sparkles. She grasped a black clutch purse in her right hand and boasted a stunning pearl watch upon the left wrist. Her makeup had been applied with the perfect shade of coral lipstick, a tiny amount blush to the cheeks and mascara on very long eyelashes. Her startling green eyes seem to smile at the sight of her first cousins.

Celia on the other hand, looked a bit stressed and disheveled. She wore a red silk blouse that outlined her shape nicely; however it was bunched on one side and loose in the back. Supple breasts were straining against the material with a bit too much cleavage. Her black slacks hugged her legs and poured into animal print boots. A large black, unattractive purse was draped over her left shoulder. Celia's hair, now short and spiky, displayed tinges of black and grey, but seemed a bit matted. Her makeup did its best to hide the wrinkles and sallow cheeks. An over abundant amount of rouge accented high cheekbones. Celia's black eyes did not seem to smile as did Eva's; they were cold and icy as she spoke to her cousins.

"Greetings to you both — on such a sad occasion." Celia adjusted her large purse and tried to stand with the same elegance as Eva.

Eva smiled. "How have you been? Its' been ages...far too long and what a shame to see each other on such a...well such a sad occasion." She hugged Marie first and then Marta. Celia simply attempted a smile and gave a nod. Eva continued. "I apologize for not being available last night. I spent the night at my partners...left my charger at my place and well...I'm sorry. I should have been there." Eva took the stance again...leaning on one hip, with her foot outstretched in front of her.

"I love your shoes!" Marta said. "Things happen...what are gonna do. I know your Mom was very upset when she couldn't reach you...you know the details now don't you?" Marta shifted her position and looked toward Marie. She threw one leg out and balanced the rest of her weight on the other hip, lost balance and then stabilized.

Eva leaned forward and widened her eyes. With a very gentle soft touch...she placed a hand upon Marie's arm and spoke. "You mean the Witches War." She whispered. After a glance toward Celia she looked to Marie and then Marta. "I know...I'm terrified. I can't believe we are all Witches with...well with powers. I have no idea what my power is...Dad thinks I'll be Sachets and Elixirs but I hear that's pretty common. Celia is Wands...not very common for a female. Celia has the advantage. She knew she was Witch...never said a thing to me. Here I thought we told each other everything." She removed her hand then lightly scratched her neck as she looked to Celia.

Eva turned her focus on Marie and then grazed a finger tip down Marie's arm. A long finger nail dusted with silver, gently caressed Marie. "You look beautiful by the way and Marta you too, honey." She then glided a nail over Marta's cheek. "You have such beautiful skin, Marta."

Marta cleared her throat and replied with a thank you. "You, you, look, you both look very nice, keeping your figures up very well." Her forehead began to sweat. She looked uncomfortable.

Celia smiled and then turned to Eva. "We are shocked and very scared. Do either of you know anything?"

Marie responded. "Well you missed quite a scene...Sabino and Stella showed...along with Uncle Carlo, Aunt Debra and that nasty Aunt Dorthea from New Orleans. It was awful, but Mom handled it very well. They scurried off like tiny rats." Marie smiled and then looked to Marta.

"Yes...yes they did...we don't know anything else. I mean, Mom keeps things quiet...you know, she still thinks of us as kids."

Eva leaned in and took Marie's hand. She looked to Marta and then back to Marie. "Do you know any...any Magick?"

Marie and Marta said, no, and then explained how their mother said it would be best not to know very much at the moment. That they knew barley enough to help them in last night's attack. Marie then leaned in toward Eva and Celia and asked. "Where are Aunt Contessa and Uncle Nathan?"

Eva and Celia looked to each other and then Celia replied. "At home, Mom and Dad are home. Mom said she was determined to make things right with your mother and was working on protective enchantments for your family…decided that they would attend the funeral tomorrow and work though the night."

"Where's your husband, Alfonso? Felicia? Fredrick?" Marta asked.

Celia replied. "He's not feeling well. I told him he had better feel well by the morning or so help me, I'll kill him." She laughed and continued. "Felicia is on her way home and Fredrick has exams." She adjusted her purse and spoke again. "I mean Mom and Dad really need to make an impression on your mother…to show her that my family is really sorry for all the hard feelings over the years. What was the fight about? I didn't know about poor Olivia."

Eva shook her head. "Where are my parents?"

Marie looked around the room. "Aunt Gabriella and Uncle Nicolai were here…maybe they stepped out for a bit of fresh air."

Just then Marta glanced out the entrance of the parlor. Olivia had run past the entrance toward the tiny room with the food, Carlotta right behind her. With a very loud voice, Marta pointed to the window and informed everyone that she could have sworn she just saw them Uncle Nicolai and Aunt Gabriella standing outside.

Eva smiled and then leaned forward and gave Marie and Marta a hug. "We really should pay our respects first. If you see Mom and Dad, tell them I'm looking for them."

Celia gave a slight bow and she and Eva walked toward the casket. Eva stopped near the casket and whispered something in Celia's ear as they knelt in front of their Aunt Arianna.

Marta placed a hand over her forehead and then lowered it and gave a small scream. She covered her mouth as Marie shushed her sister.

"Stop shushing me!" Marta whispered deeply.

"What the hell is the matter with you?" Marie asked. "You scream over everything…my God…when I get home, I swear I'm eating an entire cake!"

Marta held out her shaking hand. "The ring turned blue. It's blue Marie and it's vibrating!"

"Blue…blue, what does that mean?" Her voice raised and then lowered. "Marta blue, what does blue mean?" Marie grabbed at the buttons on her blouse. "I have explosives…tell me where to throw them?"

"Calm down Marie, enough with the explosives!" Marta slapped her sister's hand away from her blouse.

Marie took Marta by the hand and turned it in front of her face. She hissed at her sister. "It's blue Marta...blue!"

"I know it's blue. I just told you, it's blue!" She hissed.

People began to stare.

They smiled and nodded at the people. Then Marie grabbed Marta's hand and ushered her into the hall. "What color...what color is it supposed to be...what color Marta?"

"Purple! It's supposed to be purple!"

Marie violently took Marta's hand and looked at it. "Purple...Marta its purple!" Her voice was high and excited.

Marta looked down as her hand was trusted back into the room by her sister. "Marie, my arm, you're going to break my arm!"

Both their heads peered into the room as Marta's hand pointed to the casket. Before their eyes the ring turned sapphire blue.

They covered their mouths and ducked back into the hallway. "Blue... what does blue mean Marta?"

"Blue means a mortal with evil intentions!" Marta hissed and looked back to the ring as the color morphed back into purple and stopped vibrating.

Their eyes were wide as they stared at each other. "The question is...are they both evil or is just one of them evil?" Marie asked.

A voice spoke between them. "Who's evil?"

Marta and Marie screamed. Marta clutched her heart as Marie ripped a button from her blouse, hand waving frantically in the air. Marie screamed "Stay back! Stay back I tell you!"

Everyone in the hallway stopped and stared at the sisters. Dino, Carlotta's son, stood before them, brown eyes wide and mouth open. "Are you two on drugs?"

Marie and Marta lunged forward and began hitting Dino. "OK...OK I'm sorry back off already." Dino laughed and then motioned dramatically to the hallway full of spectators. "My cousins are just freaked out...funeral homes...lack of sleep...perhaps drugs...it's OK just go back to your own business."

Steven stood with Walter, Olivia's husband, and shook his head at his wife. Marie's daughter, Katherine, covered her mouth as she stared at her mother. Marta and Marie took deep breaths and looked to each other, faces red.

Dino placed his arms around their shoulders and whispered. "Are you two all worked up about the Witches War?"

Marie's eyes widened, Marta's jaw dropped.

Dino smirked. "I know everything."

* * * *

Olivia's Power

Basil looked downward as he shifted his position; he pushed his trench coat out of the way and thrust his hand into his pants pockets. He then faced Azzurra and looked into her eyes. "Mum...as I said before...the Vicar wishes the family to be safe. As to why the Higher Spirits are involved, the Vicar says we should not be concerned...you must do as he asks without hesitation and follow your instinct. That's all I can say, Mum."

Augusto shuffled forward. "If you know why the Higher Spirits are involved my boy, you need to tell us."

Katie leaned down to the small table of desserts and smelled a cannoli. "If Basil promised the Vicar that he would keep his mouth shut, well then he needs to keep his mouth shut." She looked up to her sister. "Azzurra don't stare at him like that, you're talking about a promise to a Vicar."

"Basil if it will help the family..." Nicolai began.

Katie swished a hand toward Nicolai. "No one listens to me."

"If he promised the Vicar then he promised, Nicolai." Gabriella folded her arms.

Thom shook his head. "You should never make a promise to a Vicar and then break that promise...bad idea I tell you, bad idea."

Bella spoke. "Katie, Thom and Gabriella are right. There must be a good reason as to why he wishes us to not know...we must trust the Vicar."

Dante and Franco looked to each other, then to Katie and back to Azzurra. "Basil can't Azzurra." Franco's voice became soft. "He simple can't and you shouldn't ask him too."

Katie took an Angel Wing and sniffed. "Beee Azzurra, don't be mad now. He already told you that he can't, now enough with the eyes" Katie replaced the Angel Wing with a piece of chocolate cake.

"Arianna says that you should trust the Vicar and asks that you stop looking at Basil like that." Dante interpreted over the loud buzz of the glowing white orb.

"They are right Azzurra he can't. Let's not get hairy." Anna said.

Everyone took a moment to look at Anna.

Anna continued. "What? Upset or angry don't they say hairy anymore?"

"No." Everyone replied.

Anna swished a hand toward the group. "Anyway, Augusto, he should not go against the wishes of a Vicar." She picked up a piece of pumpkin cheesecake and sniffed, her and Katie exchange words as to how good everything smelled.

Azzurra sighed. "I'm sorry Basil...they're right...but if we guess — could you tell us yes or no?"

Anna looked up, Thom shook his head and Gabriella held several fingers to the side of her temple and massaged.

Katie narrowed her eyes. "Azzurra...I'm going to get mad."

"Well Katie he wouldn't be directly telling us..." Azzurra began.

Katie plopped the cake on the table. "...you know, dirty son of a bitch. Now Basil told you that the Vicar asked him to be quite...didn't he Azzurra? He made a promise to a Vicar! Did he, or did he not?" She placed her hands upon her hips and stared at her sister.

Kimberly spoke. "Katie's right Azzurra don't get upset honey."

Drago took a few steps toward Azzurra as she looked to the floor. Katie continued. "See I was trying to be nice and not swear but then you get me mad and now I'm swearing!" Dante placed a hand on her shoulder. "Leave me alone Dante, I'm mad."

Dante rolled his eyes. "Beee now she's mad."

"Don't be mad Katie we all need to focus." Drago said.

Bella spoke. "Drago's right, let's not fight with one another; we have enough to think about."

Mateo stepped away from the wall and spoke. "My wife is dead; my son has been traumatized and nearly torn apart by Hags. Marta, Nicco and Marie as well as every living person in this room, almost lost their life last night…and here we are arguing whether or not Basil should break a promise that he made to a Vicar. This Vicar has done nothing but assist this family and here we are — wondering if the Vicar has done us a good service by keeping the reason as to why the Higher Spirits are involved with a family of Witches." He stepped toward Azzurra. The orb buzzed softly near his shoulder. "The Vicar was there for us last night. He provided moonlight when needed. That moonlight, could have very well saved our lives. He left a feathered plume behind so we could use it to communicate to others and give warning. The Vicar is a man of his word and I see no reason why Basil should not be a man of his."

Azzurra's clasped her hands over her mouth and searched Mateo's eyes. She nodded and then turned to Basil. "I am sorry my Basil. Forgive me?"

Basil held open his arms, squeezed her tightly and kissed her upon the forehead. "I forgive you Mum."

Everyone agreed and began to apologize. A moment later, Augusto looked down to Father Bernardo. "Why have you been so quiet? Normally you're bursting to say something."

Anna smelled a cheesecake with strawberry swirls. "Yea Father, the cat got your tongue?"

Father Bernardo removed his glasses and placed a hand over his eyes, resting upon his elbow. After several minutes of silence Azzurra spoke. "Father, do you know something?"

He did not answer.

Murmurs of speculation began to surface. Franco asked if anyone knew if the Degeli's were the most powerful family of Witches in the USA. Dante informed everyone that as far as he knew, the Degeli's were the most powerful family of Witches in North America. Anna suggested that the family attacked to seek revenge and insisted that the man with the white long hair had something to do with the attack. Bella insisted that the Higher Spirits would never get involved unless there was a very good reason. That it was a not simple case of revenge. Drago looked to Kimberly and advised that the family may have too much power. Kimberly nodded and then looked to Thom.

Thom poured himself a glass of wine and took a slice of carrot cake. "I agree with dear Bella. It must be something that would cause major travesty to the community at large not just a family of Witches and Warlocks seeking revenge. Drago and Kimberly have the idea."

Father Bernardo donned his glasses and stood. He placed a hand upon Basil's shoulder and cleared his throat. The room became silent. "Drago and Kimberly are right. Power...with power, comes destruction. The balance of power would be thrown off. If we lose the Witches War the balance would swoon toward evil."

"What do you mean swoon toward evil?" Azzurra asked.

"Well, my guess would be that if the family should parish in this war... the remaining family would inherit the power from those who have died. These are evil people with ill intentions of theft, greed and murder. It would spread like wild fire if they were in control. Since Azzurra is the Matriarch and has the most amount of power...she must die." Father Bernardo turned to Mateo and the orb. "Arianna must have been considered to be the next most powerful Witch, as they sent an army of demons to attack her. Not to mention that Lamia and five Spirits joined in the attack. Arianna had to be killed." He turned to Augusto. "They did not expect Augusto to survive simply because of his age. Gabby has Sachet's and Elixirs which are considered common. She should have been an easy kill with the Wolves and a Dover Demon. However, they did not realize that she was double Sachets and Elixirs and underestimated the strength and power that she inherited as a sister to the Matriarch. They also underestimated the power of Nicolai." He turned to Azzurra. "Nicco, Marta and Marie should have perished. They did not count on the help of Basil and his comrades. You saved Nicco's life, those black demons should have killed him and Tracy and devoured the Spirits that assisted...losing your son, daughters, your sisters and brother would have weakened you. There is a special bond between a mother and her son...her only son. They really wanted Nicco dead. They also did not count on Contessa calling and giving warning of the attack. This was an astronomical betrayal. Without that one phone call, Nicco, Marta and Marie would have died." Father Bernardo looked to the floor, spoke a few words to the Lord and then raised his head. "I do not use Magick and they thought I would fall easily. I am a Warlock and therefore I have powers. Their mistake was in under estimating my faith." He bowed his head and spoke thanks to the Lord. "Carlotta was not attacked and we now understand why she was left alone. Lamia has a weak spot for someone she developed a friendship with that should have never happened. Carlotta will eventually need to be killed. Olivia lives within her own nightmares. She has been tormented for years by a Cull and Spirits. The attack upon her husband, Walter, only exacerbated her misery. They would have not been concerned at the moment of her disposal. They also do not realize Olivia's power — the power of clairvoyance. They do not know for sure who shall inherit the lineage of the Degeli family. They believe, as we do, that it is Olivia's son, Michael. Why kill him if they could get him on their side. In his death they have no idea who the next in line could be. It could be a tiny infant for all they know. I believe Michael is safe for the time being…safe from being killed that is. The reason for the mass attack was to gain power so the destruction of the human race could further ensue."

Thom put his glass of wine down and dabbed both sides of his mouth. "Dear Lord…everyone in the family is in danger."

Kimberly swore softly as Drago leaned against the wall for support.

Bella placed a hand over her mouth. Katie took a few steps toward the priest. "Father, is that what you are saying? That they must kill every Witch and Warlock in our family? That everyone that is in league with Azzurra's side of the family must die?"

Father nodded as the door burst open. Carlotta and Olivia entered the room and then shut the door. Olivia spoke in rushed tones…panic stricken. "Aunt Tessa? Uncle Nathan? I think they're dead! I saw blood. The house was in shambles…I think they're both dead!"

* * * *

A Faithful Spirit

The crashing sounds of the waves gave a sense of peaceful somberness as the birds' over-head chirped in alarm and flew from one tree to another. Several seagulls flew near the shoreline, boasting their familiar calls that glided over the cool mist that caressed the air.

Deveroy produced a basin of liquid and then a white cloth. After dipping the cloth within the warm water, he rung it out and then gently wiped the blood upon the side of her face. His hand shook slightly as he laid the cloth upon her forehead and spoke the healing incantation once again.

He then stirred the contents of the cauldron and placed his palms toward the base. Crimson jets of light sprang from his palms which produced flames that surrounded the cauldron. A moment later, bubbles violently exploded against the surface; forcing steam to billow over the lip and crawl over the sand.

"A snake...I need a snake...any kind will do...hurry!" Deveroy spoke quickly to his feathered friend. Her amber eyes widened and then she gave a short hoot. A second later, she spread her brown wings and took flight.

The glint of the suns glare removed the owl from view. He looked down to Contessa; a cough escaped her lips, followed by a moan.

Deveroy brushed his long blonde hair out of his face as the breeze grew in strength. "You are going to be fine." He looked up to the sky and then whispered. "Please God…let me do this right. Let me heal her." He looked around, eyes squinting and darting in every direction. A few moments passed when a dark form of the owl approached

"Oh man…you found one. That was quick." He looked to the squirming snake. "Thank you for your sacrifice my little friend." The owl dropped the snake into the cauldron. Once again it violently erupted, spewing steam over the edges.

"Ready….it's almost ready Contessa." Deveroy rinsed the cloth and then smeared the blood away from the streak of grey hair.

A loud hoot sounded. Deveroy looked up to see a glowing white sphere hovering by the owl. It gave off a small buzzing sound. He knew at once the Spirit's identity. "Nathan…I'm sorry there was nothing I could do. Something began healing her before I got there. I don't know what happened. When I got there she was lying on the floor…and you…you were already gone. There was so much blood…I tried to heal you…I couldn't…I couldn't do it…I'm sorry"

A louder buzz came from the orb as the owl shifted in annoyance and then took flight. Deveroy turned to the orb. "Thank you…yea, yea…she should be fine. I…I made an elixir and I…I…I…I cast several healing spells. I think I did them right. Her temperature is spiked but I…I think it's under control. It's going to take a while before she is on her feet."

A giant wave splashed against the shoreline as the orb floated near Contessa's face.

"I'll tell her…but I think you should wait, wait till she can speak and then you can say your good-byes." Deveroy shifted in the sand as the orb glowed brighter.

Pale blue eyes lingered upon the orb and then Deveroy spoke; his voice became deep and cracked. "You…you've been…you've treated me…you never swore at me or called me stupid. You always took time to explain things and asked me so many questions about my thoughts…what I felt." Deveroy looked away from the orb, down to Contessa and then back to the orb. "I mean…my Dad hated me…he was so frickin' mean." The orb buzzed and hovered near him.

Deveroy nodded, clenched his jaw tight and smeared a tear away with the back of his hand. "My real name is Daniel…Daniel Wozniakowski. Achar said I needed a new name. He gave me the name Deveroy and I'm not from Europe…I'm from Georgia… Atlanta Georgia, USA. I died of TB. Achar said I needed to lose the accent. It took a while but he helped me. I never knew my mother. I had a brother…my brother and I knew my father. I knew his lies, his temper…I knew things he'd done." He smeared tears from his cheeks. "Achar said I became weak when I spoke about my family…about my dad…my brother." He lowered his head. His long blonde hair obscured his face.

Contessa moaned and rolled her head toward the young man and then once again fell silent.

He looked up to the orb and wiped his face with the sleeve of his shirt. The orb buzzed loudly. He listened for several minutes and then responded. "I think I will. The Vicar said I can have another chance and maybe I won't mess things up this time."

The orb began to rise and glowed very bright. Deveroy raised a hand to his forehead to shield his eyes and squinted. "You're right. Daniel is a good name." He looked to the sand and then back up to the orb. "I understand. I'll tell her…I promise. Thank you…I love you too."

Deveroy's pale blue eyes followed the orb as it zoomed across the blue sea. "I shall miss you Nathan and I will always be her faithful Spirit."

* * * *

The Nutcracker

*M*arta narrowed her eyes. "Dino, how in the hell do you know what's going on?"

"It was Carlotta's nutcracker, Clancy. He spilled the beans because he was mad at Grandma Katie." Dino said. He began to explain his meeting with Clancy. "It was totally freaky man...I mean I stopped over the house early this morning to do a load of laundry and steal some food. Mom was in the shower. I scooped some pasta in a *Tupperware* bowl when I heard this voice. I looked down and there was a nutcracker looking up at me. I freaked...thinking I was having a flash back or something...you know... like when I was really messed up in the head. Anyway, he had a thick cockney accent and began to explain how rude Grandma Katie was. Whoa, Grandma Katie is dead! Freaky man, real freaky. He said I had the right to know what I was. Then, two birds flew over to us...those glass birds that sit on the coffee table...they frickin' came to life man. Anyway, they tried to tell the nutcracker to be quiet and then a guy on a horse jumped out from the grandfather clock and introduced himself as Captain Morgan. I thought that was a crackup by the way. He told the nutcracker that he would be flogged for revealing such information. Clancy stuck his tongue out at the guy and began telling me all sorts of things. After a while they were all blabbing about a Witches War and how Mom and everyone are Witches and I must be part Warlock or something. That Dad doesn't know any of this. I don't do drugs anymore and barely drink so I was like whoa…this is crazy, freaky crazy. I never hallucinated like this when I was tripping." Dino's eyes widened. "I thought I damaged my brain from the one bad year in my life, but they all swore up and down that it wasn't drugs — that they were real. They said Aunty Azzurra is the big wig eh, like the most powerful Witch?" He raised his hands on either side of his head and did air quotes. "The Matriarch."

"For the love of God, that nutcracker has gone nuts!" Marta placed a hand to her forehead.

Marie grabbed his shoulders and forced him to face her. "Dino, listen to us. You have to be quite about this. You need to talk with your mother about being a Warlock. We only just found out Wednesday night. Does Elizabeth know?"

"No way man, my sister can't handle spooky stuff at all. If she found out she was part Witch…she'd freak out." Dino held his arm in front of him and waved it like he was surfing. "Booooo."

Marta slapped his arm. "Dino you better be quiet! Come on Marie, let's find Carlotta."

Marie took Dino by the arm and walked him down the hallway to the tiny room with the food. "Excuse us Tony. We have to get through." Marie said letting go of Dino.

"Nobody gets through except Carlotta and Olivia and they're already in there. Mrs. A's orders, there is something really weird going on too." Tony folded his arms and stood in front of the door. Marie and Marta began hitting him. "All right alright, but I'm telling Mrs. A. it wasn't my fault."

The door opened and they ushered Dino into the room and closed the door. "He knows everything. Some nutcracker, by the name of Clancy, told him." Marie let go of his arm. "I love you Dino…but this is not a laughing matter. We were almost killed last night."

Gasps filled the room. Azzurra threw her hands in the air. Dino's eyes widened at the sight of the Spirits. "Oh man…I'm so freaking out! Who's the cool chick from the 60's?" Dino nodded to Anna.

Carlotta moved forward. "That's your Aunt Anna…Uncle Augusto's wife." Her voice lowered and eyes narrowed. "Now you listen to me because I will only tell you this once. You had better keep your mouth shut about this. No jokes and no snide remarks. Because if I hear that you mention this once…just once…my fist is going in your face! Do I make myself clear?"

Dino's eyes widened as he backed against the wall and placed his hands in front of his chest. "I'm sorry Ma. I swear I'll keep quiet. It's not my fault Clancy told me!"

"I know it's not your fault. Don't tell your sister. She's afraid of her own shadow." Carlotta looked to Azzurra. "I'm sorry Azzurra I will speak with Clancy. Dino, honey, I'm sorry you had to hear from one of my enchantments that we're Witches."

"I don't like that Clancy. He's rude!" Katie folded her arms.

"He thinks…" Dino began.

Azzurra interrupted. "…listen to us, never mind Clancy. We think Aunt Tessa and Uncle Nathan are dead."

Marie placed a hand over her mouth. Dino blinked his eyes and then widened them, doing a quick snap of his head.

"What do we do?" Marta asked.

"Nothing, we are waiting for Basil, Franco and Dante to come back. They went to your Aunt Tessa's house. Olivia saw that the aftermath of the attack." Azzurra said.

"Can't we wipe his memory? The less he knows the better?" Augusto said, gesturing to Dino. "It's too dangerous to have him know. They'll want to kill him."

Dino took a step back and bumped into the door. "No way, man, you are not messing around with my head." Carlotta crossed her arms. "Ma, sorry I won't have Magick wipe out my memory." His eyes widened.

"Leave him be Augusto!" Anna said. "Don't freak out honey. Nobody is going to do anything to you. Carlotta you need to take a pill."

"Anna he is my son…" Carlotta began.

"…I agree with Anna. The poor thing is horrified." Bella said as she approached Dino and gave him a hug. "You're a little too rough Carlotta."

Everyone began to argue.

"He's not your son Bella."

"I agree with Bella."

"If I say I'm going knock his teeth in that's my business."

"I swear I won't say a word."

"Enough!" Father Bernardo stood and slammed a hand down on the table. "I have had it with all the arguing! Are we a family united or not?" He turned to Carlotta. "If you lay one hand on that young man…I'm going to knock *your* teeth in!" He faced Bella, raising his voice. "Bella and Anna mind your own business! And Katie, will you leave the cake alone!" Father Bernardo looked to Azzurra. "Azzurra you need to call some order to this family! I am tired of the bickering!"

Azzurra spoke with a firm voice. "Father is right. Carlotta, honey, it's not his fault that the nutcracker told him everything. Dino don't worry. No one is going to cast a spell to remove your memory and no one is going to kill you." She looked to Augusto. "And if anybody tries to wipe his memory… they'll have me to answer to."

Marta turned and spoke to Aunt Gabriella and Uncle Nicolai. "Eva and Celia are here. They're looking for you. Celia said that Aunt Tessa and Uncle Nathan were at home making protective enchantments for our family and Alfonzo is ill. Fred has exams and Felicia is out of town or something."

Marie interjected. "They acted very strange and Marta's ring turned blue — mortal with bad intentions!"

Azzurra nodded. "Now we have our answer. Celia and Eva are up to no good." She told the Spirits to hide and then opened the door. She pinched Dino's cheek and told him that they would talk to him later. Dino squeezed past his mother and left. Azzurra closed the door.

Basil appeared. The other Spirits revealed themselves.

"What is it Basil? Are they alright?" Azzurra asked.

"Nathan is dead. Franco and Dante stood behind to clean things up. They'll make it look like a heart attack. We couldn't find Contessa. When we tried a summoning charm — it didn't work. Deveroy is missing as well. Stephan said he hasn't seen him in hours. I suspect he is with Contessa he's hiding her at the moment. We think she is still alive."

Bella shook her head and covered her mouth. Thom spoke. "Dear Lord… when will this end?"

Father Bernardo stepped forward. "When you are all dead and they have assumed your powers."

"What about our kids?" Bella asked. "Are they safe?"

"I am not sure. You both married into a family of Witches and are first cousins to Azzurra. Eventually, you're kids will have to be killed. However, since they know nothing of their powers…we have time." Father Bernardo nodded. "Dino is no longer safe." He turned to Carlotta and then to Drago and Kimberly. "Drago and Kimberly, you need to tell your children. They are far too angry with you. Grandchildren or not, they will need to know how to protect themselves."

Kimberly and Drago nodded.

"I told you we should cast a spell…"Augusto began.

"…no one will cast a spell on that young man!" Father interrupted. "Carlotta, you had better speak with that nutcracker of yours and the rest of your enchantments. Tell them if they open their mouths again you'll disenchant them. I also feel you should send some of your enchantments to Dino's apartment…to help protect him. I don't think he's in immediate danger as he is Carlotta's son. However, I would feel better if all the young ones have protective amulets and enchantments."

"Doesn't that entail using Magick, Father? I thought you didn't want us to use Magick?" Augusto grunted.

"Hush, Augusto." Azzurra cut in. "Gabriella, Nicolai…go and see Eva… pretend stupid. But watch your back if you should be alone with her. My guess is that you and Nicolai are next."

Gabriella and Nicolai nodded and left the room.

"Marta and Marie…get out there. Make sure you keep an eye on Eva and Celia from afar. Let me know if anyone else shows. Stay close to Dino." Azzurra turned to Olivia as Marta and Marie left the small room. "Olivia honey, go to Walter. I think its best that he knows everything. The two of you should leave. Basil and Katie will follow you home."

Olivia nodded and left the room. Basil vanished.

Azzurra continued. "Anna, can you please keep Arianna out of sight. But stay in the parlor, close to Dino and the girls." Anna nodded and disappeared. A moment later the orb buzzed.

"She knows, Arianna. Mateo will look after Scott and Gracie. Maybe we should have one of Basil's friends look after Gracie and the kids?" Katie said.

Everyone agreed. The orb buzzed, glowed brightly and vanished.

Katie leaned down and kissed Azzurra on the cheek. "You handled that very well Azzurra…I'm proud." Azzurra smiled and said thank you.

Katie gave one last look to the desserts. "God only knows what Stephan has been teaching my Blackie." She disappeared.

Azzurra looked to Father Bernardo, Drago, Kimberly, Mateo, Augusto, Thom and Bella. "Well it looks as though we have an idea of what the Vicar told my Basil. They want us dead to gain our power. Now don't panic. We are strong Witches and Warlocks and we have Basil and Katie and most of all...the Vicar. Now, come on, we have to go out there and pretend dumb to everything in front of Eva and Celia. Let's give hugs and lots of smiles." Azzurra opened the door and took a deep breath as the eight of them left the room.

* * * *

A Good Night's Rest

Azzurra sat upon the cushioned chair in her living room. After taking a sip of tea she looked to the fountain of the Blessed Mary. "Franco, why didn't you tell me you enchanted our fountain?"

"I forgot, honey. The water will flow once the danger is over. I enchanted it to stop in case of a pending catastrophe that involved the Spirit world or Witches." Franco sat in solid form upon the sofa.

Azzurra looked to her husband. "So what did you think about Eva and Celia?"

"They are both in league with Stella and Sabino. Eva has known she's a Witch for a long time and I didn't believe a word that came out of her mouth."

"My feelings too, they are both up to something." She yawned and then spoke. "Oh Franco, I just remembered...what are those spheres for... the ones that look like they're in an egg carton on the hutch. Merek Kroll noticed them and seemed very interested in them. Maybe he thinks they can help protect us."

"Oh yea, Dante and I purchased those years ago when we were in Italy. I remember we stopped at a shop and you said they were too expensive to buy for something that you didn't know what they did. Anyway, I meant to ask Merek Kroll about them and forgot. He'll find out though. Merek can find out anything." Franco shifted, un-buttoned his suite jacked and then straightened his tie. "You didn't have to bury me a suit you know."

"Nobody likes what I buried them in! From now on...everyone gets buried in their underwear!" Azzurra stood, picked up the tea cup and saucer that Katie bequeathed her and headed toward the kitchen.

"I'm sorry honey." Franco followed. "How are you? Really, how are you?" He approached his wife and leaned against the counter.

Azzurra placed the tea cup and saucer into the sink and turned to face him. "I think I'm OK. Then sometimes I feel empty inside...like nothing is left. I feel weak and lonely. The night time brings on too many memories. I put on the purple night gown that you gave me last Christmas. I step into the slippers that you gave me and then sit on the edge of the bed and cry. I think of the years and all that has happened and wonder how much longer before it will be all over? How much more do I need to endure before the Lord takes me and releases me from this? I see our wedding picture... I look at photos of Katie and Mom & Dad, and I think to myself...where has the time gone? Why has so many people been removed from my life?" She pulled a tissue out from the sleeve of her black pant suit and dabbed at the corner of her eyes. "I feel as though sometimes it has been somebody else's life. When I look back at all the things that have happened: when did the kids get so big...when did Marie have a baby...when did Katie pass away? I think of Aunt Francine, Beatrice and Gilbert...Mom and Dad...the first Witches War...the first time I performed Magick...our wedding day... Dante's funeral, your funeral and now, I have to say goodbye to yet another sister." Tears flowed down her cheeks freely. "Arianna and I talked. I would call her at least every other day...until you passed away. I was silly to be petty about her calling me. I would call her to see if she blew anything up in the kitchen. Just last week she threw a plant through the window." She dabbed her eyes as Franco approached her and placed a hand under her chin and lifted her head to look into her eyes.

"Azzurra, honey...you have to be strong..." He began.

"...I don't want to be strong!" Azzurra brushed his hand away and stormed toward the kitchen table. "I want to cry! I want to throw something across the room! I want to lie down and stop breathing. I want to take my fist and sock Stella in that ugly face of hers! I want to see Mom and Dad. I want to hold Angelo, I want Basil to stay here and Katie and Arianna and you!" She slammed a hand on the table. "I want this war to be over! I want to make sure the kids are safe! I want Nicco to marry Tracy." She hit a fist upon the table. "I want to laugh with my lady friends over a nice game of pinochle.

I want to cast a damn spell that erases my memory! I want Marta to fall in love with Tom Buchman and I want a new pair of shoes!" She hit the back of a chair and then hit it again. It toppled over to the floor. Franco rushed to her side, took her into his arms and brought her tight to his chest. Azzurra sobbed and began hitting him "Why? Why did you leave me Franco? Why!" After several minutes she subsided and crumpled to the floor, still within his arms.

Franco rocked her back and forth for several long minutes and then she looked up into his eyes. "I'm sorry Franco."

"Sorry for what, feeling?" He brushed a tiny piece of silver hair away from her forehead. "God took me because he knew you could handle it better than I. I can't think about it…I can't Azzurra. The thought of it makes me so…I simple can't. I talk with Katie. It's good to see Dante again and I'll have Basil to help get me through. You'll have Marta, Nicco and Marie… Gabriella and well, even Augusto." He smiled. "You have Mary, Eleanor and Carol. You've been through thick and thin with them. They will be there for you. Call Bella and Thom whenever you are down. They both lost their spouses in the first battle. They know what it feels like, Carol's husbands gone…talk with her."

Azzurra nodded and dabbed at her eyes. Franco turned to the sink and spoke to the soap dispenser. "Help calm her and ready her for sleep." The soap dispenser began to ooze a purple bubble from its spout and then another. The bubbles floated over and touched Azzurra. Streams of whites, yellows and violets oozed throughout her body.

"You have a big day tomorrow. You need a good night's rest." He helped Azzurra to her feet and waved a hand over her. The black pant suit vanished, replaced by a purple nightgown and satin slippers. "Come…let's get you to bed. Basil and Katie are watching over Marta and Nicco. Dante is with Marie. Carlotta sent Clancy and the birds to Dino's and the Vicar is watching over Olivia and her family." They entered the hallway. "How are you feeling?"

"Sleepy…the bubbles took away my back pain and I feel clam and very tired." After a few seconds she spoke again. "I don't mean to be so negative Franco. You're right, I'll be strong. Things happen, that's life, and when life is over, I won't have to be so strong. However, until then I will muddle through life's triumphs and tragedies" Azzurra stopped at the entrance of her bedroom and kissed Franco on the cheek. "I miss you Franco."

Franco's eyes watered. "I'll lie with you until you fall asleep, then I'll check on Gracie and the kids. Stephan promised to look after them but I thought I'd go over and check. I'll be home shortly."

He pulled the covers back and smiled at the Cherubs who greeted them with excited tiny voices. "Play something soft for her." He whispered.

The pair of cherubs took up their miniature instruments and perched themselves upon the clock. Franco waved a hand as the lights went out. He pulled the covers up to his wife's neck as the soft music began to play. After kissing Azzurra on the forehead he lay on top of the covers and placed an arm around her. "Sleep well my love."

* * * *

The Plan

The Dining Room appeared in a soft glow of twinkling light, specks of white flicked and danced across the glass of the china cabinet. In the early morning hours, the crickets chirped.

A circular mirror with an antique 18th Century frame reflected the room's contents. The Spirit, Anna, flickered within the shadows. She adjusted her headband, while the silhouette of Dante sat beside her and shimmered. Franco's Spirit sat opposite Dante and Ritsuko's shiny black mane glistened as she stood nearby.

Basil's Spirit sat at the head of the dining room table as the grandfather clock struck two times. He looked to Katie and then nodded once. She let Blackie to the floor and stood to address the room.

Stephan's Spirit released a large sigh, opposite Basil. He glanced up to Katie and hastily placed a nail file into the blood red feathers of the Imperial Helmet. A loud clang, metal against metal, caused Katie to clear her throat. Stephan covered his mouth and then asked for forgiveness, insisting that the armor of a Roman Soldier was not very comfortable. Katie's eyes narrowed.

Michale's Spirit chuckled and then glanced to his right, at Pip. He then nodded once downward toward Stephan.

Violetta shook her head toward Pip and Michale and then gave a quick nod toward Katie. Her reflection sank into view, and then rose to the surface upon the flickering of the candles. Pip leaned against the service buffet, crossed his arms, and focused toward Katie.

Katie spoke. "Basil and I have talked, and we feel that certain measures should be taken at today's service for Arianna." Katie paused and then continued. "We also feel that Azzurra will not agree with the measures we are about to take. Now, I know she is the head of this family, however, if her instructions should conflict with Basil's or mine…you are to follow our instructions."

Anna narrowed her eyes. "Katie, Azzurra is the head of the family and has every right to make deci…"

Basil interrupted. "…Miss Anna, please hear us out. Mum doesn't feel that there is any such danger at the cemetery. She insists that within the history of the Degeli family, that there has never been an attack on the day of a funeral, that the opposing sides will respect the dead."

Anna interrupted. "But she's right. It is common knowledge that the Spirit world and Witches will respect the dead during burial. Even Sabino said as much."

Katie crossed her arms. "Anna, please let him speak." She looked to Basil.

"Now listen here everyone, Miss Katie is right. We must have a plan to protect them during the ceremony." Basil placed his hands on the table and leaned forward. "I don't believe that the family will carry on with old customs such as the respect during someone's death ceremony. I believe that when Sabino said to his family that they should give respect to the dead and then left the parlor, well that it was nothing but a ruse."

"My stars, I've never heard of a Witches War when someone was attacked at the actual burial. No respect, simply no respect." Stephan clanged again and sat upright.

"That's what I'm trying to say my friend. I think Azzurra feels as you and Anna do. That nobody would dare disgrace a burial service. But Katie and I feel that this is an exception. The entire family will be there. Mum has insisted that everyone be allowed to attend today's funeral, that in broad daylight, nothing would happen." He looked to Katie and then proceeded. "Gracie and the kids will be there. They are very young and know nothing about being Witches, and Gracie is a mortal woman. Marie will have her children there. Mum's pinochle lady friends…Miss Gabriella's neighbors and Marta's co-workers, Nicco's friends. We must take every precaution that they are not harmed. It's a good thing that Thom and Bella insisted that their children not attend the services. I also feel with so many underage children there, that if they should attack, the Vicar may intervene." Basil's Spirit dissolved into darkness and then quickly reappeared. A flame danced within his green eyes.

Katie nodded. "So because there are plenty of children attending and mortal spouses...friends and co-workers...Basil and I have come up with a plan." Blackie barked. "Hush Blackie, Muma's talking." Katie continued. "We are going directly to the church and then to the Cemetery. I want everyone to spread out. Basil and I feel that if Marta, Nicco and Marie should sit on one side, the older generation should position themselves on the other. This way we can make sure to surround friends and co-workers and the kids. They will place the more powerful Spirits and Witches near the older generation. I don't want to panic Marie or Marta so let's not tell them anything. They will react faster and more effectively if taken by surprise."

"That's horrible." Violetta spoke. "Katie we should tell them something."

"You were not at the parlor. Those two were afraid of their own shadows, ready to blow the damn place up if someone moved too quickly. Trust us Violetta." Katie swished a hand.

Basil replied. "Maybe Violetta has a point. Why don't we suggest to them to be on the lookout...just in case."

Everyone agreed as did Katie. "Grand. Now, so far, we've only seen Carlo, Debra, Dorthea, Stella and Sabino. I hardly think that they'll be a match for us but nonetheless we want to be prepared. They may use demons once again." Basil continued.

Katie spoke. "Pip and Michale, we want you two be at the back of the church, follow the Limo's and then flank the rear of the gravesite." They nodded in acknowledgement.

Basil continued. "Violetta we want you at the center of the congregation in the church and at the cemetery. Stay close to the mortals, which will be seated toward the center of the gravesite." Violetta nodded. "Anna and Dante, you will take up the front of the gravesite and church. Dante, you take stage right, Anna, stage left."

Katie added. "Franco will be near my sisters and brother, toward the front." Katie nodded to Franco, who nodded back.

Dante and Anna exchanged looks and shrugged their shoulders. "Um... stage right?" Anna asked. Dante screwed up his face in attempt to understand the stage right and left.

Basil smiled and chuckled. "Anna you're with us by the older generation, Dante take the other side."

Anna and Dante nodded.

Katie continued. "Ritsuko and I shall be up front, near the casket with Father Bernardo and the pallbearers."

Ritsuko acknowledged with a "Hi" sound. Katie narrowed her eyes toward her and meekly said hello. Ritsuko pursed her lips thin and then spoke. "I meant that I understand my position."

"Well, why didn't you say that honey? My stars, I thought you were saying hello too." Stephan shrugged his shoulders toward Katie and clanged loudly.

Basil winked at Ritsuko and then looked to Katie. "Who will be the pallbearers Miss Katie?"

Katie counted off on her fingers as she said each name. "Now let's see… there's Nicco, Dino, Nicolai, who almost tore my head off when I suggested he was too old to be a pallbearer. Then there is Gracie's son, Ryan… he insisted that he help carry his Grandmother. I think 16 is too young but what are you gonna do? He's not my son. Besides, nobody listens to me anyway." She shrugged her shoulders and continued. "And then there's Michael and David, my Grandson's. That makes six."

Basil addressed the room. "Good, now, I think we should go over some spells and defensive maneuvers."

Franco stood. "I promised Azzurra that I would lie with her while she slept. She was really upset earlier."

Stephan sung out. "Who cares? I told everyone I'd be watching over Gracie and the kids."

"Stephan!" Katie crossed her arms.

"Oh don't get so upset honey, my camel is there." He laughed loudly and then straightened his helmet when it tipped to one side. "And about a dozen really powerful enchantments!"

Katie rolled her eyes and then nodded as Ritsuko began to speak and then remained silent.

Basil once again winked at Ritsuko and then laughed with Stephan. "Mum will be fine, Franco. She won't know the difference. The Cherubs will keep her sleeping till the morning. We need you to be prepared, we do."

Franco nodded and sat. Basil spoke once again. "We should make sure that the children have protective charms around them. They need not know what they are...simply tokens left to them by Miss Arianna. So we'll have those to do as well."

Everyone nodded and agreed.

Stephan spoke. "Can I bring my camel?"

Pip and Michale laughed while Katie placed her hands upon her hips. Violetta shushed the young men as Ritsuko closed her eyes purposely and then reopened them. Basil smiled and answered. "I think that would be a grand idea Stephan. Now, as there may be danger...do you think that your camel should be there? He may not be safe my friend." Basil arched an eyebrow, his green eyes flickering within the candlelight's reflections.

"My stars I didn't think of the danger! Maybe I shouldn't be there either. He does love Egypt this time of year."

"Perhaps Egypt would be a better place. I would not forgive myself if I placed you or your camel in harm's way." Basil gave the slightest of winks to Katie. Dante and Franco narrowed their eyes as Anna rolled hers.

Stephan clanked again and then leaned forward. Blackie ran under the table and jumped upon Stephan's lap. He gave a soft cry and a sharp yelp.

"Well for heaven's sakes...aren't you a dramatic little thing? Are you going to be there Blackie?" Blackie barked. After taking a deep breath and adjusting his helmet once again, Stephan spoke. "Well, if Blackie is that brave...all right I've decided... one for all and all for one! Count me in sisters! I'll stand guard toward the middle with Violetta. Is that OK with you, pumpkin?"

Violetta smiled and nodded and then slapped Michale and Pip, who were laughing.

Basil added. "If things get too rough Stephan, I want you to leave. This is not your battle."

"Nonsense, nothing can frighten me or my camel!" He clanked loudly as he stood. "My stars...I just don't think this outfit's going to make the number."

Ritsuko closed her eyes for a brief moment and then opened them. "I think we need to focus."

"Grand, Stephan...it's good to have you with us." Basil winked to Ritsuko once again. "Now, my comrades, let's go over some spells, shall we."

* * * *

Eva's Move

Gabriella fastened the silver necklace and admired it for a moment in the mirror. Nicolai winked at his wife as he pulled the last loop of his tie into a half Windsor. They turned at the sound of a grunt. Rex lay just outside the bathroom door and began to wag his tail when they looked to him.

"Do you think it's going to rain? Maybe we should bring an umbrella." Nicolai asked.

Gabriella smiled. "No matter…I made a water repellant elixir and misted it on my hair. I'll spritz some on my clothes. I'll mist you too." She sprayed some Elixir toward her husband and laughed.

"Don't get too used to this. I bet we'll be told to not do Magick when this mess is over." Nicolai stepped over the black Labrador and left the bathroom.

Rex bolted up and began to growl…his fur standing on end. Nicolai turned and smiled at his wife. "Are you ready?"

"Ready my love." Gabriella ushered Rex to move down the hall. He sprung up on all fours and ran down the steps to the front door. He snarled and barked.

Gabriella took her husband's hand as they descended the stairs together. "Rex, come." Nicolai took him by his collar and escorted him to the basement. Rex cried and barked toward the front door. "This is for your own good my friend." He closed the door leaving Rex barking and scratching. A moment later a deep guttural howl escaped from the basement.

After a moment of looking into his wife's eyes, Nicolai smiled and spoke. "You've been the best thing that has ever happened to me. I love you."

"Oh don't be so dramatic and open the door." Gabriella swished a hand toward her husband. "Me too, sweetheart."

When Nicolai opened the door, Eva stepped through the threshold. "Hi sweetheart, don't know what's wrong with Rex…hasn't been the same since the attack the other night. Your father had to put him in the basement." Gabriella hugged her daughter hello.

"I was wondering why he was barking like that — hi Mom, hi Dad." Eva hugged her parent's. "I thought I'd stop by and we could drive together to the church." She noticed her mother's necklace. "I've never seen that necklace Ma. Where did you get it? It's beautiful."

"I just bought it last month. Thank you dear." She eyed her daughter and swished a hand through the air. "You know with the things the way they are, you're father and I have prepared for an attack. Did I tell you that I was *double* Sachet's and Elixirs? I can produce extremely powerful spells. Why, I remember actually sending this one Spirit…oh, it must have been in the first Witches War. Anyway, I sent it into the middle of the Atlantic Ocean in a sealed container that he could never escape from…probably still there." Gabriella laughed. "Oh I should have mentioned, your father and I are loaded with Sachet's and Elixirs, ready to destroy anything, mortal or other in a single heart beat, so don't stand too close dear." Gabriella smiled at Eva who took several steps back. "You're father is Sachet and Elixirs too and Enchanted Objects. I could never enchant anything. Your father most certainly can. I remember one enchantment he used. It caused this evil woman to turn inside out! Oh my, it was a mess. She just laid there and squirmed for a while…until she died, of course. Oh dear, I shouldn't have said that. You look sallow. Are you feeling well?"

Rex continued to bark through the basement door.

Eva closed the door behind her and smiled weakly. "No, no, I'm fine. Do we have time for a cup of coffee?" She walked past her parents and into the kitchen. "He won't stop barking and snarling. He acts as though he doesn't know me."

"That's because he senses danger. Something evil just entered our home." Nicolai smiled.

"What? What do you mean?" Eva placed a hand to the inside of her purse.

"Rex knows too, that's why he's fussing. Oh, see here...look at these, look closely honey." Gabriella waved her daughter toward Nicolai and pointed to a button on his black jacket that seemed to move with a picture on the inside. "Look honey. You're father enchanted his buttons to reveal the source of evil. Isn't that wonderful? Have a look, dear."

Eva began breathing heavy as she leaned into her father's jacket. Eva looked into the button only to see her reflection waving at her. She screamed and leapt back.

"Good night, sweetheart." Gabriella pulled a vial from her suit jacket and tossed it at her daughter. Eva pulled a sachet from her purse, but her mother's effect was immediate. As soon as the vial's contents broke, the mist floated rapidly around Eva. She collapsed to the floor. Nicolai pulled a sachet from his pocket as two Spirits appeared in the living room. Gabriella handed him a vial and toasted. "To us honey." They both drank as no less than twelve Hags appeared through the walls. The Hags and Spirits flew toward them and then stopped and looked around.

"Where did they go?" Medeia asked.

"I don't know." Dormava replied. "They can't have vanished to another place? I don't think it's possible."

The Hags began to howl in frustration and then turned to the basement door. "Let's eat the dog." It squawked.

A second later, the Hag blew up...then another Hag and another. Dormava was blasted off her feet and thrown into the wall. Medeia screamed as she was lifted up and spun violently into a circle and tossed from their home. Four more Hags swelled and then burst into a ball of flames only to evaporate swiftly. Other Hags began to lash blindly through the air with their sharp nails. Two more Hags expanded and then blew up. More Hags continued to enter the home. Each Hag exploded a moment after their entrance.

"Where are you? Show yourselves! Fight with honor!" Dormava demanded. Flames burst all around her. She began to scream and flail. The Spirit of Medeia zoomed through the wall, took Dormava from the room, and vanished through the opposite wall.

More Hags appeared as Rex cried from the basement, scratching at the door. Forty minutes later the remainder of the Hags fled. Nicolai appeared.

"Are they gone?" A woman's voice asked.

Nicolai looked down to his buttons. "Yes, they're gone." He hurried to the basement door and flung it open. "I'm going to put him outside. I don't want him near her when she wakes. How long will she be out?"

Gabriella began to appear...first her eyes and then hair. "About another hour — good idea...put him outside."

Nicolai ushered Rex to the door as he growled at the body lying upon the floor. "This is for your own good." Rex turned around and stared at them through the door wall.

Nicolai shut the blinds as the rest of Gabriella appeared. "Good job dear."

"Same to you, my love." Nicolai hugged his wife. "I can't say I wasn't a bit nervous."

"I know my daughter, what can I say." Gabriella looked into her purse. "I just wish we had time to make more concealing elixirs. I'm down to only one explosive and about a dozen healing Sachets and Elixirs...you?"

"I have about a dozen or so. Pockets are full" He replied.

"Good lets go...Azzurra will be worried sick." She shook her head looking down at her daughters crumpled body. "What did we do to deserve this?"

"It's the power of greed." Nicolai said. "The power of greed."

* * * *

The Eulogy

"We say goodbye to Arianna's earthy presence. However, we do not say goodbye to Arianna, for she lives on in the kingdom of heaven." Father Bernardo stood upon the altar of his church, addressing the congregation." For we know that we avoid death by accepting the Lord Jesus Christ as our savior. It is not easy to face death for those who are left behind. Death is for some, a mystery. But for those who believe, it is the beginning of eternal life." Father looked to Sabino and Stella Degeli. "For some, death will occur after death. They will not enter the kingdom of God because they are not worthy of his presence and do not ask for forgiveness. They will enter the depths of hell." His gaze followed to Debra, Dorthea and Carlo. "They will dwell in the presence of Satan and will rot there for all time."

The congregation mumbled and turned to look toward those that Father Bernardo looked upon. The priest continued.

"We do not say goodbye to Arianna's Soul today. For if we believe in the Holy Spirit that dwells within us...the Holy Spirit will exist for all time. We shall meet Arianna once again in the kingdom of Heaven. For some,

461

however, the Holy Spirit does not exist. Shut out, is the Holy Spirit, by those who seek greed, evil and power."

Father Bernardo looked to the back of the room toward another group of people. Azzurra turned around to follow his stare. Angelica's children sat in the back pew. She whispered to Bella who turned around. Theodor Dubinsky, husband of Angelica, daughter of Stella and Sabino who had been killed in the last Witches war, sat with some of his children: Larry Dubinsky and Susan Dubinsky-Flattery. Douglas, Theodor's other son, and an outcast from the family, sat with Carlotta and her X-husband, Gregory.

"Sins are forgiven for those who ask and believe in the Lord Jesus Christ as our savior. We may be tempted to do a deed that we took a vow against. This vow was meant to cast aside sin. However, if the life of a loved-one is threatened...we do what we must and always ask for forgiveness. For the Lord forgives all." He paused, looked over his glasses to his parents and continued. "Those who speak with a sincere heart will be forgiven. The Lord Jesus Christ will know if the heart is not sincere. For those with foul blackness in the depths their hearts will be seen for what they are...servants of Satan." More mumbling went on from the congregation. Father Bernardo looked once again to Azzurra and then to the opposite side of the church, toward the rear. Azzurra followed his gaze. Carlo and Debra's son...Demetrio Degeli and his wife Gina sat near her lady pinochle friends. Dorthea's children, Bradford Stewart and his wife Mary sat with his sister, Denise and her husband Richard Dombrowski. Their father, Nicholas, had been killed in the first Witches War. Their sibling, Robert Stewart and his wife Elyse remained absent.

"Arianna's violent death was the end of the pain that this world may bring upon us in our mortal forms. God takes away all pain and suffering in the death of the mortal body. Arianna felt nothing in those last moments but love and a gentle calling home. It will be difficult for she is no longer among us. The phone calls will stop. The long conversations about each other's lives will no longer exist. But in memory, she will live on forever, and in the kingdom of God. We will miss her voice, her smile, the way her face would turn beat red, hands clasped over her mouth when she laughed. To embrace what she has meant to us will be our support. Do not forget to call those who were nearest to her...to check on their well being. For in this time of mourning, we pull together and support each other and fight the onslaught of evil." More mummers erupted as people turned to the rear of the congregation. Azzurra looked over her shoulder to Kimberly and Drago and smiled at them. All of their children were seated with them; John, Chase and James Degeli. Their wives were not present. "Those who loved her must cherish what she meant to us. Arianna had a tender soul that had been reflected in her earthly bound body. She had been one of the kindest and sweetest persons that I have ever had the privilege to know. Arianna would laugh and shyly admit guilt when someone poked fun of her cooking or baking. For we all know that wasn't one of her talents. But how she reacted when someone made a fuss over cookies made with salt, or burnt pasta sauce, or a plant thrown through a window...the way she handled criticism, was her gift. Arianna smiled with humility, love for those around her and kindness. We should not hold on to petty thoughts of offending her. For in the kingdom of heaven, she is happy and will bake the world's greatest cookies." Augusto dabbed his eyes with a hanky. Azzurra patted his aged hand as she dabbed her own eyes.

"It is God, who watches over us. God, who will prevail against evil and those who attempt to inflict Satan's work upon innocent souls. Rejoice in her passing, and do not feel sorrow for Arianna. It is those left behind, that suffer." He looked to Mateo, Scott and Gracie and then eyed each of their children: Ryan, Danielle and Amanda. A moment later he looked once again to the congregation.

"Arianna is someone who will be missed by her family and friends. It is in death, that we rejoice that she is with our Lord Jesus Christ once again, in the kingdom, of God. It is with a selfish heart that we yearn for her presence that will never again be known upon this earth. It is with love, and peace, that Arianna has been called home. Amen."

* * * *

The Limo

Olivia rushed towards the second limo and approached Azzurra. "Aunty Azzurra, I saw something...but I don't know what it means. There were trees, winds and rain. I saw a bubble or something...and heard echoes... it was weird."

"Don't worry Olivia...today is a safe day. But try and focus on what you saw...concentrate on the place in which this happened...try to understand the echoes."

Olivia nodded and opened the door of the limo and helped her aunt into the car. After closing the door Azzurra turned to face Father Bernardo and Augusto. "Father, that was a beautiful eulogy...now where the hell is Gabriella and Nicolai? Thank goodness Walter stepped in for Nicolai and helped with the casket."

Augusto shook his head and looked to Father Bernardo. "I really enjoyed the constant reference to evil and Satan." He chuckled. "Never heard a eulogy quite like that."

Father Bernardo widened his eyes and looked over the top of his glasses. "Hope they got the message." He turned to Azzurra. "I am sure they are fine. They were ready for an attack. And if I know those two, they produced an arsenal of defensive enchantments and sachets. I wouldn't worry Azzurra."

Azzurra slid next to Father Bernardo and took his hand. "Well I am worried. Say a prayer Father." Father nodded and closed his eyes and said a quick prayer for Gabriella and Nicolai. She leaned toward the driver. "Pip, is that you sweetheart?"

Pip adjusted the mirror. "Good old Pip at your service, Mum."

Azzurra sighed. "Good, thank you honey...Basil?"

Basil appeared next to Azzurra near the window. "Yes Mum."

"Basil, I need you to go to Gabriella and Nicolai's, check to see if they are safe."

"Did you not notice who attended the service Mum? I don't have a good feeling about today." Basil looked out the window. He saw Carlotta speaking with Olivia and Walter. A few of the pallbearers hurried past the limo toward their own vehicles.

Azzurra looked to Basil and after a moment she tapped him on the shoulder. "Basil, honey, I need you to go and check on my sister and her husband, please."

Katie appeared on Father Bernardo's other side. "Beee I'm sure their fine Azzurra. I popped in on them early this morning. Those two did some very nice spells."

Azzurra's voice rose. "Katie I don't care. I want someone to go and check on them. Basil? What is the matter with you?"

"There is nothing the matter with me, Mum." Basil continued to stare out the window.

Azzurra narrowed her eyes. Franco and Dante appeared on both sides of Augusto. Franco spoke. "Mateo, Amanda and Danielle are in the first limo. Ryan, Gracie and Scott are talking with friends and family nearby."

"Ritsuko is driving their limo." Dante added.

"My stars, I almost went in the wrong limo! The poor kids would have screamed their adorable little heads off." Blackie barked as Stephan let him to the floor, appearing next to Franco. Augusto grunted and moved over as did Dante.

"There you are Blackie! I told you not to leave Muma's side and there you go playing with Stephan." Katie patted her lap as Blackie did what she asked and then gave a soft whine toward Stephan.

"My camel will follow us from outside the limo, thought it may be best." Stephan adjusted his Egyptian collar and smiled. "I love limo rides!"

"I know what's bothering with you, Basil. You think they are going to attack today." Azzurra adjusted her position toward Basil.

Anna appeared next to Katie. They all squished in a bit tighter. "That was a beautiful eulogy Father. It was really groovy the way you hinted at the evil members of the family…far out."

Katie adjusted toward Father Bernardo. "Can we fit any more people in this dam Limo? And nobody says groovy anymore? Sorry, Father."

"Augusto, you'll have to go over the proper slang with me. I feel so out of date, sorry, Katie." Anna said.

"Don't apologize to her. Katie has big mouth. How are you supposed to know what the proper slang is?" Augusto replied.

"I do not have a big mouth!" Katie continued to swear at him and then turned to Father Bernardo. "Sorry Father."

Father Bernardo looked over his glasses at Katie and then turned away.

Azzurra slapped her lap. "Basil is that it? Are you nervous about today?"

Katie swished a hand in the air. "We are all nervous about today. Did you see who showed up Azzurra? Douglas is the only one worth a grain of salt. Actually, he's a very nice young man. The rest of them are plain evil." She turned to Anna. "I'm sorry sweetheart, that mean bastard husband of yours, is right. How would you know proper slang? A lot has changed in forty years. I am sorry. Forgive me honey; I'm just a little nervous."

Augusto began to argue with Katie. Franco asked them to please stop as he tried to speak to Azzurra over the commotion. Anna insisted that Augusto be quite, that Katie didn't mean anything about her slang. That she understood Katie's intent.

Basil turned to face Azzurra. "Mum, I am sorry for not doing as you ask. But I won't leave you, and yes, I am very nervous about today."

Azzurra leaned across Father Bernardo. "Katie you got my Basil all upset. He thinks they will attack today — in broad daylight, with all these people around? That's ridiculous." She swished a hand past the priest toward her sister. Father Bernardo rubbed his temple. "There is no spell that I know of that can hide that many people in the middle of the day."

"Don't you swish at me, Azzurra? I think you're the one being silly to think that those evil sons of...very mean people." She smiled at Father, "Will pay any attention to some old law that forbids an attack on the day of the burial. And you haven't practiced Magick in over forty years! How do you know what kind of spells are out there?"

"I think she's right, I don't believe a Witch can produce that kind of power to conceal that many people in broad daylight." Augusto added.

"You haven't practiced either, so what the hell...heck, are you talking about?" Katie said.

"Katie, will you stop your swearing?" Dante called across the limo to his wife.

Augusto defended himself about Katie's comment.

"Oh be quiet, Dante." Katie swished a hand.

Basil continued. "Augusto, we don't know what kinds of entities they are working with. We know nothing of Lamia's abilities or if they are in the company of something that does have that kind of power. Therefore, I've instructed everyone not to leave your side." Basil leaned toward the driver. "Pip, radio Ritsuko and check to make sure everything is OK in the first limo."

"Aye aye Captain." Pip took the walkie-talkie and began speaking.

"He has a point, we don't know much about Lamia." Augusto said.

"Oh I see...what I think doesn't matter?" Azzurra folded her arms and stared at Basil.

Basil looked out the window and mumbled something under his breath.

"Ready for takeoff, Captain." Pip said.

A bright orb appeared and floated in the center of the limo. "Arianna, too bright honey, you'll blind us all." Azzurra said. She turned to Basil. "Basil, what did you just whisper under your breath?"

Basil turned quickly to Azzurra. "I simply said that *I* would be making the proper decisions...with all due respect, Mum."

Everyone alive covered their ears. "Arianna will you calm down...my hearing aid is going to break." Augusto said.

"Basil I can't…" Azzurra began.

"…yes, Mum, I am choosing to ignore any command that my not leave me by your side or the families. I have taken an oath to the Vicar to be the guardian of this family and I take that oath seriously. Nothing you can say will stop me." Basil continued to stare out the window.

"Katie will you please tell her to buzz down…my ears?" Augusto said.

Katie placed a hand toward the orb, the orb subsided. "Oh, now you want favors." She turned to her sister "I'm with Basil, sorry Azzurra.' She faced the priest. "Arianna just wanted to say what a beautiful eulogy you gave Father."

Father Bernardo nodded.

"Now, let's just enjoy the ride" Katie continued "I'm with Stephan. I do like my limo rides." She adjusted Blackie upon her lap.

A knock on the car window startled everyone. Anna lowered the window. "Oh, Hi Marta."

"Hi Aunty Anna…Ma?" Marta peeked in the window. "Ma, Aunt Gabriella just called, they are running late. But they are fine. Eva is unconscious and they fought off dozens of Hags. They said they will see you at the cemetery."

Father Bernardo made the sign of the cross. Azzurra sighed in relief and looked toward Basil. Anna said thank you and raised the window.

"Maybe Basil and Katie are right?" Anna said.

"Basil, honey?" Azzurra said with a soft voice. "I'm sorry. Maybe you have a point. Although attacking Gabriella and Nicolai at their house is different. It's not in broad daylight with dozens of people. But you may do what you wish. I won't say another word." Her eyes became focused in her thoughts.

Basil winked. "Thank you, Mum. I told you that Gabriella and Nicolai were safe."

"I said that too…but does anybody listen to me?" Katie swished a hand across Father Bernardo.

"Katie!" Father Bernardo yelled. "If one more hand swishes across my face or if you swear just one more time…so help me I will ask the Higher Spirits to remove your voice!"

The car went silent.

Several minutes later Pip interrupted the silence. "Are we set for takeoff, Captain? Ritsuko is getting antsy. The pallbearers are in the cars behind us. Violetta is driving the hearse. Should I give the OK?"

"Yes, Pip we are ready. Engage." Basil laughed. "Now, I like this silence. Thank you Father."

"Warp speed in T minus ten seconds sir." Pip acknowledged.

"What are they talking about?" Katie asked with a hint of aggravation.

"*Star Trek*." Augusto chuckled.

"Oh my stars, I love *Star Trek*!" Stephan clasped his hands together.

"I couldn't stand that show." Katie swished a hand in the air and then quickly placed it by her side. Father Bernardo rubbed his temples as the limo pulled away from the curb.

* * * *

The Gravesite

The clouds rolled into twirls of white and grays as the winds bullied their way between the large purple maples, pines and oak's. A light mist speckled the windshield of the hearse as it pulled through the wrought iron gates of *Resurrection Cemetery*. One by one, the limo's and cars passed through the gates, displaying tiny orange flags that waved in the increasing wind.

A green tarp lay over a mound of dirt, freshly uncovered for Arianna's resting place. Dozens of chairs were set up facing the casket's lowering device that stood over the gravesite. A podium, for Father Bernardo, sat to the right of the opened earth.

The doors to the limos began to open. Gracie, Scott's wife, gathered her daughters just outside the first limo. Azzurra, Augusto and Father Bernardo exited the second limo as Nicolai approached and gave her a quick hug. He pointed over his shoulder. Gabriella was rushing toward them. Nicolai looked down to the buttons of his jacket and whispered to Azzurra that there were no signs of evil. He winked and then hurried toward the hearse. Gabriella embraced her sister, smiled and then told Azzurra that she would fill her in on the details later, that she and Nicolai were fine.

Augusto approached Gabriella and gave her a tight hug, telling her that he was glad she and Nicolai were safe. Azzurra took her sister's hand and gave a slight squeeze as Father Bernardo gave his cousin a quick hug, said thanks to God and then hurried to the front of the precession.

Gracie joined Azzurra's small group and greeted them. "Azzurra, you think everything will be OK?" She asked.

"Oh Gracie...I think we're fine. I just hope the weather holds out." Azzurra leaned closer to her nephew's wife. "Who's going to do anything with all these people around?" She adjusted Gracie's shawl and then noticed something...her eyes fixed on the shawl. "Gracie? Where's the pendent that Arianna left you? Basil said he was going to have everyone wear something from Arianna. It was a protective enchantment. I don't think you'll need it, but you really should wear it in times like this."

Gracie's adjusted her shawl. "Oh...you know, I was about to put it on and then Danielle had trouble with her necklace, so I helped her. I must have left it on the table. I don't know where my head is sometimes and this is, well finding out that my husband is a war...well you know. Are the kids' half witches...? Never mind, I don't want to know...all in good time, Gracie." She said to herself and then continued. "I couldn't get my thoughts together all day...I went to feed the birds and put out cat food instead." Her son, Ryan approached.

"Honey you're supposed to be up with the pallbearers." Gracie said.

Azzurra looked at Ryan and asked him if he wore his necklace that his grandmother had left him.

"Nope, I must have left it on my dresser." Ryan smiled, gave her a quick kiss on the cheek and headed toward the hearse. Gracie hugged Azzurra and then followed her son to the hearse.

Azzurra's heart began to thud. Her palms began to sweat and her breathing quickened.

"Azzurra?" Gabriella asked.

"What's wrong? You lost your coloring?" Augusto shuffled his old bones a bit closer.

"Nothing...nothing is wrong" Azzurra looked around, taking in a deep breath. She looked down to her angel pendent, placed it in the palm of her hand and squeezed. "I'm OK. Basil said that everyone will be taking up positions within the gravesite. I don't see Stella or Sabino...do you?"

"I don't see any of them." Gabriella said as she and Augusto looked around. Bella stood nearby speaking with Kimberly and Thom.

Danielle, Gracie's daughter, greeted them. Azzurra remarked how pretty she looked and then looked down to her neckline. "Honey, do you have your necklace? The one Aunty Arianna left you?"

"Amanda has hers. The clasp on mine broke. I left it in the car." Danielle went to walk away when Azzurra grabbed her shoulder, took off her angel pendant, and placed it around Danielle. "You keep this on no matter what. Do you understand me?" Azzurra's heart sped, she took a tissue from her purse and dabbed an eyebrow.

Danielle looked down at the angel. "She's beautiful. Thanks Aunty Azzurra. I will." She ran toward her sister, Amanda.

"I think all that silly talk in the car scared you. Nothing is going to happen. Look over there." Augusto pointed. "Three more burials." He shrugged his shoulders. "It's the middle of the day. Who's going to do something?"

"What talk?" Gabriella asked.

"Basil thinks there is going to be an attack today...at the burial site." Azzurra replied.

Gabriella replied. "There has never been an attack at a burial."

Azzurra nodded and dabbed her upper lip. "I know. I know. You both brought your powers?"

"I have my Wand." Augusto replied.

"I have about a dozen healing sachets, and one explosive elixir. I had to use most of them on the Hags." Gabriella narrowed her eyes.

"Hags, dear Lord, can't they use something other than those nasty things?" Augusto grunted.

Dino and Nicco jogged up to the three of them. "Ma...here." Nicco handed Azzurra a pewter cat and a vase of water topped with foil. "I stopped by the house on the way. I forgot what the soap dispenser did, so I left it there."

Azzurra sighed with relief. "Oh, Nicco, thank you honey. Sammy and Merlin, thank you." She stowed them in her purse.

"Where is your pendant, the angel pendant?" Nicco asked.

"I gave it to Danielle. Her necklace broke in the car." She turned to Dino. "Dino honey...do you have your ring?" She took his hands that were absent of jewelry.

"Um...like you should have told me they were enchantments." Dino smirked.

"Tracy is wearing her necklace and, well, you haven't redone the enchantment on my bracelet yet." Nicco said.

"Dam it!" Azzurra hugged Dino and told him to see if his mother has any extra enchantment to give him.

Dino pointed to his temple. "I have Clancy with me and the birds." He patted the large messenger bag draped over his shoulder.

"Thank goodness." Azzurra looked down to the bag and then to Nicco. "Nicco, please remind me tonight to fix that bracelet." A loud buzzing floated next to Azzurra.

"Arianna, stop it! You'll be seen." Azzurra looked to the orb as Gabriella and Augusto looked around.

Azzurra placed her hands over her ears. "Honey I can't understand you."

Dino jumped as his messenger bag rustled. A nutcracker wearing a large red feather in a hat peeked out from under the flap. "She's talking to Nicco. Says that the brain is an object, don't be afraid to enchant the brain. You're good with people and know their weaknesses. Use it to your advantage or something like that. I'm not a messenger bird, you know."

Dino smiled. "I really like him. Thanks buddy!" The nutcracker settled back into his bag as tiny chirping erupted.

"Nicco, Arianna is right. The brain is a type of object. Enchant the brain." Gabriella said. Augusto agreed.

The voice of Father Bernardo shouted for Dino and Nicco. The two men said a quick bye, and headed for the hearse.

Michael ran past them as shouts of his name filled the area. "Michael" Azzurra shouted. He did a loop and addressed his great aunt. "Listen to me honey...do you have the ring that Aunty Arianna left you?"

"What?" Michael raised one side of his mouth.

"The ring, the ring Michael!" She took his hands. "Nobody listens anymore! Where is your ring?"

"I didn't know I was supposed to wear it. Sorry Aunty. I have to go. Father Bernardo is yelling for me." Michael smiled and ran toward the casket.

Azzurra shouted after him. "Protezione, Michael! Say it if you need to!"

Michael stopped, scrunched his face and then turned and ran toward the hearse.

Azzurra threw her hands up as her lady pinochle friends approached. She greeted them with hugs and kisses as several of Marta's co-workers greeted them as well.

After a few moments, the pallbearers were in position and Father Bernardo called for everyone to take their seats. Azzurra could see Marta and Marie guiding people where to sit. It was obvious that one of the Spirits was giving them instructions as to where people should be seated. Marta and Marie looked confused and flustered as people eyed them suspiciously as they looked in the air and gave further instructions.

Bella, Thom, Kimberly and Drago approached.

"I see some cars pulling in now." Drago said "Not sure who's in them. Everyone has something to fight with right?"

"Not you too?" Augusto grunted. "We're fine, too many people around to attack."

"Kimberly didn't have a good feeling this morning." Drago replied.

"Well, Azzurra is feeling a bit funny herself." Gabriella said.

"What is it my dear woman? They wouldn't dare attack at a burial? That would be preposterous. At the funeral home...yes...but not the burial." Thom bellowed.

"Keep your voice down, Thom." Bella asked as they began to walk up the grassy hill.

"I have a dozen or so sachets and Augusto has his wand." Gabriella said and then whispered to Azzurra if she had her wand. Azzurra nodded and took a deep breath. Gabriella faced Thom, Drago and Kimberly. "Nicolai and I were attacked this morning. My daughter Eva tried to kill us."

Kimberly gasped and swore. "Are you alright? Nicolai?

"Yes, we are both fine." She took in a breath and shook her head. "I no longer have a daughter, but yes, we are both fine.

Azzurra took Thom's arm opposite Bella and continued to walk up the grassy slope. "What did they attack with...if you don't mind me asking that is?" He shook his head.

"Hags and two of Celia's Spirits." Gabriella replied.

"Preposterous, simply preposterous!" Thom bellowed.

Augusto stopped and looked down into the grass. Olivia and Carlotta approached him and asked if he was all right.

"Azzurra!" He yelled.

Olivia and Carlotta took each arm, leaned down and looked up to his face. "Azzurra!" Carlotta yelled.

Azzurra turned. "Is he all right? What's the matter?"

Kimberly, Azzurra, Gabriella, Drago, Thom and Bella made their way back to Augusto.

"Augusto, what is it?" Gabriella asked.

Augusto shook his head. "Azzurra...Gabby...I think he's right?"

"Who's right, Augusto?" Drago asked.

Augusto raised his head, clutching the arms of Carlotta and Olivia. "Basil...dear God, he's right. I think they are going to attack. Basil and Katie are right!"

Bella placed a hand on her chest as Azzurra told everyone to be quiet. "Augusto, what do you see? Olivia...focus honey...focus with your Uncle. Pull his feelings into you."

Olivia closed her eyes and placed a hand upon Augusto's shoulder.

"Augusto, talk to me?" Azzurra demanded.

Augusto looked up to his sister and searched her face. "At the gravesite... I think they will attack at the gravesite."

"Azzurra, there are people everywhere. It's broad daylight. What are they going to do?" Gabriella said.

"She has a point, Augusto. Never, in the history of a Witches War, has there been an attack at the burial." Kimberly said with a raised inflection.

Thom and Bella began to voice their opinions. Drago spoke the loudest. "Listen to me! If Augusto and Kimberly are having feelings, Azzurra is uneasy...I say we need to be ready."

"Here here." Thom said.

"Are the kids protected?" Kimberly asked.

"David was the only one to wear his. Rose thought it wasn't pretty enough and Michael forgot his. I gave Rose my necklace. Walter tried to give Michael his ring but it was too big. So now Michael and I have no protection." Olivia answered. "I can't see anything more than what I already told you. Winds, rain…but I couldn't feel the rain." She shook her head. "I don't have a good feeling. I almost made them stay home."

Carlotta added. "Elizabeth has her necklace but Dino forgot his ring. He brought Clancy and the birds though. I am wearing my enchanted earrings. I wanted to bring Captain Morgan, but couldn't convince him to leave the fort!" She held Augusto's arm tighter as they began to make their way back up the hill. "I agree with Olivia…something is not right."

Azzurra spoke. "I agree. Something is wrong. If Augusto is feeling something…well maybe…I just don't see how." She turned to Kimberly and Drago. "You should have made your sons stay home."

Kimberly stepped around a headstone. "Azzurra, I tried to make the boys stay home. They have been practicing around the clock, been up all night. Once they found out about the Witches War and the danger we were in, they all agreed to come and fight. You know my boys…they get something in their heads and there is no talking to them. They are stubborn like their father."

"And their mother." Drago added. "The boys insisted that their wives and kids stay home. Thank God for that one."

"Let's stay calm. I think we are over-reacting to the energy that we've gone through the last couple days. Not one of them is here and there are people everywhere. I think we need to be aware and ready for an attack though." Azzurra instructed.

Thick clouds rolled over their heads as they made their way to the top of the hill. Tiny droplets of rain began to fall as several umbrellas opened.

After taking their seats, Azzurra looked to the parking lot. They were walking across the lot: Sabino and his wife, Stella, their son Carlo and his wife, Debra, their daughter, Dorthea and what seemed like all of their children. Azzurra's heart began to race as the congregation turned toward the pallbearers. They were carrying the casket up the hill as the wind picked up and light rain began to fall.

Azzurra addressed Kimberly. "Do you sense any Spirits?"

"Nothing…just our own, Basil is up front and Katie and Franco are near us." Kimberly whispered.

Azzurra looked across to the opposite aisle of chairs. Marta was seated with Tom Buchman and Tracy. She had positioned herself at the outside of the congregation. Marie sat behind Marta group with her husband, Steven and their daughter, Katherine. Barbra, JoAnn, and Tony sat behind Marie's family. Gabriella's Neighbors sat next to Barbra and behind her. Marie's book club ladies and a couple of Nicco's friends sat toward the rear. While Douglas, Theodor's son, sat next to Marie toward the aisle.

Azzurra examined who sat behind her. Kimberly and Drago sat with their three sons. Olivia sat with Rose, David and Walter behind them on the inside of the partition of chairs. Carlotta sat behind Olivia with her X-Husband and her daughter, Elizabeth. While Mary, Carol, and Eleanor, her pinochle lady friends, sat toward the back.

Mateo sat in front of the casket next to Gracie while Amanda and Danielle sat directly behind them in the center of the congregation.

"They're coming." Gabriella whispered to Azzurra.

Dorthea positioned herself next to Sabino and Stella which were seated behind Gabriella's neighbors. Dorthea's children, Denise, Robert and Bradford sat behind them. Their spouses were not with them.

Bella whispered across Augusto to Azzurra. "Carlo and Debra are here too and their son, Demetrio and his wife, Gina. They're behind your pinochle lady friends."

Azzurra turned as they were being seated. She saw Gina smile and chat with her friend, Mary. Theodor, Angelica's husband and brother-in-law to Dorthea, took his seat behind Demetrio and Gina. Theodor's children, Larry and Susan took theirs behind their father. Their spouses were not present."

Azzurra became distracted when a slim black squirrel, scuttled past her, around Gracie and then toward the back of the congregation. A fluffy red squirrel soon followed. She and Augusto leaned across to see the pair of squirrel's positioned themselves behind Stella and Sabino, near a tree. They sat upon their hind legs and faced the casket.

"Those are no ordinary squirrels." Augusto whispered.

"They were at the cemetery when I summoned Katie. A red one and a black one...just like those two." Azzurra whispered.

"Look! Look" Bella said. "Gabriella! Your daughter is here."

Gabriella, Augusto and Azzurra took notice. Eva and Celia waved and took their seats next to Carlo and Debra.

Azzurra's heart raced. Her skin felt cold and clammy. "Dear Lord...I think they're going to attack."

"Nonsense, Azzurra...look at all those people over there." Gabriella said without conviction.

Father Bernardo began speaking as the pallbearers lined themselves on opposite sides of the casket. Ryan, Dino & Nicolai stood nearest to Azzurra. Michael, Scott & Nicco stood at the far end, near Marta & Marie.

"Look! Look, Azzurra." Bella whispered. "It's your sister! Contessa! She's with a young man with long blonde hair, he's in Spirit form."

Contessa walked to the rear of the congregation with Deveroy at her side. She nodded to Azzurra and then sat behind to Carlo. She leaned over to her daughter, whispered something and then spoke to Carlo. Celia flushed as Eva placed a hand upon her arm. Carlo glared at Contessa as she smiled and waved once again to Azzurra.

Azzurra spoke. "Thank God she's OK."

A voice turned their attention to the center of the congregation. "Excuse me! Pardon me for the intrusion." Merek Kroll headed up the aisle, approached Father Bernardo, and whispered. A moment later he handed him an object and hurried to Azzurra. He placed something in her palm, forced something in Augusto's palm and then to Gabriella's. "I'm sorry everyone." He then leaned down and whispered. "Throw them at a Spirit or Demon if you need." He then took a seat next to Thom.

Azzurra opened her palm, as did Augusto and Gabriella. A milky white substance swirled within a sphere. She turned to look down the aisle at Merek. He began handing the same spheres to Thom, Kimberly, Bella and Drago.

Azzurra mouthed thank you to him as he nodded.

"Who's that?" Augusto asked as Father Bernardo began to speak again.

Everyone turned to where Augusto nodded. A man with long white hair sat behind Dorthea's children. He looked up when a woman approached from over the hill, dark skin contrasting with her entirely white attire. The man with long white hair smiled and turned to face the casket. The beautiful black woman boasted large eyes and a short pixy hair cut. Azzurra placed a hand to her chest and looked at the woman. The lady in white smiled to Azzurra and nodded. She then took a seat next to the man with the long blonde hair. Azzurra saw the squirrels dart over to the woman in white and sit at her feet. She smiled upon the two squirrels.

"Who are they and what's with those squirrels?" Gabriella whispered. "He looks like that man that Anna described. An older gentleman with long blonde hair, she thought he was creepy."

Azzurra's heart leapt. She clutched her chest and gasped.

"What is it? What's the matter Azzurra?" Gabriella asked. Kimberly leaned in as did Bella and Augusto.

"The rain...the wind...it's all round...but look...nothing is in here. It's like were in bubble." Azzurra looked up. "This is what Olivia saw." She whispered.

Gabriella gasped. Augusto swore. The trees inside the bubble were calm and not a drop of rain was felt.

* * * *

Breaking Tradition

$\mathcal{D}$roplets of rainwater spattered the outer walls of the enchantment. The regal maples, pines, birches and oaks remained calm. A petal of a white petunia gently released from its stem and dropped to the soft, green blades of grass. Flutters of a robin's wings, the waddles of ducks and the pecking of a woodpecker diminished as they sensed the powerful charm's effects.

Azzurra turned at the sound of Sabino's voice. He had risen to his feet and took a several steps toward Father Bernardo. "You will meet your God today, priest."

A jet of red expelled from Sabino's wand and shot toward Father Bernardo. Gracie leaned around to see who had spoken and caught the full effect of the spell. Her body flew into the air and thudded to the Earth. Pandemonium erupted.

Kimberly's voice dropped into a panicked whisper, eyes darting in several directions. "They're entering the gravesite — Wolves, Hags, Winged Demons and Shadows!"

Protective Enchantments triggered. Sammy leap from Azzurra's purse, Merlin soared into the air and turned into a dragon. Screams, roars, screeches, giggles and howls covered the gravesite.

Clancy sprung from Dino's messenger's bag, grew to man's height and yielded his sword. He fought two approaching wolves. The tiny glass birds zoomed and darted with lightning speed breathing a flash of freezing water that turned a Hag into a hideous ice sculpture.

Necklaces and rings encompassed their wearer, throwing back Shadow People and Vetala. Marie tossed her scarf at JoAnn, who disappeared behind its enchantment. Her husband, Steven, huddled with Katherine under her necklace's protection.

Azzurra and Augusto shouted spell after spell. Nicolai pushed Dino and Ryan to the ground, tore a button from his shirt and tossed it at a black demon. It absorbed into its slimy flesh, swelled and exploded. "Protezione!" he shouted as the ball of light encompassed the three of them. A Vetala appeared next to Nicolai's and began to absorb the shields energy as three wolves leapt upon the shield.

Azzurra hit the Vetala with spell. It exploded into green globs of goo. Thom shouted a spell that destroyed two of the wolves. Gabriella threw a sachet at Gracie. It exploded in greens and reds and whizzed throughout her body.

In her peripheral vision, Azzurra saw Father Bernardo's body lifted in the air and slam to the ground near Gracie.

"Torna all'Inferno!"
(Return to hell)

Azzurra shouted. Three Hags shrieked as they exploded.

"Fulmine luminoso!"
(Lightening bolt)

A yellow stream of light struck two wolves, they yelped and vanished.

Azzurra felt her legs lift the ground as her body hit the Earth. Flash of reds and oranges blinded her for a brief moment as she felt something warm and soothing dash in and out of her body. She began to crawl over the grass until reaching the body of Augusto. Yellow and greens lights emanated from his chest as grave stones nearby exploded into fragments of stone.

Katie's voice bellowed curse after curse. Blackie growled and snarled.

Bella's voice called for the assistance of the trees. Branches and limbs began to swat at the demons. Azzurra crawled toward Nicolai as Gabriella tossed an explosive elixir at a White Demon. It shrieked and burst into tiny dark particles.

"Torna all'Inferno!"
(Return to hell)

Azzurra shouted as she heard Drago call for his son, John. Gabriella lay before her, blood dripping from her nose and ears. "Thom! Merek! Get to Gabby!"

Azzurra moved her elbows across the grass toward Ryan and Dino. Olivia screamed for Azzurra to protect herself from above. Azzurra rolled over and pointed her wand in the air, she screamed. The Winged Demon's claws were inches from her face when it exploded! Augusto had rolled onto his belly and destroyed the Winged Demon. "Get to Ryan and Dino; I don't see Nicolai…his protection collapsed!"

Azzurra caught the sight of Walter and Rose under a protective enchantment. Gregory, Carlotta's X husband, lay on the ground as two wolves dug their jaws into him. Carlotta tossed a vial at one of them; it burst in to flames and fled. Kimberly aimed her wand and struck the other. The wolf yelped and shrunk to the size of a kitten and darted away. Olivia slumped over a chair, a green mist expelled from her mouth. Franco distracted a Black Demon from sucking the energy from David's shield of protection. Drago fought Carlo and Debra, sparks of reds and black zoomed toward each other. Chase, Drago's son, lie crumpled on the ground near him with soft greens expelling from his mouth. John was buried in a heap of chairs while James, his other son fought beside his mother, Kimberly.

Damiano and two wolves appeared behind Franco. Merek Kroll and Thom intercepted them. The Wolves exploded as a Black Demon welled in size. Merek tossed the sphere at the Back Demon while Damiano was hit by a sphere from Bella.

Damiano struggled and screamed as the silky swirl of liquid began to fill his body from his feet up. He tried to raise his body in the air as the liquid exploded into gyrating spasms that engulfed him. The Black Demon and Damiano were statues that swirled with white liquid.

Azzurra aimed her wand and destroyed another Black Demon. She turned toward Ryan and Dino and began to crawl quickly toward them.

Blackie yelped.

Nicolai was slumped against a headstone, blood dripping from his neck, eyes and ears. She used her elbows and slithered to him. Clancy, The Birds and Sammy surrounded Dino and Ryan.

"Uncle Nicolai!" Dino shouted.

Azzurra pointed her wand to Nicolai's chest and shouted the spell.

"Through the body, through the soul
Mend what's broken, heal him whole."

Nicolai remained motionless, void of the flickering lights that should have zoomed in and out of his body. Azzurra screamed for Gabriella and knelt next to the boys. Clancy was missing an arm. Three wolves and six Hags were frozen solid from the birds. A shadow took Dino's leg and began to drag him into an opening of the Earth. Dino screamed and ripped at the grass as his body slithered past Ryan, toward the giggles.

"Distruggi un demone!"
(Explode a demon!)

Azzurra shouted. The shadow burst into tiny fragments. Ryan rushed toward Dino and helped him to his feet. "Stay down!" Azzurra shouted.

Katie spoke an incantation. Vines growing on a nearby headstone slithered around a Hag, immobilizing her. Green glops of goo spattered onto Azzurra as they retracted back into a Vetala.

Blackie growled as an older woman, that Azzurra did not recognize, blasted a Dover Demon from behind. It faced the woman as orange lights sprang from its eyes. They struck her. She screamed.

"Torna all'Inferno!"
(Return to hell)

Azzurra shouted. The Demon's gaze broke as the older female Spirit stumbled backward. Azzurra saw white swirling liquid fill the White Demon's body.

Basil appeared next to her, blinking and out of focus. "Mum! Nicolai's not healing! We need a sachet!"

Gabriella crawled toward them, blood dripping from the side of her face. "Nicolai!"

A sudden explosion erupted from the ground. Dirt and grass catapulted into the air. Gabriella and Azzurra were thrown back and knocked to the ground. Basil was blasted away. More screams erupted. Sammy roared.

Corpses flew from their graves and attacked from every direction. The ducks squawked and tried to escape the enchantments barrier. Chairs, people, stone and wood became projectiles. Arianna's body leapt from the casket and dove upon the shield that protected her daughters, Amanda and Danielle. They screamed at the sight of their mother's corpse. A bright orb zoomed toward the corpse and blinded it. It screeched and began to swat at the blazing orb.

Azzurra saw red, green and purple sparks shooting from her body. Gabriella reached Ryan and Dino. Red, green and yellow sparks surrounded the left side of her head. She screamed for Azzurra and Thom as she took Ryan into her arms. A piece of wood stuck out from his stomach.

Wolves, Shadow's, Vetala and Hags screeched and giggled. Katie and Basil blasted the corpses away from Gabriella and Azzurra. The older female Spirit flicker in and out of existence as she fought two Shadows. Sammy leapt upon several Hags, shredding them to pieces. Azzurra saw a red ball of light pass her and strike a corpse that attacked from behind. Augusto cast a spell from the ground.

Azzurra heard Carlotta shout *Protezione*! Clancy lost a leg. A Wolf ice sculpture stood nearby.

Kimberly and Drago fought several corpses and Hags. Franco fought a Dover Demon while Merek Kroll stood behind his trolley tossing explosives and healing elixirs at those who had fallen. Blackie leapt upon a hags face.

Basil's voice forced Azzurra's attention toward him. He was being dragged by dozens of black shadows into the earth. Azzurra aimed her wand and exploded the Shadows. A sachet of Merek's struck Basil in the chest. Whirls of blues and crimson surrounded him, renewing his energy.

Gabriella screamed. "Azzurra help me!"

Azzurra crawled to Ryan and smeared blood away from an eye.

"I'm so cold." Ryan looked down to his stomach. "Oh God, get it out of me! Get it out!

"Ryan, stay still, you'll be fine." Azzurra said. "Pull it out." She looked to Gabriella who took the piece of wood and pulled it from his belly. Ryan screamed.

> *"Through the body, through the soul*
> *Mend what's broken, heal him whole."*

Light fizzled around the wound but did nothing. Ryan coughed up blood. Gabriella pressed on the wound to help stop the bleeding. "None of our healing spells are working! Merek!" Azzurra yelled.

"I'm out of healing sachets!" Gabriella's face was strewn with tears as she screamed for Thom and Merek. She rocked Ryan back and forth in her arms. "It's OK Sweetheart. You'll be OK." She screamed again for Thom.

> *"Torna all'Inferno!"*
> *(Return to hell)*

Azzurra shouted!

Basil, Katie, the older female Spirit, Blackie, Clancy, The Birds and the Panther surrounded them...protecting them from attacks. Tree branches struck demons, wolves, hags and corpses. Thom crawled over to Ryan and poured an elixir into his mouth. He placed his hands over the wound and began to mutter an incantation.

"Where's my Mom? I want my Mom!" Ryan whispered. His voice quivered and faltered.

Thom shook his head as the wound began to spread wider, blood seeping into Ryan's shirt.

"He's not reacting!" Thom yelled.

"Thom! Get to Dino." Azzurra cried.

"Gracie! Gracie!" Gabriella screamed. "You'll be OK sweetheart." She smoothed Ryan's hair away from his forehead. "Gracie!" Gracie began to move a few feet from her son. A mist of green softly expelled from of her mouth.

Two corpses broke into the circle. Clancy, the nutcracker, threw himself in front of Dino. The corpse tore the nutcracker in half as Bella shouted. She had sparks of greens and reds zooming around her head. A tree branch swept a Wolf off the ground and into the air. Bella spoke an incantation.

"Break the spell that came to thee, back in the ground where you ought to be!"

Bella possessed the power to negate the enchantment. Both corpses were pulled back by what seemed like an invisible rope by their mid section. They sunk back into the earth. Azzurra could see Arianna's corpse fly back into the casket.

"Carlotta!" Gabriella screamed. "Gracie!"

Carlotta crawled over to them, a thin mist protecting her. The mist flickered and then failed, energy zooming back into the enchanted earrings. She took Dino into her arms. "Dino? Dino!"

"He must have been hit by the same spell! The elixirs are not working!" Thom cried over the panthers roars.

"Thom? There has to be a counter spell or something!" Azzurra yelled as Basil fought off three winged Demons and Katie blasted six Hags into pieces. Azzurra noticed the Water Bird frozen solid.

"Palla di fuco!"
(FireBall)

A ball of fire zoomed from her wand and struck the bird. He burst into flames and then came to life. He rose into the air and began to fight the Winged Demons.

"Merek Kroll will have something! Stay with them." Thom crawled out of the circle toward Merek.

Carlotta rocked Dino back and forth. "Azzurra do something! He's not breathing! Do something!"

Azzurra stood, grasped her wand tightly and walked out of the circle. She called for Basil to enter her wand. Basil flew over Thom, around a demon and into his Witches wand. Azzurra took in a deep breath, raised her wand far above her head, made a large sweeping circle and commanded with a voice that was unlike her own.

"Torna all'Inferno!"
(Return to hell)

A bright white light shot in a gigantic ring over the entire congregation. Dover Demon's, dozens of Hags, Wolves, Vetala and Shadow's, exploded into black mist and goo.

Droplets of water spattered upon her and retracted back into Merlin. Azzurra aimed into the sky and destroyed six winged demons with one spell.

She stumbled forward, weak and drained. The tree limbs had stopped assisting them. Either Bella was dead or unconscious. Azzurra began to feel wheezy. Basil's voice and energy forced her to clear her mind. A mist of white floated in front of Azzurra and took the shape of a beautiful angel. Lamia had appeared before her.

"I'm going to kill you just like your ditzy little sister!" Lamia laughed and raised both hands. Fireballs swam across her palms. Azzurra raised her wand.

"Protezione!"

The fire hit Azzurra's shield and exploded outward. Lamia was knocked to the ground as Azzurra fell backward and tumbled to the grass. Her shield collapsed.

Kimberly stepped between them and raised her wand. Lamia pulled herself to her feet and swore. "I am far too old to be controlled by you!"

"She's not alone!" Contessa shouted from behind Lamia.

Contessa wore a gash upon her arm and blood spattered her face. Azzurra screamed for Contessa to turn around but it was too late. A Spirit with long dark hair and swirls of black robes appeared and struck her from behind. Contessa was thrown back and slammed to the Earth.

Lamia turned to the female Spirit. "Thank you, Marguerite. It's about time. I thought my sister had abandoned me."

Marguerite's black eyes narrowed. "You owe me, my sister!"

A ball of white light struck Marguerite. Marguerite turned and cast a spell of black dust at Olivia. The black engulfed Olivia, who crumpled to the ground. Kimberly twisted her wand and jabbed at Lamia in an attempt to control her.

Azzurra hit Marguerite with spell. Marguerite parried the spell and disappeared. Azzurra cast another spell. It struck Lamia in the chest but did nothing but make her swear again.

Contessa rose to her feet, swirls of light streamed in and out of her body. She moved in front of Azzurra and faced Lamia. Lamia laughed and raised a hand to Contessa. "You picked the wrong side! Even the Matriarch and her faithful Spirit cannot touch me!" Her eyes suddenly began to widen with shock as Contessa twisted her wand toward Lamia.

Kimberly fought alongside of Contessa, both concentrating on controlling Lamia. A jet of red struck Kimberly in the face. Her eyes widened as she collapsed to the ground.

Stella stood to the side of Contessa and the fallen Kimberly. "I told you I'd get you myself, my dear daughter-in-law!"

"In your mind there is but doubt
Your deepest fears are all about
You see the things you dread and fear
All around you they appear."

Nicco stood behind Stella and had cast the enchantment. Stella's eyes widened and darted back and forth as she screamed and fell to her knees. She crawled to a tree trunk, rested her back against the tree, pulled at her hair and began screaming.

Azzurra could see Contessa struggling to control Lamia. Lamia swore and fought against the control. Azzurra pointed her wand toward Lamia. Her spell struck Lamia in the chest. This time it knocked her back a few feet.

A Dover Demon appeared before Azzurra. An orange light cast from its eyes and struck her. She screamed as Franco appeared and began fighting the demon. The glow from its eyes released Azzurra.

Achar appeared between Contessa and Lamia. "Leave her alone!" Achar yelled.

"Achar no!" Contessa screamed.

Lamia laughed, raised a hand and shouted.

"Esplodi oltre spazio e tempo"
(Disburse across space and time)

Achar tried to block the spell. It struck him in the chest. He exploded into tiny particles.

"You stupid little maggot!" Lamia said.

Azzurra rushed toward Contessa as Franco dealt with the Dover Demon. Marguerite appeared before her.

Azzurra shouted a spell. Nothing happened. Once again it seemed to bounce off the Spirit. "I am very old…" Another spell hit her…this time Marguerite stumbled backward. "…ah but you are a powerful Witch." Azzurra's realized she had lost the white Sphere, panic coursed through her veins.

Augusto tossed a Sphere that hit Marguerite's foot. It began to coil up and envelope her. She struggled but couldn't move. A second later she disappeared into the Earth. White liquid spread across the grass.

A jet of black flames, from Lamia, flew toward Azzurra as Stephan and his Camel appeared between them. It struck Stephan.

"You are nasty woman!" Stephan boasted. Not seeming to be effected by the spell in the slightest.

He cast several spells toward Lamia who screamed and stumbled backward. Something in Stephan changed…his Camel reared its head as he bellowed a war cry that was so powerful, that for split second, every demon, Witch, Spirit and mortal turned toward the cry. He rushed toward Lamia, who fled.

Azzurra turned to Contessa. She was lying on the ground hit by a rogue spell. Deveroy was next to her, as was Violetta. Both destroyed several approaching demons. "She's fine! We'll watch her." Deveroy shouted.

To her right she saw Pip dragged into the earth by dozens of Shadow People. Azzurra stumbled over Carlo's body as Eva and Celia appeared before her.

"Protezione!"

Azzurra cried.

"Lontano da me!"
(Away from me)

Celia was knocked backward by a blue ball of light and lie on the ground motionless. Eva blocked the spell with *Protezione* as Michale hit her from behind with a freezing charm. Eva stood solid as ice.

Overhead, she heard the Merlin Water Bird's screech. Droplets of water fell upon her and then retracted to the bird. Sammy roared. Six Hags dove upon Michale. Azzurra blasted them away and turned toward Pip. He was gone. Michale began a battle with two wolves.

Mary, Eleanor and Carol, lay crumpled in a heap of chairs upon the grass. Phillip and Patrick, two of Debra's Spirits, appeared before Azzurra. With a flick of her wand, both floated into the air and hovered above the ground.

"Through the body, through the soul
Mend what's broken, heal them whole."

A bright light expelled from Azzurra's wand and struck her pinochle lady friends. They didn't move. However, swirls of light danced in and out of their bodies. Walter was huddled over Rose, both surrounded by his enchantment. Elizabeth, Dino's sister, crouched in a ball, her necklace's shield protecting her from three shadows. Elizabeth screamed as Azzurra cast a spell that exploded them.

Azzurra saw several swirls of oranges and violets moving in and out of Olivia's body. Carlotta's ex-husband, Gregory, lay near Olivia. Yellow and blue lights streamed in and out of him.

Drago knelt near his sons casting healing spells and protective enchantments. A glass bird flew nearby breathing a jet of freezing water toward Theodor, Dorthea's brother in law. Theodor shouted a spell at the bird. The bird parried as a sheath of ice engulfed him. Kimberly lay next to Bella, both surrounded by blue, orange and pink lights. Larry, Theodor's son, was struck by a spell and flopped to the Earth, next to sister. Both had streams of light emanating from their bodies.

Debra raised a hand toward Drago and began an enchantment. Azzurra flicked her wand as Debra flew over several chairs and hit the ground with a thud.

Azzurra turned her focus to Marta's side of the battle. She could see Marie tossing sachets and explosives. The Man sat calmly next to the woman in white. The two squirrels sat perched on their hind legs.

Stella's voice made her look down. The antique had crawled to her husband's body and leaned against another tree trunk. "Make them go away... go away...please go away." She grabbed the sides of her head and screamed as she rocked back and forth. Sabino's eyes were open and still as blood dripped along the side of his face.

Azzurra, with Basil in her wand, destroyed demon after demon. She could hear his voice and feel their energies melded as one. She saw Nicco speak to a wolf. The wolf rolled over on its back and began rubbing himself playfully in the grass. It then looked to Nicco. Nicco picked up a rock and threw it several feet within the enchanted encasement toward a group of panicked ducks who squawked and darted away from the playful fur-ball.

Marta held a wand in one hand and pointed her ring with the other. She blasted a demon with glowing green eyes. The demon dissolved into dust.

Azzurra could see Dorthea crying over her son, Bradford's body. Her daughter, Denise glared at Azzurra as she tried to revive her brother, Robert. He moaned. Denise stood, tore a button from her blazer and raised a hand toward Azzurra.

Dorthea screamed for her daughter to do nothing. Azzurra flicked her wand and before Denise could release the button, her spell stuck. Denise did a complete flip in the air and landed face down on the ground with a thump.

Dorthea and Azzurra's eyes met. Azzurra shook her head.

"I don't have my wand. Did you kill her?" Dorthea's eyes filled with tears.

"I'm not like you. She'll be fine." Azzurra began to step forward.

"Denise was out of healing sachets!" She rocked her son in her lap and moved a piece of hair away from his forehead. Robert, Dorthea's other son, moaned nearby as swirls of light streamed over him. "Azzurra…heal him. Heal my Bradford…please." She begged.

"The healing spells are not working as they should." Azzurra took a few steps toward Dorthea. Water splashed to the ground and then rose into Merlin once more.

Dorthea gasped threw sobs as she pleaded with Azzurra to try.

"Through the body, through the soul
Mend what's broken, heal him whole"

A shot of white light expelled from Azzurra's wand and hit Bradford. It did nothing. Dorthea held him to her chest and sobbed.

Azzurra turned away and saw Father Bernardo's body being dragged by a Shadow. With a flick of her wand, tiny dust particles burst into the air.

A tear rose in her eye at the sight of the dead priest. To her right, Barbra lay with her eyes open. Tracy had crawled to two of Gabriella's neighbors, the three encompassed into her shield of protection. Mateo fought several demons. Azzurra could see a bright light illuminated all around his wand. It must be Arianna; she had become his Wand Spirit.

Tony, Marta's co-worker and second son to Azzurra, lay in a heap of chairs, blood dripping from his forehead and ears as tiny sparkles of orange and reds weaved in an out his body. JoAnn was nowhere to be seen. Two of Nicco's friends lay beneath crumpled chairs. Pastels of colors darted in and out of only one of their bodies.

Marie's book club ladies lie between the tumbled chairs. Two of them breathed a soft green light from their mouths, two lay motionless, eyes opened.

Azzurra blasted a winged demon that picked up Marie. Anna caught her and released her to the grass. Dante destroyed another winged demon and three Hags. Sammy roared from the other side of the battle. "Marie, go to Dorthea...see if a sachet will heal her son." Marie ripped a button from her blouse and threw it behind her mother. A demon exploded. Marie hurried past Azzurra and knelt to the ground, next to Dorthea.

"Ma, Scott and Michael are hurt up front! Marie couldn't' get to them. She threw an elixir but it did nothing!" Marta shouted.

Azzurra nodded and made her way forward. Gracie rose from the ground and took in the sight of what had happened. Mateo grabbed her and forced her to the ground. Gracie screamed and covered her face. Douglas, Angelica and Theodor's son, cast a shield around Gabriella's neighbors, Shirley and her husband. He knelt beside them assisting Mateo and Marta.

Lamia appeared before Azzurra. "Stephan is attending to his injured Camel. Now it's just you and I."

Azzurra cast a spell, as did Marta and Douglas toward Lamia. They bounced off.

Marcus appeared next to Lamia. "The demons are fleeing! It is now or never!"

Ritsuko hit Marcus from behind. He jolted forward, rolled his eyes and flung out a hand toward her. Ritsuko parried and hit him again.

Dormava and Medeia appear next to Marcus. "Hurry, we are losing!" Dormava cried.

Lamia raised a hand toward Azzurra. The man with long white hair and the woman in white appeared next to Azzurra. The woman acknowledged Azzurra with a tilt of the head.

Azzurra blocked the first blow from Lamia and stumbled backward. Spells from Marta, Anna & Douglas were blocked by Medeia and Dormava.

Thom approached them, threw a sphere at Lamia and then fell to the ground, blood dripping from his head. Marie tossed a sachet that hit him. Sparks of gold, crimson and periwinkle swirled around him.

The sphere that Thom tossed rolled toward Lamia's foot and just before it hit, The Man made the smallest flick of his finger and deflected the sphere away.

Ashima, the woman in white, spoke. "I warned you what would happen if you interfered."

"Ashima dear...who do you think cast the concealment charm over the gravesite." The Man smiled and winked.

Ashima shook her head and called for the Vicars. Two squirrels scurried over and morphed into Vicar Thomas O'Connell and Vicar Aiden Sinclair.

Marcus blocked a spell from Mateo and Arianna.

"You both know what to do." Ashima nodded and then looked to the man with long grey hair. He was walking away in quick strides. Ashima turned into a mist of white and zoomed toward the man. He turned, smiled and dissolved into a vapor of black. The black and white collided into an enormous blast of light and then vanished.

The Vicar's stood at attention. They looked up and to the right. Their ties lit up as demons were sucked into gemstones from every direction.

Lamia turned her attention to Azzurra. She gasped as she saw that Azzurra held the Sphere. Lamia threw out her hand. However, the bright light of Arianna's orb flashed and blinded her. She screamed as the Sphere hit her in the chest. Lamia looked to Marcus, Medeia and Dormava as her body filled with milky white swirls. Her legs turned solid, then her dress, arms and chest. Her mouth opened to scream as the liquid encompassed her head and beautiful waves of dark hair.

Azzurra looked to Marcus, Medeia and Dormava. "This Withes War is over."

* * * *

The Aftermath

Marcus turned to Dormava. "Get Damiano." Dormava nodded and vanished. He then rested a hand upon the stone statue of Lamia as he, Medeia and Lamia disappeared.

"The sachet didn't work. Dorthea's son, Bradford, is dead. He wouldn't react to anything. I'm sorry Ma." Marie stood with several wounds upon her body.

Azzurra nodded and looked to Dorthea who still cradled her son's body. Denise, her daughter and her other son Robert knelt near their mother.

The Vicar turned to Azzurra. "I am sorry that we could not have done more." His hands were clasped behind his back. His deep brown eyes looked into hers. "It is with a sad heart that we will not be able to heal everyone."

"I understand, Vicar." Azzurra touched the side of his face. "I understand." A single tear rolled down her cheek. "You're a good man."

The Vicar nodded and looked to the ground at the body of Father Bernardo. "It is not your time, faithful priest. There are other plans for you." He waved a hand over the priest. A white light enveloped the body as Father Bernardo took in a deep breath. Nicco and Marta helped him to his feet." Father Bernardo took in the aftermath and made the sign of the cross. Whimpers of Gabriella's neighbors redirected their attention. Douglas had released the protective enchantment and tried to calm them. JoAnn appeared as the scarf that hid her, turned white and fell to the grass. She burst into tears and knelt next to Barbra's body, screaming "What happened!"

Vicar Thomas waved a hand and all those who were mortals fell gently to the ground. "They will not remember." He waved a hand toward Barbra as an orb flew toward her body and entered. She took a breath and lay still. Another orb flew toward Tom Buchman's body. Marta released a soft cry and hugged Nicco. Two orbs floated to Marie's book club ladies, one to Nicco's friend and one to Gabriella's neighbor.

Katherine, Marie's daughter, stood in her father's arms nearby. Tony moaned and then became silent as his wounds healed.

Tracy's necklace released its protective barrier leaving Gabriella's neighbor and his wife resting upon the grass. She staggered toward Nicco and embraced him. Mateo reached down and checked his granddaughters and nodded to Gracie.

Gracie looked up to Azzurra. "Scott? Where's Scott? My husband… where is he?" Her eyes frantically searched the battle field.

The Vicar motioned to the front of the grave site. Gracie ran toward two bodies that lay motionless, Scott and Michael's.

Anna, Ritsuko, and Dante appeared in solid form near the bodies.

Gracie screamed as Mateo ran toward his son. Mateo knelt down and leaned Scott's body in his lap. "Do something! Please Vicar, do something! I can't lose my wife and son. Please." He rocked his son back and forth.

"I am sorry." The Vicar looked down.

Mateo whaled a cry of torment. Gracie fell to the ground next to her husband and pounded the earth.

Anna spoke. "Olivia, come and be with your son, Michael."

Olivia rushed forward. Azzurra turned into Thom's arms. Bella rushed beside her and patted her hair.

Walter left his son David and Rose, who lay silent upon the grass. He slid beside his son Michaels' body and held Olivia and cried.

The Vicar appeared next to Mateo and knelt down. He touched Mateo and Gracie. They calmed. "I am sorry for your loss. It is will deep sorrow that I cannot bring him back." Mateo nodded, eyes swollen in grief.

The Vicar raised a hand and made a sweeping movement toward Mateo. An orb floated toward them and took the shape of Arianna. Arianna looked to her husband and her son as another orb floated near them and took the shape of Scott. With another hand gesture, Scott and Arianna turned solid. Mateo released Scott to Gracie as Arianna hugged Mateo.

"I'm sorry. I'm sorry I didn't make it. Dad I'm sorry, I tried. You'll take care of Gracie and the kids?" Mateo pulled Scott into his arms and whispered him.

The Vicar then turned to Olivia. "It is not his time and he knew nothing of Magick." Another orb floated to Michael's body as he took in a breath and lay quiet on the ground. Olivia and Walter cradled their son.

The Vicar turned to Gracie and spoke. "Your son Ryan needs you."

Gracie and Scott rushed to the other side of the grave site. Mateo and Arianna followed.

Gabriella rocked Ryan's body in her arms. A blank expression appeared upon her face, void of sorrow or emotion. Her face blood stained as she gazed from Ryan to Dino and then to her husband, Nicolai.

Gracie screamed and knelt to the ground. Gabriella released him into his mother's arms. Carlotta sat next to Gabriella, rocking Dino's body in her arms. Olivia rushed to her sister's side and placed her arms around her as they sunk into tears.

The Vicars' appeared next to the scene. Basil, Katie, Blackie, Franco and a woman Azzurra did not know, stood in solid form near them. Sammy, lay panting near a tiny Merlin Water bird.

The Vicar raised a hand. "I am sorry I cannot do more." An orb floated over the body of Ryan and sank into him. His wounds healed as he took a breath but remained unconscious.

Gracie burst into tears of joy as she began to kiss Ryan all over his face. Scott looked up and said thank you. Tears stung his eyes.

Carlotta and Olivia looked up to the Vicar.

"He knew of the Magick. I cannot do anything." The Vicars looked down.

A voice with a cockney accent broke through the tears. "What do you mean? He did not use Magick and refused to use Magick? I only wished I could have protected him. Please Vicar; it is my fault that he knows of Magick. Please do not punish him or Miss Carlotta. It is my fault and only my fault. Disenchant me if you must. Please bring him back." Clancy, the nutcracker, spoke as he lay torn in half upon the grass.

The Vicar looked to his fellow Vicar. "He has valid point." The Vicar Thomas O'Connell said.

The Vicar raised a hand as an orb flew into the body of Dino. "You are right, Clancy." The Vicar raised his hand toward Clancy as he repaired the nutcracker. Clancy stood, shrunk back to nutcracker size and hugged Dino under Carlotta's arm.

Carlotta kissed her son and thanked the Vicar. Gabriella stood and approached the Vicar. Azzurra, Bella, Thom and Augusto made their way near.

"May I please say goodbye to my Nicolai." Gabriella asked.

Azzurra dabbed her eyes as Augusto looked to the ground. A deep sigh escaped him.

"You may." The Vicar raised a hand and Nicolai appeared in solid form next to his wife. Gabriella collapsed into his arms. "My Nicolai, what will I do without you?" She cried into his chest. Nicolai looked up to the Vicar and mouthed thank you.

Drago and Kimberly huddled near their son's body. John lay upon the ground, his brother Chase and James stood nearby. Kimberly looked up to the Vicar, who took a few steps towards them. "We know….we know." She kissed her son upon his cold forehead.

John appeared in solid form and hugged his family. "You may say goodbye." The Vicar bowed.

A woman screamed "You Bitch! Get away! You are no daughter of ours! Get out!" Gabriella stepped away from Nicolai and slapped Eva across the face. "Get out! Get away! You will not say Goodbye to your father! Get away." Gabriella began hitting Eva over and over. Celia pulled Eva away.

"You don't understand. Mom, Dad, you just don't understand." Eva cried.

"Get out! Get out! You Bitch!" Gabriella screamed. Azzurra and Nicolai rushed forward as a blast of white light struck Gabriella. She fell back into her sister's and husbands arms and settled into soft cries.

The Vicar lowered his hand. "She will be fine. I wish I could do more."

Thom and Bella stepped forward. Thom crossed his arms and spoke to Eva and Celia. "You are both a disgrace to the name of Degeli. Now do as she says and clear away."

Celia helped Eva to a chair and sat her down. Contessa approached Celia. When her daughter looked up, Contessa slapped her hard across the face. Celia raised a hand to her cheek and smiled. Contessa slapped her again. "Wipe that smile off your face!"

Eva grabbed Celia and pushed her into the chair beside her. "Stop it!" She cried. Deveroy stood near Contessa beside Violetta.

Debra's sob averted their attention elsewhere. Azzurra saw that Debra knelt over her husband's, Carlo's body. The Vicar took a few steps and stood beside her. He looked down. "Was it worth losing your husband?"

"Please Vicar. Bring him back. Bring back my Carlo." Debra cried.

"You should ask Satan for your favor not I." The Vicar turned away. "He will laugh upon your request." Debra sobbed and kissed her husband's forehead. "Can I please say goodbye."

The Vicar stopped and looked down upon her. "Again, you should ask Satan, not I"

He turned and raised a hand toward three people that attempted to leave the site. "You three will not go until I deem you ready. The invisible barrier will need to be lifted and the mortals must be prepared for what they shall see. No outsider shall know of a Witches War." He raised a hand and a jet of red stuck Theodor and his children, Larry and Susan to the ground. They lay motionless.

A large animal grunt broke though the whimpers of the survivors. "Shush honey. People are trying to mourn." Stephan patted his camel on the top of the head as he rode up to the Vicar. Stephan leaned down and whispered something.

The Vicar nodded and made a hand movement toward the grass near a crypt. Pip rose up from the grass and took solid form.

"Thanks! That was horrifying! Why do I get such dreadful things happening to me? I'm scared for the rest of my death." Pip said as Michale rushed to his side and embraced him.

"Pip, I thought you were a gonner!" Michale hugged him again as Violetta rushed up and gave Pip a tight squeeze.

The Vicar turned to face the grave site. Vicar Thomas O'Connell appeared next to him. "We shall set things right. The enchanted bubble shall be removed revealing what has happened to the outside word. We shall make the appearance of a lightning strike. At which time those who were innocent shall rise to their feet. He looked down to Azzurra's pinochle lady friends. He and Thomas raised their hands. Chairs, dirt, stone and rocks began to move and fly into various positions. The stone statues of Wolf, Black Demon, a Dover Demon and the two floating Spirits of Phillip and Patrick vanished. Bodies began to be repositioned; wounds healed and other wounds appeared.

The Water Bird, Panther, Clancy and two glass birds disappeared. Azzurra found herself sitting between Gabriella and Augusto. Bella and Thom sat at the ends. Merek Kroll bowed and vanished with his trolley. Father Bernardo appeared behind the podium.

A voice boomed over the site. "Have faith, show love and know understanding." Ashima appeared before them. With a wave of her arm, the Spirits vanished, as did the dome that hid them from outside world.

* * * *

It's Not Goodbye

*A*zzurra pressed the button for the coffee and went to the cupboard, took out the sugar and placed it on the kitchen table. She then went to the cabinet and pulled out one of Katie's cups and saucers and placed it next to a napkin on the kitchen table.

"Katie? I made coffee. I thought we could chat a bit before heading over to Gabriella's." Azzurra took a plate from the cabinet and began to sort various Italian cookies upon the plate. Katie appeared in her blue dress with Blackie next to her.

"There you are. I slept so well last night. The cherubs played soft music and I drank Marie's sleeping draft. Franco stood with me. He just left a bit ago, said he'd be right back. Oh, I woke up and my body was so sore." She swished a hand toward Katie. "Beee I haven't seen that much exercise in years. But the soap dispenser made me feel better." Azzurra walked over to the table and placed the cookies next to the cup. "You know Katie; I still can't believe all that has happened. Basil and you were right. I just didn't think they'd attack." She turned and opened the refrigerator. "Augusto called first thing this morning. He said he just wanted to check on me. I hung up with him and Father Bernardo called. Drago called just as I picked up the phone to call him. He said Kimberly doesn't have good feelings yet. She feels something is still in the air. I told him that the fountain of the Blessed Mary is running so that as long as she works we have nothing to worry about. I told them how sorry I was about their son, John. I don't think they'll ever be the same. But you know those two, Kimberly and Drago, the whole family is tough." She set the cream on the table and turned back to the refrigerator, pulled out a loaf of bread and went to the counter. "Marta, Nicco and Marie stood till late last night and then called me early this morning. Bella and Thom called twice, once last night and once this morning. I just got off the phone with Gracie when Gabriella called. Beee I've been on the phone all morning…but what are you going to do? Anyway, Gabriella wants me to go with her today. It's going to be hard for her. Nicolai had everything planned, but she wants me to help pick out the suit and help write the obituary. I told her she should lay him to rest in his underwear. This way, no one can complain about what their wearing." Azzurra placed two slices of bread into the toaster and placed a hand upon the counter. She looked to Katie. "Katie what's the matter?"

Katie looked down and then raised her head to her sister, tears in her eyes. "Now Azzurra, don't get upset. Franco is gone sweetheart. He said you would understand." Katie's voice lowered as a tear ran down her cheek.

Something sank in Azzurra. Her heart plummeted to the pit of her stomach. It was as though someone slapped her across the face. Tears flooded at the realization of what her sister was saying.

"Arianna will be here shortly. She's saying goodbye to Mateo. Scott is saying his goodbyes to Gracie and Anna is with Augusto." Katie's voice dropped even lower. "I've said my goodbyes already…except to you." Tears welled and cascading down Azzurra's cheeks as Blackie lay on the floor and gave a soft cry.

"Katie?" Azzurra placed a small hand over her mouth and shook her head.

"Now you know I couldn't stay. Once the Witches War was over, I had to go back. I've talked with Bella and Thom. They agreed to stay for a month. They will help you through this, honey." Katie took a deep breath as Arianna appeared in solid form next to her.

"Arianna? Honey…" Azzurra shook her head, face wet with tears.

"It's not goodbye Azzurra. It's I'll see you someday." Arianna opened her arms and hugged Azzurra. She pulled Azzurra back to look upon her sister's face. "I will miss you. You always believed in me." Arianna stepped away dabbing her eyes with a tissue.

Blackie jumped up on Azzurra leg and barked. Azzurra knelt down and patted his head through tears. He gave a soft cry and jumped back to his mother. Katie stepped forward and hugged Azzurra tightly. "I will always be with you, and I will wait for you." She stepped back as an enormous rainbow of color filled the room. The back wall of the kitchen vanished into whiteness.

Azzurra staggered forward a bit and placed a hand upon the counter. "I I love you both so very much."

Katie, Blackie and Arianna turned into Spirit form. Her sister's responded with I love you and began to walk toward the bright lights. They gave a last look back as Blackie jumped into Katie's arms. She took Blackie's paw and waved as the three of them vanished.

Azzurra held onto the counter as she slid down the cabinet.

"I'm right beside you, Mum." She felt Basil's strong arm wrap around her and pull her into his chest as she let out all the emotions she felt.

* * * *

Basil's Lament

"Mum, I'm right here. I'm not going anywhere." Basil held Azzurra as she cried.

Azzurra pulled away and looked into those beautiful green eyes of his. "Why? Why are *you* not going, Basil?"

Basil helped her to her feet. "Mum, I don't have to. Not yet anyway." He looked down.

Azzurra dabbed her eyes. "Basil sweetheart, what do you mean? The others had to leave but not you?"

Basil looked up, his eyes glassy. "The Vicar gave me permission to stay with you for a few more days."

"Then you too will leave in a few days." Azzurra asked.

Basil nodded.

"Basil, come sit down." She pulled Basil to the table and sat him in a chair. "Tell me what's going on in your head."

Azzurra felt a bit of strength. She didn't know where it came from but she knew she was going to be fine. Right now Basil was in his own lament and he needed her.

"The Vicar spoke to all of us, he said the Higher Spirits demanded that we re-enter the Spirit world and leave the realm of the living. He said that if we didn't, we would be judged harshly. That we could no longer associate with Witches that are in the living." He looked down into his lap.

Azzurra couldn't help but to think of him as a little boy. He seemed lost and frightened.

"Basil is something wrong? Maybe you should think about crossing over sweetheart. You're parents must miss you dearly." Azzurra pulled a piece of dark hair away from his forehead.

Basil stood. His eyes filled with tears and then streamed down his handsome face. His voice cracked as he spoke. "Miss Katie wanted me to cross over as well. She said I ought to be with my parents."

"I agree Basil. Don't you want to see your parents?" Azzurra watched him closely.

Basil took in a deep breath and tried to fight back tears. His voice dropped an octave as he spoke. "I can't Mum...I just can't. You don't understand. All these years I've been so scared to see them. It kills me to think that they are waiting for me somewhere. But they shouldn't. I'll never cross unless I'm forced." Basil's green eyes searched Azzurra's face for some answer he didn't ask.

"Why Basil?" Azzurra's voice became kind and gentle.

"Because of things I've done. The theatre was a wild life style. The after-glow parties, the opening night parties, everyday there was some reason to get drunk and be happy. I got to know fellow actors very well. I wasn't too picky if I liked someone. If there was attraction...well then I had fun you see. My own mum used to say that it was no life for a decent young man. She begged me to go into banking or even become a rancher. She'd say that I ought to leave the theatre and work, like everyone else. My father never spoke of things. He would just say that the theatre life could lead you into bad situations. He'd shake his head as he watched me traipsing down the street with my fellow actors. I did things, even after they died in the fire. I did things that I'm sure they've seen. They know things I've done." He broke into a hard sob and then regained composure a minute later. "What they must think of me? They were right. It was no life to be had. It cost me my life, it did. Now Miss Katie thinks that I can cross over. I tried to explain to her but she shook her head and said it doesn't matter. You are their son and they will always love you and you're breaking their hearts by not crossing over. I don't want to hurt them, but the thought of them being disappointed...disgusted...angry." He searched the ceiling as tears streamed down his cheeks. "What if they hate me Mum? They will have known I've associated with Witches. What if they think you're evil or something? I can't Mum...I just can't."

Azzurra cleared her throat. "Now Basil honey, you listen to me. I don't say this because I want you to leave. I want you to be there when I pass on someday, to greet me when I die. But Katie is right. There is nothing that you have done that will take away the love of your parents. I've done things that I'm sure did not make my parents proud. We are human, and will all make mistakes and do things that may bring shame upon us." Azzurra placed the palm of her hand upon his wet cheek. "I'm telling you honey, your mother and father will be happy to see you."

Basil cleared his throat and spoke after a moment. "Maybe when it's your time...you can come with me? We can cross over together, and you can come with me to see my parents." He smeared the back of his hand over an eye.

"I promise that someday when I pass, which may be sooner than we think, I'll go with you. I'd love to meet your parents, sweetheart." Azzurra kissed him on the cheek.

"I love you Mum." Basil smiled brightly.

"I love you too...my Basil."

The End

The Degeli Family Tree

The Name "Degeli" Denotes Direct Decedent

Ciro Degeli & Wife, Adalina

Their Son's & Daughter's
Pasquale, Francine, Sabino & Bernadetta
*****

Pasquale Degeli & Wife, Luciana

Their Six Children
Azzurra, Katie, Arianna, Contessa, Gabriella, & Augusto

Azzurra Degeli & Husband, Franco Stephani

Their Daughter's & Son
Marta Degeli Stephani
Nicco Degeli Stephani & Tracy Deluca
Marie Degeli & Husband, Steven Giordano

Marie & Steven's Daughter
Katherine Giordano

Katie Degeli & Husband, Dante Marinacci

Azzurra's Sister

Their Daughter's & Son
Olivia Degeli & Husband, Walter Jasienski
Carlotta Degeli & X-Husband, Gregory O'Reilly
Angelo Degeli Marinacci

Olivia & Walter's Children
Michael, Rose & David Degeli Jasienski

Carlotta & Gregory's Children
Dino & Elizabeth Degeli O'Reilly

Contessa Degeli & Husband, Nathan Reccetti

Azzurra's Sister

Their Daughter & Son
Celia Degeli & Husband, Alfonso Marinelli

Vincent Degeli Reccetti

Celia & Alfonso's Children

Fredrick & Felicia Degeli Marinelli

Gabriella Degeli & Husband, Nicolai Pavalak

Azzurra's Sister

Their Daughter

Eva Degeli Pavalak

Arianna Degeli & Husband, Mateo Valente

Azzurra's Sister

Their Son

Scott Degeli Valente & Wife, Gracie

Scott & Gracie's Children

Ryan, Danielle & Amanda Degeli Valente

Augusto Degeli & Wife, Anna

Azzurra's Brother

No Children

Francine Degeli & Husband, Gino Acone

Azzurra's Aunt

Their Two Children

Beatrice & Bella

Beatrice Degeli & Husband, Thom Stryker

Azzurra's Cousin Beatrice, San Francisco

Their Daughter & Son's

Claudia Degeli & Husband, Daniel McFarland

Paul Degeli Stryker& Wife, Camille

Harrison Degeli Stryker & Wife, Diane

Bella Degeli & Husband Gilbert von Eisenberg

Azzurra's Cousin Bella, New York

Their Daughter & Son's
Catherine Degeli & Husband, Luke Markus
Eric Degeli von Eisenberg & Wife, Candice
Gino Degeli von Eisenberg & Wife, Jacquelyn
William Degeli von Eisenberg & Wife, Janice

Sabino Degeli & Wife, Stella

Azzurra's Uncle

Their Five Children
Bernardo, Drago, Carlo, Dorthea & Angelica

Father Bernardo Degeli

Azzurra's Cousin Bernardo, Local
Drago Degeli & Wife, Kimberly

Azzurra's Cousin Drago, Local

Their Sons'
John Degeli & Wife, Suzanne
Chase Degeli & Wife, Betty
James Degeli

Carlo Degeli & Wife, Debra

Azzurra's Cousin, Local

Their Son
Demetrio Degeli & Wife, Gina

Dorthea Degeli & Husband, Nicolas Stewart

Azzurra's Cousin Dorthea, New Orleans

Their Son's & Daughter
Robert Degeli Stewart & Wife, Elyse
Bradford Degeli Stewart & Wife, Mary
Denise Degeli & Husband, Richard Dombrowski

Angelica Degeli & Husband, Theodor Dubinsky

Azzurra's Cousin Angelica, Phoenix

Their Daughter & Son's
Susan Degeli & Husband, Pete Flattery
Larry Degeli Dubinsky & Wife, Daphne
Douglas Degeli Dubinsky & Wife, Celeste

Bernadetta Degeli

Azzurra's Cousin, Deceased
No Children

The Spirits

Katie Degeli Marinacci
Azzurra's Sister

Basil O'Bryan
Azzurra's Wand Spirit

Vicar Aiden Sinclair
Vicar to the Higher Spirits

Contessa's Household Spirits
Deveroy
Achar (Deveroy's Companion)
Lamia

Nathan's Household Spirits
Damiano
Marcus
Stephan

Celia's Household Spirits
Dormava
Medeia

Anna Degeli
Augusto's Wife

Merek Kroll
Witches' Vendor

Basil's Comrades
Michale
Pip
Ritsuko
Violetta

Vicar Thomas O'Connell
A Vicar to the Higher Spirits

Ashima
Overseer of the Higher Spirits

The Man
Lamia's Associate

Marguerite
Lamia's Sister

Debra's Household Spirits
Patrick
Phillip

Stella & Sabino's Spirits
Vida
Aleesha

Sarah
Olivia's Neighbor's Mother

Vincent
A Spirit near Olivia's

A Witches War
Tale of The Degeli Witches

Next in the series